KT-116-484

Maeve Binchy

DUBLIN 4

THE LILAC BUS

VICTORIA LINE, CENTRAL LINE

CRESSET EDITIONS

This edition published in 1998 by Cresset Editions,
an imprint of Random House UK Ltd,
20 Vauxhall Bridge Road, London SW1V 2SA

Copyright © Maeve Binchy 1998

Dublin 4 first published in 1982 by Ward Press Ltd
Lilac Bus first published in 1984 by Ward Press Ltd
Victoria Line, Central Line first published in 1983 by Century

The right of Maeve Binchy to be identified as the author
of this book has been asserted by her in accordance
with the Copyright, Designs and Patents Act 1988

All rights reserved. No part of this publication may be
reproduced, stored in a retrieval system, or transmitted
in any form or by any means, electronic, mechanical,
photocopying, recording or otherwise, without the
prior permission of the copyright owner.

Printed and bound in Germany

ISBN 0 0918 6686 3

DUBLIN 4

CONTENTS

For Gordon
with all my love

She drew the dinner table six times and it always came out the same. If you put the host at one end and the hostess at the other it didn't work out. She would sit with her back to the window and have a man on either side of her. Fine so far. Dermot would sit opposite her with a woman on either side of him. Fine again, but what about the two places in between? Whatever way you did it you would have to have man sitting beside man, and woman beside woman.

She shook her head, puzzled. It was like those problems they had always done at school; if you have three missionaries and three cannibals on an island and the boat can only hold two . . . Not that it mattered of course, and anybody who knew how much time she had spent working it out would say she should spend a week in St Patrick's, but still it was very irritating. There must be a way.

'There is,' said her daughter Anna. She had telephoned Anna to talk about something else but brought the conversation around to the perplexing dinner table. 'At a party for eight, host and hostess can't sit opposite each other. You sit opposite the most important lady . . . and put Dad on that lady's left.' Anna had gone on talking about other things, not realising that her mother was now drawing the dinner table again, with Dermot sitting facing the sideboard and the most important lady sitting at the other end of the table facing herself.

'Are you all right, Mother?,' Anna asked. Anna used to call her 'Mum' but now she said 'Mother'. She said it in a slightly jokey tone as if she had been saying Your Ladyship, it was if the word Mother were equally unsuitable.

'I'm fine, dear,' said Carmel. It irritated her when people asked was she all right. She never asked anyone else were they all right, even when they sounded most odd or distrait. Everyone felt they could patronise her, and pat her on the head. Even her own daughter.

'Oh good, you sounded a bit vague as if you'd gone off somewhere. Anyway, as I said, we're off to the cottage at the weekend so you'll have to tell me how the great entertaining went. I'm glad you and Dad are having people round. It's good to see you stirring yourself to do something.'

Carmel wondered again why Dermot could still be 'Dad' and not 'Father', and why it was good to be stirring herself. Why should things be stirred? Particularly, why should people be stirred? They should be left to simmer or cool down or even grow a crust on top of them if they wanted to. She said none of this to her eldest daughter.

'Oh no dear, the dinner party isn't this weekend. It's in a month's time . . . I was just thinking ahead.'

Anna burst out laughing. 'Mother, you *are* full of surprises. A month ahead! Not even James would insist on that much planning. Anyway, we'll have plenty of time to talk about it before then.' She made it sound like basketwork in an occupational therapy ward. Carmel hid her annoyance and hoped they would have a nice weekend. The weather forecast was good, and especially in the south-west.

She thought that Anna and James were quite insane to drive two hundred and nine miles on a Friday afternoon and the same distance again on Sunday. She could see no point in having a house and garden out in Sandycove and never getting to spend a weekend there. The cottage in Kerry had been an albatross around their necks as far as Carmel could see. She never believed that they could enjoy the five hour drive. 'Four hours thirty-five minutes, Grandmama, if you know the short cuts . . . ' James always made her feel even more foolish with his Grandmama; she felt like a grand duchess. But still Anna never complained, she spoke of it eagerly: 'Oh Mother, it's so great, we get there around nine-thirty and light a fire, take out the steaks, open the wine, kiddies half asleep already, pop them into bed . . . it's so free . . . the country . . . our own place . . . you can't believe it.'

Anna had heard the weather forecast too. 'Yes I am glad, because we're having a huge lunch there on Sunday and it will be so much nicer if we can have them all out of doors.'

A huge lunch, down at that cottage, in the wilds of Kerry, miles from her kitchen, her deep freeze, her dishwasher. No wonder Anna must think her pathetic worrying about seating people at a dinner party a whole month away. But of course Anna didn't have the same kind of worries. Anna would never let herself get into a situation where she would have those kind of worries.

Carmel drew the table plan again. She wrote in the names of the guests carefully. At one end of the table with her back to the window she wrote Carmel, and at the opposite end she wrote out Ruth O'Donnell,

Most Important Lady. She filled in the other names and wrote things under them too. Dermot, Loving Husband. Sheila, Wise Friend. Ethel, Upper Class Friend. Martin, Kind Husband of Wise Friend. David, Pompous Husband of Upper Class Friend. And then on the right hand side of Ruth O'Donnell she wrote, slowly and carefully, Joe, Life-Saver. She sat and looked at the plan for a long time. It stopped being a drawing of a rectangle with little squares around it holding names and descriptions. It became a table with glasses and flowers and good china and shining silver. She could almost smell the food and hear the conversation. She learned it off by heart, the order they sat in, just like she had learned the Great Lakes or the towns of Cavan when she was a child, by rote with her eyes tightly closed, relating not to things as they were but as they were written down.

Then she took all the bits of paper and put them into the firegrate. There were still a few old clinkers and some bits of red from last night's fire, but she didn't trust them to burn. She took out half a fire-lighter and set a match to it. And there in the room where she would give the party in a month's time, she sat and watched the flames burn the lists and the table plans. They burned away until there were only powdery ashes left on top of yesterday's clinkers.

*　　　*　　　*

'I think Carmel Murray is losing her marbles,' said Ethel at breakfast.

David grunted. He was reading his own letters and he did not want to be distracted by Ethel's chat.

'No seriously, listen to this . . . ' Ethel went back to the start of the letter.

'In a moment, Ethel . . . '

'No, you'll just leap up and go off, I want you to hear.'

He looked at her and knew he might as well give in. Ethel got her way in everything, and it made for an easy life to accept this.

'Carmel has lost her marbles? Go on from there.'

'Well, she must have. She's written to us. Written to ask us to dinner . . . next *month* . . . can you believe it?'

'Well, that's nice of her,' said David vaguely. 'I suppose we can get out of it, what's the fuss, what's so mad about that? People do ask each other to dinner. They do it all the time.'

He knew he was courting trouble to try and be smartalecky with Ethel. He was right; it had been a mistake.

'I know people do it all the time, dear,' she said. 'But Carmel Murray has never done it before. Poor Carmel that we have to be nice to because Dermot's a good sort . . . that's why it's unusual. And did you ever hear of anything so strange? A letter when she only lives five minutes away, when she may have heard of the telephone.'

'Yes, yes. It is odd. I do agree. You must do what you wish, say we're away, say it's a pity . . . some other time. What?'

'She'll know we're not away. That's what's so odd, it's on the day of Ruth O'Donnell's exhibition, she'll know that we won't be out of town for that . . .'

'How do you know it's that day?'

'Because she says so in the letter . . . she says that she's asked Ruth as well. Now do you see why I think she's losing her marbles?'

Ethel looked flushed and triumphant, having

11

proved her point. She sat imperiously at the breakfast table wearing her silk breakfast kimono and waited for the apology from her husband. It came.

'She's inviting Ruth . . . Oh my God. Now I see what you mean.'

*　　　*　　　*

Sheila hated being disturbed at school. It made the nuns so edgy and uneasy to call someone to the telephone. They hadn't moved into the modern age in terms of communications, their telephone was still in a cold and draughty little booth in the main entrance hall, inconvenient for everyone. She was alarmed when she heard that her husband wanted her . . .

'Martin, what is it, what's happened?' she said.

'Nothing. Nothing, relax.'

'What do you mean, nothing? What is it?'

'Stop fussing, Sheila, it's nothing.'

'You brought me the whole way down here from third years for nothing? Sister Delia is looking after them as a great favour. What IS it, Martin? Are the children . . . ?'

'Look, I thought you ought to know, we've had a very odd letter from Carmel.'

'A what . . . from Carmel?'

'A letter. Yes, I know it's sort of out of character, I thought maybe something might be wrong and you'd need to know . . . '

'Yes, well, what did she say, what's the matter with her?'

'Nothing, that's the problem, she's inviting us to dinner.'

'To dinner?'

'Yes, it's sort of funny, isn't it? As if she wasn't

well or something. I thought you should know in case she got in touch with you.'

'Did you really drag me all the way down here, third years are at the top of the house you know, I thought the house had burned down! God, wait till I come home to you. I'll murder you.'

'The dinner's in a month's time, and she says she's invited Ruth O'Donnell.'

'Oh, Jesus Christ.'

*　　　*　　　*

Henry shouted out to Joe, 'Hey, that letter's come from Ireland. She must have fixed the date, poor old bat.'

Joe came in and opened it.

'Yeah, in a month's time, she says it's all going according to plan. She sent the ticket and the money.'

'She's all right, isn't she?' Henry sounded approving.

'Oh, she's really fine, and I owe her, I owe her in a big way. I'll make it work . . '

'Well, if you can't, I don't know who could,' Henry said admiringly and Joe smiled back as he fetched the coffee percolator.

*　　　*　　　*

"I think Mother's coming out of herself a bit more, darling,' Anna said to James as they negotiated the early evening traffic.

'Good. It's no wonder this country's going to the dogs. Look at the build-up of traffic here and it's not even four o'clock. I mean half of them must be taking the whole afternoon off. Never mind, we'll lose them in a few minutes. What were you saying about Grand-

13

mama?'

'She's talking of having a dinner party, you know, with a proper dining table, and a seating plan. It all sounds good.'

'I've always said that she's not nearly so sleepy and dozey as you and Bernadette make out. I find plenty of things to talk to her about.'

'No you don't, you just talk at her ... she sits enthralled because you're so interesting, but it's not a real conversation.'

James didn't agree. 'You're wrong, she tells me things. No, I can't remember anything immediately ... that's silly, looking for examples. But I do get on well with her ... she just needs a bit of flattery, a few cheerful things. 'You look very dishy, Grandmama' and she blossoms ... she doesn't like people telling her she's silly.'

Anna thought for a while.

'I suppose people do tell her she's silly. Yes, you're right. I always say "Don't be silly Mother", but I don't mean it. It's just that she fusses so much, and I think that if I say she's not to be silly, then it's sort of reassuring to her. I'll be very supportive about her poor old dinner party ... I'll give her a tactful hand here and there.'

James patted her knee.

'You're marvellous, sweetheart. And talking about parties, tell me what you've arranged for Sunday .. '

Anna settled back happily in her seat and told him about all the good things that were foil-wrapped, vacuum-packed and air-tight in the huge cardboard box which they had loaded carefully into the boot of the car.

14

Bernadette said, 'That's great, Mummy. Great. I'm sure it will be marvellous.'

'I just thought you'd like to know . . . ' Carmel said.

'Well, of course I'm thrilled, Mummy. Is it tonight, or when?'

'Oh no dear, it's a dinner party . . . it's not for a month.'

'A *month*! Mummy, are you all right?'

'Yes dear, perfectly.'

'Oh. Well. I mean, is there anything . . . do you want me to come and help you plan it, or anything?'

'No, no, it's all planned.'

'Or serve it? You know, keep you calm and stop you fussing on the night?'

'No no, dear, thank you, but I won't fuss at all.'

'Well that's great, Mummy, and is Daddy pleased that you're sort of getting into entertaining and everything?'

'It's not exactly getting into entertaining . . . it's just one dinner party.'

'You know what I mean. Is Daddy thrilled?'

'I haven't told him yet.'

'Mummy, are you sure you're all right, you're not getting upset or anything like . . . '

'Like what, dear?'

'Like that time when you *did* get upset.'

'Oh no, dear, of course I'm not. That was when I had the trouble with my sleep patterns, they got out of kilter . . . No, that's all totally cured, thank God, now. You know that, Bernadette dear. I sleep like a log these nights. No no, that's not come back at all, thank heavens.'

Bernadette sounded troubled.

'No, well, good. You have to look after yourself, Mummy. You know the way you fuss about silly things, I don't want you fussing about this party . . . '

'You don't understand, child, I'm looking forward to it.'

'Good, oh and we'll come and see you soon, it's been ages.'

'Whenever you can, dear. Ring first though, I'll be out a lot in the next few weeks . . . '

'Will you, Mummy? Where?

'Here and there, dear. Anyway, it will be great to see you. How's Frank?'

'He's fine, Mummy. Take care of yourself, won't you?'

'Yes, Bernadette. Thank you, dear.'

*   *   *

Dermot thought that Carmel was a hundred miles away that morning. Twice he had said that he might be late and not to worry if he dropped into the golf club on the way home. He had to have a few chats and that was the best place to have them. Twice she had nodded amiably and distantly as if she hadn't really heard or understood.

'Will you be all right? What are you going to do today?' he had asked, uncharacteristically.

She had smiled. 'Funny you should ask that. I was just thinking that I hadn't anything to do all day so I was going to stroll down town and look at the shops. I was thinking that it was almost a sinful thing to do . . just idling away the day. . . '

Dermot had smiled back. 'You're entitled to be that sinful, enjoy yourself. And as I said, if I'm late I won't want anything to eat. We might go and have a steak ... you know. Don't fuss, don't go to any trouble.'

'No, that's fine,' she had said.

As he sat in the traffic on Morehampton Road listening to the fool on RTE telling him exactly what he knew, that Morehampton Road was blocked solid, Dermot had a vague sense of unease about Carmel. But he shook himself and decided to put it out of his mind.

'I'm becoming quite neurotic,' he told himself. 'If she does hound me about my movements and tell me detail by detail the trivia of her day I become annoyed. Now I'm uneasy because she doesn't. Impossible to please me.' He decided that everyone was being too bright on Radio Eireann and turned to the BBC where they were more solemn and in keeping with a man's thoughts in the morning as he drove in to his office.

*   *   *

Ruth O'Donnell hadn't got her invitation because she was away. She had gone to a farmhouse in Wales for a complete rest. She could have gone to an Irish farmhouse, but she wanted to be sure that she didn't meet anyone she knew. It wouldn't be a complete rest if she met people. She wanted to be absolutely on her own.

*   *   *

Carmel waited until the end of the Gay Byrne show. During the Living Word she put on her coat and took out her shopping basket on wheels. She never liked to

17

miss Gay; once she had been able to give him a small cooker for a one-parent family. She hadn't spoken to him himself but the girl on the show had been very nice, and they had sent a nice girl to collect it, or else she was from the organisation which had asked for it. It had never been made quite clear. Carmel had sent in one or two entries for the mystery voice competition too, but she had never been called on to guess it. She didn't like to leave the house before the Living Word. It seemed rude to God, to walk out just when the few short minutes of religion were on.

She knew she should really listen to programmes like Day by Day which followed it, they would make her informed, but somehow she always felt her mind wandering and she never quite understood why people got so hot under the collar about things. Once she had said to Sheila that it would be nice to have someone sitting beside you to tell you what was going on in life, and Sheila told her to shut up, otherwise everyone would say they had learned nothing after all those years with the Loreto nuns . . . She thought that Sheila had been upset that day but she couldn't be sure.

It was bright and sunny out, a nice autumn day. She pushed her tartan shopping bag on wheels in front of her, remembering when it had been a pram that she pushed. She used to know many more people in those days. She was always stopping and talking to people, wasn't she? Or was that memory playing tricks, like thinking that the summers were always hot when she was young and that they had spent their whole time on Killiney beach? That wasn't true, her younger brother Charlie said that they only went twice or three times a summer; perhaps the other memory wasn't true either. Perhaps she didn't stop at

18

the bottom of Eglinton Road when she pointed out to the girls where the buses went to sleep in the bus home, perhaps there had been nobody much around then either.

She looked at the prices of wine in the off-licence and wrote down the names of some of them so that she could make her list and selection later on. She then spent a happy hour looking at books in the big book shop. She copied down recipe after recipe in her little jotter. From time to time she got a look from one of the assistants, but she looked respectable and was causing no trouble so nobody said anything. Seared in her mind was a remark that Ethel had once made about a house where she had dined. 'The woman has no imagination. I can't understand why you ask people round for prawn cocktail and roast beef . . . I mean, why not tell them to eat at home and come round later for drinks?' Carmel loved prawn cocktail, and had little glass dishes which it would look very well in. They used to have trifle in them when she was young. She had kept them after things had been divided up between herself and Charlie but she had never used them. They stood gathering dust, eight of them, at the back of the cupboard in the scullery. She would make another kind of starter, not prawn cocktail, and she would use those selfsame glasses for it, whatever it was. She rejected grapefruit segments and worked it out methodically. You couldn't have paté, that would have to be on a plate, or soup, that couldn't be in a glass, or any kind of fish of course . . . no, it had to be something cold you ate with a spoon.

She would find it eventually, she had all day, she had twenty-nine more days . . . there was no rush. She must not get fussed. She found it. Orange Vinaigrette.

Ethel couldn't say that that was unimaginative . . . you cut up oranges and black olives and onions and fresh mint . . . sounded terrific, you poured a vinaigrette sauce over it . . . it would be perfect. Carmel smiled happily. She knew that she was doing the right thing. All she had to do was go at it slowly.

She would go home now and rest; tomorrow she would come out and find a main course, and then a dessert. She had work to do at home too. Joe had said that if he was going to come and help her he would need co-operation. She mustn't have turned into a dowdy middle-aged old frump, she must look smart and glamorous and well-turned-out. She had thirty afternoons to organise that.

*   *   *

Sheila dropped in on her way home from school. She seemed relieved to find Carmel there, and there was a look of worry on her face.

'I was a little alarmed, Martin told me you had sent us a letter.'

'It was only an invitation,' Carmel smiled. 'Come on in and we'll have a coffee. I was in the middle of tidying out some cupboards . . I've a lot of clothes that should go to the Vincent de Paul . . . but you know what always happens, you're ashamed to give them the way they are, so you get them cleaned first. Then when they come back from the cleaners they're better than anything else you have in the press so you never give them at all.' Carmel laughed happily as they went into the kitchen and put on the kettle.

'It just seemed so funny to write, when I talk to you nearly every day . . . '

'Did it? Oh, I don't know, I'm such a bad hostess I

thought you have to write things down as invitations or people didn't believe you. I suppose that's why I wrote. I'd have told you anyway.'

'But you didn't tell me yesterday.'

'No, I must have forgotten.'

'There's nothing wrong, is there, Carmel? You *are* all right?'

Carmel had her back to Sheila. She deliberately relaxed her shoulders and refused to clench her fists. Nobody was going to see just how annoyed she became when people asked her in that concerned tone whether she was all right.

'Sure I am, why wouldn't I be, a lady of leisure? It's you who must be exhausted coping with all that noise and those demons all day. I think you should be canonised.'

'Tell me about the dinner party,' Sheila said.

'Oh, it's not for a month yet,' Carmel laughed.

'I know.' Sheila's patience seemed strained. 'I know it's not for a month, but you actually put pen to paper and wrote so I thought it was a big thing.'

'No no, just eight of us, I said it in the letter.'

'Yes, Martin told me, I wasn't at home when it arrived.'

'He rang you? Oh, isn't he good. There was no need to. I mean you could have told me any time.'

'Yes, and you could have told *me* any time.' Sheila looked worried.

'Yes, of course. Heavens, we are both making a production of it! When you think how many parties Ethel goes to, and indeed gives . . .'

'Yes, well, Ethel is Ethel.'

'And you, I mean you and Martin often have people round, don't you? I often hear you say you had people in.'

'Yes, but that's very casual.'

'Oh, this will be too. Mainly people we all know well.'

'But Ruth . . . Ruth O'Donnell . . . we don't know her all that well, and honestly, do you know, I think that's the night that her exhibition opens — in fact I'm sure of it.'

'Yes, I know it is, I said that in the letter. Didn't Martin tell you? So I know we'll all be going to it . . . but it's at four o'clock . . . it will be well over by six, and even if people go to have a drink afterwards . . . well, they're not invited here until eight, for half past.'

'Yes, but don't you think on the night of her own exhibition she might want to go out with her own friends?'

'But we're her friends, in a way.'

'Not really, are we? I mean, are you? She doesn't normally come here?'

'No, I don't think she's ever been here. I thought it would be nice for her . . . and she doesn't live far away, in that new block of flats, so she won't have far to go to change.'

Sheila put down her mug of coffee.

'I don't think it's a good idea. We don't know her. Why ask someone we don't know very well to a dinner? Let's just have the six of us . . . it would be more friendly.'

'No, I've asked her anyway, and I can't think what you say that for. You're the one who tells me to go out and meet more people.'

'I didn't tell you to go out and invite well-known artists to dinner,' muttered Sheila.

'Don't lecture me,' Carmel said with a laugh, and Sheila had to admit to herself that Carmel did look more cheerful and like herself than she had in the last while. She looked a bit more like the Carmel of the old days.

'All right, I won't. Let me see your cupboard cleaning. Maybe you could give something to me instead of the Vincent de Paul. I could do with it. A teacher doesn't get paid much, God help us, when you consider how we put our lives at risk.'

'How's Martin feeling?'

'Oh, he's fine. He's great, you know, he never complains. I'm sure he's fed up but he never complains.' Martin had been made redundant two years ago when two firms had merged. He had got a golden handshake. He was still only fifty-two and he expected to get another job, then he expected to write a book. Everybody else thought he was writing a book, but Sheila never lied to Carmel. To Carmel she admitted that Martin was doing the hoovering and the shopping. They pretended that Sheila loved being back in the classroom. Not many people knew how much she hated it. Her children didn't know, not even Martin really knew. Carmel sometimes suspected, but Carmel was a long-time friend It didn't matter what she knew. It was just a bit worrying sometimes the things she did. Like inviting that woman to dinner. Was there a possibility that Carmel's nerves were bad again? She sounded so well, and she looked fine. But it *was* the act of a madwoman.

'Hey, you are doing a thorough job. You've taken everything out. Which is the good pile and which is the bad pile?'

'I don't know, they all seem the same. They're like mouse clothes, aren't they? Do you remember when we went to pantomimes years and years ago? People were dressed in mouse outfits and rat outfits . . . that's what these are like!'

'Carmel, you are preposterous! Of course your clothes aren't like that, they're smashing. Have you two of these blue cardigans?'

'I think I've three of them. Whenever I go to a shop I can never think of anything to buy except grey skirts and blue cardigans. Have one of each.'

'I mean it. Quite, quite preposterous.'

Carmel smiled happily. Other people said 'Don't be silly'; Sheila said she was preposterous. It was much, much nicer.

*   *   *

'Well?' Martin wanted to know.

'I *think* she's all right. It's hard to know.'

'You mean it was a joke about the invitation?'

'No, she means it. She's having the party, she just doesn't want to talk about it.'

'Then she's not all right.'

'I know, but she *seems* normal. She gave me a skirt and a cardigan.'

'That makes her normal?'

'No, you know what I mean. She was talking about ordinary things. She hadn't gone off on any flight of fancy or anything . . . '

'So did you talk her out of it?' Martin wanted to know.

'I couldn't, she wouldn't talk about it at all. I *told* you.'

'Oh great,' he sighed. 'That's all we need. You're her friend, for Christ's sake.'

'Martin, I've had a bad day. Not just a bit of a bad day — every single bit of it was bad. I don't want to talk about it any more. I did my best to talk to

Carmel, she wouldn't talk back, that's all. Can't you leave me alone!'

'Yes, I know I should have had a drink ready and the fire lighting and tried to soothe away your cares . . like a proper housewife. I'm sorry I'm bad at it. You don't have to tell me.'

'Jesus, Martin, if this is the night you've picked to do a wretched "I'm not a good provider" act, then you've picked the wrong night. Will you shut up and sit down. I love you, I don't want you to fart around pandering to me just because *my* outfit didn't close down . . . do you hear me?'

He was contrite.

'I'm sorry. I really am. I'm just worried, that's all.'

'So am I.'

'Do you think she knows about Ruth? Do you think she heard anything . . . ?'

'How could she have heard anything? Who does she meet? Where does she go? Unless it was on the Gay Byrne Hour or in the Evening Press Diary she'd not have heard.'

'What are we going to do?'

'I haven't a clue.'

*   *   *

'I'm sorry I'm late,' called David. 'The traffic was bloody terrible. There's no point in taking a car in these days, I've said it over and over.'

'So have I, the number ten would take you to your door.'

'I can't travel on the number ten. It never comes, or it's full when it does.'

'Anyway, why buy a big car and not show it off?'

'What?' David sounded bad-tempered in the hall.

25

'Nothing. You said you're sorry you're late, get a move on then, if you want to change or wash or anything . . . '

'For what?' David sounded even crosser. 'Oh God, I'd forgotten. Do we have to? Can't we . . . ?'

'We *do* have to and we *can't* ring and say we're tied up. We accepted two weeks ago.'

'It's all very well for you.' David was pounding up the stairs crossly. 'You have nothing to do all day but get yourself ready . . . titivate . . . titivate.'

'Thank you,' Ethel said icily.

She sat at the dressing table in their bedroom. The door to the bathroom was open and he could see the thick coloured towels piled up on the chest of drawers. He knew he would feel much better when he had a bath, he knew it was unfair to blame her.

'I'm sorry,' he said.

He kissed her at the dressing table. She smelled whiskey.

'Do they serve cocktails in traffic jams?' she asked.

He laughed. 'You've caught me out. I dropped into the club.' He looked contrite.

'Which is of course on the route home.' She was still cold.

'No, of course it wasn't, but I took the lower road. Oh hell, I only had two, but do you know who was there? You'll never guess what happened.'

She was interested. He rarely told tales of interest from the outer world; she had to prod and pry and ferret to find out anything that might be happening. She followed him into the bathroom. He flung off his coat and struggled with his shirt.

'I met Dermot, Dermot Murray.'

'Oh yes?' She was as sharp as a hawk now, pique forgotten. 'What did he say?'

26

'Well, it's amazing, it's quite amazing.'

'Yes? Yes?'

'He was sitting talking to some fellows, I don't know who they were. I've seen one of them, perfectly respectable, in the property business, I think, out the Northside . . . anyway, he was in that corner place with them.'

'Yes . . . what did he say?'

'Wait, wait, I'm telling you.' David had run the bath as he was speaking. The water gushed with powerful pressure from each tap, the room had steamed up in under a minute.

'I said to him, "How are you, Dermot?"'

David stood in his underpants tantalising his wife by the meticulous way he was repeating the trivia of the conversation. She decided not to be drawn.

'I'll sit on the loo here and when you feel like telling me, do.'

He pulled the shower curtains around him when he got into the bath. This was a modesty that had grown somewhere around the same time as his paunch. When they had been younger they had often bathed together, and had always bathed in front of each other.

'No, it's really strange,' came the voice from inside the curtain. 'I said "Thanks very much for that invitation," and he said "What invitation?" and I got such a shock I started to play the fool. You know. I said, "Come on now. You can't welch on us now, an invite's an invite."'

'What did he say then?'

'He said, "You have me on the wrong foot, David. I don't actually know what you mean." He said it so straight, I felt a bit foolish. I just got out of it. I said that I had probably made a mistake, or that you

27

hadn't looked at the letter properly.'

'Thank you very much again,' said Ethel.

'I had to say something. Anyway he said, "Letter, what letter?" I was right into it then. I said, "Oh, it's some mistake. I thought we'd got a letter from you and Carmel inviting us to dinner. I must have got it wrong." He said it wasn't very likely that she'd have invited people without telling him. Maybe it was a surprise party.'

'Boy, some surprise if it is!' said Ethel.

'That's what I thought, so I said the date. I said it's on the eighth. He said, "Well I never. Maybe it's all a birthday treat and I'm not meant to know." But he looked worried. He said, "the eighth", again, as if it was familiar. Then he said, "Not the eighth?" And I said, nervously you know, "I'm sure I got it wrong" . . .'

'He doesn't know. She's doing it without telling him. She's asking us all round there for some kind of terrible drama. That's what it's all about.' Ethel's face looked stricken rather than excited. It should be an exciting thing . . . a public row, a scandal. But not with Carmel Murray. Poor Carmel, she was too vulnerable.

David got out of the bath and dried himself vigorously in one of the big yellow towels.

'He really doesn't know she's giving the party, the poor devil. Isn't that a dreadful thing? Thank God I said something, even though I felt I had walked into it. At least it will give him a bit of time to know what action to take.'

'But she can't know about Ruth, she can't possibly know.' Ethel was thoughtful.

'Somebody may have sent her a poison pen letter — you know, "I think you ought to know" . . . ' David was still towelling himself dry.

'You'll rub the skin off your back. Come on, get dressed. She can't know. If she knew would she in a million years ask her to dinner?'

*　　　*　　　*

Joe and Henry were cooking for a party. They often did home catering; it was very easy money. They made the canapés while they watched television, and put everything in the freezer. They got lots of free perks like clingfilm and foil from the hotel where Henry worked, and the use of a car from the tourist guide service where Joe worked.

'Why won't the old bat let you do the cooking for her if she's so nervous? You could run up a dinner in two hours.'

'No, that's part of it. She has to be able to do it all herself.'

'What does she look like? All sad and mopey, is she?'

'I don't know,' said Joe. 'I haven't seen her for twenty years. She may have changed a lot since then.'

*　　　*　　　*

'Hallo, Carmel, is that you?'

'Of course it is, love, who else would it be?'

'Carmel, I'm at the club, I told you, I've had to have a few chats, I told you.'

'I know you told me.'

'So I won't be home, or I wasn't coming home. Have you had your supper?'

'Supper?'

'Carmel, it's eight o'clock. I'm ringing you from the club to ask you a simple question: have you or have you not had your supper?'

'I had some soup, Dermot, but there's steak here, and cauliflower . . . I can cook whatever you like.'

'Did you write to David?'

'WHAT? It's very hard to hear you. There's a lot of noise behind you.'

'Forget it. I'll come home.'

'Oh good. Would you like me to . . . ?'

He had hung up.

* * *

All the way home he said to himself it was impossible. She couldn't have decided to hold a dinner party without telling him, and if she had, if by some mind-blowing horror she had decided to invite all their friends around to witness a scene of marital bliss . . . how could she have chosen the eighth of October?

It was Ruth's birthday, her thirtieth birthday. He had persuaded her to hold her exhibition that day, to show everyone that she had arrived. Ruth had said that she wanted no public exhibitions, no showing the world anything, unless he could stand beside her. She didn't want to go on hiding and pretending. When the reporters were sent to interview her she didn't want to have to laugh any more and parry questions about why she had never married. She felt foolish telling people that her art was her life. It sounded so hollow, so second best and so phoney. She wanted to tell them that she loved and was loved. It was this that gave her strength to paint.

She had agreed reluctantly. The gallery had been found with no trouble. People were anxious to hang the work of Ruth O'Donnell. The work was ready. She was drained. She said she wanted time away, far away, from him. She would not spend the days planning how to walk out of his life, she assured him of that, and he believed her. She just wanted to be free, to rest, and not to hide. He believed that too. He promised he wouldn't telephone her, nor write. That would be the same as being with him, she said. There was no point in a separation if you spent hours writing a letter and waiting for the post.

She was coming back on the first, a full week before it opened, in time to see everything hung. She had only left yesterday. It wasn't possible that coincidence should be so cruel as to mar this night for him by having a weeping Carmel on his hands. Because by God if she had arranged a dinner party for the eighth she was going to unarrange it fast. That was why he had left those two auctioneers sitting like eejits in the club. This had to be sorted out immediately.

*   *   *

'I think Mummy's a bit lonely,' Bernadette said to Frank.

'We're all lonely. It's the lot of men and women to go through life alone thinking they are with friends but only brushing off people.'

'I mean it,' Bernadette said. 'She's very good to us, Frank. She pretends she doesn't mind about us living together but she does, underneath.'

'Nonsense. Just so long as we don't do anything too public in front of all those friends of hers, she's as right as rain.'

'All what friends of hers? There's no friends.'

'There must be. Posh house there in the heart of society . . . of course she has friends. Didn't you tell me tonight that she's organising dinner parties months in advance?'

'That's what I don't like.'

'God, there's no pleasing you! You're like a gnat; say out what you want and I'll debate whether we'll do it or not. Do you want us to kidnap her and keep her in the bathroom here tied by a dressing-gown cord for the rest of her life?'

'No,' she laughed.

'What do you want, Ber?'

'I wondered if we might drop in tonight, on our way to the party. Please.'

'Aw God,' he said.

'Just for a little bit,' she begged.

'We'll be there all night,' he said.

'We won't. We'll just get off the bus, run in and have a few words and then run off again.'

'That's worse than not going at all.'

'No, it would ease my mind.'

'Ten minutes then, right?'

'Half an hour, right?'

'Twenty minutes.'

'Done.'

*　　　*　　　*

'Don't say anything to the O'Briens about it, will you?' Ethel said when they were in the car.

'What would I say? I'm not a one for gossip, I never talk about people. You're the one who likes to tell and be told.'

David had his eyes on the road but he knew his wife's profile was stern. 'No, I'll say nothing to anyone. God, do you think we should do something or say something? We can't sit back and let it all happen.'

'What can we do that would help, heavens above? You sound like Superman or the archangel Gabriel stepping in. What can we do?'

'I suppose we could say to Carmel that it's not a good idea, that she might like to think again.'

'It's amazing how you manage to hold down a job, let alone run your own business,' said Ethel acerbically.

'It's all due to the loyal little woman behind me. She had faith in me when no one else had,' he said in a mock country and western accent.

'Well, if ever I meet the woman behind you I can tell you one thing, I'll not invite her to dinner with all our friends,' said Ethel, and they drove on to the O'Briens in silence.

* * *

Frank and Bernadette were just leaving when Dermot's car drew up.

'Maybe he'd give us a lift,' said Frank optimistically.

'I think that's a bit too sunny a view. I wouldn't ask him,' said Bernadette. 'How are you, Dad?'

'I see it's the annual visit,' Dermot said.

'Hi, Mr Murray,' said Frank.

'Hallo, er . . .' said Dermot desperately, stumbling over his name.

Bernadette's fist clenched in her pocket. 'We were just in having a chat with Mummy. We're off to a party.'

'Don't let me delay you,' Dermot said.

'Oh Daddy, you can be very rude,' Bernadette said. 'Why can't you be nice and easygoing, and . . . '

'I don't know,' Dermot said. 'It must be something to do with having to go out and earn a living and take on responsibilities.'

'We work too, Daddy.'

'Huh,' said Dermot.

'Nice to have talked with you, Mr Murray,' said Frank in an affected American accent.

'Sorry,' Dermot said. 'I'm in a bad mood. You do work, both of you. I'm just worried about something. Come back into the house and I'll give you a drink.'

'That's mighty white of you, sir,' said Frank.

'No Dad, we've got to be off. We just looked in to see was Mummy all right.'

'And she is, isn't she?' Dermot sounded alarmed.

'Oh yes,' Bernadette said, a little too quickly. 'She's fine.'

*   *   *

'I heard your voices. Did you meet them in the drive?' Carmel asked.

It had always irritated Dermot that she called the small distance to the gate a 'drive': it was eleven steps from the hall door to the gate if you took giant steps, and the most you could make out of it was twenty little ones.

'Yes. What did they want?'

'Oh Dermot, they just called in, it was nice of them.'

'They said they came to see were you all right. Why did they do that?'

'That's what people do, dear, when they call to see other people.'

She looked cheerful and calm. There was no resigned martyred air about her. She wasn't making little jokes which were not funny. She had no hint of tears.

'Will we have a proper meal at the table or would

you like a snack by the television?' she asked. 'The phone was so crackly and with the sound of people behind I couldn't hear whether you had a meal or you hadn't. You kept asking me had I . . . '

'Sit down, love,' he said.

'Yes, I will in a minute, but what would you . . .'

'Sit down now, Carmel. I want to talk to you, not to your back drifting out the door.'

'All right, Dermot, all right. Now will this do?'

'Have you or have you not invited a whole lot of people here on the eighth of October?'

'Certainly not.'

'You haven't?' The relief was overwhelming. It spilled all over his face. 'I'm sorry, love. There was a silly misunderstanding.'

'No. I just asked our friends and decided we'd have a nice evening and cook a nice dinner. You know you often said . . . '

'What do you mean . . . ?'

'You've often said that we should have people around more, and somehow I usen't to feel able for it, but I decided you were right, so I just asked a few people . . . for dinner.'

'When? When?'

'Oh, ages away. The eighth as you said, the eighth of October. Just a simple dinner.'

'Who have you asked?'

'Just friends. Sheila and Martin, and David and Ethel, and . . . '

'You've invited them all here on the eighth?'

'Yes. And I've asked that nice Ruth O'Donnell, you know, the artist.'

'Carmel. What are you . . . ?'

'You remember her, we met her lots of times, and

you told me how good she was. We haven't seen her for ages, but I did say when I wrote to her that there would be lots of people she'd know . . . I mean, David even knows her professionally. His company gave her a grant once, I read . . . '

'Yes . . . '

'And she'll know Sheila, because I think she came to her school to give a lecture.'

'Why didn't you ask me — tell me?'

'But, Dermot, you're always telling me to do things on my own, use my own initiative. I did for once. I sent out all the invitations . . . and now that doesn't please you either.'

'But I think you've picked the wrong night. I think that's the night she's having her opening. I thought I told you . . . '

'Yes you did, I remember. You said she was only thirty and how well she'd done. I remember the date.'

'God.'

'So I thought it would be nice for her to have somewhere to go after it. I read in the papers that she isn't married and she doesn't even have a "situation" like our Bernadette, so I thought what would be nicer than for her to have somewhere to go on the night.'

'Yes.'

'So that's what I said in my letter to her, that it would be a nice rounding off for the evening.'

'How did you know where she lives?' His voice was a gasp.

'I looked it up in the telephone directory, silly!'

'You might have sent it to the wrong person . . . '

'But she told us she lived in the new flats. Remember? I'm not such a featherbrain after all, am I?'

*   *   *

'Sheila, can I have a quick word with you before you go into the school?'

'God, you frightened the life out of me, Dermot Murray. I thought you were a guard.'

'Look, have you a minute? Can we get back into your car?'

'Half the Sixth years already think you're propositioning me! What is it, Dermot? Tell me here."

"No, it's nothing to tell. I want to ask you, ask you something.'

Sheila's heart was leaden.

'Ask on, but make it quick. That bell rings and I'm like a bolt from the blue in the door.'

'Does Carmel know about Ruth?'

'I beg your pardon?'

'You heard me.'

'I didn't. I did *not* hear you. Begin again.'

'Does Carmel know about Ruth and me?'

'Ruth? Ruth O'Donnell?'

'Sheila, stop playing around. I know you know, you know I know you know. All I want to know is does Carmel know?'

'You're assuming a great many things. What is there to know? What should I have known? Stop standing there like a guessing game.'

'Sheila, please, it's important.'

'It must be. Why else are you up here in a convent? I haven't an idea what you're talking about.'

'Think, think quickly. I know you're being a good friend and an old school chum. But think what's for the best. I don't just mean the best for me, I mean the best for everyone.'

'What am I to think about?'

'Look, I've known you for years, Sheila, I'm not a shit, now am I? I'm a reasonable human being. Would

I be up here at this hour of the morning if I was a real bum?'

Every day that Sheila had paused at her car for one moment to search for an exercise book, to write a shopping list, to listen to the last bars of some song on the radio . . . the bell had shrilled across her consciousness. Why did it not do it today?

'I can't help you, Dermot,' she said. 'I don't know anything, I really don't. I don't talk about anything, I don't listen to anything. I'm no help.'

He believed her. Not that she didn't know about Ruth. He knew she knew about Ruth. But he believed her when she said she couldn't help him. She didn't know whether Carmel knew or not. She was as much in the dark as he was.

'What am I going to do?' he asked her.

And then the bell shrilled.

*　　　*　　　*

'I just telephoned to ask you more about this party you're giving,' Ethel said.

'I explained it all in the letter,' said Carmel. 'You will be able to come? You see I know how busy you all are so I trapped you by choosing the night of Ruth's exhibition.'

'Yes, of course we'll come. You don't have to trap us. Looking forward to it . . . I was wondering whether it was a surprise — a birthday surprise for Dermot or anything David met him in the club, and I hope he didn't let anything slip.'

'No, it's not Dermot's birthday. It may well be Ruth's, I think hers is in October, but no, it doesn't matter at all. I did tell Dermot I was thinking of having a party, but you know what men are, they never listen. Their minds are elsewhere. Probably just as well that we don't know where they are half the time, don't you think?'

Ethel had the uneasy feeling that Carmel was laughing at her. Nonsense, of course, but there was that kind of a feel about the way she spoke.

*　　　*　　　*

'Oh, Dermot, I can't tell you where she is. She said the whole point was that you and she were having a separation, wasn't it?'

'Look, I'll go down on my knees to you.'

Dermot had never liked Ruth's younger sister. A know-all, a moraliser and worst of all a contemporary of his daughter Anna's when they were at UCD.

'No, I swore I would reveal nothing. Ruth only told me just in case there was any real crisis, about the gallery, you know.'

'There's a very big crisis. I can't tell you how big.'

'Honestly, Dermot, ⁀ ǝ fair. Play it by the rules. Just leave her alone, can't you? It's only a couple of weeks.'

'Listen here, smarty pants,' Dermot had lost any veneer of manners by now. 'Go into Ruth's flat, where there will be a letter with a Dublin Four post-mark addressed to her. Open it and read it. If you think then that it's serious enough perhaps you could ring your sister and ask her to ring me. That's all.' He stood up to leave the travel agency where she worked.

'Wait. It's not some awful sordid thing . . . some scandal, is it?' The girl's lip wrinkled with disgust.

'It's only a dinner invitation, but she might want to ring me about it.'

He nearly took the door off the hinges as he left.

*   *   *

Dermot telephoned his office.

'Oh there you are, Mr Murray,' the girl on the switch said with relief. 'It's not like you to be late. I didn't know what to do with your calls. We've had . . . '

'I'm not feeling well today, Margaret. Kindly inform the manager, and ask Miss O'Neill to put someone else on the Foreign Exchange and move her own things to my desk.'

'But Mr Murray . . . '

'I'll call back later, Margaret. The important thing is that Miss O'Neill sits at my desk. Put any calls for me through to her, she will know how to deal with them.'

'When will you . . . ?'

'As I said, I'll call back later, Margaret. The bank is not going to grind to a halt just because for once the manager isn't well.'

He hung up and regretted it immediately. The child on the switch didn't care whether the bank ground to a halt or not. Probably hoped it would if the truth was known. Why had he been so snappy, she was bound to gossip about it too. If only he had just taken thirty more seconds to be soothing and reassuring then it would have passed unnoticed in the minutiae of the day . . . poor Mr Murray's not well, must have that bug, oh well, Miss O'Neill's looking after his work . . . and that would be that. Now the girl on the switch would be full of indignation . . . bit my nose off, snapped at me over nothing, all I was doing was asking, what do I bloody care where he is, what he does, he can take a running jump at himself.

Why couldn't he have had the patience to exchange just two more conventional remarks? He had been so patient, so very patient about everything so far. Why couldn't he have kept his temper this morning? He frowned at his reflection in the car mirror when he got back into the driving seat. He didn't like the middle-aged tense man that looked back at him. In his mind's eye he didn't see himself that way; in his mind's eye he saw himself as Ruth's man, her strong support, the one she ran to when she was exhausted with her work, when she was full of doubts. To the little girl on the switch back at the bank, he was probably middle-aged Mr Murray, and if she knew about Ruth (which she might well in this village that they called a city) then she would think he was pathetic with his bit on the side, or a louse cheating on his wife.

Dermot didn't feel like driving anywhere. He got out of the car again and walked until he reached the canal. It was a nice crisp morning. Other people were still in their cars choking with fumes. These must be big executives, the top men, if they could come in to work as late as ten to ten, or was that right? If they were top men maybe they should have been at their desks since seven-thirty? Maybe they were the kind of men who had inherited a family business and who didn't have to work hard because they were the bosses' sons. Funny how you saw different sides of society when you stepped off your own little tread-mill for a bit.

Two women passed him on the canal path, bright laughing women in headscarfs. One was carrying a huge plastic bag and the other a large stuffed pillow-case; they were on their way to the launderette. They were the kind of women that Carmel would describe as nice poor things. And yet they weren't nearly as poor as poor Carmel. They were carting their families' washing off without a look of resentment about them. Carmel might be bending over the controls of a washing machine in her own kitchen but more likely she would just sit and stare out into the back garden. He had looked at her in off-guard moments over the last few months and this was how she was when in repose. Her face was empty as if she had left it and gone somewhere else.

He had hoped she would find interests, but he realised more and more that this was a vain hope. She had no interests. She had nothing whatsoever that would lift her out of that sad pose. When Anna and James had had the first baby Dermot thought that this would absorb Carmel's time, a grandchild out in Sandycove. He was certain she would be out there every second day, or encouraging Anna to leave the child in Donnybrook while she went about her business. But Dermot hadn't understood about modern young mothers like Anna. Cilian first, and then Orla, had just become part of her own life as if they were adults. They were constantly being strapped and unstrapped into car seats. They moved with a battery of educational toys, they were quite self-sufficient wherever they went. Doting grandmothers did not come into the picture at all.

And then of course that strap Bernadette shacked up with that Frank; 'my flat mate,' no less, she called him. She hadn't been much help or support for her mother, had she? Dermot muttered to himself about her. A lot of use it had been paying for her at the College of Art, quite happy to help friends out, to step in and sell things for someone who was stuck.

And friends? Carmel was a great one for talking about the Girls. Where were the girls now when they were needed? That Sheila, the schoolmistress rushing into the convent this morning as if her life depended on it. Great friend she'd be if anyone needed one; 'I don't talk, I don't listen, I don't know things . . .' marvellous! And who else was there? There was Ethel . . . she and Carmel had got on quite well at one stage. But there as well as anywhere else Carmel hadn't been able to cope. She had talked and talked about not returning David and Ethel's hospitality, and not accepting any more of it. Why hadn't she just said 'Come around to supper,' the way Ruth did, the way anyone did . . . anyone except Carmel.

It was fooling himself really to think she would be happier without him, fooling himself to say she wouldn't really notice if he left. She would not be able to cope. She couldn't even muster the politics of solidarity and hate, like that woman they had heard of in Ballsbridge, the wife of the man in the public relations agency. She had been so outraged when he left that she had aligned dozens of women on her side. You could hardly mention the man's name now without hearing a sibilant hiss, so blackened had it become. No, Carmel would do nothing like that.

Dermot stopped suddenly. Carmel would do nothing. And that was why he could never leave her. She would do nothing at all. For the rest of his life he would come home, tell lies, make up excuses, invent conferences, be telephoned by mythical clients who had to be seen after hours. And Ruth would do nothing. Ruth would not make a scene, demand that he choose between them, Ruth would confront nobody, insist on no showdowns. This had been the way things were for two whole years . . . everyone secure in the knowledge that nobody else would do anything; Ruth knowing she would never have to make her mind up about him fully, Carmel knowing that she would never lose him utterly and he knowing that he need never be forced to say 'I'll take this one' or 'I'll take that.'

He laughed wryly to himself. It was most people's idea of a married man's dream: an unquestioning wife and an unquestioning mistress. But it was a bad dream, he could write a book on what a bad dream it was. You were happy in neither place, you were guilty in both places. The very fact that nobody was making any move made it all the more insoluble. If Carmel had threatened and pleaded, perhaps, if Ruth had issued ultimatums, perhaps. *Perhaps* it might have been better. But nothing ever happened. Until now. Until Ruth had been invited to dinner.

*   *   *

Carmel *must* know, he said to himself for the five hundredth time. She *must* know. And yet the memory of last night had been like a vivid movie running through over and over.

'Tell me, why have you decided to ask Ruth O'Donnell whom we hardly know, whom you only met twice, to dinner? Carmel, what are you playing at?'

'I'm not playing at anything except being a better homemaker. She's nice. Everyone says so.'

'But why? Tell me, what made you think of a dinner? Why a month away?'

'To give me time to prepare to get ready. I'm not like all these marvellous women you admire so much who can have the entire golf game round for a six-course meal with no notice. I like to take my time.'

She had looked at him with a round innocent face.

44

She had prattled on about Sheila having called in, about Anna and James driving off to the cottage, about how she wished she could get the Christmas presents months ahead in September when the shops were nice and empty.

Four times he asked her in a roundabout way, four times she had answered him with a level look. She just liked the idea of having people to dinner; why was he finding fault with it? And he never answered that question, not even with a lie.

*   *   *

They went to Mass at eleven o'clock in Donnybrook church and bought the papers outside.

'Do you need anything from the shops?' Dermot asked. 'Ice cream? a pudding?'

'No, I'm on a diet, but you get some if you like,' she said pleasantly. He had looked at her face as she prayed; he had watched her come back from Communion with her head down. She never asked him why he didn't go to Communion, she never asked him anything.

*   *   *

Anna and James were happy. It had been a glorious day and they had had their lunch out in the open. Twelve of them had sat and looked out over the bay and said that this was the life and they must all be mad to live in Dublin. Anna had arranged that a local woman make fresh soda bread and they had had this with their paté. Everyone had raved about it. Cilian and Orla played at a distance with the three visiting children. Some of their friends had been staying at an hotel, others had rented a cottage . . . they all looked with open envy at the ease and comfort which James and Anna had built for themselves. This was balm to Anna and James. They stood and waved in the evening as the last guests drove off, they had cups of tea to get rid of the sleepiness the white wine had spread, and they looked at the clock. James had an iron rule: on the road back at seven. This meant an hour to wash up and tidy and pack the children and themselves — plenty of time.

They moved around the cottage gathering the bagful of educational toys. They plunged their twelve plates, twelve glasses, twelve forks and twelve knives into the hot soapy water. A rubbish sack was collected, carefully tied up and put in the boot as well. There were no dustmen in this part of heaven, they laughed to each other. Cilian and Orla, sleepy from the day in the sun, were strapped in, the cassette of James Last was at the ready and they faced the road across the country.

They spent much of it congratulating each other on the cottage. Although they would never have admitted it, even to each other, there were times when they thought it was becoming a bit much for them. But on a day like today when they could see the admiration and the jealousy of the people who sat around in the sunshine, then it was all worth it a hundred times over. They forgot the weekends they had arrived to find pipes burst, roof leaking, ants walking the kitchen floor in their thousands, mice making nests in the window boxes . . . all that was as nothing. The strings of the Last orchestra thudded and swept in the background.

James said: 'Do you know that your father's having an affair with Ruth O'Donnell, the artist?'

'Dad? Don't be ridiculous.'

'He is though, I heard it before. I heard it from someone who met them in London, of all places. Wouldn't you think you'd be safe having it away in London, ten million people, but no, spotted in flagrante.'

Anna looked around almost automatically to see if the children were asleep. If their grandfather's adultery was going to be discussed it would not be devant these enfants, she thought.

'I don't believe a word of it.'

'Honestly, sweetheart, Frances and Tim were talking about it this afternoon. They didn't like to mention it in front of you.'

'So that's what you were wittering on about. I thought it was business.'

'No, they tell me they see him often coming out of Ruth's apartment block, you know.'

'The new one . . . yes . . . heavens above.'

'Are you upset, are you upset that I told you?'

'I don't believe it, not *Dad*. I mean, he fancies her maybe and goes in and has the odd little drink. But not an affair, not sleeping with her, not Dad.'

'Um.'

'Well, don't you agree?'

'I don't know, I only tell you what I hear.'

'You think it's possible that Dad would have a real affair?'

'That's what is said.'

'But why would she? I mean she's young and well known and got her own life . . . she could have anyone or no one if she wanted. What on earth would she want with Dad?'

'Who knows? People want extraordinary people.'

'Yes.'

'You are upset. I shouldn't have told you like that straight out. It's just . . . well, it was on my mind.'

'I'm not upset. I don't know why. I suppose when I was young like everyone I was always terrified if they had a row that they were going to part. But they didn't, nobody ever did. Things just go along drifting. That's what happened to marriages in those days.'

'And in *these* days, it would appear.'

'What do you mean?'

'Well, they say that your Papa and Ms. O'Donnell have been constant companions for two to three years.'

'Never!'

'Apparently.'

'Imagine at Christmas, and the year before and the year before . . . all the family party . . . and all the time . . . I don't believe it.'

'Do you think Grandmama knows?'

'I'm certain she doesn't. Poor Mother. How odd, I don't know why I'm not all crying and thinking it's the end of everything. I suppose I just haven't accepted it.'

'I don't know why I told you.' James looked worried. 'It's only making you sad, but it seemed a big secret to keep from you . . . we don't have secrets.'

'No.'

'And you're so practical, I thought you'd want to know about it in case there's anything you wanted to do.'

'Like what, frighten her off? Please leave my Daddy alone?'

'No, but you do know her sister, don't you, Deirdre?'

'Yes, Deirdre O'Donnell, she was in college with me. God.'

'So there we are.'

'There we are all right. Are you shocked?'

'I'm a bit stunned, like you. I can't see my father-in-law in the role, but I think I'm mainly sorry for poor Grandmama. I thought that's what you'd feel most.'

'No. Mother will survive. She's very rarely living in the real world anyway. She seems a bit stoned to me a lot of the time. I wouldn't be surprised if that doctor has her on valium most of the time. That's why he's such a success with all that generation, he just prescribes it by the ton . . . takes the edge off life, that's his motto.'

'Yes, well, it looks as if your mother's going to need her supply.'

'Yes, but in a way why should she? I mean if it's been going on for years, nothing's going to change.'

'I suppose not. Check the mileage, will you, I'm turning in here for petrol.'

Anna got out the little leather covered book and wrote in 11878 under mileage, Tralee under place, and then sat with her pencil poised until she could fill in the remaining two columns, gallons and price.

*   *   *

'I'm not going to spend a month going in and out playing cat and mouse with them. I'm not going to do it,' Sheila said on Sunday evening. She had the dining-room table covered with books that she was marking for tomorrow's class.

'I suppose you could just be there, you know, if she needed you, that would be a help,' said Martin. He was doing the crossword while Sheila corrected her exercises.

'That's not the point. It's unforgiveable being drawn into other peoples' rows and scenes and disasters. I'll never forgive him for accosting me like that and forcing me to take sides and attitudes. People shouldn't drag you into their unhappinesses, it's not fair.' She looked very cross and bit on the end of her pencil in annoyance.

'No, stop being tolerant and forgiving, Martin. It's a fact. We never drag people into our marriage, now do we?'

'No,' said Martin thoughtfully. 'But then we're very lucky we don't have any problems in our marriage.'

'No,' said Sheila sharply, going back to the exercise books. She had resolved long ago that if she was going to be the breadwinner, she wasn't going to complain and ruin it all by being a martyr. The only thing that made the whole bloody business worthwhile was that Martin had no idea how tired she was and how much she hated going in to that school each day. She thought of Carmel for a moment, and a great wave of impatience flooded over her. Carmel could get up at any time she liked, she had nothing more pressing in her day than to decide which clothes she should send to the St Vincent de Paul. Carmel's children were married. Well, Bernadette was as good as married. They weren't pounding home with huge appetites for meals which had to be prepared and shopped for. Sheila tried to give the appearance of being in charge of the kitchen so that Martin's sons should not think him a sissy. They still said 'thanks, Mum' when they found their clean clothes in their bedrooms, though as often as not it was their father who had done them.

In a way Carmel had only herself to blame if she was miserable and wretched over all this business about Ruth O'Donnell. Carmel was a lady of leisure with too much time to think about the too little she had to do. Then with a jolt Sheila remembered that it was she and Martin and Dermot who were wretched. Carmel had been very cheerful, and was in fact busy organising a dinner party and smartening up her wardrobe. Not at all what this wronged wife would have been expected to do.

*   *   *

Ethel and David had people in to bridge on Sunday night. They always had what they called a curfew on Sunday nights, and every one had to have played the last card by eleven-thirty.

When the car had driven off and they were emptying the ashtrays, opening the windows and taking out the dirty glasses to the dishwasher, Ethel said: 'I have the most awful feeling, like doom, as if something dreadful is going to happen. Do you know that feeling?'

'Every day going into work, and it's always accurate,' said David.

'Don't be trivial, you love your work, and why wouldn't you? People fussing over you, fuss fuss fuss all day. No, I have a sense of foreboding and I can't think what's causing it.'

'Maybe you feel guilty about something,' David said.

'It's that kind of feeling, that sort of heavy feeling in the chest, but I've nothing to be guilty about.'

'I think it's the bank manager's bit of skirt. I honestly think that's what's making us all so uneasy. I feel a bit edgy myself.'

'But we've known about it for ages.'

'Yes, but the poor sad wife must have only just found out.'

Ethel stood looking at a plate of peanuts thoughtfully. Eventually she tipped them into the pedal bin. 'I'd only eat them,' she said as an explanation, 'and they're more fattening than large g's and t's. I suppose that is what's making us nervous. It's such a mad thing to do. Such a very men in white coats mad thing to do. Ask the woman to dinner and have a public scene.'

'She won't go of course,' said David.

'No, but the fact that poor Carmel actually asked her is so mad. That's what's upsetting. Who knows what she'll do next, walk down Grafton Street in her knickers?'

*   *   *

Deirdre O'Donnell had no trouble in getting the porter to give her a key to her sister's flat. She said that Ruth wanted her to post on some things.

She wandered around, luxuriating in being alone among someone else's possessions. Now you could look and stare and ponder to your heart's content. Everyone else in the block had their sittingrooms carefully draped and framed. They looked like the rooms in a doll's house from outside. But Ruth's sitting room was bare, it was in fact her studio, and what other people regarded as the master bedroom and decked with fitted cupboards and thick carpets, Ruth used as a secondary studio and office. The small spare bedroom was her bedsitting room; a sofa that turned into a bed sat neatly in its sofa role, and in the kitchen the saucepans sat shining in a row.

For an artist her sister was very neat, Deirdre

thought. Spinsterish she had once believed ... that was before she knew about the regular visits of Anna Murray's father. FATHER. A bank manager. Maybe she should go to him to authorise an overdraft. Seriously, that's not a bad idea at all.

On the mat there were a dozen envelopes. Some were obviously brochures or advertisements. Then she saw the letter in the neat round handwriting. She eased it out carefully. It might be full of terrible intimate things ... things that Ruth would not want her to have read. She must steam the envelope; she could stick it all back with glue if it really was too yucky and Ruth would get into a temper.

Dear Ruth,

I don't know whether you remember me or not, but we met a couple of times with David and Ethel O'Connor and you also know my friend Sheila Healy who says you gave a wonderful lecture at her school. Anyway, we are great admirers of yours and so looking forward to your exhibition on October 8th.

I'm going to try to steal you for that night to come to dinner with us. This is why I'm writing to you so far in advance; I am sure you will get many invitations nearer the time but I want to be first in with mine. We will have the O'Connors and the Healys as well, so you will be among friends.

Please let me know soon if you can come. I'm one of these middle-aged fussy sort of women who spend ages getting things organised, not like you and your friends. I'm sure you can combine about three lives successfully, but I'll be setting and resetting the table for days before you come, and then I'll pretend it all happened of its own accord.

It will give us all a great deal of pleasure if you say yes, and I know Dermot my husband would be thrilled. He has bought three of your paintings for our home. I hope you will like the way we have had them hung. So looking forward to seeing you.

Yours cordially,
Carmel Murray

Poor old cow, thought Deirdre, probably something wrong with her glands. She must know about Ruthie, half the country does. I don't think there's anything for old Dermot to get his knickers in a twist about, but I'd better ring her just in case.

Because Deirdre O'Donnell was essentially a frugal person she saw no reason why she shouldn't make the call from Ruth's own telephone. After all, it was Ruth's romance. It was Ruth's fellow's wife who had gone off her head . . . why not let Ruth pay for the call?

*　　*　　*

The farmer's wife knocked on her door and said there was a telephone call from Dublin.

'Your sister said you mustn't get alarmed. She says there is no problem.'

Ruth got up. She had been lying on the bed over the covers, reading. It was very luxurious somehow to do that, like going to the pictures in the afternoon.

'Ruthie?'

'What's happened?'

'Nothing, I told the old dame that. Nothing. Listen, Romeo asked me to contact you . . . '

'I told you I didn't want any messages. *Any.*'

'I told him that, he said that his wife has gone off

54

her head, and she's written to you.'

'Oh no.'

'It's all right, she hasn't called you the whore of Babylon. She's inviting you to dinner actually, the night your exhibition opens.'

'She's WHAT?'

'Do you want me to read it to you? "Dear Ruth, I don't know whether you remember me or not" . . . '

'Stop, stop. Is this serious?'

'Yes, but there's no abuse in it. Honestly, it's all full of admiration.'

'Oh Lord. What does Dermot say?'

'He wants to get in touch with you about it. I told him to leave you alone, but he said . . . '

'And did he say that she knows?'

'Ruthie . . . of course she knows. What are you talking about? She must know.'

'Dermot always said she didn't, or that if it came into her head she put it out again.'

'You must be mad. Do you think you're invisible or something, Ruthie? The two of you go everywhere together.'

'But if she knows, what's she inviting me to dinner for?'

'Well, that's the point, that's what Lover Boy was so much in a tizz about.'

'What does he think?'

'I don't know. I suppose he thinks that she's gone over the top, poor old thing. Do you want me to read it to you?'

'Yes, I suppose you'd better. If I've got to ring Dermot about it I'd better know what she says.'

'Right: "I don't know whether you remember me" . . . '

'Hey, Deirdre. This must be costing you a fortune.'

55

'No, it's costing you a fortune . . . the wages of sin, you know.'

'Oh go on, read it.'

*   *   *

Carmel planned her week carefully. It was nice to have so many things to do, it reminded her of being young again, when every day was so full and there seemed to be no waiting about. She would have to choose the main course and the dessert too. That would take two mornings in the bookshop reading the recipes. She was going to have a facial twice a week . . . oh, over on the North side of the city where she wouldn't be known . . . she would take the bus. She was going to spend two mornings shopping for her shoes. She had the dress already; the very good black dress which she had bought when Anna was 21 five years ago. She had worn it that evening . . . the first time . . . that first time when she had discovered about Dermot and the other girl . . . the time she had got so upset. She had never worn it again. But this time she would wear it and it would look magnificent. She would be much thinner . . . she was going to lose a stone this month. Her hair would be much more attractive . . . that man in Grafton Street who had done Ethel's hair was going to put highlights in for her a week before the party. She had telephoned and asked him what would be the best time. She had even told him she was a middle-aged lady, not a dollybird. 'I like coiffing mature ladies,' he had said.

Coiffing. It had sounded vaguely suggestive.

And there were so many other things to do. Window cleaners to come in. That firm which came and shampooed your carpet in the house. And her notebook to fill in.

She had written down anything anyone said about successful entertaining, like that thing Ethel had mentioned about the prawn cocktails and the roast beef.

She remembered Anna once talking about a house she had visited. 'They had fresh flowers in the bathroom, Mother, in the bathroom!' That had been included in the notebook. She had read an interview with a famous hostess who had said that the whole secret of successful entertaining was to have plenty of highly-polished glass and thick damask napkins on the table. That was noted, beside the advice about having a lot of salts, peppers and butterdishes so that people didn't have to keep passing them from one end of the table to the other.

Happier than she had been for a long time and armed with a list of the better cookery books, she started off for Donnybrook. At the hall door she met Anna.

'Oh dear! Why didn't you let me know you were coming, dear? I'm just off,' she said, regretfully but firmly pulling the door behind her.

'Hey, that's very welcoming,' Anna said, surprised. 'I bring your only grandchildren to visit you and that's what we get shown . . . the door.'

'Hallo Cilian . . . hallo Orla . . . ', she waved at them through the window.

Cilian struggled with his harness. 'Grandmama, Grandmama,' he called.

'Ah look, he wants to come to you,' Anna said.

'I'm sorry, darling, Granny's got to go out. Hallo Orla, blow Granny a kiss.'

'You might just ask us in for a cup of coffee.' Anna sounded huffed. 'We drove all the way in from

Sandycove to see you.'

'Oh, I am sorry.' Carmel was on her way to the gate.

'But where are you going to, Mother?'

'I'm going out dear, I have things to do. Will you still be in town this afternoon? Bring them in then and we'll have afternoon tea. Wouldn't that be nice?'

'Yes, but Mother, I wanted to have a little chat . . .'

'Grand. We'll have a little chat this afternoon.'

She was gone. Walking purposefully off towards the main road and the good brisk invigorating stretch towards the shops.

Anna looked after her, bewildered. Normally Mother was almost pathetically grateful for a visit, and fussed and ran about like an overgrown puppy. Here she was, striding off with no explanation. She looked after her, and Mother, as if she felt her eyes, turned and waved before she went around the corner. It was funny how people looked much younger when they moved quickly. Mother didn't look bad at all in her navy jacket and her check skirt. She didn't look fifty or fifty-one or whatever she was. Sometimes when she sat in that chair looking out into the back garden she looked seventy. Poor Mother, wasn't Dad awful to be fooling around with a young girl? Ruth O'Donnell too . . . but James was wrong, it couldn't be sex . . . it was just the thrill of the thing, the illicit excitement. Dad in bed with a girl? It was hard enough to imagine Dad being in bed with Mother years ago, but now . . . these days . . . Dad was so old he wouldn't even be interested in it, would he? And suppose he was, who in their right mind would go to bed with Dad?

Anna shrugged and got back into the car.

'Wasted journey,' she said to the children, who set up a simultaneous squawk of disappointment.

*   *   *

'Private call, Mr Murray, will you take it here or . . .?'

'That's all right, put me through . . . '

He knew it was Ruth from the way she spoke. She had a way of saying 'private call' that was almost lascivious.

'Dermot, can you talk?'

'Go ahead.'

'In other words you can't.'

'Not yet.'

'I got a call from Deirdre.'

'So she told you the situation . . . '

'She read me the letter, it sounded as if she doesn't have a clue.'

'Yes, well that's what I've always been saying . . .'

Dermot Murray's secretary felt she had tortured him enough. 'Excuse me,' she murmured and left the room.

'So what will I do . . . ?'

'Listen, darling love, when are you coming back?'

'In ten days, two weeks . . . '

'I love you.'

'You're alone now presumably . . . '

'No I'm in the board-room, and the board all agree. They love you too.'

She giggled. 'Dermot, what will I do, will I write and say I'm tied up?'

'It means a lot to her, it means a great great deal. She's so lively and happy since she thought of the party, you have no idea, it stops that deadness. When

I see her like this I can really imagine her living a life, a normal life of her own . . . '

'So what do you want . . . ?'

'Could you accept?'

'Say I'd love to, and then sort of opt out at the last moment?'

Dermot paused. 'Yes . . . and, well, maybe in the end, if you could come, could go to the dinner. Could you?'

'WHAT?'

'Well, it wouldn't mean all that much to you . . . to us. We have so much, and there you are, a brilliant young girl with your life before you and all that . . . '

'You can't seriously expect me to come into your house as a guest, and say how nice, how delicious, you must give me the recipe for that boiled cabbage.'

'Ruth, please.'

'No, no please about it, you're sick, that's what you are. I couldn't possibly do it. I wouldn't dream of doing it to another woman, go in triumphantly and sit down with a lot of people who are in the secret. It's monstrous!'

'You don't understand . . . '

'I don't like what I do understand. Why are you going along with it?'

Her voice was upset; the pips went.

'We can't talk on the phone, let me come to see you.'

'NO. I wanted to be alone. You set all this up as a trick didn't you . . . admit it.'

'I swear to God I didn't, I swear I only heard about it on Friday. I might never have heard if I hadn't met David in the club. I don't think she was going to tell me.'

'You mean you were going to come home and find

everyone there?'

'I don't know. I don't know.'

'But she must have known that I would have told you . . . she must have known that . . . '

'She doesn't *know* about you and me! I keep telling you!'

'Deirdre says that's lunacy . . . half of Dublin knows.'

'Deirdre doesn't know anything — anyway, Carmel never meets half of Dublin.'

'Oh God, I knew you couldn't let me have this time without spoiling it. I knew you'd have to do something to balls it up for me.'

'That is so unfair. I don't even know where you are. I won't talk to you again until you come back. I just wanted you to know what happened. If I hadn't told you, you'd have said I was being devious, wouldn't you? Well, wouldn't you?'

She softened. 'I know.'

'So if you could do one thing for me, just one. Write a note and say that you are away in the country, that the letter was forwarded to you, and that you'd love to come. Can you do that?'

'No, Dermot, I am not a puppet, I will not be manipulated into awful, sordid, cruel scenes like that. I will not do it.'

'Just say you'll come, accept, people are always accepting things they don't go to in the end. Accept, and when you come back you and I will talk, and then you'll do whatever you like . . . '

'And you won't steamroll me into doing what I don't want to do?'

'No, Ruth my love, I will not.'

'And if I write this hypocritical note saying yes, you really think this is for the best . . . ?'

'I do.'

'For all of us, for her and for me, as well as for you?'

He paused. 'Yes. Seriously I do. For her, because she can go on planning her party and it will make her, well, busy and active again, and that's what we want. We want her to have a life of her own.'

'And how will it help *me*, to accept?'

'Well, you can stop worrying about it. Once you've written a letter saying yes, then a decision is made. You can unmake it any time, but you don't have to dither.'

'And how will it help you?'

'Then I can see her absorbed in something, and that's a hell of a lot more positive than seeing her sitting staring out the window and wondering what the future has in store.'

'What does the future have in store?'

'It has you coming home to me soon. It has your exhibition and all *that* means . . . '

'I wish I didn't love you.'

'I'm very glad you do.'

'A ridiculous married bank manager, hundreds of years older than me, knowing nothing about painting . . . '

'I know, I know.' He sounded soothing. He was happy now; once Ruth got on to the groove of how unsuitable he was, he felt safe.

'I must be quite mad.'

'You are, you are. Very,' he said.

'I'll write the letter, but I won't go.'

'Good girl,' he said.

*   *   *

Dear Mrs Murray,

What a nice surprise to get your letter.

I didn't even think you'd remember that we had met. It's very nice of you to say such flattering things about my work and I am most grateful for your dinner invitation on the night of the exhibition.

I am writing this from Wales where I am spending a quiet holiday. (My post is forwarded to me, so that's how I got your letter.) I should be very happy to accept. I look forward to renewing my friendship with you, your husband and your other friends.

Sincerely,
Ruth O'Donnell

Carmel held the letter tightly in her hand after she'd read it. Relief flooded her face. She had been almost certain that Ruth O'Donnell would accept, but there had been the slight fear that she might ruin the whole plan. Now everything was all right. Everything was on target.

That night Dermot told her that she was looking very well, very healthy-looking. Carmel smiled, pleased. 'I've been walking a lot lately, I find it does me good.' That was true, she did walk and it did make her feel as if it were doing good. But she didn't tell him about the facial she had had — the second this week. The beautician had been giving her a rejuvenating mask. And she didn't tell him that she had now settled on veal with marsala for the main course, and pears baked in wine for the dessert.

She didn't tell him that she had got a letter that day from Ruth O'Donnell.

*　　*　　*

Bernadette and Anna had lunch together. Anna had a salad and a coffee; Bernadette had a huge lump of French bread and cheese, and drank a pint of Guinness.

'Only point in having lunch in a pub, really, having a pint,' she said.

Anna swallowed her disapproval. They had met to discuss what they should do about Mother and Dad, if anything. There was no point in beginning by criticising each other.

'Are you sure . . . it's not just gossip?'

'No, a lot of people know, apparently we're the last to know.'

'Well, that stands to reason,' Bernadette said logically, 'people aren't going to discuss our father's little peccadillos in company where we are sitting there listening.'

'Now, should we say anything?'

'What could we say? Do you mean ask Dad is it true?'

Anna thought. 'Yes, we could do that I suppose, and sort of say that we think it's dreadful and that it must come to an end.'

Bernadette pealed with laughter.

'Anna, you are marvellous, you're just like a dowager duchess. "I think, Father, this is quite dreadful. It must come to an end. Back to Mother. Quick quick. As you were."' She rocked with amusement at the thought of it. Anna did not rock at all.

'Why is that funny? What do *you* suggest?'

'I'm sorry, I shouldn't laugh. What *do* I suggest? I don't know. I suppose we could ask him does he intend to go off with Ruth and leave Mother, because that's the only thing we have a *right* to know really.

I mean, if he does, she'll crack up . . . '

'Yes,' Anna agreed. 'That's the point. He must be made to see that he can't do that to her.'

'He may want to do it, but he must realise that's what's going to happen, and I suppose he should be given the facts about how much he can rely on you and on me . . . to pick up the bits.'

'Well, he can't expect us to look after . . . '

'No, he probably doesn't expect anything . . . I think he should be put in the picture, that's all . . . '

Anna was surprised to see her younger sister being so firm. She always thought of Bernadette as a bit eejity, but she was being very crisp today.

'Well, Frank and I are thinking of going to Australia in the New Year . . . '

'To Australia, like Uncle Charlie? *He* didn't make a fortune.'

'That's not the point. There's a crafts co-operative we are interested in. It's not definite yet, but I don't want Mummy to be one of my reasons for going or staying . . . I mean I'll write home every week and all . . . but I don't want to go not knowing whether she'll end up in a mental ward or whether she'll be all right . . . '

'Yes . . . yes.' Anna felt left behind.

'And *you're* not really going to move in and look after her, are you, Anna, you've got your own life . . . Dad should be told this . . . just so that he knows the options.'

'Yes. But isn't it all a bit harsh . . . a bit final? Mightn't we be sort of taking too much for granted . . . '

''Yes, that's the point . . . it was you who said we must meet and discuss what to do. I think that's the only thing to do if we do anything, let him know just how far he can rely on us so that there's no misunderstanding.'

'Yes, well I don't know, maybe we should say nothing . . . Mother's probably better able to look after herself than we realise . . . '

'And you were saying that she actually seems more lively these days.'

'Yes, and she looks better, her skin looks less sort of muddy . . . and she's lost a bit of weight I think . . . '

'She always seems very cheerful when I call in or ring.'

'Yes . . . when you think how awful it was that time her nerves did get bad.'

'Oh years ago, when I was still at college?'

'Yes, it was awful, she used to go and see this psychiatrist and cry all the time . . . '

'What did they do with her, how did they cure her?'

'Oh Bernadette, you know psychiatrists, they don't do anything or cure anyone . . . they just listen and say yes, yes . . . or so I hear.'

'Why do people go on going to them then?'

'Who knows, I suppose the world's a bit short on people who will listen and say yes, yes . . . '

'But she did get better, she stopped crying and everything . . . '

'I told you, it works, all this yes yessing.'

'And we'll say nothing for the moment . . . '

'I think not, don't you?'

*　　　*　　　*

Joe arrived a week before the party. He telephoned one morning and said he was in town.

'Did I send you enough money?' Carmel sounded

anxious.

'Darling, you sent me too much money. How are you, Carmel, am I going to come and see you?'

'No, I'll come and see you. I don't want you coming here until the night . . . '

'Where will we go?'

'Let me see . . . I'll go into the hotel . . . We can have tea or coffee sent up, can't we?'

'Yeah, it's costing a fortune the hotel . . . I wonder are you putting too much money out on all this, Carmel? There might have been another way . . . '

'I have the money . . . I've always had money, that was never a problem . . . I'm so grateful to you for coming over, Joe, I'll never be able to thank you. I wish your friend had come too.'

'No, a job's a job. Henry understands . . . it would have messed things up if he'd come here. He says you're as mad as a coot but he wishes you luck.'

She laughed happily. 'Oh good, he's on our side. I'll come down to the hotel this afternoon. What room are you? I'll just slip along and get into the lift . . . '

'Oh Mrs M., you sound as if you're accustomed to this kind of racey life,' Joe laughed. He was pleased that Carmel was so cheerful, he had been afraid that it might be a very glum Carmel. A sort of doom-laden Lady Macbeth. This sounded a lot more jolly. He sat back in his bed and lit a cigarette. It was really the most extraordinary business.

*　　　*　　　*

'How nice of you to call, Ethel. No, I'm fine . . . and you? Good. And David? Great. Oh, what a pity, no, I'm just off out as a matter of fact. Yes it is a long time, isn't it? But never mind, we'll see you next week, won't we? The eighth. Oh good, good. No, not a thing, thank you, no, no, it's all under control. But very nice of you to think of it, Ethel ... What? Oh yes, everyone's coming ... but it's only a small gathering, heavens, compared to all the ones you go to. Yes, that nice Ruth O'Donnell — I had such a sweet letter from her, Wales is where she was. She's looking forward to seeing you all again, she said. Was there anything else, Ethel? I'm in a bit of a rush. Right, see you both then, love to David. Bye.'

*　　　*　　　*

'Yes, Aunt Sheila, I'm on my own. I've plenty of time to talk. She seems in great form to me, very perky. And looking very well, I think she looks better now than I've seen her looking for a long time ... good, yes I thought I wasn't imagining it. No, of course I don't mind you talking frankly. I mean I know you're her oldest friend, for heaven's sake. No, honestly Aunt Sheila I'm telling you the truth, I haven't noticed anything odd about Mother recently ... she's in very good form ... Yes, well she doesn't have much time for me either. No, I'm not actually sure what she *is* doing but whatever little things they are seem to keep her occupied. The way I look at it, isn't she far better this way all cheerful and mysterious than she was the time she got upset and her nerves were bad? Do you remember she sat there all day and we all found it a terrible drag to talk to her ... she had no interest in anyone.'

*　　　*　　　*

Anna said to James: 'You know that friend of Mother's, the one we call Aunt Sheila who went back to teaching, remember? She was on the phone whinging and whining and says that she thinks Mother's behaving oddly. How oddly, I ask, and she can't explain. Apparently Mother is too cheerful. Did you ever?'

'Poor Grandmama,' said James, 'it's bad if she's gloomy, it's bad if she's cheerful. She can't win.'

*　　　*　　　*

'You look a million dollars . . . you're *not* an old hag . . . you're smashing.' Joe was full of admiration.

'I had a make-up lesson . . . you know the kind of thing the womens' magazines advise you to do if your husband's unfaithful. "Is your make-up old-fashioned," they ask, and recommend you to try out the new shades . . . '

They both laughed, and she looked at him carefully and nodded with approval.

'You look well, Joe, really well. I'm different, I'm just painted up a bit, that's why I appear to be ok, but you're really great . . . you look like a boy.'

'An old boy,' Joe laughed. 'Oh, a very old boy . . . I'll be forty-five soon. That's not a boy these days!'

'You look still in your thirties and you look terrific . . . '

Joe was pleased that her admiration was genuine. 'Do you know what I did for us, I went out to that supermarket up in Baggot Street . . . Lord has the place all changed . . . and I got us a bottle of fizz, on me. I decided that if we're going to do this mad thing we'll celebrate it in style.'

'Do you think we should wait until it's done?'

69

Carmel was unwilling to celebrate yet.

'Hell no, if we say we'll do it, then it will be done.' He opened the bottle with a practised hand and poured into the tooth mugs. 'Of course, I still think you're as daft as a brush.'

'Why? To get what I want? To try and get what I want?'

'No.' He raised his glass to her. 'Cheers, good luck. No, that's not daft. To want it is daft.'

'Cheers,' she said, raising her glass. 'Ninety calories for four fluid ounces . . . how many in this glass?'

'I think we could say bang goes 180 calories there.'

They laughed like old times.

*   *   *

'We've done nothing but fight since you came back. It's the last thing on God's earth that I want to do.'

'We haven't been fighting,' Ruth said wearily. 'I keep asking one question and you keep asking it back. I keep saying why do I have to go to this dinner and you keep saying why not. It's not so much a fight, it's a cul-de-sac.'

Dermot sighed. 'I keep telling you that we're buying time, that's all it is . . . buying peace of mind and opportunities . . . all of these things we want, and we can get them if you just come to the house and behave nice and naturally and let everybody tell you how wonderful you are for one evening. I know, I know, you don't want to, but it doesn't seem too hard a thing to me.'

She got up and walked around her kitchen. 'And it seems amazing to me that you don't see how hard it is to do. To go and talk to her, and to smile . . . and eat the food she's been slaving over, and go to the lavatory in your bathroom, and leave my coat on your bed, your marriage bed ... really, Dermot ...'

'If I've told you once there are single beds I've told you twenty times ... this time you'll be able to see for yourself.'

'It's almost as if you felt like a big man, having us both there ...'

'Christ, God, if you knew how that is not true ... I'll feel nervous and uneasy and anxious ... and I'll feel a cheat and a deceiver. Do you think I want to draw all that on myself?'

'Please, Dermot ...'

'Please, Ruth, please ... I never asked you anything like this before and I swear I'll never ask you again.'

'Oh, for all I know it could become a weekly affair, maybe I'll be invited to move in ... put a third bed in the room.'

'Don't be coarse.'

'Isn't it bad enough to deceive her without rubbing her nose in it?'

'Ruth, I love you, don't you know?'

'I think you do, but it's like believing in God — sometimes it's very difficult to remember why you ever did ...'

*   *   *

'Aren't you having even numbers, Mother? I thought you were asking me once about how to seat eight at a table.'

It was the day before the party. Anna had dropped in to check up on Mother. Bernadette was right, Mother had never looked better, slimmer and with colour in her cheeks, or could that possibly be a blusher? And what smart shoes! Mother said she had bought them for tomorrow and she was running them in. They were super, they cost about twice as much as Anna would have paid for a pair of shoes and ten times what she thought Mother would have paid.

'No, just seven . . . I suppose I did think of getting an extra man, but people say that it's very old-fashioned nowadays making up the numbers. Ethel says that more dinners have been ruined by people struggling to make the sexes equal . . . '

'Oh yes . . . I quite agree, really dreary men being dragged in, there are more really dreary men than dreary women around, I always think . . . '

'So do I, but maybe we're prejudiced!' Mother laughed, and Anna laughed too. Mother was fine, what was all the fuss about? In order to let Mother think she was interested in the famous dinner, she asked brightly, 'Who's coming then, Mother? Aunt Sheila and Uncle Martin I suppose . . .'

'Yes, and Ethel and David . . . and Ruth O'Donnell, that nice young artist.'

Anna dropped her handbag.

'Who . . . ?'

'Oh, you must know her, the painting in the hall, and this one. And the one on the stairs. Ruth O'Donnell . . . her exhibition opens tomorrow, and we're all going to it and then coming back here for dinner.'

*   *   *

Bernadette wasn't in, but Anna told the whole thing to Frank and had a glass of parsnip wine to restore her.

'Are there bits of parsnip in it?' she asked suspiciously.

'No, it's all fermented, it's all we have,' Frank said ungraciously.

Anna told the whole story, interspersed with explanations of how her heart had nearly stopped and she hadn't known what to say, to think, to do. Frank listened blankly.

'Isn't she a fifteen-carat bitch,' Anna said in the end.

'Your mother?' Frank asked, puzzled.

'No, the woman. Ruth O'Donnell. Isn't she a smug self-satisfied little bitch? It's not enough for her to have her own exhibition which half the country seems to be going to, it's not enough for her to have poor Dad like a little lap poodle running after her . . . she has to get him to get Mother to ask her to a dinner party and make a public humiliation of her in front of all Mother's friends.'

Frank looked unmoved.

'Well, isn't it appalling,' she snapped.

He shrugged. 'To me there are two ways of looking at it, and both of them are from your Ma's point of view. Either she knows, in which case she knows what she's doing, or she doesn't know, in which case nobody's about to announce it to her over the soup, so either way *she's* all right.'

Anna didn't like the way Frank had emphasised the word *she*. If he meant that Mother was all right, who wasn't? Could it be Anna, sharp and shrill and getting into a tizz? She drained her parsnip wine and left.

*   *   *

'For God's sake, stay out of it,' James said. 'Don't

ring all those fearful old women up. Let it go its own way. You'll hear soon enough if something disastrous happens.'

'But they're my own mother and father, James. It's not as if they were just neighbours. You have to care about your own mother and father.'

'Your own daughter and son seem to be yelling for you in the kitchen,' he said.

She flounced out. James came out after her and gave her a kiss. She smiled and felt better. 'That's soppy,' said Cilian and they all laughed.

*　　*　　*

RTE rang and asked if Ruth would go on the Day by Day programme. She said she would call them back.

'Should I?' she asked Dermot.

'Definitely,' he said. 'Absolutely. Go straight out.'

Thank God, he thought, at least that will take her mind off Carmel and the dinner. This time tomorrow it would all be over, he told himself. This time tomorrow he would sit down and take stock of his life. He had all the information that anyone could ever gather about early retirement plans . . . or he could ask for a transfer.

Ruth had often said she would like to live out of Dublin, but of course in a small place it wouldn't be acceptable . . . anyway, no point in thinking about all that now; the main thing was that Carmel was quite capable of living a life of her own now . . . might even get herself a job like her friend Sheila. That was something that could be suggested, not by him, of course . . . Oh God, if she only knew how he wanted her to be happy, he didn't want to hurt her, or betray her, he just wanted her to have her own life.

74

'Your wife on the line, Mr Murray.'

He jumped physically. 'What? What?'

'Shall I put her through?'

'Of course . . . '

Carmel never rang him at the bank; what could have happened?

'Hallo, Dermot, I'm awfully sorry for bothering you, were you in the middle of someone's bank account?'

'No of course not. What is it, Carmel?'

'Do you remember Joe Daly?'

'What? Who?'

'I was asking you did you remember Joe Daly, he used to write for the paper here, then he went off to London . . . remember?'

'Vaguely, I think. Why?'

'Well, I met him quite by chance today, and he's been doing interviews with Ruth O'Donnell, he knows her quite well it turns out . . . anyway I thought I'd ask him tonight, isn't that a good idea?'

'Joe who?'

'Daly, do you remember, a mousey little man . . . we knew him ages ago before we were married.'

'Oh he's our age . . . right, whatever you say. If you think he's nice, then do. Whatever you like, dear. Will he fit in with everyone else?'

'Yes, I think so, but I wanted to check.'

'Sure, sure, ask him, ask him.'

Thank God, he thought, thank God, a mousey little failed journalist to talk about things that none of them were tied up in. There was a God in heaven, the night might not be so dreadful after all. He was about to dial Ruth when he realised she was probably on her way to the studio.

'Can you record "Day by Day", please, on the

machine over there,' he said to Miss O'Neill. 'There's going to be an item on banking I'd like to hear later.' He watched as she put on the cassette, checked her watch and set the radio tape recorder to begin at eleven.

* * *

Joe rang her at noon on the day of the party.

'Can I come up now?' he asked.

'Be very careful, look like a tradesman,' she said.

'That's not hard,' he said.

She looked around the house. It was perfect. There were flowers in the bathroom, lovely dahlias and chrysanthemums, all in dark reds, they looked great with the pink soaps and pink towels. The bedroom where they were going to leave their coats was magnificent, with the two thick Kilkenny Design bedspreads freshly cleaned. The kitchen had flowers in it too, orange dahlias and rust chrysanthemums; she had bought teatowels just in that colour. Really, it was such fun showing off. She didn't know why she hadn't done it ages ago.

* * *

He came in very quickly. She looked left and right, but the houses weren't near enough for anyone to see.

'Come in and tell me everything,' she said.

'It's worked . . . so far.'

She poured a coffee for him.

'Won't it spoil the beautiful kitchen?' he teased.

'I have five hours to tidy it up,' she laughed.

'So, I'll tell you from the start. I arrived at her flat,

your man was in there, I could hear his voice. They were arguing . . . '

'What about?' Carmel was interested.

'I couldn't hear. Anyway, I waited, I went down to the courtyard place. I sat on the wall and waited, he left in an hour. I pressed her bell. I told her who I was, that I had an interest in a gallery in London, that I didn't want to set up huge business meetings and press her in the week of her exhibition but I was very interested in seeing whether it was the kind of thing we could bring to London.'

'Did she ask why you were at the door?'

'Yes. I said I'd looked her up in the phone book . . . she thought that was very enterprising . . . '

'It is,' laughed Carmel. 'Nobody ever thinks of it.'

'Anyway I told her I was staying at the hotel but that if she liked we could talk now. She laughed and said why not now, and let me in . . . '

'And . . . ?'

'And it's very nice, all done up as a studio, not a love nest at all . . . hardly any comfort, nothing like this . . .' He looked around the smart kitchen and through the open door into the dining room with its dark polished wood. 'So we had a long talk, all about her work. She showed me what she was doing, showing, we went through the catalogue. I explained what I could do . . . Jesus, if you'd heard the way I dropped the names of galleries and people in London — I even impressed myself. I promised nothing. I said I'd act as a middleman. I even sent myself up a bit and said I saw myself as a Mister Fixit . . . she liked that and she laughed a lot . . . '

'Yes,' said Carmel before he could say it. 'I know, I know, I've heard. She's very nice. Go on.'

'Yes, well. I think I played it well. I must have.

When I was leaving I said that we must keep in touch, that I could be here for a week and perhaps she would like to have a lunch one day. She said that would be nice, and I said the next day and we picked the place you said . . . I said I'd heard it was good.'

'Was it?' asked Carmel with interest.

'It was and so it should be, it cost you an arm and a leg. I kept the receipt for you . . . '

'Joe, I don't need receipts.'

'I know, but it is *astronomical.*'

'Was it the right place . . . ?'

'Yes, we sat on and on. She doesn't drink much but they kept bringing pots of coffee . . . nobody rushed us . . . it was very relaxed and we broadened the conversation . . . she told me about how she began and how this nun at the school she went to had great faith in her even when her parents didn't really believe she had talent.'

Joe paused. 'I kept leaning heavily on the notion that I was just pass. ug through, not a permanent fixture. She was quite anxious to talk actually, I don't need much congratulation.'

'So she did tell you . . .

'Yes, I sort of squeezed it out of her bit by bit . . . not with crude questions like, "Why isn't a girl like you married?" More about Dublin being full of gossip and disapproval . . . I told her I'd never be able to live here nowadays because of my own life. She said no, it wasn't too bad . . . things had changed, but people did let others go their own way. I argued that with her, and then she had to get down to specifics. She had a false start, then she said she didn't want to be unburdening her whole life story to a total stranger.

'I said that total strangers were the only people you could possibly unburden things to. They passed like ships in the night. Sometimes it happened that you got a bit of advice from a passing ship but even if you didn't, what the hell, the ship had passed on . . . it wasn't hanging around embarrassing you every time you saw it . . . '

'And?'

'And she told me . . . she told me about her married man.'

'Was it anything like the truth? I mean, did she describe things the way things are?'

'Very like the way you told me. She met him when she was doing a job for the bank. He had taken her out to lunch, she had been lonely, he had understood . . . her father had died recently. Her mother was dead years ago. The married man was very sympathetic.'

'I'm sure,' said Carmel.

'They met a lot and he was so interested in her work and so encouraging . . . and he believed in her — and the reason she liked him so much . . . '

'Yes . . . ?' Carmel leaned forward.

'He didn't want to hurt people or do people down. He never wanted her to score over other people. He wanted her to be content in herself and with her work . . . she liked that most about him.'

Joe paused. 'So I put it to her that he must have a bit of the louse in him to maintain two ménages, he must be a bit of a crud to have it both ways . . . you know, not disturbing his own lifestyle . . . '

'What did she say?'

'She thought not, she thought he was a victim of circumstances. His wife hadn't been well, she had been — sorry, Carmel — the phrase she used was "suffering from her nerves" . . . '

'Fine, fine,' said Carmel.

'Then I talked about Henry a bit, I didn't want her to think that she was confiding too much, you know . . . people turn against people when they tell them too much.'

'Yes I know,' Carmel agreed.

'So anyway it went on from there . . . could she guide me around Dublin a bit? We had lunch at the National Gallery . . . we went in and out of the place that's giving her the exhibition, we went — oh, God knows where . . . I kept her occupied during the days, and I faded out a bit at night because I knew she'd be meeting your man after work. On Wednesday she asked me would I like to meet him. I said no.'

'Wednesday,' Carmel said softly to herself.

'Yes. I said no way did I want to get involved in peoples' private lives. That was the night she told me that she had been invited here and she was worried sick, she couldn't think why . . . She said she didn't want to come and hurt you.'

'No. No, indeed,' said Carmel.

'So she said she didn't know how to get out of it, the Man wouldn't hear of her refusing. I said the married man wanted to get a kick out of seeing you both together. She went quite white over it all . . . "He wouldn't want that," she said. "I don't know, it gives some fellows a real charge," I said, "seeing the two women there and knowing they've screwed both of them."'

'Really?' Carmel said.

Joe laughed. 'That's what she said too. Anyway, it upset her. And she said he wasn't like that. Well then, he shouldn't force you to come to the dinner, I said. It's being a real voyeur, isn't it, having the both of you there?'

Joe paused for a gulp of his coffee.

'Then I said, "I wouldn't be surprised if he forced the wife to ask you to dinner, after all why would the wife ask you? If she doesn't know about you and him it's an odd thing she should suddenly decide to pick you of all the people in Dublin and if she *does* know it's even odder." She said that's what she'd been thinking herself. She's just an ordinary woman you know, Carmel, just an ordinary female with a slow brain ticking through and working things out ... she's no Mata Hari.'

'I know,' said Carmel.

'So I said then, and the others are his friends really, maybe they're all in on it, they know about you and him, don't they?' Joe leaned over. 'So that was part one over, she really believed he was setting her up, she was so convinced. I don't know what kind of an evening they had that night, but it didn't last long. He was out of there in an hour.'

'Yes, he was home very bad-tempered and very early on Wednesday,' Carmel said, smiling.

'So Thursday I ring her and say come on, I'll buy you lunch and no gloomy chat, because isn't it a small world, I've just run into my old friends the Murrays and ha ha isn't Dublin a village? I now know who the mystery bank manager is, it's Dermot Murray. I didn't know he knew you ... She's amazed.

'"Oho," I say, "can't keep a secret in this town. No, really, isn't it a scream, I knew brother Charlie years ago, long before he went to Australia or anything, and I remember Carmel, and Carmel was walking out with Dermot Murray, a lowly bank clerk then ..." Oh she's all upset, she can't believe it, it's too much. I say stop all that fussing and fretting, I'll buy you a big lunch. I keep saying it's a scream ... '

Carmel smiled.

'I arrive and collect her. She's been crying, she's so ashamed, she wouldn't have dreamed of telling me all those intimate things if there was a chance I'd have known anyone . . . but I was a stranger in town and outside, someone who went away years ago . . . I kept laughing, the odds against it must be millions to one, forget it, anyway wasn't it all for the best? Because now that I knew that it was Carmel and Dermot I could say definitely that they weren't the kind of people who would be involved in anything sordid. Everyone had spoken very well of Dermot, and poor Carmel had always been very nice.'

'Poor Carmel,' Carmel said, smiling still.

'You asked me to play it for all I could,' Joe said.

'I know. Go on.'

'It took a lot of coaxing to get her back where she was. I reminded her of all the indiscretions I had told her, about being gay, about Henry. I told her that nobody in Ireland knew that about me, that we each knew secrets about the other. We shook hands over lunch. I felt a real shit.'

'Joe, go on.'

'She left more cheerful. I rang her yesterday morning and asked could I come by for coffee. I told her that I had heard at the hotel a man talking to a friend. I described David perfectly . . . he's not hard to describe from what you told me.'

'There's only one David,' said Carmel.

'Yes, well she identified him, and oh I wove a long tale. It could have been something else entirely, but it did sound as if it could have been Dermot he was talking about . . . I kept pretending that it might have been imagination but she saw it wasn't. She knew that if I had heard him talking like that it must be Dermot, and Dermot must indeed have told David that she was coming to the party and wasn't it all very risqué.'

Joe looked at Carmel. 'She cried a lot, she cried and cried. I felt very sorry for her.'

'I cried a lot. I cried for four months the first time, the time he went off with that Sophie.'

'But she has nobody to comfort her.'

'I had nobody to comfort me.'

'You had a psychiatrist.'

'Great help.'

'He cured you, didn't he?'

'No he didn't, he asked me to ask myself was my marriage with Dermot so important that I should save it at all costs. What the hell does he know about marriage and importance, and all costs? What else is there for me but to be married to Dermot? There *is* nothing else. It's not a choice between this and something else, it's this or nothing.'

'You're fine, you could live on your own. You don't need him. I can't see what you want him around for. He hasn't been any good to you for years, he hasn't been kind or a friend. You haven't wanted any of the things he wanted. Why didn't you let him go then, or indeed now?'

'You don't understand. Its different for ... er ... Gays, it's not the same.'

'Hell, it's not the same, of course it's not the same. I love Henry, Henry loves me. One day one of us will stop loving the other. Hopefully we'll split and go our own ways .. but the worst is to stay together bitching.'

'But your world, it's so different ... so totally different ... I couldn't do that.'

'Well you didn't. And you've won.'

'I have, haven't I?'

'Yes . . . it's all fixed up. I told her this morning that I'd been asked here, that I'd be here for moral support if she wanted to come. She said no, she didn't want to make a fool of herself in front of everyone. She'll tell you tonight at the exhibition that she can't come after all. She says she'll do it gently, she knows you are just as much a pawn as she is . . . '

'Good, good.'

'And she's not going to tell him at all. She's going to leave him stew, let him think what he likes.'

'Suppose he runs after her, suppose he won't let her go?'

'I think she'll make it clear to him. Anyway, she's already set up some other friends to go out with. She says she's sorry for you because you're a timid sort of person and you'd been planning this for a month . . . she's afraid that the whole thing will be a damp squib . . . '

'That's very nice of her.'

'It is actually, Carmel, she's a very nice person.'

'So you keep saying, but I'm a very nice person. I'm an extremely nice person, and very few people ever realise that.'

'I realise it. I've always realised it,' Joe said.

'Yes,' Carmel said.

'I'd have done this for no money, you were always good to me.'

'I sent you money because I have it, you don't. It seemed only fair that your week should be subsidised . . . '

'You were always a brick, Carmel. Always. I'd have had no life if it weren't for you.'

There was a silence. In the gleaming kitchen they sat and remembered the other kitchen, the kitchen where Carmel's brother Charlie and Joe had stood scarlet-faced in front of Carmel's father. Words that had never been used in that house were used that evening. Threats of ruin were made. Joe would be prosecuted, he would spend years and years in goal, the whole world would know about his unnatural habits, his vile seduction of innocent schoolboys ... an act so shameful not even the animal kingdom would tolerate it, and Charlie might grow up warped as a result. Joe's father who worked as the gardener would be sacked, and the man would never work again. He would be informed this night of his son's activities.

It was then that Carmel had found her voice. She was five years older than Charlie, she was twenty-two. She had been a quiet girl, her father had not even noticed her in the kitchen so great had been his rage.

'It was Charlie's fault, Dad,' she had said in a level voice. 'Charlie's been queer for two years. He's had relationships with a lot of boys, I can tell you their names.' There had been a silence which seemed to last for an hour. 'I don't like unfairness. Joe Daly has done nothing that Charlie didn't encourage. Why should his father be sacked, why should he be disgraced, why should Charlie get away with it, Dad, because Mr Daly is a gardener and you're a Company Director?'

It was unanswerable.

Charlie went to Australia shortly afterwards. Mr Daly was never told, and Joe Daly got a little assistance from Charlie's father indirectly, so that he could go to a technical school and do English and commerce and book-keeping. During that time he wrote the odd article for evening papers, and Carmel had seen him casually around Dublin. He had sent her a wedding present when she married Dermot two years after the distressing events in the kitchen. It was a beautiful cut glass vase, nicer than anything she had got from any of her father's friends, or any of Dermot's side. It would be on the dining-table tonight, with late summer roses in it.

*   *   *

'So will I leave you to rest and think over it all?' Joe said.

'I *wish* you thought I'd done the right thing,' she said.

'You know what I think. I think you should have given him away. I really do. There are other lives.'

'Not for fifty-year-old women there aren't.'

'I know what you mean, but there are. Anyway, there you go.'

'Why are you so fed up with me?'

'Carmel, I'm not fed up with you. I owed you, I'd do anything for you anytime, I told you that and I meant it. You asked me one favour. You've paid me handsomely for it. I've done it, but I don't have to approve of it.'

'Oh, Joe, I thought you'd understand.'

'You see, it's the total reverse of all that happened, years ago. Then you did something brave just . . . well . . . just so that the right thing should be done . . .'

'But this is the right thing! She's young, she'll find somebody else, a proper person, not a married man . . . not somebody else's husband . . .'

'No, you see this time you've arranged it so that the truth is hidden, lost . . She thinks that Dermot is setting her up, she thinks he's having a laugh at her, that he wanted her to come to the party as some kind of macho thing. Dermot thinks that she's let him down, promised to go through with it and then thrown him over unexpectedly. Neither believes that the other is actually honest.'

Carmel stood up. 'I know it's complicated. That psychiatrist said to me, you know, the first time, that there's no such thing as absolute right and absolute wrong. He also said that we can't control other peoples' lives, we must only take responsibility for our own. I decided what I wanted to do with mine, and I did it. That's the way I see it. I don't see it as meddling or playing God or anything.'

Joe stood up too. 'No, whatever else it is, I don't think it's playing God,' he said.

And he slipped quietly out of the house, making sure that he wasn't observed, because he wasn't meant to be a great friend of Carmel's, he was only a casual friend whom they had met luckily again, and his last job was to make sure that the dinner party was great fun.

FLAT IN RINGSEND

11

They said you should get the evening papers at lunch-time and as soon as you got a smell of a flat that would suit you were to rush out and sit on the step at the head of the queue. You shouldn't take any notice of the words 'After six o'clock'. If you got there at six o'clock and the ad had sounded any way reasonable then you'd find a line trailing down the road. Finding a good flat in Dublin at a price you could afford was like finding gold in the gold rush.

The other way was by personal contact; if you knew someone who knew someone who was leaving a place that often worked. But if you had only just arrived in Dublin there was no chance of any personal contact, nobody to tell you that their bedsit would be vacant at the end of the month. No, it was a matter of staying in a hostel and searching.

Jo had been to Dublin a dozen times when she was a child; she had been up for a match, or for a school outing, or the time that Da was in the Chest Hospital and everyone had been crying in case he wouldn't get better. Most of her friends had been up to Dublin much more often; they talked about places they had gone to in a familiar way, and assumed that she knew what they were talking about.

'You *must* know the Dandelion Market. Let me see, you come out of the Zhivago and you go in a straight line to your right, keep going and you pass O'Donoghues and the whole of Stephen's Green, and you don't turn right down Grafton Street. Now do you know where it is?'

After so much effort explaining things to her, Jo said she did. Jo was always anxious to please other people, and she felt that she only annoyed them by not knowing what they were talking about. But Dublin was a very big blank spot. She really felt she was stepping into the unknown when she got on the train to go and work there. She didn't ask herself why she was going in the first place. It had been assumed by everyone that she would go. Who would stay in a one-horse town, the back of beyonds, the end of the world, the sticks, this dead-and-alive place? That's all she had heard for years. At school they were all going to get out, escape, see some life, get some living in, have a real kind of existence, and some of the others in her class had gone as far as Ennis or Limerick, often to stay with cousins. A few had gone to England, where an elder sister or an aunt would see them settled in. But out of Jo's year none of them were going to Dublin. Jo's family must have been the only one in the place who didn't have relations in Glasnevin or Dundrum. She was heading off on her own.

There had been a lot of jokes about her going to work in the Post Office. There'd be no trouble in getting a stamp to write a letter home; what's more, there'd be no excuse if she didn't. She could sneak the odd phone call too, which would be fine, but they didn't have a phone at home. Maybe she could send a ten-page telegram if she needed to say any-thing in a hurry. They assumed that she would know the whole business of the high and the mighty in

Dublin the way Miss Hayes knew everyone's business from the post office at home. People said that she'd find it very easy to get to know people, there was nowhere like a post office for making friends, it was the centre of everything.

She knew she wouldn't be working in the GPO, but whenever she thought of herself in Dublin it was in the middle of the General Post Office chatting up all the people as they came in, knowing every single person who came to buy stamps or collect the children's allowances. She imagined herself living somewhere nearby, maybe over Clery's or on the corner of O'Connell Bridge so that she could look at the Liffey from her bedroom.

She had never expected the miles and miles of streets where nobody knew anyone, the endless bus journeys, the having to get up two hours before she was meant to be at work in case she got lost or the bus was cancelled. 'Not much time for a social life,' she wrote home. 'I'm so exhausted when I get back to the hostel I just go to bed and fall asleep.'

Jo's mother thought that it would be great altogether if she stayed permanently in the hostel. It was run by nuns, and she could come to no harm. Her father said that he hoped they kept the place warm; nuns were notorious for freezing everyone else to death just because they wore thermal underwear. Jo's sisters who worked in the hotel as waitresses said she must be off her head to have stayed a whole week in a hostel; her brother who worked in the Creamery said he was sorry she didn't have a flat, it would be somewhere to stay whenever he went to Dublin; her brother who worked in the garage said that Jo would have been better off to stay where she was — what would she get in Dublin only discontented, and she'd end up like that O'Hara girl, neither one thing nor the other, happy neither in Dublin nor at home. It had to be said that he had fancied the O'Hara girl for a long time, and it was a great irritation to him that she wouldn't settle down and be like a normal woman.

But Jo didn't know that they were all thinking about her and discussing her, as she answered the advertisement for the flat in Ringsend. It said *'Own room, own television, share kitchen, bathroom'*. It was very near her post office and seemed too good to be true. Please, St Jude, please. May it be nice, may they like me, may it not be too dear.

There wasn't a queue for this one because it wasn't so much 'Flat to Let', more 'Third Girl Wanted'. The fact that it had said 'Own Television' made Jo wonder whether it might be in too high a class for her, but the house did not look any way overpowering. An ordinary red-bricked terraced house with a basement. Her father had warned her against basements; they were full of damp, he said, but then her father had a bad chest and saw damp everywhere. But the flat was not in the basement, it was upstairs. And a cheerful-looking girl with a college scarf, obviously a failed applicant, was coming down the stairs.

'Desperate place,' she said to Jo, 'They're both awful. Common as dirt.'

'Oh,' said Jo and went on climbing.

'Hallo,' said the girl with 'Nessa' printed on her tee-shirt.

'God, did you see that toffee-nosed bitch going out? I can't stand that kind, I can't stand them . . . '

'What did she do?' asked Jo.

'Do? She didn't have to *do* anything. She just poked around and wrinkled her lip and sort of giggled and then said "Is this it?" in a real Foxrock accent.

"Oh dear, oh dear." Stupid old cow, we wouldn't have had her in here if we were starving and needed her to buy us a crust, would we, Pauline?'

Pauline had a pyschedelic shirt on; it almost hurt the eyes but was only marginally brighter than her hair. Pauline was a punk, Jo noted with amazement. She had seen some of them on O'Connell Street, but hadn't met one close up to talk to.

'No, stupid old bore. She was such a bore. She'd have bored us to death, years later our bodies would have been found here and the verdict would have been death by boredom . . . '

Jo laughed. It was such a wild thought to think of all that pink hair lying on the floor dead because it hadn't been able to stand the tones of the flat-mate. 'I'm Jo, I work in the post office and I rang . . .' Nessa said they were just about to have a mug of tea. She produced three mugs; one had 'Nessa' and one had 'Pauline' and the other one had 'Other' written on it. 'We'll get your name put on if you come to stay,' she said generously.

Nessa worked in CIE, and Pauline worked in a big firm nearby. They had got the flat three months ago and Nessa's sister had had the third room, but now she was getting married very quickly, very quickly indeed, and so the room was empty. They explained the cost, they showed her the geyser for having a bath and they showed her the press in the kitchen, each shelf with a name on it, Nessa Pauline and Maura.

'Maura's name will go, and we'll paint in yours if you come to stay,' Nessa said again reassuringly.

'You've no sitting room,' Jo said.

'No, we did it in three bed-sits,' said Nessa.

'Makes much more sense,' said Pauline.

'What's the point of a sitting-room?' asked Nessa.

'I mean, who'd sit in it?' asked Pauline.

'And we've got two chairs in our own rooms,' Nessa said proudly.

'And each of us has our own telly,' said Pauline happily.

That was the point that Jo wanted to discuss.

'Yes, you didn't say how much that costs. Is there a rental?'

Nessa's big happy face spread into a grin. 'No, that's the real perk. You see, Maura's Steve, well my brother-in-law as he now is, I hope, my brother-in-law Steve worked in the business and he was able to get us tellys for a song.'

'So you bought them outright, did you?' Jo was enthralled.

'Bought in a manner of speaking,' Pauline said. 'Accepted them outright.'

'Yeah, it was his way of saying thank you, his way of paying the rent . . . in a manner of speaking,' Nessa said.

'But did he stay here too?'

'He was Maura's boy-friend. He stayed most of the time.'

'Oh ' said Jo. There was a silence.

'Well?' Nessa said accusingly. 'If you've anything to say, you should say it now.'

'I suppose I was wondering did he not get in everyone's way. I mean, if a fourth person was staying in the flat was it fair on the others?'

'Why do you think we organised it all into bedsits?' Pauline asked. 'Means we can all do what we like when we like, not trampling on other people. Right?'

'Right,' Nessa said.

'Right,' Jo said, doubtfully.

'So what do you think,' Nessa asked Pauline. 'I think Jo would be OK if she wants to come, do you?'

'Yeah, sure, I think she'd be fine if she'd like it here,' said Pauline.

'Thank you', said Jo, blushing a bit.

'Is there anything else you'd like to ask? I think we've covered everything. There's a phone with a coin-box in the hall downstairs. There's three nurses in the flat below, but they don't take any messages for us so we don't take any for them. The rent on the first of the month, plus five quid each and I get a few basics.'

'Will you come then?' asked Nessa.

'Please. I'd like to very much, can I come on Sunday night?'

They gave her a key, took her rent money, poured another cup of tea and said that it was great to have fixed it all up so quickly. Nessa said that Jo was such a short name it would be dead easy to paint it onto the shelf in the kitchen, the shelf in the bathroom and her mug.

'She wanted to paint the names on the doors too, but I wouldn't let her,' said Pauline.

'Pauline thought it looked too much like a nursery,' said Nessa regretfully.

'Yes, and also I wanted to leave a bit of variety in life. If our names are on the doors then we'll never get any surprise visitors during the night — I always like a bit of the unexpected!'

Jo laughed too. She hoped they were joking.

*   *   *

She assured her mother in the letter that the flat was very near Haddington Road, she told her father how far it was from the damp basement, and she put in the bits about the television in each bedroom to make her sisters jealous. They had said she was an eejit to go to Dublin; the best Dublin people all came to County Clare on their holidays. She should stay at home and meet them there rather than going up and trying to find them in their own place.

*   *   *

They were having tea in the hostel on Sunday when Jo said goodbye. She struggled with her two cases to the bus stop.

'Your friends aren't going to arrange to collect you?' Sister said.

'They haven't a car, sister.'

'I see. Often, though, young people come to help a friend. I hope they are kind people, your friends.'

'Very, sister.'

'That's good. Well, God bless you, child, and remember that this is a very wicked city, a lot of very wicked people in it.'

'Yes, sister, I'll keep my eye out for them.'

It took her a long time to get to the flat.

She had to change buses twice, and was nearly exhausted when she got there. She had to come down again for the second case, and dragged the two into the room that had been pointed out as hers. It was smaller than it had looked on Friday, yet it could hardly have shrunk. The bedclothes were folded there, two blankets, two pillows and a quilt. Lord, she forgot about sheets; she'd assumed they were included. And God, she supposed there'd be no towel either, wasn't she an eejit not to have asked.

She hoped they wouldn't notice, and she'd be able

to buy some tomorrow — or she hoped she would, as she only had an hour for lunch. She'd ask one of the girls in the post office, and she had her savings for just this kind of emergency.

She hung up her clothes in the poky little wardrobe, and put out her ornaments on the window sill and her shoes in a neat line on the floor. She put her cases under the bed and sat down feeling very flat.

Back home they'd be going to the pictures or to a dance at eight o'clock on a Sunday night. In the hostel some of the girls would watch television in the lounge, others would have gone to the pictures together and go for chips on the way home, throwing the papers into the litter bin on the corner of the street where the hostel was since Sister didn't like the smell of chips coming into the building.

Nobody was sitting alone on a bed with nothing to do. She could go out and take the bus into town and go to the pictures alone, but didn't that seem ridiculous when she had her own television. Her very own. She could change the channel whenever she wanted to; she wouldn't have to ask anyone.

She was about to go out to the sitting room to see was there a Sunday paper, when she remembered there was no sitting room. She didn't want to open the doors of their rooms in case they might come in and think she was prying. She wondered where they were. Was Nessa out with a boyfriend? She hadn't mentioned one, but then girls in Dublin didn't tell you immediately if they had a fellow or not. Perhaps Pauline was at a punk disco. She couldn't believe that anyone would actually employ Pauline with that hair and let her meet the public, but maybe she was kept hidden away. Perhaps they'd come home about eleven o'clock (well, they had to get up for work in the morning); perhaps they all had cocoa or drinking chocolate in the sitting room — well, in the kitchen, to end the day. She'd tell them how well she'd settled in. In the meantime she would sit back and watch her own television set.

Jo fell asleep after half an hour. She had been very tired. She dreamed that Nessa and Pauline had come in. Pauline had decided to wash the pink out of her hair and share a room with Nessa. They were going to turn Pauline's room into a sitting room where they would sit and talk and plan. She woke suddenly when she heard giggling. It was Pauline and a man's voice, and they had gone into the kitchen.

Jo shook herself. She must have been asleep for three hours; she had a crick in her neck and the television was flickering. She stood up and turned it off, combed her hair and was about to go out and welcome the homecomers when she hesitated. If Pauline had invited a boy home presumably she was going to take him to bed with her. Perhaps the last thing she might need now was her new flatmate coming out looking for company. They were laughing in the kitchen, she could hear them, then she heard the electric kettle hiss and whistle. Well, she could always pretend that she had been going to make herself a cup of tea.

Nervously, she opened the door and went into the kitchen. Pauline was with a young man who wore a heavy leather jacket with a lot of studs on it.

'Hallo, Pauline, I was just going to get myself a cup of tea,' Jo said apologetically.

'Sure,' Pauline said. She was not unfriendly, she didn't look annoyed, but she made no effort to introduce her friend.

The kettle was still hot so Jo found a mug with

Visitor on it and put in a tea bag. 'Nessa's going to paint my name on a mug,' she said to the man in the jacket, just for something to say. 'Oh good,' he said. He shrugged and asked Pauline, 'Who's Nessa?'

'Lives over there,' Pauline said, indicating the direction of Nessa's room.

'I'm the third girl,' Jo said desperately. 'Third in what?' he said, genuinely bewildered. Pauline had fixed the tray of tea and biscuits and was moving towards the door.

''Night,' she said, companionably enough.

'Good night, Pauline, goodnight . . . er . . . ' Jo said.

She took the cup of tea into her own room. She turned up the television slightly in case she heard the sound of anything next door. She hoped she hadn't annoyed Pauline. She couldn't see what she had done that might annoy her, and anyway she had seemed cheerful enough when she was taking this boy off to — well, to her room. Jo sighed and got into bed.

*   *   *

Next morning she was coming out of the bathroom when she met Nessa.

'It's just "J" and "O", two letters, isn't it?' Nessa asked.

'Oh yes, that's right, thank you very much, Nessa.'

'Right. I didn't want to do it and then find you had an "E" on it.'

'No, no, it's short for Josephine.'

'Right on.' Nessa was off.

'What time are you coming home tonight?' Jo

98

asked.

'Oh, I don't think I'll have them done tonight,' Nessa said.

'I didn't mean that, I just wondered what you were doing for your tea . . . supper. You know?'

'No idea,' said Nessa cheerfully.

'Oh,' said Jo. 'Sorry.'

*　　　*　　　*

Jacinta, who worked beside her, asked her how the flat was.

'It's great altogether,' Jo said.

'Dead right to get out of that hostel, you'd have no life in a hostel,' Jacinta said wisely.

'No, no indeed.'

'God, I wish I didn't live at home,' Jacinta said. 'It's not natural for people to live in their own homes, there should be a law about it. They have laws over stupid things like not importing live fowl, as if anyone would want to, but they have no laws about the things that people really need.'

'Yes,' said Jo dutifully.

'Anyway, you'll have the high life from now on. You country ones have all the luck.'

'I suppose we do,' Jo agreed doubtfully.

*　　　*　　　*

If she had stayed in the hostel they might have been playing twenty-five in the lounge now, or someone might have bought a new record. They would look at the evening paper, sigh over the price of flats, wonder whether to go the pictures and complain about the food. There would be talk and endless tea or bottles of coke from the machine. There would not be four walls as there were now.

She had bought a hamburger on the way home and eaten it. She washed her tights, she put the new sheets on the bed and hung her new towel up in the bathroom on the third hook. The other hooks had 'N' and 'P' on them. She took out her writing pad but remembered that she had written home on Friday just after she had found the flat. There was nothing new to tell. The evening yawned ahead of her. And then there would be Tuesday and Wednesday and Thursday ... Tears came into her eyes and fell down on to her lap as she sat on the end of her bed. She must be absolutely awful to have no friends and nowhere to go and nothing to do. Other people of eighteen had great times. She used to have great times when she was seventeen, at school and planning to be eighteen. Look at her now, sitting alone. Even her flat mates didn't want to have anything to do with her. She cried and cried. Then she got a headache so she took two aspirins and climbed into bed. It's bloody fantastic being grown up, she thought, as she switched off the light at nine o'clock.

*   *   *

There was 'J' on her towel rack, her name was on the bathroom shelf that belonged to her, and her empty kitchen shelf had a 'Jo' on it also. She examined the other two shelves. Nessa had cornflakes and a packet of sugar and a lot of tins of soup on her shelf. Pauline had a biscuit tin and about a dozen tins of grapefruit segments on hers.

The kitchen was nice and tidy. Nessa had said the first day that they never left any washing up to be

100

done and that if you used the frying pan you had to scrub it then, not let it steep until the morning. It had all seemed great fun when she was talking about it then, because Jo had envisaged midnight feasts, and all three of them laughing and having parties. That's what people *did*, for heaven's sake. She must have just got in with two recluses, that was her problem.

Pauline came in to the kitchen yawning, and opened a tin of grapefruit segments. 'I think I'd never wake up if I didn't have these,' she said. 'I have half a tin and two biscuits for my breakfast every day, and then I'm ready for anything.'

Jo was pleased to be spoken to.

'Is your friend here?' she said, trying to be modern and racey.

'Which friend?' Pauline yawned and began to spoon the grapefruit out of the tin into a bowl.

'You know, your friend, the other night?'

'Nessa?' Pauline looked at her blankly. 'Do you mean Nessa?'

'No, the fellow, the fellow with the jacket with the studs. I met him here in the kitchen.'

'Oh yes. Shane.'

'Shane. That was his name.'

'Yeah, what about him, what were you saying?'

'I was asking was he here?'

'Here? Now? Why should he be here?' Pauline pushed her pink hair out of her eyes and looked at her watch. 'Jesus Christ, it's only twenty to eight in the morning, why would he be here?' She looked wildly around the kitchen as if the man with the studded leather jacket was going to appear from behind the gas cooker. Jo felt the conversation was going wrong.

'I just asked sociably if he was still here, that was

all.'

'But why on earth would he be still here? I went out with him on Sunday night. *Sunday*. It's Tuesday morning now, isn't it? Why would he be here?' Pauline looked confused and worried, and Jo wished she had never spoken.

'I just thought he was your boyfriend . . . '

'No, he's not, but if he was I tell you I wouldn't have him here at twenty to eight in the morning talking! I don't know how anyone can talk in the mornings. It beats me.'

Jo drank her tea silently.

'See you,' said Pauline eventually when she had finished her biscuits and grapefruit, and crashed into the bathroom.

Jo thanked Nessa for putting up the names. Nessa was pleased. 'I like doing that, it gives me a sense of order in the world. It defines things, that makes me feel better.'

'Sure,' said Jo. She was just about to ask Nessa what she was doing that evening when she remembered yesterday's rebuff. She decided to phrase it differently this time.

'Are you off out with your friends this evening?' she said timidly.

'I might be, I might not, it's always hard to know in the morning, isn't it?'

'Yes it is,' said Jo untruthfully. It was becoming increasingly easy to know in the morning, she thought. The answer was coming up loud and clear when she asked herself what she was going to do in the evening. The answer was Nothing.

'Well I'm off now. Goodbye,' she said to Nessa.

Nessa looked up and smiled. 'Bye bye,' she said vaguely, as if Jo had been the postman or the man delivering milk on the street.

*   *   *

On Thursday night Jo went downstairs to answer the phone. It was for one of the nurses on the ground floor as it always was. Hesitantly she knocked on their door. The big blonde nurse thanked her, and as Jo was going up the stairs again she heard the girl say, 'No, it was one of the people in the flats upstairs. There's three flats upstairs and we all share the same phone.'

That was it! That was what she hadn't realised. She wasn't in a flat with two other girls, she was in a flat by herself. Why hadn't that dawned on her? She was in a proper bedsitter all of her own, she just shared kitchen and bathroom facilities, as they would put it in an ad. That's what had been wrong. She had thought that she was meant to be part of a jolly all-girls-together. That's why she had been so depressed. She went over the whole conversation with Nessa the first day; she remembered what they had said about doing it up as bedsitters but not telling the landlord anything, it never did to tell landlords anything, just keep paying the rent and keep out of his way.

There was quite a bounce in her step now. I'm on my own in Dublin, she thought, I have my own place, I'm going out to find a life for myself now. She didn't have to worry about Pauline's morals any more now. If Pauline wanted to bring home a rough-looking person with studs on his jacket that was Pauline's business. She just lived in the flat next door. That's what Pauline had meant when she had said Nessa lived next door. And that's why Nessa went in for all this labelling and naming things. No wonder they had

103

been slightly surprised when she kept asking them what they were doing in the evening; they must have thought she was mad.

Happy for the first time since Sunday, Jo did herself up. She put on eyeshadow and mascara, she put some colour in her cheeks and wore her big earrings. She didn't know where she was going, but she decided that she would go out cheerfully now. She looked around her room and liked it much better. She would get some posters for the walls, she would even ask her mother if she could take some of the ornaments from home. The kitchen shelves at home were chock-a-block with ornaments; her mother would be glad to give some of them a new home. Humming happily, she set off.

She felt terrific as she swung along with her shoulderbag. She pitied her sisters who were only finishing the late shift now at the hotel. She pitied the girls who still had to stay in a hostel, who hadn't been able to go out and find a place of their own. She felt sorry for Jacinta who had to stay at home and whose mother and father interrogated her about where she went and what she did. She pitied people who had to share television sets. What if you wanted to look at one thing and they wanted to look at something else? How did you decide? She was so full of good spirits that she nearly walked past the pub where the notice said: 'Tonight — the Great Gaels.'

Imagine, the Great Gaels were there in person. In a pub. Cover charge £1. If she paid a pound she would see them close up. Up to now she had only seen them on television.

They had been at the Fleadh in Ennis once about four years ago, before they were famous. She had seen an advertisement, all right, saying that they would be in this pub, and now here she was outside it. Jo's heart beat fast. Was it a thing you could do on your own, go into a concert in a pub? Probably it was a thing people went to in groups; she might look odd. Maybe there'd be no place for just one person to sit. Maybe it would only be tables for groups.

But a great surge of courage came flooding over her. She was a young woman who lived in a flat on her own in Dublin, she had her own place and by the Lord, if she could do that, she could certainly go into a pub and hear the Great Gaels on her own. She pushed the door.

A man sat at the desk inside and gave her a cloakroom ticket and took her pound.

'Where do I go?' she almost whispered.

'For what?' he asked.

'You know, where exactly do I go?' she asked. It seemed like an ordinary pub to her, no stage, maybe the Great Gaels were upstairs.

The man assumed she was looking for the Ladies. 'I think it's over there near the other door, yes, there it is beside the Gents.' He pointed across the room.

Flushing a dark red she thanked him. In case he was still looking at her she thought she had better go to the Ladies. In the cloakroom she looked at her face. It had looked fine at home, back in her flat. In here it looked a bit dull, no character, no colour. She put on much more makeup in the dim light and came out to find out where the concert would be held.

She saw two women sitting together. They looked safe enough to ask. They told her with an air of surprise that it would be in the pub, but not for about an hour.

'What do we do until then?' she asked.

They laughed. 'I suppose you could consider

having a drink, it is a pub after all,' said one of them. They went back to their conversation. She felt very silly. She didn't want to leave and come back in case there was no re-admittance. She wished she had brought a paper or a book. Everyone else seemed to be talking.

She sat for what seemed like a very long time. Twice the waiter asked her would she be having another drink as he cleaned around her glass of orange, which she was ekeing out. She didn't want to waste too much money; a pound already coming in was enough to spend.

Then people arrived and started to fix up microphones, and the crowd was bigger suddenly and she was squeezed towards the end of the seat, and she saw the Great Gaels having pints up at the bar just as if they were ordinary customers. Wasn't Dublin fantastic? You could go into a pub and sit and have a drink in the same place as the Great Gaels. They'd never believe her at home.

The lead singer of the Great Gaels was tapping the microphone and testing it by saying, *'a haon, a dhó, a thri . . .'* Everyone laughed and settled down with full drinks.

'Come on now, attention please, we don't want anyone with an empty glass now getting up and disturbing us,' he said.

'Divil a fear of that,' someone shouted.

'All right, look around you. If you see anyone who might be fidgety, fill up their glass for them.'

Two men beside Jo looked at her glass disapprovingly. 'What have you in there, Miss?' one said.

'Orange, but it's fine, I won't get up and disturb them,' she said, hating to be the centre of attention.

'Large gin and orange for the lady,' one man said.

'Oh no,' called Jo, 'It's not gin . . .'

'Sorry. Large vodka and orange for the lady,' he corrected.

'Right,' said the waiter, eyeing her disapprovingly, Jo felt.

When it came she had her purse out.

'Nonsense, I bought you a drink,' said the man.

'Oh, but you can't do that,' she said.

He paid what seemed like a fortune for it; Jo looked into the glass nervously.

'It was very expensive, wasn't it?' she said.

'Well, that's the luck of the draw, you might have been a beer drinker,' he smiled at her. He was very old, over thirty, and his friend was about the same.

Jo wished they hadn't bought the drink. She wasn't used to accepting drinks. Should she offer to buy the next round? Would they accept, or would they worse still buy her another? Perhaps she should just accept this one and move a bit away from them. But wasn't that awfully rude? Anyway, now with the Great Gaels about to begin, she wouldn't have to talk to them.

'Thank you very much indeed,' she said putting the orange into the large vodka. 'That's very nice of you, and most generous.'

'Not at all,' said the man with the open-neck shirt.

'It'sh a pleashure,' said the other man.

Then she realised that they were both very drunk.

The Great Gaels had started, but Jo couldn't enjoy them. She felt this should have been a great night, only twenty feet away from Ireland's most popular singers, in a nice, warm pub, and a free drink in her hand, what more could a girl want? But to her great embarrassment the man with the open-neck shirt had settled himself so that his arm was along the back of the seat behind her, and from time to time it would drop round her shoulder. His friend was beating his feet to the music with such energy that a lot of his pint had already spilled on the floor.

Jo hoped fervently that they wouldn't make a scene, and that if they did nobody would think that they were with her. She had a horror of drunks ever since the time that her Uncle Jim had taken up the leg of lamb and thrown it into the fire because somebody crossed him when they had all been invited to a meal. The evening had broken up in a shambles and as they went home her father had spoken about drink being a good servant but a cruel master. Her father had said that Uncle Jim was two people, one drunk and one sober, and they were as unlike as you could find. Her father said that it was a mercy that Uncle Jim's weakness hadn't been noticeable in any of the rest of the family, and her mother had been very upset and said they had all thought Jim was cured.

Sometimes her sisters told her terrible things people had done in the hotel when they were drunk. Drunkenness was something frightening and unknown. And now she had managed to land herself in a corner with a drunk's arm around her.

The Great Gaels played encore after encore, and they only stopped at closing time. Jo had now received another large vodka and orange from the friend of the open-shirted man, and when she had tried to refuse, he had said, 'You took one from Gerry — what's wrong with my drink?'

She had been so alarmed by his attitude she had rushed to drink it.

The Great Gaels were selling copies of their latest record, and autographing it as well. She would have loved to have bought it in some ways, to remind herself that she had been right beside them, but then it would have reminded her of Gerry and Christy, and the huge vodkas which were making her legs feel funny, and the awful fact that the evening was not over yet.

'I tried to buy you a drink to say thank you for all you bought me, but the bar man told me it's after closing time,' she said nervously.

'It is now?' said Gerry. 'Isn't that a bit of bad news.'

'Imagine, the girl didn't get a chance to buy us a drink,' said Christy.

'That's unfortunate,' said Gerry.

'Most unfortunate,' said Christy.

'Maybe I could meet you another night and buy you one?' She looked anxiously from one to another. 'Would that be all right?'

'That would be quite all right, it would be excellent,' said Gerry.

'But what would be more excellent,' said Christy, 'would be if you invited us home for a cup of coffee.'

'Maybe the girl lives with her Mam and Dad,' said Gerry.

'No, I live on my own,' said Jo proudly and then could have bitten off her tongue.

'Well now,' Gerry brightened. 'That would be a nice way to round off the evening.'

'I don't have any more drink though, I wouldn't have any beer . . .'

'That's all right, we have a little something to put in the coffee.' Gerry was struggling into his coat.

'Are you far from here?' Christy was asking.

'Only about ten minutes' walk.' Her voice was hardly above a whisper. Now that she had let them know that the coast was clear, she could think of not one way of stopping them. 'It's a longish ten minutes, though,' she said.

'That'll clear our heads, a nice walk,' said Christy.

'Just what we need,' said Gerry.

Would they rape her? she wondered. Would they assume that this was why she was inviting them back — so that she could have sexual intercourse with both of them? Probably. And then if she resisted they would say she was only leading them on and insist on having their way with her. Was she stark staring mad? She cleared her throat.

'It's only coffee, mind, that's all,' she said in a schoolmistressy way.

'Sure, that's fine, that's what you said,' Christy said. 'I have a naggin of whiskey in my pocket. I told you.'

They walked down the road. Jo was miserable. How had she got herself into this? She knew that she *could* turn to them in the brightly lit street and say, 'I'm sorry, I've changed my mind, I have to be up early tomorrow morning.' She *could* say, 'Oh heavens, I forgot, my mother is coming tonight, I totally forgot, she wouldn't like me bringing people in when she's asleep.' She *could* say that the landlord didn't let them have visitors. But she felt that it needed greater courage to say any of them than to plod on to whatever was going to happen.

Gerry and Christy were happy, they did little dance steps to some of the songs they sang, and made her join in a chorus of the last song the Great Gaels had sung. People looked at them on the street and smiled. Jo had never felt so wretched in her whole life.

At the door she asked them to hush. And they did in an exaggerated way, putting their fingers on their lips and saying 'shush' to each other. She let them in and they went upstairs. Please, please God, may Nessa and Pauline not be in the kitchen. They never are any other night, let them not be there tonight.

They were both there. Nessa in a dressing gown, Pauline in a great black waterproof cape; she was colouring her hair apparently, and didn't want bits of the gold to fall on her clothes.

Jo smiled a stiff 'good evening' and tried to manipulate the two men past the door.

'More lovely girls, more lovely girls,' said Gerry delightedly. 'You said you lived by yourself.'

'I do,' snapped Jo. 'These are the girls from next door, we share a kitchen.'

'I see,' Pauline said in a huffed tone. 'Downgraded.'

Jo wasn't going to explain. If only she could get the two drunks into her own bed-sitter.

'What are you doing, is that a fancy-dress?' Christy asked Pauline.

'No, it's not a fancy-dress, wise guy, it's my night-dress — I always go to bed in a black sou'wester,' Pauline said and everyone except Jo screeched with laughter.

'I was just going to make us some coffee,' said Jo sharply, taking down three mugs with Visitor painted on them. Gerry thought the mugs were the funniest thing he had ever seen.

'Why do you put Visitor on them?' he asked Jo.

'I have no idea,' Jo said. 'Ask Nessa.'

'So that you'll remember you're visitors and won't move in,' Nessa said. They all found this very funny too.

'If you'd like to go into my bedroom — my flat, I mean, I'll follow with the coffees,' Jo said.

'It's great crack here,' said Christy and produced his small bottle from his hip pocket.

Nessa and Pauline got their mugs immediately.

In no time they were all friends. Christy took out a bit of paper and wrote Christy and Gerry and they stuck the names to their mugs — so that they would feel part of the gang, he said. Jo felt the vodka and the heat and the stress had been too much for her. Unsteadily she got to her feet and staggered to the bathroom. She felt so weak afterwards that she couldn't face the kitchen again. She went to the misery of her bed, and oblivion.

She felt terrible in the morning. She couldn't understand why people like Uncle Jim had wanted to drink. Drinking made other people ridiculous and made you feel sick, how could anyone like it? She remembered slowly, like a slow-motion film, the events of the night before and her cheeks reddened with shame. They would probably ask her to leave. Imagine coming home with two drunks, and then abandoning them in the kitchen while she had gone away to be sick. God knows who they were, those two men, Gerry and Christy. They might have been burglars even . . . Jo sat up in bed. Or suppose when she had disappeared . . . suppose they had attacked Nessa and Pauline?

She leapt out of bed, uncaring about her headache and her stomach cramps, and burst out of her door. The kitchen was its usual tidy self: all the mugs washed and hanging back on their hooks. Trembling, she opened the doors of their bedrooms. Pauline's room was the same as ever — huge posters on the wall and a big long clothes rail, like you'd see in a shop that sold dresses, where Pauline hung all her gear. Nessa's room was neat as a pin, candlewick bedspread, chest of drawers, with photographs neatly arranged; little hanging bookshelf with about twenty paperbacks on it. No sign of rape or struggle in either room.

Jo looked at her watch; she was going to be late for work, the others had obviously gone ages ago. But why had they left her no note? No explanation? Or a note asking her for an explanation?

Jo staggered to work, to the wrath that met her as she was forty minutes late. Jacinta said to her at one stage that she looked pretty ropey.

'Pretty ropey is exactly how I feel. I think I'm having my first hangover.'

'Well for you,' said Jacinta jealously. 'I never get a chance to do anything that might give me even a small hangover.'

She was dreading going home. Over and over she rehearsed her apologies. She would put it down to the drink. Or would that be worse? Would they find her even more awful if they thought she was so drunk last night she didn't know what she was doing? Would she say she had been introduced to them by a friend, so she thought they were respectable and when she found out they weren't it was too late? What would she say? Just that she was sorry.

Neither of them were there. She waited for ages but they didn't come in. She wrote out a note and left it on the kitchen table. 'I'm very very sorry about last night. Please wake me when you come in and I will try to give you an explanation. Jo.'

But nobody woke her, and when she did wake it was Saturday morning. Her note was still on the table. They hadn't bothered to wake her. She was so despicable they didn't even want to discuss it.

She made her morning cup of tea and stole back to bed. It was lunchtime before she realised that neither of them was in the flat. They mustn't have come home.

Jo had never felt so uneasy in her life. There must be a perfectly reasonable explanation. After all, there had been no arrangement to tell any of the others their movements. She had realised this on Thursday night. They all lived separate lives. But what could have happened that they had disappeared? Jo told herself that she was being ridiculous. Nessa lived in Waterford, or her family did, so she had probably gone home for the weekend. Pauline was from the country too, somewhere. Well, she had to be, otherwise she wouldn't be in a flat. She'd probably gone home too.

It was just a coincidence that they had gone the same weekend. And just a coincidence that they had gone after the visit of the two drunks.

Jo stood up and sat down again. Of course they had to be at home with their families. What else was she imagining? Go on, spell it out, what do you fear, she said to herself, that those two innocent-looking eejits who had a bit too much to drink kidnapped two big strong girls like Pauline and Nessa? Come on! Yes, it was ridiculous, it was ludicrous. What did they do, hold them at gun point while they tidied up the flat and then pack them into a van and bear them off?

Jo had often been told she had a vivid imagination. This was an occasion when she could have done without it. But it wouldn't go away. She couldn't pull a curtain over the worries, the pictures that kept coming up of Christy hitting Nessa and of Gerry strangling Pauline, and all through her mind went the refrain, 'There must be something wrong, otherwise they would have left me a note.'

It was her fourth Saturday in Dublin. The first one she had spent unpacking her case and getting used to the hostel; the second one had been spent looking at flats which were too expensive and too far from work, and which had already been taken by other people; the third Saturday she had spent congratulating herself on having found Nessa and Pauline; and now on this, the fourth Saturday, Nessa and Pauline had most likely been brutally murdered and ravaged by two drunks that she had brought back to the flat. How could she explain it to anyone? 'Well, you see, it was like this, Sergeant. I had two double vodkas in the pub bought by these men, and then when we came home — oh yes, sergeant, I brought them home with me, why not? Well, when we came home they poured whiskey into our coffees and before I knew where I was I had passed out in a stupor and when I woke up my flat-mates were gone, and they never came back. They were never seen again.'

Jo cried and cried. They *must* have gone home for the weekend. People did. She had read a big article in the paper not long ago about these fellows making a fortune driving people home in a minibus; apparently lots of country girls missed the crack at home at weekends. They must have gone off in a minibus. Please, please St Jude, may they have gone in a minibus. If they went in a minibus, St Jude, I'll never do anything bad for the rest of my life. More than that. More. If they're definitely safe and they went off yesterday in a minibus, St Jude, I'll tell everyone about you. I'll put a notice in the two evening papers — and the three daily papers, too, if it wasn't too dear. She would bring St Jude's name into casual conversation with people and say that he was a great man in a crisis. She wouldn't actually describe the whole crisis in detail, of course. Oh dear Lord, speak,

speak, should she go to the guards? Should she report it or was she making the most ludicrous fuss over nothing? Would Pauline and Nessa be furious if the guards contacted their homes? God, suppose they'd gone off with fellows or something? Imagine, if the guards were calling on their families? She'd have the whole country alerted for nothing.

But if she didn't get the guards, suppose something had happened because of those drunk men she'd invited into the house, yes, she, Josephine Margaret Assumpta O'Brien had invited two drunk men into a house, not a week after that nun in the hostel had said that Dublin was a very wicked city, and now her two flatmates, innocent girls who had done nothing to entice these men in, were missing, with no trace of them whatsoever . . .

She had nothing to eat for the day. She walked around hugging herself, stopping when she heard the slightest sound in case it might be a key in the lock. When it was getting dark she remembered how they had written their names on bits of paper: they could have taken them away with them, but they might be in the rubbish bin. Yes, there they were, Christy and Gerry, scrawled on paper with bits of sellotape attached to it. Jo took them out with a fork in case they might still have fingerprints on them. She put them on the kitchen table and said a decade of the rosary beside them.

Outside people passed in the street going about the business of a Saturday night. Was it only last Saturday that she had gone to the pictures with Josie and Helen, those two nice girls in the hostel? Why hadn't she stayed there? It had been awful since she left, it had been frightening and worrying and getting worse every day until . . . until This.

There was nobody she could talk to. Suppose she phoned her sister in the hotel, Dymphna would be furious with her; the immediate reaction would be, come-home-at-once, what-are-you-doing-by-yourself-up-in-Dublin, everyone-knew-you-couldn't-cope. And it was a temptation to run away. What time was the evening train to Limerick? Or tomorrow morning? But she didn't want to go home, and she didn't want to talk to Dymphna and she couldn't explain the whole thing on the phone downstairs in the hall in case the people in the flat below heard — the people in the flat below! *That* was it!

She was half-way down the stairs when she paused. Suppose everything were all right, and suppose St Jude had got them on a minibus, wouldn't Nessa and Pauline be furious if she had gone in and alarmed the three nurses downstairs? They had said that they kept themselves very much to themselves; the nurses were all right but it didn't do to get too involved with them. Yes, well, going in and telling them that you suspected Nessa and Pauline had been abducted and maltreated was certainly getting involved.

She went back up the stairs. Was there anything that the nurses could do to help that she couldn't do? Answer: No.

Just at that moment the big blonde nurse that she had spoken to came out. 'Hey, I was just going to go up to you lot above.'

'Oh, really, what's wrong?' Jo said.

'Nothing's wrong, nothing at all, we're having a party tonight, though, and we just wanted to say if any of you lot wanted to come, it starts at . . . well, when the pubs close.'

'That's very nice of you. I don't think . . . '

'Well, all we wanted to say is, there may be a bit of

117

noise, but you're very welcome. If you could bring a bottle it would be a help.'

'A bottle?' asked Jo.

'Well, you don't have to, but a drop of wine would be a help.' The nurse was about to walk past her up the stairs.

'Where are you going?' Jo asked, alarmed.

'I've just told you, to ask the others, the ones in the other flats, if they'd like to come . . . '

'They're not there, they're not at home, they're gone away.'

'Oh well, all for the best, I suppose,' the girl shrugged. 'I've got my meat and my manners now, can't say they weren't asked.'

'Listen,' Jo said urgently, 'what's your name?'

'Phyllis,' she said.

'Phyllis, listen to me, do the girls up here go away a lot?'

'What?'

'I mean, I'm new here, do they go home for the weekends or anything?'

'Search me. I hardly know them at all. I think the punk one's a bit odd a half-wit, between ourselves.'

'But do they go away at weekends or what? Please, it's important.'

'Honestly, I'd never notice, I'm on nights a lot of the time, I don't know where I am or whether people are coming or going. Sorry.'

'Would the others know, in your flat?'

'I don't think so, why? Is anything wrong?'

'No, I expect not. It's just, well, I wasn't expecting them to go off and they, sort of, have. I was just wondering whether . . . you know, if everything's all right.'

'Why wouldn't it be?'

118

'It's just that they were with some rather, well, unreliable people on Thursday, and . . . '

'They're lucky they were only with unreliable people on Thursday, I'm with unreliable people all the time! Maureen was meant to have hired the glasses and she didn't, so we had to buy paper cups which cost a fortune.'

Jo started to go back upstairs.

'See you later then. What's your name?'

'Jo O'Brien.'

'OK, come on down when you hear the sounds.'

'Thank you.'

*   *   *

At twelve o'clock she was wider awake than she had ever been in the middle of the day; she thought she might as well go down as stay where she was. The noise was almost in the room with her. There was no question of sleep. She put on her black dress and her big earrings, then she took them off. Suppose her flatmates were in danger or dead? What was she doing dressing up and going to a party? It somehow wasn't so bad going to a party without dressing up. She put on her grey skirt and her dark grey sweater, and went down stairs.

She arrived at the same time as four others who had been beating on the hall door. Jo opened it and let them in.

'Which are you?' said one of the men.

'I'm from upstairs, really,' Jo said.

'Right,' said the man, 'let's you and I go back upstairs, see you later,' he laughed to the others.

'No, no, you can't do that, stop it,' Jo shouted.

'It was a joke, silly,' he said.

'She thought you meant it!' The others fell about laughing. Then the door of the downstairs flat opened and a blast of heat and noise came out. There were about forty people crammed into the rooms. Jo took one look and was about to scamper upstairs again, but it was too late and the door had banged behind her. Someone handed her a glass of warm wine. She saw Phyllis in the middle of it all, her blonde hair tied in a top knot and wearing a very dazzling dress with bootlace straps. Jo felt foolish and shabby: she was jammed into a group of bright-faced, laughing people and she felt as grey as her jumper and skirt.

'Are you a nurse too?' a boy asked her.

'No, I work in the post office.'

'Well, can you do anything about the telephones, do you know there isn't a telephone between here and . . . '

'I don't give a damn about telephones,' she said and pushed away from him. Nessa and Pauline were dead, battered by drunks, and here she was talking about telephones to some fool.

'I was only making conversation — piss off,' he shouted at her, hurt.

Nobody heard him in the din.

'Which are your flatmates?' Jo asked Phyllis.

'The one in the kitchen, Maureen, and the one dancing with the man in the aran sweater, that's Mary.'

'Thanks,' said Jo. She went into the kitchen.

'Maureen,' she said. The girl at the cooker looked up with an agonised face. 'I wanted to ask you . . . '

'Burned to a crisp, both of them. Both of them burned to a bloody crisp.'

'What?' said Jo.

'Two trays of sausages. Just put them in the oven,

120

stop fussing, Mary says. I put them in the oven. And now look, burned black. Jesus, do you know how much sausages are a pound, and there were five pounds altogether. I told her we should have fried them. Stink the place out, frying them, she said. Well, what will this do, I ask you?'

'Do you know the girls upstairs?' Jo persisted.

'No, but Phyllis said she asked them, they're not making trouble are they? That's all we need.'

'No, I'm one of them, that's not the problem.'

'Thank God. What will I do with this?'

'Throw it out dish and all, I'd say, you'll never clean it.'

'Yes, you're right. God, what a fiasco. What a mess.'

'Listen, do you know the girls, the other ones, Nessa and Pauline?'

'Just to see. Why?'

'Do you know where they are?'

'What? Of course I don't. If they're here they're in the other room, I suppose, waiting to be fed, thinking there's some hot food. I'll *kill* Mary, I'll literally *kill* her, you know.'

'Do they normally go away for the weekend?'

'God, love, I don't know whether they go up to the moon and back for the weekend. How would I know? There's one of them with a head like a lighthouse and another who goes round with that dynatape thing putting names on anything that stands still . . . bells and doors and things. I think they're all right. We never have many dealings with them. That's the best way in a house of flats, I always say.'

Jo left it there. It seemed unlikely that Mary would know any more, and she decided to leave her happily with the man in the aran sweater until she was given the bad news about the sausages.

A hand caught her and suddenly she was dancing herself. The man was tall and had a nice smile.

'Where are you from, Limerick?'

'Not far out,' she said laughing. Then dread seized her again. What was she doing dancing with this stranger and chatting him up like she might have done at a dance at home? 'I'm sorry,' she said to him, 'I'm sorry, I have to go. I've got something awful on my mind, I can't stay.'

At that moment the window in the kitchen was broken by a big stone, and glass shattered everywhere. There were screams from the garden and shouts.

'I'm getting the guards, this looks like a bad fight,' said the tall boy and like a flash he was out in the hall. Jo heard him speaking on the phone. In the kitchen people were shouting to each other to move carefully. A huge lump of glass lay precariously on top of a cupboard: it could fall any moment.

'Is anybody hurt, stop screaming, is anybody cut?' Jo recognised Phyllis and felt a small amount of relief flood back into her. At least they were nurses; maybe a lot of them were. They'd be able to cope better than ordinary people. People had run out the front door and an almighty row was going on in the garden. Two men with cut heads were shouting that they only threw the stone in self-defence, people had started firing things at them from the window first; one of them was bleeding over his eye. They only picked up the stone to stop the barrage coming at them.

The guards were there very quickly, four of them. Suddenly everything was different; what had looked like a party began to look like something shameful. The room that had been full of smoke and drink and music and people dancing and people talking about nothing was now a room full of broken glass and upturned chairs and people shouting trying to explain what had happened, and people trying to comfort others, or get their coats and leave. Neighbours had come to protest and to stare: it was all different.

It didn't take long to work it out: the two men in the garden were crashers. They had tried to come in the front door and been refused admittance; they had then gone around to see if there was a back entrance. That was when the first one had been attacked with a hot weapon which had both burned and cut his face. Investigating the attack, the other one had been wounded in exactly the same way. (The weapons were, of course, Mary's burnt sausages.) They thought that everybody in the party was firing things at them so they threw one stone before leaving.

Notebooks were being put away. Phyllis said that one of the men needed a stitch, and she would go to the hospital with him, taking Mary as well, since Mary's arm had been cut by flying glass. The party was over. The guards said that too much noise was being made for a built-up area and, since two of the hostesses were disappearing to the hospital, there didn't seem to be any point in guests staying on in a flat which was now full of icy winds because of the window. Some of the men helped to pick the last bit of broken glass out, and a sheet of tin was found in the boot of somebody's car. It was a sorry end. The guards were leaving; one of them saw Jo sitting on the stairs.

'Are you all right for a lift home?' he asked.

Jo shook her head. 'I don't need one. I live upstairs.'

'You look a bit shook, are you all right?'

She nodded wordlessly.

'What a night, not much of a Saturday night in Dublin for a little country girl, is it?'

He was trying to cheer her up. It didn't work.

'Well, I'll be off, you go off too and get some sleep, you need it by the look of you.'

She nodded again.

'You are all right, you're not in shock or anything? It's all over, it was only a broken window,' he said soothingly. 'There'll be worse than that before the night's over.'

'Oh God,' she said.

'Hey, Sean,' he called, 'this one's going to faint, I think, give me a hand.'

She came to as they were getting her in the door of the flat. She had had the key in her hand and it had fallen when she fell.

'Which is her room?' Sean said.

'How would I know?' said the one who was carrying her. 'Here's the kitchen, get her in there . . . '

She saw the names on the table.

'Don't touch those, they're evidence,' she said. 'Please don't touch them.'

They decided they'd better all have a cup of tea.

*　　　*　　　*

'It's television, that's what it is,' Mickey said.

'It's that and eating too much rich food late at night,' said Sean.

'But how can you be sure they're all right?' Jo wasn't convinced.

'Because we're normal human beings,' said Sean.

Jo flushed. 'So am I. I'm normal too, that's why I'm worried. I'm just concerned and worried about them. Stop making horrible jokes about my eating rich food and having nightmares. I haven't eaten anything, I'm so worried, and that is exactly why I didn't come to the Garda station because I knew that's the kind of reception I'd get.'

She burst into tears and put her head down on the table.

'Mind the evidence,' Sean giggled

Mickey frowned at him. 'Leave her alone, she *is* worried. Listen here, those two will be back tomorrow night right as rain. Nobody abducts people like that, honestly. Nobody says please wash up all the mugs and tidy up your rooms and come on up the Dublin mountains to be abducted, now do they?' He smiled at her encouragingly.

'I suppose they wouldn't.'

'And you are kind to be concerned, and we'll say no more about it tonight now because you're exhausted. Go to sleep and have a lie in tomorrow. Those two rossies will be home tomorrow night and you'll think you were mad crying your heart out over them. Do you hear me?'

'But I'm so stupid, I'm so hopeless. I can't cope with Dublin, I really can't. I thought I'd have a great time when I got a flat, but it's all so different, and so lonely, so terribly lonely, and when it isn't lonely it's like a nightmare . . . '

'Now stop that,' Mickey said firmly. 'Stop it at once. You never talk about anyone but yourself, I this, I that. You're constantly wondering what people are thinking about you. They're not thinking about you at all.'

'But I . . . '

'There you go again. I, I, I. You think that there's some kind of gallery of people watching you, sitting there as if they were at the pictures, watching you leave the house each day, all your movements, saying, is she having a good time, is she being a success in Dublin? Nobody gives one damn. Why don't you start thinking about other people?'

'But I *am* thinking about other people, I'm thinking about Nessa and Pauline . . . '

'Oh no, you're not, you're only thinking about what *you* did to them, whether *you're* responsible for their kidnapping and disappearance, or whether they'll think *you're* silly.'

Jo looked at him.

'So, lecture over. Go to sleep.' He stood up. So did Sean.

'You're probably right,' she said.

'He's always right, known for it,' said Sean.

'Thank you very much indeed, it is a bit lonely at first, you get self-centred.'

'I know, I felt a bit the same last year.'

'Sligo?'

'Galway.'

'Thank you very much again.'

'Goodbye, Jo.'

'Goodbye, Guard, thank you.'

'Mickey,' he said.

'Mickey,' she said.

'And Sean,' Sean said.

'And Sean,' Jo said.

'And maybe some night you might come out with me,' said Mickey.

'Or me, indeed?' said Sean.

'I saw her first, didn't I?' said Mickey.

'You did,' said Jo. 'Indeed you did.'

'I'll wait a bit until the two lassies are back and installed, but I've a night off on Monday . . . '

'You're sure they'll come back?'

126

'Maybe if I called for you about eight on Monday? How's that?'

'That's grand,' said Jo. 'That's grand altogether.'

She had been reading the Problem Pages for years. One or two of them always said things about having done grievous wrong in the eyes of God and now the only thing to do was to Make Restitution. Most of them said that your parents would be very understanding — you must go straight away and tell them. You will be surprised, the Problem Pages said, at how much tolerance and understanding there will be, and how much support there is to be found at home.

Not in Pat's home. There would be no support there, no understanding. Pat's mother wasn't going to smile like people did in movies and say maybe it was all for the best and it would be nice to have another baby around the place, that she had missed the patter of tiny bootees. And Pat's father wasn't going to put his arm around her shoulder and take her for a long supportive walk on Dun Laoghaire pier. Pat knew all this very well, even though the Problem Pages told her she was wrong. But she knew it from personal experience. She knew that Mum and Dad would not be a bundle of support and two big rocks of strength. Because they hadn't been any of that five years ago when her elder sister Cathy had been pregnant. There was no reason why their attitude should have changed as time went by.

Cathy had actually finished college when her little drama broke on the family. She had been twenty-two years old, earning her own living and in most ways living her own life. Cathy had believed the Problem Pages, she thought that Mum wouldn't go through the roof. Cathy had thought that there were ways you could talk to Mum and Dad like ordinary people. She had been wrong. Pat remembered as if it were yesterday the weekend of the announcement. It seemed to have gone on all weekend, Cathy saying she didn't want to marry Ian and Dad saying Ian must be brought around to the house this minute; Mum saying this was the result of trusting people to behave like adults and like responsible people; Cathy looking frightened and bewildered. She had said over and over that she thought people would be pleased.

Pat had been sixteen, and she had been shocked to the core. She had never heard words used like the words that were used that weekend. Dad had even apologised for some of the things he had called Cathy, and Mum had never stopped crying. Cathy came and sat on her bed on the Sunday evening. 'It's not the end of the world,' she had said.

'Oh, but it is,' Pat had said, almost afraid to look at Cathy in case she saw under her waist the whole dreadful shame that was going to cause such trouble.

'It's just that I can't see myself spending the rest of my life with Ian,' Cathy said. 'We'd be ridiculous together, we wouldn't last a year. It's such a terrible way to start a marriage with anyone.'

'But don't you love him?' Pat had asked. The only possible reason you could do the things that Cathy must have done with Ian to get herself to this stage must have been love.

'Oh yes, in a way, I love him, but I'll love

other people and so will he.'

Pat had not understood, she had been no help. She had said useless things like maybe it wasn't really positive, the test, and maybe Ian might like to get married if Cathy explained it properly. Cathy had taken the whole thing very badly; she had refused to accept that Mum and Dad might have any right on their side. 'They're so liberal, they *say* they're so liberal,' she had scoffed. 'They keep saying they're in favour of getting divorce introduced and they want contraceptives, and they want censorship abolished, but they refuse to face facts. They want me to marry a man knowing it will ruin my life and ruin his life, and probably wreck the baby's life as well. What kind of liberal view is that?'

'I think they believe that it would be the best start for the .. er ... the child,' said Pat uncertainly.

'Great start ... forcing two people who should love the child most into a marriage they're not prepared for in a country which doesn't see fit to set up any system to help when the marriage breaks down.'

'But you can't have people going into marriages knowing they can get out of them.' Pat was very familiar with the argument from fourth-year debating clubs at school.

'Well, you certainly can't go into a marriage, a doubtful marriage, knowing you can't get out of it,' Cathy had said.

She had gone to London. five days later. Everyone else had been told that she was doing this wonderful new post-graduate course. It was a special qualification in EEC law; it was obviously the absolutely necessary qualification of the future. Mum had said that with all the changes that were going to come about from Brussels and Strasbourg and everything, Cathy was doing the right thing. Pat knew that Cathy would not come back. She knew that the family had broken up, and broken much more permanently than when Ethna had gone to be a nun. Ethna hadn't really left at all, even though she was in Australia: Cathy was only an hour away but she had gone for ever.

Ethna had never been told why Cathy had gone to England. At Christmas the long letter with the small slanted writing had wanted to know all about the course that Cathy was doing and what her address was and what holidays she would get for the Christmas festivities. Nobody wrote and told Ethna that Cathy hadn't come home for Christmas. Perhaps Cathy had written, but it was certainly never mentioned in the weekly letters which came and went; every week a green Irish air letter on the hall table begun by Mum, where Dad and Pat added bits; and every week, but slightly out of synch, a blue air letter from Australia with details of Sister this who had done that and Sister that who had done this. And all of the time nothing from Cathy.

At about the time that Cathy's baby should be born Pat had asked Mum for the address. 'I wanted to write and see if there was anything we could do.'

'Oh, there's nothing any of *us* could do,' Mum had said bitterly. 'If there had been anything then we would have been glad to do it, but no, we knew nothing, your sister knew everything. So she knew best and went off on her own. No, I don't think there's anything *we* could do. I don't think it would be welcomed.'

'But, Mum, it's your grandchild. Your own grandchild.' Pat had been almost seventeen and full of

131

outrage.

'Yes, and Ian's mother, Mrs Kennedy, it's her first grandchild too. But are either of us being allowed the privilege of having a grandchild, and a baby we all want, and a christening, and a fuss, and the birthright of any child? No, no, a lot of claptrap about not wanting to settle down and not wanting to be tied down. I wonder does Miss Cathy ever ask herself where she would be if I had felt that way?' Mum had got very pink in the face about it.

'I'm sure she's very grateful to you, Mum.'

'Oh I'm sure she is, very sure. Yes, she must be. Fine life *she'd* have had if she had been given away to an adoption society the moment she saw the light of day because I couldn't be tied down.'

'But you were married already, Mum, and you did have Ethna.'

'That's not the *point*,' Mum had roared.

And suddenly Pat had realised what had been said.

'Is Cathy giving the baby away, she can't be giving the baby away, can she?'

'I'm not permitted to know what she's doing. We're not in her confidence, your father and I, but I *assume* that's what she's doing. If she can't be "tied down" to a perfectly reasonable nice boy like Ian Kennedy, then it's very unlikely that she can be tied down to an illegitimate baby which she would have to rear on her own.'

Pat had gone to the firm of solicitors where Ian Kennedy worked with his father. He was a nice, red-haired boy, about the friendliest of all Cathy's boy friends; it was a pity she hadn't married him.

'I came to talk to you about Cathy,' she had said.

'Yeah, great, how is she?' he had asked.

'I think she's fine . . . ' Pat had been nonplussed.

'Good, give her my love when you write, will you?'

'I don't have her address, and Mum is being diffi-cult. You know, not being able to lay her hands on it . . . '

'Oh, I don't know where she is now,' said Ian.

'Doesn't she keep in touch?' Pat was shocked again.

'No, she said she didn't want to. Said she wanted to be free.'

'But . . .?'

'But what?'

'Doesn't she keep you informed . . . let you know . ?'

'Know what?'

Pat paused. Now, it had been definitely said, de-finitely, about six months ago, that Ian had been told of her decision to go to England on account of the pregnancy. Yes, Ian had even been in the house. He had said to Dad that he was very happy indeed to acknowledge that he was responsible for the child, and to marry Cathy if she would have him. Pat knew that he had said he wanted to support the child, and to see it when it was born; he couldn't have forgotten about all that, could he?

'I'm sorry for being silly,' Pat had said. 'I'm the baby of the family and nobody tells me anything.'

'Yes?' Ian smiled kindly.

'But I thought she'd be having the, er, baby, now and I wanted to know how she was . . . that's why I'm here.'

'But didn't she tell you? She must have told you?' Ian's face was lined with concern.

'What? Told me what?'

'It was a false alarm — she wasn't pregnant at all.'

'I don't believe you.'

'Of course! Hey, you must know this. She wrote and told everyone just after she went to London.'

'It's not true . . . '

'Of course it's true. She wrote and told us all. It was a very early test she had here, not a proper one.'

'So why didn't she come back?'

'What?'

'If it was a false alarm why didn't she come back to her job and home and to you and everything?'

'Oh, Pat, you *know* all this . . . she was a bit peeved with your Mum and Dad. She thought there'd be more solidarity, I think. And she was very pissed off with me.'

'Why was she pissed off with you? You said you'd marry her.'

'But that's not what she wanted, she wanted . . . oh, I don't know . . . anyway, it wasn't necessary.'

'So why isn't she back?'

'As I said, we all let her down. She was annoyed. She wrote, when she told me about the false alarm bit, and said she didn't feel like coming back. She must have written to your family too. Of course she did.'

'She didn't,' Pat said definitely.

'But whyever not? Why didn't she put them out of their agony?'

'*Their* agony?'

'You know what I mean. It's an expression.'

'She never wrote.'

'Oh Pat, nonsense, of course she did. Maybe they didn't tell you. You said yourself they kept things from you.'

'They don't know it was a false alarm, I know that much.'

She said goodbye to Ian, and she promised she

wouldn't make a lot of trouble for everyone, she'd be a good little girl.

'You're a real *enfant terrible*, you know. You're much too grown-up and pretty to be playing that Saint Trinian's kind of thing.'

She put out her tongue at him, and they both laughed.

*   *   *

Mum said she didn't want to discuss Cathy. Cathy had found nothing to discuss with her, why should she spend time talking about Cathy?

'But Ian says he heard from her as soon as she went. It was all a false alarm, she never had a baby, she was never pregnant at all. Aren't you pleased now, isn't that good news, Mum?' Pat pleaded with her.

'That's as may be,' Mum had said.

*   *   *

Just as she was dropping off to sleep that night, Pat thought of something that made her sit up again, wide-awake.

Now she knew why Mum hadn't been pleased. Cathy must have had an abortion. That's why there was no baby, that's why Cathy had not come back. But why hadn't she told Ian? Or Mum? And mainly why hadn't she come back?

*   *   *

'Do you think the other nuns read Ethna's letters?' Pat had asked a few days later when the green aerogramme was being sealed up and sent off.

'Very unlikely,' Dad had said.

'It's not the dark ages. They don't censor their correspondence,' Mum had said.

'Anyway she can be fairly critical of some of the other nuns; she gives that Sister Kevin a hard time,' Dad said. 'I don't expect she'd do that if they read her outgoing letters anyway.'

Pat thought that it was nice that Dad read Ethna's letters so carefully that he knew which sister was which.

*   *   *

Pat had written to Ethna; first of all a probing letter. 'I'm getting older and a bit, though not much, wiser. One of the things that upsets me is the cloak of silence that hangs over Cathy, and where she is in England and what she's doing and what the situation is. Could you tell me what the situation is as far as you know it and then I'll take it from there . . . '

She had a letter from Ethna, not on an aerogramme but in an envelope. On the outside of the envelope it said, 'The Stamps You Wanted'. That satisfied any curiosity Mum and Dad might have had. Inside it was very short.

'I really think you are making a mystery about nothing. Poor Cathy has been punished quite enough, she thought that she was indeed going to have a child. And since she was not at all willing or ready to marry the father then it is merciful that this was not so. She is happy in London, where she is doing social work. She has hardened her heart to mother and father, which is a great pity, but in time I am sure she will feel ready to open up doors of friendship again. She doesn't write to me, apart from that one letter which told me all these things; since nobody has ever mentioned anything to me about it in letters from home, I have never mentioned anything either. I pray for her, and I pray for all of you. Life is so short, it seems sad that any of it should be spent in feeling a grievance and a hurt when a hand held out would brush all the unhappiness away.'

Great help, Pat had thought at the time; punished enough, hardened her heart, brush all the unhappiness away; nun's phrases, and not a word of blame about Mum and Dad who were always writing letters to the paper protesting about letting South African rugby teams into the country. They were always talking about itinerants, and they had raised money for refugees. Why were they so hard-hearted about Cathy?

Pat had decided that she was not going to allow Cathy to disappear without trace as if some terrible crime or shame had settled on the family and people hoped that by ignoring it things would return to normal. She had tackled them at supper the night she had got Ethna's letter.

'This family is becoming a bit like nine green bottles,' she said.

'What on earth do you mean?' Dad was smiling.

'First Ethna goes off to the other side of the world, and then we are four. Then six months ago Cathy disappears without trace and now we are three. Will I go off somewhere too?'

Dad was still smiling but he looked puzzled. He stood up to fetch the coffee percolator. He looked tired and a bit beaten. Not the cheerful doctor, always in a smart suit, always optimistic, always seeing the best for patients and neighbours alike. He wore his cardigan at home, and Mum wore an old jumper that was torn under the arms. They looked shabby and a bit dishevelled as they sat in the big dining room with its good furniture and its expensive cut glass decanters. Pat felt that somehow they didn't make any effort when it was only just her. She was sure they had been far more elegant and lively when Ethna was at home and when Cathy was there.

'Are you just waiting for me to go off and that will be the hat trick?'

'What is this, Pat, what silly game are you playing?' Mum was not very amused.

'No, I mean it, Mum. It's not much of a family, is it?'

'Don't speak to your mother like that.' Dad was surprised and hurt. He had thought that talking about green bottles was going to be a joke; now it had turned into a row.

'It's not normal. People marry and have children, they don't have them just to export them off as fast as possible.'

Mum was very annoyed indeed. 'Ethna was twenty-one when she left. She had wanted to join this order for two years. Do you think we wanted Ethna to go to that outlandish place? Or to be a nun at all? Don't be so ridiculous, and have some thought for other people before you start your hurtful accusations.'

'No, I know that's Ethna, but then Cathy's gone. This house used to be full of people, now it's just us. And soon I suppose you'll want me to go. Would you prefer if I tried to get into UCC or Galway or maybe England rather than Belfield, then you wouldn't have to have me around the place and you could be all on your own?' She stood up, tears in her eyes.

'Apologise this minute to your mother, this minute, do you hear me!'

138

'Why to Mum? I'm saying it to both of you.'

She was about to leave the room when Mum had said wearily, 'Come back, Pat. Come back and I'll talk to you about Cathy.'

'You owe her no explanation, Peggy, none, not after the way she's spoken to you.' Dad's face was red with disappointment.

'Sit down, Pat. Please.' Grudgingly and shrugging, Pat sat down.

'I'm not going to fight with you. I'm going to agree with you. It's not much of a family, it certainly isn't. When your father and I got married this is not what we had in mind at all.'

'Now Peg, now Peg,' Dad said warningly.

'No, the girl is right to question what's happened. We question it ourselves, for God's sake. Not at all what we had in mind. I suppose we had in mind the practice getting bigger and going well. It has. That's all fine, that side of it. And we had in mind our friends and all the people we like being around, and that's gone well. And our health has been fine. But mainly what we had in mind was the three of you. That's what people do have in mind actually, Pat, that's what they have in mind most of the day and night when they have children. From the time that Ethna was here we've had you three in mind more than anything else.'

Pat gave a very slight shrug. It was a disclaimer. It was meant to say, you don't have to tell me all this. I know you tried. As a shrug it worked. Mum had known what she meant.

'I know you think I'm just saying this to be nice to you, or maybe perhaps that we started out with good intentions and lost them on the way. But it wasn't like that. I think some of my best times, and yours,

Hugh, were when Ethna was about six or seven, and Cathy was five, and you were a baby. Three little girls totally dependent on us, all lighting up with enthusiasm . . .'

'Sure Mum. Yes. Sure.'

'No, give me a very short minute for the sentimental sugary bit because it didn't last long. Then you were all so bright. This was another joy, some of our friends had problems. Well, we didn't call them problems but so and so's child couldn't read until he was seven, or someone couldn't settle at school, or another wouldn't manage to get on with the teachers, or failed the third Honours in her leaving. Not you three, from Ethna on we knew, top of the class, exams no real problem. Do you remember Ethna's conferring?'

'Yes . . . I got the day off school.'

'And she looked so bright . . . that's a funny word, but she did, you know, clear eyes and alert face, compared to a lot of the others. I thought, ours is very bright, there's so much before her when she gets this ridiculous nunnish thing out of her system . . .'

'But I thought you approved?'

'We had to approve in the end.' Dad spoke for the first time. 'Of course we didn't approve. Use your head, Pat, suppose you had brought up a lovely girl like Ethna, as bright as a button as Mum says, who has just got a First class honours degree in history and who wants to go with a crowd of half-educated women to a school in the outback of somewhere because she read a book about the damn place and she met a recruiting team!'

'But you never said. I don't remember . . .'

'You don't remember. How old were you — twelve, thirteen? What discussions could we have had with

140

you about it that would have helped anything except add to the argument?'

Mum had interrupted. 'We didn't even discuss it with Cathy because we didn't want gangs forming and pressure being put on Ethna. We just talked to her.'

'And what did you want her to do?' Pat wanted to know.

'I'd have liked her to do an M.A. and then a doctorate. She was very, very good. I spoke to some of the people in there, they said she had the makings of a scholar, and I'd have liked her to have had a good lively life here, instead of putting up with Sister Kevin's tantrums in a jungle.' Dad had sounded very defeated when he said that, as if remembering the whole battle and how it was lost.

'Yes, that's what I'd have liked too. I'd have liked her to go on living here, it was so near and handy, and got a small car and had friends and gone off to the West for weekends. And then married someone in her own field, some professor, and got a house near by and I could have seen the whole thing over again with her children, growing up and learning to walk . . .'

'It's a fairly normal, reasonable wish, isn't it?' Dad had asked defensively. 'Rather than see a whole life, a whole education, and talent, thrown away.'

'She's happy though, she says she is,' Mum had said.

'I suppose her letters to us are about as near the truth as ours are to her,' Dad had said. And there was a silence as they thought about the implications of that.

'So Cathy . . . ?' Pat spoke softly, hoping that the mood hadn't been broken, that she could still get her mother to talk.

'Cathy,' Mum had said.

'Cathy was no trouble either. Everyone else told us of all their sleepless nights over their terrible teenage children. We never had any,' Dad smiled at Pat as if he was thanking her. She felt a twinge of guilt.

'And Cathy did have her friends around much more than Ethna, and they used to laugh, and they were full of life. Do you remember the summer they did the whole garden, Hugh?'

Dad had laughed. 'All I had to do was provide one of those big cans of beer at the end of the day. They dug and they weeded and they cut hedges and grass.'

'It never looked back since,' Mum had said. 'It used to be a wilderness and they tamed it.'

'All for a few cans of beer,' Dad had said. They stopped talking for a moment. Pat said nothing.

'So Cathy was going to be the one who might be with us, when Ethna went. It wasn't a transfer of love. I suppose it was changing the plans or hopes. And she was so enthusiastic, about everything.'

'We felt we were qualifying with her, she was so entertaining about it all — the lectures, the course, the solicitors' exams down in the Four Courts, the apprenticeship . . it was all so alive,' Dad had said.

'And she seemed to get on so well with Ian. I kept thinking, she's only twenty-two, she's far too young to settle down but then of course I told myself I was only twenty-two when I married. Then on the other hand, I didn't have a career to decide about. Then I went back to the first hand and said since Ian and Cathy were both solicitors and Ian's father had a firm, well then, surely if they did have a couple of children and she wanted to work part-time it couldn't be too hard to arrange.'

142

Dad had interrupted. 'This is what your mother meant about you children always being in our minds. We had Cathy married to Ian in our minds long before they even kissed each other.'

'But why couldn't you accept Cathy's decision like you did for Ethna? You didn't want Ethna to go off and be a nun but when she did you sort of acknowledged it.'

'Yes,' Mum had said, 'Yes, it made her so happy and it was her life. Much as I wanted to I couldn't control it any more . . . she had to do what she wanted.'

'So why couldn't Cathy do what she wanted?'

'That was different.'

'But why, Mum, why? It's not as if you and Dad were prudes or anything, it's not as if your friends would cut you off, or as if you'd be ashamed to lift your heads. Why can't Cathy bring her baby home?'

'It's different,' Dad had said.

'I can't think why, I really can't. Nobody minds. Ian doesn't mind. I talked to him. He's very casual about Cathy — "send her my love" he said. Ethna won't mind. I wrote to her about it, but, but . . .'

'You wrote to Ethna?' Mum had said, surprised.

'Yes, to try and clear things up.'

'And did it?'

'No, not at all.'

'What did you want cleared up?' Dad had asked.

'Whether Cathy is having a baby or is not. Something very basic and simple like that, which most normal families would know.'

Dad had looked at Mum, and she had said, 'Tell her.'

'The answer is . . . that we don't know.'

'You don't *know*?'

'No. That's the truth.' Mum had continued, 'We were very shocked by Cathy's attitude. She was very harshly critical of us, and the way we lived, and thought that our attitudes were hypocritical, you know, to preach some kind of broadmindedness and then not to follow it.'

'But we didn't see it like that. You see, it was nothing to do with acceptance or reputations, we thought Cathy was being silly and making extravagant gestures, turning herself into a Protest just for the sake of it. "Look at me, I'm too modern to do like anyone else, give my child a name and a home and a background, no, I'm far too sophisticated for that!" We didn't like it, Pat, it was too studenty . . . '

'There's no need to go over all that was said, you probably heard most of it, but to cut a long story short we have only heard from Cathy once since she went to London. I always imply — well, let's be honest, I always tell people lies and say that we've heard from her, but she wrote only once two weeks after she left.'

'Did she say . . . ?'

'She said that it had been a false alarm, that her dates had been wrong, that she was only a shorter time overdue than she thought and that everything was fine.'

There was a silence.

'And did you believe her, Mum?'

'No.'

'Did you, Dad?'

'No. I didn't.'

'It was too far for there to be a mistake?'

'Well, she said she had left a specimen into Holles Street and they had said it was positive. They don't make mistakes.'

'But she says they did.'

'No, she's forgotten she told us that bit, I think.'

'Oh.'

'So we know no more than you do,' Mum had said, spreading out her hands helplessly.

'But why do you say everything's all right . . . ?'

'Because it will be one way or another, sometime, and we don't want Cathy to have to walk back into a whole lot of complications. Keep it simple, is our motto.'

'So what do you believe if you don't believe what Cathy said?'

'Well, what do you think?'

'No, what do you think?'

'Pat, either she had a termination or she is in fact having the child, and as you so rightly pointed out to me, if she is having the baby it's due this month.'

'And we don't know?'

'We don't know.'

'We don't even know where she is?'

'No.'

Then Mum had started to cry, and she cried with her arms down on the table and her head on top of them. Right into the dishes and the food. And Dad had stood up and come over and patted her awkwardly on one side and Pat had patted her awkwardly on the other.

'It's all right, Peg,' Dad had said, over and over.

'It's all right, Mum,' Pat had said, over and over.

*   *   *

It had been a hard thing to sit your Leaving Certificate not knowing where your sister was, whether she was alive or dead, and not knowing if you were an aunt or not. But Pat had gone on and done it: she had got all her Honours and plenty of points. Peggy and Hugh's third daughter was on her way to University College, Dublin, registering as a student in Belfield.

Cathy wrote home that year just before Christmas. She said she had seen enough of other people's miseries in her case-load in London to make her realise that most of life's troubles were caused by families. She would like to say very sincerely that she had been entirely to blame for any little fracas they had had. She asked forgiveness and if they liked she would love to come home for Christmas, but since she had been so difficult and stayed out of touch for so long, over a year, she could well understand if they said no. She gave her address for them to reply. It was in Hackney. Mum and Dad had sent a telegram five minutes after the letter arrived. The telegram had read, 'Welcome home, darling Cathy, to the silliest parents and the happiest Christmas ever.'

Cathy had also written to Pat.

'You may well wonder what the Prodigal thinks she's up to, and I don't want to put your nose out of joint. I ll tell you everything you want to know, if you want to know anything, when I see you, and if you have no time for me I'll understand that too. It was utterly selfish of me to go away and leave you as a teenager, in your last year at school, to cope with all the trauma and drama. But when there's a crisis people only think of themselves, or I did anyway. I hope the reunion won't be a damp squib. I haven't kept in touch with most of my friends, so can I ask you to fill the house a bit with people so that we don't become too hot-house and raise our family expectations too high? I'll stop asking and taking soon and start giving, I promise.'

Pat had thought this was very sensible. She asked her College friends in on the evening that Cathy came back. Mum had gone to the airport to meet her and by the time Pat had come home conversation was quite normal. In fact, so normal it was almost frightening. It was as if Cathy had never gone away, as if no mystery hung over the events of the past year. Cathy had said that Pat looked smashing, and that students must be dressing better than in her day, and there wasn't time for much more conversation because they had to get the mulled wine ready, which involved a lot of conversation about what you did to mull it, and how to ensure you didn't boil the alcohol out of it. Pat had been startled to see that they were all laughing quite naturally in the kitchen when Dad had said he should test each batch they made, just in case the flavouring needed adjusting. 'You haven't changed, Dad,' Cathy had laughed, and nobody made any flicker of an eyelid as the moment passed and Cathy's long absence had now sunk into the collective memory. It could be mentioned without being questioned.

It had been like that all that Christmas, and nothing seemed more natural at the end of the holiday than for Cathy to say that she would be coming back for good as soon as she had found a replacement for herself. She was going to work in Ian's office; they had a vacancy in a couple of months. Pat had been puzzled when she saw Cathy and Ian Kennedy strolling around the wintry wilderness of garden, plucking at bushes and pointing out what should be done with hard, frozen-looking flowerbeds. What was going on inside that red head of Ian Kennedy's? Did he not wonder whether Cathy had given birth to his child in London all by herself in

147

a hospital with no friends to come and visit her? Did he not worry about his child, their child, being given to an adoption society and never knowing what it should have known?

Did Ian Kennedy wonder whether Cathy had gone long, long ago to a doctor in England in order to organise a termination of pregnancy and then over-night in one of those nursing homes everyone knew about, where simple minor surgery under anaesthetic would ensure that Cathy and Ian's child didn't ever come into being? Surely he wasn't so foolish as to think that a girl could be pregnant, disappear for over a year and have some vague belief that the pregnancy was all a false alarm.

People were really behaving more and more peculiarly, Pat decided. The older they got the vaguer they became. Ethna's letters now had nice bland welcoming bits about Cathy in them. Had she forgotten all that earlier stuff about punishment, and hardening her heart, and praying for her? Once people got any way settled they seemed to lose touch with reality and built themselves a comfortable little world like a Wendy House entirely of their own creation.

* * *

She had told this to Rory a few times, and he had tried to understand it. But Rory thought that her whole life was a fraud, and that anyone who owned any kind of private house was already out of touch with society. Rory was in her Economics tutorial, by far the most brilliant student of his year, a great thorn in a lot of University flesh. Rory had economic arguments for revolution which could not be faulted.

Rory agreed with Pat that the whole Cathy business was very unreal. Rory said he loved Pat, and Pat was very sure that she loved Rory.

*　　　*　　　*

'It's a mistake to get too involved with anyone your first year in College,' Cathy had said. 'It ties you down, you should have the freedom to roam round and see who you like and who you don't. You should get to know a lot of people, not just sticking together two by two as if you were the animals going into the ark.' Pat didn't like this remark. It was too reminiscent of Cathy saying she couldn't be tied down to marry Ian. It also implied a criticism of Rory. And that was not allowed.

There was nothing that Mum and Dad could find fault with in Rory; they wanted to, but they couldn't actually put a finger on anything. He certainly didn't distract her from her work; in fact he insisted that she work harder than she was prepared to. He said her essays weren't sufficiently researched; he lent her books, he came with her to the library and sat opposite her. It was easier to do the damn stuff than to find excuses. He didn't keep her out at all night parties. He had explained to Mum and Dad that he didn't drink much so there wouldn't be any danger of drunken driving late at night in his little beat-up car. When they went away to conferences or student festivals in Cork or Galway, Rory always managed to drop the one phrase which would reassure Mum and Dad about the set-up. 'I'll leave Pat at the girls' house first and then she can settle in and I'll go off and find where they're putting the lads up . . . ' Some trivial little remark which would prevent Mum and Dad from wondering what exactly the score was.

The score was exactly as Rory described it for a long time.

'I suppose you think it's silly not to,' Pat had said.

'Silly, no. Wasteful, yes,' Rory had said. 'It's up to you entirely what you would like to do. I don't ever believe in putting on the pressure. Too much of what's wrong is wrong because people felt forced to do things for approval. But I think you're wrong. It would give us both so much pleasure and it would hurt exactly nobody. We aren't betraying anyone, we can be sure that we aren't irresponsibly conceiving a child we don't want. So wasteful is all I think I'd say it was.'

She adored Rory, his intensity and his boyish enthusiasms. She went to the Family Planning Clinic. She knew the doctor who was on duty that day. It was a friend of her father's. 'Glad to see you, that's a good sensible girl,' the friend of Dad's had said. No explanations asked for, no curiosity, no condemnation. It was all so simple. Why hadn't Cathy done this? They had clinics, even in her time.

Cathy was still a mystery. There she was, living at home so calmly. If anyone ever asked about the Common Market Legal course she was meant to have done, she would shake her head and say that she hadn't done it after all, she had worked for the Council in East London. Mum had been right in her way to have kept things simple, to have rocked no boats. Cathy came back and stepped in more or less where she had got out. It was just that time, all those months that remained as inexplicable. What had she been doing, what had she been thinking? She was so placid now, sometimes going out to the theatre with Ian, sometimes with other people. Holidaying with two girls in the Greek islands, sitting with Mum and Dad sometimes in the evenings looking at television.

Pat had insisted on Rory discussing it. 'Is it natural for them not to mention it? Is it normal? I mean, there she is at home, and nobody ever once refers to the fact that she left home pregnant and stayed away from home for fourteen months and came back and everything is as you were.'

'Um.' Rory was reading.

'But why, why do they say nothing? It's like not noticing someone is naked or not referring to someone being in a car crash or in gaol. It's not real.'

'Um. I know,' he said.

'But they don't seem to want to know, it's only me, it's only me that wants to know.'

'Well, why don't you ask her then?' Rory said.

*   *   *

'Cathy, did you have any problems with the Pill, you know, have you had to change brand or anything?'

Cathy looked up from the papers she was studying. She was sitting at the big desk in her bedroom, which she had converted into a kind of study.

'No, I was never on the Pill, so it didn't occur.'

'Never on the Pill, at all?'

'No.'

'How amazing.'

'Pat, you are twenty, going on twenty-one. You aren't actually a wise old sociologist commenting on the funny things society does.' Cathy laughed good-naturedly as she spoke.

'Yes, but . . . not ever?'

'Not ever. If I *had* been, that little incident which

you may remember would never have happened . . .'

'Yes, well, after the little incident . . . ?'

Pat felt she was treading on a minefield. She had to remain light-hearted and casual.

'Oh, after the little incident, I didn't . . . how shall I put it . . . well, I didn't actually need the services of a contraceptive.'

'Not ever?'

'No, not ever.' Cathy smiled, relaxed and calm as if they had been talking about the replanting of the herbaceous border.

'Oh.'

'So I'm not much help. But you could go to the Family Planning Clinic, tell them if it doesn't suit you. They'll change it.'

'Yes, good idea. Cathy?'

'Yes?'

'Remember that time . . . the little incident . . . what happened?'

'How do you mean, what happened?'

'I mean, did you go through with it? Did you have the baby?'

'Did I what?'

'Did you have the baby? In London?'

'Hey, what is this? A joke?'

'No, seriously. I wish you'd tell me. I hate us all pretending, it's so artificial.'

'Tell you what?'

'When you went off to London, did you actually have the baby?'

'No, of course I didn't, are you feeling all right? What an extraordinary question to ask. Have a baby? Where is it, then, if I had it, was I meant to have left it in a telephone box?'

'Well, what did you do? Did you have an abortion?'

'Seriously, is this some kind of game? Of course I didn't. What on earth are you saying . . . ?'

'But you *were* pregnant.'

'No, I thought I was. I wasn't.'

'You were, Dad knows, he said so when you were gone.'

'Oh no, he can't have, I wrote telling them it was a false alarm.'

'He didn't believe you.'

'Listen, don't start stirring up a lot of trouble over nothing. It was nothing. Why all this interrogation?'

'Is that what put you off the whole thing, fellows and making love?' Pat asked. 'They say people can get very depressed.'

'I *didn't* have an abortion, and I wasn't very heavily into fellows and making love, and I haven't gone off fellows.'

'That's all you'll say.'

'Jesus Lord, what is this, Pat, one of Rory's revolutionary tribunals? You've asked me about ten questions. I've answered all of them honestly -- which is rather good of me since *none* of them are any of your business.'

'I'm sorry.'

'No, you're not, you want some awful group where everyone sits and tells the most god-awful, self-centred, boring details of what they did and what they thought and what they felt and what they did then, and what they thought then and what they felt then . . . honestly, I can't stand that kind of thing. Even Woody Allen laughs at it, for heaven's sake. It's not going to solve the world's problems.'

'What is?'

'I don't know, but a lot of people's are solved by playing down dramas rather than creating them.'

'And is that what you're doing?'

'I'm refusing to invent them, refusing to make myself into a tragedy queen.'

'I m sorry I spoke.'

'I'm not, but I'm glad you've stopped.' Cathy grinned.

Pat gave a watery grin back.

*　　*　　*

'So you see, she's *got* to be lying. Somewhere along the line she told a lie.' Pat frowned as she ticked the items off on her fingers.

'There are times you can be very boring, Pat,' said Rory.

She was hurt and upset. 'You're often analysing what people say and why society forces us to tell lies and role-play. Why is it boring when I do it?'

'Because it's repetitive and it's slapdash.'

'How do you mean?'

'Well, you haven't even included all the possibilities, have you?'

'I *have*. Either she was not pregnant, or she was and she had either a baby or an abortion.'

'She could have had a miscarriage, you clown.'

*　　*　　*

All that had been a year ago. Pat remembered the conversation word for word. They had been all at the turning points of things somehow. The very next day, the day following the interrogation, Cathy said that she and Ian were going to get married. The news coincided with a letter from Ethna. She was leaving the order. And everyone might remember that she had spoken quite a lot of Father Fergus. Well, Fergus was in Rome at the moment and the laicisation process was well under way. She and Fergus would be married in Rome during the summer. Then they would come home, possibly try to get a teaching job. It shouldn't be hard. Both of them had a lot of qualifications and a lot of experience.

'It's all working out as you want, isn't it, Mum?' Pat had said.

'It's what all you girls want that's important, you know that,' Mum had said; she was laughing at herself a little, and she tried to take the triumphant look off her face.

That time had been a turning point for Pat too. Rory had told her about the South American woman, Cellina. Pat had liked Cellina; she had helped her to organise a solidarity campaign for fellow students back home, and she had introduced her to Rory. She had been pleased when Rory had liked Cellina. She had never seen exactly how much he had liked Cellina until he told her.

She had stopped taking the Pill. To use Cathy's marvellous, old-fashioned phrase, she felt she didn't need the services of a contraceptive. She did a lot of work on her thesis, and she did a great deal of work at home too. A family wedding for Cathy, with the Kennedys screaming their delight as loudly as Mum and Dad. Then there was the trip to Rome. Why not? If Ethna was doing something as huge as this they must all be there, and they were. Mother had Ethna back, and she had Cathy back.

But she was about to lose Pat. Temporarily perhaps, who could tell? Rory had come back from Bonn where he and Cellina had been living. He had come home alone. They had met a lot during the two weeks he was back. It seemed silly and wasteful not to go to bed with him. They were giving each other a lot of pleasure and they weren't hurting anyone, since Cellina would never know. And were they betraying anyone? The word betrayal is such a subjective one.

But now Rory had gone back to Bonn, and Holles Street, which is never wrong over such things, had said Positive. And Pat had learned enough over the years not to believe the Problem Pages. It would be best if she went to London, on her own. Connected with work. And the possibility of getting into the London School of Economics — yes, that would be a good one. She had often spoken of the LSE. Mum and Dad would be interested in that as a project.

And as long as she wrote regularly and seemed happy, that was the main thing.

Seven people woke up that morning and remembered that this was the day Gerry Moore came out of the nursing home. He wouldn't be cured, of course. You were never cured if you were an alcoholic. Four of them shrugged and thought that perhaps he wasn't really an alcoholic — these things were so exaggerated nowadays. There was a time when a man took a drop too much, but now it was all endogynous, and in the glands, and in the bloodstream, and there were allergies and addictions that had never existed before. Two people knew very well that he was an alcoholic, and the remaining one, waking up that morning, looking forward to his release, had never believed for one moment that there was anything the matter with Gerry. He had gone into that home for a good rest, and that's all there was to it.

*   *   *

Gerry's mother was seventy-three, and there had never been any scandal in her life before and there wasn't going to be any. She had reared five boys on her own. Three of them were abroad now, all of them making a good living; only two were in Ireland, and of those Gerry was easily her favourite. A big innocent bear of a man without a screed of harm in him. He worked too hard, that was the problem and in his job, Gerry had told her often, the best place to meet clients was in pubs. A grown man couldn't sit like a baby in a pub, drinking a pint of orange juice! Naturally a man had to drink with the people he talked to. They wouldn't trust him otherwise. His health had broken down from all the anti-social hours, that's what he had told her. He had to go into the nursing home for six weeks for a total rest. No one was to come and see him. He would be out in the first week of May, he had said. Now it was the beginning of May and he'd be home, as right as rain. That's if anyone could be as right as rain in the house his precious Emma ran for him. Stop. She mustn't say a word against Emma, everyone thought Emma was the greatest thing since sliced bread. Keep your own counsel about Emma. Even her son Jack had said that Emma was a walking saint. Jack! Who never noticed anyone . . .

*　　*　　*

Jack Moore woke up that morning with a leaden feeling in his chest. He couldn't identify it for a while. He went through the things that might cause it. No, he had no row going on with Mr. Power in the showrooms; no, he had no great bag of washing to take down to the launderette. No, there had been no bill from the garage for his car — and then he remembered. Gerry came home today. Insisted on taking a bus home in his own time, no, he didn't want anyone to collect him, didn't want to look like a wheelchair case. Anyway, he had to start taking control of his own life again. Jack knew that the visit to the nursing home was going to be a big talking point, a drama, a bit of glamour, just like losing his driving licence had been. Gerry had held them spellbound with his story of the young guard asking him to blow into the bag. The jokes that Gerry had made had cracked a smile even in the Gardai. It hadn't done any good in the end, of course, he had been put off the roads for a year. Emma had taken twenty-five driving lessons in ten days: she had passed her test. She drove the car, remembering to take the keys out of it when she was going to leave both the car and Gerry at home. Emma was a saint, a pure saint. He hoped her children appreciated her.

*   *   *

Paul and Helen Moore woke up and remembered that this was the day that Daddy came home. They were a lot more silent at breakfast than usual. Their mother had to remind them of the good news. When they got back from school their Dad would be sitting at home as cured from his disease as he could hope to be. Their faces were solemn. But they should be cheerful, their mother told them, everything was going to be fine now. Dad had gone of his own choice into a place where they gave him tests and rest and therapy. Now he knew that drinking alcohol for him was like drinking poison, and he wouldn't do it. Paul Moore was fourteen. He had been going to go and play in his friend Andy's house after school, but that wouldn't be a good idea now. Not if a cured father was coming back. He never asked his friends to play in their house. Well. It was only one day. Helen Moore was twelve; she wished that her mother didn't go *on* about things so much, with that kind of false, bright smile. It was better really to be like Father Vincent who said that the Lord arranged things the way the Lord knew best. Father Vincent believed that the Lord thought it was best for Dad to be drunk most of the time. Or that's what it seemed that Father Vincent thought. He was never too definite about anything.

*   *   *

Father Vincent woke wishing that Gerry Moore had a face that was easier to read. He had been to see him six times during his cure. Gerry had ended up the most cheerful patient in the nursing home; he had nurses, nuns and other patients agog with his stories of the people he had photographed, the adventures, the mistakes corrected just in time, the disasters miraculously averted. Alone with the priest, he had put on a serious face the way other people put on a raincoat, temporarily, not regarding it as anything to be worn in real life. Yes, Gerry had understood the nature of his illness, and wasn't it bad luck — a hell of a lot of other fellows could drink what he drank and get off scot free. But he would have to give it up. Heigh Ho. But then the priest had heard him tell stories about photographing film stars on location, and meeting famous people face to face. Nowhere did he seem to remember that he hadn't done a book for four years, nor a proper commission for two. He had spent most of his time drinking with that friend of his from RTE, the fellow who was apparently able to get his work finished by twelve noon and spend the rest of the day in Madigans. A hard man, poor Gerry used to call him. Des the hard man. Father Vincent hoped that Des-the-hard-man would be some help when Gerry got out of all this. But he doubted it. Des didn't look like a pillar for anyone to lean on.

*   *   *

Des Kelly woke up at five a.m. as he always did. He slipped out of the bed so as not to wake Clare: he had become quite an expert at it over the years. He kept his clothes in a cupboard on the stairs so that he could dress in the bathroom without disturbing her. In half an hour he was washed, dressed and had eaten his cornflakes; he took his coffee into his study and lit the first cigarette of the day. God, it was great that Gerry was being let out of that place at last, the poor divil would be glad to be out. He'd been up once to see him and he'd known half the crowd in the sitting room, or half-known them. Gerry wasn't well that day, so he'd scribbled a note to say he'd called. He'd felt so helpless, since his automatic response had been to leave a bottle of whiskey. Still, it was all over now, and no harm done. Pumped all the poison out of him they had, told him to lay off it for a bit longer, then go easy on it. Or that's what Des supposed they told him, that made sense anyway. If you got as reached by the stuff as poor old Gerry had been getting there over the last few months, it was wiser to call a halt for a bit. What he couldn't stand was all this sanctimonious claptrap about it being an illness. There was no fitter man in Dublin than Gerry Moore. He had been a bit unfortunate. But now he had time to take stock and get his career together, well, he'd be back on top in no time. That's if Know-all Emma, you-name-it-I'm-a-specialist-in-it Emma, didn't take control of him and crush any bit of life that was left in him right out of him. Gerry would need to watch it: with a friend like that creeping Jesus Father Vincent, with a coffin-face of a brother like Jack and with know-all Emma for a wife, poor Gerry needed a couple of real friends. One of the few things he and Clare ever saw eye to eye about these days was what a mystery it was that a grand fellow like Gerry Moore had married that Emma. Des sighed at the puzzle of it all and opened his file: he always got his best work done at this time of the morning.

*　　*　　*

Emma woke up late. She had hardly slept during the night but had fallen into one of those heavy sleeps at dawn. She was sorry now that she hadn't got up at six o'clock when she was so restless; the extra three hours weren't worth it. She tumbled out of bed and went to the handbasin. She gave herself what her mother had called a lick and a promise. She smiled at the way she had accepted the phrase for so long and never questioned it until today. Today of all days she was up late and examining her face in the mirror musing over what old childhood sayings might mean. She pulled on her pale blue sweater and jeans and ran downstairs. Paul and Helen looked at her as reproachfully as if she had handed them over to Dr Barnardo's.

'We had to get our own breakfast,' said Helen.

'You'll be late for work,' said Paul.

'The place looks awful for Daddy coming home,' said Helen.

With her lip well bitten in to stop her shouting at them Emma managed a sort of smile. They had managed to spill water, cold and hot, all over the kitchen. God almighty, it's not that hard to fill an electric kettle and then to pour hot water into cups of instant coffee, is it? She didn't say it, she didn't ask the rhetorical question which would result in shrugging and counter-accusation. They had trailed coffee powder, buttered the sink as well their bread, there was a line of crumbs from the toaster . . . calm, calm.

'Right, if you've had your breakfast, you head off, and we'll have a celebration supper tonight. Isn't it marvellous?' She looked brightly from one to another.

'Why didn't you get up in time, Mummy, if it's such a marvellous day?' Helen asked. Emma felt that she would like to slap her hard.

'I was awake most of the night and I fell into one of those heavy sleeps just a short time ago. Come on now, hoosh, you should be gone . . ..'

'Will the celebration supper last long? Can I go over to Andy's afterwards?'

'Yes!' snapped Emma. 'When supper's over you can do what you like.'

'Is Father Vincent coming to supper?' Helen asked.

'Heavens, no. I mean who would have asked him, why do you think he might be here?' Emma sounded alarmed.

'Because he's often here when there's a crisis, isn't he?'

'But this isn't a crisis. This is the end of the crisis, Daddy is cured, I tell you, cured. All the awful things about his disease are gone, there's no need for Father Vincent to come and be helpful.'

'You don't like Father Vincent much, do you?' said Helen.

'Of course I do, I like him very much, I don't know where you got that idea. It's just that he's not needed tonight.' Emma was wiping and cleaning and scooping things into the sink as she spoke.

'Would you say you like Father Vincent less or more than you like Dad's friend Mr Kelly?'

Emma put her hands on her hips. 'Right, is there anything else you'd like to do before you go to school? Play I Spy? Maybe we could have a few games of charades as well or get out the Monopoly? Will you get yourselves . . . '

They laughed and ran off. She ate the crusts of their toast, rinsed the cups and plates and ran from the kitchen into the sitting room. The children had been right, it was a mess. She took a deep breath and made a big decision. One hour would make all the difference. Please God, may she get someone who was understanding and nice, someone who realised that she wasn't a shirker.

'Hallo, is that RTE? Can you put me through to . . . .' No, suddenly she hung up. It was bad enough having one in the family who let people down: she had never missed a day since she had got the secretarial job in Montrose, she was damned if she was going to miss even an hour today. She swept up the worst of the untidiness, shoving newspapers and magazines into the cupboard, gathering any remaining cups or glasses from last night. Gerry wasn't one to notice what a place looked like.

She threw out the worst of the flowers and changed the water in the vase; then she took out her Welcome Home card and wrote 'from all of us with love.' She propped it up beside the flowers, ran out pulling the door, leapt on her bicycle and headed for Montrose. Because she was a little later than usual there was more traffic, but she didn't mind, she thought of it as a contest. She would fight the cars

164

and the traffic lights and the bits that were uphill. She would think about nice things, like how she had lost a stone and a half in two months, how she could fit into jeans again, how someone had really and truly thought she was a young woman, not the forty-year-old mother of teenagers. She thought of the great sun-tan she would get in the summer; she thought that she might get highlights in her hair if it weren't too dear. She thought of everything in the world except her husband Gerry Moore.

*　　*　　*

Gerry Moore was going to be a great loss in the nursing home. The nurses all told him that and so did the patients. The doctor had his last chat with him that morning and said that in many ways he had been one of the most successful patients who had ever done the programme because he had refused to let it depress him.

'You've been in such good form all the time, Gerry, you've actually helped other people. I must admit at the start I was less than convinced. I thought you were just marking time to get out and get at the stuff again.'

'Wouldn't I have to be half mad to do that?' Gerry said. The doctor said nothing.

'I know, I know, a lot of the lads you get in here are half mad. But not me. Honestly, I know what I'm doing now. I just have to change my lifestyle, that's all. It can be done. I once had a lifestyle, a grand lifestyle, without drink. I'll have one again.'

'You'll be in here lecturing to us yet,' the doctor laughed.

Gerry had a dozen people to say goodbye to: he

promised he'd come back to see them. 'They all say that,' people said, yet people believed that Gerry Moore would, he had that sort of way with him.

Nurse Dillon said she was surprised that a man like Mr Moore with so many friends of his own didn't want anyone to come and collect him. Gerry had put his arm around her shoulder as she walked him to the door.

'Listen here to me, I'm thinner, I'm much more handsome, I'm a sane man, not a madman. I'm a great fellow now compared to the way I was when I walked in — so don't you think I should go home my own route and let the world have a look at me?'

She waved at him all the way to the end of the avenue. He was a gorgeous man, Mr Moore, and actually he was right, he did look fabulous now. You'd never think he was an old man of forty-five.

'Mind yourself as you go your own route,' she called.

*　　*　　*

His own route. Now where would that have taken him in the old days? Stop remembering, stop glorifying . . . a taste was only a taste, it wasn't anything special. He knew that. Stop glamourising it all. These pubs, the ones he might have dropped into, they weren't welcoming corners where friends called him to join their circles; some of them were sordid and depressing. If ever he had got talking to anyone it had been a sour depressed man who might have looked at him with suspicion. It was only when he got back nearer home that he would find people he knew in pubs. Friends. Stop glorifying it. It had *not* been a constant chorus of 'There's Gerry, the very

166

man, come on over here, Gerry, what'll you have?'
No, it hadn't been like that. People had avoided him,
for God's sake, in the last months. He knew that, he
had faced it. People he had known for years. Boy,
was it going to come as a shock to them when they
saw him with his big glass of Slimline Tonic and a
dash of angostura bitters, the non drinkers' cocktail.
Ho, they'd be surprised, never thought old Gerry
Moore had it in him to change his life.

Gerry walked to the bus stop. He had a small over-
night case. He hadn't needed much in the hospital,
just his dressing gown and pyjamas and a wash bag,
really, a couple of books and that was it. Why had his
suitcases always been so heavy in the old days? Oh, of
course, booze in case he would ever be caught short,
and gear for work. No more attention to booze
EVER again, but a lot of attention to work. He was
looking forward to spending a good month sorting
himself out and seeing where he was, then another
month sending out mail shots offering specialised
work. By midsummer he should be back where he
had been, only better. A bus came and he got into it.
Happily, he reached into his pocket and got out the
money Emma had brought him. He hadn't wanted
money but of course he had been admitted to that
nursing home penniless; she had given him money for
tipping and taxis or whatever he needed. He hated
taking her money, he hated that more than anything.

He got off the bus in the City Centre. Other people
were walking about normally, it seemed to him; they
had no problems and big decisions. They looked
vacantly into windows of shops, or screwed their eyes
up against the sunlight to see whether the traffic
lights were green or red. A few early tourists strolled,
everyone else seemed to bustle a bit. He looked at

them wonderingly; most of them would have no problems handling a few glasses of spirits, a few pints, a bottle of wine with their meal, yet a lot of them wouldn't even bother to. He saw with annoyance a couple of Pioneer Pins pass by; that Total Abstinence in order to make reparation to the Sacred Heart always annoyed him deeply. Nine tenths of these fellows didn't know what they were giving up. It was as if he said that he'd give up mangoes or passion fruit, something he'd never tasted. The Lord couldn't be all that pleased with such a sacrifice; the Lord, if he was there at all, must know that these Pioneers were a crowd of hypocritical show-offs. Easy, easy. Stop thinking about drink as some wonderful happiness creator. Don't imagine that a drink suddenly turns the world into an attractive technicolour. The world's fine now, isn't it? He didn't want a drink this moment, did he? No. Well then, what was the problem?

He caught the number ten with agility just as it was about to pull out. There right in front of him was Clare Kelly. 'The lovely Clare . . . well, aren't I steeped?' he said with a mock gallant manner that played to the rest of the bus.

Clare was embarrassed and irritated to have run into him. Gerry could see that. She was a distant, cold sort of woman, he had always thought. Full of sarcasm and the witty answer. Gave poor Des a bloody awful time at home. Des had nothing to say to her these days, he had often told that to Gerry. He had said that he and Clare didn't actually talk, have real conversations; there was always a state of war, where one or the other was winning. Nobody could remember when the war had been declared but it was there, in private as well as in public, putting each other down. Not that there was much in public these days. Clare didn't have much time for her husband's friends. Des preferred it that way. Let her have her meetings and her own life, let her laugh and sneer with her own friends, mock and make little of people. That suited him fine. Gerry had been very sorry for Des, the best of fellows. No matter what things went wrong in his own life at least Emma didn't mock him.

Clare had moved over to make room for him. 'You're looking marvellous,' she said.

'Why wouldn't I, with all it cost?' he said, laughing. 'Can I get your ticket? Two to . . . are you going home or are you off to reform the world somewhere?' He paused as the conductor waited.

'Home,' she laughed at him. 'You haven't changed Gerry, they didn't knock the spirit out of you.'

'No, only the spirits,' he laughed happily, and handed her her ticket like you would give it to a child. 'Here, take this in case we have a fight before we get home and you and I separate.'

'Are you on your way home now from . . . you know?'

'Yes, just released. They gave me back my own clothes, a few quid to keep me going and the names and addresses of people who might take on an ex-con . . .' He laughed, but stopped when he noticed that Clare wasn't laughing at all.

'Wouldn't you think Emma . . . ? It's awful to have you coming out on your own, like this.'

'I wanted to. Emma said she'd come in the car after work, your Des said he'd come for me in a taxi, Brother Jack, the ray of sunshine, said he'd arrive and escort me home after work, Father Vincent said he would come with a pair of wings and a halo and spirit me home . . . but I wanted to come home on my own. You could understand that, couldn't you?'

'Oh yes,' said Clare, managing to get some lofty superiority into the two words.

'Well, how's everything been, out in the real world?'

'Quiet, a bit quieter without you.' She didn't smile as she said it. She said it as though he were a dangerous influence, someone who had been upsetting people. There was ill-concealed regret that he was back in circulation. He smiled at her pleasantly as if he hadn't understood her tone. He had to be very calm, no point in becoming touchy, no seeing insults, fancying slights, imagining hostilities; no running away to hide because people were embarrassed about his treatment; no rushing out to console himself because the world didn't understand. Nice and easy.

'Ah, if that's the case we'll have to liven it up a bit. A quiet world is no use to God, man or the devil, as they say.' He left the subject and drew her attention to some demolition work they could see from the bus. 'Hey, that reminds me,' he said cheerfully, 'did you hear the one about the Irish brickie who came in to this site looking for a job . . .'

Clare Kelly looked at him as he told the story. He looked slimmer and his eyes were clear. He was quite a handsome man in a way. Of course it had been years since she had seen him sober so that made a difference. She wondered, as she had wondered many times, what people saw in him; he had no brain whatsoever. In between his ears he had sawdust.

She smiled politely at the end of the story, but it didn't matter to Gerry because the bus conductor and three people nearby had laughed loudly. And he was really telling the joke to them as much as to Clare.

*   *   *

He was pleased to see the flowers. That was very nice of Emma. He put his little case down in the sitting room and moved automatically to the cupboard under the music centre to pour himself a drink. He had his hand on the door when he remembered. God, how strong the old habits were. How ridiculous that in all those weeks in the hospital he never found himself automatically reaching for some alcohol, but now here at home . . . . He remembered that nice young Nurse Dillon saying to him that he would find it hard to make the normal movements at home because he would be so accustomed to connecting them with drink. She had said that some people invented totally new things to do, like drinking Bovril when they came in to the house. Bovril? He had wrinkled his nose. Or Marmite, or any unfamiliar beverage, like hot chocolate. She had been very nice, that Nurse Dillon, regarded the whole thing as a bit of bad luck like getting measles; she had even given him a small Bovril last night and said that he might laugh but it could well come in handy. He had said that he was such a strong character he would go to the drinks cupboard and pour the bottles down the sink. Nurse Dillon said that he might find his wife had already done that for him.

Gerry opened the doors. Inside there were six large bottles of red lemonade, six of slimline tonic, six of Coca Cola. There was a bottle of Lime Cordial and a dozen cans of tomato juice. He blinked at them. It was a little high-handed of Emma to have poured away all his alcohol without so much as a by-your-leave. He felt a flush of annoyance creep up his neck. In fact it was bloody high-handed of her. What did all

171

this business about trusting him, and relying on him, and not pressurising him, mean if she had poured his drink away? There had been the remains of a case of wine, and two bottles of whiskey there. Money to buy things didn't grow on trees.

Very, very upset he went out to the kitchen and put his hands on the sink deliberately to relax himself. He looked at the plug hole. Without a word of consultation she had poured about twenty pounds worth of drink down there. Then his eye fell on a box in the corner of the kitchen, with a piece of writing paper sellotaped to it. 'Gerry. I took these out of the sitting room cupboard to make room for the other lot. Tell me where you want them put. E.' His eyes filled with tears. He wiped his face with the back of his hand and sniffed as he struck the match to light the gas to boil the kettle to make his cup of Bovril.

* * *

Mrs Moore had rung once or twice during the day, but there had been no reply. That Emma and her precious job. What was she except a glorified typist? Just because she was in Montrose, just because she had sat at the same table as Gay Byrne in the coffee shop, and walked down a corridor with Mike Murphy, just because she had given Valerie McGovern a lift and had a long chat with Jim O'Neill from Radio Two, did that make her special? Oh no, it didn't, just a clerk is all she was. And a clerk with a heart of stone. The girl had no feeling in her. Wouldn't any normal person have taken the day off to welcome her husband back from six weeks in hospital? But not Emma. The poor lad had to come back to an empty house.

'Ah, there you are, Gerry, how are you, are you feeling all right now, did you have a good rest?'

'Like a fighting cock, mother, grand, grand altogether.'

'And did they give you medicines, injections, did they look after you properly? I can't think why you didn't go to Vincent's. Isn't it beside you? And you have the Voluntary Health.'

'Oh, I know, mother, but they don't have the course there. I had the whole course, you know, and thank God it seems to have worked. But of course, you never know. You're never really sure.'

'What do you mean you're not sure, you're all right! Didn't they have you in there for six weeks? Gerry? Do you hear me? If you don't feel all right, you should see someone else. Someone we know.'

'No, Mother, I'm fine, really fine.'

'So what did they tell you to do, rest more?'

'No, the contrary in fact, keep busy, keep active, tire myself out even.'

'But wasn't that what had you in there, because you were tired out?'

'Don't you know as well as I do what had me in there? It was the drink.'

His mother was silent.

'But it's all right now, I know what I was doing to myself and it's all over.'

'A lot of nonsense they talk. Don't let them get you involved in their courses, Gerry. You're fine, there's nothing the matter with you, you can have a drink as well as the next man.'

'You're not helping me, mother, I know you mean well but those are not the facts.'

'Facts, facts . . . don't bother with *your* facts, with *their* facts up in that place. The fact is that your

Father drank as much as he liked every evening of his life and he lived to be seventy, Lord have mercy on him. He would have lived to be far more if he hadn't had that stroke.'

'I know, Mother, I know, and you're very good to be so concerned, but, believe me, I know best. I've been listening to them for six weeks. I can't touch drink any more. It's labelled poison as far as I'm concerned. It's sad, but there it is.'

'Oh, we'll see, we'll see. A lot of modern rubbish. Emma was explaining it to me. A lot of nonsense. People had more to do with their time when I was young than to be reading and writing these pamphlets about not eating butter and not smoking and not drinking. Wasn't life fine in the old days before all these new worries came to plague us, tell me, wasn't it?'

'It was, Mother, it was,' said Gerry wearily.

*   *   *

It *had* been fine for a while. When Gerry and Emma got married he had a good career. There was a lot of money to be made from advertising in the sixties: one day it had been a bottle and an elegant glass, another it had been a consultation about photographing new banks, the sites, and personnel, the buildings. He had known all the agencies, there was no shortage of work. Emma had been so enthusiastic about his work — she had said it was much more vibrant and alive than her own. She had taught book-keeping and ac-countancy for beginners in a technical school. She never called it a career; she had been delighted to leave it when Paul was expected, and she had never seemed to want to go back when Helen was off to

174

school and out of the way, and that was a good seven years ago. Now that the bottom had fallen out of the market in advertising and there were no good photographic jobs left, Emma wasn't able to get back into teaching either. They didn't want people who had opted out for fifteen years, why should they? That's why she was up in the television station doing typing, and thinking herself lucky to get the job.

They had said in the nursing home it wasn't very helpful to look back too much on the past; it made you feel sorry for yourself, or wistful. Or else you began to realise what had happened was inevitable, and that wasn't a good idea either. You started to think you had no responsibility for your actions. So let's not think of the past, the old days when life was fine. He made the Bovril and took it, sniffing it suspiciously, into the sitting room. Hard not to think of the old days. A picture of their wedding in the silver frame, laughing and slim, both of them. His own father and both Emma's parents, now dead, smiled out more formally. His mother had looked confident, as if she knew she would be a long liver.

Then the pictures of Paul and Helen, the series he had done; they looked magnificent, people said, on an alcove wall, a record of the seventies children growing up, turning into people before your eyes. But they had stopped turning into people photographically about five years ago. The children seemed stuck in a time warp of his making.

He looked back at the wedding picture and again he felt the prickling in his nose and eyes that he had felt when he read Emma's note in the kitchen. Poor girl, she was only a girl, she was only thirty-nine years old and she had been keeping four people for two years on a typist's salary. That's really what it boiled down to. Of course, there had been the odd cheque coming in for him, the royalties from some of those coffee table books; a little here for a print he'd taken from stock for someone's calendar, a little there for a permission to reprint. But he had cashed those cheques and spent them himself. Emma had kept the family. God, he would make it up to her, he really would. He would make up every penny and every hour of worry and anxiety. He wiped his eyes again, he must be big and strong. Gerry Moore was home again, he was going to take over his family once more.

*　　*　　*

Emma hadn't liked to make a phone call while the office was quiet. It was too important a call, she couldn't suddenly hang up if she felt that people were listening to her. Anxiously she watched the clock, knowing that he must be home by now, wishing that she had done more to make the place welcoming, mentally ticking off the shopping she had done at lunchtime; she was going to make them a celebratory meal. She hoped he wasn't regretting his decision to come home alone; going back to an empty house, to a changed lifestyle after six weeks in a hospital, it wasn't such a good idea. To her great delight the office filled up with people and she was able to turn her back and call home.

'Hallo?' His voice sounded a little tentative and even snuffly, as if he had a cold.

'You're very welcome home, love,' she said.

'You're great, Emma,' he said.

'No I'm not, but I'll be home in an hour and a half and I can't wait to see you. It's grand you're back.'

'The place is great. Thank you for the flowers and

the card.'

'Wait till you see what we're going to have tonight — you'll think you're in a first class hotel.'

'I'm cured, you know that.'

'Of course I do. You're very strong and you've got a terrific life ahead of you, we all have.'

His voice definitely sounded as if he had a cold, but maybe he was crying — she wouldn't mention it in case it was crying and it upset him that she noticed.

'The kids will be in any minute, you'll have plenty of company.'

'I'm fine, I'm fine. You're very good to ring. I thought you couldn't make calls there.' She had told him that the organisation expressly forbade private calls in or out. She had said this to stop him ringing when he was drunk.

'Oh, I sneaked one because today is special,' she said.

'I'll soon have you out of that place, never fear,' he said.

She remembered suddenly how much he hated her being the breadwinner.

'That's great,' she said. 'See you very soon.' She hung up. He sounded grand. Please, please God may it be all right. There was a man in RTE who hadn't touched a drop in twenty years, he told her. A lovely man, great fun, very successful, and yet he said he was a desperate tearaway when he was a young fellow. Maybe Gerry would be like him. She must believe. She must have faith in him. Otherwise the cure wouldn't work.

*   *   *

Paul came home first. He shuffled a bit when he saw his father sitting reading the *Evening Press* in the big armchair. It wasn't just six weeks since he had seen such a scene, it was much longer; Dad hadn't been round much for ages.

He put down his books on the table.

'You're back, isn't that great?' he said.

Gerry stood up and went and put both hands on his son's shoulders. 'Paul, will you forgive me?' he asked, looking straight into the boy's eyes.

Paul squirmed, and flushed. He had never been so embarrassed. What was Dad saying these awful corny lines for? It was worse than some awful old film on the television. Would he forgive him? It was yucky.

'Sure, Dad,' he said, wriggling away from the hands. 'Did you get the bus home?'

'No, seriously, I have been very anxious to say this to you for a few weeks, and I'm glad to have a chance before there's anyone else here.'

'Dad, it doesn't matter. Aren't you fine now, isn't that all that counts?'

'No, of course it isn't. There's no point in having a son unless you can talk to him. I just want to say that for too long this house hasn't been my responsibility. I was like someone who ran away, but I'm back, and it will all be like it was when you were a baby and don't remember . . . but this time you're grown up.'

'Yes,' said Paul, bewildered.

'And if I make rules and regulations about homework and helping in the house, I'm not going to expect you to take them meekly. You can say to me, what kind of sod are you to be ordering us about, where were you when I needed you? I'll listen to you, Paul, and I'll answer. Together we'll make this a proper family.'

178

'I wouldn't say things like that. I'm glad you're home, Dad, and that it's cured, the illness bit, honestly.'

'Good boy.' His father took out a handkerchief and blew his nose. 'You're a very good boy. Thank you.'

Paul's heart sank. Poor old Dad wasn't in good shape at all, maybe his mind had gone in that place, talking all this sentimental crap, and tears in his eyes. Oh shit, now he couldn't ask to go over to Andy's house. It would cause a major upheaval and maybe his father would burst into tears. God, wasn't it depressing.

* * *

Helen went into the presbytery on her way home in order to speak to Father Vincent.

'Is anything wrong?' The priest immediately assumed the worst.

'No, Mummy keeps saying there's no crisis, so it must all be fine, but I came to ask if you'd call in tonight on some excuse. If you could make up some reason why you had to call ...'

'No, child, your father's coming home tonight, I don't want to intrude on the family, you'll all want to be together. Not tonight, I'll call in again sometime, maybe in a day or two.'

'I think it would be better if you came in now, at the beginning, honestly.'

The priest was anxious to do the best thing but didn't know what it was. 'Tell me, Helen, what would I say, what would I do? Why would I be a help? If you could explain that to me then I would, of course.'

Helen was thoughtful for a moment. 'It's hard to say, Father Vincent, but I'm thinking of other times. Things were never so bad when you were there, they used to put on a bit of manners in front of you, you know, Mummy and Daddy, they wouldn't be fighting and saying awful things to each other.'

'Yes, but I don't think . . .'

'It mightn't have looked great to you, but if you weren't there, Daddy would be drinking much more and saying awful things and Mummy would be shouting at him not to upset us . . .'

The child looked very upset; Father Vincent spoke quickly. 'I know, I know, and a lot of homes that sort of thing happens in. Don't think yours is the only one where a voice is raised, let me assure you. But you're forgetting one thing, Helen, your father is cured. Thank God he took this cure himself. It was very hard and the hardest bit was having to admit that he couldn't handle drink. He now has admitted this and he's fine, he's really fine. I've been to see him, you know, up in the home. I know he didn't want you children going there, but he's a new man, in fact he's the old man, his old self, and there won't be a thing to worry about.'

'But he's still Daddy.'

'Yes, but he's Daddy without drink. He's in grand form, you'll be delighted with him. No, I won't come in tonight, Helen, but I'll give a ring over the week end and maybe call round for a few minutes.'

Helen looked mutinous. 'I thought priests were meant to help the community. That's what you always say when you come up to the school to talk to us.'

'I am helping, by not poking my nose in. Believe me, I'm older than you are.'

'That's the thing people say when they've no other argument,' Helen said.

*　　*　　*

Emma cycled down the road and saw Helen moodily kicking a stone.

'Are you only coming home now?' she asked, annoyed that Helen hadn't been back to welcome Gerry earlier.

'I called in to see Father Vincent on the way,' said Helen.

'What about?' Emma was alarmed.

'Private business, you're not to ask people what goes on between them and their confessor, it's the secrecy of the confessional.'

'Sorry,' said Emma. 'He's not coming round here tonight by any awful chance, is he?'

Helen looked at her mother with a puzzled look. 'No, he's not actually.'

'Good, I want us to be on our own today. You run ahead and say hello to your father, I'll be in in a moment.'

Unwillingly Helen walked on: as she turned in the gate she saw her mother take out a comb and mirror and pat her hair. How silly Mummy could be at times. What was she combing her hair for now? There was nobody at home to see her. You'd think she'd have combed it when she was in RTE where she might meet people who'd be looking at her.

*　　*　　*

Gerry gave Helen a hug that nearly squeezed the breath out of her.

'You're very grown up, you know, a real teenager,' he said.

'Oh Dad, it isn't that long since you've seen me, it's only a few weeks. You sound like an old sailor coming back from months abroad.'

'That's what I feel like, that's exactly the way I feel — how clever of you to spot it,' he said.

Helen and Paul exchanged fairly alarmed glances. Then they heard Mum's bicycle clanking against the garage wall and everyone looked at the back door. She burst in through the scullery and into the kitchen. She looked flushed from riding the bicycle; she had a huge bag of groceries which she had taken from the basket. In her jeans and shirt she looked very young, Gerry thought.

They hugged each other in the kitchen, rocking backwards and forwards as if the children were not there, as if Gerry wasn't holding a second mug of Bovril in his hand and as if Emma weren't holding the shopping in hers.

'Thank God, thank God,' Gerry kept saying.

'You're back, you're back again,' Emma said over and over.

Solemn-eyed, their children looked at them from the door into the hall. Their faces seemed to say that this was almost as bad as what they had been through before.

*   *   *

The telephone rang as they were having supper. Emma, her mouth full of prawns, said she'd get it.

'It's probably your mother, she said she'd ring.'

'She has,' said Gerry.

It was Jack. He had been kept late at the shop. Mr

182

Power had decided at the last moment that all the furniture in the show-rooms should be shifted around so that the cleaners could get at the place from a different angle. Emma spent two and a half minutes listening to a diatribe against Mr Power; she grunted and murmured soothingly. Then the tone of Jack's voice changed, it became conspiratorial.

'Is he home?' he whispered.

'Yes, thank God, he came home this afternoon. Looks as fit as a fiddle. We'll all have to go up there and be pampered, I tell you.' She laughed and sounded light-hearted, hoping Jack would catch her mood.

'And is there . . . is there any sign of . . .?'

'Oh yes, very cheerful, and he sends you his good wishes — we're just having a welcome home supper for him actually.' Would Jack take this heavy hint, was there the remotest chance that he might realise he had rung at a meal-time?

'Is he listening to you, there in the room?'

'Yes, that's right.'

'Well, I obviously can't talk now. I'll ring later, when he's asleep maybe.'

'Why don't you ring in the morning, Jack, say, late morning. Saturday's a good day, we'll all be around then, and you could have a word with Gerry himself. Right?'

'I'm not sure if I'll be able to ring in the late morning.'

'Well, sometime tomorrow . . .' She looked back at Gerry and affectionately they both raised their eyes to the ceiling. 'If only you'd get a phone, we could ring you. I hate you having to find the coins always for calls.'

'There's no point in paying the rental for a telephone, and they charge you any figure that comes into their heads, I tell you, for the number of calls. No, I'm better to use the coin box, it's not far away. It's just that there's often a lot of kids around on a Saturday.'

'Well, whenever you can, Jack.'

'You're marvellous with him, marvellous. Not many women would be able to cope like you.'

'That's right,' she laughed. He was such a lonely figure she didn't like to choke him off too quickly. 'And how are you keeping yourself?' she asked.

Jack told her at length: he told her that he had a bad neck which resulted from a draught that came through a door which Mr Power insisted on being open. He told her that people weren't buying as much furniture as they used to, and that this craze for going to auctions and stripping things down was ruining the trade. She motioned to Paul, who was nearest to her, to pass her plate. She was annoyed with Jack's timing and his insensitivity, but if she hung up she would feel guilty and she wanted to be able to relax tonight of all nights without another problem crowding her mind.

She looked over at the table as she let Jack ramble on; they all seemed to be getting on all right. Gerry looked great, he had lost weight too. The two of them were much more like their wedding photograph than they had ever been. His jaw was leaner, his eyes were bright, he was being endlessly patient with the kids, too, which was a lot more difficult than it sounded. Helen in particular was as prickly as a hedgehog, and Paul was restless. Jack seemed to be coming to an end. He would ring tomorrow and talk to Gerry, he hoped Gerry appreciated all that she did for him, going out and earning a living, keeping the family together. If only he had had sense long ago and not put so much at risk. 'But it's all fine now,' Emma said wearily. Jack agreed doubtfully and hung up.

'Was he repenting of my wicked life?' asked Gerry.

'A bit,' Emma laughed. Gerry laughed, and after a moment the children laughed too. It was the nearest to normal living they had known for about four years.

*   *   *

Gerry spent Saturday in his study. It was a four-bed-roomed house and when they had bought it they had decided at once that the master bedroom should be his study. Other men rented offices, so it made sense that the big bedroom with the good light should be where Gerry worked. The little bathroom attached to the bedroom was turned into a darkroom. Once it had been a miracle of organisation: a huge old-fashion-ed chest of drawers, a lovely piece of furniture holding all his up-to-date filing system. As efficient as any steel filing cabinet, only a hundred times more attractive. The lighting was good, the walls were hung with pictures; some of a single object, like his famous picture of a diamond; some were pictures that told a success story. Gerry receiving an award here, Gerry sharing a joke there. Then there was the huge, bulging desk, full recently of bills or handouts, or refusals or rubbish, making a mockery of the filing.

He had sighed when he saw it, but Emma had been beside him.

'Tell me what you want except a couple of black plastic sacks to get rid of the rubbish,' she had said.

'And a bottle of Paddy to get rid of the pain of looking at it,' he had said.

'You poor old divil, it's not that bad is it?' she said lightly.

'No,' he said, 'I'm only being dramatic. I'll need a dozen plastic bags.'

'Don't throw everything out,' she said, alarmed.

'I'll throw a lot out, love, I have to start again from scratch, you know that.'

'You did it once, you'll do it again,' she said and went downstairs.

* * *

Gerry made himself four big, sweeping categories: Real Rubbish; Browsing Through later Rubbish; For the Filing Cabinet, and Contacts for the New Life.

Almost everything seemed to fit into those; he was pleased with himself and even hummed as the marathon sorting work went on.

Emma heard him as she made the beds and she paused and remembered. Remembered what it used to be like, a cheerful confident Gerry, whistling and humming in his study, then running lightly down the stairs and into his car off to another job. In those days there was a big pad beside the phone where she put down the time the person called, their name, their business. She had always sounded so efficient and helpful; clients had often asked was she Mr Moore's partner and she would laugh and say a very permanent partner — they had found that entertaining. For months, years, the phone had hardly rung for Gerry, except a call from Des Kelly or a complaint from his brother Jack, or a list of complaints about something from his mother. Should she dare to believe that things were ever going to be normal again? Was it tempting fate to believe that he might really stay off the drink and build his business up? She didn't know. She had nobody to ask, really. She couldn't go to Al Anon and discuss it with other wives and families, because that somehow wasn't fair. It would be different if Gerry had joined Alcoholics Anonymous; then she would be able to join something that went hand in hand with it, but no. Gerry didn't want to go to some room every week and hear a lot of bores standing up and saying, 'I'm Tadgh, I'm an alcoholic.' No, the course was the modern way of dealing with things and he had done that and been cured.

She sighed; why was she blaming him? He had done it his way and he had done it. For six weeks in that home he had become stronger and more determined. For two days now at home he was managing. She must stop fearing and suspecting and dreading, dreading things like the first phone call from Des Kelly, the first row, the first disappointment. Would he have the strength to go on being sunny after all these?

*   *   *

Gerry had tucked three bags of Real Rubbish into the garage, all neatly tied at the neck. He insisted that Emma come up and admire what he had done. The room still looked very much of a shambles to her, but he seemed to see some order in it, so she enthused. He had found three cheques as well — out of date, but they could be re-dated. They totalled over £200.00. He was very pleased with himself for finding them and said that it called for a dinner out.

'Are you sure they weren't re-issued already? One's three years old.' Emma wished she hadn't said it. It sounded grudging. She spoke on quickly. 'If they have been, so what? You're quite right, where will we go?'

He suggested a restaurant which was also a pub. She kept the smile on her face unchanged. There was going to be a lot of this kind of thing, she'd better learn to get used to it. Just because Gerry Moore had to cut alcohol out of his life, it seemed a vain hope that the rest of Ireland would decide to stop selling it, serving it and advertising it.

'I'd love that,' she said enthusiastically. 'I'll wash my hair in honour of it.'

Des Kelly rang a bit later.

'How are you, old son?' he asked.

'Ready for the Olympics,' Gerry said proudly.

'Do they include a few jars of orange juice, or is that more than flesh and blood could stand?'

'Oh, this flesh and blood can stand anything, but not tonight — I'm taking Emma out to a slap-up meal to say thank you.'

'Thank you?'

'For holding the fort and all while I was above in the place.'

'Oh yes, of course, of course . . .'

'But tomorrow, Des, as usual. Twelve thirty?'

'Great stuff. Are you sure you won't . . .'

'I'm sure, I'm sure. Tell me about yourself — what have you been doing?'

Des told him about a script which he had sweated blood on which was refused by a jumped-up person who knew nothing, and he told him about one that had gone well and got a few nice write-ups in the paper.

'Oh yeah, I remember that, that was before I went in,' Gerry said.

'Was it? Maybe it was. The time gets confused. Well, what else? The same as usual. I've missed you, old son, I really have. There's not much of a laugh around. I tried leaving Madigan's and I went to McCloskey's and I went down to the Baggot Street area for a bit, Waterloo House, Searson's, Mooney's, but there was no one to talk to. I'm glad you're out.'

'So am I.'

'Were they desperate to you in there?'

'Not at all, they were fine, it was up to me. If I didn't want to go along with any of it I didn't have to.'

'Well, that's good.'

'And you can relax, I'm not going to be producing leaflets at you and telling you that you should cut it down a bit.' Gerry laughed as he said it. Des laughed too, with some relief.

'Thanks be to God. See you tomorrow, old son, and enjoy the second honeymoon night out.'

Gerry wished that he had found cheques for two thousand, not two hundred, then he would have taken Emma on a second honeymoon. Maybe when he got himself set up again he'd be able to do that. He'd think about it. It would be great to be out with a villa hired for two weeks in one of these places like Lanzarotte. There was a fellow in the nursing home who had bought a house there with a whole group of other Irish people, like a little complex of them out there. They made their own fun, they brought out a ton of duty-free — well, forget that side of it, but there were marvellous beaches and great weather even in winter. He went back to his sorting. It was the section on contacts that was giving him most trouble. A lot of agencies seemed to have changed, merged with others or gone out of business. A lot of new names. A lot of bad blood with some of the old names — work promised and not done, work done but not accepted. Jesus, it might be easier starting afresh in another country. Australia? This place was a village, what one knew at lunchtime everyone else knew at tea time. Still, nobody had said it was going to be easy.

*　　*　　*

Gerry was in very low form by the time it came to dress up for going out. The children were out of the house: Paul was with Andy as usual and Helen had gone to a tennis lesson. She had asked that morning at breakfast if the household budget would cover tennis lessons. She didn't really mind if it didn't, and she wasn't going to be a strain on people, but if the money was there she would like to join the group. Gerry had insisted she join, and said that he would get her a new racquet if she showed any promise. She had departed in high spirits and would stay and have tea with one of her friends who lived near the courts.

Emma was fixing her newly washed hair; she sat in a slip at the dressing table and watched Gerry come in. At first she had thought he might want them to go to bed. They hadn't made love last night, just lay side by side holding hands until he drifted off to sleep. This seemed like a good time. But no, that was the last thing on his mind so she was glad he hadn't really attended to her slightly flirtatious remarks. It didn't seem so much of a rejection if he hadn't heard what she had said. His brow looked dark.

'It will be nice to go out, I'm really looking forward to it.'

'Don't rub it in. I *know* you haven't been out for a

190

long time,' he said.

She bit back the aggrieved retort. 'What will you have, do you think?' she said, searching desperately for some uncontroversial side to it all.

'How the hell do I know until I see the menu? I don't have radar eyes. I'm not inspired by the Holy Ghost to know what's going to be served.'

She laughed. She felt like throwing the brush and every single thing on the dressing table at him. She felt like telling him what to do with his dinner invitation — an invitation she would have to pay for anyway until those out-of-date cheques were cleared — if they ever were. She felt like saying the house had been a peaceful and better place while he was in the nursing home. But she managed to say, 'I know. Deep down I'm just a glutton, I expect. Don't mind me.'

He was shaving at the small handbasin in their bedroom. His eyes caught hers and he smiled. 'You're too good for me.'

'No I'm not, I'm what you deserve,' she said lightly.

In the car he took her hand.

'Sorry,' he said.

'Don't mind about it,' she said.

'The night just seemed hard ahead of us, no wine with the dinner and all.'

'I know,' she said sympathetically.

'But you're to have wine, you must, otherwise the whole thing's a nonsense.'

'You know I don't mind one way or the other. You know I can easily have a Perrier water.'

'Part of the fact of being cured is not to mind other people. It was just that I got a bit low there, inside, in the house, I don't know. I'm fine now.'

'Of course you are, and I'll certainly have a glass or

two if it doesn't annoy you.' She put the key into the ignition and drove off.

Technically he was allowed to drive again now, but he hadn't reapplied, or whatever you were meant to do. And in the last few months he wouldn't have been able to drive. She had offered him the keys as they came to the car and he had shaken his head.

In the bar, as they looked at their menus, they met a couple they hadn't seen for a while. Emma saw the wife nudge her husband and point over at them. After what looked a careful scrutiny he came over.

'Gerry Moore, I haven't seen you looking so respectable for years. And Emma . . .' They greeted him with little jokes and little laughs; both of them patted their flatter stomachs while the man said they must have been at a health farm, they looked so well. Emma said she owed hers to her bicycle and Gerry said that, alas, he owed his to laying off the booze. It was like the first hurdle in an obstacle race. Emma knew from the whispers between the couple that there would be many more. The news would get around, people would come to inspect, to see if it was true. Gerry Moore, that poor old soak, back to his former self, you never saw anything like it, doesn't touch a drop now, made a fortune last year, back on top as a photographer, you never saw anything like him and the wife. Please. Please, God. Please let it happen.

*　　*　　*

Father Vincent called around on Saturday night and knocked for a long time at the door. The car was gone, Emma's bicycle was there, and there was no reply. He assumed they must all be out at some family gathering. But that child had seemed so white and worried, he hoped that Gerry hadn't broken out immediately and been taken back into the home. He debated with himself for a long time about whether to leave a note or not. In the end he decided against it. Suppose poor Gerry had broken out and been taken back in, it would be a sick sort of thing to leave a welcome home card. Father Vincent wished, as he often did, that he had second sight.

Paul came home from Andy's and turned on the television. Helen came in shortly afterwards; they sat with peanut butter sandwiches and glasses of milk and watched happily. They heard voices, and a key turn in the lock.

'Oh Lord,' said Paul, 'I'd forgotten *he* was back, pick up the glass, Helen, give me those plates. We're meant to be running a tidy ship here!' Helen laughed at the imitation of her father's voice, but she looked out into the hall anxiously to make sure that Daddy wasn't drunk.

*   *   *

It was very expensive having Gerry home. Emma realised this, but couldn't quite think why. She realised that he wasn't spending any money on drink; apart from that one Saturday night out they didn't entertain people. Gerry bought no clothes or household things. Why then was her money not stretching as far as it used to? A lot of it might be on stationery and stamps. Gerry was as good as his word about writing to people with ideas — just bright, cheery letters which said, without having to spell it out, I'm back, I'm cured and I'm still a great photographer. Then he liked to cook new things, things that he

193

wouldn't associate with alcohol. Together they had spent a great deal of money on curry ingredients, but then he had tired of it, and said it wasn't worth all the trouble — they could slip out and buy a good curry if they needed one. She didn't grudge it, but she had been so used to accounting for every penny carefully, putting this little bit there towards the electricity, this towards the gas, and that towards the phone. She didn't know what she was going to do when the next bills came in. And talking of bills, what the phone bill was going to be like made her feel weak around the legs.

Gerry had been talking to somebody in Limerick for nearly fifteen minutes one night, and he mentioned calls to Manchester and London. She had said nothing; she just prayed that the rewards and results of all these phone calls might be felt by the time the telephone bill came in.

*   *   *

Gerry's mother thought that he wasn't himself at all since he came out of that place. He had gone up to see her and the visit was not a success. She had bought a naggin of whiskey for him specially. It was in the glass-fronted cupboard there beside the china dogs. Ah, go on, surely one wouldn't do him any harm.

'No, Mother. That's the whole point. I've got something wrong with my insides, it turns to poison in me. I told you this. Emma explained . . .'

'Huh, Emma. High-brow talk. Allergy addiction. I'm sick of it.'

'Yes, Mother, so am I,' Gerry's patience was ebbing, 'but it happens to be true.'

'Look, have just the one and we'll quit fighting,' his mother had said.

'It would be easy for me to say Thank You Mother, to hold it here in my fist and when you weren't looking to throw it away. But I can't do that. I can't bloody do it. Can you have the wit of a half-wit and understand that?'

'There's no need to shout at me, I've quite enough to put up with,' his Mother had said, and then she had started to cry.

'Listen, Mother, give me the bottle you so kindly bought for me. I'll give it to Father Vincent for his sale of work, he can use it on the tombola or something. Then it won't be wasted.'

'I will not. If I bought whiskey it will be there to offer to someone who has the manners to take it.'

No other subject managed to bring them on to the same plane. Gerry left, and hoped that nobody who lived on earth had such a poor relationship with a parent as he had. That was the day that he went home and found Paul fighting with Emma in the kitchen. They hadn't heard him come in.

'But *WHY*, if you could tell me *WHY* I might do it. He's not an invalid, he's not soft in the head, so why does he want to play happy families sitting down to supper together every night? If I go over to Andy's after supper it's too late, then the evening's spoiled.'

'Ask Andy here.'

'No fear.'

Gerry came in and looked at them, first one and then another.

'Please spend the evening with your friend tonight, Paul. Emma, can I have a word with you in my study when you're ready?'

He walked on upstairs. He heard Helen, giggling

nervously.

'That's just the voice that Reverend Mother uses when she's going to expel someone,' she said, stifling her laughs.

* * *

'The boy is right. I am not soft in the head. I get weary of all these family meals, if you must know.'

'I thought with my being out all day and you getting back into a routine . . .'

'You thought, you thought, you thought . . . what else is it in this house except what you think?'

She looked at him in disbelief.

'I mean it, Emma, morning, noon and night . . .'

Two large tears fell down her face and two more were on the way down like raindrops on a window. She didn't even brush them aside; she didn't try to deny it, to reason with him, or to agree with him. She just looked beaten.

'Well, say something, Emma, if you don't agree with me say something.'

'What is there to say?' she sobbed. 'I love you so much and everything I do seems to hurt you, God Almighty, how can I do what will please you? I'm obviously doing all the wrong things.'

He put his arms around her and stroked her hair. 'Stop, stop,' he said. She cried into his chest.

'You're very good. I'm really a shit, a terrible shit.' She made a muffled denial into his shirt.

'And I love you too and need you . . .'

She looked up at him with a tear-stained face. 'Do you?'

'Of course,' he said.

Downstairs, Helen said, 'They've gone into the bedroom, isn't that odd?'

Paul said, 'He can't be going to expel her then.'

Helen said, 'What do you think they're doing?'

Paul laughed knowingly, 'I'll give you one guess,' he said.

Helen was horrified. 'They can't be. They're much too old.'

Paul said, 'Why else have they closed the door?'

'God, that's awful, that's all we need.'

Father Vincent called just then. Helen was so embarrassed when she recognised his shape through the door that she ran back for Paul.

'I can't tell him what we think,' she said. 'You couldn't tell a priest something like that.'

Paul let him in. 'Mum and Dad are upstairs at the moment, having a bit of a lie down. If you don't mind, Father, I won't disturb them.'

'Of course, of course,' Father Vincent looked confused. 'But can I get you a cup of tea, coffee?' The priest said he didn't want to be any trouble.

'A drink?'

'No, no, heavens, no.'

'We have drink. Dad insists it be kept there for visitors.'

Father Vincent stayed for about ten minutes with no drink and hardly any conversation. When he was at the porch again, he looked timidly at the stairs. 'If your father has taken a turn for the worse and your Mother wants any help, she only has to call on me.' Paul said that he didn't think Mother wanted any help just now, and when the door was safely closed he and Helen rolled around the sitting room floor laughing at the idea of leading Father Vincent upstairs, knocking on the bedroom door and calling out that Father Vincent wanted to know if Mother wanted any help or could manage on her own.

Gerry and Emma lay in their big bed and Gerry said, 'It's been so long, I was afraid to, I was afraid, in case . . .' Emma said, 'You were lovely as you were always lovely.' She lay counting the days since her last period; she was safe, she had to be safe. The very notion of becoming pregnant, now, was too much to contemplate. She had stopped taking the pill two years ago. It was said to have some side effects and women were warned not to stay on it for ever. And what on earth had been the point of taking the pill when there was simply no risk of becoming pregnant?

*   *   *

Jack was sorry that Gerry was back. It sort of put a stop to his Monday visits. He used to visit Gerry on a Sunday and then took the bus to their house on a Monday night after work to report on what he saw, what he said, what was said back to him and what he thought. The first couple of times they had been eager to know what he reported because they still hadn't got used to life without Gerry. Then, after that, it had become a little ritual. Emma used to cook a nice meal, and then they would all wash up. Jack would sit down in the comfort of a nice big sitting room, not his own cramped little bed-sitter. They used to watch television, while Emma sometimes did mending; the television set was turned low so as not to disturb the two children who did homework. All through April and May Jack had been involved in their life. There was no excuse for him to come any more.

He had liked those evenings sitting there with Emma; she had been so nice and interested in everything he had been doing at work. It was so cosy.

Gerry must have been a madman, stark staring mad to throw away all his money and his good living and spend time drinking with a crowd of eejits. You wouldn't mind a man who had nothing at home, but a man who had Emma. It was past understanding.

*   *   *

It seemed a very long summer for everyone. Father Vincent spent a lot of time wondering what he had done to offend the Moores; every time he went there those two young children, who had seemed nice and normal at one stage, were exceedingly silly with giggles. Gerry wanted to hear no inspiring tales of how others triumphed, he had said curtly, and Emma was too busy to say more than the time of day. She had taken some home typing and had rung him once to enquire whether there was any parish work to be done on a professional basis. He had said they would always be glad of some voluntary help, but she had said sorry, that she was not yet in a position to be able to offer that.

Mrs Moore thought that Gerry had become short-tempered and intolerant. Her grandchildren never came near her, and that Emma seemed to be too busy even to talk to her on the telephone.

Paul fell in love with Andy's sister, but Andy's whole family, sister and all, went to Greece for a month. If Paul had two hundred pounds he could have gone out to visit them. His Dad had said he could bloody earn it if he wanted it, and his Mum had said he must be a selfish little rat to think that money like that was available for a holiday for him.

Helen was very bored and very worried. She had become very ugly suddenly, she thought, after years of looking quite reasonable; now, when it was important, she had become revolting-looking. In books people's mothers helped them when this kind of thing happened, lent them make-up and bought them dresses. In real life her Mum told her to stop snivelling, there would be time enough for that later.

Des felt the summer was long too. He had nothing but admiration for Gerry — he sat there with the best of them, bought his round like any man, but it wasn't the same. Des could never relax like he had, he couldn't get it out of his head that he was waiting for Gerry to start, to catch up on the rest of them. It was restless drinking with him. God damn it, Gerry was very extreme; when he was going on that batter he was a fierce drinker, got them barred from several places, but now that he'd had a fright, instead of taking it nice and easy like any normal person and just watching it, here he was like a bloody Pioneer, sitting there with a glass of lime and soda or whatever he drank nowadays.

Gerry found the summer slow. He found the replies to his letters even slower, and the offers of any work were the slowest of all. How could the whole photography world have collapsed without his noticing it? There must be people getting work; he saw their pictures in the advertisements, on the television, in the magazines. 'Maybe,' Emma had said, 'maybe you should show them what you can do *now*, rather than old portfolios, maybe you should get a collection for another book together?' But did Emma have a clue of any sort how long it took to put a book together? You didn't go out with a camera and snap 150 things and mark them pages one to one hundred and fifty. There was a theme, there was an interest, there was a commission: a lot of the pictures had been done and paid for already in somebody else's time. Oh, it was all so slow getting back, and it had seemed so very fast, the fall down the ladder. Or was he just being melodramatic?

Emma realised one day during that endless summer that she had no friend. Not no friends but not even one friend. There was nobody she could talk to about Gerry. There never had been. Her mother had thought he was a little too flash for her and her father had wondered about security. But no matter who had asked her to marry them her mother would have seen flashness and her father suspected insecurity all around him. She never talked to her sister about anything except her sister's five children, all of whom seemed to be doing spectacularly well in exams at any given season of the year. She couldn't talk to her mother-in-law, she certainly couldn't talk to that Des Kelly, who always looked at her as if she were a particularly dangerous kind of snake. Poor Jack was so kind and anxious to help, but really the man was so limited, he couldn't have a serious conversation about Gerry's future to save his life. She had formed an unreasonable dislike of Father Vincent who used to be quite a friend of theirs ten years ago. He had always been quick with liberal attitudes and a broad spectrum but that was not what she needed now. She needed specific advice. It was now four months since Gerry had come home from that nursing home; he had not earned one penny from his trade of photography. To complain about that seemed untimely and ungracious because after all, the man had not touched one drop of alcohol either. There was no point in going to the nursing home and asking the doctors. They had asked her to be co-operative and not to boss him around. She thought that she was doing that part of it. But Lord God, how long would it go on? Already the small debts were building up — paradoxically more frightening than when he had been drinking and the bill from the off-license would arrive. Those drink bills had a terrifying unreality about them. Today's bills, high telephone charges, photography equipment, printing costs, expensive cuts of meat, they had a ring of permanency. And what Emma wanted to know was how long to go on. How long did the ego have to be flattered, the image of self restored? How soon, in other words, could she tell him that there was a job going in a photography studio in town, a very down-market photography job for the great Gerry Moore, but she knew the man who ran it needed an assistant? Did she dare yet tell Gerry, suggest it to him, say that it would be a good idea for a year or two and he could build up his contacts after work? No, it must be too soon, otherwise why would she feel sick at the stomach even thinking about it?

That September they went to a wedding. They didn't know the people well and in fact they were rather surprised at the invitation. When they got there and discovered that they were among four hundred people it became clear that the net had been spread fairly wide. It was a lavish do and there was no effort spared to see that the guests had a good time.

'Isn't it marvellous to give two kids a send off like this — they'll remember it all their life,' Gerry had said. Something about the way he spoke made Emma look up sharply from her plate of smoked salmon. She stared at his glass. He was drinking champagne. She felt the blood go out of her face.

'It's only a little champagne for a wedding,' he said. 'Please. Please, Emma, don't give me a lecture, don't start to tell me it's the beginning of the end.'

'Gerry,' she gasped at him.

'Look, it's a wedding. I don't know people, I'm not relaxed, I'm not able to talk to them. Just three or four glasses and that's it. It's all *right*, tomorrow it's back to the everyday business of drying out.'

'I beg you . . .' she said. He had held his glass out to a passing waiter.

'What do you beg me?' His voice had turned hard and the edge of it, the cutting edge, had a sneer as well. 'What could you possibly beg from me, you who have everything?'

His voice was loud now and people were beginning to look at them. Emma felt the kind of dread and panic that she used to know as a child when she was at the carnival. She hated the carnival each year — the bumpers, the chairoplane and the ghost train. Most of all she hated the helter-skelter, and this is what it felt like now. Fast and furious and not knowing what lay ahead.

'Could we go home, do you think?' she asked faintly.

'It's only beginning,' he said.

'Please, Gerry, I'll give you anything.'

'Will you give me champagne, and fun and a bit of a laugh? No, you'll give me a lecture and a flood of tears and then if I'm very good a piece of shepherd's pie.'

'No.'

'What, no shepherd's pie? Oh, that settles it, I'll have to stay here.'

She whispered, 'But the whole life, the plans . . . the plans. Gerry, you've been so good, God Almighty, five months and not a drop. If you were going to have a drink, why here, why at this place, why not with friends?'

'I haven't any friends,' he said.

'Neither have I,' she said seriously. 'I was thinking that not long ago.'

'So.' He kissed her on the cheek. 'I'll go and find us some.'

He was sick three times during the night, retching and heaving into the handbasin in their room. Next morning she brought him a pot of tea and a packet of aspirins, half a grapefruit and the *Irish Times*. He took them all weakly. There was a picture of the wedding they had been at, of the young couple. They looked smiling and happy. Emma sat down on the bed and began to pour tea.

'Hey, it's after nine, aren't you going to work?' he asked.

'Not today. I'm taking the day off.'

'Won't they fire you? Recession and all that?'

'I don't think so. Not for one day.'

'That's the problem hiring married women, isn't it, they have to stay at home and look after their babies?'

'Gerry.'

'You told them you'd no babies, but still here you are staying at home looking after one.'

'Stop it, have your tea . . .'

His shoulders were shaking. His head was in his hands. 'Oh God, I'm sorry, poor poor Emma, I'm sorry. I'm so ashamed.'

'Stop now, drink your tea.'

'What did I do?'

'We won't talk about it now while you feel so rotten. Come on.'

'I must know.'

'No worse than before, you know.'

'What?'

'Oh, it's hard to describe, general carry-on, a bit of singing. A bit of telling them that you had had the cure and you could cope with drink now, a servant not a master . . .'

'Jesus.'

They were silent, both of them.

'Go to work, Emma, please.'

'No. It's all right, I tell you.'

'Why are you staying at home?'

'To look after you,' she said simply.

'To do sentry duty,' he said sadly.

'No, of course not. It's your decision, you know that well. I can't be a gaoler. I don't want to be.'

He took her hand. 'I'm very very sorry.'

'It doesn't matter.'

'It does. I just want you to get inside my head. Everything was so drab and hard and relentless. Same old thing. Dear Johnny, I don't know whether you remember my work. Dear Freddie. Dear Everybody . . .'

'Shush, stop.'

'No thanks, I'll have a Perrier water, no, thanks, I don't drink, no, seriously, I'd prefer a soft drink, nothing anywhere, nothing, nothing. Do you blame me for trying to colour it up a bit, just once, with somebody else's champagne? Do you? Do you?'

'No, I don't. I didn't realise it was so grey for you. Is it all the time?'

'All the bloody time, all day, every day.'

She went downstairs then and sat in the kitchen. She sat at the kitchen table and decided that she would leave him. Not now, of course, not today, not even this year. She would wait until Helen's fourteenth birthday perhaps, in June. Paul would be sixteen, nearly seventeen then. They would be well able to decide for themselves what to do. She made herself a cup of instant coffee and stirred it thoughtfully. The trouble about most people leaving home is that they do it on impulse. She wouldn't do that. She'd give herself plenty of time and do it right. She would find a job first, a good job. It was a pity about RTE, but it was too close, too near, in every sense. She could rise there and get on if she had only herself to think of. But no, of course not, she had to get away. Maybe London, or some other part of Dublin anyway, not on her own doorstep. It would cause too much excitement.

She heard him upstairs brushing his teeth. She knew that he would go out for a drink this morning. There was no way she could play sentry. Suppose he said he wanted to go out and buy something; she could offer to get it for him, but he would think up a job that he could only do himself.

There were maybe another thirty-five or forty years to go. She couldn't spend them with her heart all tied up in a ball like a clenched fist. She could not spend those years half-waking, half-sleeping in an armchair, wondering how they would bring him in. And even more frightening was sitting watching and waiting in case he broke out, the watching and waiting of the last five months. She would be blamed of course . . . selfish, heartless, no sense of her duty. Could you believe that anyone would do it? Emma believed that quite a lot of people could do it, and would if the occasion presented itself, or if the situation was as bad at home as hers was.

She heard Gerry come downstairs.

'I brought down the tray,' he said like a child expecting to be praised.

'Oh, that's grand, thanks.' She took it from him. He hadn't touched the grapefruit, nor the tea.

'Look, I'm fine. Why don't you go into work? Seriously, Emma, you'd only be half an hour late.'

'Well, I might, if you're sure . . .'

'No, I'm in great shape now,' he said.

'What are you going to do this morning, follow up some of those letters?'

'Yes, yes.' He was impatient.

'I might go in.' She stood up. His face was pure relief.

'Do. You'd feel better. I know you and your funny ways.'

'Listen before I go. There's a job going in Paddy's business, only an assistant at the moment, but if you were interested he said that he'd be delighted for you to come in, for a year or two, say, until you got yourself straight.' She looked at him hopefully.

He looked back restlessly. He didn't know that so much of his future and hers rested on the reply he gave.

'An assistant? A dogsbody to Paddy, Paddy of all people. Jesus, he must be mad to suggest it. He only suggested it so that he could crow. I wouldn't touch it with a barge pole.'

'Right. I just thought you should know.'

'Oh, I'm not saying a word against you, it's that eejit Paddy.'

'Well, take it easy.'

'You're very good to me, not giving out, not telling me what an utter fool I made of myself, of both of us.'

'There's no point.'

'I'll make it up to you. Listen, I have to go into town for a couple of things this morning, is there anything you . . .?'

She shook her head wordlessly and went to the
garage to take out her bicycle. She wheeled it to the
gate and looked back and waved. It didn't matter that
people would blame her. They blamed her already. A
man doesn't drink like that unless there's something
very wrong with his marriage. In a way her leaving
would give Gerry more dignity. People would say that
the poor divil must have had a lot to put up with over
the years.

THE
LILAC BUS

For my dear Gordon, with all my love

Contents

Nancy

Nancy was early, but then she always was, and she didn't like being seen there too soon. It looked as if you had nothing else to do if you arrived far too early for the bus home. The others all arrived rushing and panting and afraid they'd miss it, because if they missed it then they really did. Tom turned the key in the ignition at 6.45 and swung the Lilac Bus out into the road. That way he had them all home before ten o'clock and that was his promise. No point in going home for a weekend if you aren't in the pub by ten, that was his philosophy. It wasn't Nancy's but she was compulsively early for everything. It was just her way. She went into a shop that sold magazines and cards. She knew a lot of the cards by heart from studying them on a Friday. There was the big one with tears falling down it: "Sorry I missed your birthday." They had the country papers in this shop too but Nancy never bought one. There'd be a paper at home and she could catch up on everything then.

She examined her new perm in the big round mirror which was not meant so much as a mirror as a deterrent to shoplifting. It was set high on the wall and at a funny angle, or she hoped it was. Otherwise the perm looked very odd indeed. She stared up at her reflection anxiously. Surely she didn't look like some small worried animal with fuzzy hair and huge terrified eyes. That's what she saw in the mirror, but of course that's not what people down at her own level would see? After all, everyone looked silly from

11

this point of view. She patted her head and had another pang about the perm. It looked to her dangerously like those old-fashioned perms that people like her mother got in Rathdoon. The summer perm and the Christmas perm. Frizz, fuzz . . . tight curls growing out into what looked like flashes of lightning or electric shocks as the weeks went by. The girls in the salon assured her that she was mad to think this. She had got a modern perm, one of the newest on the market. Think what she'd have paid if she had to pay for it! Nancy had smiled grimly. Paid for it! At that price! Nancy Morris wouldn't have paid half that price or a quarter of that price for a perm. Nancy Morris had crossed Dublin to go to a salon where she heard they needed people to practise on. *Models* was the expression, but Nancy was more realistic. They needed heads with hair and smart people like Nancy found out which were the big salons with lots of trainees and on what nights their classes and demonstrations were. She had only paid for two visits to a hairdresser since she came to Dublin six years ago. That wasn't bad going, she smiled proudly. Still it was done now, this perm, no point in peering up at herself and worrying. Better go across and get on the bus. Surely some of the others would be there by now, and it was well after half-past six.

Tom was sitting there reading an evening paper. He looked up and smiled. "Evening, Miss Mouse," he said pleasantly and lifted her big suitcase up onto the roof rack with one easy movement. She got in crossly. She *hated* him calling her Miss Mouse, but it was her own fault. When she had rung to ask for a place in his minibus she had given her name as Miss Morris. Well, she was used to being formal on the phone – that was what her job was about, for heaven's sake. How was she to know that she should have said her first name and that he genuinely misheard the Morris bit. But it was very galling that he still refused to call her Nancy, even though he always called old Mrs Hickey Judy and she could have been his mother.

"It's light for such a big case," he said pleasantly. Nancy just nodded. She didn't feel like telling him it was her only suitcase and she had no intention of going out and spending over a fiver on some kind of nylon holdall like the others had. And anyway she needed a big case: there were always things to take back to Dublin, like potatoes and whatever vegetables there were, and anything else that turned up. There was the time that her mother's friend, Mrs Casey, was getting rid of her curtains: Nancy brought them back and they were lovely in the flat.

She sat down in one of the middle seats, straightened her skirt under her so that it wouldn't crease and took out her glucose sweets. They had jars of them in the hospital, and they always told her to help herself. She didn't eat them normally but it was nice on a bus journey to have something; the others often bought barley sugar or toffees, but what was the point of spending money on sweets when they were there for the asking? She unfolded a newspaper that one of the patients had left behind in the waiting room. She got a lot of her reading material this way – people waiting for the specialists were inclined to be forgetful about papers and magazines, and there was rarely an evening she didn't have something to read. And it was nice to have a variety, she told herself. It was like a surprise. Mairead didn't understand. Nancy's brow darkened when she thought of Mairead. And all that had to be sorted out. It had been so unexpected and so unfair.

She held up the newspaper so that Tom would think she was reading and she went over it all again. Mairead coming in on Wednesday and walking round restlessly picking things up and putting them down. You didn't have to be a genius to know there was something on her mind. Nancy thought she was going to ask about the television again. They had a perfectly good black and white set which was a bit snowstormish now and then but usually got a terrific reception. What on earth was the point of paying out a fortune renting a colour set? And even a video: Mairead had once mentioned this as if they were some kind of millionaires. She had looked up from the telly, which was admittedly having one of its bad nights and you had to guess a lot from the soundtrack, but Mairead had wanted to talk about something much bigger.

"I've been thinking all week at work how to say this, Nancy, and I can't think of any proper way so I'll just say it straight out. I want to share the flat with someone else, and I am going to have to ask you to leave. In your own time of course, I'm not throwing you out on the road..." She had given a little nervous laugh but Nancy had been too astounded to join in. "You see," Mairead had gone on, "it was never permanent. It was just to see what we thought.... that was the arrangement. That was what we said..." Her voice had trailed away guiltily.

"But we've been sharing for three years," Nancy said.

"I know," Mairead said miserably.

"So why? Don't I pay the rent in time always and the electricity? And I contribute to the food from home and I got curtains for the hall windows and...?

"Of course, Nancy, nobody's saying you didn't."

"So why?"

"It's just... no there's no reason, can't we do it nice and easily now without quarrels and questions. Can't you just find another place and we'll still meet now and then, go to the pictures, you come over here one evening, me go to your place. Come on, Nancy, that's the grown-up way to do things."

Nancy had burned with rage. Mairead, who worked in a flower shop, telling her what was the grown-up way to do things. Mairead who hadn't got one honour in her Leaving Certificate ordering Nancy out of her flat. *Her* flat. True, she had found it, and when she needed someone to share the rent her aunt Mrs Casey, the friend of Nancy's mother, had suggested Nancy. Where had Mairead got these notions and more important, why? Who did she want to share with?

The worst thing was that Mairead didn't seem to know

or care, she just said she would like a change. At this point Nancy had turned off the flickering telly and had settled in for what she thought was going to be a heart-to-heart where Mairead would tell her all about some star-crossed love. But no. Mairead was busy looking at the calendar. Would we say just over a month, like the middle of October? That would surely give her time to find somewhere.

"But who will I share with?" Nancy had wailed.

Mairead had shrugged. She didn't know, maybe Nancy could get a bed-sit on her own. She didn't do much cooking or entertaining, a bed-sit might be just as good. But they cost a *fortune*! Mairead had shrugged again as if it didn't concern her.

The following morning Nancy was having her tea in the kitchen – she never bothered with a breakfast since there was always food in the hospital, and what was the point of being a receptionist for all these doctors unless you got some perks like a canteen and glucose sweets? Mairead rushed in late as usual and Nancy asked her had she forgiven her.

"Forgive you, Nancy? What for? What in heaven's name for?"

"Well I must have done something, otherwise you wouldn't be asking me to leave our flat."

"It's *my* flat and don't be such a clown. We're not married to each other, Nancy. You came in here to share my rent, now that bit's over. Right? Yes. That's all there is to it." She was gulping down a bowl of cornflakes and trying to pull on her boots at the same time. Mairead loved these boots; they horrified Nancy – they had cost a week's salary. For a pair of boots.

"What'll I tell them in Rathdoon?" Nancy asked solemnly. Mairead was startled.

"About what?" she had asked, bewildered.

"About us breaking up?"

"Sure who would want to know? Who even knows we share a flat?"

"Everyone: your mother, my mother, your aunt Mrs

Casey, everyone."

"Well, what do you mean what will you tell them?" Mairead was genuinely surprised.

"But your mother, what will she think? What will I tell her?"

Mairead had lost her temper suddenly. Nancy still felt a shock just thinking about it.

"My mother is a normal woman; she's like everyone else's mother, including your mother. She doesn't think anything. She wants to know that I'm not pregnant and I'm not on drugs and I'm still going to Mass. That's all any mother wants to know in the name of God, those same three things. In India mothers want to know that or Russia or wherever, and it may not be mass for them but it's something. People's mothers don't give two flying damns about their daughters sharing flats with people and whether they get on well or whether as in our case they drive each other up the wall. They just want to be told the essentials."

"We don't drive each other up the wall," Nancy had said quietly.

"No, well, irritate each other. What's the difference. Why bother your head explaining and telling and reporting back. People aren't bloody interested."

"Do I irritate you?"

"Yes."

"How?"

"Oh Nancy, *please*." Mairead was stricken. "We agreed last night to be grown-up and not to have pointless rows and recriminations. We agreed. Now look what you're starting. Of course people irritate each other: I probably drive you mad. Listen, I must go."

Nancy had a terrible day: she had looked at the prices of flats and bed-sitters and they were sky high. The further out you went they came down a bit of course, but she had to be within cycling distance of the hospital. There was no way she was going to spend her hard-earned money on bus fares. She had thought too about what Mairead had said. She couldn't think why she was irritating. She didn't smoke, she never invited rowdy people in like Mairead often did, people who brought a bottle of wine each and then went out for chicken and chips. She didn't play records loud – she didn't have any records. She did everything to help. Often she cut special offers out of the paper and collected vouchers for foods or detergents. She suggested often to Mairead that it would be cheaper to come home every weekend to Rathdoon because people spend a fortune at weekends in Dublin and you could live free at home. How had she been so irritating?

Even this very morning she had asked Mairead if it was definite, and Mairead had nodded wordlessly. Nancy had offered to let Mairead have the weekend to consider her decision but in a low soft voice, unlike her harangue of the previous morning, Mairead had said there would be no considering and she realised that Nancy would be co-operative and start looking for another place straight away.

She looked up at the sound of voices. Dee Burke had arrived; she wore her college scarf even though she had left UCD two years previously, and she carried a canvas grip which she threw up on the roof herself. Tom was laughing at her.

"You'll be a discus champion yet," he said.

"No, it's to show you that women are genuinely liberated, that's all – besides there's nothing in it except a couple of pairs of knickers and some law books I'm meant to be studying."

Nancy was amazed that Dee, who was Dr Burke's daughter and lived in a big house covered with creeper could talk about knickers to Tom Fitzgerald in such a relaxed way. It didn't even sound rude the way she said it. Dee was a law unto herself though and always had been. You'd think she'd have her own car but she said that she wasn't earning much as a Solicitor's apprentice. Still Nancy would have thought that this minibus would have been beneath the Burkes. They were people of such standing in

Rathdoon, they must find it strange that their daughter travelled with anyone and everyone. Dee never seemed to notice. She was friendly with everyone, with that tinker of a fellow Kev Kennedy that you'd try to cross the road to avoid, with desperate Mikey Burns and his dirty jokes. Dee was specially nice to Nancy; she came and sat beside her and asked, as she often did, about Nancy's work.

It was quite extraordinary the way Dee remembered the names of the doctors she worked for, and knew that one was an eye specialist, one an orthopaedic surgeon and one an ear, nose and throat man. She knew there was Mr Barry and Mr White and Mr Charles. Even Nancy's mother wouldn't know that, and as for Mairead she could hardly remember the names of her own bosses let alone Nancy's.

But then Dee was nice and she had great breeding. People like that were courteous, Nancy always thought and they had the manners to be interested in other people.

Rupert Green arrived next. He was wearing a very smart jacket.

"Merciful God, Rupert, is that Italian? Is that the real thing?" Dee asked, feeling the sleeve as Rupert got in.

"Yes it is actually." Rupert's pale face flushed with pleasure. "How did you know?"

"Aren't I worn out looking at them in magazines. It's gorgeous."

"Yes, it's a second, or a discontinued line or something, but a friend got it for me anyway." Rupert was very pleased that it had caused such a stir.

"Well, they'd need to be a second or something, otherwise your father would have to sell his practice to buy it," Dee laughed. Rupert's father was the solicitor, and it was through Mr Green she had got her apprenticeship in Dublin. Nancy looked at them enviously. It must be great to have such an easy way of going on. It was like a kind of shorthand in professional families, she noticed, they could all talk to each other at the drop of a hat. She felt a twinge of annoyance that her father, long dead, had been a postman and not a lawyer. The annoyance was followed by a stronger twinge of guilt. Her father had worked long and hard and had been pleased to see them all do well at their books and get secretarial or clerical jobs.

Rupert went to the back seat and almost on cue Mrs Hickey arrived. Suntanned even in winter she looked healthy and strong and as if she might be any age. Nancy knew she must be in her late fifties, but that was only by questioning people and piecing it all together. Judy Hickey worked in some kind of mad place that sold herbal cures and grain and nuts, and she even grew some of the things herself which was why she came home every week end to harvest them and bring them back to this shop in Dublin. Nancy had never been to the shop; Dee told her it was marvellous, that everyone should go and see it just for the experience of it but Nancy took her position as receptionist to three of Dublin's leading consultants very seriously. It wouldn't do for her to be seen going in and out of some quack's shop, would it?

Judy went to sit beside Rupert in the back and Mikey Burns had begun to squeeze himself in to the front seat. Laughing and rubbing his hands he told them a joke about hairy tennis balls. Everyone smiled and Mikey seemed to be able to settle down now that he had told at least one dirty story. He looked out eagerly.

"Will I be lucky and get the beautiful Celia beside me or do I get Mr Kennedy? Oh dear, just your luck Mikey, here comes Mr Kennedy."

Kev sneaked into the bus looking over his shoulder as if he expected a guard to lay a hand on him and say *Just a minute* like they do in films. Nancy thought she had never seen anyone who looked so furtive. If you spoke to Kev Kennedy he jumped a foot in the air, and he never said much in reply so he wasn't spoken to much.

And lastly Celia came. Big and sort of handsome in a way, though Nancy didn't admire those kind of looks. She often wore tight belts; as she wore them when she was nursing, she had probably got used to them. They made her figure very obvious. Not sexy, but it certainly divided it for all to see: a jutting out top half in front and a big jutting out bottom half at the back. Nancy would have thought she might have been wiser to wear something more floppy.

Celia sat in beside Tom: the last person always sat beside the driver. It was only twenty to seven and they set off with five minutes in hand.

"I have you very well trained," Tom laughed as he nosed the minibus out into the Friday evening traffic.

"Indeed you have. No wee-wees until we're across the Shannon," said Mikey looking round for approval, and since he didn't hear any he said it again. This time a few people smiled back at him.

Nancy told Dee all about Mr Charles and Mr White and Mr Barry and how they saw their private patients on certain days of the week and how she kept their appointment books and shuffled people around and how patients were often very grateful to her and gave her little presents at Christmas. Dee wanted to know were they well thought of, the doctors, and whether people praised them. Nancy tried to dredge examples but couldn't. She was more on the administrative side, she kept insisting. Dee wanted to know whether she met them socially, and Nancy had laughed to think such a thing was possible. That was the joy of being a doctor's daughter, you didn't think class distinctions existed any more. No, of course she didn't get involved in their home lives. Mr Barry had a Canadian wife and two children, Mr White's wife was a teacher and they had four children, and Mr Charles and his wife had no children. Yes, she sometimes spoke to their wives on the phone; they all seemed very nice, they all remembered her name. "Hallo Miss Morris," they would say.

Dee fell asleep when Nancy was explaining about the hospital switchboard which was very awkward and how they had been looking for a separate switchboard for the

20

consultants for ages, but maybe things would get better with the new set-up in the phone headquarters. Nancy was a bit embarrassed at that. Maybe she had been rabbitting on, possibly she did irritate people by talking too much about little things; sometimes her own mother got up and went to bed in the middle of one of their conversations. Mairead might be right. But no, that couldn't be, Dee had been positively pressing her for details of her working life, she had asked question after question. No, Nancy couldn't blame herself for being boring. Not this time. She sighed and looked at the fields flying by.

Soon she nodded off too. Behind her Judy Hickey and Rupert Green were talking about someone they knew who had gone to an Ashram in India and everyone had to wear yellow or saffron. In front of her Kev Kennedy was half-listening as Mikey Burns explained a card trick with a glass of water. Mikey said that it was better if you saw it done but you could still grasp the point if you concentrated.

In front of them Tom was saying something to Celia; she was nodding and agreeing with it, whatever it was. It was very comfortable and warm, and even if she did lean over a bit in sleep and slump on top of Dee, well it didn't matter. She wouldn't have let herself doze if she were beside one of the men. Or indeed beside Judy Hickey: there was something very odd about her.

Nancy was asleep.

Her mother was still at the kitchen table when she got in. She was writing a letter to her daughter in America.

"There you are," she said.

"All in one piece," said Nancy.

It wasn't much of a greeting between mother and daughter when the whole country had been crossed. But they had never been a demonstrative family. No hugging and kissing, no linking arms.

"How was the journey?" her mother asked.

"Oh, the same. I had a bit of a sleep so I have a crick in

my neck." Nancy rubbed it thoughtfully.

"It's great to be able to sleep on that road, with maniacs screeching past you in all directions."

"Oh, it's not that bad." Nancy looked around. "Well, what's been happening?"

Her mother was poor at handing out news. Nancy would have liked her to get up, wet a pot of tea and come back full of detail and information. She wanted to hear the week's events and who had been home, who had been heard from, who had revealed what. But somehow it was never like that.

"Whatever happens? Nothing's been happening – weren't you here until Sunday night?" Her mother went back to the letter, sighing, "Do you never write to Deirdre at all? Wouldn't it be a Christian thing to write to your own sister in America and tell her what's going on? She loves to hear little things you know."

"So do I, but you can never remember anything to tell me!" Nancy cried in complaint.

"Ah, will you stop that nonsense, sure aren't you here the whole time? You only go up to Dublin for a couple of days in the week. Poor Deirdre's on the other side of the Atlantic Ocean."

"Poor Deirdre has a husband and three children and a freezer and an icebox and a sprinkler in her garden. Poor Deirdre indeed."

"Couldn't you have all that yourself if you wanted to? Stop grudging things to your sister. Have some bit of niceness in you."

"I've plenty of niceness." Nancy felt her lip tremble.

"Well stop giving out about Deirdre then, and go on, take a sheet of paper and put it in with mine. It'll save you getting a stamp and everything."

Her mother shoved a writing pad across the table. Nancy hadn't even sat down yet. The big suitcase with the hard corners was in the middle of the floor. She felt this was a shabby welcome home, but she was also a practical person. If she scribbled off a page to Deirdre now, well it

22

would save her having to do it some other time, and it would please her mother who might go and bring out some soda bread and apple tart if she was in a good humour. Nancy wrote a few lines hoping that Deirdre and Sean and Shane and April and Erin were all well, and saying she'd love to come over and see them all but the fares were desperate and it was much easier for them to come over this way because of the pound and the dollar. She told Deirdre about Mr White's new car, and Mr Charles going to Russia on his holidays and Mr Barry's wife having a new handbag that was made from the skin of a baby crocodile and had cost what you wouldn't believe. She added that it was nice to get back to Rathdoon at weekends because... She paused at this point. It was nice to get back to Rathdoon because... She looked at her mother sitting at the table frowning over the letter writing. No, that wasn't why she came home. Her mother was only mildly pleased, and if she wasn't here there was the television or Mrs Casey or the bingo or half a dozen other things. Sometimes on the long summer evenings, Nancy had come home and found the house empty and her mother out at ten o'clock. She didn't come home for the dance like Celia did, or Kev or Mikey on the bus. She had not got what you'd call friends in Rathdoon.

She finished the letter, "It's nice to get back at the weekends because the Lilac Bus is really very good value and you'd spend a small fortune in Dublin over the weekend without even noticing it."

Her mother was packing up for bed. No tea, no apple tart.

"I think I'll just make myself a sandwich," Nancy said.

"Did you have no tea? Aren't you very disorganised for a high-up receptionist?" said her mother, who went to bed without a word of goodnight.

It was a bright sunny September Saturday. The tourists were mainly gone but there were always a few golfers around. Nancy wandered up the street with no plan. She

23

could have bought a newspaper and gone to the hotel to have coffee, but apart from the money altogether she wouldn't do that. It was being uppity going in there sitting as if you were the type. No. She saw Celia's mother washing the step of the pub. She looked older, her face was lined like that gypsy-looking Judy Hickey's. She called out a greeting, but Celia's mother didn't hear, she kept scrubbing. Nancy wondered was Celia still in bed or was she helping to clean up inside. Celia worked weekends in the pub, that's why she came home. Her mother must have made it worth her while, because it was a hard job to stand on your feet all weekend there after having stood on your feet as a nurse all week. But you'd never know the time of day with Celia, she was so tight with information or anything at all. It was odd to see her talking away to Tom on the bus last night; usually she looked out the window with a moon face. Not like Dee, who was so full of life and so interested in everything. Nancy often wished that things were different, and that she could call on Dee at the weekend, or go off somewhere with her. But she wouldn't dream of going up to Burkes. Not in a million years would she call on the house. The surgery was a different matter, that was the way things were.

She passed Judy Hickey's cottage and saw signs of great activity out in the back. Big packing boxes were laid all round, and Judy was wearing old trousers and had her hair tied up in a scarf. The house itself was shabby and needed a coat of paint but the garden was immaculate. It was odd that so many people watered and weeded and kept the birds off for Mrs Hickey, Nancy thought; she wasn't the kind of woman that you'd think people would like at all. She only went to Mass one Sunday in four, if that. She never spoke of her husband and children. They had gone away years ago when the young lad was only a baby; Nancy could hardly remember the time there was children in that house. Anyway, up and away with the father and the two children and not a word out of the mother. She never got the court to give them back to her ; people had said there must be some fine secrets there that they didn't want to come out, otherwise she would surely have gone to law. And for years her working in this shop which sold things gurus used out in the East and things that must be disapproved of, ginseng and all that. Still Judy Hickey seemed to have more friends than a few. Even now there were two of Kev Kennedy's brothers helping her, and last week Mikey Burns was there with his shovel. Young Rupert would probably have been in the team but his father was very sick and that's why he had been coming home every weekend.

Nancy sighed and passed on. A half-thought that she might help too had come in one side of her mind but flashed quickly out the other. Why should she dig and get dirty in Judy Hickey's garden for nothing? She had better things to do. When she got back home and there was a note on the kitchen table, she wondered what better things she meant. Her mother had scribbled that Mrs Casey had called to take her for a spin. Mrs Casey had learned to drive late in life and had a dangerous-looking old car which was the joy of her heart. It had brightened life for many people including Nancy's mother; indeed there was talk of a few of them coming the whole way to Dublin in it. The plan had been that Mrs Casey and Mrs Morris would stay at the flat. After all, Mrs Casey was Mairead's aunt. Now there would be no flat and no Mairead. Nancy's heart lurched at the memory of it all.

And nothing for the lunch and no mention of when the spin would be over, and nothing much in the press or in the little fridge, nothing you could eat. Nancy put on two potatoes to boil and went across to Kennedys' shop.

"Can I have two small rashers, please?"

"Two pounds is it?" Kev Kennedy's father didn't listen much to people: he was always listening to the radio in the shop.

"No, just two single ones."

"Huh," he said picking two out and weighing them.

"You see my mother hasn't done the shopping yet so I

don't know what she wants."

"You can't go far wrong on two slices of bacon," Mr Kennedy agreed, morosely wrapping them in greaseproof paper and putting them in a bag. "She'll never accuse you of getting the family into debt over that."

She heard a laugh and to her annoyance noticed that Tom Fitzgerald was in the shop. For some reason she didn't like him hearing her being made fun of like that.

"Oh, Miss Mouse is a great one to live dangerously," he said.

Nancy managed a smile and went out.

The afternoon seemed long. There was nothing on the radio, and nothing to read. She washed her two blouses and put them out on the line. She remembered with great annoyance that nobody, not even her mother, had remarked on her perm. What was the point of getting one if people didn't notice? Paying good money for one of the newest perms. Well, paying money if she had had to: fortunately she hadn't. At six she heard the banging of car doors and voices.

"Oh, there you are, Nancy." Her mother always seemed surprised to see her. "Mrs Casey and I've been for a great drive altogether."

"Hallo Mrs Casey. That's nice," Nancy said grumpily.

"Did you get us any supper?" Her mother looked expectant.

"No. Well, you didn't say. There wasn't anything there." Nancy was confused.

"Oh, come on Maura, she's only joking. Surely you've something made for your mother, Nancy?"

Nancy hated Mrs Casey's arch voice treating her as if she was a slow-minded five-year-old.

"No, why should I have? There was no food there. I presumed my mam was getting something."

There was a silence.

"And there was nothing for lunch either," she said in an aggrieved tone. "I had to go over to Kennedy's to get rashers."

"Well we'll have rashers for our supper," Mrs Morris brightened up.

"I've eaten them," Nancy said.

"'All of them?" Mrs Casey was disbelieving.

"I only got two," she said.

There was another silence.

"Right," Mrs Casey said, "that settles it. I wanted your mother to come back with me but she said no, that you'd probably have the tea made for us all and she didn't want to disappoint you. I said it was far from likely, judging from what I'd heard. But she had to come back, nothing would do her." She was half way back to the door. "Come on, Maura, leave the young people be . . . . They have better things to do than getting tea for the likes of us." Nancy looked at her mother, whose face was set in a hard line of disappointment and shame.

"Enjoy your evening then, Nance," she said. And they were gone. The car was starting with a series of jumps and leaps.

What could Mrs Casey have heard, what did she mean? The only person she could have heard anything from was Mairead, or Mairead's mother. What could they have been saying – that Nancy was irritating? Was that it?

She didn't want to be in when they came back but where could she go? She had arranged no lift to the dance: she would as soon be hanged as to go out on the straight road and hitch all the way to the night entertainment which she wouldn't enjoy anyway. She supposed she could always go to Ryan's pub. She'd be bound to know people and it was her own home town and she was twenty-five years of age so she could do what she liked. She put on one of her freshly cleaned blouses which she ironed with great care. She decided the perm was an undoubted success and gave herself a spray of the perfume she had bought her mother last Christmas and set out.

It wasn't bad in Ryan's; some of the golfing people were buying big rounds, shouting at each other from the counter: what did you want with the vodka, Brian, did you want water with the Power's, Derek? Celia was behind the counter helping her mother.

"You don't usually come in here," Celia said.

"It's a free country and I'm over twenty-one," Nancy said snappishly.

"Oh Jesus, take it easy," Celia had said. "It's too early for the fights."

There was a phone in a booth and she saw Dee Burke making a call; their phone must be out of order at home. Nancy waved but Dee didn't see her. Biddy Brady who had been two classes below Nancy at school had got engaged and she was celebrating with a group of the girls. The ring was being passed around and admired. She waved Nancy over to the group, and rather than sit on her own she went.

"We're putting a sum into the kitty each and then the drinks keep coming and we pay for it until the money runs out," said one girl helpfully.

"Oh, I don't think I'll be here all that long," Nancy said hastily, and noticed a few odd looks being exchanged.

She waved at Mikey Burns who was carrying two drinks over to a corner.

"Have you any pub jokes?" Nancy asked, hoping he might stop and entertain them for a moment.

"Not tonight, Nancy," he said, and didn't even pause. Mikey! Who would do anything for an audience! He was heading for the corner, a woman with her head down sat there, it looked like Billy Burns' wife.

Billy was Mikey's brother, the one that got the looks and the brains and the luck people said.

There was a bit of commotion behind the bar and Celia's mother seemed to be shouting at her. It was hushed up but Celia looked very anxious. One of the Kennedy brothers had stepped in behind the bar to help wash glasses.

Nancy felt a bit dizzy. She had drunk two gins and

28

orange which she had bought for herself and two as part of Biddy Brady's celebration. She had had nothing to eat since lunchtime. She decided to get some fresh air and some chips in that order. She could always come back. She sat on the wall near the chip shop and ate them slowly. You could see the whole town from here: the Burkes' house with all that lovely creeper cut away from the windows so neatly. She thought she saw Dee leaning out a window smoking but it was darkish, she couldn't be certain. Then there was the Fitzgeralds' drapery, Tom's family's business. His two brothers and their wives worked there, as well as his father. They had a craft shop now attached to it, and they made up Irish tweeds into skirts for the visitors. Mrs Casey lived about a mile out so she couldn't glare at her windows and imagine her mother eating lamb chops and looking at television, counting the days with Mrs Casey until the *Late Late Show* came back from its summer break. When they had been planning the Dublin trip they had wanted Mairead and Nancy to get them tickets for the show, and Mairead had actually written and found out what the chances were. Nancy had thought it was madness of the first order.

It was chilly and the last chip was gone. She walked back to Ryan's and thought she would go in the side entrance and visit the Ladies' on the way. She nearly fell over Mrs Ryan who was sitting on the step.

"Oh, it's *Miss* Morris," the woman said with a very snide little laugh.

"Goodnight, Mrs Ryan," said Nancy a bit nervously.

"'Oh Miss Morris, Miss Mean Morris. Mean as all get out, they say about you."

She didn't sound drunk. Her voice was steady and cold.

"Who says that about me?" Nancy was equally cold.

"Everyone. Every single person who ever speaks your name. Poor Biddy Brady's crowd of girls, just to mention a few. You sat down and took a couple of spirits off them and walked off. That's class, Miss Morris, strong men have

29

wanted to be able to do that and they're not."

"Why do you call me Miss Morris?"

"Because that's what you call yourself, that's what you think you are. And by God that's the way you're going to stay. No man would take you on, Miss Morris, a mean woman is worse than a nag and a slut put together...."

"I'll be off, I think, Mrs Ryan."

"Oh I would, Miss Morris; those little girls in there have had a few drinks now and if you haven't come back to put a couple of fivers into their kitty, I think you'd be far better to be off."

"Put *what* into their kitty?" Nancy was stunned.

"Oh, be off, Miss Morris, I beg of you."

But her blood was up now. She pushed past the woman and went into the smoke and heat.

"Sorry Biddy," she said loudly, "I went home for change. I hadn't my money with me. Can I put this into the kitty and I'm having a gin and orange when the round comes."

They looked at her in disbelief and with some guilt. Those who had been loudest against her were abashed.

"A large gin and orange for Nancy," they called and Celia who was working alone with only Bart Kennedy to help her raised her eyebrows. Nancy Morris ordering large ones.

"They cost a fair whack nowadays, Nancy," she said.

"Oh, for Christ's sake, will you give me a drink not a sermon," Nancy said and the others all laughed.

They were singing "By The River of Babylon, where I sat down," but Nancy was only mouthing the words.

Mean, Mean, Mean. That was what Mairead thought, what she told her mother and her aunt, why she wanted her out of the flat; that's what Mrs Casey thought, that's what her mother had felt tonight, that's what the Kennedys' father had been jeering at in the shop. That's what Celia meant now, talking about the price of a drink. That is what

Mrs Ryan, who must have gone stone mad tonight, meant, sitting on the floor of her own public house in the side entrance.

Mean.

But she wasn't mean: she was careful, she was sensible, she was not going to throw away her money. She was going to spend it on what she wanted. Which was... which was... Well, she didn't know yet. It certainly wasn't clothes, or a holiday or a car. And it wasn't on dear things to furnish rented accommodation, and it wasn't on going to dances or discos or to hotels with fancy prices. And it wasn't on smart hairdressers or Italian shoes or fillet steaks or a stereo radio with headphones.

They had linked arms now and they were singing "Sailing" and swaying from side to side. Mrs Ryan had come back and was singing with the best; in fact she was standing up in the middle of the circle and playing the Rod Stewart role with somebody's golf club as a microphone.

Celia was pulling pints still; she looked at her mother with neither embarrassment nor pride – it was just as if she were another customer. Tom Fitzgerald was talking to her over the bar. They were very thick, those two. Tears came down Nancy's face at Mrs Ryan's words. A mean woman. She wasn't at all mean. But if people *thought* she was, then she must be. Mustn't she?

Deirdre had once said she was a bit tight with money, but she had thought that was Deirdre being all American and accusing people face to face of things. Her brother in Cork had once said that she must own massive property up in Dublin now, what with her earning a good salary and paying hardly a penny out a week except her rent and the Lilac Bus. She had said nonsense, that it cost a packet to live in Dublin. He had pointed out that she had a bicycle and she got a three-course meal in the hospital at midday, and what else did she spend it on? The conversation had ended fairly unsatisfactorily, she had thought. Now she realised that he was saying she was mean. Mean.

Suppose people *really* thought she was mean? Should she explain that it wasn't meanness, and she was only making sure she didn't throw money away? No, somehow it was one of those things that you couldn't explain. It was either there, the belief, or it wasn't there. And so, unfair as it was, she was now going to have to go overboard the other way.

Tomorrow she would suggest to her mother that she take them both to a nice Sunday lunch in the hotel as a treat. It was too late to do anything about Mairead, there was no promising to be more generous or to spend more or whatever it was people wanted. And maybe she could get some posters of Ireland and send them to Deirdre's children. Happy birthday Shane or April or Erin from your Auntie Nancy in the Emerald Isle. And to the silent brother in Cork, some book about fishing and a pressing invitation to visit her when next he came up for the Spring Show.

It must work: look at Biddy Brady's party, they were delighted with her. But why shouldn't they be, she had put ten whole pounds into their bowl on the table. But it seemed to please them a lot and they were raising their glasses a bit crookedly and saying Nancy Whiskey and things to her that they'd never have said otherwise.

There was no sign of Mrs Ryan; she had gone out again after her party piece. Nancy would like to have thanked her. Because now she had a lot of problems licked. And the great thing, the really great thing was this: it needn't cost a lot of money. In fact, if she was very careful it need cost hardly anything. She could take a lot of those glucose sweets and put them in a box, say, that could be a present for her mother one week. And she could give as presents those paperweights which she got from the drug companies – sometimes you could hardly see the name of the medicine they were advertising. And wasn't it just as well she had told nobody about the rise in her wages. She had negotiated it herself quietly, so no one need ever know about that at all.

Dee

They often had a drink on a Friday night in the pub beside the office. Dee would only stay for half an hour. The Lilac Bus wouldn't wait, she knew that. She knew too that a lot of people in the practice were surprised that she went home every weekend. It was so far, and there was so much to do in Dublin. Wasn't she very dutiful? Oh no, she had denied, no. It was selfishness: she went home because it was peaceful, there were no distractions, she could study at home. But the law books that crossed Ireland in her canvas bag came back again unopened as often as not. Dee Burke spent much of her weekends sitting at her bedroom window and staring out at Rathdoon. Until it was time to go back to Dublin again on Sunday evening.

And of course her parents were pleased. She could get off the bus at the corner and walk up to the golf club, waving cheerily as the Lilac Bus went on into town. For every Friday night in human memory Dr and Mrs Burke were at the golf club, and if there was a birth or a death or something untoward in between, people knew to phone the club and the Doctor would take the call.

They had been surprised at the beginning of the summer when she began to come home so regularly. Surprised but glad. It was great to have company round the house, and Dee was always the liveliest of the family. They would jump up with pleasure when she put her face around the door on a Friday night to join them and whoever else in the club bar.

35

Her father would get her a toasted sandwich and put his arm around her shoulder if she stood beside him at the bar counter. Her mother would smile over from the table. They were so delighted to have Dee home again. Sometimes her stomach rose and fell at their innocence and their kind welcome. What did people do when they didn't have the Burkes to go back to, Dee wondered? Went mad maybe? Went to discos? Got sense? Pulled themselves together? Oh, who knew what other people did? Who cared?

Tom Fitzgerald was quite handsome; she had never thought of it until tonight when he was laughing at her for flinging her own bag up on the roof rack. He had a lovely grin. He was an odd fellow – you could never get a straight answer out of him on anything. She knew nothing about him, nothing at all, and she had grown up fifty yards from him and his brothers. She didn't even know what he did for a living. She had asked her mother once.

"Don't you travel across the country sitting beside him? Why don't you ask him yourself?" her mother had said, not unreasonably.

"Oh, he's not the kind you could ask," Dee had said.

"Well then, you'll have to remain ignorant," her mother had laughed.

"At this stage of my life I'm not going to go into the drapery and ask personal questions to the Fitzgeralds about what occupation their son follows."

Nancy Morris was sitting in the bus, first as usual. She looked different somehow. Was it a new blouse or her hair? Dee wasn't sure – she wouldn't ask in case Nancy would start bewailing the cost of everything as she usually did. And yet she was getting a fine big salary, so Sam had told her. Far more than any of the receptionists or clerks were getting in the Solicitors' office. Maybe I won't sit beside her tonight, Dee resolved, but she knew she would. Who else knew Sam, who else could tell her about Sam Barry and his daily life except Nancy? Imagine being able to travel home with Sam's receptionist every weekend. It was like having a bit of

Sam with her. It took a lot of the loneliness away just to be able to talk about him. Even very indirectly, even if it meant talking about Mr Boring White and Mr Boring Charles as well. Because Nancy must never, never know that it was only Mr Sam Barry that she was interested in.

Nancy would talk for ever: she explained the routine and the kind of problems the consultants had, not being able to get beds quickly enough in the hospital, and all the complications of the Voluntary Health Insurance and the forms and people not understanding them. But she knew nothing about their lives outside the hospital. Nothing except what they told her and what the nurses told her, and that was little.

"Do their wives ever ring them at work?" Dee asked. It was like probing a sore tooth; she knew she shouldn't ask.

"Oh yes, sometimes they do." Nancy was maddening.

"And what do they say?"

"They're all very nice, they call me by my name."

That surprised Dee: Nancy was so unforthcoming and businesslike, you couldn't imagine anyone chatting to her.

"Oh yes, 'Hallo Miss Morris,' they say. All of them: Mrs White, Mrs Charles, Mrs Barry."

So that's what she meant by calling her by her name!

"And has Mrs Barry much of a Canadian accent?"

"Gosh, Dee, you do have a great memory for them all. No wonder you're so brainy and going to be a solicitor. Imagine you remembering she was a Canadian. No, not much of an accent, but you'd know she was from over there. American sounding."

Imagine my remembering she was Canadian? Imagine my being able to forget it! She doesn't know many people here ; she's far from home; it's not as if she grew up here and has her own circle of friends; she needs time to make a life for herself, we have to wait until things settle down.

Dee could never understand the logic of that. If they were going to wait until Candy Barry settled into Irish life they were building up more and more trouble for themselves. Why didn't they settle her back into Canadian life, she wanted to know? Before she had become isolated from her roots there. Why? Because of the children of course, the two little Barrys, small clones of their father, five and seven. He wasn't going to let those go four and a half thousand miles away and see them once a year on a visit.

But what about the children that he and Dee would have together? That would be different. Wonderful but different. You didn't parcel away your two lovely sons because you were going to have a new family with somebody else. No indeed. Dee was immature to suggest it.

Sam used that word as a great insult. He said it had nothing to do with age. People younger than Dee could be mature and people much older than both of them would never achieve it. She didn't like the word, it seemed to mean whatever he wanted it to mean. Like when you're playing poker and the two is wild, the two can be any card you want it to be.

She didn't know why she asked Nancy about his work. She never learned anything new, but it was like seeing a photograph of some scene that you knew well; it was always interesting to see it again from another angle. The only bit she shouldn't have asked was about their wives ringing up. That had made her uneasy now.

Sam said that Candy never called him at work and yet Nancy Morris said she did. Nancy probably wanted to show off about how well she knew them all. Boasting. She was in the middle of some complicated diatribe about the telephone system now. Dee felt her eyes closing. She slept and dreamed that she was getting her parchment from the Chief Justice and Sam was there congratulating her, and a photographer from the *Evening Press* had the three of them lined up and was writing their names down in his notebook.

Dee often dreamed that Sam was part of her life: she felt that this must signify that she was not guilty about him and that everything they had together was above board and out in the open. Not too much out in the open of course, but not

hole-in-the-corner either. For example, her flat-mate
Aideen knew all about Sam, and met him when he called.
And Sam's friend Tom knew too: he used to go out to meals
with them sometimes. So it wasn't as furtive as you might
think. Sam had wanted to know why her parents didn't cop
on, but Dee had said it would never cross their minds, and
anyway she was softening them up for the future by
insisting she had no romantic interests yet but would
certainly fall for somebody highly unsuitable when the time
came. Dee had pealed with laughter over this, and Sam had
looked sad. She had stopped laughing suddenly and he had
been very quiet.

"The future mightn't be perfect," he said. "Not for us:
you shouldn't hope too much, you know."

"The future's not going to be perfect for most people,"
she had said cheerfully. "But they have to keep hoping,
otherwise what's the point of anything?"

That had seemed to cheer him a little, but he had been
quieter than usual.

Dee wasn't sure why she came home so often now.
Aideen couldn't understand it either.

"Sure if you're down there, he'll never see you. Can't he
ring you here, if he has a free minute?"

True. But he was having less and less free minutes.
Candy's parents were over from Toronto. They had to be
shown round. One of the little blonde boys had fallen off a
bicycle and opened his forehead; he had to be visited in
hospital, and looked after when he got home.

There was the family holiday on the Shannon, on the
cruiser, and the hurried phone calls from coinboxes when he
was meant to be buying drinks or going to the Gents'.

And recently there were times that weren't explained at
all, but they were times that seemed to have no minutes in
them all the same. It was easier in Rathdoon, he *couldn't*
ring her there, even if he wanted to. Her father would
recognise his name, the phone was in the hall, it would be
hopeless. Perhaps that's why she went, because anything

was better than sitting in a place where he could ring and didn't.

Aideen said she should fight harder for him, force him to leave that Candy. He had been so keen on Dee at the start that he would have done anything for her, now she had let him believe that he could have it both ways. But Dee thought she might want it both ways too. She didn't want a huge scandal, and having to leave her apprenticeship and end up half-qualified, half-married, half-home-wrecker and half-disgraced. Aideen said that was nonsense and that Dee's parents had been able to accept that her brother was living with a girl, so why couldn't they accept what she planned to do. Dee thought there was a lot of difference between Fergal living with his girlfriend when everyone knew that they would get married soon anyway, and her making off with a well known Dublin consultant and forcing him to abandon his wife and two little boys. It was a matter of degree. Aideen had said that was nonsense, it was all Sin and it was all not Respectable. So why not do it?

Why not? It wasn't really up to her any more: Sam was not nearly so ardent. In fact once or twice he had made excuses that seemed just like the things he had said to Candy on the phone a year ago. "Sorry love, I tried, but it's useless, there's this meeting, it's the only time they can get all the people together. I pulled out last time. I can't be seen to do it again." Very familiar. Frighteningly familiar. But was he making excuses to his young mistress so that he could be with his middle-aged Canadian wife? Or was there another young mistress? Someone even younger than twenty-three? Someone who didn't sigh and groan when he cancelled an arrangement? Someone who never suggested that Candy be sent back to Toronto?

Dee was remarkably calm about the possibility of a rival. She couldn't take it seriously. He really *was* a busy man, by anyone's standards; he worked long hours and there were still more people straining to see him. He had barely time for one relationship, not to mention two. To think of three would be ridiculous. Nobody could juggle that many romances and promises and endearments in the air. Nobody.

She was glad when they stopped, just for the chance to stretch her legs. Tom gave them ten minutes and not a minute more in the pub beside the garage where he filled up the Lilac Bus. The men usually had a half-pint each and sometimes Dee bought Nancy a gin and orange and Celia a bottle of Guinness. She would have a little brandy herself if her stomach felt cold and nervous. But tonight she felt all right. Sam was away on his conference.

He had rung her from the airport to say goodbye. He had said he loved her and that he'd see her on Monday night, late when he got back from London. He'd tell Candy the conference went on until Tuesday. That was fine, it was ages since he had been able to stay a full night, she would make sure that there'd be no confrontation and scenes. Just like it had been in the beginning.

They were settling back in the bus. Poor Mikey Burns, the bank porter, who was so nice apart from all his lavatory jokes, said that he felt much better now that he'd shaken hands with the wife's best friend. He said it twice in case people hadn't got it. Kev Kennedy still hadn't.

"You're not married, Mikey," he had said.

Mikey looked defeated.

Dee said she mustn't sleep too much on the bus, it gave her a cramp in her shoulders, and Nancy said there was a great way of getting rid of tension in the neck you had to hang your head down as if it was a great weight and then roll it around. Judy Hickey joined in the conversation unexpectedly and said that this was one of the principles of yoga and seemed greatly in agreement. Dee thought Nancy was put out by this, as if she didn't want to join up with yoga over anything.

He would be in London now, staying in that big posh hotel near the American Embassy where she had once spent a weekend with him as Mrs Barry. It had been so racy, and she kept thinking she'd meet someone from home as if anyone from Rathdoon would ever go inside a place like that. He had said there would be a reception at 8.30 and they would all wear name badges. It would have begun now. She felt an urge to talk about him again. This would be her last chance since she wouldn't be able to mention him at home.

"I expect they go away a lot on conferences, professional sort of things," she said to Nancy.

"Sometimes." Nancy was vague. "Not often. Of course they've all had their holidays in August, and you've no idea how hard it is to fix appointments; people don't understand that doctors, specialists, have to have holidays like anyone else. More than anyone else," she added righteously.

Dee wasn't going to go down that martyr road; she wanted to hear about Mr Barry being invited to this very prestigious gathering in London. She wanted to hear what he said when he got the invitation, and she wanted to hear Nancy say that he was coming back on Tuesday, so she could hug that to herself like a little secret.

"Yes, but didn't you say one of them was off to a conference this weekend?" she said.

"No." Nancy was puzzled. "No, definitely not."

"Maybe they'd go and not tell you?" Dee's heart had started to move in a very unacceptable rhythm.

"I don't think so," Nancy was lofty. "But anyway it wouldn't be this weekend, because I know where they're all going, as it happens. It's a big do. Mr and Mrs Barry – she's a Canadian you know – well, they're having their tenth wedding anniversary party tomorrow, and it's going to be a big barbecue. Mr Barry asked me to pray specially that it wouldn't rain."

She didn't hear anything else for the rest of the journey home. But she must have managed to nod or smile or something because she certainly didn't notice Nancy looking at her puzzled or anything. She felt as if somebody had opened her throat just under the gold horseshoe he had

42

bought her as a pendant that time in London, and poured in a jug of iced water. The water was freezing up again. Why? That was all she wanted to know. Why the elaborate lies? Filled with such detail, about the name badges, the names of Americans and French and Germans that he was going to meet? Did these people exist at all, or had he picked names out of a phone book or out of literature? Why? If he and his wife had such a good marriage that they were gloating publicly with a big babyish barbecue over the whole thing . . . then why did he need Dee as well?

She went over it all, from the very start, when they had met at a party on the day of a Rugby International. It had been a big lunch where people had been invited to pre-match snacks and most people had such a good time they had stayed on and watched the match on telly instead. Dee had felt guilty about their tickets and all the young disappointed hopefuls who could have used them and Sam had gathered up half a dozen and run out on the road and given them to the first crowd of passers-by he saw. They had looked through the window and laughed at the waving kids and the eager way they had run towards Lansdowne Road. She and Sam had laughed a lot that afternoon, Candy was at the other end of the room talking about recipes. When they were leaving, Sam had said, "I must see you again," and she had laughed a peal of delight, and told him it was pure Hollywood.

"I am pure Hollywood," Sam had said, and somehow it had sounded endearing and nice. She had given him work and home numbers and he had called the next day. He had pursued her, yes, that wasn't too strong a word for it. *Pursued.* She had said she didn't want to get involved with a married man, and he said that he knew it was more pure Hollywood and pure corn and pure things-that-married-men-said, but actually his marriage was empty and a great mistake and something he should never have done but he had been in Canada and lonely and far from home; and that, apart from Dee altogether, he and Candy would undoubtedly drift their separate ways when the children were old enough to understand, and that he would be very gentle and careful, and that he would love her always. Now why would someone do that? If you loved one person and thought they were smashing and lovely and fresh why would you then have big parties and hand-holding and a lot of bullshit with another person? What was the point? Or suppose you loved the other person and enjoyed being married to her for ten years and adored the two little boys and everything then why would you tell lies about being fresh and lovely and tell tall tales about conferences in London with name badges to someone else? It was beyond understanding; and Dee felt that something in her head was about to break with the effort of understanding. She bent forward a little. Tom's eyes in the mirror caught the movement.

"Are you OK Dee?" he called.

"Sure," she muttered.

"Right, coming to your corner in five minutes," he said. He must have thought she was car-sick.

"We're never home already?" She was genuinely shocked. She thought they were seventy miles from Rathdoon. "You should try driving Concorde," she said, managing a sort of joke for him.

"Sure that would be child's play after the Lilac Bus," Tom grinned back at her.

She wondered should she go straight home and not get off at the golf club. But that would be worse, back to an empty house on her own. No, better join in and be with people who would talk and laugh and be pleased to see her.

She opened her bag and got out a mirror before she went in. Unbelievably she was not too bad, her face tanned from all those weekends at home, her hair straight and shoulder length – Sam said it was like an advertisement for shampoo, which was high praise. Her eyes normal looking, not wild. No, she wouldn't frighten her parents and their friends. In she would go and when they asked her what she'd have she'd say she had a stomach upset and could she have a brandy and port. Someone told her once that this was a great drink and it cured every ill. Or most ills anyway.

They were delighted to see her as always, but they were bursting with news. They couldn't wait for the drink to be in her hand so that they could drink a toast. They had had a phone call from Fergal – what do you think, he and Kate had bought the ring, they were getting married just before Christmas, wasn't it marvellous? And Kate's parents had been on the phone too and they had all said wasn't it wonderful the way things turned out, and maybe young people nowadays were much wiser than their parents and didn't rush into things. Dee Burke raised her glass of port and brandy and drank the health of her brother Fergal and her new sister-in-law-to-be, Kate, and she wondered with her mother what they both would wear to the wedding. And the drink went down through that channel where there had been iced water before, and it sort of burned it with a fiery anaesthetic and she began to think that whoever said it cured all ills might have had a point.

But it didn't bring sleep. And she had to move gently if she moved at all. The big old house was full of creaks and bumps. If you went to the lavatory during the night you woke the whole house. It was considered courteous to arrange your functions so that you didn't have to. Her parents talked on long downstairs. They had been married for thirty years, she realised. They never made much of anniversaries and when her mother was fifty last year it had been very politely ignored. No showy barbecues for them, no public displays.

But that didn't matter. What was she going to do? Was she going to pretend that she knew nothing, let him lie on about London? No, that would be living out a total dishonesty. But then wasn't he prepared to do that with her? Some of the time. And with Candy some of the time. He didn't have this high regard for total honesty. How had he not known that Nancy would prattle about it? She had told him that she travelled home on the same minibus every weekend as his receptionist. But Sam didn't know that she talked to Nancy about the consultants, and Sam would never believe for one moment that Nancy would mention something as trivial as his party to someone who was not meant to know him. Would she ring him at home and confront him? What earthly good would that do? None.

She would try to be calm and wait until daylight. What was that thing you were meant to do to your neck and shoulders? She tried what she remembered of the instructions but it just made her feel worse.

An hour later she understood what insomnia was about. She had never understood why people didn't just turn on the light and read if they couldn't go to sleep.

Another hour later she laughed mirthlessly to herself about her lack of sleeping pills. There she was, a doctor's daughter, and another doctor's lover and she hadn't one little Mogadon to call her own. A bit after that she started to cry and she cried until she fell asleep at twenty to eight just as her mother was creaking down the stairs to put on the coffee.

She woke after one o'clock: her mother was standing by the bed.

"Is your tummy better?"

Dee had forgotten the so-called gastric attack to excuse the ports and brandy.

"I think so," she said bewildered.

"If you're well enough, can you do me a favour? We've had another phone call from Fergal," her mother paused expectantly.

"The wedding's off?", Dee said rubbing her eyes.

"No, stupid, but they're coming this evening, about six o'clock. Can you run me into town, I'll want to get things."
"Into town" meant the big town seventeen miles away.
"Down town" meant Rathdoon itself.

46

"What do we want to go into town for?"

"You can't get anything nice here, anything different."

"Mummy, in the name of God, isn't it only Fergal? Why do we want anything *nice*, anything *different* for Fergal?"

"But it's Kate as well."

"But hasn't he been living with Kate for a year? Are you losing your marbles or something, what would she want anything nice and different for? Can't we go to Kennedy's and get some ham or lamb or whatever we'd be having anyway?"

"Well if you don't want to drive me, you need only say so. I'm sure your father won't mind giving me a quick spin into town," her mother was huffy now and annoyed.

"It's not a quick spin, you know it, it's seventeen miles. It's a bad road, it's jam packed with shoppers on a Saturday in there, we'll never get a parking place, the whole thing will take three hours."

"Well, don't *you* worry about it, Madam: you're so busy you can sleep on into the broad daylight – I see what a demanding life *you* have. No, your father may be able to give up his one game of golf a week to take me."

Dee got out of bed, and picked up a dressing gown.

"I'll have a bath and I'll take you now, but I want you to know that there's a grave danger you're going mad. Next week you'll be going into town to get something nice and unusual for me."

"If you were bringing home a fiancé I'd be glad to," her mother said. "And by the way, do you never wear pyjamas or a nightdress or anything? Isn't it very peculiar to wear nothing at all in bed?"

"It's very peculiar Mummy – I'd say I'd be locked up if anyone knew."

"Oh there's nothing like a smart aleck, nothing as lovely as your own daughter turning into a smart aleck," said her mother and went downstairs happily to make a list.

Mrs Burke bought a new tablecloth and six napkins to

match. Dee cast her eyes to heaven so often her mother asked her not come into the next shop to be making a show of her. She was moved on three times by guards, hot harassed men who could never have dreamed that this is what it would be like when they joined the force. She saw a woman slap her three-year-old hard on the legs until he roared in fright and his father thought she had gone too far and gave the woman a hard shove. Marriage! Dee thought. Family life. If a Martian were looking at us, he would think we must be insane to run towards it like a crowd of lemmings. And it's all we want, everywhere: romantic books, *Dallas* on the telly, everyone we know. Nobody seems to learn any lessons on the way.

Her mother came out weighed down with parcels just as a guard was coming at her again; she dragged the parcels and her mother into the car with one movement.

"You're becoming very rough Dee, very ill-mannered," Mother said, annoyed and flustered.

"It's all this naked sleeping," Dee said, smiling up at the guard. "That's the cause of it, I'm certain."

Half-way home Dee realised what had happened. That stupid Nancy had got the weekend wrong. That was it. Hadn't Sam said he'd be tied up with the family, *next* weekend. Imagine believing the daylight from Nancy Morris. She really was going mad, it wasn't just a joke she made to her mother, of course that was it. Nancy was fussing and filling in her appointment book and complaining about the cost of living and she hadn't heard.

The relief was immense: it was the joy of getting an exam, it was like going to confession, not that there had been much of that lately – it was like passing your driving test.

She laughed happily and her mother looked at her in alarm.

"Mummy, I was just thinking of the day I passed my driving test," she began.

"Well I don't know whether you'd pass it if you had it to do again," her mother said. "You've been hitting those potholes at a great rate, your father wouldn't like his car to be belted about like that."

"No, I was just thinking of the lovely feeling when the man said I passed. Would you like me to teach you to drive, Mummy, seriously?"

"I would not," her mother said. "And what's more I don't think I'll ever sit in a car with you again. Will you look at the *road*, Dee!"

"It's an open invitation. One lesson on a Saturday, one on a Sunday — sure you could drive us all to Fergal's wedding."

She felt light-headed and happy. If she saw stupid Miss Mouse as Tom called her, she would have mown her down.

When Fergal and Kate arrived, Dee thought they both looked slightly touched. They were a revolting mixture of over-talkativeness and utter wordlessness. They explained at tedious length how they had become mature in the last few months and both of them had developed this sense of their immaturity and lack of responsibility at exactly the same time. They wanted to make their commitment now in front of everyone, rather than shilly-shallying any longer. Doctor Burke, who looked as if he wouldn't have minded if they never married, nodded and grunted appreciatively. Fergal's mother gasped and pounced on every word, and reminded them of every detail of John's wedding five years before, every detail that is except the one that his bride was four months pregnant. Dee switched off for a little and thought of Sam in London. He had said there would be papers all of Saturday afternoon but that he was going to skip the official dinner. Together they had looked at an English newspaper and circled plays or shows he might see. She wondered was it a nice warm night in London as it was here. Then it hit her like a tennis ball coming suddenly into her stomach. He had asked Nancy Morris to pray for a fine weekend for the barbecue. *This* weekend.

She wasn't able to eat the meringues which her mother had filled so carefully with a coffee flavoured cream to impress Fergal and Kate. She asked to be excused for a few minutes because she had remembered there was something she had to give Celia Ryan down in the pub.

"Won't it do later?" her mother had asked.

"No, she wants it now." Dee was standing up.

"Will I come down with you and have a pint?" She shooed Fergal away. "What a thought, after all this lovely meal Mummy's got for you. No, I'll be back in a few minutes."

"What does Celia want at this time of night?" Her father asked mildly. "Won't she be pulling pints and trying to help that poor mother of hers to cope?"

"See you," Dee called.

She ran up to her room for her handbag and swung down the road.

"Can you give me a pound of change for the phone, Celia?" she asked.

"God you're a great customer, if we had more like you we could open a singing lounge and have a cabaret on the profits," Celia laughed.

"Piss off, Celia. I'll have a brandy in a minute, I just want to make a call to Dublin."

Celia's level glance never changed, she never enquired whether the Burke phone was out of order, she just gave her the money.

"Could I get a call back in that box?" Dee wanted to know.

"Yes, I'll give you the number but I don't put it up – I don't want other people to know."

"You're a pal," Dee said.

"Barry residence," said the Canadian voice she hadn't heard since the one and only time she met its owner at that rugby party which was only a year and a half ago but felt like a lifetime.

"May I speak to Mr Sam Barry, please."

"Well, it's a little awkward just at this very minute. Who is this please?"

"It's Miss Morris, his receptionist."

"Oh Miss Morris, I didn't recognise your voice. I am sorry. Sam is just getting the barbecue going, it's a very delicate moment." There was a little laugh. "Once the thing has taken we can all relax. Can I ask him to call you, Miss Morris, I assume it's urgent?"

"I'm afraid it is, Mrs Barry." She sounded apologetic. "It's just a short message, but I should speak to him. It won't take a moment."

"Well, listen, I know he says that you are a rock of stability in a changing world, can I have him call you?"

"In the next half hour, if he could." Dee gave the number that Celia had written down.

"Rathdoon, what a pretty name!" Mrs Barry was determined to be charming to the rock of stability. Or else she was so happy about the anniversary barbecue she was at peace with the world. Dee didn't wait to find out.

"Very pretty. Bye, Mrs Barry." She hung up; she was shaking. She sat on a stool at the bar. Celia made it a large brandy but charged only for a small one. Dee made a move to protest.

"Nonsense, you're always buying me drinks."

"Thanks." She held the glass with both hands. Celia must have noticed the shake.

"They tell me your Fergal's engaged," Celia said.

"Lord, that didn't take long." Dee grinned.

"Oh, it's stale news, I heard last night when I came off the bus."

"So did I: the parents are over the moon."

"Well, they don't have to pay for the wedding," Celia laughed.

"Celia, stop that, you sound like Nancy Morris."

The phone rang. Celia refilled her glass wordlessly and Dee slipped into the booth.

"Hallo," she said.

"A call for you," exchange said.

"Miss Morris?" Sam asked.

"No, Miss Burke," Dee said.

"What?"

"Miss Burke speaking, can I help you?"

He wasn't sure. "I'm sorry, I was asked to ring a Miss Morris at this number . . . "

"No, you weren't, you were asked to come in from the barbecue and talk to your mistress Miss Dee Burke. That was the message I gave your wife."

"DEE. DEE." He was horrified. There was actual fear in his voice.

"Oh, she was very nice about it, she got a pencil from her purse and wrote down the number. She said Rathdoon sounded a pretty place."

"Dee, what are you doing?" His voice was a whisper.

"I'm at home for the weekend, like I told you I would be. The question is, what are YOU doing. Did they cancel the conference? Let's see, you were leaving the airport about four thirty – gosh, did they tell you at London airport or did you have to get into town?"

"Dee, I can explain exactly what happened but not here and now; what did you really say to Candy?"

"Oh just that, and she really did say that Rathdoon sounded pretty – ask her."

"You didn't . . . but why?"

"Because I felt it was all so confusing, all this business of lies and saying one thing and everyone knowing it wasn't true. Everyone. I thought it would be easier not having to pretend so much."

"But . . . "

"I mean she knows, Candy does, that you'll be spending Monday night with me, and so now you don't have to lie to her about that, and I know that you and Candy are having a marvellous tenth anniversary barbecue and that Mr Charles is there and Mr White and all your friends and they were all watching you start up the fire. She told me all that, so

52

there's no more pretending: it will be much easier from now on."

"You didn't, Dee. You didn't really say those things to Candy."

Her voice was very hard now. Very hard. "You'll have to find out now, won't you."

"But she said it was Miss Morris on the phone."

"Oh, I told her to say that." Dee sounded as if she were explaining things to a child. "Much simpler for your guests; I mean I don't know what you want to tell other people, but we'll talk about it all on Monday, won't we?"

"Dee, please don't go, you've got to explain."

"I have explained."

"I'll ring you back."

"Ring all you like, this is a pub."

"Where are you going now?"

"I see the real Miss Morris over here in a corner. I think I'll buy her a gin and orange and tell her all about us. That will make it easier for me to ring you at work; you see, I couldn't before because she knew me, but now with all this new honesty . . . "

"What new honesty?"

"What Candy and I have been talking about."

"You're a bitch, you told Candy nothing; this is a game, some vicious little game."

"Hush hush, don't let them hear you."

"Where will you be tomorrow?"

"I'll see you on Monday night, as arranged: come any time, straight from work if you like now that there's no need to hide things any more."

"I beg you, tell me what you told Candy."

"No, YOU must ask Candy that."

"But if you told her nothing then . . . "

"That's right, you'll have walked yourself into it."

"Dee."

"Monday."

"I'm not going to be blackmailed into coming round to

you on Monday."

"Suit yourself. I'll be at home then, if I don't get called away or anything." She hung up.

"If he rings again, Celia, will you say you never heard of me and I haven't been in all night?"

"Sure," said Celia.

She went back to the house. Fergal was explaining that there came a time in your life when you couldn't play any more – you had to face up to things.

"Jesus Mary and Joseph, Fergal, you should have been a philosopher!" Dee said admiringly.

"Did you have a drink with Celia Ryan?"

"I had two large brandies, mother dear," Dee said.

"How much was that?" Fergal the man saving for a mortgage was interested now in the cost of fun.

"I don't know, I only paid for one small one when I come to think of it." There were sudden tears in her eyes.

"Dee, why don't you and I go for a walk for a bit and let the wedding talk go on to a crescendo here?" Doctor Burke had his blackthorn stick in his hand.

They walked in silence. Down past the chip shop and over the bridge and on to the fork in the road.

It was only coming back that there was any chat.

"I'll be all right, Dad," she said.

"Sure I know you will, aren't you a great big girl and won't you be a solicitor one day, a fierce terror making them all shake in the district court?"

"Maybe."

"Of course you will, and all this other stuff will sort itself out."

"Do you know about him?" She was genuinely surprised.

"This is Ireland, child. I'm a doctor, he's a doctor, well a sort of one – when they get to that level it's hard to know."

"How did you hear?"

"Somebody saw you and thought I should know, I think,

54

a long time ago."

"It's over now."

"It may be for a while . . . "

"Oh no it is, tonight."

"Why so suddenly?"

"He's a liar and nothing else; he lied to her and to me –
why do people do that?"

"Because they see themselves as having lost out and
they want some of everything, and society doesn't let us
have that so we have to tell lies. And in a funny way the
secrecy keeps it all going and makes it more exciting at the
start."

"You know what it's like all right; I don't know how you
could."

"Oh, the same way as your fellow does."

"DADDY. No, not you. I don't believe it."

"Oh years and years ago. You were only a toddler."

"Did Mummy know?"

"I don't think so. I hope not. But she never said
anyway."

"And what happened to the girl?"

"Oh she's fine; she hated me for a bit, that was the
worst part – if she had been just a little bit understanding.
Just a small bit."

"But why should she?" Dee was indignant.

"Why, because she was young and lovely like you are
and she had the world before her, and I had made my way
and it was nice but a bit, you know . . . a bit samey."

"She should have shook your hand like a chap and said
'No hard feelings, Johnny Burke, you'll be a treasured
memory'," Dee was scathing.

"Something like that," her father laughed.

"Maybe she should have." Dee linked her father
companionably. "Because you're a much nicer man than
Sam Barry will ever be. I think he deserves a bit of roasting,
actually."

"Ah well, roast away," her father said goodnaturedly.

"You've never listened to me up to now – there's no reason why you should now."

Dee sat in her room and looked down at the town. She thought she saw Nancy Morris sitting on the wall near the chip shop, but decided that it couldn't be. Nancy . . . pay for a whole portion of chips . . . ridiculous.

Mikey

Mikey always said that you couldn't come across a nicer crowd of girls than the ones who worked in the bank. The men were grand fellows too but they were often busy with their careers and they wouldn't have all that time to talk. And one of the men, a young buck who'd be some kind of a high manager before he was thirty had taken it upon himself to say to Mikey that it would be appreciated if he watched his sense of humour since the bank ladies had found it rather coarse on occasions. Mikey had been very embarrassed and had said nothing all day. So silent was he that the nice Anna Kelly who was pure gold asked him if he felt all right. He had told her what the young buck said, and Anna Kelly had said that banks were stuffy old places and maybe the buck had a point: jokes were fine with friends, but God the bank, it wouldn't know how to laugh if you were tickling its funny bone for a year.

So he understood now and he never uttered a pleasantry within the bank walls again. If he met them on the street that was different; he could pass a remark or make a joke like anyone then because they were all on neutral ground. And he used to tell the girls about his family in Rathdoon, well, about the family that Billy and Mary had really. The twins with the red hairs and the freckles and then Gretta with the pigtails and the baby, a big roll of butter with a laugh you could hear half a mile away. He told Anna Kelly that sometimes on the summer evenings when it would be very bright the twins wouldn't have gone to bed, and they'd be sitting at their window waiting till the Lilac Bus turned into the street and Uncle Mikey would get off. They collected stamps and badges, any kind of badges, and he had them all on the lookout for anything of that order so as he never went home empty-handed.

He was the only one of the bank porters who came from the country. The rest were all Dubliners: they used to laugh at him and say there'd have to be an official enquiry as to how he got the job. But they were a very good-natured lot, and there was great chat all day as they manned the doors, or wheeled the big boxes on trolleys where and when more money was needed or had to be put away. They delivered letters and documents up and down the street. They knew a lot of the customers by name and they got great Christmas presents altogether.

The Lilac Bus had started just when Mikey had needed it. His father was getting senile now, and it was hard on poor Billy and Mary to have the whole business of looking after him. But it would have been a long way to come back without Tom FitzGerald and the little minibus that dropped you at the door. Imagine having to get yourself to the town by a crowded train, packed on a Friday night and maybe not a seat, and then after that to try and organise the seventeen miles home. It would take all day and all night and you'd be exhausted.

His old father was pleased to see him sometimes, but other times the old man didn't seem to know who he was. Mikey would take his turn spooning the food, and combing the matted hair. He would play the Souza marches his father liked on the record player, and put the dirty clothes in the big buckets of Dettol and water out in the back. Mary, who was Billy's wife and a sort of a saint, said that there was no problem to it if you thought of it all as children's nappies. Into a bucket of disinfectant for a while, throw that out, into a bucket of water a while and throw that out and then wash

60

them. Weren't they lucky to have space out the back and a tap and a drain and all. It would be desperate altogether for people who lived in a flat, say.

And the nurse came twice a week and she was very good too. She even said once to Mikey that he needn't come back *every* weekend, it was above the call of duty. But Mikey had said he couldn't leave it all to Billy and Mary, it wasn't fair. "But they'd be getting the house: what would Mikey be getting?" the nurse had pointed out. Mikey said that sort of thing didn't come into it. And anyway, wasn't it a grand thing to come back to your own place.

The twins told Mikey that there was never any fighting when he came home and Mikey was surprised.
"Why would there be fighting in this house?" he asked.
The twins shrugged. Phil and Paddy were afraid of being disloyal.
"Sure you couldn't be fighting with your poor old grandfather, he would never harm the hair of your heads," Mikey said.
The twins agreed and the matter was dropped.

They loved Mikey around the house and he had a fund of jokes for them. Not risky ones of course, but ones they could tell anyone. Gretta even wrote them down sometimes so that she'd remember them to tell them in class. Mikey never told the same one twice; they told him he should be on the television telling them one after another with a studio audience. Mikey loved the notion of it. He had once hoped that he might be asked to do a turn for the bank's revue but nobody had suggested it, and when he had whispered it to that nice Anna Kelly, she said she had heard that you had to be a member of the union to be invited, that only members of the IBOA were allowed to perform. He had been pleased to know that, because otherwise he would have felt they were passing him over.

61

He had his doubts about the Lilac Bus when he arrived the very first Friday. Tom Fitzgerald had asked them to be sure not to wave any money at him, because the legalities of the whole thing were what you might call a grey area. He did have the proper insurance and everything, and the Lilac Bus had a passenger service vehicle licence, but there was no point in courting disaster. Let them all give him the money when they were home in Rathdoon where it would be nice and calm. None of them had understood the ins and outs of it but they all agreed. Mikey wondered if people like Doctor Burke's daughter and Mr Green's son Rupert would fancy sharing a journey home with Mikey Burns the bank porter and the son of poor Joey Burns who before he lost his wits had been a great man for standing waiting till Ryan's pub opened and nothing much else. But Dee and Rupert were the salt of the earth, it turned out. There wasn't an ounce of snobbery between the pair of them. And Mrs Hickey, she was a lady too but she always seemed pleased to see him. Nancy Morris was the same as she always had been since she was a schoolgirl, awkward and self-conscious. Nothing would get her out of that, she'd be an old maid yet. Celia Ryan was another fish altogether: it was a mystery she hadn't married someone by now. She always looked as if her mind was far away, yet she was meant to be a powerful nurse. He knew a man who'd been in Celia's ward, and he couldn't speak highly enough of her. He said she was like a legend in the hospital.

Nowadays he enjoyed the journey home, after he had got over his shyness of the first few runs. He would tell them a joke or two; they weren't a great audience, not like Gretta and Phil and Paddy, but they did smile and laugh a little and didn't it cheer them up?

Sometimes he sat beside Celia and he would tell her tales of the world of banking. He told her of all the new machines, and the days of bank inspections, and how the tourists would drive you mad, and how in the summer you'd have a line half a mile long of Spanish and French students

62

all wanting to change about £1 each of their foreign money. Celia didn't tell many tales of the hospital, but she often gave him helpful advice about his own father, all in a low voice so that the others didn't hear her talking about incontinence pads and velcro fastenings for clothes.

But tonight it was the young Kennedy fellow sitting beside him. There was something seriously wrong with that boy. His brothers Bart and Eddie were the nicest fellows you could meet in a day's walk, but whatever had happened to young Kev he looked as if he had seen the Day of Judgement. You only had to address a civil word to him to have him leap out of his skin. Try to tell him a good story and he'd miss the point altogether. Mikey thought he'd teach him a few tricks that might be of use to him, to be able to do a trick in a pub. But the young fellow looked at him with the two eyes staring out of his head and didn't take in a word of it. In the end Mikey let him be, staring out the window as if the goblins were going to leap out of the hedges and climb into the bus after him.

Mikey nodded off. It was easy to sleep in the bus. The two girls behind him were already asleep, dreaming of fellows probably. Mikey dreamed that his father was well and strong again and had opened some kind of import and export agency in Rathdoon and that he, Mikey, was the manager and that he was able to give grand summer jobs to Phil and Paddy and Gretta delivering letters to people up and down the street. He often dreamed of the children. But he never saw a wife for himself in the dream. Mikey Burns had missed the boat as far as wives were concerned. Too nervous and eejity at the time he should have been looking for one, and now at forty-five he wasn't the kind of forty-five year old that would be in the race at all. Better not make a fool of yourself going to dances or picking up fast-knowing women in pubs and being made to look thick altogether.

When they crossed the river and were really in the West they paused for the ten-minute comfort stop, and the half pint to open the throat a bit. Celia came up to him quietly and put an envelope into his hand.

"That's for the bedsores: it's all written on it, keep him moving as much as you can."

"Aw Celia you're terribly good, can I pay for this?"

"Are you mad Mikey? Do you think I paid for it? Dublin Health Authority would like you to have it as a little gift." They laughed. She was very nice.

What a pity he hadn't found a grand girl like Celia when he was young and promising looking. After all, he had a grand well-paid job now, he'd be able to make a home for anyone. The reason he didn't really have one wasn't money, it was lack of interest. He couldn't be buying a place and furnishing it and getting tables and chairs in it all for hmself. The room he rented was grand and comfortable and he denied himself nothing. He had a grand big telly and he had bought a mirror himself to fix to the front of the wardrobe the way he'd go out properly dressed. He had a lovely radio beside the bed which was a lamp and a clock and an alarm all in one. When he went out to people's houses, and the Dublin fellows often invited him up to their places, he was always able to bring a big box of chocolates, a fancy one with ribbon on it. He was able to give a good account of himself.

But when he'd been a young lad, who were they except the sons of poor Joey Burns and his mother had taken in washing and cleaned people's floors? It hadn't held Billy back: Billy strutted round Rathdoon as if he owned it, as if he were as good as any other citizen of the place. And wasn't he right? Look where he was now, he had all kinds of business interests, he employed five people in Rathdoon. He had the take away shop; nobody believed there was a need for it until it appeared. Half the families in the place ate Billy's chicken and chips on a Saturday night, and they had fried fish too, and hamburgers. And they sold cans of lemonade, and stayed open late to get the crowds going home from Ryan's, and Billy had put up two huge mesh litter bins at his own expense and everyone was delighted with him.

And he had an insurance business as well. Not a big one but anyone who wanted cover went through him – it could all be filled in quickly in the house. And he had some kind of a connection with a fellow who came to do tarmacadaming. If you wanted the front of a place all smartened up then Billy would get other people with their places facing the same way to agree and the man with the machine and the tar would come and it was cheaper for everyone, and the place looked a king to what it looked before. A whole section of the main street looked really smart now, and Billy had got a tree planted in a tub and it was like something you'd see in a film. Billy had the brains and Billy never ran away the way Mikey ran off up to Dublin after his mother had died. Billy had stayed to marry Mary Moran who was way beyond anyone they'd ever have thought about. Or that Mikey would have thought about.

He was looking forward to being home tonight. He had a computer game for the twins' birthday. It was several cuts above the Space Invaders they had tried out once, and it could be plugged into any kind of television; he had been playing it on his own television all week but the shop assistant said it would work as well on a smaller set. The twins had their birthday on Monday and he was going to give them the game on Sunday afternoon. He would set up the room with the curtains pulled and pretend they were going to watch something on the television, and then would come the surprise. He had got a smart red girl's handbag for Gretta, even though it wasn't her birthday, because he didn't want her to be left out, and a yellow rabbit for the baby in case it might have feelings of discontent in its pram.

Mary would never let him near his father on the Friday night, she'd have a supper warm for him, or if it had been a busy day she'd run across the road to the family take away and get him fish and chips as soon as she saw the Lilac Bus pull up. She used to thank him so much for coming back to help with his father, and she'd tell him funny things about

65

the children and what they had done during the week. They were back at school now so there would be tales of what divilment Phil had got up to and the threatening messages that came home about him from the Brothers.

Mikey was the second to get out. They would leave Doctor Burke's daughter up at the golf club entrance; her parents were always there of a Friday night and she'd go and join them. Then when it came to the end of the street the first drop was Mikey. He would take down Nancy Morris's huge suitcase which weighed as light as a feather and leave it inside the bus because she and Kev Kennedy would be next out, and Kev had nothing with him ever except a parcel which he kept under his seat.

Mikey advised them all to be good and if they couldn't they should be clever and if they couldn't be clever then they should buy a pram. He laughed happily and closed the door behind him.

There was no light in the kitchen and no meal on the table. There was no sign of Mary and no note either. He didn't mind not seeing Billy – his brother was usually up at the take away or in Ryan's doing some deal with someone. But Mary?

He looked in the other rooms. His father was asleep, mouth open, wheelchair near the bed, on the chair a large chamber pot, optimistic since the old man was never able to time things so accurately.

There was a smell of disinfectant mixed with better smells. Mary had big bunches of flowers round the room. She always said that she thought it cheered the old man up, and sometimes she had seen him stretch out and touch the flowers gently. He snored lightly, there was a night light, and a Sacred Heart lamp as well.

Then he went up the stairs quietly. The twins had bunk beds; their toys and clothes and books were all around. Phil slept in a ball with his fists clenched; Paddy was more peaceful, lying on his side. Gretta looked funny with her long straight hair brushed out. He remembered her with

66

plaits for as long as she had been old enough to force her hair into them. She had a smile as if she was dreaming. She was a thin little thing, gawky and plain-looking but she had a smile that would tear the heart out of you. Even when she was asleep.

The door of Billy and Mary's bedroom was open: they weren't there. The baby round and soft like a cream bun lay in its cot near the bed. There was a lovely white lacy bedspread, and on the wall there was a picture of Our Lady in a field of flowers. It had a blue lamp lighting under it. It was called "Queen of the May". Mary told Mikey once that the day she and Billy got engaged he had won a competition at a carnival where you had to throw rings over things and he had chosen that picture for her because she liked it so much.

Mikey put his small bag in his own room which was neat as anything. She always had a bright clean pillowslip on the top as if he was the highest quality coming for the weekend. Sometimes Mikey's mind went back to what the house had looked like in his mother's day when they hadn't any such style or time for it.

It was puzzling, but maybe she had gone to get him fish and chips. He waited downstairs and listened to the news on the television. And eventually he began to get worried. They never left the children all alone in the house, even though they were perfectly safe, but it was just the way they were. His anxiety increased. He walked across to the take away and to his surprise there was Mary serving. There were four people waiting for their order and only one of the young girls who worked there was behind the counter. They were working flat out.

"Mikey, Lord is it that time already?" She was pleased but flustered to see him.

"Will I get behind there and give you a hand?" He knew the way he had done it with them a few Saturday nights during the summer when they had been very busy. And the prices were on the wall.

67

"Oh Mikey, would you?" She was very grateful.

He hung up his jacket and took an apron from a drawer. In a few moments they had the crowd thinned, and Mary was able to draw breath again. She spoke first to the girl who worked there.

"Treasa, would you take off your apron like a good child and run up to Ryan's. Tell them that we're short-staffed tonight and we'll be closing early. Tell them if they want anything to come down in the next half hour for it otherwise they'll be disappointed."

"Who will I tell, mam?" the child seemed worried.

"That's a point – not much use telling poor Mrs Ryan these days. Let me see, if there's anyone behind the bar helping, like Bart Kennedy, anyone like that, someone who looks in charge."

"Celia's home: she was on the bus, she'll probably have got behind the counter by now," Mikey said.

"That's it, tell Celia."

Treasa skipped off up the road, pleased to be out of the heat.

"Where's everyone?" Mikey looked around.

"Oh there's been a lot happening, I'll tell you all when we get back. Keep a brave face on it for half an hour more and then it will be done." A trickle of people came in, and Mikey served them, and just as Mary had guessed would happen a great influx came from Ryan's pub. They were full of good-natured abuse about it being against the law of the land to close the chipper before the pub. Mary had laughed good-naturedly and said wasn't she going above and beyond the call of duty to let them know now rather than have them going home with stomachs full of beer and nothing to soak it up.

She didn't want a portion for herself, so Mikey wrapped up his own choice, and when they had drained the fat, scrubbed the tops and swept up anything that could be swept up into black plastic bags which were tied with little wires at the top, they crossed the street and went home.

Mary heated a plate under the hot water tap, got out the tomato sauce and some bread and butter.

"Will I wet you tea or would you like a drop of anything?"

They got a bottle of Guinness each and sat down.

"Billy's gone. Gone for good."

He stared at her, fork half-way to his mouth.

"He went this day before lunch, he'll not be back. Ever."

"Ah no, Mary. That's not possible."

She took a sip of her drink and made a face.

"I never like the first sip, but it tastes grand after that." She smiled a weak little smile.

Mikey swallowed and said:

"It was just a bit of a row, that's all. People have rows, they get patched up."

"No, there was no row, there was no difference of opinion even."

Mikey remembered the way the twins had said there was no fighting when he was around the place.

"But just a bit of a barney now and then, these things sort themselves out, really they do." He was pleading now.

"No, I'll tell you it from start to finish – there was no row. Back there early on in the summer we did have rows all right: he was very touchy, I thought, bite the head off you as soon as look at you, but he said that's the way I was too. The children even noticed us."

"So what happened?"

"Well I don't know, honestly. But anyway we had a great summer, as you know, business was booming. He used to be tired but he was never cross any more, and what with the baby getting to be so grand – you know they're like divils for the first few weeks – anyway we hadn't a worry under the sun." She stopped and looked away beyond him.

Mikey was silent.

"Eat up your fish and chips, Mikey, you can eat and listen."

"I can't."

69

She lifted the plate from him and put it into the oven very low down. "You'll eat it later then. Today was when it all happened, and if I hadn't come back I wouldn't have known: I wouldn't have known at this moment. I wouldn't have known until the end of next week. And the whole of Rathdoon would have known before me."

"Known what, for God's sake?"

"He's gone off with Eileen Walsh, you know the one we said was too good to be working in a chipper. Well, she was far too good, she was only biding her time to go off with the owner of the chipper. That was the little plan. Could you beat it?" The voice was steady but the eyes were over bright.

"But it's only a fancy isn't it, it's a bit of madness. I mean where would they go, and what would they do? And how could he leave you and the baby and the whole family?"

"He's in love with her. That's the word: *In Love.* Isn't it marvellous? He was never *In* love with me; he loved me, of course, but that was different apparently."

Mikey stood up, but he didn't know what to do so he sat down again. Mary went on with the story.

"I was meant to be going into the town. There's always a lift in on Fridays and I had a list of things we needed for the take away, not things we get from the suppliers, but stupid things, big ashtrays for example and a couple of tins of bright red paint – we were going to paint the windows to match the geraniums, can you believe? But to go on with what happened: You know old Mrs Casey who's only just learned to drive, well she was giving me the lift and as soon as we were out on the road beyond the golf club, didn't the engine splutter and make these desperate sounds.

"Ah well, I said to myself, there's my day in town gone for its tea. But she's such a nice woman, Mrs Casey, you couldn't offend her. I told her it was a blessing in disguise and I could get the things next week and maybe I'd go home and make an apple tart since Mikey'd be coming back on the bus tonight."

A big lump came up in Mikey's throat.

70

"And I said to her to sit tight, I'd walk back and tell the Brennans in the garage to go out for her."

Mary took another sip.

"It was a gorgeous day, and I picked wild flowers from the hedges, and when I came in there was Billy at the table with a whole load of papers all round him. And I was delighted because he was meant to have been gone for the day. So I said wasn't this grand and we'd have a bit of lunch the two of us – something we hadn't done in years – and I saw that there was 'Dear Mary' on one piece of paper and on another and only two or three lines on each. And I *still* didn't know anything was wrong so I said 'Are you writing me love letters at my age?' as a kind of joke. You see I thought he was just back unexpectedly and was writing me a note to explain that he'd been in."

"Oh Mary, isn't this terrible," said Mikey, believing it for the first time since the saga had started.

"And this is the awful bit: he started to cry, he started to cry like a child. Well, I nearly dropped dead – Billy Burns crying. I ran to him to try and put my arms around him and he pushed me away. And he was sobbing like a baby that's getting teeth, so I said to him to hush it down or his father would hear. I'd left the baby next door but your father would have been having a doze and it would have frightened the daylight out of him like it was doing to me." She paused for a moment.

"Then he said about Eileen, and her expecting and all."

There was a silence and the clock ticked and the soft snoring sound of the old man could be heard from the back room.

"And he said he couldn't face me, and he was leaving a letter. And I said that he didn't have to go now, not at once, that surely he could stay and we could talk about what was to be done. But he said there'd been too much talking and that was it, now he was going." Mikey put out his big hand and patted Mary's arm hopelessly.

"And there was a lot of this and that, but funny no fight,

71

no shouts or me saying he was a bastard or him saying he couldn't bear me any more, that I was an old nag or anything."

"Well, no one could think that," Mikey cried loyally.

"No, he said I'd been the best wife and mother in the world, and that he couldn't tell me how sorry he was, he was just heartbroken, he said. All the papers were to show me that the chip shop is in my name, and the thousand pounds in the building society is for me, and the name of a solicitor who'd be able to find him, who'd pass letters on."

"And where does he think he's going?"

"To England. Where else?"

"And how will he earn a living for himself and this floosie?"

"She's not a floosie – Eileen a floosie? Billy would earn a living on the planet Mars, don't worry about that."

Mikey was struck dumb.

"But the thing that upset him most was his father, your father."

"Billy never gives much time to poor old Dad."

"No, but he thought it wasn't just for me to be left with him – to have to look after an old man who isn't my own father. I said that Da was the least of the problems, what I wanted to know was how he could leave me, his wife, his friend for years and years, for fourteen years married, and a year before that mad about each other. That's when he explained all this *In Love* business."

"What did you do?"

"What could I do? His mind was made up, he was leaving. He had a list of things he wanted me to do. There was a special sum of money left in one envelope that was for me to have driving lessons. I was to find out who taught Mrs Casey: whoever taught her could teach the divil himself. He was leaving the van. I was to ask Bart Kennedy to give me a hand and pay him a proper wage, I was to decide whether he should write to the children or not and what I should tell them, if anything. He thought I should say he had gone

72

away for a bit and then they'd grow used to it."

Mary stood up to get another bottle of stout.

"He had been packing his things too, it nearly broke my heart to see his good shirts stuffed in all creased, and he had forgotten all his shoes. I asked him to say goodbye to your father – he's been very clear the past couple of days, knows all of us – but no, he wouldn't. I said he might never see him again and he said that he'd never see any of us again. That's when I got a bit frightened about it all. I knew there's never any changing his mind. So I decided I'd let him go, without screaming and roaring and begging."

"You let him walk out . . . "

"No, I said I'd go out and let him finish at his ease. I said he needn't bother about the letter now, he'd said it all, that I'd go out and get more flowers and things and keep out of his way for an hour or two until he left. That he could leave all the insurance papers where they could be found, and the solicitor who would pass on the messages to him if there was anything we hadn't thought of. He was SO relieved: you should have seen his face – you see he was afraid there'd be this big scene. He said that maybe I'd be glad of the change too, and I said, oh no, I wouldn't, I would miss him every day of the year and so would his children, and on the days when his father was clear his father would miss him too. I wasn't going to give him the nice comfortable feeling that he was doing us any favours. And out I went. I crept along the back way and he finished his packing and his leaving things out on the table, and your one came along in her car and he put the boxes and cases in and she kissed him just standing at our door and they drove off.

"When I came in it was all in neat piles on the table and a piece of paper saying 'Thank you very much, Mary. All the best, Billy.' So now you know everything, everything that's to be known."

"Isn't he a callous bastard, isn't he the biggest most selfish . . . "

"That won't bring him back."

"I'll bring him back, I'll get him back. He's not going to desert you, there's ways of bringing him back."

"Not if he doesn't want to come back! Will you have your fish and chips now, they'll go all hard otherwise?"

He hardly slept all night; it was only when the dawn came that he fell off and it wasn't long after that the twins were in the room followed by Gretta carrying a cup of tea. That was always their excuse to wake him: it was called bringing him his tea in bed. Most of it was in the saucer and some of it was on the stairs but it was still an excuse. They were full of plans for the day. They'd come down and wait while he was feeding grandpa and changing him: they accepted that routine as part of life like sunsets or having to wash your hands before meals. They wanted to show him a new game that had arrived in Brophy's shop. It was a huge thing like a Space Invaders but it cost twenty pence a time and they could only have three goes altogether unless of course Uncle Mikey wanted an extra game. And Mammy had said they could go on a picnic in the afternoon because since daddy was gone to Dublin for a bit there'd be no work to be done around the house and no one coming in about Insurance who had to have tea. And hadn't he better get up now in case all the good went out of the day.

Matty felt the day was very heavy on his hands, that things kept happening as if he were outside looking in at all the things that were happening instead of being part of them. He saw himself feeding his father slowly with a spoon, he saw himself cutting crusts off the sandwiches for the picnic, and climbing for the blackberries. It was like playing a part in a play.

He was glad when it was evening and the children went to bed; they went easily because he had promised them the most monstrous surprise of their lives tomorrow. Something that he absolutely guaranteed they would never expect. He assured Gretta that it was something she could share too and that there was a small non-birthday present for her as well.

"I don't know what I'd have done without you and that's the truth," Mary said. "The day just flew by for me." He was glad it had. He had arranged for two girls to help Treasa in the chip shop.

"Will Eileen not be in again?" Treasa complained. Her tone was guileless, she didn't know.

"No she won't, she's gone off somewhere; we'll get you these two young ones you've had in there before on bank holidays and high summer," he said firmly. "Mrs Billy and I are going to be down in Ryan's for a bit, so you'll know to send one of them down there if there's any problem, but a big bright girl like you, Treasa, you'll manage it. Don't you know it all like the back of your hand?"

Treasa was delighted with him.

"Oh go on, Mr Mikey, you and your Dublin chat" she said.

"Are we going off down to Ryan's?" he asked her.

He was going to make a joke and say something about stepping out together or hitting the high spots but he felt it would have been the wrong thing to do. She looked up at him, pleased and surprised that he seemed so eager.

"I'm not much company for you."

"I think we should go out though, don't you? From the start like. No hiding away in corners, no crawling out when people think you've got two heads. Be out there from the word 'go'. After all YOU haven't done anything."

"I've failed to hold onto my husband, that's a great crime around these parts."

"Oh I don't think so; aren't they all stuck into television every night here? I think you'd have to do far more than that to be a disgrace."

"I hate you to be involved in it, Mikey, you've been nothing but kindness itself, every weekend as nice as anything and look what happens to you: caught up in all the scandal, all the gossip."

"There won't *be* scandal and gossip, and that's up to you

75

to make sure of." He heard his own voice in his ears. He thought it sounded very confident, very sure. Mary must have thought so too.

"You're a great help to me taking all these decisions, I'm like one of those things in films that just walk about not knowing what they're at."

"Zombies," he said.

"Imagine you knowing that," Mary said.

"I see a lot of films," Mikey said. "What else have I to do?"

Ryan's was crowded. He put Mary in a corner and went up to the counter. Celia was going full strength and Bart Kennedy was giving her a hand. Mikey remembered his brother's instructions about paying Bart a proper wage and bile against Billy rose in his throat. To be able to calculate like that, to plan for her desertion, to deceive her so long.

"It's not like you to be short of a word, Mikey Burns." Celia was standing in front of him. She must have asked him his order and he hadn't heard.

"I'm sorry." He had to force his sense of outrage down before he could speak.

"Are you all right?" Celia's voice was concerned.

Mikey shook himself. He was full of brave words to his sister-in-law about how SHE was to behave, now he must do the same for himself. He could speak again, but he hadn't the heart for jokes.

He gave his order and carried the pint and the glass of Snowball across to Mary. As he was passing young Biddy Brady's engagement party, Nancy Morris of all people put her hand out as if to stop him. Wanted him to come and tell them some funny stories. And he always thought she was such a superior acting kind of a one, always looking in on herself and never having time for other people. Well, well.

"Not now, Nancy" he had said and he saw her face turning away embarrassed. He hadn't meant to be so short with her, but honestly, *now* of all times.

"Here we are" he said.

She had her head down looking at the floor.

"Look up Mary Burns, look up and smile."

She looked up and gave a watery smile.

"That's marvellous but it isn't a patch on your daughter's." She gave one of Gretta's sudden grins, the kind of grin that split a face in half, they both laughed.

"That's better," said Mikey, "now let's see what we'll do."

They got out a writing pad and made out a list of things she had to do this week. Ring suppliers – their names were all on some kinds of bits of paper on various spikes around the office. Billy Burns hadn't kept any books that would gladden the heart of a taxman but at least there was some method in his ways. They wrote out a kind of notice which she could give to anyone who called about insurance: "Mr Burns' policies are all being dealt with by the following office . . . " followed by the name of the solicitor's. She would give these to anyone with a laughing explanation that unfortunately as a mere woman she was never kept informed of the Master's doings. It seemed fairly sure that he hadn't absconded with other people's money, so his Book had been passed on or sold to some other agent by now. The solicitors would know. They listed the people they could call on to work in the take away, and how much they should be paid. He went for two further pints and two further Snowballs, and by that time they had covered every eventuality and worn themselves out.

"I'll sleep tonight, I'm that exhausted," Mary said, letting out that she hadn't slept the previous night.

"I'll sleep too: I'm less frightened," Mikey said. She looked at him gratefully: "You're very very good to me, but there's one thing you haven't mentioned at all."

"What's that?"

"What about you? Will you still be coming home on the

bus at weekends?"

"I'll get off the Lilac Bus before ten every Friday with the help of God," he said.

"You're very different tonight, you're not always cracking jokes and making games out of things people say. I find it much easier to talk to you, but hard to believe it IS you, do you know what I mean?"

"I think so" he said.

"Like I want to ask you do you want to come home to Rathdoon even more than at weekends, but I don't know how to put it. If I say, will you come back altogether, it looks as if I want you to come back and look after us all and take it all on, and that's NOT it. And then, if I don't ask you, you might get the notion you're not welcome."

"I've thought all that out too," Mikey Burns said.

"And what did you arrive at?" She leaned over the glass with its rim of froth. She couldn't wait to hear.

"You're still hoping in your heart he'll come back. That it's only a bit of summer madness. That it'll be all forgotten by the end of the month."

"I'd like it, but I don't think it's going to happen," she said simply.

"So, suppose I came home and settled myself in and Billy Boy came over the hill one fine day, where would that leave us all?"

"As we were, wouldn't it?" She looked at him enquiringly.

"No. I'd have to run away again, there wouldn't be room for us all in the one nest."

"So are you not coming back to us. I always thought you had a great soft spot for us altogether." She sounded sad.

"I'll come back for good if he isn't back for Christmas. That's the best way. That's the way to do it." He looked proud of his deductions.

"It's your home," she said gently. "You were always as welcome in it as the sun coming in the windows."

"You say that because you're like that. My brother Billy

didn't say it, did he, when he was leaving. He told you to get Bart Kennedy and pay him a proper wage."

"He did say it but I didn't repeat it. I didn't want to be making you think you had to do anything." She looked troubled now.

"What did he say?"

"He said . . . ah it doesn't matter what he said. He made it clear he thought of the place as your house too."

"I want to hear it."

"Why? What does it matter? We know he hardly knows what he's doing: he's half mad these days, he couldn't string words together."

"Well I'd like to know anyway, please," he said simply but firmly. This wasn't the giggling, jokey man of last weekend.

"He said something like: 'Mickey's not likely to settle down anywhere with anyone at his age, and he's very good to the old man, and the children love him. Maybe if he could find something for himself round here, he'd be in the place. Sure the house is half his anyway, he has a right to it.' It was something along those lines."

She didn't look at him, and he looked hard at the beermat which had a puzzle on it.

"Full of charm, my little brother, isn't he?"

"That's what he is: your little brother, don't ever forget that."

"And would it suit you, Mary, if I were to be about the place?"

"Would it suit me? Wouldn't I love it, isn't it what I always wanted? There's always been a living for us all in that take away alone, you've seen the takings, and if we were working in it together . . . "

"Well then, I'll come back at Christmas, that's the best. I might even get myself made redundant up at the bank, and have a lump sum. Those fellows up in the bank, the porters, are fierce organised, you'd never know what kind of a deal they'd get for me."

79

"And wouldn't it be dull for you, after Dublin?"

"No, don't I come home for nearly half the week as it is?"

"And maybe finding yourself a girl?" She was hesitant.

"I think brother Billy was right on that one, the time is past." He smiled an ordinary smile, not a screwed up one.

Rupert Green passed the table. "Did you see Judy Hickey at all?" he asked.

"No, I'm afraid we were talking, I didn't notice," Mary said.

"She could be round the corner behind the pillar there," Mikey pointed. Biddy Brady's party had linked arms and were singing "Sailing" and Celia's mother was arriving with a golf club as if she were about to brain them but as they all watched horrified it turned out that she had no such intention: she was about to join in the singing, and was in fact calling for one voice only, her own.

"I've met everyone from the Lilac Bus except the one I set out to meet," grumbled Rupert. "Dee Burke was just flying out the door, Miss Morris looks as if she's had a skinful, Kev is cowering in a corner, and the rest of the cast is at the counter canoodling."

"If she comes in what I'll tell her?"

"Oh I'll find her, I have to tell her something extraordinary."

Mary and Mikey looked politely interested.

He was gone.

"It's probably about some toadstool or mushroom; they're always talking about herbs and elderflowers and things," Mikey said. Mary laughed and tucked her bag under her arm.

"Won't you want another man?" he said suddenly. "I mean you're still young. Won't living with a brother-in-law cramp your style?"

"No," she said, "No, I won't. I mean, even if I could have one and I can't. But I think I'm through with all that sort of

80

thing. I think I just want a bit of peace and for the children to be able to grow up happily enough and for me to have a place here, you know, just like you said, not running away. That will do me."

He remembered the dream that he had on the bus: the dream where there had been no wife but he was in charge of the children sending them on little messages up and down the street. He realised now there had been no Billy in the dream either. Some of the details were different, of course, but the central part was the same. He would be safe at home with them all. And there would be no demands made on him as a man. He could be just himself, and he'd be as welcome as the sun that came in the windows.

Judy

There had been four customers in the shop that afternoon, Judy had been taking note recently and writing it down in a little book. After lunch two students came in and spent almost half an hour reading books on herbalism and the art of home-made wines. An elderly man bought a copper bracelet for his arthritis and said that when the savages who came into his house and robbed him blind were leaving they pulled his copper arm band off in case it had been valuable. A woman with a tight hard face bought some Evening Primrose oil and asked could you dilute it with ordinary vegetable oil or baby lotion to make it go further.

It was a matter of weeks now before they had to close. Judy's heart was heavy as she walked toward the Lilac Bus. She was tired too, and not in form for a long drive to the West. She had been tempted to opt out. To go back to her little flat and have a long long bath listening to some nice music on the radio. Then to put on her caftan and her soft little slippers and lie there until the aches in her limbs and the build-up of a headache behind her eyes was gone. Fine advertisement I am for a health shop . . . she smiled to herself as she strode on towards the bus. Aching and creaking and bankrupt. No wonder people live such unhealthy lives if they see what good living leads to!

She hoped that Mikey Burns wouldn't be too loud tonight with his schoolboy jokes. He was a decent poor fellow but he was hard to take at any length. The trouble was that if you made no response to him he thought you hadn't heard and said it all again, and if you did manage a laugh he got encouraged and told you a few more.

She arrived just at the same time as Rupert: that was good, they could sit together in the back seat. It looked a bit standoffish if you were to keep a seat for anyone, but she really couldn't bear to be nudged by Mikey the whole way to Rathdoon or, even worse, to hear that solemn tedious little Nancy Morris telling her how to get free soap by buying toothpaste on a Wednesday or some such hare-brained scheme.

He was a good boy, Rupert: yes that was exactly how she would describe him if anyone asked her. Good. He was an only child of parents who were middle-aged when he was a toddler and who were old now that he was a man of twenty-five. His mother was sixty-seven and his father was seventy this year. But Rupert said there were no celebrations, his father was bedridden now and was failing by the week. Rupert said it was harder and harder each time he came home because he had this vision of his father as a hardy man with views of his own on everything, and then when he got into the big bedroom on a Friday night it was the same shock, the same readjustment – a paper-thin man with a head like a skull, with nothing alive except the big restless eyes.

Judy had known Rupert since he was a baby and yet she had only got to know him since the bus. He had always been a polite child. "Good morning, Mrs Hickey. Do you have anything for my pressed flower collection?" Protestants were like that, she had always thought in her good-natured generalisations: pressed flowers, politeness, neat haircuts, remembering people's names. Mrs Green was so proud of her Rupert, she used to find excuses to walk him down the town. The Greens had been married for twenty years when Rupert was born. Celia Ryan's mother in the pub had whispered that she gave Mrs Green a novena to St Anne that had never been known to fail, but because of her religion she had delayed using it. The moment she had said it, Catholic or no Catholic, St Anne had intervened and there you were, there was Rupert.

Judy told him that one night on the Lilac Bus and he laughed till the tears came down his face. "You'd better tell me about St Anne and what class of a saint she is. I suppose I should be thanking her that I'm here, or speaking sharply to her when times are bad."

Judy often smiled at Rupert's quaint ways. He was wonderful company and the same age as her own son, Andrew, miles away in the sun of California. But she could never talk to Andrew like she talked to Rupert – in fact she could never talk to Andrew at all over the years. That was the legal agreement.

Judy wondered would you recognise your own child.

Suppose she went to San Francisco now and walked through Union Square, would she immediately know Andrew and Jessica? Suppose they passed her by? They would be grown man and woman, imagine, twenty-five and twenty-three. But if she didn't know them and they didn't know her, what was all the point of giving birth and holding a child inside you for all that time? And suppose they did recognise her, that something like an instinct made them stop and look at this fifty-year old woman standing in the sunshine . . . What would they do? Would they cry "Momma, Momma" and run to her arms like a Hollywood film? Or would they be embarrassed and wish she hadn't turned up? They might have their own idea of a momma back in Ireland. A momma who was just not suitable. That's what Jack said he would tell them. Their mother hadn't been able to look after them – no other details. And when they were old enough to hear details and understand them, they would be given Judy's address to write to and she could send them an explanation if she felt able to. She never felt able to because they never wrote. For years and years she had been rehearsing it and trying out new phrases, like practising for a job interview or a school essay.

Little by little she realised they were eighteen, nineteen, twenty. Well old enough to ask about an unsuitable mother. Well old enough to be told. But no request ever came.

She didn't even write to Jack's brother after a while. Jack's kind big brother who had given them all a home on the West Coast of America but who had always tried to patch up the split. He had told her nothing in his letters except to assure her that the children were settling in to their school and that all was for the best.

This evening she wondered about them both, Andrew and Jessica – golden Californians now. Were they married? Very probably. Californians married younger, divorced sooner. Was she a grandmother? Very possibly. His name might be Hank or Bud or Junior. Or were those all old names? Why did she think it was a grandson, it might be a girl, a little girl in a sunhat like Jessica had been the day they took her away. She had a Californian clock in her mind always, ever since they left twenty years ago. She never paused and said, "I wonder what time it is out there," she always knew. It was coming up to a quarter to eleven in the morning for them. It was always that when she came round the corner to the Lilac Bus. And she didn't know if they were married or single, working in universities or as domestics. She didn't know if they were happy or wretched, she didn't even know if they were alive or dead.

She slipped neatly in beside Rupert on the back seat, passing young Dee Burke who had been looking so troubled for the last Lord knows when, it was amazing she hadn't cracked up. Past the odd young Nancy Morris. What a cuckoo in the nest that little one was – her mother was a grand little woman altogether, and Deirdre who had gone to the States was very nice, whenever she came back, full of chat. The brother in Cork was a nice lively fellow too. What had come over Nancy to make her so prissy or whatever it was she had become?

Rupert was wearing a new jacket which obviously thrilled him to the core. It just looked like an ordinary teddy boy jacket to Judy, but then she was the first to admit she knew nothing about smart clothes. Dee Burke had gone into ecstasies over it and Rupert had flushed with pleasure.

"It's a birthday present," he whispered as the bus started. "I'll tell you all about it later."

She didn't want to hear all about it on the bus, not while her hip was aching and her head was throbbing, and that young Morris girl might well pretend not to be listening but was only two feet away from them. She felt old tonight. She was years older than everyone on the bus except Mikey Burns and she was a good few years beyond him too. She was twenty years older than the young couple who had set up the health shop and who would be dismantling it within six weeks unless there was a miracle and they discovered the Elixir of Youth and bottled it in expensive but appealing packaging. Surely she was past all this rattling backwards and forwards across the country. Surely she should have some peace and settle down, in one place or the other.

She rooted in her big bag and gave Rupert a small parcel. "It's Green Tea," she said, "Just a little to see if you like it."

His eyes lit up. "This is what you make the mint tea, the proper mint tea with?" he said.

"Yes, a handful of fresh mint, a little sugar in a glass, and you make the tea separately in a silver pot if you have one and then pour it on the mint leaves."

Rupert was very pleased. "I'd been making it with tea bags since we came back from Morocco, and it tasted really terrible, but out there it was like heaven. Oh I AM grateful to you Judy."

"It's only a little," she said warningly.

"Look on it as a sample. If we like it we'll come in and buy kilos of the stuff and make your shop do a roaring trade."

"It would need it." She told him about the kind of trade they were doing. He was reassuring, it was the same everywhere.

He worked in an estate agency. Things were very slow. Houses that would have leaped off the books weren't moving at all. And there were shops closing down all over the place. But these things went in phases, he said. Things had to get better soon, the kind of people who knew about these things were confident, that's what you had to remember. Judy said wryly that the kind of people who knew about such things could probably still afford to be confident, they had so many irons in the fire. It was the rest of the world that was the problem.

They felt like old friends the way they talked. She asked him to come and advise for a bit at the cutting of the elderflower, and to help choose some of the dried rosemary and lemon balm for the little herb pillows she was making. Rupert said that for the Christmas trade she should make dozens of those and sell them herself to big shops in Grafton street – they would make great Christmas gifts. Fine, Judy said, but what about her own shop, the shop she worked in? That's the one she wanted to help, not big stores which would make money anyway.

He told her about a politican's wife who had come into the auctioneer's and enquired politely about the location of her husband's new flat. Somehow they all knew that this flat was not a joint undertaking and that the wife was trying to find out. Everyone in the place had copped on and they all became vaguer and more unhelpful by the minute. Eventually the woman had stormed out in a rage. And they had drafted an immensely tactful letter to the politican pointing out that his nest had not been revealed but was in danger of coming under siege.

"Poor stupid woman," said Judy. "She should have let him install a harem in there if it kept him happy."

"You wouldn't have let him do that, you'd have too much spirit," Rupert said admiringly.

"I don't know. I let a man walk away with my two babies twenty years ago. That wasn't showing much spirit, was it?" Judy said.

Rupert gasped. Never had Judy Hickey mentioned the amazing happening that the whole town knew about in garbled versions. He had asked his mother who had said that nobody knew the whole ins and outs of it, and that Rupert's father who had been the local solicitor then also, had been very annoyed because nobody consulted him, and he was the obvious person to have been brought in on it. But there had been something about a Garda charge and a lot of conversation and a solicitor from Dublin coming down for Jack Hickey and then documents being drawn up and Jack and the two children going to America and never coming back.

"But people must know WHY," Rupert had insisted.

His mother said there were more explanations than there were days in the year.

She had been only six years married and twenty now without her man and her children, but she always kept the name Hickey. It was in case the children ever came back, people said. There was a while when she used to go into the town seventeen miles away and ask at the tourist office if you could get the lists of American tourists or just those with children. There was a while she would go up to the bus tours that sometimes came through Rathdoon and scan the seats for nine year old boys with seven year old sisters. But all that was long in the past. If it was so long in the past, why had she mentioned them now?

"Are they on your mind then?" Rupert asked gently. She replied as naturally as if she was in the habit of talking about them. She spoke with no more intensity than she had talked of the mint tea.

"They are and they aren't. We'd probably have nothing to say to each other at this stage."

"What kind of work does he do now? He's not retired, is he?"

"Who? Andrew, he's only your age. I HOPE he hasn't retired yet." She looked amused.

"No, I meant your husband. I didn't know whether your

children were boys or girls." Rupert felt he had put his foot in it.

"Boy and girl, Andrew and Jessica. Andrew and Jessica."

"Nice names," he said foolishly.

"Yes, they are nice names aren't they? We spent ages choosing them. No, I've absolutely no idea whether Jack Hickey is working or whether he is lying in a gutter being moved on by big American cops with sticks. And I don't know if he ever worked in California or whether he lived off his brother. I never cared. Honestly I never gave him a thought. It sounds like someone protesting, I know it does, but it's funny: I have great trouble remembering what he looked like then and I never until this moment wondered how he's aged. Possibly got fatter. His elder brother Charlie was a lovely man, he was fat, and there was a family picture I remember, and the parents were fat."

Rupert was silent for a moment. Such obvious indifference was chilling. You could understand hate or bitterness even. You could forgive a slow fire of rage and resentment. But she talked about him just as you would about some minor celebrity who had been in the news one time. Is he dead or alive? Who knows, who remembers? On to another topic.

"And do the children, well . . . do Andrew and Jessica keep in touch even a little bit?"

"No. That was the agreement."

If he was ever to know, it would be now. He inclined his head slightly to see if anyone else was listening. But no, Dee was fast asleep with her head at an awkward angle, and that awful Morris girl was asleep too. The others were too far ahead to hear.

"That was a harsh sort of agreement," he said tentatively.

"Oh they thought they were justified. People used to think it was quite justifiable to hang a sheep stealer, don't forget."

"Is that what you did?" he asked smiling, "Steal a

92

sheep?"

"Would that it had been so simple. No no, I thought you knew, I thought your father might have told you. No, I was a dope peddler. That's even worse than anything, isn't it?"

She looked like a mischievous girl the way she said it. He felt she couldn't be serious.

"No, what was it about really?" he laughed.

"I told you. I was the local drugs person." She spoke without pride or shame. Just as if she was saying what her name was before she was married. Rupert had never been so startled. "You do surprise me," he said hoping he was managing to keep the shock out of his voice. "But that was YEARS ago."

"It was the sixties. I suppose it is years ago, but your lot aren't the first to know about drugs, you know – the sixties had their own scene."

"But wasn't that only in America and England? Not like now."

"Of course it was here too, not in huge housing estates, and not kids and not heroin. But with brightish, youngish things, at dances, and people who just left College who had been abroad, and it was all very silly, and to this day I think perfectly harmless."

"Hash, was it?"

"Oh yes, Marijuana, pot, a few amphetamines, a bit of LSD."

"You had acid? YOU had acid?" He was half-admiring, half-shocked.

"Rupert, what I had was everything that was going, that wasn't the point. The point was that I was supplying it, and I got caught."

"Why on earth were you doing that?"

"Out of boredom in a way, I suppose. And the money was nice, not huge but nice. And there was a lot of fun too, you met great people – not dead-wood people like Jack Hickey. I was very stupid really. I deserved all that happened. I often think that." She had paused to muse.

Rupert mused with her for a bit. Then he spoke again:

"Were you doing it for long? Before you were caught?"

"About eighteen months. I was at a party and we all smoked something, Lord knows what it was called – I thought it was great, Jack had said nothing at the time, but when we got home he roared and shouted, and said that if this ever happened again, and what he'd do and what he wouldn't do."

"Had he refused it then?"

"Ah you didn't know our Jack, not at all, he had passed the poor little cigarette with the best but he had kept his mouth closed and only pretended to inhale. He was sober and furious. Oh, there was a barney that went on all week, then the ultimatum: if I ever touched it again . . . curtains, he'd take the children off to America, I'd never see them again, no court in the land . . . you could write it out yourself as a script and it would be right, it would be what he said." Rupert listened, fascinated. Judy's soft voice went on:

"Well, Jack was dealing with the livestock. It wasn't like a farm, you know, the house then, it was like a ranch: there were only livestock – no milking, no hens, no crops, just beasts in the field – buy them, graze them, sell them. We had poor old Nanny, she had been my Nanny in the days of old decency and she minded Andrew and Jessica, I used to go here and there. Gathering material for a book on the wild flowers of the West. Gathering bad company more likely. Anyway, because I had my little car and because I went here and there what could be more natural than I go to Dublin or to London as I did twice to get some stuff for people. Others suggested it, I took it up like a flash."

"It's like a story out of a book," Rupert breathed admiringly.

"A horror story then. I remember it as if it was yesterday: acting on information received, warrant, deeply embarassed Mr Hickey, a person of such importance as yourself, absolutely sure there's nothing in it, but have to apply the same laws to the high as to the low, and if we could get it all over as quickly as possible wouldn't that be for the best? Dear, dear, heavens above, what have we here, in MRS Hickey's car, and MRS Hickey's briefcase in the bedroom. And hidden away behind MRS Hickey's books. Well, he was at a loss for words and perhaps Mr Hickey could come up with some explanation?"

She was like an actress, Rupert thought suddenly. He could see the Sergeant or the Superintendent or whoever it was. She could do a one-woman show, the way she was telling the story, and it was without gesture or emphasis since it was being told in a low voice not to wake the others as the minibus sped through the evening.

"It took for ever. And there were people down from Dublin and there was a TD, someone I didn't even know Jack knew. And Jack said that the whole place was becoming too much for him anyway and he had been thinking about selling it for a while, but if there was this scandal then people would know he was doing it under a cloud and the price of the place would drop right down. They were all businessmen, even the guards, they could understand that.

"Then the documents. Jack was going to take the children to his brother unless I signed a sworn statement that I agreed I was an unfit person to act as their mother any longer. The Sergeant could charge me, as soon as Jack had the place sold, his plans made and was off to California with the babies. He begged me to think of the children."

"He did that and yet took them away from you?" Rupert was confused.

"Yes, you see his point was that I was a drugs criminal, that wasn't a good start for any child: they'd be better without me. A deal had been done, kind wise people had seen extenuating circumstances, it was up to me to make the most of them."

She looked out the window for a while.

"I didn't think it would be for ever. I was frightened, I was sure it would all die down. I said yes. He sold the place, well he sold it to that gangster, remember, who conned everyone and went off with a packet. Then the Liquidator or whatever sold it to the nuns and they made it into the conference centre. So now you know the story of the Big House and all the bad people who lived there until the present day." He hadn't realised that she was once mistress of the big Doon House where she now lived in the gate lodge. Today the house had priests, nuns and laypeople coming to do retreats, have discussions. And sometimes there were ordinary conferences that weren't religious at all: that's how the community made the costs of the place. But it was usually a very quiet type of conference where the delegates weren't expecting much of a night life. Rathdoon could offer Ryan's Pub and Billy Burns' chicken and chips; people usually expected more if they came a long way to a conference.

"I had to leave Doon House within a month. But he tricked me in one way. Even with the slightest hint of a drugs offence in those days you couldn't get into the States. They wouldn't give me a visa. And in order to make the distance as great as possible between poor Andrew and Jessica over there and their mad mother over here Jack arranged that I be charged with a minor offence: possession. It was a nothing, even here, and compared to what I could have been charged with, which was dealing, it was ludicrously light. But then the deal had been done, don't forget. And even being charged with possession kept me out of the States."

There was another silence.

"Wasn't that a bad trick to play on you?" Rupert said.

"Yes. Yes. I suppose he thought like the people who burned people in the Inquisition . . . that they were doing the right thing. You know, rooting out evil."

"It was very drastic, even for the sixties wasn't it?"

"Will you stop saying the sixties as if it was the stone age. YOU were born in the sixties, don't forget."

"I don't remember much about them," Rupert grinned.

"No. Well I suppose you'd call it drastic; Jack would have called it effective. He was a great man for getting the job done." She spoke with scorn: "That's all he cared about. That's done, he'd say proudly. It was the same coping with me. But Rupert, did you not know all this before? I mean, I don't want to make out that the whole town talks of me morning, noon and night, but I would have thought that you must have heard some drift of it?"

"No, never. I knew that the children had gone away with their father and I think I asked why but I was never told."

"That's because you're so nicely brought up! They're too well bred in your house, they'd never talk of other people's business."

"I think my mother'd be glad to if she knew about it. And it's not only us. I once asked Celia why you didn't have your children, and she said there was some desperate row years ago when judges were even worse than they are today. That's all, nobody knows about the . . . er . . . the smoke and things."

"I don't know whether to be pleased or disappointed," Judy laughed. "I always thought people believed I was up to no good with all the herbal remedies, bordering on the witch doctor nearly."

"I'm afraid people think that's very worthy, we'll have to make your image more villainous for you," Rupert said.

"Oh for ages the unfortunate guards used to come and inspect my herb garden. I had a map of it for them in the end, and told them they must come in whenever they liked and that I would explain anything that looked a bit amiss. Then by the time I went to Dublin, they'd more or less written me off as a dangerous drugs pusher."

"You mean you're in the clear at last, after twenty years?"

"I don't know: sometimes I see the imprint of heavy boots round the camomile beds. Eternal vigilance."

"Do you hate Jack Hickey for it?"

"No, I said to you I never think of him. But you'd

97

probably find that hard to believe, especially when I think of the children a lot, and to all intents and purposes I don't know them at all. They're strangers to me."

"Yes," Rupert obviously did find it hard to understand.

"It's the same with your mother, you know. Even though she doesn't let on, she thinks of you every day up in Dublin, she is aware of you in a way that it's hard to explain."

"Oh, I don't think so."

"I know it, I asked her once, just to know whether I was odd. She said that when you were away at school it was the same and at university and then when you went into the company. She says that often in her day she pauses and wonders what Rupert's doing now."

"Heavens," he said.

"Not for long, just for a second, you know, not brooding. But I expect you don't pause and wonder what she's doing."

"No, well I think of them a lot, of course, and since Father's been so badly and everything. I DO think of them of course," he said somewhat defensively.

"Stop getting upset, I was only using you as an example. Even if Andrew and Jessica had lived with me until they were grown-up they might still be away and not thinking about me any more. It's the way things happen."

"You're dead easy to talk to, I wish I could talk to my mother like I talk to you. She's much older of course," he added tactfully.

"She is indeed, she could nearly be *my* mother too, but that's not the point... You can never talk to your own mother, it's a law of nature."

She smiled and looked out the window, and when that Nancy Morris started talking sense for once about how to relax neck muscles she joined in. She was afraid that young Rupert Green had too much of the Meaning Of Life and the Wronged Woman's viewpoint. She decided to let him snuggle back into his expensive Italian jacket and dream whatever his dreams were.

She always got on better with young people. Someone once said she should have been a teacher but she said no, that would have been putting herself on the other side of the desk from them. But she had much more young friends than people her own age. Bart Kennedy, for example. She could talk to Bart till the cows came home, and she only exchanged the time of day with his father. Kev Kennedy up there in the front of the bus, he was another story: it was very hard going having a chat with Kev. He'd remind you of a young lad who'd been posted at a doorway to give a warning when the master was approaching. And she liked Celia and Dee, she thought, looking round the bus. And young Tom Fitzgerald, he was a great lad. You couldn't like Nancy Morris but she wasn't young anyway. Despite her years she was an old woman and always had been.

And the young people of Rathdoon had always been a great help to her with the things she grew in the small bit of land that Jack Hickey had given her twenty long years ago. She was DIFFERENT to other people, they told her: she didn't pass judgement on them all, she didn't tell them they should be married, or settled down, or more provident or less drinky. And even though they may have thought she was half cracked they came and helped her dig and pick and dry and pack.

She never found the house lonely, no more than the flat in Dublin. Not after all this time. She liked her own company, she ate meals at odd times, she would listen to music at midnight if she liked. In the flat she wore padded earphones and thought she must look like some ageing raver if anyone could see her, but it was a house with many bedsits and flats and you couldn't wake civil servants and people who worked in big office blocks by playing your music through their walls. She did not feel the need of headphones in the lonely little lodge that was all Jack Hickey gave her from the big house. There was nobody near enough to hear, and the birds seemed to like hearing concertos and symphonies. They came and sat on the fence to listen more carefully.

The first time Tom had dropped her there he said he'd wait till she turned on the light. She had been pleased. He had enough nature in him to make sure that she got in safely. But then he was like all the youngsters she knew nowadays, far more natural and a lot more decency in them than the bombasts of her time. Like young Chris and Karen who ran the health shop. They cared so much about it, they never wanted to be rich, to find a good line in anything which would be a snazzy seller and move quickly. They knew none of the jargon of the middle aged businessman, and because they *were* idealistic and simple about things they were going to go to the wall. Her heart was heavy thinking about them. Maybe over in California somewhere Jessica and her husband, if she had one, were starting a health shop. Suppose they were in difficulties, wouldn't it be great if some kind older person were to help?

Judy only had a life interest in her gate lodge, she couldn't sell it even if she wanted to. She only rented her bedsitter in Dublin, she had no savings. Once she had saved the fare to America and kept the post office book thumbed and touched so often it was almost illegible. She had it always in her handbag and would finger it as if it were the ticket to the States. But not now. And she would love so dearly to be able to contribute to Chris and Karen and their dream. Because it was her dream, that shop too. They could make her a director or some such nonsense. If only she had a small lump sum and a regular little subsidy for them instead of taking a small wage from their very sparse little till.

She told Rupert not to waste his weekend coming up to help her in the garden. He had come home to be with his parents and he might as well stay in Dublin if he didn't spend his time with his dying father and give his mother some lift by being in the house all weekend. She was very firm about this, even when he said he'd like the work and the exercise. There'd be plenty of time for all that later. Let him not waste the last months or weeks of his father's life digging and hoeing in a stranger's garden.

"You're not a stranger, Judy, you're a friend,' Rupert had said. She had been pleased at that too.

It was a bright sunny September Saturday. The place seemed to be full of activity. You got weekends when that happened, when Rathdoon seemed to hum with excitement and you got other weekends when not even a tornado coming down Patrick Street would shake them up. She saw Nancy Morris prowling up and down as if she was looking for lost treasure, Kev Kennedy was in and out of his father's shop with a face on him that made it clear the Mafia had put out a contract on him that morning. Every time you stepped out on the road there was someone driving into town that would nearly mow you down. Mrs Casey's ramshackle car with Nancy Morris's mother in it, Mikey Burns going round the place with a set face on him, either doing messages or taking his brother Billy's children blackberrying. He was preoccupied to a degree she had never known. She saw Celia too during the day driving a car with the intent look of someone in a rally. Her mother was beside her and the back of the car was filled with some kind of luggage under a rug. Tom FitzGerald came in for a couple of hours to help in the garden, saying that since he hadn't had one single cross word from any member of his family or their spouses he felt things were too good to be true and he wouldn't risk staying in their company one more minute in case the whole thing would fall apart. She saw Dee Burke driving her mother to town, her face empty and sad, her mother talking away without seeing any emptiness at all beside her. Imagine anyone thinking the country was quiet. Some weekend she must ask Karen and Chris to come and stay – some bank holiday, if they were still in business.

Red Kennedy come in to help his brother Bart.

"Would these make a lot in Dublin?" he asked, looking at the little boxes of seeds.

Judy reflected: "Not a lot, in a way, we're just the wrong size. If it were a one-woman operation selling them at the side of the road, yes there's a living; otherwise it should really be huge nurseries and big chain stores and all that. Still we struggle on."

But it underlined to her the fruitlessness of it all, and the waste of effort not just from her but from decent young fellows like Bart and Red, like Mikey last week and Tom Fitzgerald's nephews when they were home from school. Was it really fair asking them to help in such a doomed business venture. They never did it for money, there wasn't any, but even in terms of their enthusiasm was it wrong to take so much of that as well? She thought of Chris and Karen in Dublin, anxious and also anxious on HER behalf. They felt they owed her a place and a living because she had been so solidly supportive for them. How she wished that there had been a letter from a firm of American solicitors saying that the late James Jonathan Hickey of San Francisco, California had left her a legacy and that her two children were going to fly over and deliver it personally. She often had fantasies about the children arriving, but this was the first time she had thought about the money. Yes, she'd even take a legacy from Jack even if the children didn't deliver it. Anything to help Chris and Karen.

Soon she called a halt to the work. Judy's great success was that she stopped her helpers before they got tired.

There were huge glasses of her elderflower wine which some said was better and reached you more powerfully than anything that was pulled as a pint down in Ryan's. They sat on a wall in the sun and drank it, and the Kennedys went home.

It was dark in the small house and she felt well when she had washed the earth off. She lay out on her window seat with her hands behind her head.

"You look like a cat," Rupert said as he came in. The

door was never closed in summer, never locked in winter.

"That's good. Cats are very relaxed," Judy said.

"Are you relaxed?" he wanted to know.

"Not in my head. My head is worrying about inessential things like money. I never worried about money before."

"I suppose it was always easy to get it before."

"Yes, well in the old days I told you how I got it, but since then I haven't needed it much. Now, I'd like to keep the shop open, that's all."

Rupert sat down on a rocking chair that squeaked. He got up immediately and went for the oil.

She thanked him, but said his mother had a rocking chair, he should be sitting on that.

"There's nothing to say; I had to escape for a little bit," he pleaded.

"Only a little," Judy said.

"It's just that he tried to talk. He asks are there many houses on the market and things." Rupert had a face full of pain.

"But isn't that good? He's well enough, alert enough to know. Kind enough to care."

"And mother says, that he really likes having me home. But it's nothing. Nothing at all."

"Only if you make it nothing for them." Judy lost her sympathy. She stood up and stretched.

"Listen to me Rupert Green, not one more minute of your father's time am I taking. I'm going for a walk in Jack Hickey's woods." He looked hurt.

"Please boy, please. Think of all those years when you'll say if only I could have just sat there and talked about any old thing. And for your mother, please. I'll meet you and you can buy me a pint of that synthetic stuff they call chilled wine down in Ryan's." He brightened up.

"Will you? That would be nice."

"When he's asleep, when he's had some return from you."

"I'm not THAT bad."

"No, but he was nearly fifty years of age when you arrived in his life and he had to be wokén up with your teething and your screaming and then you didn't come into his office: he couldn't put Green and Son. It's Green and MacMahon. Go on, sit with him, talk about anything. It doesn't matter if it seems formal and meaningless, you're there, you're trying . . . that's all that matters."

"And what time will we go to Ryan's?" He was eager.

"RUPERT! Will you give over, this is not a date. Ryan's is not a cocktail lounge, it's the only bar in Rathdoon, I'll be down there when I feel like it and you come when your father's well asleep and you've had a bit of time with your mother."

"Around nine or so?" he said desperate to be specific.

"Around nine or so," she said resignedly.

She put on her boots. It was a long time since she had walked the woods. The three nuns who ran the ecumenical conferences and the diocesan seminars in the big house knew vaguely that Mrs Hickey in the gate lodge had once lived in the big house. They were always polite to her and encouraged her to wander around if she ever felt like it. They were possibly relieved that the wildish looking woman in the gypsy style headscarves didn't take them up too often on their offer. She never went anywhere near the house but she had told them it was nice to be able to feel free to walk under those old trees and pick flowers. Sometimes she would leave a great bunch of bluebells at their door, wrapped up in damp leaves. She never rang or asked to be entertained in the parlour. It was an ideal relationship.

Today she walked more purposefully. She didn't just stroll following a whim or a line of young saplings. No, today she knew where she was heading.

It was still there in among the ivy covered trees. Wild now, but hidden from the most determined searchers because of that old fallen tree. It looked as if there was nothing beyond. She eased herself over the tree and stood once more in her own little marijuana grove. She saw the cannabis plants that she had begun twenty-two years ago, many dead, many seeded and wasted. Some living though, some needing only a little attention.

It wouldn't take her long to find a proper outlet in Dublin. It must be done well away from the shop, Chris and Karen must never know.

She felt as strongly about this as her husband had felt that Andrew and Jessica must never know.

She felt the old quickening under her heart. It would be exciting to be back in the business again after all these years.

Kev

Kev thought he'd never get away from the Pelican. The Pelican was in one of those good moods, very rarely seen of late, where he'd ramble on about people known only to himself. There was a cast of thousands in the Pelican's stories and the same people never appeared twice. Kev listened attentively because if you missed the bit where your man came in one day and your other man was already in there and your old fellow came out the other door then you lost the whole grasp of it, and the Pelican might easily snap some kind of a question at you to make sure you were on the ball.

Kev was only afraid of the Pelican; he was *terrified* of some of the others. But even though the Pelican was not the highest in the terror stakes Kev would have let the Lilac Bus go to Rathdoon without him rather than risk insulting this man whose big hooked nose was the cause of his name. You didn't mess with the Pelican, Kev didn't know much, but he knew that much.

Fortunately the Pelican was hailed by someone more interesting and Kev was released; he sprinted round the corner. The bus was almost full. But he wasn't the last. Mikey Burns was rubbing his hands: oh please may he not have any quiz games tonight. Mikey was perfectly nice when he quietened down, but all this "I say I say I say" like one of those comics on a music hall show on telly. And he was no GOOD at it, that was what was so hopeless, he always laughed in the wrong place. It would have been nice to sit beside Celia; that's what he liked best: she'd address about five civil sentences to him and then she'd leave him to his own thoughts, as she looked out the window. Or Rupert, he was a quiet fellow too, and not toffee-nosed or anything. Kev's brothers Bart and Red were always surprised that he didn't seem to know Mrs Hickey better. They were mad about her: in fact his Da was always saying that they'd go over to her place and dig her witch's brews in the garden and her lavender and her forget-me-nots and they wouldn't dig their own potatoes like men. Mrs Hickey was nice enough, but she had a disconcerting way of looking right through you when she was talking, as if she didn't want any small talk. Neither did Kev of course want any small talk, but he didn't want that dark intense face with those X-ray eyes looking at him either. He always got the feeling that she saw just a little bit too much.

Kev worked in Security, well not real security with helmets and coshes and alsatians and vans with no hand signals. More like being a porter really or a commissionaire but it was called security. When anyone phoned down to the front desk to ask if a letter had been delivered by hand or if a visitor had arrived Kev answered the phone with the words, "Hallo. Security?"

Once he had got a phone call from his father asking him to bring down boxes of some new potato crisp that had been advertised on the television and the place was going mad looking for it. Kev's father had been so entertained by Kev calling himself Security that he had threatened to telephone every day just for the sheer pleasure of it. Kev had told him anxiously that they had been told to keep personal calls down to the minimum. But he shouldn't have worried, his father wasn't going to waste good money on hearing the same joke over and over.

Bart and Red didn't know what he came home for every weekend. It wasn't that they didn't want to see him, they were just as happy that he was back as not. But why *every* weekend? That was what would fox you. And he didn't even go to the dance on a Saturday night. And he didn't have a crowd to drink with in Ryan's; he'd go in and out for a couple but he wouldn't have a session there. The Kennedys had little or no conversation with their Da who had a cigarette in his mouth and the radio on full blast from morning to night. It was unlikely to be for company.

Kev knew that he was a bit of a mystery to them. And to Tom Fitzgerald who had explained that the bus only made a profit if he could be sure of his seven passengers on a Friday. That's why he could do it so cheaply. You agreed to come on the bus every Friday for ten weeks, or if you couldn't you'd send someone in your place – not to Rathdoon of course, but part of the way or as far as the big town seventeen miles from home. Or if you could find nobody you still paid for your seat. That way it was half the cost of any other bus going that route and what's more it brought you to the door. Kev was getting out of the bus before ten o'clock and saying goodnight to Nancy Morris who only lived across the street. He was home in Rathdoon safe. He would take a big breath of air and let it all out in a long sigh of relief. Tom often looked at him puzzled, and his father would nod welcomingly over the radio and tell him it was just coming up to the news. A mug of tea might be handed to him and a slice of shop cake cut. They had never known any other kind of cake, Kev and his brothers. Their mother had died long ago and even Bart, who could remember her, never knew her when she was well enough to make bread or cakes. When the news was over his father might ask had it been a hard week and were there any savages with crowbars in. He said there were more cases of violence in Dublin than there were in Chicago and he would never set his foot in the city again without an armed guard. Kev had tried to argue with him in the beginning, but now he didn't bother. Anyway, nowadays he was beginning to think his father was right.

Nobody at work knew where Kev went at weekends: they all thought that he was some kind of lay monk or something and that he went to do good works but part of the goodness was that you didn't talk about it. The kind old Mr Daly, one of the nicest people Kev had ever met, would shake his head in its uniform cap full of admiration.

"I don't know why they give out about the younger generation," old Mr Daly would say, "I really don't. There's that young Kev who works with us in the front hall, and he's off giving soup to winos and praying in front of the Blessed Sacrament, and teaching illiterates to read. Gone out of here like a bow from an arrow at six o'clock and we never hear hair nor hide of him until Monday morning."

Kev had never told one word of this fabrication to Mr Daly or to anyone else. But having heard it, and seen that it was accepted he let it pass. After all if anyone came nosing around and asking questions, wasn't it better that old Mr Daly and John and the others thought he was with the Simon Community or the Legion of Mary rather than knowing he caught a lilac-coloured minibus as regularly as clockwork and sped out of Dublin and all its danger every Friday night.

Just suppose for one sickening minute that Daff or Crutch Casey or the Pelican came round upset over something, well there was nothing they could be told. Nobody knew where Kev went at weekends.

He had always had this secrecy, even when he was a young fellow. He remembered Bart telling a total stranger in the shop that their mother was dead, that she had died in the hospital after two months and a week. Kev would never have given that information to a woman who had come in to buy bars of chocolate and ice cream for the children in the car. No matter how nice she had been, no matter how much she had praised the three young lads serving in the shop because their father was out getting the shed at the back built to hold the gas cylinders and the briquettes. Kev would have told her nothing and put his arm in his mouth which was a great way to stop having a conversation. But Bart and Red would tell anyone anything . . . Bart even told about the time when Kev was seventeen and he had tried to get Deirdre Morris, who was the much nicer sister of Nancy, to come into a field with him and swore it was to show her a nest of small birds.

Deirdre Morris had thrown back her head laughing, pushed him over so that he fell in the mud and had gone home laughing. "A nest of small birds – is that what they call it nowadays?" Kev was shocked. To admit to such a lustful thing and even worse to admit to such a defeat. But no, Bart thought it was a scream, and that time that Deirdre had come back from America married with a baby called Shane, Bart was still able to laugh over it with her. And Red was the same, a demon dancer and he'd tell half the country their business, and about how they should have got an agency for tarmacadamming the place but his Da hadn't moved quick enough and Billy Burns had got it first. Kev told nothing. But then Kev had much more to hide.

Celia arrived just after him and the doors were closed. They were off. Round the corner and through the open door of the pub he could the Pelican holding a pint in one hand and a rolled up newspaper in the other. A rolled paper was a great thing for making a point, for emphasising something, And that was the Pelican's style. Emphasising things.

Mikey was unfortunately in top form tonight: tricks with matches and a glass, have them rolling in the aisles in a pub. Didn't poor Mikey realise that it was only drunks that suddenly started doing match tricks in a pub, or lonely people, or madmen. Not ordinary people unless they were all in a group of friends, and if you had a group of friends why would you need to do tricks anyway? He was explaining how to weight the matchbox, Kev looked out the window and saw the housing estates outside Dublin flashing by. Old Mr Daly said to him that any day now Kev would find himself a young woman and they'd save for a house in a place like that and there'd be no knowing him ever after. People like Mr Daly and Mikey knew nothing about the real world. There was Mikey going on about how you weighted the matchbox deliberately with a twopenny piece in it and it always fell over on the side you'd put the coin in, so you could bet someone that it would always fall on the side you said. Kev had looked at him vacantly.

"I bet you Bart or Red Eddie would love a trick like that," Mikey muttered. Kev knew they would. They had the time and the peace of mind to enjoy it.

Kev never told Mikey that he was a porter too in a way. Well security really, but it was the same field. He never told any of them where he worked, except that it was in the big new block. You could be doing anything there, literally anything. They had civil servants and they had travel agencies, and airlines and small companies with only two people in them, they had a board in the hall with a list a mile long of the organisations who were tenants of the building. Kev just said he worked there; when anyone asked him what he did, he said this and that. It was safer. One morning he was standing there in his uniform and he saw Dee Burke coming. She was going with some papers to a solicitor on the fifth floor. Mr Daly phoned up and announced her and Kev had sorted furiously on the floor for something so she didn't see him. Later he wondered why. It couldn't matter whether Dee Burke knew that he worked at the front desk of the big new office block. She hardly thought when she went to buy her cigarettes at the Kennedy shop that their youngest son was the chairman of some company up in Dublin. He didn't even want her to think he was in a clerical job. Why hide then? Wiser. Like not walking on cracks in the road. No reason but it just *seemed* the right thing to do.

Of course in a way it was all this secrecy that had him where he was. If he had been a different type he'd never have got into this mess at all.

It began on his birthday, he was twenty-one. It was an

ordinary working day. His father had sent him a ten pound note in a card with a pink cat on it. Bart and Red Eddie had said that there would be great drink in Ryan's next Friday on account of it. Nobody else knew. He hadn't told Mr Daly in case the old man might get a cake and embarrass him; he didn't tell anyone back up in the house where he had a room. They kept to themselves a lot and if they heard him saying he was twenty-one they'd feel they had to do something for him. He didn't tell anyone up at the pigeons either. In the lofts they didn't have time for birthdays and such things. So that day nobody in Dublin knew that Kevin, youngest son of Mr Michael Kennedy, shop proprietor, and the late Mrs Mary Rose Kennedy of Rathdoon had now reached twenty-one. He thought of it a lot all morning and somehow it began to seem over-important to him. Other people had records played for them on radio programmes, other people who were twenty-one had cards, lots of them, not just one. Dee Burke had a party in a hotel – he remembered hearing about it just a couple of months back; Bart and Red had been invited and Bart said he couldn't get into a monkey suit but Red the demon dancer had hired one and had a great time. And even his own brothers had bits of celebration. Bart and all his pals had a barbecue down by the river; those were before every Tom, Dick and Harry were having barbecues. They roasted a bit of beef and ate it between doorsteps of bread and it was gorgeous, and there'd been great singing and goings on. And when Red was twenty-one two years back there had been a crowd of them who had all come to the house for a few drinks and a cake then they'd got into a truck and driven off to the dance. But nothing at all for Kev.

It got in on his mind. He made an excuse to Mr Daly and said that he wanted to go out the back for a half an hour. He didn't feel well. Mr Daly was so concerned that he immediately felt ashamed. Those were the days before he had been a regular disappearer at weekends, before Mr Daly had assumed that he was an unsung and uncanonised saint.

He sat out in the loading area as it was called, a place where vans could come with deliveries of paper, or messengers on those big motor bikes with speaking handlebars could leave their machines. He took out a cigarette and thought about other fellows his age and wondered why he had been so anxious to get away and why he had ever thought it would be any better. Four men were loading a van efficiently. A fifth was standing leaning on a crutch and staring around him idly. Into the van were going sanitary fittings, handbasins, lavatories, small water heaters. Without haste but with commendable speed they loaded.

Kev dragged his cigarette. They must be getting new fitments somewhere upstairs, that looked like a big contract. Wait. He hadn't seen any of them come through security, and everyone had to come to the front desk. Even if they went straight out the door again and were sent round to the loading bay. The rules said desk first.

His eyes took on the merest flicker of interest but it was enough to alert the man with the bent leg leaning so casually on the crutch.

"Not wearing a cap, didn't notice him," he said out of the corner of his mouth.

A big man with a beak-shaped nose paused momentarily and then slid from the human chain which was stacking the fitments. He strolled over to Kevin whose stomach knotted in fright. He realised like a shower of cold rain coming down his gullet that this was a Job, these were five men taking fitments OUT of the new building, fitments that would turn up again in houses all over the city. He swallowed hard.

The Pelican walked slowly: he didn't look a bit furtive, nor did he look worried.

"Can I have a smoke?" he asked casually. Behind him the loading continued regular as clockwork, innocent as anything.

"Yes. Um," Kev handed him the packet.

"What are you doing with yourself here?" The Pelican's

116

eyes narrowed.

The question was perfectly polite. It could have been a gentle enquiry of any fellow lounger on a summer morning. He might even have added something like "on this fine day". But he hadn't. The Pelican and all of them were waiting to know what Kevin would say and Kevin knew that what he said now was probably going to be the most important question he ever answered in his life.

"It's my twenty-first birthday," he said. "And I got annoyed sitting inside there in Security and nobody knowing, so I thought I'd come out here and have a bit of a smoke anyway to celebrate."

There was absolutely no doubt that what he said was true. You didn't need a lie detector or the experience of years with truth drugs to know that Kev Kennedy had given a perfectly accurate account of why he was there, and something about him made the Pelican believe that there was going to be no trouble here.

"Well, when we're finished here maybe we'll buy a drink at your lunch hour. A fellow shouldn't be twenty-one and have nobody know."

"That's what I think," Kev said eagerly, averting his eyes from the biggest and most barefaced theft from the building where he was meant to be part of Security. It seemed to be winding up now, the convoy were closing the doors and getting into the van.

"So, what is it? One o'clock?" the Pelican's nose was like a scythe so large and menacing did it appear, and his eyes were like two slits.

"It's a bit difficult at lunchtime, you see I only get forty-five minutes and I suppose you'll be moving on out of the area," Kev's face was innocent.

"But where would you like your birthday drink then and when?" There was no area for argument in the proposal, only a small margin of latitude for the time and place.

"Well, wherever you like of course, and at about six. Is that all right?"

Kev was eager. The Pelican nodded. He named a city centre pub.

"We'll give you a drink each, and as you no doubt saw there's five of us, so that's five drinks."

"Oh, God, that would be great altogether," Kev said. "Are there five of you? I didn't notice."

The Pelican nodded approvingly. He swung his way back to the van and in beside the driver who looked like a champion wrestler.

"Six o'clock," he called cheerfully out the window.

It wasn't discovered until four thirty. A lot of offices on the sixth floor weren't occupied yet. Some people just assumed that the bathrooms were being refitted, and sighing had gone to other floors. It was only when one of the secretaries said she was getting dropped arches and told Mr Daly that it was an extraordinary thing to think that brand new cloakrooms should be redone within three months that any kind of alarm was raised. The broad-daylightness of it all staggered them. The guards were called, the confusion was enormous. Kev had difficulty in getting away by six. He was ninety per cent sure that they wouldn't be there. They could be walking into a trap for all they knew. How were they to know that they were dealing with Kev Kennedy who never told anybody anything? They might have assumed he would have plain-clothes guards drinking pints of shandy all round the pub. But just in case. And just in case they came back and dealt with him. After all they knew where he worked, he knew nothing about them.

They were all there.

"There was a bit of commotion at work, I got delayed," he said.

"Ah, you would all right," said the Pelican generously. He was introduced to Daff and John, and Ned and Crutch Casey.

"What's your real name?" he asked the man with the twisted leg.

"Crutch," the man said, surprised to be asked.

They each bought him a pint and they raised their glasses solemnly and said Happy Birthday at each round. By the fourth round he was feeling very wretched. He had never drunk more than three pints in Ryan's and never more than two anywhere else. Ryan's led you to be daring because even if you fell down you got home on all fours without too much difficulty.

Daff was the man like a wrestler. Kev wondered why he was called that but he decided it might not be wise. Daff bought the last drink and handed Kev an envelope.

"We were sorry to see a culchie all on his own with no-one to wish him a happy birthday, so that's a small present from Pelican, Crutch, John, Ned and me." He smiled as if he were a foolish, generous uncle dying for the nephew to open the electric train set and begin to call out with excitement.

Kev politely opened the envelope and saw a bundle of blue twenty pound notes. The room went backwards and forwards and began to move slowly around to the left. He steadied himself on the bar stool.

"I couldn't take this, sure you don't know me at all."

"And you don't know us," Daff beamed.

"Which is as it should be," the Pelican said approvingly.

"But I'd not know you, without . . . without this, you know."

He looked at the envelope as if it contained explosives. There were at least six notes, maybe more. He didn't want to count them.

"Ah but this is better, this MARKS the day for all of us, why don't we meet here every week around this time, and if you've that invested properly then you could buy us a drink, and slowly we could sort of GET to know each other."

Kev's mouth felt full of lemon juice.

"Well I'd love to . . . sort of keep in touch with you all . . . but, honestly, this is too much. Like, I mean, I'd feel bad."

"Not at all, you wouldn't," smiled the Pelican and they

were gone.

Every Tuesday since he had met them; sometimes it was just a drink. Sometimes it was more. Once it had been a driving job. He would never forget it to his dying day. They went into a new block of flats and carefully unrolled the brand new stair carpet. They had heard that the fitting men were coming that afternoon so they had anticipated the visit by removing every scrap of it. The timing had been of the essence on that one. The expensive wool carpet had arrived that morning; there was only a four-hour period when it could be removed, and that meant watching the flats very carefully in case any untoward enquiries were made. It was all completely successful, of course, like all their enterprises seemed to be. Kev had taken a day off work for the carpet heist but the carpet heist had taken years off his life. He felt as if he had been put down on the street and the whole crowd coming out of Moran Park had walked over him. He couldn't understand how they remained so untouched. Crutch Casey told of horses that had fallen at the last fence. Ned and John were more dog people, they talked of evil minded and corrupt greyhounds who KNEW how to slow down through some instinct. The Pelican told long tales full of people that nobody knew, and Daff seemed to say nothing much but he was as relaxed as a man coming out after a swim about to light his pipe on the beach on a sunny day.

They never told him he HAD to join in, and they didn't ask him so much that he felt he should run away to America to escape them. Often he didn't have to do anything except what they called "re-sorting". That might mean wrapping a whole load of Waterford Glass which arrived from a hotel before it got time to get out of its boxes, into different kind of containers. Each glass to be held carefully and sorted according to type, wrapped in purple tissue paper in gift boxes of six. He became quite an authority on the various designs, or suites as they were called, and decided that the Colleen Suite was his favourite; and that when he got married he would have two dozen Colleen brandy glasses and use them around the house as ordinary everyday glasses, or in the bathroom for his toothbrush. Then he remembered what he was doing and the fantasy would disappear. He would look around the garage and keep parcelling in the nice anonymous gift boxes. He never knew where they went, and what happened to them. He never asked. Not once. That's why they liked him, that's why they trusted him utterly. From that very first day in the loading area they thought he was one of their own, and it was too late now to tell them that he wasn't. The longer it went on, the more ludicrous it would be trying to get out.

On calmer days Kev asked himself what was so terrible. They never took from individuals, they didn't do people's houses and flats: it was companies who had to replace miles of red wool carpet, boxes of prestigious glassware, rooms full of sanitary fittings. They never did over old women, young couples, they never carried a weapon, not even a cosh. In many ways they weren't bad fellows at all. Of course they never actually went out to work in a normal way, and they did lie to people, with their clipboards and their air of being perfectly legitimate. And people did get into trouble after they'd visited places, like poor old Mr Daly who'd been hauled in by everyone and though it was never said, the thought had been in the air that he might be getting too old for the job. And they stole. They stole things almost every week and by no standards could that be a thing that Kev Kennedy from Rathdoon wanted to be in. Or worse, caught in. It was unthinkable. They still talked about that young fellow who was a cousin of the FitzGeralds and worked in their shop for a bit; he was given three years for doing a post office in Cork. The whole of Rathdoon had buzzed with it for months and Mrs FitzGerald, Tom's mother, had said she hoped everyone realised that he wasn't a first cousin, he was a very far out one, and they had tried to give him a start and look at the thanks they got. Could you imagine what old Da would have to go through? And all Red's hopes of getting some gorgeous wife would go for their tea, and poor Bart was so decent and helpful, wouldn't it be a shame on him for ever?

But how did you get out? He couldn't live in a city that contained the Pelican and Daff and Crutch Casey if they thought he had ratted on them. There was no point trying to pretend that he had left town or anything. They knew everything: it was their business to know things, to know when deliveries were expected, when watchmen went for their coffee, when regular porters were on holidays, when managers were young and nervous, when shops were too busy to notice their furniture being loaded into private vans. They knew where Kev lived and worked; he wouldn't dream of lying to them.

But he got out of weekend work. That's when they did some of their bigger jobs, and he wanted to be well away from it. He told them vaguely that he had to go out of town. He had been going home that very first weekend after they met him and so it had seemed a natural continuation, not a new pattern of behaviour. He didn't say it was Rathdoon, he didn't say it was home, but they knew he wasn't lying when he was saying that he went out of town for weekends, Crutch Casey had said goodnight to him one Sunday night outside the house where he had a room, and Kev knew that it was just a routine inspection. He had been cleared now, even the Pelican whom he had met by accident just on the corner knew that he was leaving Dublin for the weekend – he didn't even bother to check.

But how could he get out of working for them mid-week? Some of the jobs were getting bigger and Kev was getting tenser. Once or twice Daff had asked him not to be so jumpy – that he was like some actor playing a nervous crook in an old black and white B movie. It was fine for Daff who didn't have a nerve in his body. Simply fine for him. Others didn't find it so easy. The very sight of a guard was enough to weaken Kev's legs, even the shadow of anyone fairly big was enough to make him jump. Oddly enough it hadn't made him feel guilty about religion: he went to Mass and at Christmas and Easter to communion; he knew that God knew that there wasn't much Sin involved. No Grievous Bodily Harm or anything. But he had never been much of a one for talking to God individually like you were meant to: he didn't feel like putting the question personally. And there was nobody else really BUT God when all was said and done because everyone else would have a very strong view one way or the other, and mainly the other. Like get out of that gang at a rate of knots, Kev Kennedy, and stop acting the eejit.

Mikey's poor kind face was there a few inches from him, Mikey Burns who'd be the kind of bank porter that would get shot in a raid, certainly not like Kev, the kind of security man who had become best buddies with the gang that had ripped off all the fittings from the place he worked. Mikey Burns sleeping with a little smile dreaming about something, jokes with glasses of water and coins maybe, and there was he, Kev, who had driven get-away vans and done watch duty and helped to reparcel stolen goods. Kev felt alien as he looked out at the darkening countryside. Lonely and guilty as hell.

His father told him after the news that Red had notions about a farmer's daughter and was going to bring her to tea during the weekend no less, and they were all to keep their shoes on, talk nicely and put butter on a plate and the milk in a jug. He said that he thought Bart might as well join the Franciscans and put on sandals and carry a begging bowl for all the good he was ever going to do with his life and his share of the business. When he wasn't digging up Mrs Hickey's foxgloves and hemlocks or whatever it was she grew he was helping Mrs Ryan in the pub to stand on her own two shaky legs and serving the customers from behind the bar and not a penny piece was he getting from either of them. He was surprised that Bart hadn't gone into Fitzgerald's shop and said that if they'd like someone to stand there and serve for a few days a week without wages he'd be happy to do it. Kev didn't know what to say to this. He nibbled a slice of cake and thought about the difference between people. There was Daff who had a nice big open face like Bart, organising the transfer of twenty microwave ovens from one warehouse to another by a deceptively simple scheme which involved Ned who was the most forgettable of them all going up with a sheaf of papers, an air of bewilderment and an instruction that they were apparently to go back to have something checked. And there was Bart Kennedy who had a big open face like Daff digging Judy Hickey's garden for her and helping Celia's mother to stay upright in Ryan's. God, what different worlds he moved in; Kev thought with a shudder at the danger of it all.

"Are you not going down to the pub?" his father asked.

"No, I'm tired after the week, and the long journey, I'll just go up and lie on my bed," he said.

His father shook his head: "I really wish I knew what brings you home, you do so little when you arrive, and you've lost your interest in football entirely. You could have been a good footballer if you'd put your mind to it."

"No, I was never any good. You only say that because you wanted a son a county footballer, I'm no good."

"Well what does bring you back here, what are you running from . . ?" He hadn't finished but the cup was in pieces on the floor and Kev's face was snow white.

"Running, what do you mean?"

"I mean is it the violence up there or the dirt, or those blackguards roaming in tribes or what? Haven't you good wages and you're always very generous giving me the few quid here . . . but a young man of your age, you should be up to all kinds of divilment and diversions, shouldn't you?"

"I don't know, Da, I don't think I was ever much good at anything, football, divilment, anything." He sounded very glum.

"Haven't you got a fine job up in one of the finest buildings in the land, and you earn your own living which is more than those two boyos there – oh they're a great pair I have on my hands. One a sort of Martin de Porres going round the place giving half his cloak to everyone he meets, one a dandy who has the bright red hair nearly combed off his scalp and the mirrors nearly cracked in bits staring into them. You're the best of them, Kev, don't be running yourself down."

Kev Kennedy went up to bed without a word, and he lay there as the sounds of Rathdoon which were not very loud went past his window, a small window over the shop, which looked out on the main street.

Red's girl was coming the very next day it turned out, so they all had to do a spring clean on the back room. There were to be cups instead of mugs, a clean cloth was spread and bread was cut on a tray and then put onto a plate to avoid all the crumbs. They took ham and tomatoes from the shop, a bottle of salad cream and Red hardboiled three eggs.

"This is a feast, she'll marry you immediately," Bart said when he saw Red looking speculatively at some of the frozen cakes in the cold food section.

"Quit laughing and keep looking round the room to see what it would look like to a new eye." Red had it bad this time. Her name was Majella and she was an only child, she was used to much greater style than the three Kennedy brothers and their father could provide even if they had been trying seriously. But none of them except Red was making much of an effort: their father wanted to be in his shop, Bart wanted to get over to Judy Hickey and Kev wanted to go off down by the river where he felt nice and quiet and miles from all that was happening at this very moment to microwave ovens in a warehouse in Dublin.

Majella was arriving at five o'clock: her father would give her a lift, but he wouldn't call in, it was much too early for that yet. They did a deal, the brothers. Bart and Kev agreed to wear proper ties and jackets and have polished shoes. Red agreed to go over to Judy Hickey's and put in two hours because she needed it this weekend particularly and because it would keep him calm. There would be no bad language, eating with fingers and picking of teeth, but in return Red would not embarrass them by giving moon faced sick calf impersonations, not would he ask them to delight Majella with stories of their exotic lives. When the bell rang to say that somebody had come into the shop they would go in order of seniority. Da first, then Bart, then Kev, then Da and so on. Red was not to abandon them to talk to Majella on their own.

She was a lovely big girl with no nonsense in her and by the time they had sat her down she was like part of the family. She said they must be great fellows altogether to have the butter on the place and the milk not in a bottle but in a jug. Whenever she went over to her cousin's place they were all putting their dirty knives into the butter at once, they needed a woman to civilise them. Red began to look like a sick calf when she talked of the civilising influence of a woman and he had to be kicked until he dropped it again. Majella said she was going to do the washing up and they could all dry, and seeing out of the corner of her eye that the dishcloths were not all they might be she called to Red to bring a packet of J-cloths out of the shop.

"Isn't it paradise to be here!" she said with a big smile at them all. "Who could want anything better than a shop right off your own living room?"

They had dried up in no time; the big room looked better somehow than it had done for years. Majella said that maybe she and Red might go for a bit of a tour round Rathdoon now and get out of everyone's way. By half past six she had a blushing delighted Red firmly by the arm and was linking him on her own little lap of honour around the community she had decided to join.

"Oh there's no escape there, that knot will be tied, poor Red." Bart laughed good-naturedly about the fate that could well be happening to his brother.

"Will you stop that nonsense: poor Red, my hat!

Wouldn't a girl have to be half mad or have the courage of a lion to marry any one of the three of you." He sounded very pessimistic indeed.

"Would you say she IS mad?" Kev asked interestedly. "She was a very nice class of a girl I thought."

"Of course she's nice, she's far too good for him: the thing is will she realise it in time?" Bart and Kev exchanged glances. Their father seemed to be torn between the delight of having the lovely laughing Majella around the place and the strictly honest course of action which was to warn the girl that his son was a bad bargain.

"Let her work it out for herself maybe?" Bart suggested and his father looked relieved.

Bart had a lot of sense, Kev realised, suddenly. He wasn't just a do-gooder and a big innocent. But he was the other side of the tracks now, he wasn't in the Underworld like Kev was, there could be no talking to him about the problem.

"Would you fancy an early pint down in Ryan's before the mob gets in there?" Bart said to him. Kev was pleased.

"That'd be the way to do it" he said sagely. Their father had gone back to the shop and was twiddling the dial for the news.

They walked down the road. It was quiet – most people were in at their tea; the sound of the half past six news that their father was listening to back in the shop came from several windows. Down past Billy Burns' chip shop. Billy wasn't there today, Mikey and that bright little Treasa who worked there, no sign of the new girl Eileen, well she had always looked too good to spend her day lifting pieces of cod or wings of chicken out of a deep fryer in Rathdoon. They came to the bridge. Bart leaned over and looked at the river. They used to race sticks under the bridge here when they were kids, and there were always so many arguments about whose stick had won Bart invented a system of tying different coloured threads on to each one. It seemed very long ago.

"What's eating you?" Bart asked.

"I don't know what you mean?"

"I'm not the world's brainiest man but I'm not blind either. Tell me, Kev. Can't you? It can't be any worse when you've told me. It might even be a bit better. Like I'm not going to be saying aren't you an eejit or blame you or anything, but there's something terrible wrong up in Dublin, isn't there?"

"Yes" Kev said.

"Before Red fell so much in love that he can't think of anything else, he and I were going to go up there one day on the excursion and try and sort it out, whatever it was."

Kev gulped with gratitude at the thought of his two brothers taking on a heavy gang like Daff, the Pelican, Crutch Casey and their team.

"What did YOU think the problems might be?" he asked nervously, fishing to see had Bart any notion of how bad things were or was he still in a world like the playground of the infants' school.

"I thought it might be a girl you got into trouble, but it's going on too long for that. I thought it might be a debt – you know, poker or the horses – but you don't seem to have any interest in either."

Bart's big innocent face looked puzzled. Kev drew a long breath. Well it seemed that Bart could take on that much anyway. What about the next step, could Bart listen to the story that had begun on his twenty-first birthday a year and a half ago, or would he run for the guards. Kev didn't know. Bart was shaping a stick and tying a bit of string round it.

"Here," he said to Kev, "Let this be yours: I'll beat you any day with my one." They threw the sticks over the side and rushed across to see them coming through. Kev's stick was in front.

"Would you beat that?" Bart seemed surprised. "I've been up here practising and I thought I had the shape of stick that ran best with the flow."

128

Kev began to tell him, in fact once started it tumbled out of hm: a mixture of names and commodities, Crutch Caseys and Microwaves, Daffs and cut glass, Pelicans and Axminster carpet. Kev had no starring role the way he told it, his only stroke of genius had been to go home every weekend on the Lilac Bus to avoid even more major crime in the city at weekends. He was in now and there was no getting out. Bart must know that, they'd all seen the films, they knew the plot. If Kev said to Daff that he'd had enough, thank you, he couldn't answer for the consequences but he knew it'd be awful. He didn't think they'd beat him up: they never used violence, he said almost pleadingly to Bart. But they would punish him. They'd send the guards round to his house or to work, or they'd send a note to Mr Daly accusing Kev of giving the tip-off about the cloakroom fittings that time. It was a nightmare: he was in it for ever.

He hardly dared to look at Bart during some of the confession, and once or twice he gave the odd glance and got the feeling that Bart was half smiling. Maybe he didn't understand the hugeness of it all. Once he was almost certain he got a smile and Bart had hastily put his hand over his face.

"So now, you see I'm caught entirely," he ended.

"I don't think so," Bart said slowly.

"But it's not LIKE here, Bart; you don't know, they're diferent to us. They're not our type of people."

"But they must have thought you were their kind of person otherwise they wouldn't have pulled you in," Bart said.

"But I TOLD you how that happened. I'm not a thief by nature, I'm fairly happy to work for my wages. Not very, but fairly. I'm not any good as a criminal."

"No I don't mean their type as a thief, you're secretive like they are. That's what they liked about you – you're not a blabber about who you know, what you do: that'll make them think you won't blab about them."

"Well I don't – haven't until now, that is."

"So that's how you get out if you want to. Tell them you're in with another lot now. No hard feelings, handshakes, pints all round, and that's it."

"Bart, you haven't any idea . . . "

"But you see, you keep up this hard man image with them except once or twice when you've had a fit of the shivers. You never try to talk them out of it, or discuss what they do with the stuff. They probably think you're a silent pro and someone has made you a better offer."

"They wouldn't have such a high regard for me as that."

"They must have a very high regard for you if they let you in on all their jobs. No, leave them as you joined them, with no chat, no explanations except the one they are owed. That you've got a new scene."

Bart talking about scenes, Bart saying that these gangsters are owed an explanation – it was like the end of the world.

"I don't think I'd be able to go through with it."

"You were able to join them, that was harder."

"And should I give them back the money?"

"Give them WHAT?"

"My share, I mean, if I'm not staying on like?"

"Your share. You have it still?"

"Of course I do, I didn't spend any of it, in case . . . you know . . . the guards and everything and a court case and I'd have to give it all back."

"Where is it?"

"It's upstairs in the room."

"In Dublin?"

"No here, back at the house. Under the bed."

"You're not serious."

"But what else would I do with it, Bart? I carry it with me home and back each weekend in a parcel with my clothes."

"And how much is it at all? Your share?"

"I'm afraid it's about four thousand, two hundred pounds," Kev said with his eyes cast down.

130

Eventually he raised his glance and Bart was smiling at him with pride.

"Isn't that the direct intervention of God?" Bart said to him. Kev would never have seen it like that; however confused his relationship with God was and however non-personal it had become, he couldn't imagine that the Almighty was delighted with such a sum of stolen money arriving under a bed in Rathdoon.

"This solves all our problems," Bart said.

"When Romeo back there went courting Majella the only fly in the ointment was would we have enough to build on a bit at the back. We were afraid it would get a bit crowded with us all on top of each other, and we saw the very thing we wanted, a kind of ready-made extension that they dig foundations for and then sort of plant on top of. Do you follow?"

Kev nodded nervously.

"But Red and I were afraid you were in some kind of financial trouble and we'd better not get ourselves too far into a loan. But here you are, a millionaire. Now we can go ahead, and if you'd like to contribute a bit . . . "

"Yes, well of course I would but don't you think if I'm getting out of their gang I should *offer* them the share back?"

"What kind of criminal are you at all?" roared Bart. "Won't they know immediately you're a ninny if you start a caper like that. You've got to consider that your wages, your share of the deal, now you're meant to be going on to a bigger one, you eejit: you're not meant to be giving them conscience money."

"No."

"And there's no way you can give it to the carpet people or the lavatory makers or the microwave people . . . "

"I wasn't in on the microwave – that's this weekend."

"See?" Bart felt this proved some point. "So what are you going to do with it, wouldn't building up the family home be as good as anything?"

Kev was astonished. No blame, no lecture, no accusation. Sheer hard practical advice, as if he knew the kind of people that Daff and the Pelican were. Because when you thought of it that was EXACTLY the way to go about it. And then he need never see them again.

"I'll give it all to you tonight, Bart," he said eagerly. "Where will we say we got it? Like if anyone asks?"

"You'll keep some of it, put it in the post office, but we'll say nothing to anyone, like you've been doing all your life. We'll get in touch with those people about the extension on Monday. What could be more natural than that country eejits like us would have money in a paper bag under the bed, they'll only be delighted – no VAT, nothing."

Kev was stunned. Saint Bart, in the black economy.

"And thanks to your very generous donation, we'll be able to get the bigger extension, and there'll be plenty of room if Majella produces a brood of Kennedys."

A stone fell off the bridge and into the water and Kev Kennedy didn't jump at all, and his eyes didn't widen with anxiety.

Rupert

He bought a packet of mints because Judy Hickey had told him last week that he reeked of garlic and much as she loved all good herby smells she didn't want to sit cooped up beside a porous sponge of garlic for three hours on a small minibus. Funny, Judy: if he had met her in Dublin, he would never have suspected that she came from home. She wasn't a Rathdoon sort of person. He had told her that once and she had retorted that neither was he – a thin, pale, artistic young Protestant: what could be more unlikely?

But she was wrong. There were handfuls of Protestants in every town in the West; they were as much part of the place as the mountains and the phone boxes and the small beautiful churches with hardly any attendance standing dwarfed by the newer Catholic churches which were bursting at the seams. No use explaining that to Judy, trying to tell her that she was much more unusual, dark and gypsy-like, living in a small gate lodge at the end of the drive from Doon House, growing herbs and working all week in a health food shop in Dublin. In another time she'd have been burned as a witch without any discussion, he had once told her. Judy had said gloomily that the way the country was going it could happen yet, so he shouldn't joke about it.

He smelled of garlic because he had eaten a very good lunch. He always did on a Friday; that was because he wouldn't be back again until late on Sunday night when it was the wrong time to have a meal. So Friday lunchtime was the only opportunity they could get to have anything approaching a relaxed weekend meal before he went back to Rathdoon for the weekend. Of course there *was* the rest of the week but it wasn't quite the same, as there was work next day, and anyway there was something about a weekend that gave you more time – more anticipation. He hated not having his weekends in Dublin. He hated going home on the Lilac Bus.

Rupert had never had an argument with his father in his whole life. And he could remember only three differences of opinion with his mother. Those went back to the time he was away at school and she had written three times to the headmaster to receive assurances that the beds were aired. He knew nobody else in the world who had such a relationship with their parents. Everyone else fought and forgave and loved or hated and stormed and railed or became fiercely protective. Nobody had this polite courteous distance based entirely on gratitude and duty. Nobody else who felt such irritation couldn't express it.

They didn't really need him, that was his whole point, and he wished them well, but he didn't need them either. So why should the pretence be kept up? It made it so much harder on all of them. Not only on Rupert – but maybe it was a little harder on him, he felt, after all their lives were ending. His hadn't really begun and couldn't begin as things were.

There hadn't even been a row when Rupert had decided to give up his law studies. He had been apprenticed to a firm in Dublin, begun his lectures with the Incorporated Law Society and at the same time read for a degree in Trinity. It wasn't a superhuman load – a lot of people did it easily – but Rupert never took to it. Not any of it. The bit he liked best oddly was the office. He was quite happy doing the clerical work, the part that Dee Burke, who worked there now said she hated. Rupert had made few friends in Trinity which surprised him; he thought it would be like school, which had

136

been fine. But it was very different and he felt totally outside it all.

He had come home the weekend he knew he had failed his First Law with a heavy heart. He hadn't tried to excuse himself, he just apologised as if to a kind stranger, and his father accepted the apology as if it had been given by a kind stranger. They had sat one on either side of the table while his mother looked left and right at whoever was speaking.

Rupert said it was a great waste of his father's money and a disgrace to him in his profession. His father had brushed these things aside: heavens no, people often failed their first examination, there was no cause for alarm, some of the greatest lawyers claimed that they had never been showy scholars. No need for any regrets, it should all be written off as part of sowing wild oats, part of getting your freedom. Next year it would be more serious, head in book, down to it, wasn't that right?

On into the night Rupert had talked, saying that he wasn't cut out for it. It wasn't what he wanted. He didn't believe he would love it when he was in his father's office: he didn't love the office he was apprenticed to in Dublin, he only liked the more mechanical parts. He couldn't get interested in the theory of the law or the way it was administered. He was so sorry it had turned out like this, but wasn't it better that they should know now rather than discover later. They agreed logically that it was. They asked him what DID he want. He didn't know; he had been so sure that he would like Trinity, and like studying law, he had never given it much thought before. He liked thinking about the way people lived and their houses and all that. But wasn't it going to be very hard to try and get accepted to study architecture? his father wondered. He didn't mean study it, he didn't know, Rupert said desperately. He would get a job, that's what he'd do. His parents didn't understand this: they thought you had to have a degree to get a job, the kind of job Rupert would want. When he found the position as a junior in the estate agent's they said they were pleased if that's what he wanted. They didn't sound displeased, they sounded remote as they always had been.

His father was remote when he told Rupert that the time had come to get someone else into the office and that if Rupert were absolutely sure that he didn't intend to come into the profession he was going to offer a position to David MacMahon's son. Rupert assured him it would be fine, and got only a minor start when he realised that young MacMahon would have to be offered a partnership and the name of the office would be repainted to read Green and MacMahon. Once or twice they had asked him whether he had thought of coming back to Rathdoon and setting up his own little auctioneering business. There must be plenty of sites being sold and garages and people liked to keep things local. "It might be no harm to get in before Billy Burns sets one up, he's started everything else in the town," his mother had said, but firmly and politely he had assured them that this was not going to happen. He left them in no doubt that his plans involved staying in Dublin. This had happened on the day his mother had said that she wondered whether they should put a new roof on the house or not. Sometimes she felt that the one she had would do for their time and wasn't that all it would be needed for . . . ? Rupert had answered her levelly as if she had been asking no deeper question or making no last desperate plea. He talked of roofs and the value they added to houses and gave the pros and cons as he knew them, bringing himself no more into their plans than if he had been asked by a passing tourist.

His mother asked a bit coyly once or twice if he met any nice girls in Dublin. She didn't ask that any more. He must have given her some fairly firm answers, because he was only twenty-five, an age when you might be assumed to be still meeting girls. If people didn't know that you never met girls, you only met Jimmy.

Rupert's throat tightened just thinking of Jimmy. They had

met for lunch this Friday; it had now become a bit of a ritual. Jimmy had no classes on a Friday afternoon: they had found the boys didn't study too well and had given them games or art or music. So Jimmy could jump into his little car and drive off to meet him. Rupert had noticed with an alarm mixed with pleasure that Dublin was becoming very slap-happy on Friday afternoons anyway, and not just in schools. At the office they did very little business and people seemed to be leaving for home – even if it was just the suburbs – earlier and earlier. If the noise in a nearby pub was anything to go by those particular workers of the world weren't going to do much to change it when they got back to their desks – if they got back. Still it was nice for Rupert. He could take a long lunch hour with no questions asked. They had found a restaurant that both of them liked (not easy as they had such arguments about food), and it was a very happy couple of hours.

Jimmy insisted that he go home every weekend; it was even Jimmy who found the Lilac Bus for him. Jimmy said it was a pity that they couldn't have weekends but it wouldn't be for ever, and since the old man had always been so undemanding wouldn't it only be right to go back to him now in his last few months? And it must be desperate on his mother waiting all week for him: of course he had to go. Jimmy wouldn't even let him pretend he had flu, not even for one weekend. He was very definite about it.

Jimmy was definite about everything, it was part of his charm. He never wondered about anything or deliberated or weighed things up. And if as it turned out sometimes he was utterly wrong, then he was equally definite about that.

"I was all wrong about the man who invented those cats' eyes for the road at night. I was thinking about somebody totally different. I couldn't have been more wrong." Then he would go ahead with the new view. But he had never changed his view about Rupert going home at weekends; that was an absolute.

Jimmy didn't have any home to go off to on a Friday.

139

Jimmy's home was right there in Dublin. He was the youngest of six, and his two sisters and three brothers had gone exactly the way their father wanted which was into the newspaper vendor business. Some had pitches on good corners, others had roofs over their heads and sold ice creams and birthday cards as well. But Jimmy's father was in the habit of saying gloomily, "There's always one arty farty cuckoo in the nest, one who won't listen to reason." Jimmy had been a bit of a pet when he was a youngster: they all encouraged him at his books, and then to university and into teaching in a very posh school. They made jokes about him being gay but it was never said straight out whether they believed he was or not. Anyone over-educated as they regarded him would have had the same abuse, the accusations of being limp-wristed, the mockery of his clothes, the vain search for an ear ring and the camp clichés from the television: "Ooh Jimmy, you are awful."

But he went there every Wednesday evening. They all called in on the small crowded house; they talked about rivals and which magazine would be seized by the censor as soon as somebody in authority had a look at it. They talked of how the dailies were doing and how there was no point in taking this magazine because it wouldn't survive to a second issue. They told each other how they had long narrow sticks and bet the hands off any kid stealing a comic. Jimmy would join in by asking questions. He always brought a cake, a big creamy one from the nice delicatessen where they often went. His family would have a communal coronary arrest if they knew how much the cake cost. His mother used to say it was a nice piece of cake even though the smallest bit soggy just in the middle. Jimmy would scoop up the bit where the Cointreau or Calvados had concentrated and eat it with a spoon. His brothers said it was a very fair cake, and reminded them of children's trifle.

It would be so easy to have a family like Jimmy's. They asked so little of him, they were so complete in themselves. If Jimmy were to disappear from their lives for ever, he would be spoken of affectionately, but if Rupert were to forgo just one weekend going home on the Lilac Bus it would be a national crisis for the Green family. Sometimes he thought that this was very unfair, but Jimmy would have none of it.

"You're a difficult sensitive plant, Roopo," he'd say. "Even if you had my family, you'd feel threatened and anguished – it's the way things are."

Rupert would laugh, "Don't call me Roopo, it sounds like some exotic bird in the zoo."

"That's what you ARE: like a dark brooding exotic bird that finds almost every climate too difficult for it!"

He had met Jimmy one great lucky day in the office. There was a picture of what they called a "charming unconverted cottage" in the window. It was a bit far out too, not in the more fashionable direction and it could not be described as trendy, even by the most optimistic of those who wrote the descriptions.

Jimmy came in, a slight figure in an anorak, wearing tinted glasses. He had blonde hair that fell over his forehead and he looked a bit vulnerable. Rupert didn't know why he moved over at once to him even though Miss Kennedy was nearer. He didn't feel any attraction to him at that stage – he just wanted to see that he got a fair deal. He had been studying the picture of the cottage, and had an eager smile on his face.

Rupert had told him the good and the bad: the bad being the roof and the distance and awful boulders of rocks in what had been loosely called the garden. He told him the good, which was that it was fairly cheap, that it was nice and private, and that if you had any money now or later there was another building attached to it which was a sort of an outhouse but which could easily be made into another small dwelling. Jimmy listened with growing interest and asked to see it as soon as possible. Rupert drove him out there, and without anything being said they knew they were planning their future as they stood in the wild overgrown rocky ground around the little house and climbed the walls of the outhouse to find that the roof there was perfect.

"It's not handy for where you work," Rupert pointed out, as Jimmy had said where he taught.

"I don't want to live handy to where I work, I want to live miles away. I want to have my own life away from the eyes of the school."

Rupert felt an unreasonable sense of exclusion.

"And will you share it, do you think? That is, if you take it," he had asked.

"I might," Jimmy had said levelly. "I have no plans yet."

He bought the house. He had been saving with a building society for four years and he was considered reliable. The estate agency was pleased with Rupert: they had had the cottage on their books for rather too long. When all the negotiations were over, Rupert felt very lonely. This small smiling Jimmy was going to be off now living his own life in the windswept place. He would build that wall that they had discussed as a shelter, he would do up the second part of the house, paint it white, paint a door bright red maybe, grow some geraniums and get a suitable tenant. It would pay his mortgage. And Rupert would hear no more of it. Or of him.

He phoned on the Friday.

"Rupert, will you help me? I've lost all the fire for the place. I can't SEE it any more, what it's like, what's going to be so great about it. Will you come out and remind me?"

"Yes." Rupert said slowly. "Yes, that's what I'd love to do."

He sat in a kind of trance all that Friday; if people spoke to him he only heard them vaguely. It was all so clear now: the confusions, the guilt, the hope that it would all settle down and sort itself out and that one day a woman would come along who would make him forget all this short-term stuff – which frightened him rather than making him satisfied. But all the time knowing there would be no woman, and not really wanting a woman. But had he read the signs right? Suppose Jimmy was just a charming fellow with nothing on his mind but a good cheery chat with that nice fellow from the estate agent's? Suppose Jimmy said he had a fiancée or some married lady that he wanted to meet in secret. He drove out, noting that it would take him half an hour from door to door should he ever need to go that way again. Jimmy was standing at the gate. Waiting.

He knew it was going to be all right.

And it had been more than all right for three years now. They had done the two little houses up with such love that now they really *did* merit a glowing description on an auctioneer's books. But they would never be for sale. They were separate enough to pretend that they were two dwellings if it were ever needed. But it never was. When Jimmy invited his family out to see the place they all thanked him and said they must get round to it but they never arrived. Rupert didn't press his elderly parents to come to Dublin, and just showed them pictures of his part of the house. And of the garden. They made it all into a giant rockery and knew as much about alpines and rock plants as anyone for miles around. They had a big kitchen with a sink and work area on each side so that they could both cook if they wanted to. Every penny they had went into their little place. They had friends soon, people who came to dinner and admired or offered advice but mainly admired. It was so ideal and they were so happy.

That's why he hated leaving it at weekends. It was on Saturdays that they used to be most peaceful there, often shopping and cooking a meal – not only for Martin and Geoff or other gay friends but for the nice young married couple who lived nearby and who kept an eye on their garden that time they went to Morocco. These were people to relax with. These and one or two people in the estate agency didn't have to have any pretences arranged for them. It was only in Jimmy's school and Rupert's home town that the acting was essential.

Jimmy said it was so ludicrous in the 1980s not to be

able to say that he was gay. And he would have at once it if were remotely possible. But no, apparently the boys' parents would think he had designs on them: they would think he was looking at them speculatively.

"I don't want any of those horrible ink-covered filthy ignorant kids," Jimmy would wail. "I want you, Rupert, my beautiful dark Rupert that I love."

And Rupert would fill up with pleasure and pride that Jimmy could be so natural and open and say all that to him. He tried to say spontaneous things too but they came out with greater difficulty. He was a bit buttoned up as Judy Hickey had once said to him. He wondered often if Judy knew that he was gay. Probably. But it had never been the right time to tell her or to invite her out to see the rock plants and alpines that she would love.

Of course he could tell Judy Hickey: after all, she was a scandal herself in some way, wasn't she? There had been some really murky business years ago. She would be pleased to know there was another Great Secret in Rathdoon. But he could never tell Judy that one of the real reasons he hated so much leaving every Friday for these empty weekends was that he was so afraid Jimmy would find someone else. Or maybe even had found someone else.

At lunch this very Friday he had asked Jimmy what he would do all day Saturday, and there had been no satisfactory answer. Martin and Geoff were having people in for drinks – he would go to that in the evening. He'd mark exercise books, he'd try and fix up the hi-fi which had never been satisfactory. It was all very vague. Suppose, suppose, Jimmy had begun to like somebody else? His heart was cold inside like the unexpected bit you find when you take a loaf out of the freezer and it hasn't properly thawed. He could never tell anyone that fear. Not anyone in the whole world.

It was easy to talk to Judy. She told him about her little herb pillows; he told her all the fuss over the TD with the love nest. They both laughed at that and for some reason that he couldn't quite see it brought her into talking about her own past. He was astounded at her story, a young wife and mother dealing in drugs all those years ago. And the husband doing deals with the law as if he was part of the Wild West. Imagine her not seeing the children, but imagine even more her getting supplies of LSD for the huntin' shootin' fishin' set! And hash! Jimmy would go wild when he heard. He could have listened for ever but suddenly she decided she was boring him and launched into chat with that half-mad Nancy Morris. She had also said that his mother thought about him every day. That couldn't be so. Mother thought about father, and the house, and the vegetable garden and the hens, but mainly father and how she was afraid that young Mr MacMahon didn't have the respect due to the senior partner and founder of the firm. Mother hardly showed any interest in Rupert's life in Dublin which was of course a relief, but it did mean that it was most unlikely that Mother would think about him every day. Surely Judy was being fanciful? She probably hoped no matter what she said her lost children thought of her every day. That was it.

Their house was small and white with clematis growing up over the porch. Jimmy thought that a Protestant solicitor's family would live in a manor house, heavy with creeper and inspiring awe among the peasantry. Rupert had said that only two houses had proper creeper. One was Dr Burke's, which was beautifully kept and one was the old vicarage, which was so neglected it now looked like a huge stone covered with ivy. They had a service each Sunday in Rathdoon in the beautiful church, but had no vicar, no rector; he came out from the big town seventeen miles away and had Matins in Rathdoon, and another, later Matins another fifteen miles down the road. Jimmy was fascinated, but Rupert had never asked Jimmy home to meet the family. Jimmy had asked him to his house many a time. Rupert had gone once and felt awkward even though nobody else had and they had all button-holed him about the price of property.

His mother was waiting just inside the door. That always annoyed him too and he got annoyed with himself over the very annoyance. Why shouldn't she wait to stop him ringing or knocking and disturbing his father's sleep. But it always made him think she had been standing waiting for his shadow to fall through the glass panels. He said goodnight with a much lighter tone than he felt, and braced himself. The soft leather of the magnificent jacket touched the back of his neck. It was Jimmy's birthday present to him. A few days early but Jimmy said it would cheer him up for the weekend. Dee Burke had been right, they did cost a fortune. Again the niggling worry: how had Jimmy been able to spend that much money even if it was a second? Put these doubts away, Rupert, he told himself firmly. Jimmy is good and true. Why pour vinegar onto it all with your stupid suspicions. Jimmy is at home tonight marking books and looking at television, Jimmy is not in a bar in town cruising someone. Why destroy EVERYTHING?

"He's very well, very clear," his mother whispered delightedly.

"What?"

"Your father. He's very clear. He's awake; he asked several times what time would the Lilac Bus be in. Every time he heard anything change gear on the corner, he said 'Is that the bus?' "

Rupert put his carrier bag down on the hall floor. "That's great Mother, that's really great," he said with heavy heart and went up the little stairs slowly to see the man with the head like a skull and the skin like cling-film. The man he had never been able to talk to in his life.

It was a sunny Saturday but his father's room was darkened and the dim light hurt his eyes. His mother was bottling fruit downstairs. Jimmy said Catholics never bottled fruit or preserved eggs – it was something their religion didn't go along with. Jimmy had told him more lies about Roman Catholicism than he ever believed anyone could invent. He had always been brought up carefully to

146

respect it at a distance by his parents, and even though they thought it definitely held the people back they were impressed by the piety and the crowds going to Mass. His parents had gone to Galway to see the Pope. Jimmy said that his parents had made a small fortune the weekend the Pope arrived since the whole of Dublin wanted to buy every newspaper twice in case they missed anything.

Back at home in the cottage, Jimmy would be drinking freshly brewed coffee and reading the *Irish Times*. Then he might go out to the garden and do some transplanting. September was the month to move the evergreens if you wanted to change the plan a bit. But no, Jimmy would wait for him to come back for that. Maybe he would be puzzling over the hi-fi. Please may he not be driving into town just because he's bored; please may he meet nobody at lunch over a drink and smoked salmon sandwich.

"You're very good to come down every weekend," his mother said suddenly as if she could read the homesickness for his real place written all over his eyes. "Your father really does like talking to you. Do you notice that? Can you see it?"

Jimmy had begged him not to cross the whole of Ireland and then have a row. How could Jimmy understand that there were NEVER rows, and there never would be. Well, a coldness then, Jimmy would say. If you are going to go to all that trouble, it's silly to balls up your weekend: if you're making the gesture, make it properly.

"I think he *does* seem to like talking," Rupert said. "It doesn't tire him too much does it?"

"No, he plans all week what he's going to say to you. Sometimes he asks me to write it down, or just headings. I want to talk to Rupert about this, he'll say, and I write it down. Often he forgets what it was he was going to say about it, but it's there at the time."

Rupert nodded glumly.

"Like he was going to ask you about those flats you sell in blocks; he was very interested in how they work out the

147

leasehold. He said that there was never any of that in the conveyancing he had to do. But all he asked me to write down was 'Block of Flats,' you see, and then he couldn't remember last week what it was he wanted to say about them."

"I see," Rupert said, trying to sound more sympathetic than he was afraid he might appear.

"But this week, he seems very much brighter and more aware, doesn't he?" she was pleading.

"Yes, much more. Oh indeed. He was talking about this house here and what we would say if we had it on an auctioneer's books. I was giving him funny descriptions and he smiled a bit at it."

Rupert's mother was pleased. "Good, he hasn't smiled a lot. That's nice."

"Why don't you have a bit of time off, Mother, when I'm here. Why can't you go into town, maybe, you'd like that. I can keep an eye on father and be here if he wants anything."

"No no, I want you to enjoy yourself," she said.

"But really Mother, I mean I'm not doing anything anyway." He shrugged. "I might as well look after father and let you have a few hours to yourself." He meant it generously, but he knew it had come out all wrong.

"But you're home for the weekend," she cried. "I wouldn't want to miss that by going off to the town. I can do that any day. Mrs Morris or young Mary Burns, Billy's wife, would sit with him. No, I want to get value out of your being here."

"Sure. Of course," he said, appalled at his own insensitivity. Jimmy would never in a million years have said anything like that. Jimmy would have brought life and laughter into the house the moment he got back. Jimmy. Oh Jimmy.

They had lunch, the kind of lunch that only his mother could serve: endless preparation and toasting of bread and cutting of crusts and spreading of cheese and slicing of tomatoes. And yet it was nothing – it managed to be both stodgy and insubstantial. If only she would let him cook. But then he had never asked her. Perhaps it might be giving something away to say that he could have made them a light and delicious lunch in a quarter the time. It was his own fault like everything.

His father struggled all afternoon. And Rupert struggled back.

Sometimes his mother was there, sewing. She was always making little things for her sister who was married to a vicar and who always needed things for parish sales. His father would struggle and concentrate. His efforts to please meant that he could even be re-routed back to his own old days as a solicitor coming first to the town, when things were different and better. There was a time when his father had been happy to ramble through the times gone by. But not now: it was as if he was determined to show a guest in his eyes that he *was* interested in whatever kind of strange thing the guest did for a living. All afternoon Rupert's soul was crying out, "It's all RIGHT father. Look, can't you rest: I have an okay life and I wish you and mother well but why do we go through all this meaningless chat. There is nothing to say any more."

The sun was almost going down when he could bear it no more; he said he had promised Judy Hickey he would do something for her and he had better dash over to her.

"A brave woman, Judy Hickey – she held her head high in this place for two decades," his father said in a surprisingly strong voice.

"Yes, well, why not?" Rupert was defensive. "She got a harsh punishment."

"She took it, and she didn't run away and hide. She stepped down from being lady of the manor and lived in the gate lodge."

"And lost her children," Rupert's mother added. "That was the worst bit."

"Yes, well, I won't be long." He felt he could breathe again when he was out in the air; he left the square and went off towards the gate lodge of the big Doon house.

Judy was lying curled up like a cat. She wasn't pleased to see him – in fact she nearly sent him back straight away. She was like Jimmy really but without the persuasive charm: Jimmy made it seem reasonable; Judy made it seem like a duty.

But she meant it: she got up and stretched and said she was going to go out and walk in her husband's wood. Jack Hickey's wood she called it. She said he should talk about anything, anything to show his father that he was trying too.

But what could he say? He couldn't tell him that his heart was tearing with the barbed wire of jealousy in case his male lover might have been unfaithful. Then NOBODY could tell a father that about a lover of any sex. But Rupert was worse off: he couldn't talk about his life, about the beautiful gentians that he and Jimmy had planted and how the willow gentian had burst into a whole pool of dark blue flowers last July and they had taken photographs of each other admiring it. He found it hard to talk about the garden without mentioning Jimmy because the two were twined together, like the house, like cooking, like holidays and reading and laughing and the things people did for heaven's sake.

Annoyed with Judy for being short with him, he walked home. He passed the Kennedys' shop and saw a big handsome girl being ushered in. The red-headed Kennedy boy, Eddie, was looking at her with a foolish grin: they must be courting. She was very attractive; how simple life would have been if only he had been born to court a big handsome girl who would bring life and laughter into his quiet house.

Suddenly he thought of Jimmy in the house. Jimmy pausing at the door to touch the clematis and cup it in his hands with admiration. Jimmy saying to Rupert's mother that she should sit down and put her feet up and let her big ugly son and himself make the meal for a change. Jimmy telling Rupert's father tales of the boys' school where he taught, and the fees and the extras and the awful school concerts. Jimmy walking casually down the road with him to Ryan's for a drink before dinner while the carbonade was in the oven. Jimmy would lighten their house better than any strapping girl from a well-to-do farm outside town.

"I was just thinking," he said to his mother when she let him in the door again as if she had been hovering. "Could I bring a friend home next weekend?"

After that it was easy. His mother said she was glad that she had got good notice because she would clear out the guest room. It had been something she had meant to do for a long time but never had the heart somehow. And his father said that it would be very interesting to meet someone who taught in that school because he had known a lot of people in his time who had been there and they were all united in never having a good word to say for it but having done extremely well as a result of being there.

Then a sudden shock. Suppose Jimmy didn't want to come?

"I hope he'll be able to make it; I didn't think of asking him," he stammered.

"Why don't you ring him?" his mother suggested. His mother. Who made trunk calls as one might try to get in touch with another planet. Cautiously and without much hope of success.

"God, isn't that lovely to hear you?" Jimmy said.

"I'm ringing from home," said Rupert.

"Well, I hope so. I did think sometimes you went off to exotic places without me, but I decided to trust you." Jimmy's laugh was warm. Rupert swallowed.

"It's lovely here this weekend and I was wondering . . . I was wondering . . . "

"Yes?"

"I was wondering if you'd like to come down next week and stay, you know?"

"I'd love to.'"

There was a pause.

"You would? You would, Jimmy?"

"Sure I thought you'd never ask," Jimmy said.

Celia

Her friend Emer used to call it the Dancing Bus. All over Dublin people got on buses on Friday night to go home to great dances in the country. It had been a revolution, they said – culchies choosing to go home because the crack was better there than in Dublin. And they had the advantages of a bit of freedom in the city during the week and not losing touch with the home place either.

Celia laughed at the thought of her bus being a Sweetheart Special. She told Emer when they had cups of tea in the day room about the cast that turned up at a quarter to seven every week. Emer had sighed in envy. It sounded great, a nice spin across to the west, a weekend with no washing and housecleaning and trying to tell the three teenagers that there wasn't enough money for anything and trying to tell her husband who had been out of work for three years that there was plenty of money for everything. Emer had a sister married in the town that was seventeen miles from Rathdoon. Wouldn't it be lovely to go off there once in a while? Oh Lord, she'd love it.

And so that's what happened. Celia had to work weekends, one in every four. So she gave her place on the bus to Emer. It had suited them all, and Emer said her family in Dublin were so grateful to see her back on a Sunday night that they never complained about anything, they just made her a coffee and said they'd missed her. Of course Celia did go to the dances at one time, and they were great altogether: you got a first-rate band to come to a place where the people drove in for miles and there would always be a big crowd. She used to dance with Kev Kennedy's brother, Red, sometimes, but she much preferred Bart, the eldest of that family. He was so solid and reliable. You never quite knew what he was thinking but he was always there. In fact you never had to ASK him to help, he seemed to know when it was necessary and turn up. Emer said he sounded a very suitable sort of man indeed, but Celia thought not. She said he wasn't interested in settling down and she wasn't going to set her sights on another one who was a permanent bachelor. She'd had enough trouble getting over the first. Emer had sighed supportively and wondered why as a married woman she was trying to encourage others to join the club. It certainly wasn't what it was cracked up to be, and in many ways it wasn't much good at all.

But Celia only laughed at her. Emer was thirty-eight and sounded tough and cynical but deep down she would die for that handsome, whinging husband of hers and those tall rangy kids who got bigger and needed more clothes every time you looked at them. Celia wasn't going to be put off love and marriage by any of Emer's protests; it was what she wanted. Not urgently, not immediately, not at any price, but she wanted it sometime. Despite what she had seen of it in her own family.

She could hardly remember a day at home when there hadn't been some kind of a row. A lot of them were in public too because if the whole of Rathdoon was coming into the pub from eleven o'clock in the morning on, then they would have to be aware of the shouts and the disagreements and the sight of Mr or Mrs Ryan coming flushed with anger from the back room into the bar and serving a pint, only to disappear again and fight the point further. Celia had often heard that children grew anxious and withdrawn when their parents fought in the home. But that's not what happened to the Ryans. They grew up and went away, that was all. As

156

soon as they were able to get out, out they got. Her eldest sister had joined a band of Australian nuns who had come to Ireland looking for vocations. Looking for very young vocations, since Celia's sister had only been sixteen. But the offer of further education had been attractive as well. She wrote home from time to time incomprehensible letters of places and things that were never explained. Then the boys had gone too. Harry to Detroit and Dan to Cowley in England. They wrote rarely, hard sorts of letters with a kind of graspingness they never had as youngsters – how a bar in Ireland must be a gold mine now. Harry had read in Detroit that Ireland was booming since the Common Market, and Dan had been told in Cowley that having a publican's license in the west of Ireland was like having a licence to print money. These letters hurt Celia: there was much more than a hint, there was a direct statement that Celia and her mother were doing very nicely out of the family business, thank you. When she saw how things really were she felt she should laugh, but before she laughed she should weep.

Five years ago when her father died people said that at least one blessing was that Kate Ryan had always been more or less running the business single-handed and so there'd be no doubt at all that she'd be able to carry on. It wasn't like some establishments where the wife had always been in the background. No, poor Kate had been managing on her own while the husband drank down at one end of the bar with his own little circle.

And poor Kate had carried on for a good bit. In the summer she'd hire a young fellow to wash glasses and there was always Bart Kennedy to give a hand if things got very busy. No, she was fine. There was no shortage of customers, and mercifully drink wasn't the kind of thing that came and went in fashions – people always loved drink. Apart from the first week of Lent, the custom was always steady and at weekends it was roaring. There was no opposition, and you'd never get another licence for a place as small as this.

Rathdoon was unusual in that it had only one pub; other places might have had three. There had been talk once that Billy Burns was thinking of applying for a licence; he had been interested in buying a place about twenty miles away and asking to transfer that licence to Rathdoon, but nothing had come of it.

Celia had been thinking about Billy Burns during the day for some reason. She had woken with that silly tune on her mind, "Where have you been all the day, Billy Boy, Billy Boy?" and she thought it fitted Mikey's brother down to the ground. Mikey was such an innocent old eejit, and there was something a bit too smart about Billy. Nothing to do with his setting up another pub or not. In fact if he did that might be a solution to a lot of their problems. If her mother's pub went downhill due to legitimate competition that would be an honourable way out. If her mother drank Ryan's into the ground that was a less honourable way altogether.

But you couldn't say anything even vaguely like this to Celia's mother. Other people were hitting it a bit hard these days, other people were making fools of themselves and running up debts: there were men in Rathdoon who had big pores in their noses and red and blue veins in their cheeks from drink; there were women in Rathdoon who went into the big town seventeen miles away to do the shopping, but Kate Ryan could tell you that it was little shopping they did except half a dozen half-bottles hidden under the teatowels or whatever they bought as an excuse. Half bottles were easier to hide and they were easier to dispose of. Kate Ryan could tell you of those who came in at night for just one drink, Mrs Ryan, and she had seen them topping it up from their handbags. They didn't want to be seen ordering more than the one. But Celia's mother would have no tales of a woman who didn't even have to hide it because she had it there on her own shelves, and she was surrounded by it as her way of earning a living for twelve hours a day.

It had been such a shock the first time she saw her mother

drunk. Mam had been the one who didn't and Da had been the one who did. It was like left and right and black and white. To hear those slurred words, to have to cope with an inarticulate argument – Celia had been quite flustered and not at all the calm Nurse Ryan that could cope with anything on her corridor. The next day her mother had made great excuses, frightening excuses. It was food poisoning: she had eaten some of that chicken paste out of a jar, she was going to write to the manufacturers and enclose the label. Not only had it made her sick several times during the night but it had also affected her mind in some way. She couldn't remember clearly, she couldn't piece everything together. When Celia said agreeably enough that the chicken paste might well have been bad but it was probably the drink that made her forget the night before, she flew into a rage, one of those real rows like there used to be when Da was alive. It was NOT drink. Could Celia kindly tell her what drink she was referring to? Had Celia seen her mother sitting down to have a drink even once last night? Celia shrugged. She thought it might have been just this one time. Let it pass.

Three weeks later she came home for the weekend, and her mother was mixing up the gin and the vodka, forgetting to take the money from people and letting the pints overflow while she went to deal with someone else. It was then that Celia decided she had better book herself onto the Lilac Bus and come home every weekend that she could. This had been going on for a year now and her mother was getting worse and worse. And the really bad thing was that she wouldn't admit it, not for one moment. Not even to herself.

In the hospital Celia had seen dozens – more than dozens, probably hundreds – of people who were trying to help people who wouldn't help themselves. There had been endless conversations about old men who wouldn't go into sheltered accommodation and had set fire to their kitchens three times and old women who had broken their hips over and over because they wouldn't ask anyone to help them across a street. There were shrivelled anorexics who wouldn't eat, there were ashen-faced coronary patients who had insisted on doing overtime in stress-filled jobs and eating huge meals filled with cholesterol. There were women worn out with the fourteenth pregnancy, there were the mothers of the schoolchildren who had overdosed, there were the wives of the men whose livers had packed up despite a hundred arguments that alcohol was poisoning them slowly to certain death. Always she had sounded sympathetic, always she had appeared to understand. But inside there was a bit of her which said that they couldn't have tried hard enough. If Celia had a daughter who was desperately unhappy at school and who had lost four stone in weight, she wouldn't hang around – she'd try to cope with it. If she had a father who couldn't cope, she'd have him to live with her. Only now was she beginning to realise that it was not to be so simple. People had minds of their own. And her mother's mind was like a hermetically sealed box in the vault of a bank.

Emer had been in high good humour: she had won a hundred pounds on the hospital draw. Each week they all had to buy a ticket for the building fund. It cost fifty pence, and they *had* to buy it – there wasn't any choice. Three hundred fifty pences aded up to £150 and every second week the prize was £50 and every other one it was £100. It kept people interested and that small weekly contribution to the building fund was assured. Even if you were going to be on holidays you had to give someone else your sub. The winning ticket was announced on a Friday afternoon by number and you went to Wages to collect the prize. Emer was going to say nothing about it at home. Not one word. They would never hear. They would want jeans, they'd want a holiday, they'd think you could go on a holiday for a hundred quid. They'd want to go to Macdonalds every night for a month, they'd want a video. Her husband would say it should go into the building society, it should be saved in case he never worked again. No, much better to keep it for herself. She and Celia would have a night out next week. Celia had laughed at her affectionately. "Sure," she had said. "People do what they want in the end, isn't that what you always say?"

She knew that what Emer would want despite all the protestations of independence and keeping the money to herself was totally different. She would want to arrive home this Friday night bursting with the news. She would want to send out for chicken and chips and plan endless treats which would indeed include jeans and a bit saved to please her anxious husband and a promise to look into the economics of a down payment on a video. That's what Emer would want and that's what she would do in the end. They both knew it.

And if Celia had a husband and kids she hoped that's what she would want too. Otherwise what was the point of the whole thing?

She was tired. It had been a long day. In other hospitals they worked twelve hour shifts: eight in the morning till eight at night. Celia thought she'd be ready to strangle some of the patients, most of the visitors and all of the staff if they had to have that routine. It had been quite enough to have eight hours today. A young woman had become desperately upset because at visiting time her a brother, a priest, had said that he was saying a special Mass for her in their house. He had thought she would be pleased; she had thought that this meant it was the end. Then her husband told the priest that he had a neck to come in and upset the wife and there was a row of such proportions that everyone in the ward stopped talking to their own visitors and began to listen. Celia had been called. She pulled the curtains round the bed, she organised some light sedation, she explained in a crisp cool voice that the woman's diagnosis had been entirely optimistic, that nothing was being hidden from her or from anyone. She said that since priests had the power to say the Mass, what could be more natural than he would say one in the family home as a thanksgiving for her recovery so far and a hope that it would continue?

She also said with a particularly pointed look at the priest that it was a pity some people couldn't explain things sensibly without using voices laden with doom and ritual, and have some sensitivity about people's association of having Masses said with being very ill indeed. Then with a reprimanding glance at the husband she said that the whole point of a visiting hour was for the patient to be made more comfortable and happy and not to be plunged into the middle of a huge family row with accusations being hurled for the whole ward to hear. They were all younger than her except the priest, and he was probably under thirty. They took it very well and nodded their apologies to her and to each other. She drew the curtains open again and busied herself around the ward until she was sure they were all properly calm again. When the priest and the husband had gone she sat with the woman and held her hand and told her not to be an eejit: priests would want to say a Mass in a house at the drop of a hat. And after all it was their life. If they didn't believe it was important, who did? It was only the rest of the world, Celia explained, who thought that Masses and God were only brought in when all else had failed. For priests they were there all the time. She hit the right note exactly and the woman was laughing by the time she left the ward.

Would that it were going to be so easy at home.

Last weekend Bart Kennedy had let slip that he had been there several nights during the week as well as the weekends. She was alarmed. She and Bart never spoke of the reason for him being there. He never said that her mother was drunk, he would say she needed a bit of a hand. He never said that her mother had insulted one of the customers, he would say there had been a bit of a barney but it was probably all sorted out now. She had asked him to take wages for himself, and he had laughed and said not at all. He was only helping out and how could he go and sign on if he was getting a regular salary? He assured her that he took the odd pint for himself and offered one to a friend occasionally but it was peanuts and couldn't go on. Emer wondered had he perhaps any hopes of marrying into the establishment, but Celia said that was nonsense – Bart wasn't the type. Nothing funny about him, mind you, but just one that would never marry. Don't forget, Celia knew all about those: she had served her time for five years on a hopeless cause. She could spot them a mile off now.

But enough: she wasn't going to think of that fellow any more. That was all behind her and at least the humiliations weren't known in Rathdoon. It was to another town that she had followed him hopefully at weekends, thinking that there was much more to it than there was, being there, being available; eventually because it seemed the one thing he was sure he wanted she had slept with him. That was what he had called it but there was no sleeping involved: it was guilt for fear of discovery, and not very much pleasure for either of them. She hadn't lost him because she had been too easy to get; she hadn't lost him at all because he was never hers to lose; he had no intention of disturbing the very even pattern of his life by a wife and house and children. No no, no, he would stay on with his parents while they lived and maybe with a sister later. There would always be girls – girls now and later women – who would believe that they had the secret and the key to unlock his independence. No, Celia could write a book on the Irish bachelor if she wanted to, but she hadn't time: she HAD to sort it out this weekend, otherwise she'd better leave the hospital and come home. It wasn't fair on everyone else in Rathdoon.

She was glad that Kev Kennedy was a little bit ahead of her. That meant that he would sit beside Mikey. Tonight she was not in the mood for Mikey's jokes; some evenings she could take a few and then turn to her own thoughts but

163

there was too much on her mind, and Mikey was so easily hurt. It was good not to have this battle between offending him or going mad herself. She slipped easily in beside Tom the driver. He leaned over her and slammed the door shut.

"It's only twenty to seven. I have you all very well trained," he said and they all laughed with him as the bus went out into the traffic and headed for home.

Tom was a fine companion. He always answered agreeably and gave long answers if he were in the mood to chat and short ones if he weren't. The silences were companionable. He never talked to the people behind because it distracted him, and he liked the person sitting beside him to tell him if it was all clear on the left as they nosed onto main roads from side roads. Much nicer than the rest of the FitzGeralds up in the craft shop, but then it was silly to expect families to be the same. Look at Billy Burns: he'd buy and sell Mikey a dozen times before breakfast. Nancy Morris – there was something wrong with her, Celia thought. She had a very fixed look, a look that really was fixed on nothing. Celia had seen it in hospital sometimes. Nancy was as different from that laughing Deirdre, her sister in America, as she was different to a Martian. And there was poor Kev, Bart's young brother behind her there in the bus. And possibly she was different to her own brothers and sister. At the thought of her own family her brow darkened. Why would none of them do a thing to help? How had it happened? She *could* write them a round robin: "Dear Maire and Harry and Dan, Sorry to have to tell you but Mam is hitting the bottle worse than ever Dad did. What will we do? Looking forward to hearing by return from New South Wales, Cowley, Oxfordshire, and Detroit, Michigan, Your loving sister, Celia, Dublin." That was the point: Dublin. It was only up the road as far as they were concerned, and she wasn't married, that was even more the point wasn't it? If she had been a wife then none of them would have expected her to abandon that and look after her mother, no matter how near she was. But being a nurse, an

164

angel of mercy, helping the sick and earning her living . . . that would be written off.

And what's more they wouldn't understand, any of them. Maire would write from Woolowogga or wherever she had gone on a course – she was always going to ludicrous places on courses – and she would say it was Blessed to give and Blessed to help. Great. Harry would write from Detroit and say she must do what she thought was best as she was the one on the ground. He would add something about it being a nice tidy living for her, and probably put in a really sensitive bit about not wanting his share out of the family business yet. Dan would write, he might even ring from England: he'd encourage her like mad to go home, he'd say that nursing wasn't a REAL career or anything, and that it was all for the best. His bit of tact might be to hope that now she was known as the landlady of a pub in all but name perhaps Celia might get a few offers of marriage. She was only twenty-six, why had they written her off in three countries? She was their baby sister; she remembered them as big and strong and great fun, but in their letters and their rare appearances they were selfish and they were strangers. And they thought of her as an old maid.

"Do your family drive you mad?" she asked Tom as they had just overtaken a huge dangerous-looking lorry that seemed about to shed everything it had on everything that was near it.

"Oh yes, of course they do," Tom said. "I mean that IS what drives people mad actually, families. It's not strangers in the street or the Bomb or the economy, it's always their relations."

"Or love, I suppose, or lack of it?" Celia was impersonal, interested in talking about ideas. So was Tom. That's why they found their chats easy and never found their long silences threatening.

"Yes, love, but love usually involves some idea of family: you love someone, you want her to be your wife; she won't, you go mad. That's family. You hate your wife, you don't

165

love her any more, you wish she'd fly off on the next space shuttle. That's family."

Celia laughed. "God you'd be great in one of those family counselling places with psychiatrists and all."

"I'm always surprised they never asked me in on one," said Tom, and they didn't speak for another fifty miles.

She was glad to get out and stretch. She had heard of other buses where they got stuck into a pub like this one for a real session and maybe it would be an hour and half before people got back on the road. But Tom Fitzgerald ruled his Lilac Bus very firmly, it was time to visit the Ladies' and a very quick drink. There really wasn't even time for a coffee because they always took such ages to make it in pubs, and indeed in Ryan's of Rathdoon they wouldn't make it at all.

"What'll you have Celia?" Dee had a knack of getting to the counter quickest and an even better knack of getting served. Celia had a bottle of Guinness and a few words. Dee had never changed, not since she was a schoolgirl bursting with pride at her new uniform and coming into the bar to show it off to the Ryans. She had been everywhere to show it off, and everyone had given her a lemonade, or a bar of chocolate or even half a crown. Nobody had anything but good wishes for the doctor's daughter off to her posh convent boarding school. Dr Burke was part of every life and death in Rathdoon, nobody would have a jealous thought about his children and what they had. Who would deserve it more?

She slipped Mikey some ointment that they used up in the hospital to ease bedsores. She didn't want to let Dee see her in case it was thought that she might be trying to improve on the doctor, but Dee would probably never think that in a million years. She was a grand girl with a very infectious laugh, and of course she had the patience of Job that she could talk to Nancy Morris so animatedly about Nancy's boring job and her endless tales of Mr This the consultant and Mr That the consultant. How did Dee put up with it and even look interested and remember their

166

bloody names? The ten minutes were up and they were back in the dark comfort again.

She saw that Tom had tapes in the van; she had never noticed them before.

"Is that a player as well as a wireless?" she asked with interest when they were on the road again.

"Yes, do you wonder I have to guard this vehicle with my life? All I own is tied up in her," he laughed.

"You don't play any, while we're driving?"

"No. I thought about it: everyone would have a different taste and I wouldn't want to inflict my choice on all of you."

"Oh, it would have to be yours, would it?" Celia threw back her head of thick brown hair, laughing at him. "Where's the democratic bit then? Why couldn't everybody choose their own, even bring one each week?"

"Because if I had to hear any more of the Nashville sound than I already hear by accident in my life, I think I'd drive off the road and into the deepest bog that would close over us," he said.

"Let's have no music then," Celia said agreeably and they drove on thinking their own thoughts. Celia was wondering what time she would catch her mother at the most receptive. There must be *some* moments in the day when the unfortunate woman was not suffering from a hangover or withdrawal or had got stuck into it again. There must be a time – late morning maybe – when she could ask Bart to man the place. Not that anyone came in much on a Saturday until it was well into lunchtime. She could always put CLOSED on the door, Father Reilly put closed on the presbytery for heaven's sake when he simply had to have an hour to himself, or maybe it was for some poor divil that couldn't be disturbed. That was it, no more drawing on poor Bart. Anyway he liked to work with Judy Hickey during the daytime when she was home for the weekend. She could put CLOSED on the door for an hour or two, but apart from chaining her mother by both wrists and ankles how was she going to get her to stay and listen to the very unwelcome view that she was now incapable of managing her own pub and must get herself into an alcoholic unit before it was too late? It was gone beyond false promises now, and assurances and little games. Celia had been present when a surgeon told a forty-two year old man last month that he had terminal cancer and had less than two months to live. This is what it felt like again. That sense of dread and half hoping the world would end before you had to say it. Of course it had turned out very oddly in the hospital; they had thought the shock might be intense and that was why Celia was there as part of a back-up. But he had been very quiet, the man, and said, "Is that a fact?" They had stood dumbfounded, Celia, the great surgeon and the anaesthetist. Then the man had said, "And I never went to America. Imagine in my whole life I never saw America. Isn't it ridiculous in this day and age." He had said that several times before he died; it seemed to disturb him more than death itself and leaving his wife and three young children.

Suppose her mother were to say something equally unexpected like that she had been wondering was this what was wrong with her, and she would like to go at once as a voluntary patient to some kind of place that would dry her out. Stop thinking like Alice in Wonderland, Celia told herself sternly. You're a grown-up, it's no use shutting your eyes wishing things would happen.

"There's a lot of rags tied to a bush coming up now. I think it's a holy well or a wishing tree or something," Tom said suddenly. "Maybe we should all get out and tie our shirts to it," Celia said. They passed it, and indeed there were ribbons and what looked like holy pictures pinned onto it.

"I never saw that before, and all the times we must have driven past it," Celia said, looking back over her shoulder. She thought she saw Dee Burke crying, her face was working in that sort of way a child's does to keep off the sobs. But Nancy Morris was yammering on as usual so there couldn't be anything really wrong.

"I never saw it before. Maybe it's a new saint, you know the way they get crossed off like St Philomena, maybe one got put on."

"Why DID St Philomena get crossed off, I wonder?" asked Celia.

"I don't know, maybe they found her out," Tom grinned. "I know my sister Phil was very annoyed indeed at the time, she felt it was an attack of some sort."

"Oh yes, Phil, that would be her name. How is Phil by the way? I haven't seen her for a while."

"She's fine," Tom said shortly.

Celia went back to the tree for conversation. "Are they pagan or are they religious, I wonder?" she said.

"A mixture, I think." He was still short.

Celia thought about the tree. Wouldn't it be great to go there and pray to some saint who had a special interest in drunken mothers, leave an offering or whatever they left and then go home and discover that it had worked. Bart Kennedy would be serving behind the bar and her mother would be sitting with a packed suitcase and face full of optimism.

"See you during the weekend," Tom said with a friendly smile.

She nodded. He had been a bit moody tonight, she thought. She didn't mind their stops and starts normally, in fact she liked it. But tonight she had wanted to talk. Actually what she had really wanted was Emer. You could say anything to Emer and you knew she would think about it but she wouldn't bring it out again on every occasion and ask you how you felt about it. Emer would give you advice but not be annoyed if you didn't take it. "Everyone does what they want to in the end" she would say. She wasn't as specific when it came to knowing how to convince someone else to do the right thing. Or the best thing. Celia had long discussions with her over this. Did you wire the jaws of fat kids who were compulsive eaters? Did you have medical cards for smokers and only those who were certified as

169

having good strong lungs and no trace of emphesema would be allowed to buy a packet – they'd have to show the card first. That would save life wouldn't it? Celia might suggest. Emer would shrug. Temporarily only: the child with the wired jaw would wait eagerly until the contraption was removed; the smoker would get the cigarettes somehow or smoke butts. But then why were drugs banned? Why not just sell heroin by the kilo in Quinnsworth and be done with it. Those who wanted to kill themselves would and there would be no drugs racket and pushers and people having to turn to prostitution or theft for it.

Emer said that drugs were different: they were poison, they killed. You wouldn't sell arsenic or strychnine would you?

What about alcohol: that killed, they had seen enough rotted livers to know that; they could see the slow death around them. Emer said that if Celia felt as strongly as that she shouldn't own a pub, and she should have a temperance banner. Then they would both have a bottle of Guinness and talk about something else. But she was such a comfort; no wonder that her handsome husband and her three giant children were always waiting so eagerly for her to come home from work. And she wasn't a Superwoman either. There were bad times and low times in Emer's life as well as in everyone else's. That's why she was so good to talk to.

"Goodnight," she nodded, and added "Thanks for getting us here." She didn't want to be curt with Tom just because he hadn't been like Emer! That would be unfair.

"Best to the West, as Mikey would say," Tom laughed.

"Don't encourage him – he has enough catchphrases already." She went in the door and knew from the loud greeting that her mother called across the bar that it was going to be a long hard hour and a half. She put her bag in the kitchen, she hung up her jacket and came out quietly to stand beside Bart Kennedy who patted her on the arm as she wordlessly began to pull the pints.

Her mother shouted for two hours when the pub eventually closed. She sat at one of the tables and hurled abuse as Celia methodically emptied the ashtrays and wiped the surfaces. She would NOT be patronised in her own pub, she cried, she would not have Celia coming off the bus and taking over as if she owned the place. Celia did NOT own the place and in fact the place would never be hers. She hoped that Celia knew this. She had made a will with that nice young Mr MacMahon in Mr Green's office, and she had said that after her death the pub should be sold and the money divided equally in four and shared out between Maire and Harry and Dan and Celia. So now. Celia said nothing. She washed the glasses under hot water first, then under cold, then turned them upside down to drain on a plastic grid: that way the air got at them from all angles and dried them without smears.

Her mother had a brandy bottle on the table beside her. Celia made no attempt to touch it. She just moved past her and locked the door. The place was now ready for the next day. She gulped a bit at the thought of the conversation she was going to have in the morning when the closed sign would appear on Ryan's door for the first time since her father's funeral.

"Aren't you going to have the common manners to say goodnight, Miss High and Mighty?" her mother called.

"Goodnight Mam," said Celia as she went up the narrow stairs wearily to the small white bedroom with the iron bed. She lay awake for a while. Long enough to hear her mother stumbling up the stairs and hitting off the chest of drawers on the landing. She must have known it was there: it had been there for thirty-eight years, all her married life.

It was very sunny, too sunny. Celia woke with a jump. The curtains had been pulled back, and there was her mother with a cup of tea.

"I thought you might like this, after your week's work,

and you must have stayed up late last night doing the glasses." The voice was steady enough and the hand wasn't shaking as it passed the tea-cup and saucer.

Celia sat up and rubbed her eyes. "You were with me when I washed the glasses," she said.

"I know, I know, of course," her mother was flustered, she hadn't remembered. "Yes well, naturally, but thanks for ... um ... organising it all the same."

There was no smell of drink but Celia realised that she must have had a cure, maybe a vodka. That's why she was able to cope. She had smartened herself up too, combed her hair and worn a dress with a white collar. Apart from her eyes which looked terrible, Mrs Ryan didn't cut too bad a figure at all.

This might be the time. Celia swung her legs out of the bed, and took a great swig of the tea.

"Thanks Mam. Listen, I wanted to say something to you. I've been trying to get a good time ... "

"I have a kettle on downstairs; I'll come back up to you when I have a minute."

She was gone. There was no kettle on. Celia got up and dressed quickly. She decided against jeans and put on a skirt and blouse and a big wide belt. It made her look more authoritative, more nurse-like in a way. There was no sign of her mother in the kitchen. Where could she have gone? There was a sound of scrubbing out the side entrance, and there was Mrs Ryan on hands and knees with bucket and scrubbing brush working away.

"I was noticing this last night: it's in a very bad way, we mustn't let the place go to rack and ruin around us." She was sweating and puffing. Celia let her at it. She went back into the kitchen and made more tea. Eventually her mother had to come back in.

"There, that's much better," she said.

"Good," said Celia.

"I saw that Nancy Morris, a proper little madam that one. 'Hallo Mrs Ryan' if it suits her, and wouldn't give you the time of day if it didn't. I pretended I didn't hear her. She has her mother scalded coming home every weekend."

"I'm sure," Celia said. Mrs Ryan's jaw dropped.

"Oh not like you. I mean it's grand that you come home, and you're such a help."

"I'm glad you think so this morning. It was a different tune last night," Celia said.

"Oh you wouldn't need to mind me on a Friday night, the place gets so crowded and they're coming at you from all sides. I probably sounded a bit impatient, but didn't I thank you for doing the glasses, didn't I bring you a cup of tea in bed?" She was pleading now, almost like a child.

Celia took the bucket and the brush away from her gently and closed the door behind her. She lulled her to the table with soft talk. She didn't want the woman to bolt from the room.

"Of course you brought me a cup of tea in bed, and I *know* that deep down somewhere you are grateful to me for coming back and helping out, but that's not the point, Mam, not the point at all. You don't remember anything about last night, not from about nine o'clock on, that's what I'd say."

"What are you talking about?"

"You were well gone when I arrived – that was before ten. You fought with a man and said he'd only given you a fiver not a ten. You told young Biddy Brady that you didn't want a whole crowd of her girl friends cluttering up the pub tomorrow – fortunately Bart got us out of that one. You spilled a whole bottle of lime juice and you wouldn't let anyone wipe it up so that the counter was sticky all night. You couldn't find the tin of potato crisps and you told a group who had come here for the golfing that you didn't give a damn whether you found them or not, because they smelled to you like a child's fart. Yes, Mam, that's what you said."

Her mother looked up at her across the table. She showed no signs of getting up to run away. She looked at Celia quite calmly.

"I don't know why you are saying all this," she said.

"Because it happened, Mam." Celia begged her. "Believe me, it all happened, and more and much more other nights."

"And why would you make this up?"

"I didn't. It was like that; it will be like that again tonight, Mam, you're not able to cope. You've had a drink already today, I can see. I'm only telling you for your own good."

"Don't be ridiculous, Celia." She was about to stand up. Celia reached out and held her there. Hard by the wrist.

"I haven't written to the others yet: I didn't want to alarm them, I thought it might pass. I thought it was only weekends when you were under a bit of pressure. Mam, you have to accept it and DO something about it."

"Others?"

"Maura, Harry, Dan."

You're going to write all over the world with these tales?"

"Not if you can help yourself first. Mam, you're drinking far too much, you can't control it. What you're going to have to do is . . . "

"'I'm going to have to do nothing, thank you very much indeed. I may have had one too many sometimes and all right I'll watch that. Now will that satisfy you? Is the interrogation over? Can we get on with the day?"

"PLEASE Mam, listen. Anyone will tell you, will I get Bart in here to tell you what it's been like? Mrs Casey was saying, Billy Burns was saying, they were all saying . . . it's getting too much for you here . . . "

"You were always prudish about drink, Celia, even when your father was alive. You didn't realise that in a bar you have to be sociable and drink with the customers and be pleasant. You're not cut out for a pub the way we were, the way I am. You're too solemn, too sticky for people. That's always been your mistake."

There was no point in putting *Closed* on the door, she

wouldn't talk. The most she would admit was a drop too much on some occasions. She denied all the scenes, she remembered none of the conversations.

People started drifting in around lunchtime. Celia watched her mother accept a small whiskey from Dr Burke who had come in to get some drink to celebrate his son's engagement. Celia wished that Dee's father would lean over the counter to her mother and say "Mrs Ryan, your eyes are all bloodshot and there are big lines under them; for your health's sake you must give up drink." She wished that Father O'Reilly would come down from the presbytery on a home visit and tell her that for the good of her soul she must go and have some treatment and then take the pledge. But doctors and priests didn't interfere enough these days maybe.

The phone box was way at the end of the bar, quiet and discreet. No wonder half of Rathdoon made their calls from there rather than beside the eager ears of the post office people.

Emer was just getting the lunch. They had all been to the pictures last night on her winnings and tonight they might go again. Videos had gone through the roof: even the kids realised that a video was out of the question.

"What will I do with her?" Celia asked.

"She doesn't admit it to herself?"

"No. I gave her chapter and verse – what she said, what she spilled and broke, who she insulted. Not a word does she believe."

"And you can't get support troops in."

"Not really. Bart will be too polite and anyone else would be embarrassed."

"I suppose you'll have to wait."

"I can't wait any more and neither can she. It's terrible. There MUST be some way. How do people come to see things? Is there no way of hurrying it up?"

"Well, I did hear of a man who signed himself in for treatment the moment he saw himself on a video of his

175

daughter's wedding. He had no idea that he was so bad until . . . "

"That's it. Thanks Emer."

"WHAT? You're going to turn a video on your mother in Rathdoon? Have sense."

"I'll tell you about it on Monday." Celia was gone.

Mrs Fitzgerald invited her in. Yes, Tom was here. They were having a pot of coffee – would Celia join them? She felt they had been having a chat, that she shouldn't interrupt. She said she'd only be a minute. Yes he did have a small cassette recorder, and yes a blank tape . . . or a tape that she could record over. What was it – something from the radio? No, OK, it didn't matter. Look, it was easy to work. No, he didn't mind being without it until they were on the bus again. He was puzzled, but he didn't ask any more. She took it back to the pub.

There was so much clutter under the pub counter that the small tape recorder passed unnoticed.

Celia used it judiciously, half an hour on one side and half an hour on the other.

She even moved it out in her hand to be closer to her mother when the solo singing began and Mrs Ryan was screaming a tuneless racy version of a song which she hardly knew. She let it play for the insults to Bart Kennedy and for the bad language.

At one stage Tom Fitzgerald came into the bar, he saw his recorder and said "Is that fair?"

"You have your standards, I'll have mine," she snapped, and then much more wearily: "She doesn't know, you see, she really doesn't know."

"She's not going to like it," he said.

"No."

"When will you . . . ?"

"Tomorrow morning, I'd say."

"I'll come in around lunch and pick up the pieces," he smiled. He had a very, very nice smile.

Her mother sat stonily through the first few minutes. She railed with anger at the arguments and the bad language. Then she decided it was a fake and when she heard her maudlin conversation about what a great man her husband had been, tears of shame came into her eyes.

She folded her hands on her lap and sat like some timid employee waiting to be fired.

Out of the little tape recorder came the voice of Mrs Ryan as it called on Biddy Brady's engagement party to shut up and let HER sing. Tears fell from her closed eyes as the voice came out in its drunken, tuneless wail. Celia started to turn it off.

"Leave it," her mother said.

There was a long silence.

"Yes," said Mrs Ryan, "I see."

"If you wanted to, we could say you had pneumonia or that you were off to see Dan in Cowley. That would sort of cover it up."

"There'd be no point in covering it up. I mean, it's only more lies isn't it? Might as well say what it is." Her face was bleak.

"Sure you're half way there, Mam, if that's the way you think – you're nearly better," said Celia, leaning across the small dark tape recorder to hold her mother's hand.

Tom

He remembered the day he painted the Lilac Bus. It had been a sort of dirty beige before, and there was an exhilaration about pointing the spray can at it and seeing it change before his eyes. His mother had been appalled. It looked so vulgar and called attention to itself. That was about the worst crime in her book – attracting attention. The good went by unnoticed and understated; the bad were flashy and loud and painted their vans this silly mauve colour. Tom's father just shrugged. What could you expect? he asked his wife in a tone that meant the one thing he really didn't expect was an answer. Tom's father hardly ever spoke *to* Tom anymore: he spoke about him, in his hearing.

"I suppose that boy believes that money grows on trees . . . that boy thinks we should have the itinerants living in our garden . . . that boy feels that work is beneath him." Sometimes Tom answered; sometimes he let it pass. It didn't really matter which he did. His father's mind was fixed anyway: that boy was a waster, a left-wing long-haired layabout. A purple minibus was only what you'd expect.

It wasn't what Tom expected. He just decided one day on a whim, one day when the washing didn't seem to be making the van look any better. And he LOVED it now that it was lilac-coloured: it had much more personality and more life. That was when he decided to go into the transport business. It wasn't *exactly* legal of course, but suppose they did have

181

an accident: an insurance company would have a hard time proving that he wasn't driving seven friends home for the weekend. No money was ever seen to change hands in Dublin. He didn't stand at the door selling tickets as the bigger bus people did. They were the same people all the time, give or take one or two a month. It wasn't a moneyspinner or anything; he paid for his petrol and cigarettes out of it, that was all. But it did mean he could smoke as much as he liked and he could come home every weekend to Rathdoon, which was what he wanted to do. The Lilac Bus had made all this possible.

Tom knew all about his passengers' lives in Rathdoon, but very little about what they did in Dublin. He had thought of finding out where they all lived and dropping them home rather than leaving them in the city centre at ten o'clock on a Sunday night but something told him that they might prefer the anonymity of the city to be kept absolute; they mightn't want the others to see their digs or their rooming houses or their set-up. More than once Tom had noticed a small fair-haired fellow in tinted glasses in a car parked near where the bus began and ended its weekend run. He would wave eagerly to Rupert Green. Now Rupert very clearly might not want that known. It was only because Tom had X-ray eyes that he had noticed the car. And his eyes had sometimes caught Dee Burke slipping into a big car and the arms of an older man. The older man had never been mentioned by Dee or by anyone in Rathdoon, so it was safe to assume that he was a secret older man not a legit one. No amount of watching or guessing could tell him what young Kev Kennedy was so afraid of. It hadn't always been that way: he used to be a very nice young fellow, and the only one of that family to get up from the kitchen table and leave their father and their slices of bread and ham and the radio on from Goodmorning to Closedown. But for the past year or so he was in bits.

Celia lived in a nurses' house. Six of them shared a place which was apparently highly successful. They had two television sets, a washing machine and an ironing board always in position in the back room. Celia had said there was never a cross word exchanged in that house – it was an ideal way to live until they married and had homes of their own. Nancy Morris shared a flat with that nice bouncy Mairead Hely; how Mairead stuck it was a mystery. He had met her one night at a party and she told him that Nancy's newest trick was to watch out for food tastings in supermarkets and rush in before they closed and have paper cups of soup or bits of cheese on toothpicks and then to come home triumphantly to the flat and say "I've had my supper." That night, and it was about three months back, Mairead had said that she was gathering up her courage to ask Nancy to leave, but she couldn't have gathered it yet. Poor Mikey was so nice Tom would have driven him home willingly, but he just laughed and walked to a bus stop with the never failing sense of good humour that was so hard to take. Judy Hickey took a bus the same direction and Tom often saw them talking together as he turned the Lilac Bus and drove off home.

None of them knew where his home was, that was certain. Long ago he had developed a gift for not answering direct questions so skilfully that people thought they had been given some kind of answer but didn't ask again. When Nancy Morris had asked him how much he paid a week for his flat, he said it was hard to work out, and that was that from Miss Morris. Rupert once asked him which side of the city did he live, and Tom had said that he was sure Rupert must know the trends in what people wanted. He often thought that it was interesting looking at people in cinema queues for example and wondering where they lived; he suposed that if he were working in an auctioneer's like Rupert, he'd think it even more interesting. Rupert agreed and had talked cheerfully about the unexpected ambitions of a lot of the people who came into his office. He never again asked Tom where he lived, and he didn't sound as if he had been rebuffed.

Dee Burke had told him that her brother was living in sin and wasn't it monstrous that boys could get away with it and girls still couldn't really. She had asked him suddenly, "Maybe you live in sin too. Do you?" "I don't know," he had said, "I'm very confused about sin; they never explained it properly at our school, what about yours?" Dee had said gloomily that they never stopped explaining it at her school and they were all so sick of it by the time they left, they had hardly the energy to commit any, which might have been the aim all along. But she still didn't find out what his lifestyle was. And down in Rathdoon he was spoken of as the one Fitzgerald boy that didn't join the family firm, the only one who didn't want to build an empire. He did something arty up in Dublin. But in any gathering of three if his name came up there would be three different theories on what he did. It gave the lie to the obsession with gossip that small towns were meant to have automatically, Tom thought. There was Dee with her older chap, Rupert with his boy friend, Kev with his gambling debts or whatever it was and no one back home knew a thing about any of them. Or about Tom. In Rathdoon only one person knew how Tom lived and why: his mother.

Nobody would guess that in a million years. His mother tutted with the best, sighed over his clothes and bus – genuine sighs. She really would have preferred a nice inconspicuous bus and more conservative clothes: nice neutral colours, stone-coloured trousers and brown jackets like her other sons wore. Suits, white shirts, restrained ties for Mass on Sunday. When his father railed about the young generation in general and That Boy in particular Tom's mother was gentle in her reproach. Anyone looking on might have thought she agreed with her husband. Who could have known that Tom was her lifeline?

She was a handsome woman, Peg Fitzgerald. Fifty-two, very well groomed; you never saw a hair out of place on Mrs Fitzgerald. She wore knitted suits, in lilacs or dark green, and a good brooch to tone in with whatever colour it was. In summer she wore lighter linen suits but they were the same colours and she had looked the same for years. She had three perms a year in the big town, and she had a shampoo and set every Friday morning of her life with little Sheila O'Reilly, the niece of the Parish Priest. Sheila didn't do much business in Rathdoon, but she never seemed to mind. She was always cheerful and if there were no heads of hair to deal with she did knitting instead and made a little out of that as a sideline. She wished there were more regular customers like Mrs Fitzgerald, who wanted their hair done the same way at the same time every week.

Mrs Fitzgerald was in the shop every day. The craft shop side of it had been her idea and was very successful. Any time a tour bus stopped there was a heavy electronic buzzing of tills in the Fitzgerald Craft Centre. There were shawls, lengths of tweed, pottery – a very wide range to suit all tastes. It was also the place where the whole of Rathdoon bought birthday presents for each other. Peg had difficulty persuading the family that it was a good idea, but now they looked at her with a new respect. She was a firm believer too that things should be kept in the family. When the boys married it was understood that their wives would work there. In fact one potential daughter-in-law broke off the engagement because she said all she would get from the marriage contract was to be an unpaid shop worker instead of the bank official that she was. Tom had thought that showed some spirit but the rest of the family including the jilted brother all combined in thinking they had a lucky escape if that was going to be her attitude.

From the outset Tom had said he wouldn't work in the shop; there had been no fight about it, only scorn. He had said reasonably he thought that it was better for his three brothers and two sisters if they *knew* from the word go that he would not be joining them. Then they could make their own plans without any question marks hanging over him. He decided this as long ago as his school days. But they had thought it was like being an engine driver and took no notice. What he would like to do was go to Dublin and live. Just live, not necessarily DO anything until he found something he'd like to do, and then maybe America or Paris or Greece. If you didn't have high living standards and want a comfortable house and a lot of possessions and rich food you could live very cheaply. They had thought it was a phase.

He had got a lot of honours in his Leaving, much more than the brothers who were well on their way to being merchant princes: expanding to other towns, opening new branches, developing their mother's much mocked idea of a craft shop in other centres all over the west. Tom was pronounced brighter than any of them by the masters who had taught all the Fitzgeralds, but he was adamant and very firm for an eighteen year old. He had all these bits of paper to prove he was educated, now could he get on with his own life? He thanked his father as warmly as he could for the grudging offer of university fees, but still it was no. All he wanted was to be left alone. He wouldn't go to the bad, he would come home regularly if they liked so that they could see him and satisfy themselves that he was still normal. He would hitch. He would sign on for the dole each week, and NO that would not be an almighty disgrace in Dublin. Who would see him or know him for God's sake, and NO it was not unfair, that's what people did nowadays: the rich paid taxes and there was at least bread and a roof for those who weren't rich. We didn't let them die in the streets today, stepping over them saying wasn't it a pity they didn't have the get up and go to find a good job and earn their living. NO, he did not intend to stay on national assistance for ever. And, YES, he was very grateful for the offer of a place in the family firm but we only had one life and that was not how he was going to spend his.

And wasn't it lucky that this is what he had decided to do? What on earth would have happened if he hadn't been around?

It had been very easy to live cheaply in Dublin. For a

while he lived with a young couple who gave him a bed and some food; they didn't have all that much themselves. He taught their children every evening, two nice bright little boys. He went over everything they had done at school and helped them with their homework. But he didn't really like it because he felt they should be out playing instead of doing more and yet more. They knew enough, he kept telling their worried young parents, they're fine: don't pack their heads with facts and more and more. The parents didn't understand. Surely the best thing was to get a good start, to be in there with a better chance than the others? But they were only ten and nine, it was YEARS before they would need to be in there fighting the others for places and points and positions. No, the pale mother and father hadn't got on in their lives because they had nobody to guide them; they weren't going to let the same thing happen to the children. He left them amicably. He worked as a gardener for an old lady and slept in her garden shed for a year without her knowing. She never knew in the end, and he had moved his camp bed and primus stove long before the funeral so nobody ever knew.

He worked in a night club as a sort of bouncer. He was slim and not the typical bouncer material but he had a look in his eye that was as important as muscle. His boss who was one of the sharpest men in Dublin was anxious to keep him on, promote him even, but it wasn't the life Tom wanted. He left again amicably and before he left he asked the sharp boss what was good about him. He'd like to know just for his own record. The Boss said he owed him no explanation if he was leaving but OK, Tom had a look in his eye that said he would go the distance. People didn't mess with him. Tom liked this reference just as he had liked the old lady saying he was a loving sort of gardener, and the nine year old boy saying that he made Latin so much more interesting than they did at school because there was none of this treating it as a language – more as a puzzle really. But these were not written references. Each new job had to be found on charm or effort; each time he had to go in cold.

He had a summer in Greeece driving a minibus, not unlike the lilac bus, over mountainy roads, taking holidaymakers to and from airport and hotels. He had a summer in America working at a children's camp with seventy discontented youngsters who would all rather have been at home. He had a winter in Amsterdam working in a souvenir shop. He had a funny three months in London working in market surveys – going up to people on the street with a clipboard and asking them questions. He had a different kind of three months in London working as a hospital orderly; he found it harrowing, and his respect for nurses went way, way up. He had been on the point of telling Celia about those months, several times, but he never told stories about what he had done – it led to questions and questions often needed answers.

He didn't think of himself as a drifter, and yet for nine years, since he had left school, he had done nothing with any purpose or any permanence. Still, he wouldn't have missed any of it, not even those strange days in the hospital pushing elderly frightened people on trolleys through crowds, all speaking different languages, all the nationalities under the sun working in the hospital and coming in as patients. And now it meant that he could look after Phil, for he had no job to give up, no real lifestyle to interrupt.

Phil was the nicest in his family, there was no doubt about it. They all agreed on that, just as they all agreed that Tom was the oddest and the most difficult. Phil was the nearest to him in age: she was almost a year to the day older than he was. All the six Fitzgeralds arrived within seven years, and then the young Peg stopped producing a new baby every season. There were pictures of them all when they were toddlers and Tom always thought it looked like a nursery school rather than one family. But his mother had always said it was great to get it all over at once. You had a period when they all seemed to be unmanageable and then suddenly they had all grown up. Anyway Phil had always been his special friend, and in the great sixteen and seventeen year old arguments about Tom not joining the firm Phil had been very supportive. She had been in the big town seventeen miles from Rathdoon learning shorthand and typing at the time, it had been agreed that she should work in the office rather than the shop. But she used to come home at weekends during her commercial course and encourage Tom to live his own life. She had a big round face, Phil had, and she was always laughing. Years ago he remembered her dancing with Red Kennedy and getting a lecture that the Kennedys were perfectly nice, not a thing wrong with them, but she should set her sights a little higher. Phil had said indignantly that she wasn't setting her sights at Red Kennedy or at anyone, she was just dancing with him, but there had still been a lot of head shaking.

Phil was what they called a fine girl in Rathdoon, Mrs Fitzgerald used to say that she'd slim down when the time came. Hadn't Anna, the eldest of the family had a lot of puppy fat too. But Mrs Fitzgerald always thought that there was some kind of law which said that a girl needed to be nice and slim and attractive when she was thinking of choosing a husband and settling down. It was just the way things were. But Phil didn't notice some magical trick of nature: she remained plump and round-faced and never developed the hollow cheeks and small waist which were generally agreed to have been important when her sister Anna attracted and married the very suitable Dominic whose family made tweeds.

Tom had never thought she was too fat; he had told her that several times when he came home for the weekend. He said she must be losing her marbles to think she was a fatty, and cracked to think that she had no friends because of this.

"Who are my friends then? List them," she had cried.

Tom couldn't, but he said he couldn't list any friends of his family for God's sake, he was away, he didn't live here. She MUST have friends. No, she claimed, she didn't. That was when meaning to be helpful he had suggested this

Singles type of holiday. Everyone went on their own, there were no loving couples to start out with but hopefully plenty of them on the way back. Phil had read the brochure eagerly and decided that she should go on it.

"Don't tell anyone it's a singles special," her mother had advised. "It looks a little pathetic. Say it's an ordinary holiday in Spain."

Tom never knew quite what happened, but it wasn't a success. Phil said that Spain was all right, and the weather had been fair, but nothing else. Later, much later, he heard that all the girls except Phil had been topless on the beaches, that almost everyone on the group charter had enjoyed a close physical relationship with one or more other people on the same group charter – again, everyone except Phil – and that there was no question of meeting people and dancing with them and talking to them and getting to know them. This was apparently a much more swinging type of holiday than some singles outings, and swinging meant going to bed with people, people who were total strangers.

But Tom didn't know all this at the time. Phil had come back quiet and non-communicative. He noticed shortly after this that she seemed to have lost weight, but he didn't say anything, because he had been the one to tell her that weight wasn't important. If he admired her now, she would believe that he had only been kind before. Phil didn't go to the dance any more and she didn't go out to the sea with a crowd of girls like she used to. But to be honest, he didn't notice these things at the time; it was only afterwards he remembered it all.

Phil had come to Dublin on one of the day excursions by train from the town. It was a bit of a killer: the train left at 9 a.m., you were in Dublin at noon and then the train back was at 6 p.m. So it was some concentrated shopping before they all fell back with sore feet and bulging parcels to go home again that night. Phil always rang Tom if she went on one of these marathons, and he came to meet her at the station in his minibus which was a dirty beige in those days.

She looked very pale, and said that she had been having really terrible pains like a knife on the train, so bad that the people in her carriage said she should go to a hospital or a doctor since she had been crying out with the sharpness of them. Tom looked concerned and just at that moment she bent over again doubled up with pain and letting out a long low scream, so his mind was made up. He drove her to the out-patients of a hospital. He was quiet and firm. He got her seen before anyone by saying it was an emergency. As her brother, he signed the permission to operate for a burst appendix and he was there when she woke up to tell her that it had all been fine, and it was over and all she had to do now was to rest. Her troubled face smiled at him sadly. Their mother came up the next day with a suitcase of things that Phil would need, a lot of reassurance, sighs of how good God was to let it all happen when Tom was there to take charge, and messages of love, boxes of chocolates, bottles of lavender water from the rest of the family.

She was recovering quite well Tom thought. Well, her strength was coming back quickly and he was very startled when one of the nurses said she would like to talk to him about his sister. Privately. She had made a report to the people who should know already, like the matron and the surgeon who had operated, but this was now something that must be taken further, through Miss Fitgerald's own doctor perhaps.

He was alarmed. The nurse spoke reprovingly, as if poor Phil had been caught stealing in the wards. What was it? Well, the nurse had noticed she spent a long time at the lavatory, and she had asked her about constipation or diarrhoea. Apparently neither, but she was still in there for a considerable time, so the nurse had listened at the door. Tom felt his heart beating: what horror was he going to be told?

It was what the nurse had suspected. Vomiting, retching. Two or three times a day.

"What's causing it?" Tom cried. He had no idea what

the tone of shock was all about. Why wasn't he being told this by a doctor?

"She's doing it herself," the nurse said. "Eating chocolates, biscuits, banana, slices of bread and butter. You should have seen the papers and the empty boxes. And then vomiting it all up."

"But why on earth would she do that?"

"It's called Bulimia; it's like anorexia nervosa – you know, where people starve themselves to death if they can. It's a form of it. They binge and gorge and then they make themselves sick to get rid of the food they've eaten."

"Phil does this?"

"Yes, she's been doing it for some time."

"And did this cause her appendix to burst?"

"Oh no, not at all, that was something totally unconnected. But maybe lucky in a way. Because at least now you know and the family will know and help her try to fight it."

"Can't you just tell her to stop. Can't we all tell her it's . . . it's revolting – it's so senseless."

'Oh no, that's not the way, that's not what they'll say at all when she goes in."

"Goes in where?"

"To a pyschiatric hospital. It's a mental condition, you know, it's got nothing to do with us."

The nurse wasn't quite correct. It did have a little to do with them because Phil was admitted to the psychiatric wing of that same hospital and there was a medical side to her treatment as well as all the therapy and group discussions on the psychiatric side. She had been very relieved at the beginning to know that other people did the same thing. She thought she was the only person in the world who had ever done it, and she felt a great burden of guilt taken off her shoulders. She never felt guilty about the self-induced vomiting: she said it was the easiest thing in the world. If you just put your finger in the right place down your throat it happened automatically. But she did feel guilty about stuffing herself with the food. Especially eating in a lavatory – that was the thing she felt shameful about. She wasn't ready at all to talk about why she did it. Tom was told that she would undoubtedly do it again and again before she was cured. Before she came back to reality and accepted that she was perfectly fine as she was. The help and support of a family at a time like this was crucial. If Phil was to see that she was a person of high esteem in her own family that would go a very long way towards helping her have a good image of herself again. The family, yes. But Lord God the Fitzgerald family. At this time.

Poor Phil couldn't have picked a worse time to call on them, Tom thought grimly. It was the very period that the newspapers were full of the case about the armed raid on the post office in Cork and the subsequent conviction and sentencing of Teddy Fitzgerald their cousin, who had worked in the business with the family. That had been a heavy cross. Then there was the infidelity of Dominic, the highly suitable husband of Anna the eldest. There had been many a tale of a relationship and finally the birth of a child which Dominic grudgingly acknowledged as his, even though it was born not to his wife but to one of the most unsuitable women in the west of Ireland, tinkers who had settled down and according to Mrs Peg Fitzgerald the only thing worse than a tinker on the road was a tinker who had settled down. So there was that disgrace. And there had been a few other things too, none of them as shocking but all of them adding up to a general family anxiety. It was the wrong time to hear that a member of the family was now entering on to a long period of psychiatric treatment and would need their support.

Mrs Fitzgerald made her point of view absolutely clear. There would be no talk about Phil whatsoever. This was final. Phil had recovered from her burst appendix, she had been convalescing, she had been visiting friends, she would come back shortly. Meanwhile they would get a temporary girl for the office. Mrs Fitzgerald would go to Dublin once a month to give this support that the hospital said it needed, Tom would go to see her as often as he could, and that was it. It would not be discussed; they had quite enough problems already without adding this one. And what would it do to Phil's chances of getting a husband if it was widely known she had been in a mental institution? No more arguments.

Tom was sure that this was not what the doctors meant by family support: hushing it all up, making it into a greater shame than Phil already felt it was. He was certain that his mother's monthly visits – full of assurances that nobody knew, no one suspected, people had been fooled and hoodwinked, cover stories had been invented – were all the worst thing for his sister who would listen with stricken face and apologise for all the trouble she had caused. Sometimes his mother would reach out awkwardly and take Phil's hand.

"We love you . . . um . . . very much. You are much loved, Phil." Then she would draw her hand back, embarrassed. She had been told by the psychiatrist that this was a good line to emphasise, but she recited it as if it were learned by heart. They were not a demonstrative family, they had never hugged or kissed each other. It was hard for his mother to reach out and say that to Phil. And bewildering for Phil to hear it, just before her mother gathered her gloves and handbag and started to leave.

He went to see Phil every day, every single day and he telephoned her on each Saturday and Sunday. His mother said that she would telephone except that there was nothing to say, but Tom found things. After all he knew her much better: they had been meeting each other constantly, and he was able to pick from a variety of things to say. He never felt as if he were talking to someone who wasn't well. He didn't talk down to her, he would never apologise profusely if he hadn't been able to ring or visit, just briefly. He wouldn't let on that he thought his presence was essential to her. He treated her as if she were as sane as he was.

They talked about childhood a lot. Tom remembered his as happy enough, too much talk about the business, a bit too much of covering over and not letting the neighbours know this or that, and keeping our business to ourselves. Phil remembered it quite differently. She remembered that they were always laughing, and that they had all been sitting round the table together talking to each other, though Tom said they couldn't have been. There would have to have been either their mother or their father in the shop. Phil remembered them going on great outings to the sea and picnics; Tom said he honestly could only remember one. Phil said they used to play games like I Spy and the Minister's Cat, and Sardines, where one person had to hide and when you found them you squeezed in like a sardine beside them. Tom said that was only at parties. But they didn't fight over the memories; they talked them over like an old film that you'd seen years ago and everyone could remember bits of, but nobody could remember all of.

They talked about boyfriends and girlfriends and sex. Tom wasn't surprised to hear that she was a virgin, and she wasn't surprised to hear that he was not. They talked easily and without guilt, sometimes for hours in the day room or in the garden, sometimes just for short times because Phil was silent and withdrawn, or because Tom had to work. He was working in an auction showroom these days, helping to carry furniture in and out, put lot numbers on things and write them up in a catalogue. He had been thinking of moving on, but the hours suited him and it was near the hospital so that he could come and go easily. One of the other patients asked if Tom was her boyfriend. She had laughed uneasily and said she never had a boyfriend. The other girl had shrugged and said she was probably as well off: they were a barrel full of trouble that's all they were. She hadn't assumed for a moment that Phil COULDN'T have a boyfriend. It made Phil feel a lot more cheerful. She asked Tom what kind of girls he liked, and he said unusual ones, not people who talked about houses and engagement rings and the Future. He had a very nice girlfriend once but unfortunately she met a really dull guy and he offered her all this other business – security, respectability – and she came and told Tom straight out she was going to take it. Phil had been very sympathetic.

"You never told us any of this," she said.

"True, but you never told us that you half fancied Billy Burns, even though he was a married man," he said laughing.

"You dragged that out of me" she laughed too. He thought it was all too slow, she MUST be better now.

He said this more than once to the psychiatrist and was depressed to hear that Phil was still not happy, still not at ease with herself and sure of her place in the world. They all thanked Tom for coming and said he was invaluable. Not only in his own visits but in the lifeline he offered back to Rathdoon. She never minded his going back home at weekends. In fact she liked it because it brought her closer to the family and because he always brought back news of them all and, better still, a cheerful letter from her mother.

Every Saturday morning he forced his mother to write her a letter. He literally sat there while she wrote. He wouldn't accept that she had nothing to write about, and he refused to let her wriggle out of it.

"Do you think I'd be doing this, do you think I'd sit here every Saturday morning unless it was important?" he had shouted. "She is desperate to know that we are fond of her, and that her place is here; she won't be ABLE to come back unless she knows this."

"But of course it's here, naturally we want her back. For heaven's sake, Tom, you're making a big drama out of it all."

"It is a big drama. Phil is in a psychiatric hospital and mainly because we can't let her know that she is important here."

"Your father and I think that's all mumbo jumbo. She was never made to feel anything but important; we treated her with great respect, people loved having her in the office. She was always so cheerful, and she knew everyone's names: wasn't she the life and soul of that place?"

"Write it. Write it down on paper," he would order.

"I'd feel stupid saying that to Phil. It's silly, it's treating her as if she's not all there. She'll know I'm only acting."

"But you said you meant it, a minute ago."

'Yes, of course I mean it, but it's not something you say, not something you write down."

"Since you're not there to say it, you have to write it. Since you won't let her come home and be treated in the town where you'd only be seventeen miles away, where you could see her every day, then you're going to have to write it. Otherwise how is she to know, how in God's earth can she KNOW that she's important here?"

"It's not that I won't let her come back here. It's for her own good, to keep things quiet, to keep our business to ourselves." He had heard it so often, maybe he would hear it for ever. Perhaps Phil would never get better.

He was in the middle of yet another Saturday confrontation when Celia Ryan came in. He was surprised to see her, and in a way relieved. His mother had been very hard to pin down today. She had escaped him in the morning by saying she was needed in the shop, and it was only when he brought her a cup of coffee and a writing pad that he could get her to listen. She had been going through one of her Phil-must-pull-herself-together phases. Tom felt a mad urge to ask Celia to sit down and explain to his mother her own first-hand knowledge of Anorexia and Bulimia, mentioning casually that Phil was in a psychiatric ward with the latter. His mother would probably fall senseless to the ground if he were to tell the family disgrace to Mrs Ryan's daughter. The temptation had only been a flicker.

Celia wanted a loan of his tape recorder, of all things,

and a blank cassette. She wanted to record something. She seemed flustered. She didn't tell him what she wanted it for, but then he rarely told people anything, whether they asked him or not, so he couldn't fault her there. She said she'd give it to him on the bus.

"Terrible time she has with that mother of hers," Mrs Fitzgerald said.

Tom nodded. He thought he didn't have a great time with his own mother but it was not in him to say it; he just wanted the letter to give to Phil on Monday.

"She'll probably marry Bart Kennedy, and they can keep an eye on the place that way," Tom said.

"Bart Kennedy? Not at all. Sure nobody will marry Bart Kennedy, he's not the type that marries." Mrs Fitzgerald was positive.

"Bart, a fairy? Go on out of that."

"No, I don't mean that or anything like it. He's just not the kind of man who marries, you must see that. Maybe men don't notice these things: women do. Red Kennedy now, he'll be married within the year I'd say, I hear he's courting. But Bart – not at all."

"I thought that's what she came home for," Tom said.

"She comes home to stop that place going down the drain, that's all."

"Really?" Tom felt pleased. He didn't know why but he felt a sense of relief.

He went into the pub that night and discovered why she had wanted the tape recorder. It seemed a bit sneaky somehow. Like taking advantage of the poor woman who was slobbering and messing around behind her own bar. Even more humiliating was the thought that Mrs Ryan's daughter was recording the tuneless singing.

"She doesn't know, she really doesn't know," Celia said as an explanation when he had asked her was it fair. He imagined Celia trying to tell her mother about the excesses of the night before and Mrs Ryan brushing it away with that busines-like cheerful manner she had when sober. It wasn't the kind of thing anyone else would say to her so she would be bound to believe that Celia was making it up at worst or at the very least exaggerating it.

"I'll come round tomorrow and pick up the pieces," he said. She smiled back at him, a warm grateful smile. He looked at Bart Kennedy. Bart was pulling pints and laughing with the lads – he and Celia didn't have eyes for each other at all. Tom must have been mad to have thought it in the first place.

There were no pieces to pick up next day. Celia's mother had taken it very well. She was sitting in the back room while Celia and Bart dealt with the Sunday lunchtime trade.

"She's coming to Dublin. I thought it would be easier. I'd be able to get to see her."

"When?"

"Tomorrow. I won't come back on the bus tonight. I'll wait and go with her. I've a great friend, a nurse in Dublin – she'll work for me tomorrow even though it's meant to be her day off."

"Does she live in your harem of nurses?"

"Emer? Not at all: she's a respectable married woman with a family."

"Would you work if you were married?"

"Bloody sure I would. Catch me giving up a job to cook meals and clean a house for a man. Anyway everyone has to nowadays. How would you have any life at all if you didn't? And nursing's fine, I'd hate to lose it."

"How long will it be . . . " he nodded towards the back room where Mrs Ryan sat waiting in a chair.

"I don't know. It depends on her – you know, if she wants to."

"Doesn't it depend on her family too, and support?"

"Well there's only me; she can't have the beauties in Australia and Detroit and England, so she'll have to make do with me."

"My sister Phil isn't well, she's got the same problem,"

he said suddenly.

"I never knew Phil had a drink problem." She said it without censure or shock.

"No, not that, I meant she has the same problem: she only has me in Dublin. She's got an anorexic thing, you know, but she does eat and makes herself vomit."

"She's a better chance with that; so many of the anorexics die, it's desperate to see them, little wizened monkeys, and they think that this is the best way to be. But bulimia is very stressful, poor Phil. Isn't that very bad luck."

He looked at her gratefully. "Will they be any help, the ones who've gone away?"

"I shouldn't think so, will yours?"

"No. I'm beginning to realise it now. I kept thinking I could change them, but it's all head in the sand, pretend it isn't happening, don't tell anyone."

"In time, in their time maybe. Not yours." She was very gentle.

"Well they'll have to make do with us then," he said, "your half mad Ma and my half mad sister."

"Aren't they lucky they've got us," said Celia Ryan and laughed like a peal of bells.

"I'll miss you going back on the bus tonight," he said.

"Well maybe you might come and console me when I've got my mother in. And if it would be any help I could come and see Phil with you, if you'd like it, that is?"

"I'd like it a lot," said Tom Fitzgerald.

VICTORIA LINE,
CENTRAL LINE

CONTENTS

Victoria Line

Central Line

To Gordon with all my love

VICTORIA LINE

Tottenham Hale

Amy watched six taxis avoid her and go deliberately towards other people. Then she began to realise she was suffering from advanced paranoia and that she had better cut her losses and take the tube home. She was already so late and angry, that the lurching crowded journey couldn't make her much worse. And there was the danger that if she stood much longer on the side of the street being ignored by rush hour taxi drivers she might lose her small remaining ration of sanity. And she needed to hold on to what she had for tonight.

Tonight Ed's sister and her husband were coming to dinner. Tonight, for the first time, she would meet the Big Mama figure in Ed's American family, the one they all bowed to, the one Ed had practically written to for permission to marry Amy. At the time Amy had thought it funny; she had even suggested that her dental reports and photostats of her GCE certificates be sent to New York. But three years later, after a period of watching Ed write his monthly letter to his big sister Bella, she found it less funny. She was never shown these letters and in pique she had opened one before posting it. It was an infantile report on how their life had been progressing since last month: childish details about the floor covering they had bought for the kitchen, aspirations that Ed's salary would be reviewed and upped. Praise for a new dress that Amy had bought, minutiae about a picnic they had had with another couple. It had made Amy uneasy, because it had made Ed seem retarded. It was the kind of letter that a mother might expect from a small son who had gone off to summer camp, not something that a sister in far away America should need or want.

Ed had been euphoric about the visit. It had been planned for over three months. Bella and her husband Blair were coming to London for three days as part of a European tour. They would arrive in the morning; they did not want to be met, they preferred to recover from their jet lag alone in the privacy of a good hotel with a comfortable bedroom and bathroom. Fully refreshed, at seven p.m. they would come and see their beloved Ed and welcome their new sister Amy to the family. Next day there would be a tour to Windsor and an evening at the theatre, with a dinner for the four of them; and on the Saturday morning, Amy might kindly take her new sister Bella shopping, and point out the best places, introduce her to the heads of departments in the better stores. They would have a super girly lunch, and then Bella and Blair would fly out of their lives to Paris.

Normally, on any ordinary Thursday, Amy came home from Harley Street, where she worked as a doctor's receptionist, took off her shoes, put on her slippers, unpacked her shopping, organised a meal, lit the fire and then Ed would arrive home. Their evenings had begun to have a regular pattern. Ed came home tense and tired. Little by little, in front of the fire, he would unwind; little by little he relaxed his grip on the file of papers he had brought back from the office. He would have a sherry, his face would lose its lines; and then he would agree really that there was no point in trying to do too much work in the evening.

With a glass of wine, he would say that the Labourer was worthy of his Hire, and he would expand about people being entitled to their leisure. And afterwards, he would carve away happily at the table he was making, or watch television, or do the crossword with Amy; and she realised happily that she was essential to him, because only her kind of understanding could make him uncoil and regard his life as a happy, unworrying thing.

That was all before the threatened visit of Bella.

For three months now, he hadn't been able to relax. No matter how many blandishments and encouragements Amy put in his way, he seemed stressed and anxious. He was anxious on all fronts: Bella would think it strange that he hadn't moved out of sales into middle management before this; he must show Bella what the structure of the company was, he must prove to her that he had done as much home work and extra work as he could possibly do. Every night his briefcase bulged with sheets of incomprehensible figures. But this wasn't all. He couldn't even concentrate on the office work, he would jump up and spot some defect in the house.

'Heavens, Amy, that curtain rail is missing three hooks, can you fix it darling? Please.'

Sometimes he said: 'Before Bella comes', sometimes he didn't. He didn't even need to, really. Amy knew.

The phone mouthpiece was dirty, the bath-mat had got worn-looking, the window boxes needed repainting, the carving dish had one of its feet twisted the wrong way, the ice trays in the refrigerator were both cracked.

About a dozen times, Amy had reacted and explained that Bella was not coming on a mission of inspection; she hadn't flown the Atlantic to check the curtains, the telephone or the ice trays, she had come to see Ed. But his face just became more worried and he said that he would like things to be right.

So right was everything, that Amy was almost a nervous wreck. The house had been polished within an inch of its life. A magnificent casserole was waiting to be reheated, good wine had been chosen, the table had been set before she left the house that morning. If Bella were to go through the house with a fleet of police specially trained in house-searches, nothing damaging could be revealed. No hidden mounds of rubbish or unsorted paraphernalia in any cupboard. If Bella decided to pull back the sitting-room carpet and examine the underlay she would not be able to find fault.

Magazines and newspapers praising the excellence of this part of North London had been laid around strategically, so that Bella's gaze could be diverted to them should she disapprove of the suburb where Ed and Amy lived. They had even alerted one set of neighbours of the possibility that they might take Bella and Blair over for a drink if they wanted to say 'Hi' to some local people.

Amy had asked for the afternoon off, and she had spent it at the beautician's. She had suggested it herself and Ed's kind, worried face had lit up.

'It's not that you don't look lovely already, Amy,' he had said, afraid to offend her. 'It's just that . . . well, you know, I told Bella you were so groomed, and you know the photographs we send . . . well, we always send ones that make us look good.'

Bella was no oil painting, Amy often thought in rage. She was downright plain; she was tall and rather severe. Her clothes in the pictures that Ed had shown her – photographs taken some years back – had been simple and neat with no concession to fashion. Why, then, had Ed spent nights deliberating over Amy's wardrobe and planning what she should wear? Bella was a teacher, and Blair had some unspecified job in the same school, administration Ed thought, but he didn't really give it any time. None of the family gave Blair any time, he was good to Bella as a consort. He was mute and supportive. That was all that was needed. Bella's four younger brothers owed her everything. They would never have gone through school if she hadn't urged them; they wouldn't have got good jobs, and married suitable women without her wise influence; they would be no-things, hopeless orphans, rudderless, had not Bella persuaded the authorities to let her play Mama at the age of fifteen. Ed had only been five then, he couldn't even remember the mother and father who went into a lake in a drunken motor-accident.

Sometimes Amy wondered about the other sisters-in-law. Wasn't it odd that the sons had all gone so far afield from beloved Bella? There was a brother who had gone to California – that was about as far as you could get from New York State; and one was in Vancouver, and one in Mexico, and Ed was in London. Amy suspected that her three sisters-in-law and she would get along famously. She felt sure they were united in a common hatred of Bella and what she was doing to their men.

But no hint of this escaped in any of the family letters, all of which seemed to be full of Bella. When she had been in bed for three weeks with influenza, letters posted in San José, Vancouver and Mexico City had crashed on to the mat in Tottenham Hale giving the latest bulletins. The three brothers had written to Ed in terms of congratulation and encouragement once the visit of Bella to England had been announced. Bella's own letters were short and terse, and offered little news of her own life, only praise or enquiry about the life of the recipient. The more Amy thought about her, the more she became convinced that Bella was mad.

Now, beautifully coiffed, elegantly made-up, manicured, massaged at a cost which left her seething with rage, Amy stood on the platform waiting for the train to take her home to meet this monster. She got a couple of admiring looks which pleased her; a student pinched her bottom hard, which hurt her and annoyed her; but with confidence gained from parting with the huge sum of money to the beauty salon she said clearly and loudly, 'Please don't do that again,' and everybody looked at the student who went scarlet and got out at the next station. Two men congratulated her and she felt pleased that she was becoming mature.

She worked out that she would have two hours at home before the dreaded Bella arrived. That would be time to do the final fixing of the meal, have a bath and dress. Ed had taken the afternoon off and he was going to have arranged fresh flowers and done any last minute things.

'Won't she think it strange that you took time off work to do housework?' asked Amy.

'If she doesn't ask, we mightn't have to tell her,' he said, giggling like a schoolboy.

Amy told herself firmly that she was not a criminal, she hadn't kidnapped Ed, she had loved him and married him. She looked after him well by any standards, she encouraged him when he felt down but she didn't push him on to impossible heights. This appalling Bella couldn't fault her on her performance, surely? And if that was all true, which it undoubtedly was, then why did she feel so apprehensive? The train gave a great lurch which flung all those still standing into each other's arms. Carefully, they disentangled themselves, with little laughs and apologies; and it was a few moments before they realised that the train had actually stopped and they were not at a station.

'That's all we need,' said a florid-looking man with a briefcase. 'Told the wife I'd be home early, and now we're going to be stuck here all night.'

'Surely not?' asked a woman who looked tired and miserable. She was carrying a heavy bag of shopping. 'There'll be nobody to let the children in,' she added in a worried tone.

Amy began to realize the situation. Every minute here was a minute less in the elaborate count-down for Bella's arrival. If they were fifteen minutes delayed, then she might have to go without a bath. If they were half-an-hour delayed she might have to lose bath, and decorating the trifle. Her mind couldn't take in anything longer than half-an-hour's delay.

Very soon, a uniformed man came through the carriage assuring them that there was no danger, no crisis, but that there had been a fault which must be corrected, and that London Transport apologised infinitely but there would be a delay.

No, he didn't know how long the delay would be.

Yes, he could assure them that there would be no danger.

No, there was no possibility of another train running into them.

Yes, he understood that it was a great inconvenience.

No. There was no way of doing anything more quickly than it was already being done.

Yes, people would be electrocuted and die if they stepped out on to the rails.

'That would appear to be that,' said the florid man. He looked at Amy appreciatively. 'I suppose if we are to be marooned, I'm to be congratulated on finding such an elegant shipmate. I'm Gerald Brent by the way.'

'I'm Amy Baker,' said Amy smiling.

'Mrs Baker, would you care to have a drink with me?' said Gerald Brent. He took a bottle of wine out of his briefcase, a penknife with a corkscrew attachment, and the top of his vacuum flask.

Laughing, Amy accepted.

'I'll drink from the other side,' said Gerald.

The well-known patience and docility of Londoners was beginning to be evident around the compartment. People were settling down to read the *Standard* and the *News*; one man was even having a little sleep of sorts; the worried woman had taken out a woman's magazine and resigned herself.

'Wife's mother is coming to dinner,' said Gerald. 'Terrible old bat. I'm not sorry to miss her, really. Anyway, this wine is much too good for her. Have another drop.'

Amy took the refill and looked at him to see if he was joking.

'You don't really think we'll miss dinner, do you?' she asked.

'Bound to,' said Gerald. He explained what must have gone wrong on the line, how a safety mechanism had worked properly but it would mean that it now had to be rewound by hand. They would have to bring personnel into the tunnel to do this.

'Three or four hours, at least,' he said.

It just wasn't possible, that in the whole of London, one tube line should have a mechanical failure, and she should be on it. It was simply beyond belief that this should happen on this one day out of the thousand or so days she had been married to Ed. It was quite inconceivable that Bella, the big black shadow over all their lives, was going to become like a mushroom cloud of menace and disappointment ever more. Ed would never recover from it. The evening would be a shambles, he would run out into the street looking for her. He might believe that she had left him as some kind of protest about Bella. Amy felt a wave of nausea at the horror of her situation, her face whitened and she looked as if she was going to fall.

'Steady,' said Gerald. 'You mustn't rush that wine, it's very good, full bodied, rich. Here. Sit on this corner.' He moved her to the corner of someone's seat. A London mateyness had now begun to develop and people who would have travelled unspeaking for years became animated and friendly through shared disaster.

Amy told Gerald all about Bella: she told him about opening the letter, she told him that Bella had strong-armed all her brothers into a forced, humble, gratitude. As she told him, it became even clearer to her just how destructive Bella had been; and how in Vancouver, San José and Mexico City, as well as London, four normal men were working like nervous beavers to thank this woman for giving up her youth to rear them. While in fact, Amy realised suddenly, all that Bella had done was give full vent to normal maternal instincts, and got in return praise from authorities and social services. From four brothers she had got a slavish devotion.

Amy and Gerald finished the bottle of wine. Gerald muttered an occasional word of encouragement, and, whenever Amy began to panic at the thought of the ruined evening, he offered reassurance.

'Nonsense, of course he'll know where you are. They'll have it on the local news.'

'Heavens, girl, relax, he'll ring the station, they'll tell him.'

'Good God, woman, Bella doesn't expect you to get a pickaxe and hack your way out!'

He told her that his wife thought he drank too much, and that he did. He had once had an affair with his secretary, which his wife had never discovered, or he *thought* she'd never discovered; but he hadn't enjoyed the intrigue side of it, so he ended it, and his secretary called him a chauvinist bastard in front of three senior partners in the firm. It had been very distressing.

Coffee and sandwiches were brought in from the next station and a real party atmosphere began to develop. There was even a sing-song and by the time they did get out at ten p.m. to the flashing of photographers' light-bulbs and the attention of waiting crowds, Amy was quite unconcerned about Bella and the whole, ruined evening.

It was with a shock that she recognized Bella's features on the platform. Peering into the crowds emerging from the train she looked worried, and anxious for Amy's safety. Behind her were a worried Ed and a worried Blair.

'There she is,' cried Bella running forward, arms out. 'Amy, my little sister, are you all right? Are you hurt? Have you been looked after? My poor Amy, what an ordeal, what a catastrophe, for you!' She released her to let Ed hug her, and Blair hold her in a manful, silent grip.

Gerald watched the scene, and raised his hat before going on his way with a quizzical laugh.

Together the four of them went out of the station. Bella didn't look severe or plain, she looked aglow with interest and concern. She had telephoned the police four times, she had made sure that the train had been in no danger, she had taken first aid things to the station just in case. But now how wonderful, it had all ended happily and they were on the way back to Ed and Amy's lovely home. It had looked so really beautiful when she had arrived, those really cute window boxes, and my, how nice Amy sure kept everything, when she had to telephone she noticed just how fresh and dainty the whole house was. Well now, they could all go back and have that really delicious-looking dinner that she knew was there.

Blair smiled a great stalwart and supportive smile. And Ed looked like a child who got the candy; and Amy wondered why she could have resented Bella coming, she was so pleased that she was here. And even more pleased that she liked everything. Now, Amy would really go out of her way to give her a good shopping trip on the Saturday morning After all, the only important thing was to please Bella.

Seven Sisters

It was very odd that they should live in Seven Sisters, Pat thought for the hundredth time. It seemed too much of a coincidence that anyone who was giving a wife-swapping party, with uninhibited fun and carefree swinging for sophisticated couples, should just happen to live in a place with the group name of Seven Sisters. She had said so to Stuart as well.

'They have to live somewhere,' he said unhelpfully.

Pat had studied the *A to Z*.

'I don't really see why they call it Seven Sisters, it's more Hornsey really,' she complained.

'If they'd called it Hornsey you'd probably say that that was even more suggestive,' said Stuart mildly.

For two weeks before the party, Pat lived on a high level of anxiety. She examined her new set of underwear with a worried frown. It was red and black, the black bits were lace and, in one instance, a rosette. Again and again she tried them on in the bathroom and examined herself critically in the mirror. She looked so very white, and the dark colours made her look almost dead. She wondered whether this would fire all the men with lust, whether they would be driven insane by the combination of dead white skin, red silk and black lace, or whether one of the women would take her aside and advise her to use a fake tan lotion. The awful thing was that there was no one to ask. Even if she were to write to this appalling magazine where Stuart had first seen the article about wife-swapping and had replied to one of the box numbers, she still wouldn't get a reply in time.

Over and over she rehearsed what she would say:
'Hallo, *lovely* of you to ask us . . . what a super house.'
No, she couldn't tell this terrifying harlot who owned the
house in Seven Sisters that it was lovely of her to have
invited Pat and Stuart, since Pat and Stuart had in their
corrupt and pleasure-seeking way told the Seven Sisters
lot that they wanted to come and take off their clothes to
go to bed with a load of strangers. The more she reminded herself that this is what they had arranged to do,
the more faint and foolish she felt.

Even though she tried to put it from her mind, she
wondered if there would be time for any conversation
before they got down to action. Would she find herself
stark naked in a corner talking to some other naked
housewife about the children's drama group or the new
supermarket? Would Stuart stand naked laughing
with new people about the tomatoes they grew in their
allotment?

That was the kind of thing that happened at the
ordinary parties they went to . . . tame little evenings
where people kept their clothes on, and didn't mate with
each other, and discussed how expensive the season
tickets on the train had become, and how hard it was to
find a doctor who could spend two minutes listening to
you. Tame evenings, dull evenings. Getting in a rut,
becoming old before their time, suburban even though
they hadn't yet reached their middle-class suburbia, no
excitement, nothing very different, nothing that made
them gasp.

Two children, the national average, Stuart working in a
bank . . .

God Almighty! – Suppose some of the bank's clients
were at the party! It wasn't so ridiculous. People don't
live beside their banks, some of them could easily live off
the Seven Sisters Road. Had Stuart thought of that? She
had better tell him, they could call it all off. It would be
foolish to imperil his whole career . . . No. He must have

thought of it. He was utterly set on going to this party now. He would only think she was groping around for some excuse.

. . . nice little flat, no garden unfortunately, but then they went to the allotment at weekends. Children very strong and happy, love their school. Debbie in the school play again this term, and Danny hoping to be picked for the third team. Lots of friends at school always running in and out of the neighbours' houses too and playing in the adventure playground at the end of the road. Not an earth-shaking life, but a happy one . . . even the school Principal had said the other day . . .

Sweet God! – Suppose the school ever got to hear of this! How utterly shaming for Debbie and Danny to be branded the children of perverts, sexual freaks. They might even be asked to leave lest their family shame might taint the other children. Relax. How could the school hear of it, unless other parents, or indeed some of the staff, were there being uninhibited and swinging in sophisticated adult fun? . . . Yes, of course, if anyone was there, a conspiracy of silence would have to be maintained.

. . . anyway the school Principal had said that he had enormous admiration for the parents of today, since they made so many sacrifices for their children and were so supportive and aware of all their needs. But he felt sure that this effort was repaid in a thousand ways by the fact that they lived in a peaceful community, far away from the wars and tensions and differences that rend other countries.

Stuart had said that people who went to these parties were normal, ordinary, good, respectable citizens like everyone else. He said that all they were doing was trying to push forward the frontiers of pleasure. They were trying to add to the delights of normal sexual love between a married couple . . . and be less selfish about it . . . by offering to share that love with other married couples. He had read, and he believed that there was a lot of truth in it, that this kind of generosity, this giving of your rights in your partner to other friends, was an act of love in itself. And, even more important in these treacherous days, it completely by-passed the need to be 'unfaithful' to the other partner – there would be no forbidden lovers, or illicit affairs. It would all be out in the open. It would be healthy and good.

Stuart talked about it with the enthusiasm he had when he first talked about his allotment. His eyes had that gleam that they once had when he had planned a life of self-sufficiency. The rest of London might starve, might poison itself with nuclear fall-out, but Stuart and Pat and Debbie and Danny would grow what they needed for survival on their little allotment, and, aha, who'd laugh then? Pat had asked mildly how Stuart would protect his runner beans and cabbages against twelve million starving Londoners, if they were the only family which had managed to be self-sufficient. Stuart had said it was a technicality.

The Saturday and Sunday gardening continued, it had lost its first flush of real excitement, but nowadays it brought them a gentle pleasure. Perhaps this would happen with wife-swapping too, Pat thought. Soon the heady excitement and flush of enthusiasm would pass, and they would settle into a weekly wife-swap happily and resignedly travelling to Seven Sisters, or Barking, or Rickmansworth, or Biggin Hill.

Stuart seemed so alarmingly calm about it all. This as much as anything disturbed Pat. She had asked him, did he think he should get new jockey-shorts.

'No, love, I've plenty up in the wardrobe,' he had said mystified.

'For the *party*,' she had hissed.

'Why should I need new jockey-shorts?' he had asked, as puzzled as if she had said he should buy a new transistor radio. 'I have nine pairs upstairs. I tell you, I have plenty.'

As the event drew nearer, Pat worried more about Stuart. Did he have no nerves, no feelings, that he could take it all so calmly . . . the fact that he had written to a box number and a woman with a voice like a circular saw had telephoned?

She had never given too much thought to their sex life. It had always seemed very pleasant and adequate, and she certainly didn't regard herself as frigid, not in the sense of the women's magazine articles on the topic. She couldn't remember saying that she had a headache, or that she didn't feel like it. There was, she supposed, a sort of sameness about it. But then, for heaven's sake, some things *are* the same. The taste of a bar of chocolate or a gin and lime is always the same. The sound of Beethoven's Fifth or Johnny Mathis is always the same. Why this great urge for something different?

Pat was hurt and puzzled. She had read about women who discovered that their meek and conventional husbands actually liked bondage or violent pornography . . . so perhaps she should feel relieved that Stuart had suggested only nice old middle-class wife-swapping. Still, Pat felt aggrieved. If she were prepared to live for the rest of their days with their life as it was now, saving for the house, going on a caravan holiday once a year, and making love comfortably in the darkness and privacy of their own room twice a week, then it was somehow ungrateful of Stuart not to feel the same about it.

Pat had an appointment with the hairdresser on the afternoon of the Terrible Day.

'Going somewhere nice?' asked the hairdresser in her bright, routine way.

'Eer . . . yes,' said Pat.

'Oh, to a function is it?' asked the hairdresser.

'Um. No, no. Not a function. Private house. Old friends, and new friends. A party. An ordinary party,' Pat screamed defensively.

The hairdresser shrugged.

'Very nice, I'm sure,' she said huffily.

The baby-sitter arrived on time. Pat had hoped that she might ring and say she couldn't come. That would mean the end of this ludicrous outing across London to copulate with strangers. The only tingles of excitement she felt were the ones which ran through her brain asking her if she were certifiably insane.

Debbie and Danny barely looked up from the television.

'Goodnight, Mum. Goodnight, Dad. Come in and see us when you get back.'

Pat's eyes filled with tears.

'Stuart love . . .' she began.

'Goodnight, you lot.' Stuart said firmly.

She had assumed that they would take the car and was startled when Stuart said that it was much simpler than driving to take the tube.

'Only one change,' he said. And to Pat the words seemed sinister and fraught with meaning. She wondered if he was saying that they would only swap with one couple when they got there. She felt nausea rise in her throat. Suppose it were like a dance in the tennis club years ago, when nobody asked you to dance and you ended up grateful for some awful person who eventually did suggest a shuffle around the floor. Could this happen tonight? Suppose some appalling, foul couple rejected by everyone else nodded encouragingly at them? Would they have to say yes? Did the house rules say that there was no opting out?

'Yes, but wouldn't it be nice to have the car coming home?' she asked.

'Mightn't feel like driving on the way back,' said Stuart succinctly.

Worn out with pleasure? Exhausted? Asleep on some strange other wife's bosom? Going home with someone else? Staying with the awful woman in Seven Sisters? What could he mean, he mightn't feel like driving? The whole nightmare was now quite frightening. Why had she ever agreed to this wicked, and silly thing? Why had Stuart ever suggested it?

The tube came immediately, as trains always do when you are going to the dentist or a wife-swapping party. The stations flashed by. Stuart read the back of someone else's evening paper. Pat examined her face three times in her compact mirror.

'You look fine,' Stuart said to her when she got the compact out a fourth time.

'I suppose you're right. Anyway, it's not my face they'll be looking at,' she said resignedly.

'What? Oh. Oh yes,' said Stuart smiling supportively, and going back to reading the late football results.

'Do you think we'll take off our clothes immediately?' Pat asked wretchedly as they walked out of the station and towards the house.

'I don't know, I expect it depends on whether they have central heating,' Stuart said matter of factly.

Pat looked at him as if he were a total stranger.

'Did she give you any indication of how many people were going to be there?' Pat asked shrilly after another minute of walking. 'I mean, they're not very big houses. They can hardly have dozens.'

'No, she said just a few friends,' said Stuart. 'A few friends, she didn't say how many.'

'But we're not friends, we're sort of intruding on them in a way aren't we?' she begged. There were tears in her eyes. They were only one corner away from the house now. Right-turn that and they were in the road and there was no going back.

Stuart looked at her, moved by the tears he could hear in her voice.

'It'll be lovely, Pat dear. You'll love it. You're always a bit nervous at times like this.'

She looked at him, her eyes flashing.

'What do you mean at times like this? What "times like this" have there been before? When have we done anything remotely like this. It's the only time like this . . .' To her horror, she burst into tears.

Stuart looked very distressed. He tried to touch her, to put his arm around her, but Pat pushed him away.

'No, stop saying it's all right, and that I'll love it. I'll hate it. I'm not going. That's final.'

'Well why didn't you say this before? Why did you wait until we're nearly there?' Stuart asked, his innocent, round face looking both foolish and puzzled at the same time. 'I can't understand why you didn't say to me that you thought it wasn't on, then we'd never have set it all up. I thought you wanted to come too.'

Pat gave a snort into her tissues.

'You *said* it sounded an adventurous thing . . .' he said.

Pat coughed loudly.

'You *said* we'd try it once and if we didn't like it we'd have got it out of our system,' he went on.

Pat blew her nose.

'Why, love? Why have you changed your mind now? Just tell me. We'll do whatever you want to. We won't go if you really hate the idea. Just tell me.'

Pat looked at him through her red eyes. His face was indeed very round and innocent. She wondered that she had never noticed that before. He was simply another disappointed young bank clerk. Another man in a deadend job, with an average wife, a few drinks on a Saturday, two nice, but time-consuming and money-swallowing children, a car that needed a lot of money spent on it, or else needed to be replaced. They had a loan of a caravan each year, but he would never feel the sands of the West Indies or the Seychelles between his toes.

She began to speak and then stopped. She must be

very careful now. It was as if he had been a negative, and
now somebody had shown her the developed print. She
could see all the frustrations, the hours of commuting,
the thickening of his waist. Those things were far from
the James Bond or Wild West books he read for a half-
hour before he went to sleep each night.

A surge of understanding went out from her. He just
needed some excitement, something out of the ordinary,
some proof that he wasn't a mouse, that he was going to
do something daring in his life before he grew old and
retired and walked with a stick and crumpled and died.

Quite calmly she looked at him and said:

'I'm jealous. That's it. That's the truth.'

'You're what?' he said.

'I don't want them, to have you, to see you. I don't
want those girls to . . . you know, make free with you. I'd
be very jealous. I love you. I don't want them loving you.'

'But Pat,' he said desperately. 'We've been through all
this; it's got nothing to do with love. It's got to do with
swapping. It's got to do with excitement, and frontiers
. . . and not doing the same things always . . . till the end
of our days.'

She had been right. She resolved that she would do
everything her feeble imagination and some sex manuals
could dream up if only they got home unscathed from
Seven Sisters.

'You're too great,' she said hesitantly. They didn't use
flowery endearments, they never paid each other extravagant compliments. It was hard to begin on a street in
the middle of the evening in North London on the way to
a wife-swapping orgy. But people have to begin somewhere.

'You're too . . . important. Too precious, and exciting.
I love it when we . . . er . . . screw. I don't want other
women to share it. It's my . . . er, pleasure.'

'Do you love it?' he asked innocently.

'Oh I do,' she closed her eyes, a sigh of genuine

pleasure that she might in fact be going to win escaped her, and it sounded like genuine desire.

'I didn't think you minded all that much one way or another,' he said.

'If you knew how I do,' she said. And then firmly, 'But I wouldn't feel at all the same if you let all these women crawl over you . . .'

She paused. It was a calculated risk. In fact she had given little thought to Stuart's part in the whole sorry business, she had been obsessed with her own role. But she thought that to say this would have been to confirm Stuart in thinking that he had married parochial, puritan riff-raff and that his excitement would be between the covers of books for the rest of his days.

'I often . . . er . . . get panicky in case some of the women who come into the bank might . . . er, proposition you,' she said.

Stuart looked at her.

'There's no need to worry like that. That's kind of paranoid that jealousy,' he said soothingly. 'I've always been faithful to you. Even this business tonight is *with* you.'

'I don't want to share you with them,' she said. 'I'm not going to. They've got lousy old husbands, awful fellows. I've got you. Why should I be so generous?'

He paused. He looked up the road, he looked down the road. Her eyes never left his face. Down the road won.

'Suppose we got a couple of kebabs . . .'

'And a bottle of wine.'

As they turned to go back to the station, a middle-aged couple stopped in a car to ask them where the Road was.

Pat asked them what number they wanted.

As she had suspected, it was number 17.

'Have fun,' she said as she gave them directions, and she and Stuart dissolved in laughter.

'They were a bit old,' said Stuart. 'Do you think it would have been very sordid and sort of pathetic?'

Pat wasn't going to let him think that.

'No there were probably fabulous birds there. Anyway, older ones are more passionate. She'd probably have had you pinned to the hearth rug the moment we got in the door.'

Under a street lamp, she thought his face looked a bit foolish. As if he had seen how tatty and grubby it might all have been. He was very gentle. In a great wave of affection she realised that indeed she would not have liked sharing him with anyone, and that an evening in bed with a bottle of wine, and a nice spicy donar kebab and all that black and red underwear might be the most exciting kind of thing that she had experienced for some time as well.

Women are so much more sensible about sex, she thought cheerfully as Stuart bought the tickets home. She had forgotten the weeks of anxiety, the endless examinations in the mirror, the ceaseless fears lest anyone should discover. Heady with relief she even allowed herself the indulgence of imagining what that elderly woman in the car might look like naked, and she smiled at Stuart who looked like a tiger now that his wife was too rabidly jealous to allow him to indulge in the wife-swapping party to which they had been invited. Horizons had been broadened without anyone having to do anything.

Finsbury Park

Vera hated to see television plays about poverty. She even disliked seeing working-class women, babies in their arms, hair in rollers, explaining some social problem to a concerned television reporter. It reminded her too much of her youth. In those shuffling, whiney women she could see her mother, cigarette always hanging from the corner of her mouth, cardigan held together with a safety pin, the door of the flat never closed since people were always coming in and out, the place smelling of clothes drying . . . clothes that had not been properly washed so it was really dirty clothes drying.

Vera hated to hear women laugh loudly, they reminded her of her mother and her elder sister, cackling away when things were at their worst, cheering each other up with bottles of ginger wine and announcing that they would be dead long enough. Vera never liked to think of anything that reminded her about life as it was lived before she was fifteen.

On her fifteenth birthday she was taken to the hospital with rheumatic fever, and during the long weeks there she got to know Miss Andrews, the gentle school teacher in the next bed who changed her life.

'Ask them to bring you lavender water not sweets.'

'Ask your school friends for hand cream not comics.'

'I'll choose some nice books for you from the library.'

'We'll tell the social worker you'd like a hairdo to cheer you up. . .'

The Vera who came out of hospital was slimmer and attractive looking. And she had changed inside too. Miss

Andrews had taught her a very important lesson – even awful things and unhappy times can have their uses, they can be a kind of apprenticeship. Vera must stay at school, she must pass some kind of exams even if school was hell and home was worse than hell.

She had closed her eyes to the dirt and depression around her. She had dreamed of the day she would live in a clean house with no frying pans encrusted with the remains of a thousand meals. She dreamed of having a room to herself where no noise and no shouting could be heard, where no younger sister with nits in her hair would bounce on her bed saying:

'It's half my room, you can't throw me out.'

'Don't leave too soon,' Miss Andrews had begged. 'Don't go until you are sure you can support yourself. It would be too depressing to have to return there. That would break your spirit.'

Vera found it difficult to remember the two years she stayed on in her mother's flat. She knew that her father must have come home from time to time . . . the period seemed to be punctuated with screaming and violence. She must have learned something at the school because she had managed to escape with some 'O' levels. And during those two years she must have formed the habit of visiting Miss Andrews once a week, some hundred calls must have been made to the quiet apartment with its piano, its dried flowers, its cabinets of china and its purring Persian cat.

As an apprenticeship it must have worked, but it was blotted out. By the time Vera had finished, she could type, she could take shorthand, she could spell. Miss Andrews had taught her to smile and to speak nicely. Not in actual lessons, but by example. Vera's voice was less shrill, her vowels less extreme, her reactions less speedy – so much so that her mother was totally unprepared for her flight from the tenement. It was done without fuss, without argument and without heed to the pleas.

'You'll come back often to see us, you'll come home every weekend,' begged her mother.

'Of course,' said Vera, and never did.

She sent her mother an envelope with a card and a pound in it three times a year, Christmas, birthday, and mother's day. No details of how she was or where she was. No plans about coming back for a visit. No enquiries about the rest of the family. They had no way of telling her, when Margaret died. And no way of appealing to her when Colin was lifted by the police. And when the pound had reduced to a fifth of its value she still sent it. Crisp and green, attached by a paper clip to a non-committal card of good wishes. Once her mother tore it up and threw it into the fire. But Vera was never to know that.

Miss Andrews had been too genteel, too ladylike to reveal to Vera what she later discovered to be a major truth in life – that money was the solution to almost every problem. If Miss Andrews had known this she hadn't thought of passing it on, and after Vera had cut her ties with the family she also stopped seeing Miss Andrews. To the teacher she sent more thoughtful cards, and sometimes a lace handkerchief or a little sachet for her drawer. She never said what she was doing or where she was, and soon, or at some time anyway, the lonely teacher put Vera out of her mind. There was a finality about her three-line notes . . . they said goodbye.

Throughout her first five years of freedom, which also meant five jobs and five different bed-sitters, Vera still regarded herself as in apprenticeship. There was no time for dalliances like every other girl she worked with seemed to have. There was no money to waste on silly things – the cinema, yes, sometimes, if it was the kind of film that might teach her something, about style, clothes, manners. Mainly British films, American style was too foreign, it might be outrageous, it might not even *be* style. Lunch hours spent in fashion stores, or in bookshops, reading but not buying the magazines; money, after the rent was paid, spent on evening classes in everything from Beginner's French to Grooming.

Suddenly she was twenty-three, and nicely spoken and well informed and living in an attractive bed-sitter. She had collected some pretty ornaments, not unlike those that Miss Andrews had in her glass-fronted cabinet. She knew extremely important things about not mixing styles in her decor. She had learned as if by rote some rules of elegant living and if she had ever given herself the opportunity to entertain anyone she was absolutely confident about how the table should be set and what wines to serve with each course.

She had never relaxed about her background, and was amazed that other girls, the kind she met at work, would talk so freely about the uncouth habits of their parents . . . and joke about the vulgarity of their backgrounds. Vera would never be drawn. Once or twice when people did press she said that it hurt her to talk about the past. And people assumed that there had been some tragedy or some unpleasantness and left it at that.

Because of her interest in china she got a job running the gift shop of a smart hotel and it was here that she met Joseph. Twenty years her senior, with his big anxious eyes and his worried face, he was the ideal catch, one of the giggling receptionists had told her. A lonely widower, no children, pots of money, so broken up after his wife's death that he had sold the house and moved into a hotel. He had been living in this hotel for three years. He was apparently looking for a wife, since hotel life had its drawbacks. Sometimes he called at her little shop to buy gifts for clients, always she advised him with charm and taste. He was very attracted to her. Soon he managed to find the courage to ask her out. Vera's own hesitation was genuine. In her effort to become her own version of a lady, she had given very little time to recognising that she was a woman. She knew little of men, and was very shy on their first few outings. This pleased Joseph more than anything else she could have done . . . In a matter of weeks he was telling her of his dream house, but his fears of being lonely in it if he bought it for himself alone. She agreed with him enthusiastically, she thought that a big place was bad if you were alone. That's why she only had a tiny bed-sitter.

Joseph wondered if he could come and call at her bed-sitter some time. Vera agreed and asked him for afternoon tea the following Saturday. The sunlight caught the beautiful china, and the gentle highlights in Vera's hair, and the shining wood of the one small table . . . and Joseph's eyes filled with tears. He started to apologise for being forty-five, and to excuse himself for his arrogance in supposing that a beautiful young girl could possibly . . . She let him babble on for some minutes and then just as he was about to retract everything he had said from sheer embarrassment, she laid a finger on his lips and said,

'Don't say any more, Joseph. I should love to see your dream house in Finsbury Park, and we'll make it the most wonderful palace in the world.'

She had heard dialogue a little like that in some old movie, and it seemed right for the occasion. It was indeed. Utterly right. The months passed in a flurry of inspecting the house, giving in her notice at the hotel, accepting a small marriage settlement from Joseph, a complete refusal on her part to have anything to do with her family, a quiet wedding, an undemanding honeymoon in the sunshine of the South of France and then Vera's apprenticeship ended and her life began.

The small scullery attached to the great kitchen in Finsbury Park became her headquarters. Here she sat and studied the plans, here she returned after great measuring trips around the rooms, here she studied fabrics, paint charts, samples of tiles, wood pieces. It was in this scullery that the catalogues began to mount up as she debated, and wondered and frowned, and pouted, and looked at the first ones again. Joseph began to fret after a few weeks.

'Is it proving too much for you, my little darling?' he asked anxiously. 'You know we can have a designer, and a consultant if you like. Someone who will take the donkey work from you.'

'Donkey work?' cried Vera in genuine amazement. 'But this is the best bit. This is what we want, to decide it ourselves, to have it perfect. To have a perfect house which we get for ourselves!' Her eyes looked almost wild with enthusiasm, so Joseph decided not to point out that they slept on a bed in a bedroom, and ate meals in the little scullery while a fourteen-room house awaited them. It was like a naked house waiting to be dressed.

It got dressed. Amazingly slowly. It took months for the painting, months for the curtains, the furniture to build up. Two years went by and it still looked as if they had just moved in. Joseph was deeply disappointed.

He worked hard all day as a company lawyer. He had thought that his life had taken a new and almost miraculous turn when the flower-like Vera had agreed to marry him. True, his evenings were less lonely than when he lived in the hotel. But they were a lot less comfortable. In the hotel he had room to rest, to relax, room to work. In the hotel he had excellent food. At home, in the future palace, he had no room. He lived from a box in their bedroom, since Vera would allow no furniture anywhere until it had been finally agreed and settled and each item took months. The cooking was negligible since they had to wait for all the equipment to be installed. Vera didn't seem interested in food, she didn't seem to think he needed it either. She rushed to greet him on his return each day with a peck on the cheek and a sheaf of leaflets and swathes of fabric.

'Oh there you are, my dear. Dearest, do you think this

flower is too large. I'm not quite certain, I'm almost certain but not quite.'

He began to try and guess what she wanted him to say, but knew that he had to give the pretence of ruminating over it, otherwise she would not be satisfied. Often, faint with tiredness and hunger after two hours of studying design, he wondered whether she might in fact be having some kind of nervous trouble that he hadn't noticed before. Then he would banish the thought guiltily, and tell himself that he was a selfish swine to expect his young wife to have a glass of scotch ready, a meal cooking and a lively interest in his day.

Sometimes he called at the hotel and ate before he came home. Vera never seemed to mind. Yes, of course she had plenty to eat, she made herself cups of soup and sandwiches she said vaguely.

Joseph's hope that they would have children was also doomed. It was a long time before he realised that Vera had been taking the contraceptive pill. All this time he had been hoping that she would tell him she had conceived.

'But darling we can't *think* of children in this beautiful house. I mean how could you have children with this wallpaper?' Her hands caressed the wallpaper almost sensuously.

'But not ever?' gasped Joseph shocked.

'Perhaps sometime,' Vera said distantly aware she might have gone a little too far.

Vera was twenty-eight, they had been five years married when he dared to say to her that the house was perfect. He had admired every single item, rearranged every piece of furniture with her and now he hoped that the endless business was over. To his increasing alarm he noted that she didn't seem too anxious to spoil the kitchen by cooking, and she didn't want to fade the colours in the sitting room by letting the light in. There was no comfortable fug in the study she had designed for him, because she begged him not to have the heating too high lest it blister the paint. His cigar smoking was done outside his own home.

That was the unhappiest year of Joseph's life, because he now realised that the completion of the house did not signal the start of a normal life together. Her attractive face was still bent over magazines and fabric charts. They had never entertained anyone. He had taken his mother, an elderly woman there once . . . for a drink before Sunday lunch. Vera said she couldn't possibly cook a huge Sunday roast if they were to show the kitchen at its best.

'But why do we have to show it, at its best?' he begged.

'Why spend all this time and money unless we want things at their best?' she answered.

He hoped that if he got her some regular help she might become more relaxed about it. Together they interviewed seventeen applicants, the wages he offered were high. Eventually she settled on a Filippino girl with as much interest in the house as she had herself. Together they cleaned and polished all day. Together Vera and the little Filippino washed woodwork, and held the fitments of glass lights in soft dusters rubbing gently till they shone. The little girl from Manilla saved every penny she earned, and drank packet soups with Vera all day to keep up her strength. At night she went to her own room, and watched a portable television. Vera had bought her this in order to keep her at home. She told Joseph that if Anna went out at night she would lose her energy for polishing.

Joseph suggested a cook as well, but Vera asked why did they want someone to mess the place up. She would however like a daily woman to do the heavy work so that Anna and she could be free to do the finer chores.

The cleaning woman came five days a week. She thought Vera was daft and told her so. Vera didn't even listen. She certainly didn't feel insulted.

'If you don't like the job and the money, I'll get someone else,' she said reasonably, without any offence in her voice.

The cleaning woman was called Mrs Murray, and she lived in a block of flats not at all unlike the ones where Vera had grown up. Sometimes Mrs Murray feeling a bit sorry for this poor madwoman she worked for, would tell tales of Life in the Buildings. Vera's face contorted with near spasms. She almost ran from the room if Mrs Murray began to evoke the life and sounds.

'Please, Mrs Murray, I beg you, go on with your work. I don't want to delay you. Another time.'

Behind her back Anna and Mrs Murray pointed to their own foreheads and shook their heads.

'I think she must have had nothing when she was young,' said Mrs Murray one day in a burst of confidence to Anna.

'I always think she very wealthy lady,' said Anna.

'Wouldn't you feel sorry for her old man?' Mrs Murray went on. 'He'd be better off down with us, coming in to a bit of a laugh and a good meat pie, and a block of ice cream with a glass of port after it, and his slippers. I think that's what he'd prefer, to tell you the God's honest truth.'

Anna gave it some thought.

'Yes, and when I think of my family back in Manilla . . . where there is little money . . . and little food and little furniture . . . but when the father comes in . . . all stops and there is smiling and welcoming and he is an important man.'

Mrs Murray nodded sagely.

Outside the door, where she had paused, not to eavesdrop but to polish the corner of a picture frame which had escaped them all, Vera stood and listened. Her body was flooded with a great pity for them. Two poor women, not much older than herself. One from a drunken Irish family, living now in slum conditions in a London council flat, one a poor Asiatic whose family and country were so wretched they had to export her to clean floors and send them back her wages.

And these two women pitied her. Vera gave a high-pitched little laugh at the wonderful way that nature allows people to bear their burdens so easily by considering themselves better off than others. Happily she moved from the door and knelt down to examine the ball and claw feet of the table which were known for their ability to trap dust.

Highbury & Islington

'I hope you'll like them all,' he said for the fourth time.

'Oh, I'm sure I will,' said Heather without looking up.

'I think you'll get on with them,' he said, anxiously biting his lip.

Heather raised her eyes from the magazine.

'I said I'm sure I will, funny face. Even if I don't it's not the end of the world. They don't have to live with me, I don't have to live with them.' Cheerfully she leaned over and kissed him on the nose. Then she took off her shoes, settled her feet in his lap and applied herself seriously to her magazine. A very colourful looking one with a lot of Sin and Passion and Frenzy in capital letters on the cover.

Adam hoped that she might have finished the magazine and, better still have thrown it away before they got home. He could see his mother's amazement – Frenzy and Sin magazines weren't forbidden at home, it was just that nobody would contemplate buying them. He could imagine his sister's sarcastic comments. Louise was always a little sardonic about strangers but he felt unhappily that Heather might give plenty of ammunition.

'*A trifle bookish I see, your Heather?*' Louise would shout as she retrieved the offending magazine. And, oh God, would Heather relax so thoroughly that she would actually sit in her stockinged feet as she was doing now?

Adam looked out of the train window, and fixed his face in what he hoped was a calm, pleasant expression while he tried to work out some of the more glaring problems which faced him at the weekend. He had explained to Heather that there could be no question of sharing a bed under his mother's roof. She had accepted it good-naturedly.

'No point in terrorising the poor old darling is there? I'll wait until they've all had their Ovaltine then I'll slip along to wherever you are.'

He had even managed to tell her that this would not do either. He painted a picture of a home with three women, Mother, Louise and old Elsie; this was the first time any guest had been invited to stay; there would be enormous excitement. There would be amazing scrutiny. Heather had sounded disbelieving but shrugged.

'Well, two nights' denial won't kill us.'

Adam had read a lot about love before he had met Heather. He knew only too well that love was often unreturned – as in the case of his loving Jane Fonda for a while. She had simply been unaware of his existence. And nearer home there had been a severe case of unreturned love when he had yearned for that stuck-up girl in the dramatic society. Of course, he too had been loved, by that mousey friend of Louise's; the quiet little girl with the irritating cough and nervous laugh. She had loved Adam for a bit and was always pretending that she had been given two theatre tickets and asking him would he like to come to plays with her. He hadn't loved her even a little bit.

Heather was his first experience of Real Love, and Adam frowned as he looked into people's houses from the train window. Real love often ran into problems, well, from Romeo and Juliet onwards. There were cases of families refusing to countenance young lovers. He didn't think this would happen at home. Mother and Louise wouldn't summon old Elsie from the kitchen and face him with an ultimatum. It would be very different and much harder to take . . . they would laugh at Heather, and ridicule his taste. In little ways they would call attention to her shortcomings; they would assume that she was a tasteless little dalliance on his part. They couldn't know that he loved her and wanted her more than he had ever wanted anything in his life.

He moved her feet slightly, she looked up and smiled at him over her torrid magazine.

'Dreaming?' she asked him affectionately.

'A bit,' he said and felt a wave of disloyalty flooding him. Love wasn't meant to be like this, it had nothing to do with trying to get two sets of people to make allowances, to change, to bend in order to accommodate each other. Love was meant to be straightforward. If things got in the way of love, then the Lover had to remove them, honestly and with integrity and dignity. The Lover wasn't meant to sit gnawing his fingers about the confrontation of those that he loved.

He had known Heather for a year and he had loved her for eight months, but this was the first time he had ever raised enough courage to take her home for a weekend. It hadn't been easy.

'But of course you can have a friend to stay, darling,' Mother had said. 'Who is he? Anyone we know?' Mother had an idea that she might know anyone of substance in London. Among the twelve million people Adam could meet, she felt sure that the one chosen to be a friend might be someone she knew.

'A girl. How dramatic!' screamed Louise pretending to be a Victorian Lady overcome with shock. Adam could have wrung her neck with pleasure. 'Is she a débutante? Do tell, do tell.'

Adam had explained that Heather had a bed-sitting-room in the same house in Islington. He did not go into the fact that for the past few months they actually shared the same bed-sitting-room so as to save rent. To the eager faces of Mother and Louise, and of Elsie who had come in from the kitchen at the noise of all the excitement, he announced that she really *was* just a friend, and that he would love to invite her for a weekend. He begged them not to ask people around for sherry on Sunday morning. He implored Elsie not to give the place a thorough spring clean before young Mr Adam's young lady came; he said that honestly Louise shouldn't save her supper party for the tennis club people until Heather arrived. Short of going on bended knees he couldn't have done more to ask for a quiet, normal weekend. It had, of course, been useless.

It was only natural that they should be so interested in his doings, Adam thought forgiving them, loving them for caring so much. Since Father died he was the only man in their life; Louise was too bookish, too brisk for men. Well, she was nineteen and had never shown any real interest in men. She worked in the local library, she never mentioned boyfriends. She couldn't have any secretly, could she? After all she lived at home. Every second weekend Adam arrived home to the Sussex town, and told them tales about his life in London. The work in the bank, his prospects. His squash games, his walks on the Heath. The little pub theatres he went to, his French classes preparing for big banking opportunities in the EEC.

He mentioned lots of friends by name, but never Heather. He said nothing about the discos they went to on the Saturdays he stayed in London. He thought Mother might find discos a bit, well, lower class, and Louise would ask in her penetrating voice: 'But why, Adam, why do people go to rooms with loud music and funny lights which eventually ruin their eyesight – I mean, do they enjoy it, Adam?' He told Elsie that he was learning a little bit more about cooking, but he didn't explain that it was Heather who taught him, Heather who said: 'I made the supper last night, you'll bloody do it tonight mate or I'll find myself a bloke who believes in equality.'

His worlds were so different that he had put off for as long as he could the date when they had to be brought together. Adam who sat down with a linen table napkin to tasteless, overcooked, plain food served from cracked china plates behind heavy net curtains . . . and Adam who sat on the bed with a great wooden bowl of highly spiced chili, a bottle of red wine on the floor, his arm around Heather as they laughed and watched television. In the summer evenings the window of their basement flat was often open for all to see . . . He could hardly believe they were the same person.

Heather had invited him to her home several times. Her stepfather had asked Adam for a loan of a pound on each occasion and Heather had cheerfully shouted at him not to be so daft. On one occasion Adam had secretly slipped the man a pound, hoping to buy his affection, but in fact it only worsened relations between them as Heather had said it would. Heather's mother was a hard-working Scot. She looked Adam up and down and said she hoped that he was a man who could hold down a day's work. Adam explained nervously that although he was still a lowly bank official he was indeed a regular worker and had great ambitions. Heather's mother said she approved of that because she herself had been unlucky in that she had married two wasters and two scroungers and two men who would drink the Thames Estuary dry if they got a chance. 'There were only two altogether, Mam,' Heather had said laughing. 'She always makes it sound as if there were six!'

Adam couldn't understand the casual bond that held the mother to her daughter. It wasn't love, it had nothing to do with duty. There was no need involved, it didn't seem to matter whether Heather went home for months or not. There were no recriminations, no interrogations. There didn't even seem to be a great deal of interest. Heather's mother could hardly remember the name of the department store where Heather worked. Adam marvelled at that: Mother and Louise and Elsie knew the name of every under-manager and a great many of the customers in his bank.

Heather had always seemed amused about his tales of home. But then, Adam wondered with mounting horror as the train was taking them ever nearer, had he told accurate tales? Had he let her know just how very formal Mother could be? Heather hadn't thought of taking a gift for the weekend, so Adam had bought a potted plant.

'You can give that to Mother,' he had said.

'Why? I don't know her. She'd think it was silly,' said Heather.

'No, first time meeting her, she'd think it was nice,' he insisted. 'It's what people do, honestly.'

'You didn't take a plant to my Mum,' she said reasonably.

Adam was furious. He hadn't taken a plant to Heather's mother because she lived forty minutes away on the tube, because they had gone there for tea one Saturday, because Heather had said that her mother hated airs and graces and he hadn't wanted to be considered a young dandy. Now it was being used against him.

He thought about the kind of weekend they could have had if they had stayed in London. The cinema tonight, perhaps, and a fish and chip supper. Saturday morning poking around antique shops and second-hand stalls. Drink a few pints with some of Heather's friends at lunchtime . . . the afternoon would pass in a haze of doing up the room they lived in, sweeping the leaves away from the basement gutters; they might carry on with that picture framing; they might go and drink a bottle of wine with other friends until they went to the disco; and instead he had this torture ahead.

The train stopped and his heart lurched; they couldn't be there yet. Surely there was another half-hour.

'Are we there?' Heather yawned and rooted for her

shoes. She hadn't a hint of nervousness or anxiety. She reached for his carefully chosen potted plant.

'Don't forget your geranium,' she said.

They hadn't arrived, but they had reached a situation which called for their having to change trains. That was how the guard put it.

'Has this one broken down?' Heather asked him.

'It is a situation where you have to change trains, Madam,' he said again.

'I'd love it if he was in charge of any crisis,' grumbled Heather getting out on to the platform. Her eyes lit on the Ladies Room. 'I'll take advantage of the change of train situation to have a relief of bladder situation,' she said happily and scampered off to the lavatory.

Adam stood glumly wondering why he thought everything that Heather said was funny and endearing at home in London and he thought it was coarse and offensive when he was starting to get into Mother's orbit. He leaned against a telephone box waiting for Heather to come back from the Ladies and for the next train to come and rescue them. On the opposite platform stood lucky people going to London. They would be there in time to go to a theatre perhaps, they might be salesmen coming home from some conference in Brighton. None of them had forty-eight hours of anxiety lying ahead of them as he did. None of them had to worry about Mother asking Heather, 'And what school were you at my dear?' and Louise asking Heather, 'You mean you actually sell things to the public? Heavens!', Elsie asking Heather, 'Would you like Earl Grey or English breakfast in the morning?' He winced and felt a real pain at the thought of it. And there was no way he could muzzle Heather and ask her to remain completely silent, so she was bound to talk about times when they had both been pissed and to let slip that they had smoked pot, and lived in the same room, and that her father had died in an alcoholics' home and her step-father was bankrupt . . .

Adam heaved a very deep sigh.

Love was turning out to be full of problems that the poets and the movie makers never spoke of.

Suddenly he thought he couldn't stand it. Not now, not yet. He wasn't ready to take the weekend now. Perhaps later when he and Heather were so sure of each other and of their happiness that a weekend like this wouldn't matter. Perhaps later when he didn't seem like a small boy wet behind the ears to the Mummy and the Sister and the Old Retainer . . . perhaps then Adam's Bohemian lifestyle and friends would be much more acceptable. Perhaps when he was more of a man.

He knew he had to act in the next minute if he was going to stop the disastrous visit. A quick phone call . . . he was most most dreadfully sorry but he had just come down with this dreadful flu, and Heather had sent her regrets and would so look forward to meeting Mother and Louise and everyone another time. Yes, yes he could do it now quickly. And to Heather? Well imagine how funny life is! He had just phoned home to explain that they were going to be late and, fancy, Mother had come down with this dreadful flu and had been trying to contact him, could they possibly put off the visit? Then he and Heather had only to cross the platform, jump on a London bound train. In an hour or two they would get off at their tube station, and, hand in hand, clutching their weekend bags and the geranium, they would go home . . . there would be no hurts, no confrontations. Love would remain separate and self-contained. He could be a loving son every second weekend until he was mature and manly enough not to care.

With one hand on his ear to cut out the noise of the trains he told the tale first to Elsie and, gritting his teeth trying to put out of his mind her tones of disappointment, he agreed to tell it all again to Mother.

'We had everything so nice,' Elsie said, 'We even had a

fire in Miss Heather's bedroom. Your mother had the chimney swept during the week.'

Mother was concerned about his imaginary flu, but he had the strangest feeling she didn't entirely believe him. She gave the merest of hints that she thought something more exciting and glittering had turned up for Adam and Heather.

'Don't go out to any parties or occasions now, if you have flu.'

There was something about the way his mother used the work 'occasions' that brought a prickle of tears to Adam's eyes. It was as moving as Elsie being disappointed not to see Miss Heather's pleasure at the fire in her bedroom. Mother thought that bank clerks and shopgirls were good worthy people in service industries . . . but she thought of her son Adam as being 'in banking' and she assumed that his nice friend Heather was a young lady who would indeed be invited to glittering functions.

'I'm sorry, Mother,' he said.

'Adam my dear, you can't help having influenza,' said Mother, and he could hear Louise in the background saying: 'Oh no, you don't mean after all this they're not coming. It's too bad.'

Fiercely he told himself that it was better this small hurt than two days of misunderstanding and misery. Then Heather came swinging easily along the platform.

'Any news on the train?' she asked.

He told her about his sudden call, his mother's flu, her deep regrets, he added that there had been a fire in her bedroom. Heather looked at him levelly.

'Yes, really, a fire in your bedroom, Mother had got the sweep to come in and do the chimney specially during the week,' he said, desperate that she should understand how much welcome had been prepared. After Elsie and Mother's pain he couldn't bear it if Heather were flippant.

'I see,' she said at last.

'So, we can just go back, back to London, we can cross the footbridge there,' he said reading the sign aloud.

'Yeah, that's right,' said Heather.

'And we're really only losing the cost of the ticket,' he said eagerly looking at her. 'That's all we're losing.'

'Sure Adam,' she said, but he knew from her voice that he was losing a great deal more. He had known that from Mother's voice too. For once in his life, Adam wondered if there were a danger that he might *never* grow up.

King's Cross

Eve looked around the office with a practical eye. There was a shabby and rather hastily put together steel shelving system for books and brochures. There were boxes of paper still on the floor. There was a dead plant on the window, and another plant with a Good Luck in Your New Job label dying slowly beside it. The venetian blind was black – there was so much clutter on the window ledge it looked like a major undertaking to try and free the blind. One of the telephones was actually hidden under a pile of literature on the desk. In the corner was a small, cheap and rather nasty-looking table . . . which would be Eve's if she were to take the job.

And that's what she was doing now, as she sat in the unappealing room . . . deciding if she would take the job of secretary to Sara Gray. Sara had rushed off to find somebody who knew about holidays and luncheon vouchers and overtime. She had never had a secretary before and had never thought of enquiring about these details before she interviewed Eve. She had pushed the hair out of her eyes and gone galloping off to personnel, which would undoubtedly think her very foolish. Eve sat calmly in the room waiting and deliberating, by the time Sara had bounded back with the information, Eve had already decided to take on Sara Gray. She looked like being the most challenging so far.

Sara heaved a great sigh of relief when she heard that Eve would stay and work with her. She had big kind brown eyes, the kind of eyes you often see shown close up in a movie or a television play to illustrate that someone is a trusting, vulnerable character and therefore likely to be hurt. She looked vague and bewildered, and snowed-under. She sounded as if she needed a personal manager rather than a secretary – and this is where Sara Gray had hit very lucky because that's what Eve was.

From the outset she was extraordinarily respectful to Sara. She never referred to her as anything but Miss Gray, she called her Miss Gray to her face despite a dozen expostulations from Sara.

'This is a friendly office,' Sara cried. 'I can't stand you not calling me by my name. It makes me look so snooty. We're all friends here.'

Eve had replied firmly that it was not a friendly office. It was a very cut-throat company indeed. Eve had asked Sara how many of the women secretaries called their male bosses by their first names. Sara couldn't work it out. Eve could. None of them. Sara agreed reluctantly that this might be so. Eve pressed home her point. Even the managers and assistant managers on Sara's level were not going to escape, they all called Sara by her first name because she was a woman, but she felt the need to call many of them Mr. After two days Sara decided that Eve must be heavily into Women's Lib.

'There's no need to fight any battles on my behalf, Eve,' she said cheerfully. 'Look at how far I've got, and I'm a woman. Nobody held me back just because I'm a downtrodden put-upon female. Did they? I've done very well here, and I get recognition for all I do.'

'Oh no, Miss Gray, you are quite wrong,' said Eve. 'You do not get recognition. You are the assistant promotions manager. Everyone knows that you are far better and brighter and work much harder than Mr Edwards. You should be the promotions manager not the assistant.'

Sara looked upset. 'I thought I could say I'd done rather well,' she said.

'Only what you deserve, Miss Gray,' said Eve who

seemed to have acquired a thorough familiarity with the huge travel agency and its tour operations in two days. 'You should have Mr Edwards' job. We all know that. You *must* have it. It's only fair.'

Sara looked at her, embarrassed.

'Gosh Eve, it's awfully nice of you, and don't think I don't appreciate it. You're amazingly loyal. But you really don't know the score here.'

'With great respect, Miss Gray, I think it's you who doesn't know the score,' said Eve calmly. 'It is absolutely possible for you to have Mr Edwards' job this time next year, I'll be very glad to help you towards that if you like. I have a little experience in this sort of thing.'

Sara stared at her, not knowing what to say.

'Miss Gray, I'm going for my lunch now, but can I suggest you do something while I'm gone? Can you telephone one or two of the people on the list of references I gave you? You will notice they are all women; I've never worked for men. Ask any one of them whether she thinks it's a good idea to trust me to help. Then perhaps you might add that you will keep all this very much in confidence . . .'

'Eve,' interrupted Sara, her good-natured face looking puzzled, 'Eve, honestly, this sounds like the mafia or something. I'm not into power struggles, and office back-stabbing . . . I'm just delighted to have someone as bright and helpful as you in the office . . . I don't want to start a war.'

'Who said anything about a war, Miss Gray? It's very subtle, and very gradual and – honestly the best thing is to telephone anyone on that list, it's there in the file marked Personal.'

'But won't they think it rather odd. I mean, I can't ring up and ask them what do they think of Eve trying to knock Mr Edwards sideways so that I can get his job.' Sara sounded very distressed.

'Miss Gray, I have worked in five jobs, for five women,

I chose them, they thought they chose me. At the very beginning I told them how a good assistant could help them get where they wanted. Not one of them believed me, I managed in a conversation like this to convince them to let me.'

'And . . . what happened?' asked Sara.

'Ask them, Miss Gray,' replied Eve, gathering her gloves and bag.

'They won't think I'm er . . .'

'No, all of them – except the first one, of course – rang someone else to check things out too.' Eve was gone.

Sara wondered.

You often heard of women becoming a bit strange, perhaps Eve was a bit odd. Far too young to be meno-pausal or anything, heavens Eve wasn't even thirty, but it did seem an odd sort of thing to suggest after two days.

Was there a wild possibility that she might have had a secret vendetta for years against Garry Edwards, the plausible head of promotions, who indeed did not de-serve his job, his title, his salary or his influence, since all of these had been made possible only by Sara's devoted work?

Sara reached for the phone.

'Sure I know Eve,' said the pleasant American woman in the big banking group. 'You are so lucky, Sara, to have her. I offered her any money to stay but she wouldn't hear of it. She said her job was done. She acts a bit like Superman or the Lone Ranger, she comes in and solves a problem and then sort of zooms off. A really incredible woman.'

'Can I . . . er . . . ask you what problem she . . . er . . .' Sara felt very embarrassed.

'Sure. I wanted to be loans manager, they didn't take me seriously. Eve showed me how they would, and they did, and now I'm loans manager.'

'Heavens,' said Sara. 'It's a teeny bit like that here.'

'Well naturally it is, otherwise Eve wouldn't have picked you,' said the loans manager of a distant bank.

'And how did she . . . um . . . do it?' persisted Sara.

'Now this is where I become a little vague,' the pleasant voice said. 'It's simply impossible to explain. In my case there was a whole lot of stuff about my not getting to meet the right people in the bank. Eve noticed that, she got me to play golf.'

'*Golf?*' screamed Sara.

'I know, I know, I guess I shouldn't even have told you that much . . . listen, the point is that Eve can see with uncanny vision where women hold themselves back, and work within the system without playing the system properly so – she kinda points out where the system could work for us, and honestly honey, it worked for me, and it sure as hell worked for the woman who Eve worked on before me, she's practically running industry in this country nowadays. In her case it had something to do with having dinner parties at home.'

'What?' said Sara.

'I know, it sounded crazy to me too, and I got real uneasy, but aparently she needed to show people that she could sort of impress foreign contacts by having them to a meal with grace and style and all pizzazz in her country home. Eve sort of set it up for her with outside caterers and it worked a dream. You see, it's different for everyone.'

Sara was puzzled. She walked down to the local snack bar and bought a salami sandwich. She ate it thoughtfully on the road coming back to the building. In the lift she heard that Garry Edwards was going to a conference in the Seychelles next week. It was a conference for people who brought out travel brochures, a significant part of promotions for any travel firm. Sara had done all the imaginative travel brochures, Garry Edwards had okayed them. Yet he was going to the Seychelles and she was eating a tired salami sandwich. When she opened her office door Eve was sitting there typing.

'I'll do it,' she said. 'Whatever it is, play golf, give foolish dinner parties . . . I'll do it. I want his job. It's utterly unjust that he's going to that conference, it's the most unjust thing I've ever known.'

'He won't be going to it next year,' said Eve. 'Right, Miss Gray, I have a few points ready to discuss with you, shall we put this sign on the door?'

'What is it?' Sara asked fearfully.

'It merely says, "Engaged in Conference", I made it last night.' Eve produced a neat card which she then fixed on the outside of the office door.

'Why are we doing that?' whispered Sara.

'Because it is absolutely intolerable the way that people think they can come barging in here, taking advantage of your good nature and picking your brains, interrupting us and disturbing you from whatever you are doing. We need a couple of hours to plan the office design, and it's no harm to let them see immediately that you are going to regard your job as important. It may only be half the job they should have given you, but don't worry, you'll have the right job very soon.'

'Suppose that the really big brass come along, or Mr Edwards or you know, someone important.' Sara was still unsure.

'We are having a conference, about the redesign of your office.'

'But there isn't any money to redesign it . . . even if they'd let me.'

'Yes there is, I've been up to the requisition department, in fact they looked you up on the book, and wondered why you hadn't applied. Whenever you're ready Miss Gray, we can start.'

Together they worked out how the office should look. It was a big room, but it was in no way impressive; apart from the inferior furniture, its design was all wrong. Eve explained, that a separate cubicle should be built for her near the door. Eve should act as a kind of reception area for Sara, she should call through to announce visitors, even though it was only a distance of a few yards.

'They'll walk past and come straight on in,' said Sara.

'Not if I walk after them and ask can I help them. They won't do it twice, Miss Gray,' said Eve and Sara realised that most of them wouldn't even do it once.

The costing of the partition was not enormous, and it left a reasonable amount for the rest of the furnishings.

'We'll have the filing section in my part since you shouldn't really have to be looking things up your-self, Miss Gray, but it will of course be kept in a very meticulous way so you can always find anything.'

'What will I have in my part of the office then?' asked Sara humbly.

Eve stood up and walked around. 'I've been giving it a lot of thought, Miss Gray. You are really the ideas woman here. I'm sorry, I know it's jargon, but that's what you do for the promotions department. You thought up that whole idea about choosing a holiday from your stars in the zodiac and that worked, you thought of having a travel agents' conference in that railway station which suited them all since they had to come from all over the country and go back again by train. You thought up the scheme of having children write the section for children's holidays, so I think that this is what you should be doing really. Thinking. And let me handle the routine things, you know, the letters about "Can you trace what we did about Portugal two years ago?" If the filing system works properly then anyone will be able to do that for you. I'll set it up so that at least four-fifths of your incoming mail can be handled by any competent secretary. That should give you a great deal more time to do what you are really good at.'

Sara looked hopeful but not convinced.

'Me just sit in here with a chair?' She shook her head. 'I

don't think it's on Eve, I really don't. You know they'd think I'd gone mad.'

'I wasn't suggesting a chair. I was going to suggest a long narrow conference table. Something in nice wood, we could look at auctions or in an antique shop. And about six chairs. Then, for you a small writing desk. Again something from an old house possibly, with your telephone and your own big diary and notebook, a few periodicals and trade magazines or directories you need, that's all.'

'Eve, in God's name, what is the long conference table for. Eve, I am the assistant promotions manager, not the chairman of the board. I don't give conferences, call meetings, ask my superiors to come in here with the hope of blinding them about policy.'

'You should,' said Eve simply. 'Listen,' she went on. 'Remember that children writing the brochure idea? It was marvellous. I've been looking through the files, you got not one word of credit, no letter, no mention, no thanks even. I would not be at all surprised if you, Mr Edwards and I are the only people who know you thought it up, and the only reason I know is that I see entries in your diary about going to schools and talking to children and spending a lot of your free time working on it. Edwards got the praise, the thanks and the job, for not only that but for everything you did. Because you didn't do it right.'

'It worked, though,' said Sara defensively.

'Miss Gray, of course the idea worked, it was brilliant, I remember seeing those brochures long before I ever knew you, and I thought they were inspired. What I mean is that it didn't work for you, here within the company. Next time, I suggest you invite Mr Edwards and his boss and the marketing director and one or two others to drop in quite casually – don't dream of saying you are calling a meeting, just suggest that they might all like to come into your office one afternoon. And then, at a nice table where there is plenty of room and plenty of style, put forward your plans. That way they'll remember you.'

'Yes, I know, in theory you're right, Eve . . . but honestly, I'm not the type. I'm jolly old Sara Gray, with a nice, jolly, hopeless lover who comes and goes at home – and who is gone at the moment. And they all say to themselves, "poor Sara, not a bad old thing" – none of them would take me at a rosewood conference table for one minute Eve, they'd either corpse themselves laughing or else they'd think I was having a breakdown, they'd fire me. And you.'

Eve didn't look at all put out. 'I wasn't suggesting calling a conference tomorrow, I was suggesting having the furniture right. If you are someone who is valuable to the company for her ideas, you should have a space to think up these ideas, a platform to present them on, and the just recognition for them.'

'You're right,' Sara said suddenly. 'What else?'

'I think you should get into the habit of having Mr Edwards and others coming to this office, by appointment of course, rather than you rushing to theirs. It makes you more important. That's why we need the right furniture. Mr Edwards has an office like an aeroplane hangar, and very well laid out, I've inspected it. But yours could have a charm, it could become the place where ideas were discussed say on one particular evening a week, a Thursday, before people left. It would be relaxing, and pleasant, and *you* would be in control.'

As they talked on, it got darker outside, and they switched on the bright neon overhead light.

'That'll have to go for a start,' said Eve. 'It's far too harsh, there's no style, no warmth.'

A few times the door had been half-opened, but whenever people saw the two heads bent over the desk and lists, they muttered apologies and backed out.

'I never thought a notice would do that,' said Sara admiringly.

'Wait till we get things going properly, you'll be amazed.' said Eve.

Eve refused a drink, a girly chat and the offer of a share in a taxi. Instead she took out her notebook again.

'You should have an account with a taxi firm,' she said briskly. 'I'll set that up tomorrow, when I'm organising the flowers and your dress allowance.'

Sara stared at her in the windy, wet street as if Eve had gone completely mad.

'*What* are you organising . . .?' she began.

'Plants, flowers for the office, all the male senior executives have them, and they also get a special expense allowance for clothes because they have to travel, it being a travel company, and . . .'

'Eve, I'm not a senior executive, I can't have free flowers paid for by the office.'

'As assistant manager you are technically a senior executive. The other two assistant managers are elderly men who have been pushed upstairs, so if you equate your title with theirs then you can have flowers, nothing extravagant, about six nice flowering plants. I think we can choose them from a brochure, they'll arrive tomorrow.'

For the first time for a long time Sara sat back contentedly in her chair at home and didn't think about Geoff and wonder when his new obsession would end. Often she felt lonely and sad during his absences, so that she would hide from the feeling by having the television on or listening to music for long hours. But tonight she just sat calmly drinking her tea and looking into the fire. Eve's arrival meant that a lot of the tension in the office had been eased. It was like someone massaging your shoulders and taking away the stiffness – you didn't know how tense you had been until the massage was over – Eve was going to make things a lot better, and she was going to force Sara to take herself more seriously too. It was a bit exciting in a way.

Next morning was a Friday and Eve wanted to know whether Sara had any important plans and engagements for the weekend. Sara shrugged 'I was going to sort out those figures for Mr Edwards, you know the ones he wanted on the breakdown of age groups on the coach holidays. We need to know where to direct some of the coach tour promotions this year.'

'Oh, that's done.' said Eve. 'I did it this morning, I saw his note. I've two copies here for you to sign, one for Mr Edwards and I thought you should send one to the head of marketing, just to let him know that you are alive and well and working harder than Mr Edwards.'

'Isn't that a bit sneaky?' asked Sara looking like a doubtful schoolgirl.

'No, it's standard office procedure. Mr Edwards is the sneaky party, by not acknowledging your part in all the work that is being done.'

With a weekend free Sara agreed happily to go to look at second-hand furniture and office fittings. Eve had already organised the office partition, and it began with great hammering and activity after lunch.

'I suggest you go and check out a few new outfits for yourself, Miss Gray,' said Eve. 'You can't possibly work here with all this noise.'

'Could you come with me, I'm not exactly sure what I . . . ?'

'Certainly, Miss Gray, can you wait five minutes while I tell these gentlemen I shall be back in two hours to see how they are getting on?'

Eve managed to make three large men look as if they knew she was going to have them fired unless the partition was perfect. Then she went to the shop with Sara.

There was a brief objective discussion about what clothes Sara already possessed. Eve explained that she had only seen two tweed skirts and one black sweater in the three days she had been working there. Shame-facedly, Sara said she thought there were a couple of other sweaters and perhaps two more workable tweed skirts.

Eve seemed neither pleased nor put out; she was merely asking for information. In the store she suggested three outfits which could interchange and swap and make about a dozen between them. They cost so much that Sara had to sit down on the fitting-room chair.

'I took the liberty of getting you a credit card for your expenses, Miss Gray,' said Eve. 'I rushed it through, and what you are going to spend now is totally justifiable. You have to meet the public, you have to represent the company in places where the company may well be judged by the personal appearance of its representatives. What you are spending on these garments is half what Mr Edwards has spent in the last six months, and you have been entitled to expenses of this kind for over a year and never called on them.'

By Monday Sara could hardly recognise either herself or her new surroundings. On Eve's advice she had had an expensive hair-do; she wore the pink and grey wool outfit, put the pink cyclamens on her window sill, near the lovely old table with its matching half-dozen chairs which they had eventually found for half nothing since it was too big for most homes, and nobody except Eve would have thought of it as office furniture

Eve was living in her purpose-built annexe surrounded with files and ledgers. She had just begun to compile a folio of Sara's work so far with the company, a kind of illustrated *curriculum vitae* which would show her worth and catalogue her achievements. Nobody was more sur-prised than Sara by all she seemed to have done during her years in the company.

'I'm really quite good, you know,' she said happily.

'Miss Gray, you are very good indeed, otherwise I

wouldn't work with you,' said Eve solemnly, and Sara could detect no hint of humour or self-mockery in the tone.

Towards the end of the second week, Eve pronounced herself pleased with the office. She had bought an old coat-stand which ideally matched the table and chairs, and on this she urged Sara to hang her smart coat so that the whole place just looked as if it were an extension of her own creative personality. If anyone gasped with amazement at the changes in the room, Sara was to say that there was all this silly money up in requisitions for her to decorate the place, and she did hate modern ugly cubes of furniture so she had just chosen things she liked – which had in fact been cheaper. People were stunned, and jealous, and wondered why they hadn't thought of this too.

Remarks about her appearance Eve suggested should be parried slightly. No need to tell people that she now had regular twice weekly sessions with a beautician. Eve had booked her a course of twenty.

So on the second Friday of her employment Eve came into Sara's part of the office and said she thought that they were ready to begin.

'Begin?' cried Sara. 'I thought we'd finished.'

Eve gave one of her rare smiles. 'I meant begin your work, Miss Gray. I've been taking up a lot of your time with what I am sure you must have considered inessentials. Now I feel that you should concentrate totally on your work for promotions and let me look after everything else. I shall keep detailed records of all the routine work that I am doing. Each evening I'll leave you a progress report, too, of how I think we have been getting on in our various projects. These I think you should take home with you or else return to my personal file. We don't want them seen by anyone else.'

Sara nodded her thanks. Suddenly she felt overwhelmed with gratitude for this strange girl who was behaving not as a new secretary but as if she were an old family retainer blind with loyalty to the young Missie, or a kindergarten teacher filled with affection and hope for a young charge.

She felt almost unable to express any of this gratitude because Eve didn't seem to need it or even to like it.

'Are there any, er, major projects you see straight away?' she asked.

'I think you should look for an assistant, or a deputy, Miss Gray,' said Eve.

'*Eve*, you can't go, you can't leave me now!' cried Sara.

'Miss Gray, I am your secretary, not your assistant. I certainly shall not leave you for a year. I told you that. No, you need to train someone in to do your job when you are not here.'

'Not here?' Sara looked around her new office which she was beginning to love. 'Where will I be, why won't I be here?'

'Because you will be away on conferences, you will be travelling abroad to see the places the company is promoting, and of course, Miss Gray, you will be taking your own vacation, something you neglected to do last year I see.'

'Yes, but that'll only be a few weeks at most. Why do I need to have an assistant, a deputy? I mean it's like empire building.'

'You'll need to train an assistant to take over when you get Mr Edwards' job at the end of the year. One of the many reasons why women fail to get promotion is because management can say that there is nobody else to do their job on the present level of the ladder. I suggest you find a bright and very young, extremely young man.'

'But I can't do that. They'd know I was plotting to get Garry Edwards' job'.

Eve smiled. 'I'm glad you are calling Mr Edwards by his first name at last, Miss Gray. No, you need an assistant to do your work for you while you are away, of course.

Otherwise, if this whole office is seen to tick along nicely without you in your absence, people will wonder why your presence is so essential. If on the other hand, it turns into total chaos, they will blame you *in absentia*. So you need a harmless, enthusiastic, personable young man to sign letters which I will write and to postpone anything major until your return.'

'Eve, why do you have to go away in a year?' Sara said suddenly. 'Why can't you stay and together we'll take over the whole place. Honestly it's not impossible.'

'Oh, Miss Gray, there'd be no point in taking the place over. It's not what either of us want, is it?' asked Eve, accepting naturally that it would be perfectly feasible to takeover the largest travel company in Britain if she put her mind to it.

'You never tell me what you want,' Sara said, impressed by her own daring.

'I like to see women getting their work recognised. There's so much sheer injustice in the business world – I mean really unjust things are done to women. I find that very strange. Men who can be so kind to stray dogs, lost strangers, their own children, contribute generously to charities and yet continue appalling unfairness towards women at work.'

She stopped suddenly.

Sara said, 'Go on.'

'Nothing more,' Eve said firmly. 'You asked me what I wanted. I want to see that injustice recognised for what it is, and to see people fight it.'

'You should write about it, or make speeches,' said Sara. 'I never even saw it in my own case until you came. I do agree now that I've been shabbily treated and now I've got a bit of confidence to demand more. And that's only after ten days with you. Think what success you'd have if you were to go on a lecture tour or on television or something.'

Eve looked sad.

'No. That's just the whole trouble. It doesn't work that way, damn it. That's why it's going to take so long.'

Politely she extricated herself from further explanations, from any more conversation, from having a drink at a near-by pub with Sara. She had to go home now.

'You never tell me about your home,' said Sara.

'You never tell me about yours, Miss Gray, either,' said Eve.

'I would if I got a chance,' Sara said.

'Ah yes, but you and I would not get on so well if I knew about your worries and problems!'

Sara took it as a very faint warning. It meant that Eve didn't want to hear about Sara's problems and worries either. She sighed. It would have been very helpful if Eve could apply her amazing skills to Sara's disastrous relationship with Geoff. He had been gone now three weeks. No, it couldn't be three weeks. It was. She could hardly believe it. The last ten days had passed so quickly she had scarcely missed him. She was so stunned by this that she hadn't heard what Eve had said.

'I was only saying that I left your invitation for the supper party tomorrow night there on your desk,' Eve repeated as she gathered up her things. 'I hope you enjoy it. I heard that all senior executives were normally invited to meet the chairman and board members so I made sure your name was on the list. Nice chance to wear that black dress too, Miss Gray, I expect you're thinking.'

Sara's eyes were big with gratitude. As if by magic Eve seemed to have known that another lonely weekend was looming ahead. But she knew not to admit to any emotion.

'Great. I'll go in there and knock them dead. And on Monday we'll be ready to begin the campaign.'

'Excellent,' said Eve. 'I suggest you find out whether any of the board have young and hopefully stupid sons who might want to start in the business. As your assistant, you know. We need someone rather over-educated with no brains.'

'What are you going to do for the weekend?' asked Sara.

'This and that, Miss Gray. See you Monday,' said Eve.

Sara spent Saturday reading the company's reports which Eve had left thoughtfully on her desk. She took Eve's advice and wore the black dress to the party where Garry Edwards' surprise at seeing her was as exciting as any romantic flutter. 'I can see how people can become obsessed with all this infighting and competitiveness,' thought Sara.

She was charming to the chairman, she was respectful to Garry Edwards and risked calling him Garry once or twice: she caught him looking at her sideways several times. She was very pleasant to a middle-aged and lonely woman who was the wife of a noisy extrovert board member. The woman was so grateful that she positively unburdened her life story. Eve's face came like a quick flash across the conversation; Sara remembered how she had implied that people don't really want to be bogged down with personal life stories, particularly of a gloomy nature. She murmured her sympathy for the details and disclaimers of the woman's tale about neglect and being pushed into the background.

'All he cares about now is our son, he's coming down from Cambridge soon, with an Arts Degree: no plans, no interests.'

Eve would have been proud of her. She geared the conversation gently to her own office, to how she would be delighted to meet the boy – she even gave the woman her card with a little note scribbled on it. How amazing that she should suddenly find a need for those nice new cards which Eve had ordered for her and produced within days of her arrival. Garry Edwards came across at one stage to find out what she was up to; Sara steered the conversation away again.

'Where's that chap that you are seen with sometimes – and sometimes not?' asked Edwards, determined to wound.

'If he's not here, it must be one of the evenings I'm not seen with him,' said Sara cheerfully.

That night she went to sleep in her big double bed, hoping that Geoff would not come home. She had too much to think about.

The weeks went by, two more of them. She had already held three successful and supposedly impromptu gatherings in her office. Always she had included several people higher in the pecking order than Garry Edwards.

Everyone had thought it was a splendid idea to have the handsome young son of their important board member and his lonely wife in the department. He worked most of the time in the general promotions department and two afternoons a week he got what was described as a training from Sara. What it really was was an access to her files, permission to sit in her room as she worked out schemes with some of the other promotions executives, and he learned an almost overpowering respect for Miss Gray from Eve who stood up and expected him to do the same. Eve almost lowered her voice in awe when she spoke of anything Sara had done, and the well meaning, over-educated and not very bright Simon did the same.

Simply because Eve kept him under such an iron rule Simon did learn something. So much in fact that his parents were utterly delighted with him, and the head of marketing, who had opposed his appointment as the nepotism it undoubtedly was, had to admit that that young Miss Gray was able to do the most extraordinary things. He took to dropping in to her pleasant office occasionally, and once or twice that strange colourless secretary had told him very firmly that she couldn't be disturbed. When he implied that he was more important than whoever she could be talking to, the secretary had said very flatly that her instructions were to ask everyone to make appointments, or at least to telephone in advance if they intended to drop in. Since the head of marketing had been saying long and loud that too much socialising and twittering went on in his department in the name of work he could not be otherwise than pleased.

Geoff came back. His latest lady decided that she must go back to her husband and children. This she said was where her duty lay. She said it when all Geoff's money had run out. Geoff had shrugged and come back to Sara. Amazingly she wasn't at home. He let himself in one night with a bottle of champagne, a single rose and a long explanation, but there was nobody to receive any of these things so he just went to bed.

She wasn't there in the morning either. He checked her wardrobe, most of her sweaters and skirts seemed to be there. The place looked neater somehow, and there were no work files strewn about. She had a lot of much more expensive cosmetics in the bathroom too. He wondered what had been happening. He couldn't have been gone more than a month. She hadn't run out, surely? She couldn't have decided to end with him, surely? After all she hadn't changed the lock or anything. His key still opened her hall door.

He called her next morning, and a very cool voice that was not Sara's answered him. 'Miss Gray's office.'

'Oh we have gone up in the world,' giggled Geoff. Loyalty to Sara and building her up to her colleagues was never his strong suit.

'I beg your pardon?' said the voice.

'Listen, it's Geoff here, can I talk to Sara?'

'Can I know who wants to speak to Miss Gray please?' asked Eve.

'Hell, I've just told you. It's Geoff. Sara's chap, Geoff. Put me onto her will you, sweetheart.'

Eve answered very pleasantly. 'I'm afraid you must have the wrong number.'

Geoff sounded annoyed, 'Sara Gray's office, right?'

'Yes this is Miss Sara Gray's office, now will you kindly tell me who this is speaking?'

'Geoff. Geoff White, for Christ's sake, who is that?'

'I am Miss Gray's secretary. Mr White can you please tell me your business. You're taking up a lot of time.'

She didn't actually lie when Sara asked had Geoff phoned. She said that a totally inarticulate man had called but it could hardly have been Geoff. Sara had only paused momentarily to wonder. She had spent five days at a sales conference in Paris, and had told Eve excitedly how she had been asked to address the meeting twice about new brochure ideas. Mr Edwards – or that buffoon Garry as she was now calling him – looked positively yellow with rage. He had tried to make a pass at her which she had rejected with amazement and something akin to distaste. Eve was full of praise.

Next day Sara said: 'The inarticulate man must have been Geoff. His things were in the flat, but I couldn't bear to be woken at three a.m. with champagne and tears and all, so I bolted my door and didn't hear whether he called or not.'

Eve nodded in her cool way. She wanted to hear no more, not one word of Sara's private life. Yet she looked pleased. Things were going as hoped for. Sara was now too busy to worry about Geoff, and soon she would be too confident to accept his amazing behaviour which was already a legend in office gossip. The new Sara would either throw him out or make him behave in a civilised way. Very satisfactory.

The weeks passed again. By now it was already office gossip that Sara would shortly take over from Garry Edwards. People who hadn't rated her much before, were saying now that she had been holding back. Others said that she was always brilliant and that it was only a matter of time before it was recognised.

Garry Edwards blew it. He tried to drop Sara into great trouble for one of his own mistakes. Unlucky Garry Edwards that he had joined battle with Eve's filing system, the relevant documents were produced in a matter of minutes; quite obviously Sara had dealt with the problem, had recommended a correct course of action.

It was shortly after this that Eve asked Sara to come into her small cubicle and go over the filing system with her.

'Let's do a test,' Eve said. 'Suppose you had to find Press Comment on Senior Citizen Campaign, where would you look?' Sara checked first under 'publicity' then under 'Senior Citizens'. It took her five minutes.

'It's too long,' said Eve firmly. 'Perhaps you should have a look for something every day for the next month or so. Just to familiarise yourself.'

'You're going to leave me aren't you?' asked Sara.

'I think so,' said Eve.

'It's not the year, it's not even half a year,' Sara complained.

'But there's nothing left to do, Miss Gray. We get you a new efficient typist, we both explain to her and to Simon what the routine is, you'll be leaving shortly anyway for Mr Edwards' job, we'll just make sure that any change-over here goes smoothly.'

'Can't you come with me, upstairs?' Sara nodded in the direction of the promotions manager's office. 'Please.'

'No, you can do it better on your own really. And it's better for you.' She was like a swimming instructor encouraging a bright but apprehensive pupil.

'The office, Eve, how will I do up the office so that its like this . . . I mean I hate his furniture, I hate his style.'

'You choose, Miss Gray. A few months ago you wouldn't even have noticed his office or his style.'

'Eve, a few months ago you know very well nobody would have noticed me.'

'You underestimate yourself, Miss Gray. Shall I advertise for a secretary, I'd be happy to advise you on any points during any interview.'

'God, yes Eve,' Sara looked at her. 'I won't keep asking you but you know there's no problem about salary.'

Eve shook her head.

Sara put her face into a bright smile. 'In a few months I suppose I'll get a telephone call from some bewildered woman asking me do I know Eve and can I possibly recommend her insane notions.'

Eve looked solemn. 'Well, yes, if you don't mind. I should like your name as a reference.'

'And I'll say Miss whoever you are . . . Eve is not from this planet. Let her have her way with you and you'll be running your company in months.'

Eve stood up briskly. 'Yes, if you think it was all worth it.'

Sara put out her hand and held Eve's arm.

'I know you hate people prying but why, just why? You're far brighter than I am, than the woman in the bank, than the other woman – the one you told to have dinner parties. I mean, why don't *you* do it. Why don't you do it for *you*. You know better than any of us how to get on. It's like a kind of crusade for you but you stay in the background all the time. I don't know what you're at. What you want.'

Eve shrugged politely. 'I like to see you do well, Miss Gray, that's enough reward for me. You deserve it. You were being passed over. That wasn't just.'

Sara nodded. 'Now I promise, all the rest of the time you are here, I'll never ask again. Never. Just tell me. Why this way? If you feel there's discrimination against women there must be better ways to fight it.'

Eve leaned against the beautiful table and stroked it. 'If there are I can't find them. I simply know of no better way to fight it than from within. You have to use the system. I hate it but it's true.'

Sara didn't interrupt. She knew that if Eve was ever going to say anything it would be now. She let the pause last.

'How do you think I, as a feminist, like asking intelligent, sensitive women like you and like Bonnie Bernstein in the bank, and Marrion Smith in the ministry to dress properly? As if it mattered one goddamn whether you wore woad to the office . . . all three of you are worth more than any man I ever met in any kind of business. And I could say that for seven or eight other women, too. But women don't have a chance, they don't bloody know . . .'

Sara sat breathless.

'It's so *unjust*.' Eve stressed that word heavily. 'So totally unjust. A married man has a woman to look after his appearance and his clothes and his meals and his house, a woman does not. A single man has a fleet of secretaries, assistants, manicurists, lovers to look after him. A single woman is meant to cope. A man is admired for sleeping with people on his way up, a woman is considered a tramp if she does. A man . . .' She paused and pulled herself together, almost physically. 'Miss Gray, you must excuse me. I really don't think I should be taking up your time with all this. I do apologise. I feel ashamed of myself.'

The moment was gone, the spell was broken.

'I don't suppose you'll tell me why you feel like this? I mean was there some experience in your life, Eve, you are so young, too young to be bitter about things.'

Eve looked at her. 'No, of course I'm not bitter, I'm very constructive. I just try to get some justice for strong, good women who deserve it. When I've got it I move on. It's very satisfying. Slow but satisfying. Now, about this advertisement. I don't think we should phrase it "travel business", it will attract the kind of woman who thinks in terms of cheap flights and free holidays.'

Sara played along. She owed Eve that much.

'Oh yes, of course. Let's word it now, and put it in whenever you want to. The later the better of course. You know I don't want you to leave here ever.'

'Thank you very much, Miss Gray. But I think really if you agreed I'll get it into tomorrow's papers.'

Sara looked up.

'So soon?'

'There's a lot to be done,' said Eve.

Euston

Elizabeth marvelled at the changes in Euston. She remembered the station much more clearly as the fairly gloomy and barracks-like place where she had gone with Mother and Father to meet Dara each year when she came over from Ireland on holiday. And here she was years later in the huge revamped place with its shops and its flashing lights and escalators waiting for Dara again. Dara who could well afford to fly but who decided that it would be more fun to retrace the old tracks and come on boat and train; Dara who had always made the holidays turn into technicolour for Elizabeth, the only child; Dara who was so quiet and gentle but somehow managed to make things cheerful in a house where there was little love; Dara who had been able to say things to Mother and Father even after one of their dreadful rows – something that would ease the atmosphere – while Elizabeth would sit mute and tight-lipped, afraid that by opening her mouth she would drive her parents further from each other than they already were.

Even after the divorce, when she and Dara were fifteen, there had been a visit. Mother and Elizabeth had waited in this very spot and when Dara got off the train and ran up to them, she had hugged Mother and said, 'You poor old thing, it must be desperately lonely and sort of low for you these days,' and Mother had hugged her back and cried. Mother crying in public and hugging Dara.

Elizabeth had felt her heart lift for the first time since

the divorce. Dara always had this gift of saying what people didn't say and it all worked perfectly.

During that particular visit Dara had suggested that she would like to see Father. Dara said she had a present for him from Ireland. Mother had pursed her lips and looked disapproving. Elizabeth had feared that everything was going to turn sour again. 'Aw, come on out of that,' Dara had said. 'Now for the rest of your life you can't be expecting that nobody except Elizabeth is going to want to be friends with both of you. It's not a battle for us.'

And because of Dara the visit to Father had been marvellous instead of stilted, and Dara had said 'Aw, come on out of that, of course you've got a new lady friend, why can't we meet her? It's silly to ask her to be out all day, or hidden away as if she were in disgrace.' So Father, delighted, had suggested that Julia join them for lunch, and it had been a memorable meal with wine and a sip of brandy afterwards, and Dara said that there was no purpose in carrying tales from one household back to another, it only made things worse on everyone . . . and with her carefree attitude she had brought some kind of happiness into that troubled summer also.

Dara lived in Ireland with an old grandmother, a housekeeper and a gardener. Her parents, who had been friends of Mother and Father in the old days, had been killed in a car crash and so now Dara's life was a matter of cycling to a local school each day, coming home and making sure her hands were nice and clean and that she came in to lunch or dinner when the gong sounded. She told her old grandmother little tales about what happened at school or with her friends, or during the holidays about what she had read. She seemed to lead an idyllic existence, wandering around the countryside exploring and reading in her large sunny bedroom which looked out on purple mountains. Once a year she came to spend two weeks in London, her annual treat.

The friendship lasted long after schooldays. Dara had trained as a nurse in an Irish hospital at the same time as Elizabeth was doing her training in London. They still holidayed in each others' homes, and as they became more adventurous they even went as far as Spain and Italy together. When Dara's grandmother died there was even talk of her coming to London to share a flat with Elizabeth but she said she would miss the purple mountains and the narrow roads, which she now drove along in her little car instead of pedalling on her creaking bike.

There was also a question of Dara marrying some doctor near-by. Elizabeth had become very excited about this and hoped the romance was going well.

'Do you think he's interested? Do you really think he's contemplating it?' she had asked Dara eagerly when she went to spend a spring week in the Irish countryside and had met the handsome doctor two or three times.

Dara had astonished her by saying: 'Oh, that's not the point. I mean it's easy enough to make him interested, it's just that I don't know yet if *I* want him or not. That's the only problem.'

Elizabeth had been mystified. She assumed in some vague way that Dara must be talking about sexual favours, but despite their years of friendship this was not an area that they discussed. The young doctor was dropped from conversation and from Dara's life, and always Elizabeth had a suspicion that Dara may have loved him a lot, but had failed to attract him. That her conversation had merely been bravado. Still, Dara seemed to have few regrets. She had transformed her grandmother's crumbling old house into an excellent old people's home. The housekeeper and the gardener lived there in style and comfort to work out their old age in payment for all they had given to the place. This gave Dara a very high reputation in the community. Many a young one who came into money might have been hoity-toity, but Miss Dara was different. A very kind

young woman indeed. She employed a small staff, all
of whom seemed to have been chosen on grounds of
their pleasant personalities. It wasn't surprising that the
place had a waiting list of several years. Dara kept a
supervisory eye on the place but she still worked some
hours in the local hospital and still took time to travel.
People often wondered why she didn't marry. By the
time she was thirty-five they assumed that she was a
career woman. It couldn't be from lack of suitors or
opportunities.

Elizabeth, too, wondered from time to time, why Dara
had never married. But it had not been a serious worry.
She assumed it was because of the gentle fulfilling pace
that Dara's life always seemed to have been lived at. She
had never been searching or seeking. She was always
perfectly content with her lot. That's what had made her
such a delightful companion. Perhaps these Irish men
who must surely have fancied her had been too diffident,
too unsure in their own minds about the whole concept
of marriage to force Dara to change, to insist that barriers
be broken down. Dara would have made a great wife and
sailed through all the storms of matrimony, Elizabeth
sighed as she waited at the station.

And there were many. Oh dear Lord, there were
many. It was a simple fact that when you get married
there are not enough hours in the day. Nothing more or
less. There are not sufficient slots of time to be a wife, full
of interest and concern, and dying to make love, and up
to date with every aspect of Derek's work in research. To
be a mother, wiping dirty faces, washing clothes, playing
creative games, spotting incipient infections, participat-
ing meaningfully in the playgroup scheme, arranging
baby-sitters that will get on well with the children. To be a
worker, to put in thirty-eight hours a week in the nursing
agency. To be a home maker, that awful American word
which seemed to cover a full-time job polishing, shining,
making curtains, cooking, entertaining, gardening.

Even if she slept only two hours a night, Elizabeth thought, it would be too much. There were not enough *hours*.

She needed the job, they both needed her to have the job. Derek's job was not well enough paid for the kind of lifestyle they wanted. Anyway, she liked the job. What she didn't like was the constant guilt, the foolish wearying feeling of being behind at everything. She hated taking the children's mending to work to try and do it in the crowded bus, but where else could she find that spare half-hour? She hated shopping at lunch hour, she hated having to rush and pick the children up from a neighbour's house and have them at home demanding her time and attention before she had time to unpack the groceries and have a shower. It would only take her half an hour, that extra half-hour would give her so much more freedom and energy, but it was impossible. Her bus passed the neighbour's house at five-thirty so it made sense to pick the children up there and walk the ten minutes home with them rather than coming back and having an extra twenty minutes added to the evening at the other end of a half-hour's peace at home. Or so Derek had said. Derek came home at seven, when the house was invariably a mess, the children and herself locked in some struggle about bed, toys, bath, supper. It had become so wildly unsatisfactory that Elizabeth was feeling severe strain, and because of her small medical knowledge she knew it was teetering near the edge of a breakdown.

She wrote it all out in a long letter to Dara, wondering whether she should just collapse and let it all take care of itself. Dara said she would come for a month. Elizabeth could spend a week in a nursing home, two weeks in a health farm and one week at home picking up the threads.

'I'll come at the beginning of February,' Dara had written. 'By March 1st you will be right as rain.'

It was as if a Messiah had announced an imminent coming. Elizabeth was happy already.

When Dara came bouncing up the ramp, her short brown hair ruffled and attractive, Elizabeth felt an almost physical pain of relief. Here was the one person who would make the household happy again. The great restorer of peace as she had been in Mother and Father's time, doing it over twenty years later for Elizabeth herself. She hugged her and clung to her with tears starting to flow.

Dara was obviously startled to see her friend in such poor shape. She put her hand professionally on Elizabeth's forehead.

'I see I'm just in time,' she said. She waved them into a taxi airily. 'You're in no shape to battle with the tube, silly,' she said. 'Anyway we can make our plan of campaign in comfort. Have you booked the nursing home?'

'Yes,' gulped Elizabeth. 'I think they must think I am not all there. It's very dear.'

'That's my wedding present to you, I never gave you a proper one,' said Dara. Elizabeth had a vague memory that Dara had given her some huge fluffy towels but she said nothing.

'Now, the health farm the next week.'

'Yes, yes. I booked it. I know you said to take it from Mother's legacy, I have. Do you think two weeks is too long?'

'No,' said Dara. 'Now Derek. Have you told him yet?'

'Well, yes and no,' said Elizabeth, her face becoming twisted in an effort to explain.

'That means no,' said Dara.

'He'd think I was silly, he'd think I was weak and self-indulgent.' Elizabeth began to stutter in her eagerness to defend Derek's attitude. 'You see, I've been so hopeless recently. So tired. And so complaining. I don't want to let him think he married a dud.'

'Tell him your doctor insisted on it,' said Dara. 'I'll back it up, and say in my professional opinion, which is true by the way, I never saw anyone so much on the verge of collapse. I'll run the house, mind the kids, give Derek his bowl of porridge now and then, and when you come back glowing and well you'll be as right as rain.'

That lovely expression, 'as right as rain', Elizabeth had used it a million times, without ever thinking about it She thought suddenly of the soft gentle rain in Ireland. She thought about the constancy of rain. She felt vastly cheered.

'I don't know why you came to meet me,' said Dara. 'I could easily have made my own way to the house, you know. It would have given you another couple of hours to yourself.'

'Oh we always meet you at Euston,' said Elizabeth, and Dara patted her hand affectionately.

The house was indeed in poor shape. Dara looked around with a practised eye. The children were sweet little three- and four-year-olds, Benny and Nell, but they had obviously worn Derek to a frazzle.

'What *do* they eat at this time darling?' he said in a harrassed tone to Elizabeth. 'They seem very restless. I've no idea what you would have given them.'

Dara gave Derek a peck, and vanished to her room. She returned in ten minutes dressed for work in a simple pinafore of green corduroy.

'You look very business-like,' said Derek with approval. Elizabeth felt even more foolish in her best silk suit, which she was hoping might escape the strains and dangers of Benny and Nell.

'Well, your wife is going to leave us together for three weeks, I'll tell you all about it later,' she said. 'So meanwhile, I suppose I'd better dress to please you.'

Already the tension was lifting.

Already the atmosphere was lighter.

Dara was working her familiar magic.

'Lie down, Elizabeth my love, I'll call you when the meal is ready. Do, there's a good girl,' said Dara.

And Elizabeth went up to her room, where she rested with a great sense of relief. Dara would explain it all to Derek. Dara would make him see that she wasn't a non-starter. Not a weakling. She closed her eyes. At peace for the first time for ages. It was nine o'clock when Dara came to waken her with a cup of consommé with sherry.

'This will liven you up,' she said.

Elizabeth drank it gratefully.

'What's happening? I must get up,' she said suddenly.

All her guilt came flooding back. The meat hadn't been unfrozen for the goulash, the dish-washing machine hadn't been emptied. Heavens. There might well be no clean linen. She had been asleep for two hours.

'It's under control,' said Dara. And indeed it was. Derek had been banished with a drink to the television, the children had been bathed and given cornflakes, the goulash had been designated tomorrow's dinner, while Dara's smoked salmon from Ireland had been carved and sliced and laid on beds of vegetables, the table had been polished and old mats with hunting prints had appeared. In the kitchen the soft whir of the washing machine meant that all the table linen as well as the children's clothes were purring around in a low suds detergent. Elizabeth sighed with pleasure. It was a delightful dinner, and Derek said to her tenderly that he felt very selfish for not having noticed her strain. All three of them made great plans for the week in the nursing home. They drank a toast to the joy of hospitalisation without any disease, or any terror of waiting for results. For the first time in months Elizabeth slept a long peaceful sleep.

Elizabeth went to the nursing home early in the morning. Derek drove her there before he went to work. Dara said she knew well the running of the house, and insisted that she could also replace Elizabeth at the nursing agency so that no extra cash would be lost. The real reason she wanted to do it was to ensure that nobody there could regard Elizabeth as a malingerer. Dara's nursing qualifications were even superior to Elizabeth's, there would be no problem.

And indeed there *were* no problems.

Dara realised quickly that a great deal of problems could be solved by buying food in bulk. So she made a master list and suggested that she and Derek buy this early on Saturday morning. She settled him with the children in a café and had the shopping ready to be collected from the supermarket door in forty minutes. Then she settled in to sit with the children while she sent Derek with a list to buy the week's drink and gardening requisites. 'That's a man's job,' she said when Derek demurred, and he felt very important.

On Sunday she arranged to have the neighbour's children for the day, mainly so that they would entertain Benny and Nell in the bedroom which she had made into a play room for them. But it also made the neighbour feel that she wasn't being taken for granted. It meant she could go to the pub and even have a leisurely lunch with her husband and a bit of slap and tickle. She agreed readily to hold on to Benny and Nell until whatever hour the family liked to collect them on work days. 'I think Derek should pick them up in his car. Their little legs get tired walking home,' said Dara. Derek wondered why nobody had ever thought of this.

She spent a half-hour each day in the garden, but always in places where it showed. The front looked weeded and cared for. Dara even organised funny winter window boxes which looked cheerier than anything else on the road.

When Derek arrived home with the children, she was there, cheerful, fire lighting, and drink in her hand. Derek relaxed while she bathed the toddlers, and together they read them funny stories while they had their supper and went to bed. Then Derek and Dara played chess or looked at television while she mended clothes. Dara told Derek funny tales of the people she nursed. She always made the people sound tender or witty or eccentric, never demanding or tiresome. He loved to hear of them. She was very interested to know where his research was going and why so much money was being given to the Americans while so little went to the British.

Each night they telephoned Elizabeth and listened to what she said. Sometimes she seemed very defensive, and self-justifying. 'You don't have to explain to us,' said Dara over and over. 'We know why you're run down. It's a killer running a job and a home.' Yet, Dara didn't look killed by it, she glowed with happiness, and the house seemed to turn on oiled hinges.

The day of Elizabeth's return was to be fêted, Dara decided. There would be a special celebration meal. Elizabeth was to come back at seven o'clock on a Friday.

'Be sure to take a taxi from the station, darling,' said Derek. He was beginning to believe that a small expense on taxis could save a lot of wear and tear and a lot of time.

Benny and Nell made a banner with 'Welcome Home Mummy' on it. There was to be a bottle of champagne and a cake. They all sat until nearly eight o'clock when Derek became worried and rang the health farm.

'Oh, she left here this afternoon,' the director said. 'She should be with you by now.'

The key turned in the lock and in from the wet sleet came Elizabeth dripping on the newly vacuumed floor.

'I took the tube, a taxi seemed such a waste. Then there were no buses,' she said.

There were cries of welcome, she looked less tired but very bedraggled from her long wait and walk in the rain. She gazed around the house admiringly, it looked very well kept somehow. There was much more peace than there had been three weeks ago when, weary and beaten, she had left it.

'I'll only have a very little piece of cake,' she said proudly. 'I've lost nearly a stone.' They all cooed over her, and Derek put his arm protectively around her shoulder and said he was delighted to have her back and her old self.

Dara tactfully went to bed early after dinner to leave them together. Derek began to tell Elizabeth about the new turn in his work but from habit her mind wandered, and she said she must think of tomorrow's lunch.

'It's done,' he said irritably.

'Done? How can it be done?' she asked mystified.

'Well it's Saturday tomorrow darling. We'll be going out shopping early, and then home to soup and sandwiches, like we do every Saturday.'

'Well, I'll make the sandwiches, if we're going to leave early,' said Elizabeth, a bit discomfited to hear him say 'like every Saturday', when there had only been three Saturdays.

'Oh, darling. They're made. We always have something on Friday night that can end up as sandwiches next day. Dara has mashed up the chicken with some mayonnaise I expect, and we'll get nice crusty bread tomorrow and that's lunch.' He said it with such confidence and sense of repeating the obvious that Elizabeth felt both amused and yet chilled. How very well the house had managed without her.

'It's a good idea this Saturday shopping then?' she asked timidly.

'Well, it makes sense doesn't it?' said Derek, making nothing of five years of her standing in line at delicatessens and greengrocers during lunch hours and carrying them home on crowded buses.

But the week was sheer pleasure. She went back to work and was oohed and aahed over by the other nurses and by her patients who all praised that nice Irish nurse who had been there during her illness.

Each evening when she got back the house seemed like

a welcoming palace; Dara had used the time to do a thorough spring clean and a reorganisation of the linen cupboard.

'Can you give me a list of all the things you buy on a Saturday?' Elizabeth asked humbly.

'Could you explain what exactly you do in the garden?' she begged.

'How are the clothes always clean when you are here?' she implored.

Dara always answered helpfully. She never implied that Elizabeth was an incompetent.

The day before she left Elizabeth said, 'I don't think I'm as right as rain.'

'You're nearly as right as rain,' said Dara as they sat in the sparkling kitchen and had a cup of tea. The children were gurgling happily in their bedroom-cum-playroom, and Derek was having a shower before his evening sherry and chat before dinner.

'What'll I do, Dara?' she asked.

'You *could* quit work, take a lodger to make up some of the dough.'

'No, no.'

'You could do extra hours for the agency and employ a home help.'

'No, no,' said Elizabeth.'

'Well, just keep sort of going I suppose,' said Dara. 'I mean it's not anyone's fault that you're not as right as rain. It's not Derek's fault, he's smashing, and the kids are lovely, and the work's fine, and that neighbour of yours is a real pal, if you take her kids on a Sunday she'll do anything for you. She loves her Sundays.'

'Don't go,' Elizabeth begged.

'Aw, come on Eliza,' Dara always called her that. For over twenty years it has been 'Come on Eliza'.

Eliza looked at her, hoping for a solution.

'Of course I've got to go. Take it easy, take it nice and easy. There aren't any problems at all you know.'

Elizabeth looked at her friend carefully. Dara had said that about Mother and Father. 'Aw, come on Eliza they're only having a bit of a barney with each other . . .' then they had got divorced.

'Aw, come on Eliza, it's not the end of the world, they're both nice happy people, don't make them into old miseries by your own attitude. Enjoy both of them.' Fine until Father had committed suicide and Mother had joined that funny religion of nutters leaving a small legacy to Elizabeth as a gesture towards sanity and family life.

'Aw, come on Eliza, everyone works and runs a home these days – why do you think you're going to be the one who won't manage?' she had said when Elizabeth had first complained of finding it all a little too much.

'Eliza, you'll be as right as rain,' she had said only four weeks ago. And Eliza wasn't.

It had always been the same, when Dara had left, Mother and Father had looked at her and each other, expecting something that Elizabeth wasn't able to give, and being disappointed with her, unreasonably disappointed, because she couldn't. She realised that everyone – Derek, Benny, Nell, that tiresome neighbour, the people at the agency – would all look expectantly at Elizabeth and wish that there was something there, something that Dara's presence had led them to believe was there.

She looked at her friend, and wondered for the first time why she hadn't had a duller friend, one against whom she could be measured and come out winning. Someone dull who would make her shine. Someone messy who would make her seem organised by comparison.

It had been a bad thing to have had Dara to stay. It had been a bad thing for twenty-six years, but she only realised it now, when she was as far as she ever was from being as right as rain.

Warren Street

Nan had had another god-awful day. Nobody seemed to use any under-arm deodorant any more. She had been wincing from whiffs of sweat all day, as people flung off their garments to try on her designs.

That maddening Mrs Fine had, of course, noticed the seam that wasn't exactly right; while that stupid, stupid woman – who apparently worked in some important position in an estate agents – had forgotten again what she wanted made out of the woollen material but was absolutely certain that it wasn't the poncho that Nan had cut out for her.

'Why would I have said a poncho, when I have one already?' she asked wide-eyed.

'That's what I asked you at the time,' hissed Nan.

But the thing that was making Nan's heart leaden was that she had had a row with Shirley.

Now nobody had rows with Shirley. She had a face so like the rising sun you expected rays to stick out from her head like in a child's drawing. If Nan had rowed with her, it had to have been Nan's fault and that was that.

Shirley had been coming to Nan for two years now, ordering maybe five garments a year. Nan remembered the first day she came she had been pressing her nose against the window rather wistfully, looking at a little bolero and skirt outfit on display. The skirt wouldn't have gone over Shirley's head, let alone made it to her waist.

Nan pulled back the curtain and waved her inside – she still wondered why she did it. Normally she never encouraged customers. She had enough enquiries she couldn't deal with, and this was obviously not a fashion-conscious girl whom it would be a pleasure to dress.

Shirley's great, happy face and bouncing, bulging body arrived in Nan's little shop.

'I think I have the wrong place,' she began. 'Lola who works with me and who's eight months pregnant said she got her smocks here, and I was wondering if you have any more smocks. I mean, they might fit me, even though I'm not pregnant.'

Nan had liked her cheerful face so much she'd encouraged her.

'Sit down. I'll go and see. I've very few things really – I mainly make clothes up for people you see.'

'Oh, are you a designer?' asked Shirley innocently.

She had touched on something very near to Nan's heart. She would have liked to think of herself as a designer and she had a flair for ideas and style. She sold things to classy boutiques from time to time. But something about Shirley's face made her answer, to her own surprise: 'No, more a dressmaker.'

'Oh, that's great,' Shirley had said. 'I thought that they'd disappeared. I wonder, would you be able to make me a smock . . . ?' She broke off, seeing a refusal beginning to form itself on Nan's face.

'Oh, please, please do!' she said. 'I can't find anything in the shops that doesn't have white collars or tiny, thoughtful, mum-to-be prints on it.'

'It's just that I'm very busy . . .' Nan began.

'It would be very easy to do,' said Shirley. 'You wouldn't have to put any shape in it, and you wouldn't have to waste time wondering if the fit was right.' She grinned encouragingly, and that did it. Nan couldn't bear her to go around the world as vulnerable as that, and indeed, as badly dressed in that hideous, diagonally-striped garment she had on.

'You win,' Nan had said, and they spent a happy

half-hour planning what Shirley would wear for the winter.

Away went the belted grey army issue-type coats – the only one that fitted Shirley – and on came a cape. Away, too, the men's warm sweaters and on with a rosy red dress and a warm pink one.

Nan also made her a multi-coloured evening dress, which had all the shades of the rainbow in it. It was, she thought, a pleasure to design a dress for Shirley. She was so grateful, so touched and happy when it was finished. Sometimes she would whirl around in it in front of the mirror, her fat little hands clasped excitedly like a child.

Shirely was one of the few clients who didn't seem to have a list of complaints and personal problems, which was another bonus. Nan thought of Mrs Fine, always running down her husband. Shirley never complained about men at all.

Miss Harris was always bitching about traffic or work, or how you couldn't get a taxi or a waiter who spoke English, or proper wholemeal bread. Shirley never seemed in the least upset by such deprivations.

In fact, Nan knew little of Shirley's life, except that she fancied her boss in an advertising agency. Or maybe she didn't – Shirley was always so jokey. The last garment she had made Shirley was a really lovely dress. Nan had spent hours on the very fine wool, with its embroidery, ruffs and frills, its soft blues and yellows. Shirley looked like an enormous, beautiful baby.

It was for some gala evening and Shirley had said: 'If he doesn't tear the clothes off me when he sees me like this, he never will.'

Nan worked on a system of appointments that meant you had to come and see her on the hour, and she only saw eight people a day. That way, she said, the job was manageable. People didn't stay longer than twenty minutes at the most. The rest of the hour Nan worked away with her quiet, little machinist burring on in the background.

She would never be rich, never be famous, but it was a living. She couldn't see a life where she would be finishing buttonholes at three a.m. for a show next day. Her own life and her own lover were far too precious for that. Colin and she had lived together happily for ages and often thought of getting married but they'd never actually got the details organised.

That's what they said. The truth was that Colin would have disappeared very sharply if Nan had suggested marriage. She didn't mind much; although sometimes she felt he had it all ways since they both worked. She did the housework and paid the rent; but then it was her place, and he did share the bills.

And he loved the fact that she worked downstairs. Sometimes if he had a day off he would come in and give her a rose in the workroom, and on one never-to-be-forgotten occasion he had asked the machinist to go for a walk, locked the door and made love to her there and then, to the accompaniment of Miss Harris pounding on the door.

One day Colin had seen Shirley leaving with a finished dress. 'Who on earth was the beach ball bouncing out a minute ago?' he asked. Shirley wasn't the usual mould of Nan's clients.

'That's our Shirl whom I talk about sometimes,' Nan said.

'You never told me she looked like a technicoloured Moby Dick,' said Colin. Nan was annoyed. True, Shirley was enormous; true, she was dressed extremely brightly – mainly at Nan's insistence. But because she had such a lovely face, she looked well in colourful clothes and Nan didn't like Colin's joke.

'That's a bit uncalled for, isn't it?' she said sharply. Colin was amazed.

'Sorry to tease her – let me hold out my hand for a

smack,' he mocked. 'Yes it was very uncalled for, teacher, nobody called for it at all.'

Nan retorted: 'It's cruel to laugh at somebody's shape.'

'Aw, come on, come on,' said Colin reasonably. 'You're always saying someone's like a car aerial or the Michelin Man or whatever. It was just a remark, just a joke.'

Nan forgave him. 'It's just that I feel, I don't know, a bit protective about her. She's so bloody nice compared with almost anyone who comes in here, and she's literally so soft – in every way. I just feel she'd melt into a little pool if she heard anyone making a remark like that about her, honestly.'

'She was halfway down the street before I opened my mouth,' said Colin.

'I know – I suppose I just hope that nobody says such things whether she hears them or not,' said Nan.

That conversation had been a few months ago, Nan reflected, as she sat, head in hands. Funny that it all came back to her now. She did remember exactly how protective she had felt, as if Shirley had been her favourite sister and their mother had entrusted Nan with the care of seeing that nobody ever laughed at the fat girl.

Nan could hardly believe that, not half an hour ago, Shirley had banged out of the door and shouted from the street that she would never come back. It was like a nightmare where people behave completely out of character.

Shirley had come along for a final fitting for the wedding outfit. Her best friend was getting married and Shirley and Nan had been through reams of ideas before setting on the emerald green dress and matching hat.

Nan had been delighted with it and Shirley's face was a picture of happiness as they both looked at the outfit in the mirror: the tall, slim, slightly wary-looking dressmaker in her elegant grey wool tunic and the short, mountainous client in her metres and metres of glittering emerald.

'You'll need green eye-shadow, not blue,' said Nan. 'I'll lend you some for the wedding if you like.' She looked around for her bag. 'Do you know, I was running out of some, and then I thought of you and this colour, so I asked Colin to get me some. He's in the trade, you know, so it's a little perk. I can't find the wretched thing anywhere.' As she hunted for the parcel which wasn't in her handbag after all, Nan felt a strange, unnatural, silence descend behind her.

'Is that it?' asked Shirley, holding up an envelope that was on a table. The envelope had writing on it. It said 'Green eye-shadow for burly Shirley.'

The two women looked at the inscription in silence for what must have been only four seconds or so, but seemed never-ending. Nan could think of only one thing to say.

When it was obvious that Shirley was going to say nothing either, she tried, but her voice only came out like a squeak. What she had been going to say was, 'I didn't write that', and that didn't seem a very helpful thing to say at that moment.

She thought she would kill Colin. She would physically hurt him and bruise him for this. She would never forgive him.

Shirley's face had turned pink. Her fat neck had gone pink too, which didn't go very well with the emerald.

'Is that what you call me: "Burly Shirley"? Well I suppose it has the advantage of rhyming,' she said. She was so hurt she was almost bleeding.

Nan found her words finally. 'Colin has rude, destructive nicknames for all my clients. It amuses him – it's childish, immature and senseless,' she snapped fiercely.

'How does he know I'm . . . burly? He's never met me,' said Shirley.

'Well, you see he makes up these nicknames without knowing who people are. You do see that it's not an insult and it's not a comment. He could have written anything.' Nan nearly laughed with relief. How marvellous to get out of it in this way. But Shirley was looking at her oddly.

'So I expect he just chose the word because it rhymes with your name. If you had been called Dotty he might have said Spotty.' Nan was very pleased with herself, at the unknown powers of invention that were suddenly welling up within her.

Shirley just looked.

'So now that's cleared up, why don't you take the eye-shadow and put a little on to see how it looks with the outfit?' urged Nan.

Shirley politely started to put it on, and Nan released her breath and foolishly didn't leave well, or nearly well, alone.

'I mean it's not as if anyone would deliberately make a joke about being fat to anyone, not that you are very fat or anything, but one wouldn't mention it even if you were.'

'Why not?' asked Shirley.

'Why? Well, you know why – it would be rude and hurtful to tell someone they were fat. Like saying they were ugly or . . . you know . . .'

'I didn't think being fat was on the same level as being ugly, did you?'

Desperately Nan tried to get back to the comparatively happy level they had just clawed their way to a few moments ago.

'No, of course I don't think being fat is the same as being ugly, but you know what I mean – nobody wants to be either if they can possibly avoid it.'

'I haven't hated being fat,' said Shirley. 'But I wouldn't like to think it was on a par with being ugly – something that would revolt people and make them want to turn away.'

'You're not very fat, Shirley,' Nan cried desperately.

'Oh but I am, I am very fat. I am very short and weigh sixteen stone, and no normal clothes will fit me. I am very, very fat, actually,' said Shirley.

'Yes, but you're not really fat; you're not fat like . . .' Nan's inventive streak gave out and she stopped.

'I'm the fattest person you know, right? Right. I thought it didn't matter so much because I sort of felt I had a pretty face.'

'Well, you do have a pretty face.'

'You gave me the courage to wear all these bright clothes instead of the blacks and browns . . .'

'You look lovely in . . .'

'And I didn't worry about looking a bit ridiculous; but you know, ridiculous was the worst I thought I ever looked. I didn't think it was ugly . . .'

'It isn't, you understood . . .'

'It's always disappointing when you discover that someone hasn't been sincere, and has just been having a bit of fun, that she's just been pitying you.'

'I don't pity you . . . I wasn't . . .'

'But thanks anyway, for the outfit.' Shirley started to leave. 'It's lovely and I'm really very grateful. But I won't take the eye-shadow, if you don't mind.'

'Shirley will you sit down . . . ?'

'The cheque is here – that *is* the right price, by the way? You're not doing it cheaply just for me, I hope.'

'Please, listen . . .'

'No, I'm off now. The life has gone out of it here, now that you pity me. I suppose it's just silly pride on my part, but I wouldn't enjoy it any more.'

'Shirley, let me say something. I regard you as my most valued customer. I know that sounds like something out of a book, but I mean it. I looked forward to your coming here. Compared with most of the others, you're a joy – like a friend, a breath of fresh air. I enjoyed the days that you'd been. Now don't make me go down on my knees. Don't be touchy . . .'

'You've always been very friendly and helpful . . .'

'Friendly . . . helpful . . . I regard you as some kind of

kid sister or daughter. I had a fight with Colin about you not three months ago, when he said you looked like Moby Dick with stripes or something.'

'Oh yes.'

'Oh God.'

Shirley had gone. The bang of the door nearly took the pictures off the walls.

'I'll miss her dreadfully,' thought Nan. 'She was the only one with any warmth or life. The rest are just bodies for the clothes.' To hell with it. She would telephone Lola, the friend who had sent Shirley to her in the first place.

'Listen, Lola, this sounds trivial, but you know that nice Shirley who worked with you . . .'

'Shirley Green? Yeah, what about her?'

'No, her name is Kent, Shirley Kent.'

'I know it used to be till she married Alan Green.'

'Married?'

'Nan, do you feel okay? You made her wedding dress for her, about a year ago.'

'She never told me she got married. Who's Alan Green? Her husband?'

'Well, he's my boss, and was hers. Nan, what is this?'

'Why do you think she didn't tell me she got married?'

'Nan, I haven't an idea in the whole wide world why she didnt' tell you. Is this what you rang up to ask me?'

'Well have a guess. Think why she mightn't have told me.'

'It might have been because you and Colin weren't getting married. She's very sensitive, old Shirl, and she wouldn't want to let you think she was pitying you or anything.'

'No, I suppose not.'

'Anyway, it was the most smashing wedding dress – all that ruffle stuff and all those lovely blues and lace embroidery. I thought it was the nicest thing you've ever made.'

Oxford Circus

Once she had decided to write the letter, Joy thought that it would be easy. She had never found it difficult to express herself. She found her big box of simple, expensive writing-paper and began with a flourish: 'Dear Linda . . .' and then she came to a sudden stop.

Joy didn't want to use any clichés about Linda being surprised to hear from her, she didn't want to begin by explaining who she was, since Linda knew. She had no wish to start by asking a favour since that would put her in a subservient role, and Joy wanted to have the upper hand in this whole business. She didn't want it to seem like girlish intrigue; both she and Linda were long past the age when schoolgirl plots held any allure.

Eventually she wrote a very short note indeed and regarded it with great pleasure before she put it into the envelope.

Linda,
  I'm sure my name is familiar to you from the long distant past when Edward was both your friend and mine. There is something I would very much like to discuss with you, something that has little bearing on the past and certainly nothing to do with either nostalgia or recriminations! Perhaps if you are coming to London in the next few weeks, you could let me know and I can take you to lunch?
  Sincerely, Joy Martin.

Linda re-read the letter for the twentieth time. Everything, every single warning bell inside her told her to throw it away, to pretend she had never read it. Joy Martin must be mad to want to reopen all the hurts and deceptions and rivalries of ten years ago. They had never met, but she had read all Joy's passionate letters to Edward, she had sneaked a look at the photographs of Joy and Edward taken on their illicit weekends, the weekends when Edward had said he was visiting his elderly mother. Linda could feel her throat and chest constricting with the remembered humiliations and injustices of a previous decade. Throw it away, burn it. Don't bring it all back. It was destructive then, it can only be destructive again now.

Dear Joy,
How intriguing! I thought this kind of thing only happened in glorious old black and white movies. Yes, I do come to London fairly often and will most certainly take you up on your offer of lunch. Can we make it somewhere near Oxford Circus? That way it will leave me right in the middle of the shopping belt. Simply mystified to know what all this is about.
Regards, Linda Grey.

Joy breathed a great happy sigh. She had been so afraid of rejection. A whole week had passed without acknowledgement, and she had almost given up hoping for the Hampshire postmark. Her first hurdle had been cleared. She knew now that Linda Grey must feel exactly as she did about Edward. She had not been wrong. There had been a huge amount of caring, almost passion, in her love letters to him – those letters which Joy had sneaked from his wallet to read. There had been purpose and serious intent in her threats of suicide. No, her fear that Edward might have been forgotten in Linda's cosy Hampshire life was . . . unrealistic. Edward was never forgotten.

Linda came to London the night before this rendezvous.
In her handbag she had Joy's card with the name of the
restaurant: '. . . only a few minutes from Oxford Circus,
as you requested.' She checked in at an inexpensive hotel
and ordered a cup of tea to wash down her two sleeping
pills. A night in London with the possibility of some
showdown involving Edward on the morrow would
keep her awake for hours, and she had no wish to arrive
looking flustered. She had made appointments for hair
and facials. She was going to buy herself some very
expensive shoes and a handbag. Joy Martin could not sit
elegantly and pity poor Linda who had lost Edward all
those years ago. Still, she thought as her body began to
relax with the mogadon. Still, Joy had lost him too. He
had left Joy very shortly after he had left Linda.

She felt very guilty about Hugh. He had been concerned about her visit to London and wanted to come
with her. No, she assured him, just a check-up. She really
thought she needed the little break as much as the
check-up. She begged him not to come. She would
telephone him tomorrow and tell him that she felt perfect
and that the doctor had confirmed it. He would be
pleased and relieved. He would arrange to meet her at
the station and take her out to dinner. He was so kind and
good. She didn't know why she was making this ridiculous pilgrimage to dig up the hate-filled ghost of Edward.

Joy woke with a headache and a feeling that something
was wrong. Oh God! This was the day. Linda Grey
would be getting on her train somewhere in the countryside telling her mouse-like husband that she was going to
look at some fabrics in Oxford Street, and was on her way
panting with excitement at the very mention of Edward's
name. She made herself a health drink in the blender and
a cup of china tea. But the headache didn't lift so she took
some pain-killers very much against her will. Joy liked to
believe that she didn't need drugs. Drugs were for weak

people. Today that belief didn't seem so clear. She also thought that only weak people stayed away from work when they felt a little below par. But today that wasn't a theory that she could substantiate. She telephoned her secretary. No, of course she wasn't seriously ill, just a little below par. Her secretary was alarmed. Crisply Joy gave instructions, meetings to be rearranged, appointments to be cancelled, letters to be written. She would be back tomorrow morning. Perhaps even this afternoon.

She felt alarmed that it was all taking so much out of her. She had planned it so very carefully. She had allowed no emotion, no waverings. It was now absolutely foolproof. Why did her stomach feel like water? Why did she think she couldn't face her job at all during the day. Full of annoyance she put on her smart sheepskin coat and set out for a long healthy walk in Hyde Park.

As she walked she saw people with their dogs. She would have liked to have a dog; she didn't disapprove of people having dogs in London if they gave them enough exercise. When all this business was over, Joy thought to herself, she might get a dog. A beautiful red setter, and she could walk him for hours in the park on a bright cold morning like this.

It was five to one and Linda was determined not to be early. She gave herself another admiring look in a window. Her hair was splendid. What a pity that nobody in the village at home could do that sort of thing with scissors and a comb. They really only liked you to have rollers and a half-hour under the dryer. Linda smiled at herself with her newly painted lips. She looked in no way like a woman of nearly forty. She supposed that Joy Martin probably spent days in beauticians. After all, she had a very glamorous job running an art gallery and an art dealing business. Linda had even seen her photograph once talking to a royal person. Facials and expensive handbags would be no treat for Joy.

She forced her feet to go slowly and only when she saw that she was a nice casual six minutes late did she allow herself to enter the restaurant, take two deep breaths and enquire about a table for two booked by Miss Martin.

'You look smashing,' said Joy warmly. 'Really glamorous. Much younger than you did years ago actually. I always think we improve in our thirties really instead of going off.'

'How on earth did you know what I used to look like?' asked Linda settling herself into the corner chair.

'Oh I used to look at the pictures of you in Edward's wallet. Now, will we have a gin or would you prefer a sherry?'

'A gin,' gulped Linda.

'What do you think of me? Have I aged or gone off do you think?'

'No, in fact you look very unsophisticated, sort of wind blown and young,' said Linda truthfully. 'I thought you'd be much more studied, obviously groomed, over made-up. A bit like me,' she giggled.

Joy laughed too. 'I expect you went to a beautician's just to impress me. I was so nervous at the thought of meeting you, I've been out walking all morning in the park. That's why I'm so windswept and rosy. Normally I'm never like this.'

Linda smiled, 'Isn't it funny?' she said. 'After all these years, and we both find it very anxious-making and . . . and well . . . disturbing.'

'Yes,' said Joy. 'That's exactly what it is. Disturbing.'

'Then why did you suggest it, I mean if it's going to make us both anxious and act out of character, what's the point?' Linda's face looked troubled.

Joy paused to order two gin and tonics and to tell the waiter that they would like a little time before they made up their minds about the lunch menu.

'Well,' she said, 'I had to. You see I want you to help

me. I want you and I together to murder Edward. Seriously. That's what I'm hoping you'll help me to do.'

Most of Linda's omelette aux fines herbes lay untouched. But Joy had managed to eat much of the wholewheat pizza. Linda had managed one sip of the dry white wine but it had tasted very sour. The longer Joy talked the more Linda realised that she was indeed perfectly serious.

'Well, it stands to reason that he's a man the world would be much better off without. We all agree about that. Well, Linda, be reasonable. There was my divorce. I haven't seen my son for nine and a half years because of Edward. If it hadn't been for Edward I would have a perfectly normal and happy relationship with my son who is now sixteen. As it is I am not allowed to visit him at school; everyone agrees it is less distressing for Anthony if his mother is kept away. Later when he's an adult I shall have some ridiculous "civilised" meeting with him, where we will have nothing to say. So that was one thing Edward destroyed.'

'But you were willing to divorce your husband, to leave everything for Edward. Wasn't it your fault too?'

'No it was not my fault,' Joy was calm and unemotional. 'I was twenty-eight and bored with marriage and a demanding child and Edward lied to me, used me, filled my head with nonsenses, betrayed me and then would not stop by me after I had done what he begged and implored me to do – leave home, leave my husband and child and run away with him. He laughed at me.'

Linda said: 'I didn't know that.'

'And look what he did to you. A nervous breakdown. A serious two-year depression. Two years out of your life because you believed him, and couldn't accept his betrayals, his double life, his endless pointless lies.'

Linda said: 'I didn't think you knew that.'

'There were people before us, Linda, there were people after us. Mine wasn't the only divorce he caused, yours wasn't the only nervous illness. And nobody has punished him. Nobody has said this man is evil and he must be stopped. He mustn't be allowed to roam the world destroying, destroying, turning good to bad and dark, turning simple things to twisted and frightening.' Joy's voice hadn't raised itself a decibel but there was something in it that was a little like a preacher, like some Southern Baptist in a movie describing Satan. It chilled Linda and forced her to speak.

'But it's all over Joy, it's all done. It's all finished. Other people are being silly and foolish nowadays, like you and I once were stupid. They're making mistakes now. Not us.'

Joy interrupted her. 'We were not silly, we made no mistakes, neither do his women of today. We all behaved normally as if Edward were normal. When we said things we meant them. When we told him tales they were true, when we made promises they were sincere.'

Once more her voice was uncomfortably like a preacher. In the busy crowded restaurant Linda felt frightened.

'But you don't seriously want to . . . er . . . get rid of him?'

'Oh yes,' said Joy.

'But why now? Why not years ago, when it hurt more?'

'It hurts just as much now,' said Joy.

'Oh, but it can't,' Linda cried sympathetically. 'Not now.'

'Not for myself,' said Joy. 'But now he has gone too far. Now he has done something he can't be forgiven for. He's taken my niece to live with him. She is, of course, utterly besotted with him. She's given up her job for him like you gave up yours, she's given up her fiancé like I gave up my marriage. She will shortly give up her sanity like you did, and her happiness like I did.'

Linda felt a little faint. The smart restaurant seemed somehow claustrophobic.

'Are you very concerned about your niece?' she asked, her voice coming from a long way away. She wanted to keep Joy talking. She didn't want to have to say anything herself.

'Yes, she lives with me. She's all I've got. I've had her since she was seventeen, three years. I thought that if, well if I did a good job looking after her, they might let me have Anthony back too. Anyway, I'm very attached to Barbara, I've told her everything, she's learning the trade in our company, she's studying art history as well. The one thing I couldn't foresee in a city of twelve million people was that she might meet Edward.'

'Does she know? Does he know?' Linda's voice was still weak: there was a coldness in Joy's tone now that terrified her.

'Barbara doesn't know. I've never seen any reason to tell her about my relationship with Edward. And Edward doesn't remember me.'

'What?'

'He came to the house, to my house last month to collect Barbara, she introduced him to me proudly. His eyes rested on me easily. He doesn't remember me, Linda. He has forgotten me.'

Linda was swept by sympathy for the woman ten years previously she would have like to have killed.

'He pretended. It was another ploy. He *can't* have forgotten you. Joy, don't get hurt over it, you know what he was like. He's just trying to wound you. Don't let him.'

'He had forgotten me, Linda. I am certain he has forgotten you too, and Susan or whoever came after us. I will not let him use Barbara. She took her things last week and has gone to him!'

'She's twenty years of age Joy, these days that's old enough . . '

'No day is anyone old enough for Edward, or cruel

enough,' said Joy. 'Oh, Barbara is sure she is doing the right thing:

"You know how it is, Auntie Joy.

"You were wild once they say, Auntie Joy.

"If you knew how he makes me need him, Auntie Joy."'

Linda looked across the table. 'Don't tell me what you want to do,' she said.

Joy reached for her hand. 'Please, please. It needs two. You know, you understand, you and I were the same age, we went through the same things. We know. No one else can do it.'

'Don't tell me. I don't want to hear,' said Linda.

'We need two. Nobody can ever connect you with it. You can come up to London for a day, just like today, to buy curtains or whatever. It's in two parts. You needn't even look at him I tell you. He'll be unconscious anyway. I shall have given him the tablets first.'

Linda stood up shakily. 'I beg you not to think about it any more. Do something, anything. Go away. Come and stay in the country with me. Just stop planning it.'

'It has been planned. It's all planned. You are to come to my house, I'll leave the key and the gun.'

'I won't listen,' said Linda. 'I can't listen. You don't want to kill him, you want him back. You don't give two damns about your niece. You want Edward. You want him dead if you can't have him. It gives you a wave of pleasure just thinking of his head on one side, dead. His mouth still, his eyes open but not seeing things, not darting . . .'

'How do you know? How can you know that it's like that?' Joy's eyes were bright.

'Because I planned to kill him ten years ago. Ten years ago when you went to live with him. I planned it, too. But I had to plan it on my own. I wasn't confident enough.'

'You what?' Joy looked at her in disbelief.

'I planned it all, I would tell him I needed to see him

once. I would assure him there would be no scenes, I would ask him to my flat but in fact I would have some friends there and when he came I would pretend that he had attacked me and that I was fighting him off in self-defence. In the mêlée a knife would be used.'

'Why didn't you do it?' asked Joy.

'Because of you. I knew that you would have known it was murder. You would know Edward didn't care enough for me to attack me. You could have had me convicted.'

'How far had you got?' whispered Joy.

'As far as organising the knife, the friends in my flat, and asking him to come and see me.'

'And what happened?'

'Oh when he called, I told him I had changed my mind, I didn't want to see him after all. He stayed for one drink, long enough to bewitch Alexandra, my friend.'

'Alex. Oh God! She was your friend?'

'So you saved me from doing it. Let me save you.'

Joy pulled herself together. It was almost a visible thing. First her spine straightened. Then her brow became unlined. A small smile came to her mouth.

'We are being very dramatic, aren't we?' she said in a brittle voice.

'Very,' agreed Linda politely.

'Shall we have coffee, or are you in a hurry to get on with your shopping?'

'Rather a hurry actually,' said Linda.

'So you're off back to Hampshire then and the peaceful life,' said Joy waving for the bill.

'Yes, nothing much to do,' said Linda.

'Very quiet and tranquil I expect,' Joy said producing her credit card for the waiter.

'Only excitement I get is reading the papers, seeing who's saying what and doing what. Reading about the things that happen in London, sudden deaths, scandal. You know the kind of thing.'

A small and almost genuine smile came to Joy's eyes. 'I see,' she said.

Linda left, pausing to ask the waiter if there was a phone she could use. She told Hugh that she was very pleased with her check-up and she might catch the earlier train home. He sounded very pleased. And, for the first time in a long time, his pleasure gave her pleasure too.

Green Park

They had both sworn that they would not dress up. They had assured each other that it would be ridiculous to try to compete with Jane after all these years and considering all the money she had. Very immature really to try on fine feathers and glad rags – like children dressing up and playing games. Yet when they met at the station they were almost unrecognisable from their usual selves.

Helen had bought a new hat with a jaunty feather, and Margaret had borrowed a little fur cape. Both of them wore smart shoes and their faces normally innocent of powder had definite evidence of rouge and even eyeshadow. After much mutual recrimination they agreed that they both looked delightful and settled themselves into the train to London with more excitement than two schoolgirls.

How extraordinary to be heading off for tea at the Ritz with Jane. Helen whispered that she would love to tell everybody in the railway compartment that this was where they were heading. Margaret said it would be more fun to let it fall casually in conversation afterwards: 'How nice you look today, Mrs Brown, what a sensible colour to wear, lots of people in the Ritz last week seemed to be wearing it.'

And of course they giggled all the more because, in spite of sending themselves up, they actually were a little nervous about going to somewhere as splendid as the Ritz. They were over-awed. The very mention of the Ritz made them nervous. It was for perfumed, furred people not people who had dabbed some of last Christmas's perfume behind the ears and borrowed a sister-in-law's well-worn Indian lamb.

In some way both Helen and Margaret feared they might be unmasked when they got there. And they giggled and joked all the more to stifle this fear.

None of their fear was directed towards Jane. Jane was one of their own. Jane had trained to be a children's nanny with them all those years ago. You don't forget the friends made during that kind of apprenticeship. It was far more binding than the services were for men. It was almost like having survived a shipwreck – the eighteen girls who survived that particular obstacle race in the school for nannies, which had long since closed down, had forged a friendship which would last for life. Some of them had gone to the Gulf states and they wrote regular newsletters saying how they were getting on. Some, like Helen and Margaret, had married and applied their nanny training to their own children; only Jane had become spectacular and famous. But because she was Jane from the nanny training school it didn't matter if she became head of the United Nations, Helen and Margaret would never be in awe of her.

They changed trains, twittering happily at Euston and took the underground to Green Park.

'Perhaps people think we are career women, dropping into the Ritz for a business conference,' whispered Helen.

'Or wealthy wives up for a day's shopping,' sighed Margaret.

Neither Margaret nor Helen were wealthy. Margaret was actually married to a vicar and lived in a draughty vicarage. She was so much the vicar's wife now that she felt quite guilty about wearing the Indian lamb in case any of her husband's parishioners saw her and wondered about her showiness. Helen, too, was far from wealthy. Jeff, her husband, had a flair for backing things that went wrong and that included horses. Yet never had a hint of envy been spoken or indeed felt by the two women about the wealthy friend they were en route to meet.

Jane was the mistress of a very eccentric and extraordinarily wealthy American industrialist. He had bought her many gifts, including a ranch and a small television station; she was one of the world's richest and best known kept women.

For the twentieth time Margaret wondered if Jane could possibly look as well as she appeared in the photographs, and for the twentieth time Helen said it was quite possible. If you didn't have to do anything each day except make yourself look well, then it was obvious you could look magnificent. Suppose each day when Margaret got up she didn't have to clean the vicarage, take her children to school, shop, cook, wash, go to coffee mornings, sales of work, cookery demonstrations and entertain the doctor, the curate, the headmaster – think how well she could look. Margaret had a very good bone structure, Helen agreed grudgingly, she could look very striking if only she had time to lavish on herself. Margaret felt a bit depressed by this; she knew that Helen meant it as a compliment but it left her feeling as if she were in fact a great mess because she didn't have this time, and that her good bone structure was wasted.

As they came up from Green Park tube station into the sunlight of Piccadilly the two women giggled again and reached for their powder compacts before they crossed the road to the Ritz.

'Aren't we silly?' tittered Helen. 'I mean we're forty years of age.'

'Yes, so is Jane of course,' said Margaret as if that was some kind of steadying fact. Something that would keep their feet on the ground.

Jane had been attractive twenty years ago, but she was a beauty now.

'You look ridiculous,' gasped Helen. 'Your face, your

whole face, it's the face of a twenty year old. You look better than when we were all teenagers.'

Jane gave a great laugh showing all her perfect teeth.

'Aw, for Christ's sake Helen, I bought this face, and bloody boring it was, I tell you. It's easy to have a face like that. Just give it to someone else to massage it and pummel it and file the teeth down and put caps on, no the face isn't any problem.'

Margaret felt that she wished the foyer of this over-powering hotel would open and gulp her into the basement area. She had never felt so foolish, in her ratty overdressed, over-done bit of Indian lamb.

'Come on, we'll go to the suite,' Jane said, an arm around each of their shoulders. She noticed how impressed Helen and Margaret were with the tea lounge and the pillars and the little arm chairs beside little tables where only the very confident could sit waiting casually for their friends. She knew they would love to sit in the public area and drink it all in with Jane herself there to protect them.

'We'll come back and do the grand tour later, but now we go and meet Charles.'

'Charles?' Both women said it together with the alarm that might be generated at a dorm feast if someone mentioned that the headmistress was on her way. It was obvious that neither of them had thought that the ordeal of meeting Charles was included in the invitation of tea.

'Oh yeah, the old bat wants to make sure I really am meeting two old chums from the college. He has a fear, you see, that I'll have hired two male go-go dancers from some show. I want him to get a look at you so that he can see you are the genuine article, not something I made up. Come on, we'll get it over with, and then we can settle down to cream cakes and tea and gins and tonics.'

Because Jane had shepherded them so expertly towards the lift, Margaret and Helen hadn't even had time to exchange a glance until they found themselves outside a door where two tall men stood.

'Are they bodyguards?' whispered Margaret.

'They speak English,' laughed Jane. 'I know they look like waxworks, but that's part of the qualifications. If you came in here with a machine-gun to kill Charles you wouldn't get far.'

They were nodded in by the unsmiling heavies at the door, and Charles was visible. He stood by the window looking out at the traffic below. A small, old, worried man. He looked a bit like her father-in-law, Helen thought suddenly. A fussy little man in an old people's home who didn't really care when she and Jeff went to see him, he only cared about what time it was, and was constantly checking his watch with clocks.

When Charles did give them his attention he had a wonderful smile. It was all over his face, even his nose and chin seemed to be smiling. Margaret and Helen stopped being nervous.

'I'm a foolish old gentleman,' he said in a Southern States drawl. 'I'm jes' so nervous of my Jane, I always want to see who she goes out with.'

'Heavens,' said Margaret.

'Well, I see, how nice,' stammered Helen.

'You ladies jes' must understand me. I guess you know how it is when you only live with someone, you aren't so sure, it's not the same binding thing as marriage,' he looked at them winningly, expecting some support.

Margaret found her vicar's wife's voice: 'Honestly, Mr . . . er . . . Charles . . . I'm not in any position to know what you're talking about. I don't know any couples who live together who are not married.'

She couldn't in a million years have said anything more suitable. Jane's mouth had a flicker of a smile and in two minutes Charles had taken his briefcase, his personal assistant, and his bodyguards and having made charming excuses he left for a meeting that had been delayed presumably until he had satisfied himself about Jane's activities and plans for the afternoon.

'Is the place bugged?' Helen whispered fearfully when he had gone. Her eyes were like big blue and white china plates.

Jane screamed with laughter: 'Darling Helen, no of course not. Hey, I'm really very sorry for putting all that on you both but you see the way he is.'

'Very jealous?' suggested Helen, still in a low voice.

'A little paranoid?' Margaret offered.

'No, dying actually,' said Jane flatly, and went to get a jewelled cigarette box. 'Yeah, he only has two months, poor old bat. He's half the size he was six months ago. They said well under a year, now it's getting quicker.'

She sounded as if she were talking about a tragedy in some distant land, a happening in a country where she had never been. Everyone is sad about far floods and droughts but they don't concern people like near ones do. Jane spoke of Charles as if he were a figure she had read about in a Sunday paper, not a man she had lived with for ten years. She seemed neither upset nor relieved by his terminal illness, it was just one of the many sad things that happen in life.

'I'm very sorry,' said Margaret conventionally.

'He doesn't look as if he had only a short time to live,' said Helen.

'I'm sure that if he's not going to get better it's all for the best that it should happen swiftly,' said Margaret being a vicar's wife again.

'Aw shit, that's not what I wanted to see you about,' said Jane. She looked at their shocked faces.

'Look, sorry, sorry for the language, and this, well, lack of feeling. I *am* sorry for the old bastard, he's been very brave, and he's very frightened, you know. But hell, Margaret, Helen, we are not fools. I mean, be straight. He's hardly the love of my life.'

There was a silence. Whatever they had expected from

afternoon tea with Jane in the Ritz, it certainly was not this.

Jane appealed to them: 'I thought that being in the nanny school was blood brothers, you know, for life? I thought that those of us who survived could say anything, anything and it wasn't misconstrued.'

Margaret said: 'Jane, of course you can say anything to me but remember we've all lived a life since we came out of nanny school. Mine has been very sheltered. I'm a vicar's wife for heaven's sake. What can be more sheltered than that? I ask you. It's the kind of thing people make jokes about, it's so well, so different from yours. Can you really expect me to take all this in my stride?'

'All what?' Jane wanted to know.

'Well your wealth, your lifestyle, the fact that your husband, your common-law husband is dying of cancer and you say awful words and . . .' Margaret looked genuinely distressed. Helen took up the explanation.

'You see, Jane, it's not that either Margaret or I are trying to be distant. It's just that we don't really live in the same world as you any more and I expect after a few minutes or an hour we'll all settle down and be the same as we used to be. It's just hard to expect us to act on your level.'

Jane walked around the room for a moment or two before she replied:

'I guess I was taking things a bit too much for granted. I guess I was reading too much into all that solidarity we had twenty years ago.'

She was silent, and looked perplexed. She looked young, beautiful and puzzled, the two matrons stared up at her from their sofa in disbelief. It was if they were watching a film of their youth where only Jane had stayed young. She used to look just like that when she was nineteen and thinking of a way to avoid detection by the nanny college principal.

'You needn't think the friendship isn't there,' said

Helen. 'In fact it is, enormously. I can tell Margaret things about my private life, my worries with Jeff and money. Susie was back from Kuwait and when we met she was telling us all about how she discovered she was lesbian and she could tell nobody.' Helen looked like a big innocent schoolgirl trying to join the senior girls by revealing secrets and showing herself to be mature.

'Oh I know, Susie wrote to me,' said Jane absently.

'I feel we've let you down, Jane,' said Margaret. 'I feel there was something you wanted us to do for you, and just by racing the wrong way at the outset we've made that impossible.'

Jane sat down.

'You were always very astute Margaret,' she said. 'There was indeed something I wanted to ask you. But now I don't know whether or not I can. You see I can only do it if I am utterly frank with you. I can't go through any charade with anyone from nanny college. There are rules I break in life but never that.' She looked at them.

'Of course,' said Helen.

'Naturally,' said Margaret.

'Well, you see, I wanted to stay in England until Charles kicks it. No, sorry, if we are going to be frank, I simply will not use words like "passes away", he's dying, he's riddled with cancer, he's not going to see Christmas. I don't wish him any more pain, I wish he were dead. Dead now.'

Their faces were sad, less shocked than before but still not understanding.

'So if we stay here till the end, I want Charles to see that I have friends, good decent normal friends like you two. I want to take him to your homes. He'll probably insult you and buy you new homes but we can get over that. I mean he'll buy you and David a new parsonage certainly Margaret, possibly the bishop's palace, and as for Jeff he'll either buy him a bookmaking business or he'll send him to a Harley Street specialist to have what he will consider compulsive gambling cured in some clinic at three hundred quid a day.'

There was a ghost of a smile passing over the faces of the two on the sofa.

'I wanted to ask your support in these last weeks. There's nobody else I could trust, and I've worked so goddamn hard for ten years I can't lose it all now.'

'What will you lose?' Margaret asked. 'You've already said you won't miss him. I don't see how our inviting him to our homes can help anything at all.'

'Don't you see?' Jane cried out. 'He is going mad, he has premature senility, he's paranoid. He thinks I'm unfaithful to him, he thinks I'm cheating on him. He's busy trying to dispossess me of everything.'

'He can't do that,' Helen gasped.

'You can't think that,' Margaret gasped at the same time.

'He can, he can do a lot of it, and I can and do think it because I know it,' said Jane.

In simple terms she told them a tale of stocks and companies, of the properties she owned absolutely which could not be repossessed, of the shares that had been bought back. The two women sat mutely listening to companies which were merged and stock transferred. They heard of the invalid wife whom Charles would never divorce because in his part of Georgia only cads and men who were not gentlemen divorced invalids. They heard of his suspicions, none of them founded on any truth, that Jane was in fact using his riches to buy herself young lovers.

'Even so, even if he does dispossess you,' said Helen, trying to find a word of consolation, 'You'll still be very rich.'

Margaret thought of the corridors upstairs in the vicarage which would never have a carpet on them because they could only afford to carpet to the top of the stairs.

'You'll still be young Jane, and wealthy compared to

almost everyone,' she said. 'I can't see how anything will be so terrible.'

'It's terrible to be denied over ninety per cent of what I could have had,' said Jane. 'If the old bat had stayed sane. That's why I want to try and recoup as much as I can. I can't chain him to his bed. The lawyers for his various trusts are slobbering with greed. They're helping him each bloody hour to get more away from me. My lawyers say it's an unequal struggle. They even want to be paid in advance in case I'm left with nothing at the end.'

She looked like a thwarted child.

'How would coming to visit us help?' Helen asked trembling at the thought of bodyguards and Charles and huge cars in her small terraced house.

'He'd see I was normal, came from some normal sinless background. He's heavily into sin now that he can't commit any any more. He'd see heavy respectability in your homes. We could act out a pantomime till he snuffs it.'

Margaret gave her a look of great distaste.

'You can't mean it, Jane.'

'I do.'

Helen looked at her as if she had been someone apologising for a drunken scene.

'You can't have been aware of what you were asking us to do. That's why you feel you can no longer ask it,' she said.

Jane slooked at them slowly.

'I'm asking you to join in a little deception with me, I'm telling you the whole score, I'm explaining why, and why I need it.'

'But Jane, it's so dishonest, it's so phoney, so high-powered,' said Margaret.

'I think it's only because you imagine it's *high-powered* you're asking me to drop it,' said Jane. 'We went in for a lot of things that were phoney and dishonest in the old days. No holds were barred when you two were landing your men but now that we're older and the stakes are higher, it's high-powered as well as dishonest, we can't do it.'

With a very swift movement she lifted a telephone and cancelled afternoon tea asking room service to make sure it was set for them downstairs instead.

'My guests will prefer to eat in the tea lounge instead,' she said crisply.

Her eyes were bright, she dismissed any further discussion of the matter, she shepherded them neatly downstairs, past another bodyguard at the door who plodded discreetly after them and eventually positioned himself in the hotel lobby where he could see them at all times.

As she poured tea, Jane insisted on hearing of all their happenings, and little by little the guard relaxed sufficiently for them to talk about their homes and lives. She told them, too, about some of the things she had done. Nothing relating to Charles and his short future or his pathetic paranoia.

She told how she had met a famous film star, and she described what it was like to have a beautician arrive every morning at seven a.m. and not to allow you to face the world until after nine. She ate no cream cakes but urged the others to finish the plate.

They parted at the door under the admiring glance of many people who thought Jane quite startlingly attractive, and under the watchful glance of the bodyguard who had instructions not to let Jane out of his sight. There were little kisses and assurances of further letters and visits and meetings, there were clasps and grins and pronouncements that it would all turn out fine in the end.

Helen and Margaret went down into the tube again. Green Park station looked less full of promise and giggles and a day out.

'Everything they say about money not bringing

happiness is true,' said Helen as she fumbled in her shabby purse for the coins for her ticket.

'You would have thought that with all that money and high life she would have been contented, but no, it's more, ever searching for more,' said Margaret.

They were very silent going home. It was unlike them to be silent. Such a long friendship meant that they could say things which others wouldn't broach. But even the apprenticeship in the nanny college and all that it involved was no help to them now.

Helen thought about how Jane had helped her to raise the money for her wedding to Jeff, when Jeff had lost the whole three hundred pounds on a horse. Jane had been efficient and practical and dishonest. She had sold tickets for a charity that did not exist. She delivered the money to Helen without a comment.

Margaret was thinking of the early days when she had fallen for Dave, the handsome divinity student. Jane had helped her then, so well had Jane helped her that David's fiancée had been dislodged. There was just a rumour here and tittle tattle there so that poor David thought that he had become engaged to a Jezebel. While the same process in reverse was worked about Margaret. A blameless innocent was how Margaret appeared.

In those days it had seemed the normal thing to do, to support your friends. After all, everyone knew that men were notoriously difficult and could cause all kinds of hurtful problems. They were always misunderstanding things. It was only right that friends should help each other when there was a problem of that sort. Those were their thoughts, but they didn't share them.

Victoria

Rose looked at the woman with the two cardboard cups of coffee. She had one of those good-natured faces that you always associate with good works. Rose had seen smiles like that selling jam at fêtes or bending over beds in hospitals or holding out collecting boxes hopefully.

And indeed the woman and the coffee headed for an old man wrapped up well in a thick overcoat even though the weather was warm, and the crowded coffee bar in Victoria Station was even warmer.

'I think we should drink it fairly quickly, Dad,' said the woman in a half-laughing way. 'I read somewhere that if you leave it for any length at all, the cardboard melts into the coffee and that's why it tastes so terrible.'

He drank it up obediently and he said it wasn't at all bad. He had a nice smile. Suddenly, and for no reason, he reminded Rose of her own father. The good-natured woman gave the old man a paper and his magnifying glass and told him not to worry about the time, she'd keep an eye on the clock and have them on the platform miles ahead of the departure time. Secure and happy he read the paper and the good-natured woman read her own. Rose thought they looked very nice and contented and felt cheered to see a good scene in a café instead of all those depressing, gloomy scenes you can see, like middle-aged couples staring into space and having nothing to say to each other.

She looked at the labels on their suitcases. They were heading for Amsterdam. The name of the hotel had been neatly typed. The suitcases had little wheels under them.

Rose felt this woman was one of the world's good and wise organisers. Nothing was left to chance, it would be a very well-planned little holiday.

The woman had a plain wedding ring on. She might be a widow. Her husband might have left her for someone outrageous and bad-natured. Her husband and four children might all be at home and this woman was just taking her father to Amsterdam because he had seemed in poor spirits. Rose made up a lot of explanations and finally decided that the woman's husband had been killed in an appalling accident which she had borne very bravely and she now worked for a local charity and that she and her father went on a holiday to a different European capital every year.

Had the snack bar been more comfortable she might have talked to them. They were not the kind of people to brush away a pleasant conversational opening. But it would have meant moving all her luggage nearer to them, it seemed a lot of fuss. Leave them alone. Let them read their papers, let the woman glance at the clock occasionally, and eventually let them leave. Quietly, without rushing, without fuss. Everything nearly stowed in the two bags on wheels. Slowly, sedately, they moved towards a train for the south coast. Rose was sorry to see them go. Four German students took their place. Young, strong and blond, spreading German and English coins out on the table and working out how much they could buy between them. They didn't seem so real.

There was something *reassuring* she thought about being able to go on a holiday with your father. It was like saying, thank you, it was like stating that it had all been worthwhile, all that business of his getting married years ago and begetting you and saving for your future and having hopes for you. It seemed a nice way of rounding things off to be able to take your father to see foreign cities because things had changed so much from his day. Nowadays, young people could manage these things as a matter of course; in your father's day it was still an adventure and a risk to go abroad.

She wondered what her father would say if she set up a trip for him. She wondered only briefly, because really she knew. He'd say, 'No, Rose, my dear, you're very thoughtful but you can't teach an old dog new tricks.'

And she would say that it wasn't a question of that. He wasn't an old dog. He was only barely sixty, and they weren't new tricks, since he used to go to Paris every year when he was a young man, and he and Mum had spent their honeymoon there.

Then he would say that he had such a lot of work to catch up on, so it would be impossible to get away, and if she pointed out that he didn't really have to catch up on anything, that he couldn't have to catch up on anything because he stayed so late at the bank each evening catching up anyway – well, then he would say that he had seen Europe at its best, when it was glorious, and perhaps he shouldn't go back now.

But he'd love to go back, he would love it. Rose knew that. He still had all the scrapbooks and pictures of Paris just before the war. She had grown up with those brown books, and sepia pictures, and menus and advertisements, and maps carefully plotted out, lines of dots and arrows to show which way they had walked to Montmartre and which way they had walked back. He couldn't speak French well, her father, but he knew a few phrases, and he liked the whole style of things French, and used to say they were a very civilised race.

The good-natured woman and her father were probably pulling out of the station by now. Perhaps they were pointing out things to each other as the train gathered speed. A wave of jealousy came over Rose. Why was this woman, an ordinary woman perhaps ten years older than Rose, maybe not even that, why was she able to talk to her father and tell him things and go places with him and type out labels and order meals and take pictures?

Why could she do all that and Rose's father wouldn't move from his deck-chair in the sun lounge when his three weeks' holiday period came up? And in his one week in the winter, he caught up on his reading.

Why had a nice, good, warm man like her father got nothing to do, and nowhere to go after all he had done for Rose and for everyone? Tears of rage on his behalf pricked Rose's eyes.

Rose remembered the first time she had been to Paris, and how Daddy had been so interested, and fascinated and dragging out the names of hotels in case she was stuck, and giving her hints on how to get to them. She had been so impatient at twenty, so intolerant, so embarrassed that he thought that things were all like they had been in his day. She had barely listened, she was anxious for his trip down the scrapbooks and up the maps to be over. She had been furious to have had to carry all his carefully transcribed notes. She had never looked at them while there. But that was twenty and perhaps everyone knows how restless everyone else is at twenty and hopefully forgives them a bit. Now at thirty she had been to Paris several times, and because she was much less restless she had found time to visit some of her father's old haunts – dull, merging into their own backgrounds – those that still existed – she was generous enough these days to have photographed them and he spent happy hours examining the new prints and comparing them with the old with clucks of amazement and shakings of the head that the old bakery had gone, or the tree-lined street was now an underpass with six lanes of traffic.

And when Mum was alive she too had looked at the cuttings and exclaimed a bit, and shown interest that was not a real interest. It was only the interest that came from wanting to make Daddy happy.

And after Mum died people had often brought up the subject to Daddy of his going away. Not too soon after the funeral of course, but months later when one of his old friends from other branches of the bank might call.

'You might think of taking a trip abroad again sometime,' they would say. 'Remember all those places you saw in France? No harm to have a look at them again. Nice little trip.' And Daddy would always smile a bit wistfully. He was so goddamn gentle and unpushy, thought Rose, with another prickle of tears. He didn't push at the bank which was why he wasn't a manager. He hadn't pushed at the neighbours when they built all around and almost over his nice garden, his pride and joy, which was why he was now overlooked by dozens of bed-sitters. He hadn't pushed Rose when Rose said she was going to marry Gus. If only Daddy had been more pushing then, it might have worked. Suppose Daddy had been strong and firm and said that Gus was what they called a bounder in his time and possibly a playboy in present times. Just suppose Daddy had said that. Might she have listened at all or would it have strengthened her resolve to marry the Bad Egg? Maybe those words from Daddy's lips might have brought her up short for a moment, enough to think. Enough to spare her the two years of sadness in marriage and the two more years organising the divorce.

But Daddy had said nothing. He had said that whatever she thought must be right. He had wished her well, and given them a wedding present for which he must have had to cash in an insurance policy. Gus had been barely appreciative. Gus had been bored with Daddy. Daddy had been unfailingly polite and gentle with Gus. With Gus long gone, Rose had gone back to live in Daddy's house. It was peaceful despite the blocks of bed-sitters. It was undemanding. Daddy kept his little study where he caught up on things, and he always washed saucepans after himself if he had made his own supper. They didn't often eat together. Rose had irregular hours as a traveller and Daddy was so used to reading at his supper, and he ate so early in the evening. If she stayed out at night there were no explanations and no questions. If she told him some of her adventures there was always his pleased interest.

Rose was going to Paris this morning. She had been asked to collect some samples of catalogues. It was a job that might take a week if she were to do it properly or a day if she took a taxi and the first fifty catalogues that caught her eye. She had told Daddy about it this morning. He was interested, and he took out his books to see again what direction the new airport was in, and which areas Rose's bus would pass as she came in to the city centre. He spent a happy half-hour on this, and Rose had looked with both affection and interest. It was ridiculous that he didn't go again. Why didn't he?

Suddenly she thought she knew. She realised it was all because he had nobody to go with. He was, in fact, a timid man. He was a man who said sorry when other people stepped on him, which is what the nicer half of the world does, but it's also sometimes an indication that people might be wary and uneasy about setting up a lonely journey, a strange pilgrimage of return. Rose thought of the good-natured woman and the man who must be ten or fifteen years older than Daddy, tonight they would be eating a meal in a Dutch restaurant. Tonight Daddy would be having his scrambled egg and dead-heading a few roses, while his daughter, Rose, would be yawning at a French restaurant trying not to look as if she were returning the smiles of an ageing lecher. *Why* wasn't Daddy going with her? It was her own stupid fault. All those years, seven of them since Mum had died, seven years, perhaps thirty trips abroad for her, not a mention of inviting Daddy. The woman with the good-natured countenance didn't live in ivory towers of selfishness like that.

Almost knocking over the table, she stumbled out and got a taxi home. He was actually in a cardigan in the garden scratching his head and sucking on his pipe and looking like a stage representation of someone's gentle, amiable father. He was alarmed to see her. He had to be reassured. But why had she changed her mind? Why did it not matter whether she went today or tomorrow? He was worried. Rose didn't do sudden things. Rose did measured things, like he did. Was she positive she was telling him the truth and that she hadn't felt sick or faint or worried?

They were not a father and daughter who hugged and kissed. Pats were more the style of their touching. Rose would pat him on the shoulder and say: 'I'm off now, Daddy,' or he would welcome her home clasping her hand and patting the other arm enthusiastically. His concern as he stood worried among his garden things was almost too much to bear.

'Come in and we'll have a cup of tea, Daddy,' she said, wanting a few moments bent over kettle, sink, tea caddy to right her eyes.

He was a shuffle behind her, anxiety and care in every step. Not wishing to be too inquisitive, not wanting, but plans changed meant bad news. He hated it.

'You're not *doing* anything really, Daddy, on your holidays, are you?' she said eventually, once she could fuss over tea things no longer. He was even more alarmed.

'Rose, my dear, do you have to go to hospital or anything? Rose, my dear, is something wrong? I'd much prefer it if you told me.' Gentle eyes, his lower lip fastened in by his teeth in worry. Oh what a strange father. Who else had never had a row with a father? Was there any other father in the world so willing to praise the good, rejoice in the cheerful, and to forget the bad and the painful?

'Nothing, Daddy, nothing. But I was thinking, it's silly my going to Paris on my own. Staying in a hotel and reading a book and you staying here reading a book or the paper. I was thinking wouldn't it be nice, if I left it until tomorrow and we *both* went. The same way, the way I go by train to Gatwick, or we could get the train to the coast and go by ferry.'

He looked at her, cup halfway to his mouth. He held it there.

'But why, Rose dear? Why do you suggest this?' His face had rarely seemed more troubled. It was as if she had asked him to leave the planet.

'Daddy, you often talk about Paris, you tell *me* about it. I tell *you* about it. Why don't we go together and tell each other about it when we come back?' She looked at him; he was so bewildered she wanted to shout at him, she wanted to finish her sentences through a loud speaker.

Why did he look so unwilling to join? He was being asked to play. Now don't let him hang back, slow to accept like a shy schoolboy who can't believe he has been picked for the team.

'Daddy, it would be nice. We could go out and have a meal and we could go up and walk to Montmartre by the same routes as you took in the Good Old Days. We could do the things you did when you were a wild teenager.'

He looked at her frightened, trapped. He was so desperately kind, he saw the need in her. He didn't know how he was going to fight her off. She knew that if she were to get him to come, she must stress that she really wanted it for her, more than for him.

'Daddy, I'm often very lonely when I go to Paris. Often at night particularly I remember that you used to tell me how all of you . . .'

She stopped. He looked like a hunted animal.

'Wouldn't you like to come?' she said in a much calmer voice.

'My dear Rose. *Some time*, I'd love to go to Paris, my dear, there's nothing in the world I'd like to do more than to come to Paris. But I can't go just like that. I can't drop everything and rush off to Paris, my dear. You know that.'

'Why not, Daddy?' she begged. She knew she was doing something dangerous, she was spelling out her own flightiness, her own whim of doubling back from the station, she was defining herself as less than level-headed.

She was challenging him, too. She was asking him to say why he couldn't come for a few days of shared foreign things. If he had no explanation, then he was telling her that he was just someone who said he wanted something but didn't reach for it. She could be changing the nature of his little dreams. How would he ever take out his pathetically detailed maps and scrap-books to pore once more with her over routes, and happenings if he had thrown away a chance to see them in three dimensions?

'You have nothing planned, Daddy. It's ideal. We can pack for you. I'll ask them next door to keep an eye on the house. We'll stop the milk and the newspaper and, Daddy, that's it. Tomorrow evening in Paris, tomorrow afternoon we'll be taking that route in together, the one we talked about for me this morning.'

'But Rose, all the things here, my dear, I can't just drop everything. You do see that.'

Twice now he had talked about all the things here that he had to drop. There was *nothing* to drop. What he would drop was pottering about scratching his head about leaf curl. Oh Daddy, don't you see that's all you'll drop? But if you don't see and I tell you, it means I'm telling you that your life is meaningless and futile and pottering. I will not tell *you*, who walked around the house cradling me when I was a crying baby, you who paid for elocution lessons so that I could speak well, you Daddy who paid for that wedding lunch that Gus thought was shabby, you Daddy who smiled and raised your champagne glass to me and said: 'Your mother would have loved this day. A daughter's wedding is a milestone.' I won't tell you that your life is nothing.

The good-natured woman and her father were probably at Folkestone or Dover or Newhaven when Rose said to her father that of course he was right, and it had just been a mad idea, but naturally they would plan it for later. Yes, they really must, and when she came back this time they would talk about it seriously, and possibly next summer.

'Or even when I retire,' said Rose's father, the colour coming back into his cheeks. 'When I retire I'll have lots of time to think about these things and plan them.'

'That's a good idea, Daddy,' said Rose. 'I think that's a very good idea. We should think of it for when you retire.'

He began to smile. Reprieve. Rescue. Hope.

'We won't make any definite plans, but we'll always have it there, as something we must talk about doing. Yes, much more sensible,' she said.

'Do you really mean that, Rose? I certainly think it's a good idea,' he said, anxiously raking her face for approval.

'Oh, honestly, Daddy. I think it makes *much* more sense,' she said, wondering why so many loving things had to be lies.

Pimlico

Olive sat in her little office making her weekly lists. First she balanced her books. It didn't take long. Her guests paid weekly and usually by banker's order. Her staff bills were the same every week. The laundry was always precisely the same – thirty-two sheets, thirty-two pillow-cases, thirty-two towels, seven large table-cloths, seven smaller teacloths. Olive had costed the business of getting a washing machine and a dryer and in the end decided that the effort, the space, and the uncertainly in case of breakdowns were simply not worth it. Her food bills were fairly unchanging too; she hadn't been twenty years in the hotel business for nothing. And other bills were simple as well, she transferred a regular amount weekly to meet the electricity, telephone, gas, rates and insurance demands when they arrived. Olive could never understand why other people got into such muddles about money.

Then she made her list of activities for the noticeboard. This involved going through the local papers, the brochures from musical societies and theatres, appeals from charitable organisations for support for jumble sales. When she had a good selection, she would pin them up on her cork board and remove those which had become out of date. She took care to include some items that none of her guests would dream of choosing like Wagner's Ring or a debate about philosophy. But she knew that they liked to be thought the kind of people who might want to patronise such things and it flattered them.

Then she would take out her loose-leaf file, the one she had divided into twelve sections, one for each guest, and in her neat small handwriting Olive would make some small entries under each name. It was here that she felt she could find the heart of her hotel, the memory, the nerve centre. Because Olive knew that the reason her twelve guests stayed with her, was not the great comfort, the food, the value, the style; it was simply because she knew all about them, she remembered their birthdays, their favourite films, their collar sizes, the names of their old homes or native villages. Olive could tell you quite easily the day that Hugh O'Connor had come to live there, all she had to do was open Hugh's section in the file. But it warmed him so much to hear her say: 'Oh, Hugh, don't I remember well the day you arrived, it was a Wednesday in November and you looked very tired.' Hugh would beam to think that he was so important that his arrival had seared itself into Olive's mind.

She never saw anything dishonest or devious about this. She thought it was in fact a common courtesy and a piece of good sense in what people nowadays called 'communications and relating'. In a way it was almost a form of social service. After all, if she was going to go and spend a half-hour with Annie Lynch on a Saturday afternoon, with Annie retired to her bedroom with what looked like the beginnings of a depression, then Olive thought how much more considerate to look up Annie's file and remember the little farm in Mayo and how it had to be sold when Daddy took to the drink, and how Annie's mother who was a walking saint had died and the boys were all married and the only sensible thing for Annie to do was to come and work in London. Olive had filed the kind of things that seemed to cheer Annie up, and would trot them out one by one. Yes, perhaps she should remember everything without writing it down, but really she lived such a busy life. It would be impossible to manage without her little Lists.

Nobody knew of Olive's filing system; they weren't even aware that she seemed to have a better than average memory. Each one of her guests simply marvelled at his or her own good fortune at having found a woman who ran such a comfortable place and who obviously understood them so well. Even the three Spaniards who had been with Olive for five years thought this too. They didn't question their money or their small living quarters, they just appreciated that she could remember their names and their friends' names and the village in the south of Spain where they went back once a year when Olive closed for her two-week break. She was determined that nobody would ever know and had even made preparations that after her death her executor should arrange to have her private records of her years in the hotel business destroyed unread. A solicitor had told her that such a request was perfectly in order.

She was only thirty years of age when she bought the small and then rather seedy hotel in Pimlico. Everyone had assured her that she was quite mad, and that if clever boys who knew about making money hadn't made a go of it, how could an innocent Irish girl with ten years' experience working in a seaside Irish boarding-house hope to do any better? But Olive was determined; she had saved since her teens for the dream of a hotel of her own, and when her uncle's legacy made it actually within her reach she acted at once. Her family in Ireland were outraged.

'There's more to it than meets the eye,' said her mother who foresaw gloomy summers without Olive's considerable help in the boarding-house.

'Maybe she'll find a fellow in London, she hasn't found one here,' said her sister cattily.

Olive's father was enthusiastic that she should try working in London for a little bit before actually committing herself to the buying of a hotel. He had worked there himself for ten years and found it a lonely place.

'When you've seen Piccadilly Circus and Buckingham Palace and you've said to yourself, this is me here sitting listening to Big Ben strike, well that's it. You've seen it then. It's time to come home. It's a scaldingly lonely place.'

As determined as any young woman about to enter religious life and take vows as a nun, Olive went ahead with her plans.

Ten years in a third rate boarding-house had given Olive more of an insight into the psychology of hotel work than any amount of professional courses. She saw the old and the lonely who could barely endure the sea winds and the bracing air and who hardly left the sun lounge during their two-week visit. She knew they came for company, and that the anticipation was much better than the holiday. She saw the couples with their children hoping that the two-weeks vacation would be a rest, a bit of peace, a time to get to know each other again, and she saw her mother disappointing them year after year by frowning at the children, complaining about noise and in general making the parents much more anxious than they would have been had they remained at home in the normal daily round. Oh, the number of times Olive would have loved to have been in charge, she knew what she would have done. She would have had a special room for the children with lino on the floor, a room where it didn't matter if they kicked the furniture or made a noise. She would have offered the guests a welcoming drink when they arrived instead of making an announcement about what time she expected them to be in.

But in the years of watching the visitors come and go, Olive gained what she thought was an insight into the returned emigrants, those who lived the greater part of their life in big English cities. What they seemed to appreciate so much when they came back was the smallness of the place, the fact that people saluted other people and knew all about them. These might have been the very things that they fled to London and Birmingham and Liverpool to avoid, but it certainly seemed to be something their souls cried out for now. Olive knew that when she had enough money she would run a place for Irish people in London, and she would make a small fortune. Not a big fortune, she didn't want that, just a little fortune. So that she could live in comfort, and could surround herself with nice furniture, nice pictures, so that she needn't worry about having two bars of the electric fire on. The kind of comfort which would mean she could have a bath twice a day, and take a taxi if it were raining.

And in her terraced house in Pimlico she built up the hotel of her dreams.

It had taken time. And a great deal of effort. For a year she lost money – heavy, frightening sums, even though she regarded it as an experiment. She advertised in local papers in boroughs where there were large Irish populations, she attracted lonely people, certainly, but not the ones she could help. Too many of her guests turned out to be working-on-the-Lump men who had forgotten their real names because they used so many in so many different jobs, men who appeared on no social welfare list, men who knew that if they got a bad dose of pneumonia or broke a leg that the other lads would pass a hat round for them, but there would be no pension, no insurance, no security.

They didn't stay long in Olive's little hotel, and she made them uneasy, asking where they were from and what they did.

'Sure the police wouldn't ask me that, Mam,' a man had replied to her once when she had asked some simple and she thought courteous question about his origins.

Then she had the con-men. The charmers, the people who were expecting money shortly, who cashed cheques, who told tales. It was an apprenticeship, she was learning. Soon she thought she was ready and she advertised again. By this time she had the hotel the way she wanted it. Not splendid, nothing overawing, but comfortable. There wasn't a hint of a boarding-house about it, no sauce bottles appeared with regularity on stained cloths. She arranged a weekly rate which included an evening meal, with no refund if the meal were not taken. She knew enough about her future clients to know that they were the kind of people who would like to be expected home at a quarter to seven. They could always go off out again afterwards.

She implied that those she was accepting were people of good manners and high standards. This was done very cunningly and without any hint of appearing restrictive. Whereas her mother would have said: 'I want no drink brought into the bedrooms', Olive said: 'I want you to consider this house very much as your home. I know you don't want to be in the kind of place where people have bottles in bedrooms.'

She chose the guests carefully. Sometimes after several interviews where she always gave them tea and managed to explain that it was simply a matter of having promised the place to somebody else who was to let her know by Thursday. It took her a year to build up to twelve and she sat back satisfied. They were right. They were the correct mix. They depended on her utterly, they needed her, and for the first time in her life she felt fulfilled. She felt she had got what other people got from teaching or nursing or maybe the priesthood. People who needed them, a little flock. She never included marriage and children in her list of fulfilling lifestyles. She had seen too many less than satisfactory marriages to be impressed by the state. And anyway she was too busy. You didn't run the perfect hotel without a lot of work.

There had been a question of marriage two years ago. A very nice man indeed. A Scot, quiet and industrious. She had met him at a hoteliers' trade fair, when she was examining a new system of keeping coffee hot. He had told her that it didn't really work, he had tried one in his own hotel and it had been wasteful. Their friendship got to a stage where her twelve guests were rustling and ruffled like birds in a coop fearing the intrusion of an outsider. Alec came to tea so often on Sundays that there were definite fears he might either join the establishment or else spirit Olive away. The ruffled feelings were balm to Olive, the ill-disguised anxiety among those men and women who paid her hefty sums of money to live with her was almost exhilarating. Olive kept them and Alec in suspense for some weeks and finally sent Alec away confused, wallowing in the luxuriating relief and happiness of the civil servants, bank clerks, book keepers, shop assistants and bus driver who were now her family.

She finished her list of entries in the ring file with the information that Judy O'Connor, the nice girl who worked in the chemist shop, had a brother who was a missionary and that he was coming back from Africa and through London on his way home to Ireland for Christmas. Olive thought it might be a nice occasion to have a mass in the hotel.

Well, why not? They were all Irish, they were all Catholic. Even the three little Spaniards, José, his wife Carmen and her sister Maria, they were Catholics, they would love a Mass in the dining-room. It would make it all much more like home. She must start putting it in Judy's mind soon. Olive was careful for people not to think that all the good ideas came from her. She let the guests think that it was their idea to strip their own beds on Monday mornings and leave all the dirty linen neatly ready for the laundrymen. The guests thought that they had suggested pooling fifty pence a week each to have wine with Sunday lunch.

Hugh O'Connor was absolutely certain that *he* had broken off his engagement to that rather forward hussy who had no morals and wanted to come in and share his room saying that it was perfectly all right since they were engaged. Annie never realised that it was Olive who suggested she should break her ties with Mayo, she thought she had done it herself. The guests thought that it had just come about that they all stayed in the hotel for Christmas, they saw nothing odd about it. Olive had carefully managed to distance herself from those who had been rash enough to go to relations or friends. They had felt lacking in some kind of spirit and had felt deeply jealous when they returned afterwards to hear about the wonderful turkey, and the presents and the carols by the Christmas tree and the Pope's Blessing in the morning and the Queen's speech in the afternoon – a combination of what was best about both cultures.

The last thing that Olive did on her List day was to write home. Her father was in hospital now, her mother almost crippled with arthritis. She sent them regular small contributions with pleasant cheering letters. She had no intention of returning home. They were nothing to her now. She had a real family, a family that needed her.

Vauxhall

On the first Sunday of the month Andrew's parents came to lunch. They arrived winter and summer at midday precisely . . . and every single time Andrew's father would rub his hands and ask his son how he felt about a spot of fresh air. In response Andrew would rub his own hands, pretend to consider it and then nod as if finding it a satisfactory idea.

'Back around two-fifteen – that all right dear?' he would call in to the kitchen where his mother and June were oohing and ahhing over some little gift of home-made tea cakes or tray cloths, then he and his father set off, rain or shine, for a twenty-minute walk to the pub, two and a half pints and a twenty-minute walk back home. Twelve times a year for fifteen years. That was thirty pints a year, a total of four hundred and fifty pints, but little communication shared with his father in the crowded pub which was always filled with jaded young people recovering from last night's swinging south-of-the-river party.

Then, looking at their watches anxiously in mock fear of great punishment, they left carefully at the time when last orders were being shouted and others were begging for that final injection to see them through the Sunday afternoon in Vauxhall. Andrew and his father walked back, more expansive about the roses in people's gardens, the value of property and the increase in hooliganism. When they let themselves into the flat, June and her mother-in-law would give little cries of mock relief, that the men hadn't disappeared for ever, that the lunch had not been spoiled and that they could all now sit down and have Sunday lunch.

At this point June or Andrew would go nervously to Cora's door and tap gently.

'Time for lunch, darling, Gran and Gramps are here.'

There was always a rising note at the end of the statement, questioning. It was as if they didn't know whether or not she would emerge. But she always did. Cora, their only daughter. Cora their tall fourteen-year-old only child.

The years had passed so inevitably, Andrew thought to himself that particular Sunday, as he felt the familiar relief surging through him when Cora came out, her long hair neatly held with a blue ribbon, her soft navy sweater coming well down over her jeans so that it actually looked some kind of formal attire. A huge smile for both grandparents, a kiss, an exclamation of pleasure over the joint – it was always lamb, beef or pork on a first Sunday but since Cora had been old enough to exclaim she had done so. Andrew looked at her with his constant bewilderment. How had he and June produced this lovely, blonde, distant creature? What went on in her head? What did she think of him really as she sat at his table and ate a Sunday roast with his wife and his parents? Would he ever know?

This Sunday was no different to any other. Mother had a hilarious tale about some new people who had moved into their road and had decided to invite all the neighbours in for drinks. The neighbours had disapproved strongly of such over-familiarity but had accepted, and everything had gone wrong – episode after episode of disaster from burst pipes, and clogged loos and stone cold cocktail sausages, to running out of sherry, were revealed to peals of laughters from June, grunts of recollection from father and a polite attention from Cora. To Andrew it seemed suddenly a cruel, heartless tale, unlike his mother's normal generosity, but then he remembered she often told little stories of the discomfiture of others. It made her own position more satisfactory.

June followed it with stories of the Residents' Association in the block of flats, and how they had forced the landlords to do up the entrance, and forced the council to improve the street lighting, and how they had forced the family in the top floor not to cook dishes which could be smelled all over the block.

Even though they often talked about the Residents' Association Andrew thought that today the chat seemed very militant; he got a momentary vision of all those old ladies and retired bank officials who seemed to be its inner circle, dressed up with arm bands and high boots. He smiled to himself.

Father was brought into the conversation by the two chatty women – his wife and daughter-in-law didn't want to monopolise the conversation: did he think that it was worth buying a cover for those plastic bags where people grew vegetables in cities, or should they be left to breathe, or would they look nice covered with attractive stones like a mini rockery or was there a danger that this might suffocate the tomatoes? To every one of these points Father gave his usual attention. His years of being a diplomatic clerk in chambers made him unwilling to come down too firmly on any side even in something as untendentious as this. He weighed everything happily and the audience listened respecfully.

It was a wet Sunday, which meant that they would not go for the little stroll down to the Albert Embankment, or the little walk to the park. When it rained they played Scrabble, looked at gardening catalogues, or Mother sometimes read an entire letter from Andrew's sister in New Zealand, full of people that none of them knew; but Mother would speculate happily and say: 'I think Vera is the one married to the Scottish chap, the couple they went camping with.' Then at four-thirty they had tea, and at five they were in their car, thanking and explaining that they had to go, because of the light in the winter and because of the traffic in the summer. Six times a year Andrew's father said to him: 'We'd better push off so's we can get home in the light, you know.' Six times a year: 'Have to leave now, otherwise we'll get into a hell of a mess with all the traffic building up.' Over fifteen years each phrase must have been said ninety times with an air of newness and discovery, and they had all nodded sagely. Since Cora had been old enough to nod she had always looked politely disappointed that they had to leave, but understanding as well.

'They were in very good form weren't they?' said June brightly as she pushed the tea trolley to the kitchen. Cora had disappeared to her room.

'Yes,' said Andrew getting the tea-cloth.

'Oh, will you? Thank you, love,' said June, even though Andrew had wiped the dishes after one hundred and eighty lunches and afternoon teas attended by his parents. There had always been a tradition that the lunch table was cleared and stacked neatly in the kitchen, not washed up at once.

'Andrew and I enjoy doing it later,' June always said.

'Next month is birthday month,' June said cheerfully. 'We'll have to think of what to get.'

By an odd coincidence all their birthdays fell in the same month, and this year his parents would both be seventy-five, he and June would be forty-five and Cora would be fifteen.

They had always celebrated it as a big family feast, one birthday cake for everyone, lots of presents and cards; and his mother and father always brought the cards that they had received from all their friends as well, and Cora had to say which of her school friends had given her a card.

'We've only got to hold out another fifteen years, and then we can have four generations,' Andrew said thoughtfully. 'Father and Mother could well make it to ninety don't you think?'

'What on earth do you mean?' June paused in the violent scrubbing of a difficult saucepan.

'Well, they're thirty years older than us, we're thirty years older than Cora . . .'

The same pang that always struck him when Cora was mentioned hit him sharply in the chest. He knew so little about her. Was it possible that this girl would soon be loved by a man, or desired by one?

He felt a chill at the thought. It wasn't a question of thinking her too young and innocent. In fact he had been pleased rather than distressed when he had seen one of her schoolfriends, an attractive boy, with his arm across Cora's shoulder one day walking from the bus. She had been carefully instructed in the Facts of Life by June with the help of an illustrated booklet. June had said that it was far more difficult than actually giving birth to her in the labour ward. Cora had read the pieces with interest and said; 'Oh, I see, thank you very much.'

June had tried to leave the door open for more discussion but it never came from Cora. So, from time to time she tried to add little helpful hints.

'You see, there's nothing *wrong* with feeling sexually attracted to someone. In fact it's all absolutely right if you see what I mean. The problem is that we start feeling these, um, feelings when we are rather too young to do anything about them. But they're not wrong or shameful you know.'

'Oh no,' Cora had agreed. 'I didn't think they were.'

'It's just that, economically, it would be silly for boys and girls to get married to each other and what not at thirteen and fourteen because they have no wages or money for a house, you do see?'

'Oh, yes, I see, it would be ridiculous,' Cora had said.

'I think she understood,' poor June had whispered. 'But she didn't sort of react or anything, so I can't be certain.'

Andrew knew exactly what she had meant.

Of course he was quite insane to think that because he and June had followed his parents so precisely in what they had done, Cora would do the same. She might even become part of a commune with lovers all over the house, he shuddered to himself. But then he dismissed that. It could involve a jollity, an intensity too, things that didn't characterise his cool, young daughter. An attractive young teenager, almost a young woman.

'I wonder,' he said tentatively, 'I wonder whether Cora should have her own party next month? You know, teenagers, records, dancing. She might like that. After all girls of fifteen seem grown up to each other these days.'

'A party? Here?' June was not aghast, but it was something that had never occurred to her. 'Do you think she'd like that?'

'Well, teenagers do,' said Andrew. 'Don't they?'

'And she has been to other people's birthday parties I suppose,' said June.

They looked at each other across the draining rack, their faces showing not so much shock that their daughter was turning into a young woman, but total confusion about what kind of young woman she might become. Neither of them knew.

'Shall I ask her, or will you?' asked June.

'I will if you like,' Andrew replied.

They finished the wiping and tidying in silence. Later on Cora would emerge from her room around seven and they would have a light supper. This was Cora's little job. She had been doing it now for about three years. Baked eggs, or sardines on toast, or cold meat and tomatoes if there had been a lot left over from the Sunday joint. She always prepared it quietly with no complaints, and washed up after it. She had been no trouble. Ever. Andrew wondered why he was defending her to himself. Nobody had attacked her.

This Sunday it was sardines. He joined her in the kitchen as she was cutting the crusts from the bread.

'Do you mind doing this Cora, would you prefer to be out with your friends?'

'No, of course I don't mind, Dad,' she smiled at him remote as a stranger who has done you a small service, like giving you more room in a bus or picking up a parcel you have dropped.

'Would you like your own party next month, when you're going to be fifteen?' he said straight out. 'With music and lights and beer for the boys and a kind of wine cup for the girls.'

She looked at him for a couple of seconds.

He tried to read what was on her face.

'Dad,' she began. He had never seen her at a loss before.

'Dad. No. I think I won't. It's very kind of you and Mum, but honestly.'

'But why, love? We'd like you to have a party, a real party for your friends. Perhaps it isn't beer and wine cups. You tell us, and we'll do it right.'

She looked wretched.

'Or you do it . . . you know we won't interfere, we'll be so much in the background we'll have faded into the wallpaper,' he laughed nervously.

With the knife she was using for the toast still in her hand she started to fasten up the buttons of his cardigan and unfasten them and fasten them again. She was as tall as he was, her hair fell over her face and she left it there.

'Dad, it's really very nice of you, but I've got everything I want. Honest. I don't want a party. Honestly.'

She seemed to feel that his buttons were now satisfactory and she moved back to the table.

He felt more hurt than he had ever felt and it must have shown in his face.

'We'd do it right, you know,' he said childishly.

'Of course you would, but there's no right way or wrong way. It's just not on Dad.'

'Other people have parties. You go to other people's

houses when their children have birthdays.'

'But it's such a waste, I mean, Dad, people do so much damage and they don't appreciate it, and the parents are always let down. Always. I don't know anyone who's had a party whose parents didn't get upset for about six months after it. I don't want it. Dad, not for you and Mum, you're not the type.'

'What type do we have to be to give parties that are good enough for your friends, Miss?' he said almost roaring with the pain of it.

'What do we have to do, hire a bloody disco on the King's Road, is that it?'

She had put down the knife, timidly she came over to him and went at his cardigan buttons again.

'I did them wrong,' she said. It took a great effort not to shy away from her, but he stood rigid, while she opened them and refastened them, the most intimate thing she had done since she was a toddler.

'It's not that I don't want my friends to meet you and Mum, that they won't think you're good enough – they won't see you, they won't know what you're like, they won't notice you. Can't you understand? I don't notice my friend's parents, I don't listen to them. I'm not thinking you're not good enough, Dad, you're too good to have your nice lounge all mucked up. You should be grateful to me, not all hurt.'

He felt numbed. His anger and hurt were gone but they hadn't been replaced by anything. Perhaps this is a breakthrough, he thought to himself. At least she acknowledges the possibility that I do have some feelings.

'Well, it's up to you, love,' he said. 'Your mother and I only want you to have what you want.'

She had arranged the sardines neatly, two on each piece of bread, head to tail, was putting the plates in to warm and turned on the grill.

'Honestly Dad, lunch here like always, you know, the cake and everything, that's what I'd like.'

'But it isn't much, Cora love, we'd like to do more for you, you know lunch with old fuddy duddies . . . a bit dull.'

'It's what people *do*, Dad, isn't it? I mean, you might want something different for you too when it's your birthday but that's not the point is it? I mean you don't go off and do what you want to do, you have a lunch and a cake here for Gramps and Gran. You always have, it's the way things *are*.'

He watched her put the sardines under the grill and start to make the coffee. Everything was ready on the tray. It was the way things were, it was what people did. He wondered what his old father might really like to do to celebrate being seventy-five.

Too old for a belly dancer, or a weekend in Paris probably. Father most possibly liked coming to the flat and having his walk, his two and a half pints, his lunch, his gifts, his doze over Scrabble, his tea and his drive home before the crowds. Andrew didn't know. Andrew didn't even know how he wanted to celebrate his own birthday. How did he want to spend the day? A slap-up lunch in a hotel? No. It would hurt June to think that she couldn't produce something as good as a hotel. Champagne on ice? No, he liked bitter. With a crowd of people his own age from the office and the golf club? No. It wasn't done in their set, he'd feel awkward. What he really liked was the family day, the feeling that it was everyone's birthday, and they had got through one more year, the five of them, with no disasters. That's what he really liked to do, or he supposed it was.

And if that was so for the man of seventy-five and the woman of seventy-five and the couple of forty-five, perhaps the young woman of fifteen felt the same. It was safe, it was the known thing.

It wasn't exciting, it wasn't imaginative but, by heavens, it was what people did. It was the way things were.

Stockwell

Mona had vomited when the news was given to her. It was the last thing she had expected would happen and she was very ashamed. She helped the doctor and his young aide to clean the carpet, brushing aside any of their cries that she leave it alone.

'I wouldn't hear of it. These things have to be done quickly. Have you any Borax? Good, and then I find a quick squirt with a soda syphon is good. I really am most frightfully sorry.'

The doctor finally got her to sit in a chair again. Gave her a glass of water, a pill and his hand.

'I didn't put it well. I probably gave you a far worse impression of the situation . . . you must excuse me, Mrs Lewis. I have been very crass.'

His hand tightened on hers and his kind brown eyes were filled with concern. Mora Lewis looked at him gratefully.

'Dr Barton, I can't thank you enough. You have been exactly what I needed in every way. You could not have been more supportive. It's not your fault that the diagnosis was so bad. You must realise that I am completely in your debt.'

The doctor took off his glasses and wiped his eyes. He looked at this handsome woman in front of him again and marvelled. He had told her that she had inoperable cancer of several glands. In response to her calm question, he said that he had been told it was a matter of months and probably not as many as six months. It was when he had added 'Before Christmas' that her stomach muscles had reacted even though her face had not.

How could he have been so heavy-handed, so thick-skinned, so leaden? Why did he have to mention Christmas to this glowing woman? Why remind her of the one most emotive date in the year and let her picture a family scene without her? He could have cut out his tongue.

But she encouraged him to talk calmly. She had talked calmly throughout their whole odd professional relation-ip. She had come to him four months previously saying that she was staying with friends in Stockwell and giving a local address. After her third visit, however, she explained that she really lived in a different part of London, it was just that she wanted a doctor far away from her friends, far away from people who might know her business. Mona Lewis lived in Hampstead and all her friends went to the same doctor. It wasn't that she didn't trust him, of course she did, but if what she suspected was wrong with her was indeed true, then she didn't want his pity, his sympathy, his concern, until she knew how she was going to cope with it.

It had seemed reasonable. He had referred her for all the tests, he had liked her breezy matter-of-fact ways. He had even had nice little chats with her which were rare for him to have with patients, since his was a largely immigrant practice and much of his work seemed to him to consist of trying to understand worried young Indian mothers who could not come to see him on any matter without the husband there to interpret and act as Chaperone. Mona Lewis with her light-hearted sense of mocking him was a special treat.

She had told him that her fingers were simply itching to re-pot the tired busy lizzies and ferns in his waiting-room. She had even bought him some plant food and left him a book on simple plant care which he had read to please her. even when she had gone for the biopsy she had remained cheerful. He had got her into a local hospital.

'Where do your family think you are this week?' he had asked, worried.

She had mentioned a husband and twin daughters of sixteen.

'I've told them I'm on a course.'

'Why?' he had asked gently. 'Why don't you tell your husband? He'd want to know.'

'Don't be ridiculous, Dr Barton, nobody would want to know that his wife was having a biopsy. Come now, that's not worthy of you.'

'Very well, let me put it another way. He would like to share these things with you, if they have to be undergone, he will want to be part of them.'

'I want to go through the first bit by myself,' she said. 'Later, later I'll talk to the others. Please let me do it this way.'

He hated having to give her the news, but there was no ethical way he could involve anyone else. He was, as she said, being supportive.

She finished her glass of water, examined the damp patch on the carpet and shook her head ruefully as if a favourite puppy, not herself, had made the mess.

'I am sorry again about that, Dr Barton, very shaming. Now, can I just settle up with you as usual, and then I'll leave you to the rest of your waiting room.'

She had established early on that she would like to be considered a private patient even though she always came in surgery hours, and she paid in cash. He hadn't liked the whole arrangement, and particularly as her diagnosis looked worse and worse. Today for the first time he was adamant about the money.

'Please, Mrs Lewis. Just pause and think about me as a human being, not just a doctor with a hand out for money from a private patient. I have given you distressing news today.'

She looked at him politely, her hand already on her wallet.

'It's quite bad enough for me to know that a charming and vital woman like you has a terminal disease and it is doubly hard to have to be the one who tells you this, can you please let me have the dignity of telling you and seeing you to a taxi or telephoning your husband, or calling a friend for you, without having to take your goddamn bank notes?'

She snapped her bag shut.

'Of course. And how considerate of you. I didn't pause to think. But no. I'd prefer to walk. I usually do walk around her, when I come to you. And take buses. I'd like to do that today. Please.'

As he shook her hand, and she assured him that she felt perfectly fine, he knew he was seeing her for the last time. She would not now come back to him. She didn't want to discuss remissions, radium treatment. She wanted to know nothing of drugs or palliatives. She implied that if anything were to be done, it might be done back in Hampstead.

'You have been exceptionally good to me. I know that professional people hate things to be irregular, and you have been wonderful at hiding your irritation that I didn't go through the more conventional channels.'

The doctor didn't know why he said it but it was uppermost in his mind so it just came out.

'People often try to . . . you know . . . beat it, get there first. It's not a good idea. They bungle it, and even if they don't . . . well . . . you know, nature does it in its own rotten way. It would be a pity to take your own life . . .'

'Oh no,' she smiled at him. 'No, I agree it would be a mess. Anyway, why would I go to all these measures to find out, if I were going to do something so feeble as take a bottle of pills and a bottle of vodka?'

'I'll keep feeding those plants in case you come back to

see me,' he grinned taking his tone from hers. She liked that.

'Of course I'll come back to see you,' she smiled. 'One day when you least expect it, when all the shoots need to be trimmed.'

He watched until she had turned the corner, then he pressed his buzzer and saw a malingering workman who claimed he had a bad back, and barked at him so fiercely that the man left in terror demanding to know when Dr Barton's relief doctor would be on duty.

Mona felt dangerously calm. It was a sunny July afternoon, and everything looked quite normal. Like it often looked in this strange part of London, less planted, less cared for than her own neighbourhood. Funny that she liked it so much. She was certain that Jerry would like it too, but it was something she would never share with him. What she had to do now was go through the whole sham of tests again. It seemed silly and wasteful, but this was how she had planned it. Tomorrow, tell Jerry that she felt below par, fix an immediate appointment with Franz, allow Franz to send her for tests at the clinic, follow through, slowly and remorselessly everything she had just done.

And at every step of the way now she could be clearsighted and calm because there was going to be nothing hanging in the balance, no doubts, no waiting to know. Because she now knew the very worst she could behave with her customary calm. Reassuring everyone, allowing no panic, being utterly fatalistic. She even had a little sentence ready. 'Don't be silly, darling, it's not a question of knowing that I'm going to die, after all we all know we are going to. I just know *when* I'm going to die. That gives me the advantage over all of you.'

She was going to be perfectly frank with the girls also. There was no hiding and whispering and pretending as there had been when her own mother had died. Six

months of confusion, and hope and counter hope, and
bewilderment. Mona was going to be authoritative in
death as she had been in everything in life. It was sad, it
was obviously very regrettable since she was only forty-
six. But to look on the bright side, she had had an
excellent life, she would leave behind not a dependent,
unsupported family, but a husband whose every comfort
had been catered for, whose house ran smoothly and
easily, two attractive sixteen-year-olds who had always
been able to discuss their future plans with their mother
and who would not cease to do so now. She would
redouble her efforts to get Marigold into art school, and
to direct Annabelle towards a career in social work. She
would see that they both had advisors, separate ones,
and contacts. She would also establish a proper social life
for Jerry so that he wouldn't be left high and dry. If only
she could persuade him to learn bridge. He had with-
stood it so long, and yet as a widower it would be his
instant passport to people's houses. Nobody would say,
we must have poor Jerry around, poor chap is utterly
broken up since Mona's death, instead they would think
more positively and say: 'We need a fourth for bridge.
How about Jerry?'

Mona hated the thought of telling Sally, her dearest
friend. Sally was so utterly sentimental and emotional,
she could ruin everything by arriving around at their
house with flowers and autumn bouquets saying that she
wanted Mona to see one more bunch of dahlias or a last
autumn crocus.

She had several plans also for the school where she
taught. She would explain to the principal that a new
teacher must be found for the autumn term, but she
would ask if she could stay on as an advisor for the first
two months or so, or until her strength gave out. She also
felt she should like permission to discuss some aspects of
death and facing it with the older girls, since they were
unlikely to have the chance again of meeting someone

who was going to face it as calmly as Mona was about to do.

And as for dear Jerry, she was going to try to explain to him how essential it was that he should marry again, lest he become eccentric and absent-minded and his whole lovely antique business fall apart. If she could find the right words to explain that posthumous jealousy cannot exist. She would be in a great sleep and nothing could hurt her or touch her. Mona realised that not everyone else felt as peaceful about facing death as she did, and she wondered whether she should give talks on the subject on the radio or to women's groups.

Thinking of women's groups reminded her of old Vera North, her mother's friend of many years, now bedridden and in a wheelchair. Mona usually went to see her once a month, but with all the tests and waiting and examinations she hadn't seen Vera for some time. I'll go today, she thought. It will give everyone an explanation of why I was out all day, and should my face look a bit gloomy in spite of myself then they'll think it was because of seeing Vera.

Vera called for tea, she had a faithful slave who had looked after her since childhood. Mona always admired the set up, they needed each other, Vera and the old retainer Annie. She didn't think it was shameful to have a maid, not if you were Vera, not if you were kind and considerate, and paid Annie a just wage.

'I've been busy,' she explained to Vera.

'I know,' Vera said. 'You look more cheerful now. You looked worried when I saw you last. Were you having a medical examination?'

'How on earth did you know?' asked Mona amazed.

'Is it a hysterectomy?' asked Vera.

'No, lymph glands,' said Mona before she realised.

'Poor Mona, you are so young, yet so courageous.' Vera did not look put out.

'I am brave, but by other people's standards, not my

own. I just feel that we should take the mythology out of cancer. I mean, people are afraid to mention its name. They call it silly names, they won't acknowledge it. Such huge strides have been made in, say, attitudes to mental illness, it seems strange that we cannot admit to cells going rogue which is all that cancer is.'

'I know, Mona,' said Vera gravely.

'So as a last gesture, as some kind of, I don't know, some kind of statement I suppose – I'm going to talk about it, I'm going to make it normal. Acceptable even.'

She smiled triumphantly at Vera. She just got a steady glance in return.

'You see since I *am* going to be gone by Christmas at least I know that there's some end to my courage, some defined end. It's not going to be all that hard . . . and it will make it so much easier for everyone else.'

'Do you think it will make it easier for other people?' Vera asked mildly.

'Well it stands to reason . . . if they see that I'm not terror stricken, if they see that if the one who has the bloody disease can accept it, then they will too. It will save so much time, it will cut through all that pretence, we needn't make all those absurd plans for holidays next year, when everyone knows that I won't be around next year . . .'

She was rather put out by Vera's refusal to be impressed, her unwillingness to admire such amazing bravery.

'They'll prefer to pretend. And they will definitely prefer you to pretend,' Vera said firmly.

'But that's nonsense. I'm doing it for them, I'm not going to have them go through what we went through with Mother. Vera, you must remember that, how dreadful it was.' Vera sat very still.

'How old were you when Clare died . . . seventeen, eighteen?'

'I was eighteen, Vera, and I won't put my family

through such an experience. We were constantly going to the Church and lighting candles in front of statues so that Mother's illness should turn out not to be serious. The word Cancer was simply not allowed to be mentioned, there was no honesty. All the things I would like to have said to my mother but never did because we were prevented from admitting it was goodbye by some confused code of keeping quiet. If mother even knew she was dying, which I doubt, none of us had a chance to ask her if she had any last things to discuss.'

'Oh she knew,' said Vera. 'She knew very well.'

'Did she talk to you about it?' Mona was startled.

'She began by wanting to talk to everyone, you are so like her it's uncanny. She wanted to face it . . . do all the things you want to do.'

'But *why* did she not do that?'

'It caused too much pain. Simply that,' Vera said. 'She saw after a couple of days that people couldn't take it. Your father for one: "Clare, stop this, there is hope, nothing is definite. I won't have you speaking as if you are a condemned woman".'

'And other people?'

'Just the same. Me too. I wouldn't look her in the eye and discuss the fact that her body was rotting, no, even though she wanted to laugh and tell me that it was nothing special, mine would rot too. I wanted to believe there was hope. I wanted not to see her getting thinner and comment that the disease was taking its toll. I wanted to say, "Yes you have lost a lot of weight and it does suit you". You see Mona, you're going to find the same thing. I know what I'm talking about.'

'But that was nearly thirty years ago,' Mona pleaded. 'Things have changed now. They must have.'

Vera touched her gently. 'Go and see if you like, and if they haven't changed, come back and talk to me.'

Mona looked at her stonily.

'I mean it, Mona, my brave young girl. Really I do. I

wasn't able to do it for your mother, and I don't want to do it for you. But if I couldn't face one generation being brave, if I let her go to her death with hypocritical exclamations of how well she looked, I won't do it a second time.'

Mona smiled at her and stood up to go.

'I mean it,' Vera said. 'Come back any time. And think before you bare it all to the others. You and your mother are unusual in this world, the rest of us aren't so strong.'

Mona kissed her goodbye. The first time she had done that.

'And I'll tell you more about Clare too . . . you'll like her,' said Vera.

'I'll come back anyway,' Mona said. 'You don't have to bribe me. And Vera, I'll try and tell the others, it would be very good if someone made a stand. Wouldn't it?'

'Clare wanted me to marry your father,' said Vera.

'I wish you had,' said Mona.

'Perhaps I'll marry Jerry instead,' said Vera with a tiny little laugh.

And Mona left quickly before she saw the tears that were going to come from it.

Brixton

The woman in personnel was about fifty and had a silly perm, all grey bubbles like an ageing Harpo Marx. Sandy looked at her without much hope.

'Well, of course, I can try and fix you with hostels or shelters organisation addresses, Miss Ring. But quite frankly I feel sure you would do better just to find accommodation for yourself.'

'How can I do that?' Sandy asked. It was so very different to the hospital where she had trained. There, the rules about where nurses had to live were still strictly enforced. There had been a list of approved lodgings and apartments, and only in these were the nurses permitted to stay.

'The nurses seem to play musical chairs with each other,' said the Harpo Marx personnel officer disapprovingly. 'You'll be very unlucky not to see about a dozen tattered notices on the board downstairs offering accommodation.'

'That sounds great,' Sandy said eagerly. 'And if I share with someone who works in the hospital, then I'll learn the ropes a bit more quickly.'

She got a watery and unenthusiastic smile. The personnel officer obviously found as little satisfaction in her job as she had found success with her hairdresser.

There were eight notices offering accommodation. Four were too expensive, two specified that the applicant must speak Spanish. That left two. One of them had a phone number, so Sandy dialled it at once. In her hand she had her *A to Z* so that she could identify where the place was.

'It's SW9,' the girl said.

'Clapham?' asked Sandy studying her map intently.

'More east of it,' the girl said.

'Near the tube?'

'Yeah, four minutes.'

'How many of you in the flat.?'

'Just me.'

'That's not a bad rent for a flat for two.'

'You ain't seen it, lady.'

'Shall I come over and look, and let you look at me?'

'Sure. Come now I'll make you tea.'

'That's very nice, I'm Sandy Ring.'

'That's funny. I'm Wilma Ring.'

'Hey, we might be cousins.'

'Yeah. Are you black?'

'Err . . . um . . . no. Are you?'

'Yeah, we most likely ain't cousins. See you for tea.'

It was certainly shabby, though nothing that paint and a new hall door could not have cured, Sandy thought to herself, but the street didn't have too much smart paint and new hall doors. There were three bicycles in the hall and a lot of very loud music came up from the basement.

What the hell, Sandy thought, I'm not going to be on nights for the first six months, and if I can't sleep after a day's hospital work because of a few bars of music I must be in bad shape. Wilma was standing at the door.

'Come in, cousin,' she called with a laugh. 'Have some nice English tea to get you over the culture shock of a walk through the Brixton West Indies.'

It was agreed in ten minutes. The room, the rent, the lifestyles.

'I don't have friends in, because I'm studying, see,' Wilma said. 'But I study in my own bedroom, so you can have people in so long as they don't shout through the walls. And if your guys don't eat all the food in the fridge and take all the hot water, they can stay all night.'

'What are you studying?' Sandy wanted to know. She didn't feel like telling Wilma yet that there would be no guys for a long time, not after the guy in Wales, the one she was running away from.

'Open University. I am reading for a university degree,' said Wilma. 'When you come back tonight, remember to get yourself a lamp and bulb for your room, there's only a centre light, it makes it even worse than it need be.'

'I can come back tonight?' Sandy said.

'I can't see why you should pay a hotel and pay me. You've only got one body and it can only sleep in one bed.'

For a few weeks they rarely saw each other. Wilma worked strange hours on the admission shifts, so that she could have appropriate time off for her studying and to watch the programmes on television. Sandy worked a day shift on the neuro-surgical ward. It was demanding and sometimes depressing. She often wished that Wilma were there to chat to when she got back. Bit by bit she got used to the area; they even joked with her in the corner store as she refused ackee and salt fish and other Jamaican treats.

'I only like the patties,' she said firmly.

'You wait till you go out to the island and have goat curry,' Nelson, the good-looking man who ran the shop, used to say to her. 'Then you never eat anything else.'

'I can't imagine going to Jamaica,' she said truthfully. 'It must be such a contrast between the rich tourists and the poverty of the people who live there.'

'What makes you think that?' Nelson wanted to know.

Sandy was about to say that if so many Jamaicans came to Britain to live in what she considered relative poverty, things must be in a very bad state back home. But she was unsure if that would be offensive, so instead she muttered vaguely about something she had seen on television.

'You don't take no notice of that Wilma,' Nelson had said. 'Wilma is a no-good communist, she is always finding something wrong with every society.'

The day she heard this new slant on her flat-mate, Sandy climbed the stairs and found Wilma at home. She had washed her hair and was sitting in an unaccustomed relaxed mood with her feet on the window box, a towel around her head and a beer in her hand.

'Come on, pretend we're in the sun-soaked Caribbean. There's a beer for you in the fridge,' she called to Sandy and they sat in the summer evening listening to the sounds from the street below, the planes overhead, the distant traffic, and the general hum of city noises.

'I hear you're a communist,' Sandy said lightly.

'That pretty boy Nelson has a big mouth an' no brain,' commented Wilma, unperturbed.

'I think he fancies you. He always mentions you,' probed Sandy.

'Yeah, he should fancy Margaret, the mother of his three children. She works sixteen hours a day for him. He should discuss her politics and her tits, not mine,' retorted Wilma, this time with more spirit.

'But *are* you a communist?' persisted Sandy. In a way she hoped Wilma was. It was quite outrageous enough to share with a Jamaican woman, that had them all whispering back in Wales, but a Jamaican communist, would be over the top.

'Of course not, dope,' said Wilma. 'Would I be lying here talking chicken shit to a silly little nurse like you, drinking beer, if I were a communist? No, I would be fighting the good fight somewhere and overturning things. Not planning to become rich and middle class and have a university degree.'

'I think you are mad to try and do all that studying,' said Sandy, stretching her tired muscles. 'It's bad enough

doing what we do. I only want to sleep and look at telly
when the day is over. Study! I couldn't even think of it.'
'I had always heard they were ambitious in Wales,'
Wilma said.
'They may be. I'm not any more. Anyway, being a
nurse isn't that far below being a teacher, you know, they
rate about the same. And teachers don't get all that much
more money. I don't know why you're killing yourself if
all you'll do is teach in the end.'
'I'll do both,' said Wilma.
'How can you do both?' Sandy became suddenly
irritated at the calm way this tall girl had everything
planned. Even her short burst of leisure was carefully
planned, hair shampooed, fresh air by the window,
lounging in a robe, instead of sitting there, tired and hot,
like Sandy was.
'I'll be a teacher during the day, and then some nights a
week I'll do a night shift, and I can work full-time nursing
in the long holidays. Teachers have vacations of three to
four months, you know, when you add it all up. It is a
ridiculous life . . . they get paid . . . I don't know.' She
shook her turbanned head from side to side in amazement.
'My sister married a teacher in Wales. They don't get
well paid I tell you, and he's knackered come the summer
when the exams are over. You've got it wrong,' Sandy
said. She didn't like to hear of people doing two jobs. She
felt quite proud of herself, having managed to drag
herself unwillingly from Wales, from a man who walked
on her to a big strange city and find a job and a flat. She
thought that Wilma was pushing it.
Wilma got them more beer.
'Ohh,' she sighed. 'Ohh, Sandy girl, if only you knew
what my mother had to do for me, and what she and her
sisters have had to do for all our family. I'll *never* stop
getting degrees, every letter I have to my name is a shaft
of sunlight for them. It's a reason to go on scrubbing

floors, to go into offices and shops at five a.m. where the air is stale and the baskets are full of yesterday's sour milk cartons, but the letters after my name will make it worth while.'

'Oh, for heaven's sake, Wilma, you're far too intelligent to go along with that crap,' cried Sandy, annoyed now and tactful no longer. 'If you really wanted to help your mother, then you'd give her money, for God's sake. I mean, I send my mother money each week, not much, but a little, for her to get herself something nice, maybe a hair-do or a night at the bingo and a fish supper. My Dad keeps her very short.'

'Oh yes?' said Wilma.

'Yes, bloody yes. And that's what you should do instead of filling your poor Mam's head up with ideas and nonsense, and degrees and airy-fairy letters after your name. If you can't bear her being down on her knees then take her off them. You can send her ten quid a week – better, you can go and give it to her. She only lives an hour away. I can't understand why you don't go to see her more. My Mam lives hundreds of miles away, otherwise I'd go and take her out on a Saturday night for a bit of a laugh. That's what a daughter is for.'

Wilma sat up and looked at her.

'No, Sandy my little sister, that is *not* what a daughter is for. A daughter must never be for that. That means the system never ends. A daughter must be something better, something stronger, she must give hope and reason for what is being done. She must make some sense out of all the scrubbing, bring some logic to all that lavatory cleaning. Otherwise a daughter is just yourself again, on and on for ever.'

Sandy saw why Nelson thought that Wilma wanted to overturn society.

And because she thought of Nelson she mentioned him.

'But the other Jamaicans don't feel that way, Nelson

and those girls in the store for example, they have a laugh and they go to parties and they sing songs, and they say it's not too bad. Isn't that better for a mother, to see she has happy children?'

Wilma stood up and rested her hands on the window box. She looked as if she were about to make a speech to a crowd below but instead she spoke in a very gentle voice.

'My mother told me that before she came here she never knew that white women were poor too, when she saw poor white women in Britain she thought they had done something bad and were being punished. She came from a family where the women were strong.

'*Her* mother remembered being a Mammy and remembered having to lie down and let a white boss screw her. But that had all gone by my mother's time, she had five jobs, five different jobs to get her fare to England, and when she came here she had six jobs to make the money for us to come, but she didn't mind having six jobs because she lived in luxury. She had electricity, not kerosene, she had water in a tap, down the corridor but in a tap. She had a house where the food didn't melt, or rot, or go bad, she didn't have to buy expensive ice to keep food fresh for twenty-four hours. And one by one she sent for us. One by one we came.'

Her voice began to sound a little like a preacher's. Sandy could imagine her putting a few 'Yea, verrilys' into her conversation.

'You see, what was so wonderful was that we knew she would send for us. I was only nine when she went, only a child of nine when she got on the bus to Kingston that day, and I knew she would send for us one by one. That when I came first, part of her sending for Sadie and sending for Margaret and the others was that I should work hard at school. It was team work, it was solidarity like you've never known. If we had the homework done and our Mother's supper ready when she came in from one job, that gave her strength to go out to another. If she didn't have to worry about us, if we cleaned the house, then she could stay healthy, in her jobs and not fret. You have to scrub a lot of floors and get a lot of bonus and overtime to pay five airfares from Jamaica and for a home for them to live in.'

Wilma smiled seraphically.

'But we were a lucky family because it was the woman who came. No danger of the woman finding a fancy man and forgetting us like happened to some of the men who came. A woman with five children will not forget them. That Nelson you admire so much in the corner store, he has a wife and two children in Ocho Rios, as well as Margaret and the three children here. Nice for Nelson to be chatty and to have a laugh and a drink and a song. Very nice. My mother would spit on him. A disgrace to Jamaica, every song and every bit of a laugh which you said I should be having is a mockery.'

'But, Wilma, surely you can have both. I mean the pride in your doing well *and* a bit of a laugh, that's all I was suggesting. That's all I was saying, your Mam has to have some relaxation, some happiness.'

'I write to her and I tell her what I am studying, sometimes she looks at the television when the Open University programmes are on. She can't understand them, but that's her happiness.'

'What does she do on her time off?'

'She sleeps. And when she wakes to work again she remembers that her mother couldn't read but she can read and write, and she knows that even though she can read and write she will never have qualifications but I will have a university degree, and that sends a big surge of happiness right through her and she is glad that she didn't just sit and laugh with her mother while the chickens ran around the dusty yard, and that I did not sit and laugh with her, while we both went out to play bingo.'

'I see,' said Sandy, who didn't see at all.

'You don't see, because for you it has always been a possibility, a good life. You don't have to prove anything to your mother nor she to hers.'

'Oh I don't know. I've had more education, a better job, more freedom than she did.' Sandy didn't want anyone to think that there had been no progress. Life hadn't been a bed of roses in the small Welsh town.

Wilma sighed. Sandy was by far the nicest of the girls who had shared her flat, but she would leave, she would leave soon. Without a proper explanation. And Nelson would say that she left because she was too toffee-nosed for the area, and Old Johnny, the man from Barbados two floors down, would say that it was good riddance to that young whitey anyway, and only Wilman would know that it had nothing to do with colours of skin or area, or smells of curry or steel bands in the basement. It had everything to do with life being short and most people wanting to have a laugh and a good time.

CENTRAL LINE

Shepherd's Bush

People looked very weary, May thought, and shabbier than she had remembered Londoners to be. They reminded her a little of those news-reel pictures of crowds during the war or just after it, old raincoats, brave smiles, endless patience. But then this wasn't Regent Street where she had wandered up and down looking at shops on other visits to London, it wasn't the West End with lights all glittering and people getting out of taxis full of excitement and wafts of perfume. This was Shepherd's Bush where people lived. They had probably set out from here early this morning and fought similar crowds on the way to work. The women must have done their shopping in their lunch-hour because most of them were carrying plastic bags of food. It was a London different to the one you see as a tourist.

And she was here for a different reason, although she had once read a cynical article in a magazine which said that girls coming to London for abortions provided a significant part of the city's tourist revenue. It wasn't something you could classify under any terms as a holiday. When she filled in the card at the airport she had written 'Business' in the section where it said 'Purpose of journey'.

The pub where she was to meet Celia was near the tube station. She found it easily and settled herself in. A lot of the accents were Irish, workmen having a pint before they went home to their English wives and their television programmes. Not drunk tonight, it was only Monday, but obviously regulars. Maybe not so welcome as regulars on Friday or Saturday nights, when they would remember they were Irish and sing anti-British songs.

Celia wouldn't agree with her about that. Celia had rose-tinted views about the Irish in London, she thought they were all here from choice, not because there was no work for them at home. She hated stories about the restless Irish, or Irishmen on the lump in the building trade. She said people shouldn't make such a big thing about it all. People who came from much farther away settled in London, it was big enough to absorb everyone. Oh well, she wouldn't bring up the subject, there were enough things to disagree with Celia about . . . without searching for more.

Oh why of all people, of all the bloody people in the world, did she have to come to Celia? Why was there nobody else whom she could ask for advice? Celia would give it, she would give a lecture with every piece of information she imparted. She would deliver a speech with every cup of tea, she would be cool, practical and exactly the right person, if she weren't so much the wrong person. It was handing Celia a whole box of ammunition about Andy. From now on Celia could say that Andy was a rat, and May could no longer say she had no facts to go on.

Celia arrived. She was thinner, and looked a little tired. She smiled. Obviously the lectures weren't going to come in the pub. Celia always knew the right place for things. Pubs were for meaningless chats and bright, non-intense conversation. Home was for lectures.

'You're looking marvellous,' Celia said.

It couldn't be true. May looked at her reflection in a glass panel. You couldn't see the dark lines under her eyes there, but you could see the droop of her shoulders, she wasn't a person that could be described as looking marvellous. No, not even in a pub.

'I'm okay,' she said. 'But you've got very slim, how did you do it?'

'No bread, no cakes, no potatoes, no sweets,' said Celia in a business-like way. 'It's the old rule but it's the only rule. You deny yourself everything you want and you lose weight.'

'I know,' said May, absently rubbing her waistline.

'Oh I didn't meant *that*,' cried Celia horrified. 'I didn't mean that at all.'

May felt weary, she hadn't meant that either, she was patting her stomach because she had been putting on weight. The child that she was going to get rid of was still only a speck, it would cause no bulge. She had put on weight because she cooked for Andy three or four times a week in his flat. He was long and lean. He could eat for ever and he wouldn't put on weight. He didn't like eating alone so she ate with him. She reassured Celia that there was no offence and when Celia had gone, twittering with rage at herself, to the counter, May wondered whether she had explored every avenue before coming to Celia and Shepherd's Bush for help.

She had. There were no legal abortions in Dublin, and she did not know of anyone who had ever had an illegal one there. England and the ease of the system were less than an hour away by plane. She didn't want to try and get it on the National Health, she had the money, all she wanted was someone who would introduce her to a doctor, so that she could get it all over with quickly. She needed somebody who knew her, somebody who wouldn't abandon her if things went wrong, somebody who would lie for her, because a few lies would have to be told. May didn't have any other friends in London. There was a girl she had once met on a skiing holiday, but you couldn't impose on a holiday friendship in that way. She knew a man, a very nice, kind man who had stayed in the hotel where she worked and had often begged her to come and stay with him and his wife. But she couldn't go to stay with them for the first time in this predicament, it would be ridiculous. It had to be Celia.

It might be easier if Celia had loved somebody so much that everything else was unimportant. But stop, that wasn't fair. Celia loved that dreary, boring, selfish Martin. She loved him so much that she believed one day he was going to get things organised and make a home for them. Everyone else knew that Martin was the worst possible bet for any punter, a Mammy's boy, who had everything he wanted now, including a visit every two months from Celia, home from London, smartly-dressed, undemanding, saving away for a day that would never come. So Celia did understand something about the nature of love. She never talked about it. People as brisk as Celia don't talk about things like unbrisk attitudes in men, or hurt feelings or broken hearts. Not when it refers to themselves, but they are very good at pointing out the foolish attitudes of others.

Celia was back with the drinks.

'We'll finish them up quickly,' she said.

Why could she never, never take her ease over any-thing? Things always had to be finished up quickly. It was warm and anonymous in the pub. They could go back to Celia's flat, which May felt sure wouldn't have even a comfortable chair in it, and talk in a business-like way about the rights and wrongs of abortion, the pro-cedure, the money, and how it shouldn't be spent on something so hopeless and destructive. And about Andy. Why wouldn't May tell him? He had a right to know. The child was half his, and even if he didn't want it he should pay for the abortion. He had plenty of money, he was a hotel manager. May had hardly any, she was a hotel receptionist. May could see it all coming, she dreaded it. She wanted to stay in this warm place until closing-time, and to fall asleep, and wake up there two days later.

Celia made walking-along-the-road conversation on the way to her flat. This road used to be very quiet and full of retired people, now it was all flats and bed-sitters.

That road was nice, but noisy, too much through-traffic. The houses in the road over there were going for thirty-five thousand, which was ridiculous, but then you had to remember it was fairly central and they did have little gardens. Finally they were there. A big Victorian house, a clean, polished hall, and three flights of stairs. The flat was much bigger than May expected, and it had a sort of divan on which she sat down immediately and put up her legs, while Celia fussed about a bit, opening a bottle of wine and putting a dish of four small lamb chops into the oven. May braced herself for the lecture.

It wasn't a lecture, it was an information-sheet. She was so relieved that she could feel herself relaxing, and filled up her wineglass again.

'I've arranged with Doctor Harris that you can call to see him tomorrow morning at 11. I told him no lies, just a little less than the truth. I said you were staying with me. If he thinks that means you are staying permanently, that's his mistake not mine. I mentioned that your problem was . . . what it is. I asked him when he thought it would be . . . em . . . done. He said Wednesday or Thursday, but it would all depend. He didn't seem shocked or anything; it's like tonsillitis to him, I suppose. Anyway he was very calm about it. I think you'll find he's a kind person and it won't be upsetting . . . that part of it.'

May was dumbfounded. Where were the accusations, the I-told-you-so sighs, the hope that now, finally, she would finish with Andy? Where was the slight moralistic bit, the heavy wondering whether or not it might be murder? For the first time in the eleven days since she had confirmed she was pregnant, May began to hope that there would be some normality in the world again.

'Will it embarrass you, all this?' she asked. 'I mean, do you feel it will change your relationship with him?'

'In London a doctor isn't an old family friend like at home, May. He's someone you go to, or I've gone to anyway, when I've had to have my ears syringed, needed antibiotics for flu last year, and a medical certificate for the time I sprained my ankle and couldn't go to work. He hardly knows me except as a name on his register. He's nice though, and he doesn't rush you in and out. He's Jewish and small and worried-looking.'

Celia moved around the flat, changing into comfortable sitting-about clothes, looking up what was on television, explaining to May that she must sleep in her room and that she, Celia, would use the divan.

No, honestly, it would be easier that way, she wasn't being nice, it would be much easier. A girl friend rang and they arranged to play squash together at the weekend. A wrong number rang; A West Indian from the flat downstairs knocked on the door to say he would be having a party on Saturday night and to apologise in advance for any noise. If they liked to bring a bottle of something, they could call in themselves. Celia served dinner. They looked at television for an hour, then went to bed.

May thought what a strange empty life Celia led here far from home, miles from Martin, no real friends, no life at all. Then she thought that Celia might possibly regard her life too as sad, working in a second-rate hotel for five years, having an affair with its manager for three years. A hopeless affair because the manager's wife and four children were a bigger stumbling-block than Martin's mother could ever be. She felt tired and comfortable, and in Celia's funny, characterless bedroom she drifted off and dreamed that Andy had discovered where she was and what she was about to do, and had flown over during the night to tell her that they would get married next morning, and live in England and forget the hotel, the family and what anyone would say.

Tuesday morning. Celia was gone. Dr Harris's address was neatly written on the pad by the phone with instructions how to get there. Also Celia's phone number at work, and a message that May never believed she would hear from Celia. 'Good luck.'

He was small, and Jewish, and worried and kind. His examination was painless and unembarrassing. He confirmed what she knew already. He wrote down dates, and asked general questions about her health. May wondered whether he had a family, there were no pictures of wife or children in the surgery. But then there were none in Andy's office, either. Perhaps his wife was called Rebecca and she too worried because her husband worked so hard, they might have two children, a boy who was a gifted musician, and a girl who wanted to get married to a Christian. Maybe they all walked along these leafy roads on Saturdays to synagogue and Rebecca cooked all those things like gefilte fish and bagels.

With a start, May told herself to stop dreaming about him. It was a habit she had got into recently, fancying lives for everyone she met, however briefly. She usually gave them happy lives with a bit of problem-to-be-solved thrown in. She wondered what a psychiatrist would make of that. As she was coming back to real life, Dr Harris was saying that if he was going to refer her for a termination he must know why she could not have the baby. He pointed out that she was healthy, and strong, and young. She should have no difficulty with pregnancy or birth. Were there emotional reasons? Yes, it would kill her parents, she wouldn't be able to look after the baby, she didn't want to look after one on her own either, it wouldn't be fair on her or the baby.

'And the father?' Dr Harris asked.

'Is my boss, is heavily married, already has four babies of his own. It would break up his marriage which he doesn't want to do . . . yet. No, the father wouldn't want me to have it either.'

'Has he said that?' asked Dr Harris as if he already knew the answer.

'I haven't told him, I can't tell him, I won't tell him,' said May.

Dr Harris sighed. He asked a few more questions; he made a telephone call; he wrote out an address. It was a posh address near Harley Street.

'This is Mr White. A well-known surgeon. These are his consulting-rooms, I have made an appointment for you at 2.30 this afternoon. I understand from your friend Miss . . .' He searched his mind and his desk for Celia's name and then gave up. 'I understand anyway that you are not living here, and don't want to try and pretend that you are, so that you want the termination done privately. That's just as well, because it would be difficult to get it done on the National Health. There are many cases that would have to come before you.'

'Oh I have the money,' said May, patting her handbag. She felt nervous but relieved at the same time. Almost exhilarated. It was working, the whole thing was actually moving. God bless Celia.

'It will be around £180 to £200, and in cash, you know that?'

'Yes, it's all here, but why should a well-known surgeon have to be paid in cash, Dr Harris? You know it makes it look a bit illegal and sort of underhand, doesn't it?'

Dr Harris smiled a tired smile. 'You ask me why he has to be paid in cash. Because he says so. Why he says so, I don't know. Maybe it's because some of his clients don't feel too like paying him after the event. It's not like plastic surgery or a broken leg, where they can see the results. In a termination you see no results. Maybe people don't pay so easily then. Maybe also Mr White doesn't have a warm relationship with his Income Tax people. I don't know.'

'Do I owe you anything?' May asked, putting on her coat.

'No, my dear, nothing.' He smiled and showed her to the door.

'It feels wrong. I'm used to paying a doctor at home or they send bills,' she said.

'Send me a picture postcard of your nice country sometime,' he said. 'When my wife was alive she and I spent several happy holidays there before all this business started.' He waved a hand to take in the course of Anglo-Irish politics and difficulties over the last ten years.

May blinked a bit hard and thanked him. She took a taxi which was passing his door and went to Oxford Street. She wanted to see what was in the shops because she was going to pretend that she had spent £200 on clothes and then they had all been lost or stolen. She hadn't yet worked out the details of this deception, which seemed unimportant compared to all the rest that had to be gone through. But she would need to know what was in the shops so that she could say what she was meant to have bought.

Imagining that she had this kind of money to spend, she examined jackets, skirts, sweaters, and the loveliest boots she had ever seen. If only she didn't have to throw this money away, she could have these things. It was her savings over ten months, she put by £30 a month with difficulty. Would Andy have liked her in the boots? She didn't know. He never said much about the way she looked. He saw her mostly in uniform when she could steal time to go to the flat he had for himself in the hotel. On the evenings when he was meant to be working late, and she was in fact cooking for him, she usually wore a dressing-gown, a long velvet one. Perhaps she might have bought a dressing-gown. She examined some, beautiful Indian silks, and a Japanese satin one in pink covered with little black butterflies. Yes, she would tell him she had bought that, he would like the sound of it, and be sorry it had been stolen.

She had a cup of coffee in one of the big shops and watched the other shoppers resting between bouts of buying. She wondered, did any of them look at her, and if so, would they know in a million years that her shopping money would remain in her purse until it was handed over to a Mr White so that he could abort Andy's baby? Why did she use words like that, why did she say things to hurt herself, she must have a very deep-seated sense of guilt. Perhaps, she thought to herself with a bit of humour, she should save another couple of hundred pounds and come over for a few sessions with a Harley Street shrink. That should set her right.

It wasn't a long walk to Mr White's rooms, it wasn't a pleasant welcome. A kind of girl that May had before only seen in the pages of fashion magazines, bored, disdainful, elegant, reluctantly admitted her.

'Oh yes, Dr Harris's patient,' she said, as if May should have come in some tradesman's entrance. She felt furious, and inferior, and sat with her hands in small tight balls, and her eyes unseeing in the waiting-room.

Mr White looked like a caricature of a diplomat. He had elegant grey hair, elegant manicured hands. He moved very gracefully, he talked in practised, concerned clichés, he knew how to put people at their ease, and despite herself, and while still disliking him, May felt safe.

Another examination, another confirmation, more checking of dates. Good, good, she had come in plenty of time, sensible girl. No reasons she would like to discuss about whether this was the right course of action? No? Oh well, grown-up lady, must make up her own mind. Absolutely certain then? Fine, fine. A look at a big leather-bound book on his desk, a look at a small note-book. Leather-bound for the tax people, small note-book for himself, thought May viciously. Splendid, splendid. Tomorrow morning then, not a problem in the world, once she was sure, then he knew this was the best, and wisest thing. Very sad the people who dithered.

May could never imagine this man having dithered

in his life. She was asked to see Vanessa on the way out. She knew that the girl would be called something like Vanessa.

Vanessa yawned and took £194 from her. She seemed to have difficulty in finding the six pounds in change. May wondered wildly whether this was meant to be a tip. If so, she would wait for a year until Vanessa found the change. With the notes came a discreet printed card advertising a nursing home on the other side of London.

'Before nine, fasting, just the usual overnight things,' said Vanessa helpfully.

'Tomorrow morning?' checked May.

'Well yes, naturally. You'll be out at eight the following morning. They'll arrange everything like taxis. They have super food,' she added as an afterthought.

'They'd need to have for this money,' said May spiritedly.

'You're not just paying for the food,' said Vanessa wisely.

It was still raining. She rang Celia from a public phonebox. Everything was organised, she told her. Would Celia like to come and have a meal somewhere, and maybe they could go on to a theatre?

Celia was sorry, she had to work late, and she had already bought liver and bacon for supper. Could she meet May at home around nine? There was a great quiz show on telly, it would be a shame to miss it.

May went to a hairdresser and spent four times what she would have spent at home on a hair-do.

She went to a cinema and saw a film which looked as if it were going to be about a lot of sophisticated witty French people on a yacht and turned out to be about a sophisticated witty French girl who fell in love with the deck-hand on the yacht and when she purposely got pregnant, in order that he would marry her, he laughed at her and the witty sophisticated girl threw herself overboard. Great choice that, May said glumly, as she dived into the underground to go back to the smell of liver frying.

Celia asked little about the arrangements for the morning, only practical things like the address so that she could work out how long it would take to get there.

'Would you like me to come and see you?' she asked. 'I expect when it's all over, all finished you know, they'd let you have visitors. I could come after work.'

She emphasised the word 'could' very slightly. May immediately felt mutinous. She would love Celia to come, but not if it was going to be a duty, something she felt she had to do, against her principles, her inclinations.

'No, don't do that,' she said in a falsely bright voice. 'They have telly in the rooms apparently, and anyway, it's not as if I were going to be there for more than twenty-four hours.'

Celia looked relieved. She worked out taxi times and locations and turned on the quiz show.

In the half light May looked at her. She was unbending, Celia was. She would survive everything, even the fact that Martin would never marry her. Christ, the whole thing was a mess. Why did people start life with such hopes, and as early as their mid-twenties become beaten and accepting of things. Was the rest of life going to be like this?

She didn't sleep so well, and it was a relief when Celia shouted that it was seven o'clock.

Wednesday. An ordinary Wednesday for the taxi-driver, who shouted some kind of amiable conversation at her. She missed most of it, because of the noise of the engine, and didn't bother to answer him half the time except with a grunt.

The place had creeper on the walls. It was a big house, with a small garden, and an attractive brass handle on the door. The nurse who opened it was Irish. She checked May's name on a list. Thank God it was O'Connor, there were a million O'Connors. Supose she had had an unusual name, she'd have been found out immediately.

The bedroom was big and bright. Two beds, flowery covers, nice furniture. A magazine rack, a bookshelf. A television, a bathroom.

The Irish nurse offered her a hanger from the wardrobe for her coat as if this was a pleasant family hotel of great class and comfort. May felt frightened for the first time. She longed to sit down on one of the beds and cry, and for the nurse to put her arm around her and give her a cigarette and say that it would be all right. She hated being so alone.

The nurse was distant.

'The other lady will be in shortly. Her name is Miss Adams. She just went downstairs to say goodbye to her friend. If there's anything you'd like, please ring.'

She was gone, and May paced the room like a captured animal. Was she to undress? It was ridiculous to go to bed. You only went to bed in the day-time if you were ill. She was well, perfectly well.

Miss Adams burst in the door. She was a chubby, pretty girl about twenty-three. She was Australian, and her name was Hell, short for Helen.

'Come on, bedtime,' she said, and they both put on their nightdresses and got into beds facing each other. May had never felt so silly in her whole life.

'Are you sure we're meant to do this?' she asked.

'Positive,' Helen announced. 'I was here last year. They'll be in with the screens for modesty, the examination, and the pre-med. They go mad if you're not in bed. Of course that stupid Paddy of a nurse didn't tell you, they expect you to be inspired.'

Hell was right. In five minutes, the nurse and Mr White came in. A younger nurse carried a screen. Hell was examined first, then May, for blood pressure and temperature, and that kind of thing. Mr White was charming.

He called her Miss O'Connor, as if he had known her all his life.

He patted her shoulder and told her she didn't have anything to worry about. The Irish nurse gave her an unsmiling injection which was going to make her drowsy. It didn't immediately.

Hell was doing her nails.

'You were really here last year?' asked May in disbelief.

'Yeah, there's nothing to it. I'll be back at work tomorrow.'

'Why didn't you take the Pill?' May asked.

'Why didn't you?' countered Hell.

'Well, I did for a bit, but I thought it was making me fat, and then anyway, you know, I thought I'd escaped for so long before I started the Pill that it would be all right. I was wrong.'

'I know.' Hell was sympathetic. 'I can't take it. I've got varicose veins already and I don't really understand all those things they give you in the Family Planning clinics, jellies, and rubber things, and diaphragms. It's worse than working out income tax. Anyway, you never have time to set up a scene like that before going to bed with someone, do you? It's like preparing for a battle.'

May laughed.

'It's going to be fine, love,' said Hell. 'Look, I know, I've been here before. Some of my friends have had it done four or five times. I promise you, it's only the people who don't know who worry. This afternoon you'll wonder what you were thinking about to look so white. Now if it had been terrible, would I be here again?'

'But your varicose veins?' said May, feeling a little sleepy.

'Go to sleep, kid,' said Hell. 'We'll have a chat when it's all over.'

Then she was getting onto a trolley, half-asleep, and going down corridors with lovely prints on the walls to a room with a lot of light, and transferring onto another table. She felt as if she could sleep for ever and she hadn't even had the anaesthetic yet. Mr White stood there in a coat brighter than his name. Someone was dressing him up the way they do in films.

She thought about Andy. 'I love you,' she said suddenly.

'Of course you do,' said Mr White, coming over and patting her kindly without a trace of embarrassment.

Then she was being moved again, she thought they hadn't got her right on the operating table, but it wasn't that, it was back into her own bed and more sleep.

There was a tinkle of china. Hell called over from the window.

'Come on, they've brought us some nice soup. Broth they call it.'

May blinked.

'Come on, May. I was done after you and I'm wide awake. Now didn't I tell you there was nothing to it?'

May sat up. No pain, no tearing feeling in her insides. No sickness.

'Are you sure they did me?' she asked.

They both laughed.

They had what the nursing-home called a light lunch. Then they got a menu so that they could choose dinner.

'There are some things that England does really well, and this is one of them,' Hell said approvingly, trying to decide between the delights that were offered. 'They even give us a small carafe of wine. If you want more you have to pay for it. But they kind of disapprove of us getting pissed.'

Hell's friend Charlie was coming in at six when he finished work. Would May be having a friend too, she wondered? No. Celia wouldn't come.

'I don't mean Celia,' said Hell. 'I mean the bloke.'

'He doesn't know, he's in Dublin, and he's married,' said May.

'Well, Charlie's married, but he bloody knows, and he'd know if he were on the moon.'

'It's different.'

'No, it's not different. It's the same for everyone, there are rules, you're a fool to break them. Didn't he pay for it either, this guy?'

'No. I told you he doesn't know.'

'Aren't you noble,' said Hell scornfully. 'Aren't you a real Lady Galahad. Just visiting London for a day or two, darling, just going to see a few friends, see you soon. Love you darling. Is that it?'

'We don't go in for so many darlings as that in Dublin,' said May.

'You don't go in for much common sense either. What will you gain, what will he gain, what will anyone gain? You come home penniless, a bit lonely. He doesn't know what the hell you've been doing, he isn't extra-sensitive and loving and grateful because he doesn't have anything to be grateful about as far as he's concerned.'

'I couldn't tell him. I couldn't. I couldn't ask him for £200 and say what it was for. That wasn't in the bargain, that was never part of the deal.'

May was almost tearful, mainly from jealousy she thought. She couldn't bear Hell's Charlie to come in, while her Andy was going home to his wife because there would be nobody to cook him something exciting and go to bed with him in his little manager's flat.

'When you go back, tell him. That's my advice,' said Hell. 'Tell him you didn't want to worry him, you did it all on your own because the responsibility was yours since you didn't take the Pill. That's unless you think he'd have wanted it?'

'No, he wouldn't have wanted it.'

'Well then, that's what you do. Don't ask him for the money straight out, just let him know you're broke. He'll react some way then. It's silly not to tell them at all. My sister did that with her bloke back in Melbourne. She never told him at all, and she got upset because he didn't know the sacrifice she had made, and every time she bought a drink or paid for a cinema ticket she got resentful of him. All for no reason, because he didn't bloody know.'

'I might,' said May, but she knew she wouldn't.

Charlie came in. He was great fun, very fond of Hell, wanting to be sure she was okay, and no problems. He brought a bottle of wine which they shared, and he told them funny stories about what had happened at the office. He was in advertising. He arranged to meet Hell for lunch next day and joked his way out of the room.

'He's a lovely man,' said May.

'Old Charlie's smashing,' agreed Hell. He had gone back home to entertain his wife and six dinner guests. His wife was a marvellous hostess apparently. They were always having dinner parties.

'Do you think he'll ever leave her?' asked May.

'He'd be out of his brains if he did,' said Hell cheerfully.

May was thoughtful. Maybe everyone would be out of their brains if they left good, comfortable, happy home set-ups for whatever the other woman imagined she could offer. She wished she could be as happy as Hell.

'Tell me about your fellow,' Hell said kindly.

May did, the whole long tale. It was great to have somebody to listen, somebody who didn't say she was on a collision course, somebody who didn't purse up lips like Celia, someone who said, 'Go on, what did you do then?'

'He sounds like a great guy,' said Hell, and May smiled happily.

They exchanged addresses, and Hell promised that if ever she came to Ireland she wouldn't ring up the hotel and say, 'Can I talk to May, the girl I had the abortion with last winter?' and they finished Charlie's wine, and went to sleep.

The beds were stripped early next morning when the final examination had been done, and both were pronounced perfect and ready to leave. May wondered fancifully how many strange life stories the room must have seen.

'Do people come here for other reasons apart from . . . er, terminations?' she asked the disapproving Irish nurse.

'Oh certainly they do, you couldn't work here otherwise,' said the nurse. 'It would be like a death factory, wouldn't it?'

That puts me in my place, thought May, wondering why she hadn't the courage to say that she was only visiting the home, she didn't earn her living from it.

She let herself into Celia's gloomy flat. It had become gloomy again like the way she had imagined it before she saw it. The warmth of her first night there was gone. She looked around and wondered why Celia had no pictures, no books, no souvenirs.

There was a note on the telephone pad.

'I didn't ring or anything, because I forgot to ask if you had given your real name, and I wouldn't know who to ask for. Hope you feel well again. I'll be getting some chicken pieces so we can have supper together around 8. Ring me if you need me. C.'

May thought for a bit. She went out and bought Celia a casserole dish, a nice one made of cast-iron. It would be useful for all those little high-protein, low-calorie dinners Celia cooked. She also bought a bunch of flowers, but could find no vase when she came back and had to use a big glass instead. She left a note thanking her for the hospitality, warm enough to sound properly grateful, and a genuinely warm remark about how glad she was that she had been able to do it all through nice Dr Harris. She said nothing about the time in the nursing-home. Celia would prefer not to know. May just said that she was fine, and thought she would go back to Dublin tonight. She rang the airline and booked a plane.

Should she ring Celia and tell her to get only one chicken piece. No, damn Celia, she wasn't going to ring her. She had a fridge, hadn't she?

The plane didn't leave until the early afternoon. For a wild moment she thought of joining Hell and Charlie in the pub where they were meeting, but dismissed the idea. She must now make a list of what clothes she was meant to have bought and work out a story about how they had disappeared. Nothing that would make Andy get in touch with police or airlines to find them for her. It was going to be quite hard, but she'd have to give Andy some explanation of what she'd been doing, wouldn't she? And he would want to know why she had spent all that money. Or would he? Did he even know she had all that money? She couldn't remember telling him. He wasn't very interested in her little savings, they talked more about his investments. And she must remember that if he was busy or cross tonight or tomorrow she wasn't to take it out on him. Like Hell had said, there wasn't any point in her expecting a bit of cossetting when he didn't even know she needed it.

How sad and lonely it would be to live like Celia, to be so suspicious of men, to think so ill of Andy. Celia always said he was selfish and just took what he could get. That was typical of Celia, she understood nothing. Hell had understood more, in a couple of hours, than Celia had in three years. Hell knew what it was like to love someone.

But May didn't think Hell had got it right about telling Andy all about the abortion. Andy might be against that kind of thing. He was very moral in his own way, was Andy.

Holland Park

Everyone hated Malcolm and Melissa out in Greece last summer. They pretended they thought they were marvellous, but deep down we really hated them. They were too perfect, too bright, intelligent, witty and aware. They never monopolised conversations in the taverna, they never seemed to impose their will on anyone else, but somehow we all ended up doing what they wanted to do. They didn't seem lovey-dovey with each other, but they had a companionship which drove us all to a frenzy of rage.

I nearly fainted when I got a note from them six months later. I thought they were the kind of people who wrote down addresses as a matter of courtesy, and you never heard from them again.

'I hate trying to recreate summer madness,' wrote Melissa. 'So I won't gather everyone from the Hellenic scene, but Malcolm and I would be thrilled if you could come to supper on the 20th. Around eightish, very informal and everything. We've been so long out of touch that I don't know if there's anyone I should ask you to bring along; if so, of course the invitation is for two. Give me a ring sometime so that I'll know how many strands of spaghetti to put in the pot. It will be super to see you again.'

I felt that deep down she knew there was nobody she should ask me to bring along. She wouldn't need to hire a private detective for that, Melissa would know. The wild notion of hiring someone splendid from an escort agency came and went. In three artless questions Melissa would find out where he was from, and think it was a marvellous fun thing to have done.

I didn't believe her about the spaghetti, either. It would be something that looked effortless but would be magnificent and unusual at the same time. Perhaps a perfect Greek meal for nostalgia, where she would have made all the hard things like pitta and humus and fetta herself, and laugh away the idea that it was difficult. Or it would be a dinner around a mahogany table with lots of cutglass decanters, and a Swiss darling to serve it and wash up.

But if I didn't go, Alice would kill me, and Alice and I often had a laugh over the perfection of Malcolm and Melissa. She said I had made them up, and that the people in the photos were in fact models who had been hired by the Greek Tourist Board to make the place look more glamorous. Their names had passed into our private shorthand. Alice would describe a restaurant as a 'Malcolm and Melissa sort of place', meaning that it was perfect, understated and somehow irritating at the same time. I would say that I had handled a situation in a 'Malcolm and Melissa way', meaning that I had scored without seeming to have done so at all.

So I rang the number and Melissa was delighted to hear from me. Yes, didn't Greece all seem like a dream nowadays, and wouldn't it be foolish to go to the same place next year in case it wasn't as good, and no, they hadn't really decided where to go next year, but Malcolm had seen this advertisement about a yacht party which wanted a few more people to make up the numbers, and it might be fun, but one never knew and one was a bit trapped on a yacht if it was all terrible. And super that I could come on the 20th, and then with the voice politely questioning, would I be bringing anyone else?

In one swift moment I made a decision. 'Well, if it's not going to make it too many I would like to bring this friend of mine, Alice,' I said, and felt a roaring in my ears as I said it, Melissa was equal to anything.

'Of course, of course, that's lovely, we look forward to meeting her. See you both about eightish then. It's not far from the tube, but maybe you want to get a bus, I'm not sure . . .'

'Alice has a car,' I said proudly.

'Oh, better still. Tell her there's no problem about parking, we have a bit of waste land around the steps. It makes life heavenly in London not to have to worry about friends parking.'

Alice was delighted. She said she hoped they wouldn't turn out to have terrible feet of clay and that we would have to find new names for them. I was suddenly taken with a great desire to impress her with them, and an equal hope that they would find her as funny and witty as I did. Alice can be eccentric at times, she can go into deep silences. We giggled a lot about what we'd wear. Alice said that we should go in full evening dress, with capes, and embroidered handbags, and cigarette-holders, but I said that would be ridiculous.

'It would make her uneasy,' said Alice with an evil face.

'But she's not horrible, she's nice. She's asked us to dinner, she'll be very nice,' I pleaded.

'I thought you couldn't stand her,' said Alice, disappointed.

'It's hard to explain. She doesn't mean any harm, she just does everything too well.' I felt immediately that I was taking the myth away from Malcolm and Melissa and wished I'd never thought of asking Alice.

Between then and the 20th, Alice thought that we should go in boiler suits, in tennis gear, dressed as Greek peasants, and at one stage that we should dress up as nuns and tell her that this was what we were in real life. With difficulty I managed to persuade her that we were not to look on the evening as some kind of search-and-destroy mission, and Alice reluctantly agreed.

I don't really know why we had allowed the beautiful couple to become so much part of our fantasy life. It wasn't as if we had nothing else to think about. Alice was a solicitor with a busy practice consisting mainly of battered wives, worried one-parent families faced with eviction, and a large vocal section of the female population who felt that they had been discriminated against in their jobs. She had an unsatisfactory love-life going on with one of the partners in the firm, usually when his wife was in hospital, which didn't make her feel at all guilty, she saw it more as a kind of service that she was offering. I work in a theatre writing publicity-handouts and arranging newspaper interviews for the stars, and in my own way I meet plenty of glittering people. I sort of love a hopeless man who is a good writer but a bad person to love, since he loves too many people, but it doesn't break my heart.

I don't suppose that deep down Alice and I want to live in a big house in Holland Park, and be very beautiful and charming, and have a worthy job like Melissa raising money for a good cause, and be married to a very bright, sunny-looking man like Malcolm, who runs a left-wing bookshop that somehow has made him a great deal of money. I don't *suppose* we could have been directly envious. More indirectly irritated, I would have thought.

I was very irritated with myself on the night of the 20th because I changed five times before Alice came to collect me. The black sweater and skirt looked too severe, the gingham dress mutton dressed as lamb, the yellow too garish, the pink too virginal. I settled for a tapestry skirt and a cheap cotton top.

'Christ, you look like a suite of furniture,' said Alice when she arrived.

'Do I? Is it terrible?' I asked, anxious as a sixteen-year-old before a first dance.

'No, of course it isn't,' said Alice. 'It's fine, it's just a bit sort of a sofa-coverish if you know what I mean. Let's hope it clashes with her décor.'

Tears of rage in my eyes, I rushed into the bedroom and put on the severe black again. Safe, is what magazines call black. Safe I would be.

Alice was very contrite.

'I'm sorry, I really am. I don't know why I said that, it looked fine. I've never given two minutes' thought to clothes, you know that. Oh for God's sake wear it, please. Take off the mourning gear and put on what you were wearing.'

'Does this look like mourning then?' I asked, riddled with anxiety.

'Give me a drink,' said Alice firmly. 'In ten years of knowing each other we have never had to waste three minutes talking about clothes. Why are we doing it tonight?'

I poured her a large Scotch and one for me, and put on a jockey necklace which took the severe look away from the black. Alice said it looked smashing.

Alice told me about a client whose husband had put Vim in her tin of tooth powder and she had tried to convince herself that he still wasn't too bad. I told Alice about an ageing actress who was opening next week in a play, and nobody, not even the man I half love, would do an interview with her for any paper because they said, quite rightly, that she was an old bore. We had another Scotch to reflect on all that.

I told Alice about the man I half loved having asked me to go to Paris with him next weekend, and Alice said I should tell him to get stuffed, unless, of course, he was going to pay for the trip, in which case I must bring a whole lot of different judgements to bear. She said she was going to withdraw part of her own services from her unsatisfactory partner, because the last night they had spent together had been a perusal of *The Home Doctor* to try and identify the nature of his wife's illness. I said I thought his wife's illness might be deeply rooted in drink, and Alice said I could be right but it wasn't the kind of thing you said to someone's husband. Talking about drink reminded us to have another and then we grudgingly agreed it was time to go.

There were four cars in what Melissa had described as a bit of waste land, an elegantly paved semi-circular court-yard in front of the twelve steps up to the door. Alice commented that they were all this year's models, and none of them cost a penny under three thousand. She parked her battered 1969 Volkswagen in the middle, where it looked like a small child between a group of elegant adults.

Malcolm opened the door, glass in hand. He was so pleased to see us that I wondered how he had lived six months without the experience. Oh come on, I told myself, that's being unfair, if he wasn't nice and wel-coming I would have more complaints. The whole place looked like the film set for a trendy frothy movie on gracious modern living. Melissa rushed out in a tapestry skirt, and I nearly cried with relief that I hadn't worn mine. Melissa is shaped like a pencil rather than a sofa; the contrast would have been mind-blowing.

We were wafted into a sitting-room, and wafted is the word. Nobody said 'come this way' or 'let me introduce you' but somehow there we were with drinks in our hands, sitting between other people, whose names had been said clearly, a Melissa would never mutter. The drinks were good and strong, a Malcolm would never be mean. Low in the background a record-player had some nostalgic songs from the Sixties, the time when we had all been young and impressionable, none of your classical music, nor your songs of the moment. Malcolm and Melissa couldn't be obvious if they tried.

And it was like being back in Andrea's Taverna again.

Everyone felt more witty and relaxed because Malcolm and Melissa were there, sort of in charge of things without appearing to be. They sat and chatted, they didn't fuss, they never tried to drag anyone into the conversation or to force some grounds of common interest. Just because we were all there together under their roof . . . that was enough.

And it seemed to be enough for everyone. A great glow came over the group in the sunset, and the glow deepened when a huge plate of spaghetti was served. It was spaghetti, damn her. But not the kind that you and I would ever make. Melissa seemed to be out of the room only three minutes, and I knew it takes at least eight to cook the pasta. But there it was, excellent, mountainous, with garlic bread, fresh and garlicky, not the kind that breaks your teeth on the outside and then is soggy within. The salad was like an exotic still-life, it had everything in it except lettuce. People moved as if in a dance to the table. There were no cries of praise and screams of disclaimer from the hostess. Why then should I have been so resentful of it all?

Alice seemed to be loving every minute of her evening, she had already fought with Malcolm about the kind of women's literature he sold, but it was a happy fight where she listened to the points he was making and answered them. If she didn't like someone she wouldn't bother to do this. She had been talking to Melissa about some famous woman whom they both knew through work, and they were giggling about the famous woman's shortcomings. Alice was forgetting her role, she was breaking the rules. She had come to understand more about the Melissa and Malcolm people so that we could laugh at them. Instead, she looked in grave danger of getting on with them.

I barely heard what someone called Keith was saying to me about my theatre. I realised with a great shock that I was jealous. Jealous that Alice was having such a nice time, and impressing Melissa and Malcolm just because she was obviously not trying to.

This shock was to physical that a piece of something exotic, avocado maybe, anyway something that shouldn't be in a salad, got stuck in my throat. No amount of clearing and hurrumphing could get rid of it and I stood up in a slight panic.

Alice grasped at once.

'Relax and it will go down,' she called. 'Just force your limbs to relax, and your throat will stop constricting. No, don't bang her, there's no need.'

She spoke with such confidence that I tried to make my hands and knees feel heavy, and miracles it worked.

'That's a good technique,' said Malcolm admiringly, when I had been patted down and, scarlet with rage, assured everyone I was fine.

'It's very unscientific,' said the doctor amongst us, who would have liked the chance to slit my throat and remove the object to cries of admiration.

'It worked,' said Alice simply.

The choking had gone away but not the reason for it. Why did I suddenly feel so possessive about Alice, so hurt when she hadn't liked my dress, so jealous and envious that she was accepted here on her own terms and not as my friend? It was ridiculous. Sometimes I didn't hear from Alice for a couple of weeks; we weren't soul mates over everything, just long-standing friends.

'. . . have you had this flat in the City long?' asked Keith politely.

'Oh that's not my flat, that's Alice's,' I said. Alice was always unusual. She had thought that since the City would be deserted at weekends, the time she wanted a bit of peace, that's where she should live. And of course it worked. Not a dog barked, not a child cried, not a car revved up when Alice was sleeping till noon on a Sunday.

'No, I live in Fulham,' I said, thinking how dull and predictable it sounded.

'Oh I thought . . .' Keith didn't say what he thought but he didn't ask about my flat in Fulham.

Malcolm was saying that Alice and I should think about the yachting holiday. Keith and Rosemary were thinking about it, weren't they? They were, and it would be great fun if we went as a six, then we could sort of take over in case the other people were ghastly.

'It sounds great,' I said dishonestly and politely. 'Yes, you must tell me more about it.'

'Weren't you meant to be going on holiday with old Thing?' said Alice practically.

'That was very vague,' I snapped. 'The weekend in Paris was definite but the holiday . . . nothing was fixed. Anyway weren't you meant to be going to a cottage with your Thing . . . ?'

Everyone looked at me, it was as if I had belched loudly or taken off my blouse unexpectedly. They were waiting for me to finish and in a well-bred way rather hoping that I wouldn't. Their eyes were like shouts of encouragement.

'You said that if his wife was put away for another couple of weeks you might go to their very unsocialistic second home? Didn't you?'

Alice laughed, everyone else looked stunned.

Melissa spooned out huge helpings of a ten thousand calorie ice-cream with no appearance of having noticed a social gaffe.

'Well, when the two of you make up your minds, do tell us,' she said. 'It would be great fun, and we have to let these guys know by the end of the month, apparently. They sound very nice actually. Jeremy and Jacky they're called, he makes jewellery and Jacky is an artist. They've lots of other friends going too, a couple of girls who work with Jeremy and their boy friends, I think. It's just Jeremy and Jacky who are . . . who are organising it all.'

Like a flash I saw it. Melissa thought Alice and I were lesbians. She was being her usual tolerant liberated self over it all. If you like people, what they do in bed is none of your business. HOW could she be so crass as to think that about Alice and myself? My face burned with rage. Slowly like heavy flowers falling off a tree came all the reasons. I was dressed so severely, I had asked could I bring a woman not a man to her party, I had been manless in Greece when she met me the first time, I had just put on this appalling show of spitely spiteful dikey jealousy about Alice's relationship with a man. Oh God. Oh God.

I knew little or nothing about lesbians. Except that they were different. I never was friendly with anyone who was one. I knew they didn't wear bowler hats, but I thought that they did go in for this aggressive sort of picking on one another in public. Oh God.

Alice was talking away about the boat with interest. How much would it cost? Who decided where and when they would stop? Did Jeremy and Jacky sound madly camp and would they drive everyone mad looking for sprigs of tarragon in case the pot au feu was ruined?

Everyone was laughing, and Malcolm was being liberated and tolerant and left-wing.

'Come on Alice, nothing wrong with tarragon, nothing wrong with fussing about food, we all fuss about something. Anyway, they didn't say anything to make us think that they would fuss about food, stop typecasting.'

He said it in a knowing way. I felt with a sick dread that he could have gone on and said, 'After all, I don't typecast you and expect you to wear a hairnet and military jacket.'

I looked at Alice, her thin white face all lit up laughing. Of course I felt strongly about her, she was my friend. She was very important to me, I didn't need to act with Alice. I resented the way the awful man with his alcoholic wife treated her, but was never jealous of him because

Alice didn't really give her mind to him. And as for giving anything else . . . well I suppose they made a lot of love together but so did I and the unsatisfactory journalist. I didn't want Alice in that way. I mean that was madness, we wouldn't even know what to do. We would laugh ourselves silly.

Kiss Alice?

Run and lay my head on Alice's breast?

Have Alice stroke my hair?

That's what people who were in love did. We didn't do that.

Did Alice need me? Yes, of course she did. She often told me that I was the only bit of sanity in her life, that I was safe. I had known her for ten years, hardly anyone else she knew nowadays went back that far.

Malcolm filled my coffee cup.

'Do persuade her to come with us,' he said gently to me. 'She's marvellous really, and I know you'd both enjoy yourselves.'

I looked at him like a wild animal. I saw us fitting into their lives, another splendid liberal concept, slightly racy, perfectly acceptable. 'We went on holiday with that super gay couple, most marvellous company, terribly entertaining.' Which of us would he refer to as the He? Would there be awful things like leaving us alone together, or nodding tolerantly over our little rows?

The evening and not only the evening stretched ahead in horror. Alice had been laying into the wine, would she be able to drive? If not, oh God, would they offer us a double bed in some spare room in this mansion? Would they suggest a taxi home to Fulham since my place was nearer? Would they speculate afterwards why we kept two separate establishments in the first place?

Worse, would I ever be able to laugh with Alice about it or was it too important? I might disgust her, alarm her, turn her against me. I might unleash all kinds of love that she had for me deep down, and how would I handle that?

Of course I love Alice, I just didn't realise it. But what lover, what poor unfortunate lover in the history of the whole damn thing, ever had the tragedy of Coming Out in Malcolm and Melissa's lovely home in Holland Park?

Notting Hill Gate

Everyone knew that Daphne's friend Mike was a shit and to give us our due most of us said so. But she laughed and said we were full of rubbish. She agreed, still laughing, to take the address of the battered wife place, just in case, then we gave her a lovely fur jacket that Mike wouldn't be able to share, and she left us and married him. We never saw her again. But we had to find a new secretary.

Nowadays nobody thinks any more that you meet a lot of interesting people on a newspaper, so you don't have breathless, over-educated, anxious-to-please Oxford graduates rushing around doing all the dirty work willingly as well as all the ordinary work efficiently. Nowadays you have temps earning a fortune, but with no security, and no plans and no interest in what they're doing. My woolly, right-minded, left-thinking views thought that this was unfair on the girls . . . they had no career structure, no dignity, and the agencies made all the money. But then from time to time my wrong-minded right-wing views made me wonder what the country was coming to when you couldn't get a girl who could spell, read, take orders and be grateful for a good job. It was a month of temps before Rita came.

Rita was big and black and tough about luncheon-vouchers, and wanted us to buy her a season ticket on the tube. She walked not like other people walk . . . she rolled along as if she had wheels in her shoes. She had a lot of low-cut purple or green blouses and she wore a series of desperately tight orange or yellow skirts. Marian, who deals with readers' letter, said she thought that Rita's skirts must rip open every evening after the strain of the day, and she would throw them away.

She looked slow and lazy, and as if she was thinking of something else almost all the time, but she was far better than anyone we had had up until then. You didn't have to tell Rita twice that there were ten hopeless people who kept coming into the office with ideas for stories, and that none of the ideas were ever any use. Rita just nodded vaguely, but she knew how to deal with them. She would write down what they said, type it out and put it in a file. The people would go away satisfied that things were underway, and Rita had all the ideas neatly put in the H file, under Hopeless.

After three weeks, we realised two things, firstly that Rita was still there, that she hadn't walked out at 11 a.m. one day like the other temps were in the habit of doing, and secondly that she didn't need to be watched and advised all the time. Martin, the features editor, asked her if she would like a permanent job, and Rita looked as if she had been offered a potato crisp at a bus-stop, and said she might as well. But only if he would pay for a monthly ticket on the underground for her.

Rita lived in Notting Hill but that's all she said. This was a change too, because normally whoever sat in the desk seemed to unburden themselves of a long and complicated life history. There was nothing about Daphne's Mike that we didn't know, his deprived childhood, his poor relationship with Daphne's mother, his disastrous early marriage . . . even Daphne's black eyes were explained away by some incredible misunderstanding, some terrible mistake for which Mike was now heart-broken. All the useless temps had told us tales about their flats being too far out, or their fellows thinking they owned them, or distant boyfriends in Cumbria or on sheep-stations in Australia who wanted them to throw up the job and come home and marry them. Rita never told us anything.

'Do you live in a flat or with your family?' Marian asked her once.

'Why?' asked Rita.

'Oh well I just wondered,' said Marian a bit confused.

'Oh that's all right,' said Rita quite happily, but didn't answer the question.

She used her luncheon-vouchers to buy a huge sandwich and a carton of milk, and she ate it quietly reading a trashy magazine, or at least one that was marginally more trashy than our own features pages. Because she was so uncommunicative, I suppose we were more interested in her. She got the odd phone call, and I found myself listening to her side of the conversation with all the attention of a village postmistress. She would speak in her slow flat tone, smiling only rarely, and seemed to be agreeing with whoever was on the other end about some course of action.

Once she said, 'He's a bad bastard I tell you, he used to be a friend of my husband . . . get out of it if you can.' Full of secret information I told Marian and the others that Rita had a husband. Martin said he had always supposed she did; nothing about Rita would suggest she was a lonely girl who went home to an empty bed, she was too sexy. We had long arguments about his attitudes, like that only sexy women had husbands and that all single women went home to empty beds . . . but it was an old and well worn line of argument. I was more interested that he thought Rita sexy. I thought she was overblown, and fat, and very gaudily dressed, but assumed that West Indians might like brighter colours than we would because of all their bright sunlight back home. Sexy. No.

I was waiting one night in a pub for my sister who's always late and I had forgotten to bring anything to read. So I looked around hopefully in case anyone had abandoned an evening paper. There was one on the floor near a very good-looking blond lad and I went over to pick it up. He put his foot on it immediately.

'That's mine,' he said.

He was very drunk. When someone's very drunk you don't make an issue about nicking their evening paper. I apologised and said I thought it was one that someone had finished with. He looked at me coldly and forgave me. Irritated, I went back to my seat and wished that my sister could for once in her life turn up at something approaching the time arranged. The blond boy now stumbled over to my table and in exaggerated gestures began to present me the paper. He managed to knock my gin and tonic over my skirt and the contents of the ashtray on top of that. I could have killed him I was so annoyed, but before I had time to do anything, a big shadow fell on the whole scene. It was of all people Rita.

She didn't seem embarrassed, surprised, or apologetic. She said, 'You drunken bum,' pulled him away back to a distant seat, ordered me another gin and tonic, brought a cloth, and a lot of paper napkins, all in what looked like slow movements, but they only took a minute or two all the same.

I was so surprised to see her that I forgot about the disgusting mess seeping into my best cream-coloured linen skirt. What was even more amazing, she offered no explanation. I'd have said I was sorry about my friend, or made some nervous joke about it being a small world. Rita just said, 'Hot water, and if that doesn't work, dry cleaning tomorrow, I suppose.' She said it in exactly the same way she'd say, 'We can try the usual photographer for the fashion pictures, and if he's busy get the agency ones I suppose.' With no involvement at all.

Hot water didn't work very well, the whole skirt now looked appalling. When my sister Trudy came in, I was in such a temper that it frightened her.

'You can wear a coat,' she said trying to placate me.

'I haven't got a bloody coat,' I said. 'It's the middle of bloody summer. My coat's at home on the other side of London, isn't it?'

Rita asked with the mild concern of a bystander and not the sense of responsibility of someone whose drunken boyfriend had just ruined an expensive skirt:

'Do you want something to wear? I'll give you something.'

Trudy thought she was an innocent concerned bystander and started to gush that it would be perfectly all right thank you . . .

Rita said, 'I live upstairs, you can come up and choose what you'd like.'

Now this was too good to miss. Firstly I had discovered that Rita had a white boyfriend who looked like a Greek God, that he was as drunk as a maggot, and that Rita lived over a pub. Now I was going to see her place . . . this would be a great dossier for the office.

'Thanks, Rita,' I said ungraciously, and left Trudy open-mouthed behind me.

As we went out the pub door and almost immediately through another, I wondered, Was I mad? Rita's clothes would go around me four times. How could she or I think that any skirt of hers would fit me?

She opened the door of a cheaply furnished, but neat and bright, apartment. Two small and very pigtailed girls sat on a big cushion looking at a big colour telly.

'This is Miss that I work with,' said Rita.

'Hallo Miss,' they chorused, and went back to looking at bionic things on the screen.

We walked into a bedroom also very neat and bright, and Rita opened a cupboard. She took out what looked like two yards of material with a ribbon around the top.

'It's a wrap-around skirt, it fits any size,' she said. I got out of the dirty dishcloth I was wearing, and wrapped it around, and tied the ribbon. It looked fine.

'Thank you very much indeed, Rita,' I said, trying at the same time to take in every detail for the telling tomorrow in the pub, while Rita would be sitting at her desk. There were big prints on the wall, Chinese girls, and horses with flying manes. The bed had a beautiful patchwork quilt, it looked as if it could sleep four people comfortably.

'Are those your little girls?' I asked, a question brought on indirectly by the bed I suppose.

'They're Martie and Anna, they live here,' said Rita.

I realised immediately she hadn't told me whether they were her daughters, her sisters, her nieces, or her friends. And I also realised that I wasn't going to ask any more.

'You can leave the other skirt,' said Rita and then, for the very first time volunteering some information, she added, 'Andrew has quite enough money to pay to have it dry-cleaned, and I'll bring it into the office for you on Friday.'

Oh, so he was called Andrew, the young beautiful boy, and he had plenty of money, oh ho. I was learning something anyway. I didn't dare to ask her whether he was her boyfriend. It wasn't that Rita was superior or distant, but she drew a shutter down like someone slamming a door, and didn't find it rude or impolite. It left you feeling rude and impolite instead.

I thanked her for the skirt. Martie and Anna said 'Goodbye Miss' without removing their eyes from the screen. Somehow *they* seemed so much at ease with the goings-on that it made me very annoyed with myself for feeling diffident because this was a black house and I was a white woman. Who creates these barriers anyway, I argued with myself, and, taking a deep breath, said to Rita on the stairs:

'Why do they wear their hair in those tight little pig-tails? They'd be much prettier if their hair was loose.'

'Maybe,' Rita shrugged, as if I had asked her why she didn't move the coffee percolator to another table in the office to give herself more room. 'Yeah maybe,' she agreed.

'Do you like them with their hair all tied up like that?' I asked courageously.

'Oh it has nothing to do with me,' she said, and we were out on the street and into the pub again.

Trudy had a face like thunder when I came back but she greeted Rita pleasantly enough, and asked her if she would like to join us.

Rita shook her head. 'This drunken baby has to be taken to bed,' she said enigmatically, and she frog-marched the handsome Andrew out the door without a good-bye. I ran to the window to see whether she was taking him up to her own flat, but they had gone too quickly. There was no way of knowing whether they had gone in her door or turned the corner, and I didn't really want to run out into the street to check.

Trudy wasn't very interested in my speculation.

'I don't suppose I should have been so surprised to see her,' I reflected. 'I knew she lived in Notting Hill. This is a very black area around here too, I suppose.'

'Quite a few white people live here as well,' said Trudy acidly, and I forgot that she had just paid what seemed like an enormous sum of money for a very small, very twee house around the corner.

The others were interested at lunch-time the next day. They wanted to know what Andrew looked like.

'Like that actor who plays the part of Henry in that serial,' I said, meaning an actor whose dizzying looks had sent people of all ages into some kind of wistful speculation as to what a future with him might be like.

'You mean Andy Sparks,' said Marian, and with a thud I realised it *was* Andy Sparks. It was just that his face seemed so contorted, and he hadn't worn the boyish eager look nor the boyish eager anorak he always wore in the serial.

'My God, it was definitely him,' I said. By this time the others were losing interest, they thought I had gone into fantasy. Large lumbering black Rita, who read rubbishy

magazines, who never seemed interested in anything,
not even herself . . . she could never have been the petite
amie of Andy Sparks.

'We did a feature on him about three weeks ago,' said
Martin. 'No, it can't have been the same guy, you only
think so because they had the same name.'

'You did say Rita was sexy,' I pointed out, trying to
bolster up my claim that she might be so sexy that
she could have been seen with the superstar of the
moment.

'Not *that* sexy,' said Martin, and they began to talk
about other things.

'Don't tell her I told you,' I said. I felt it was important
that Rita shouldn't think I had been blabbing about her. It
was as if I had gone into her territory by being in that pub,
and I shouldn't be carrying back tales from it.

I looked up the back pages surreptitiously. It *was* the
same guy. He had looked unhappy and drawn compared
to the pictures we used of him, but it was the same
Andrew.

On Friday Rita handed me a parcel and an envelope.
The parcel was my skirt, which she said the cleaners had
made a lovely balls of. They were sorry but with a stain
like that it was owner's risk only, and she had alas agreed
to owner's risk. They were, she said, the best cleaners
around. I looked at the docket and saw she was right. I
also saw the name on the docket. It said 'A. Sparks'. She
took the docket away and gave me the envelope. It was a
gift-token for almost exactly what the skirt had cost, and
it was from the shop where I had in fact bought it. Not a
big chain-store but a boutique.

'I can't take it,' I said.

'You might as well, he can afford it.' She shrugged.

'But if it had been a stranger, not a . . . er . . . well
someone you knew, then I wouldn't have got it replaced,' I stammered.

'That's your good luck, then,' said Rita and went back

to her desk. She hadn't even left me the docket so that I could show the others I was right about the name.

At lunchtime I invited Rita out with me.

'I thought you were having lunch with that woman who wrote the book about flowers,' she said, neither interested nor bored, just stating a fact.

'She rang and cancelled,' I said.

'I didn't put her through to you,' said Rita.

'No, well I rang her on the direct line actually,' I said, furious to have my gesture of taking her out to lunch made into an issue. 'I didn't feel like talking to her.'

'And you feel like talking to me?' asked Rita with one of her rare smiles.

'I'd like to buy you a nice lunch and relax with you and thank you for going to all that trouble over my skirt,' I snapped. It sounded the most ungracious invitation to lunch ever given.

Even if I had been down on my knees with roses I don't think Rita would have reacted differently.

'Thanks very much, but I don't think I will. I don't like long boozy lunches, I have too much work to do in the afternoons here anyway.'

'For Christ's sake it doesn't have to be long and boozy, and though you may not have noticed it, I work here in the afternoons myself,' I said like a spoiled child.

'Okay then,' she said, took up her shoulder bag, and with no coat to cover her fat bouncing bottom and half-exposed large black breasts, she rolled down the corridor with me, into the lift and out into the street.

I chose a fairly posh place, I wasn't going to have her say I went to less expensive places with her than with the journalists or people I interviewed.

She looked at the menu as if it were a list of cuttings we needed her to get from the library. I asked her if she would like pâté and said that they made it very well here.

'Sure,' she said.

I could see it was going to be hard going.

We ordered one glass of wine each, she seemed to accept that too as if it were extra dictation. The few starts I made were doomed. When I asked her whether she found the work interesting in the office, she said it was fine. Better than where she had worked before? Oh yes she supposed so. Where had that been? Hadn't I seen it on her application? She'd been with a lot of firms as a temp. I was driven to talk about the traffic in London, the refuge of all who run out of conversation.

Just then a bird-brained rival of mine on another newspaper came over. Normally I would have walked under buses to avoid her. Today she seemed like a rescue ship sent to a desert island.

She sat down, had a glass of wine, wouldn't eat because of some new diet, wouldn't take her coat off because she was in a hurry, and looked at Rita with interest. I introduced them just name by name without saying where either worked.

'I expect you're being interviewed,' the bird-brain, highly-paid writer said to Rita. Rita shrugged. She wasn't embarrassed, she wasn't waiting for me to give her a lead. She shrugged because she couldn't be bothered to say anything.

At least now I didn't have to do all the talking. Rita and I heard how hard life was, how long it took to get anywhere these days because of the traffic, how hopeless hairdressers were, how they never listened to what you wanted done, how silly the new summer clothes were, how shoes didn't last three months, how selfish show-biz people were making big productions out of being interviewed, instead of being so grateful for all the free publicity. Then her eyes brightened.

'I'm doing Andy Sparks,' she said. 'Yes I know, your lot had him last week, but he's promised to tell me all about his private life. I'm taking him to dinner in a little club I've just joined, so that people won't keep coming over to disturb us. He's meant to be absolutely as dumb as anything, only intelligent when he gets lines to read. Anyway we'll see, we can't go far wrong if he tells a bit about the loves of his life, I only hope it won't be religion or his mother or a collie dog or something.'

Rita sat half-listening as she had been doing all along. I started to say about three different things and got a coughing fit. Finally it dawned on the world's most confident bad writer that she was losing her audience so she excused herself on the grounds that she wanted to go and get herself smartened up at the hairdresser, just in case this beautiful man by some lovely chance wasn't in love with his mother or the man who directed the series.

'Do people usually talk about him like that?' I asked Rita.

'About who?' she said.

'About Andy Sparks,' I said relentlessly.

'Oh, I suppose they do,' she said uncaringly. 'I mean he's quite famous really, isn't he? In everyone's homes every night – as they say.'

'Did you know him before he was a star?' I asked.

'No, I only got to know him a couple of years ago,' she said.

'Are you fond of each other?' I asked, again amazed at my bravery.

'Why?' she said.

'Well, I thought that he seemed very dependent on you the other night.'

'Oh, he was just pissed the other night,' she said.

There was a silence.

'Look,' I said. 'I don't want to talk about him if you don't. I just thought it was interesting, there you are knowing him very well while we just had to do bits and pieces about him to make up that feature. I suppose I wonder why you didn't say anything.'

'And have my picture in the paper you mean? Like Andy Sparks and the girl he can't have . . . that sort of thing.'

'No, of course we wouldn't have done anything like . . .'

'Of course you would,' she said flatly. 'You work on a newspaper.'

'There might have been a bit of pressure yes, but in the end it would have been up to you. Come on, Rita, you work with us, you're part of our team, we wouldn't rat on you that way.'

'Maybe,' she said.

'But why can't he have you . . . ?' I went on. 'You said Andy Sparks and the girl he can't have.'

'Oh well, I'm married to someone else,' she said.

'I see,' I said, though I didn't.

Another silence.

'And does he want to marry you, Andy, I mean?'

'Oh yes, I think Andrew would like to, but I don't think he really knows what he wants.'

'Do you not want to leave your husband?' I asked, remembering suddenly that there had been no sign of a man around that little flat.

'He's inside, served four years of fifteen, he'll probably have to do two more anyway.'   .

'Oh God, I'm sorry I asked.'

'No you're not, if you hadn't asked you wouldn't know. You want to know, it's partly you yourself, it's partly your job. You all like to know things.'

It was the longest speech I'd heard her make. I didn't know what to say.

She went on.

'Listen, I'm not coming back to the office. I don't want to go back now, because everyone already knows I know him. Oh yes they do, you told them, but you told them not to mention it, I'm not a fool. I can't bear offices where everyone knows everything about everyone else, that's why I stayed so long with you lot . . . you didn't talk too much about your own lives, and you didn't pry into mine. I thought you'd like me being fairly buttoned up

. . . but no, it's all of you who've been doing the prying . . .'

'I understand what you mean, Rita, honestly I do. The girls who did your job before were always so boring about their boyfriends and their life's history . . . but seriously I understand if . . .'

She looked at me.

'You understand nothing if I may say so. You don't understand the first little thing. And because it isn't clear to you at once, you turn it all into a little mystery and have to solve it. You don't understand why Andrew fancies me, you don't understand why I wait for a husband to come out of prison, you don't understand whether those kids Martie and Anna are mine or not.'

'It's none of my business,' I said, distressed and unable to cope with the articulate and very, very angry Rita. 'I can't say anything right now.'

Rita calmed down. Her eyes didn't flash, but they were not back to the dead dull look they normally held.

'Well, I could tell you a few things which would give you information, but you still wouldn't *understand*. Martie and Anna aren't my girls, they're Nat's. Nat is my husband. Nat is in gaol because he beat Myrtle to death. Myrtle was my best friend. Myrtle always loved Nat. Nat never loved Myrtle but he had two children by her. Even after he married me, he would see Myrtle. I knew, I didn't mind, that's the way Nat was. I knew it at the time, I know it now. Myrtle found this other fella, he wanted to marry her, take the kids and all he would. Myrtle told Nat, Nat said no, he didn't want another man raising his kids. Myrtle asked me what she should do. I said I thought she should marry the other fella, but then my advice was prejudiced.

'Myrtle said I was right, and she told Nat. They had a great row. Nat he lost his temper and he beat Myrtle and he beat her, and she died. I telephoned the police and they came, and they took him, and he got fifteen years and I look after Anna and Martie.'

She paused and took a drink of her wine, and though I didn't understand I could approach an understanding of how strong she must have been, must still be.

'And you won't understand either why Andrew wants me to go away with him. He just needs me. I don't know whether he loves me or not, or whether he knows what love is, but he needs me, because I . . . well I'm what he needs. And he doesn't understand either, he can't understand that Nat don't mind me seeing him. He knows that Nat has a lot of friends who tell him or his friends what's going on. But Nat doesn't mind me going about with a white man, a white actor from the television. Nat thinks that's just company for me. Now can you understand any of that at all?'

At the end of the week when the bird-brain's story appeared it was pretty tame stuff. She did have an angle that Andy Sparks had some mystery woman in his life, someone he leaned on, someone he needed, but was not prepared to discuss.

Rita came around that day to collect some things she'd left in the drawer of her desk, and to pick up her salary. She came at lunch-time when there was nobody there, except her replacement, who was full of chat and said that she had told Rita all about her fiancé being mean with money. She asked Rita if she thought that was a bad omen. Rita had said that she couldn't care less.

'Odd sort of woman, I thought,' said the replacement. 'Very untidy, sort of trampishly dressed really. Funny that she wasn't more pleasant. Black people are usually happy-looking, I always think.'

Queensway

Pat wished that she didn't have such a lively imagination when she was reading the advertisements. When she saw something like 'Third girl wanted for quiet flat. Own room, with central heating' she had dark fears that it might be a witches' coven looking for new recruits. Why mention that the flat was quiet? Could central heating be some code for bonfires? But she couldn't afford a flat of her own, and she didn't know anyone who wanted to share, so it was either this or stay for ever in the small hotel which was eating into her savings.

She dreaded going for the interview, which was why she kept putting off answering any of the offers. What would they ask her? Would they give her a test to see whether she was an interesting conversationalist? Might they want to know all about her family background? Did they ask things like her attitude towards promiscuity, or spiritualism, or the monarchy? Or would it be a very factual grilling, like could she prove that she wouldn't leave a ring around the bath or use the phone without paying for her calls?

There were about twenty women working in the bank, why did none of them want to share, she complained to herself. At least she knew something about them, that they were normal during the daytime anyway. But no, they were all well-established in London, married to men who wouldn't do the shopping, or living with blokes who wouldn't wash their own socks, or sharing flats with girls who wouldn't clean up the kitchen after them. There was no place in any of their lives for Pat.

Three months was all she was going to allow herself in the hotel, three months to get over the break-up of her home, to calm herself down about Auntie Delia being taken away to hospital and not recognising anyone ever again. It was better, the doctors said, that Pat should go right away, because Auntie Delia really didn't know who she was any more, and would never know. She wasn't unhappy, she was just, well there were many technical terms for it, but she was in a world of her own.

If you have worked in a bank in Leicester, you can usually get a job working in a bank in London. But if you've lived with Auntie Delia, funny, eccentric, fanciful, generous, undemanding, for years and years, it's not so easy to find a new home.

'What should I ask them?' she begged the small, tough Terry who knew everything, and who had no fears about anything in this life. 'I'll feel so stupid not knowing the kind of questions that they'll expect *me* to ask.'

Terry thought it was so simple that it hardly needed to be stated.

'Money, housework and privacy, are the only things girls fight about in flats,' she said knowledgeably.

'Find out exactly what your rent covers, make sure there aren't any hidden rates to be paid later, ask how they work the food – does everyone have their own shelf in the fridge, or do they take it in turns buying basics? If you are all going to have a week each in charge of the food, get a list of what people buy and how much they spend. Stupid to have you buying gorgeous fresh-ground coffee or expensive tea, when they only get instant and tea bags.'

'And what should I ask about the housework?' Pat wondered.

'Do they have a Hoover, if so who uses it and when? It would be awful if they were all manic house cleaners, washing down paintwork every day. And examine the place carefully, they might be so careless that the place is full of mice and rats.'

Privacy meant that Pat was to inquire what arrangements they had about the sitting-room: did people book it if they were going to ask anyone in, or did everyone eat, play, watch telly together, or did people entertain in their own bedrooms?

So, armed with all this intelligence, she dialled the 'Third Girl wanted, lovely flat, near park, own room, friendly atmosphere' advertisement. Auntie Delia would have snorted at the ad, and said that they sounded like a bunch of dikes to her. Pat still couldn't believe that Auntie Delia didn't snort and say outrageous things any more.

The girl who answered the phone sounded a little breathless.

'I can't really talk now, the boss is like a devil today, he says I shouldn't have given this number. Can I have your number and I'll phone you back later when he leaves the office? It's a super flat, we wouldn't want to leave it in a million years, it's just that Nadia went off to Washington and we can't afford it just for two.'

Pat didn't like the sound of it. It seemed a bit fast and trendy. She didn't like people who said 'super' in that upward inflection, she didn't like the thought of people suddenly dashing off to Washington, it was too racy. And she thought the name Nadia was affected. Still, she might use them as a rehearsal. There was no law saying you had to take the first flat you saw.

The breathless girl rang back ten minutes later. 'He's gone out for an hour,' she confided. 'So I'm going to make use of it, ringing all the people back. I thought I'd start with you because you work in a bank, you might get us all an overdraft.'

Pat took this little pleasantry poorly, but still you had to practise flat-getting somewhere, and she arranged to call at eight o'clock. She made a list of questions, and she promised herself that she would take everything in, so that she would go better equipped to the next and more serious interview.

It was an old building, and there were a lot of stairs but no lift. Perhaps they all became permanently breathless from climbing those stairs. Feeling foolish to be feeling nervous, Pat rang the bell. It had a strange echoing chime, not a buzz. It would have, thought Pat. Nadias, and Washingtons, and Supers, naturally they'd have to have a bell that pealed, rather than one which buzzed.

Joy wasn't at all breathless now that she was home. She wore a long housecoat, and she smelled of some very, very expensive perfume. She was welcoming, she remembered Pat's name, she apologised for the stairs but said that you got used to them after a month or so. There were eighty-three steps, counting the flat bits between floors, and they did encourage you not to be forgetful about things like keys.

Pat stared around the hall. It was literally covered in pictures and ornaments, and there were rugs on the walls as well. At one end there were a couple of flower baskets hanging and at the other a carved hall-stand full of dried flowers.

'It's far too nice to sit inside,' said Joy, and for a wild moment Pat thought that they would have to go down all the stairs again before she had even seen the flat.

'Come into Marigold's room, and we'll have a drink on the balcony.'

Marigold! thought Pat. Yes, it would have to be Marigold.

A big room, like one of those film-sets for an Anna Neagle movie, with little writing-desks, and a piano with photographs on top. There were flowers here too, and looped lacey curtains leading out to a balcony. There in a wheelchair sat Marigold. The most beautiful woman that Pat had ever seen. She had eyes so blue that they didn't really seem to be part of a human body. She could have played any number of parts as a ravishing visitor from Mars. She had so much curly hair, long, shiny and curly, that it looked like a wig for a heroine, but you knew it wasn't a wig. She smiled at Pat, as if all her life she had been waiting to meet her.

'I wish Joy would tell people I live in a wheelchair,' she said, waving at Pat to get her to sit down. She poured some white wine into a beautiful cut crystal glass and handed it to her. 'I honestly think it's so unfair to let people climb all those stairs and then face them with what they think will be a nursing job instead of a home.'

'Well I don't, I never, you mustn't . . .' stammered Pat.

'Rubbish,' said Joy casually. 'If I said you were in a wheelchair nobody would ever come at all. Anyone who has come, wants to move in, so I'm right and you're wrong.'

'Have you had many applicants?' asked Pat.

'Five, no six including the lady with the cats,' said Joy.

Pat's list had gone out of her head, and she had no intention of taking it from her handbag. They sat and talked about flowers, and how wonderful that in a city the size of London people still had a respect for their parks, and rarely stole plants or cut blooms for themselves from the common display. They talked on about the patchwork quilt that Marigold had made, how difficult it was to spot woodworm in some furniture, and how a dishonest dealer could treat it with something temporary and then it all came out only when you had the thing bought and installed. They had more wine, and said how nice it was to have an oasis like a balcony in a city of ten million or whatever it was, and wondered how did people live who didn't have a view over a park.

'We must have a little supper,' Marigold said. 'Pat must be starving.'

No protests were heeded, a quick move of her wrist, and the wheelchair was moving through the pots and shrubs of the balcony, the flowers and little writing bureaux of the bedroom, the bric-à-brac of the hall, and they were in a big pine kitchen. Barely had Joy laid the table for three before Marigold had made and cooked a cheese soufflé, a salad had been already prepared, and there was garlic bread, baking slowly in the oven. Pat felt guilty but hungry, and strangely happy. It was the first evening meal anywhere that seemed like home since they had taken Auntie Delia away.

She felt it would be crass to ask how much did people pay and who bought the groceries, and what kind of cleaning would the third girl be expected to do. Neither Marigold nor Joy seemed to think such things should be discussed, so they talked about plays they had seen, or in Marigold's case books she had read, and it was as if they were just three friends having a nice dinner at home instead of people trying to organise a business deal.

At eleven o'clock Pat realised by the deep chiming of a clock that she had been there three hours. She would have to make a move. Never had she felt socially so ill at ease. She wondered what she should say to bring the visit to an end and the subject of why she was there at all into the open. She knew quite a lot about them. Marigold had polio and never left the flat. Joy worked in a solicitor's office as a clerk, but next year was going to go into apprenticeship there and become a solicitor too. Marigold seemed to have some money of her own, and did the housework and the cooking. They had met some years ago when Marigold had put an ad in the paper. Marigold had found the flat.

Nadia was mentioned, a little. There were references to Nadia's room and Nadia's clock, which was the big one that chimed, and some chat about the time they had made the curry for Nadia's dinner-party and everyone had gone on fire from it.

Resolutely Pat stood up and said that her little hotel closed at midnight and she had better get back, as they didn't have a night-porter.

'Well, when shall we expect you?' asked Marigold.

Pat, who hadn't even been shown her room, hadn't been informed about how much rent, what kind of lifestyle was to be expected, was stunned.

'What about the five other people, and the lady with the cats?' she asked desperately.

'Oh no,' said Marigold.

'No indeed,' said Joy.

'Well, can I think about it?' Pat asked, trying to buy time. 'I don't know whether I could afford to live here, and you mightn't like my friends, and we haven't really sorted anything out.'

Marigold looked like an old trusted friend who has suddenly and unexpectedly been rebuffed.

'Of course you must decide for yourself, and perhaps you have somewhere else in mind. We are terrible, Joy, not to give Pat details of rent and things. We're simply hopeless.'

'The rent is £20, and we usually spend about £10 a week each on food, and flowers and wine,' said Joy.

That was expensive, but not for what you got. You got a magnificent home, you got lovely meals, you got two very bright nice women to live with.

Pat heard her own voice saying, 'Fine. Yes, if you think I'd fit in here with you, that's fine. Can I come at the weekend?'

That night she wondered what she had done. Next morning she wondered whether she had been insane.

'I don't know,' said tough little Terry. 'If the food's as good as all that, if the one in the wheelchair does all the work, if the place is like something out of *Home and Garden*, I think you're laughing. If you don't like it you can always move out.'

'I didn't even look at my bedroom.' said Pat with a wail.

'They'll hardly give you a coal-hole,' said Terry practically.

Joy rang her breathlessly that day.

'It's super that you're coming. Marigold's so pleased. She asked me to tell you that there's plenty of room in your bed-sitting-room for anything you want to bring, so don't worry about space. Any pictures or furniture you like.'

Pat wondered why Marigold didn't ring herself. She was at home, she didn't have to avoid a spying boss. Pat also wondered whether this was a polite way of telling her that there were four walls and nothing else in her room.

On Saturday she arrived with two students who ran a flat-moving service. They carried up her little tables, her rocking-chair, and her suitcases. They had cluttered up her hotel bedroom ridiculously, and she wondered whether there would be any more room for them where she was going. As they all puffed up the eighty-three steps, Pat felt very foolish indeed.

Joy let them in, with little cries of excitement. They paraded through the bedecked hall to a huge sunny room, which had recesses for cupboards, a big bed and a washbasin. Compared to the rest of the flat it looked like an empty warehouse.

Joy fussed along behind them. 'Marigold said we should empty it so that you wouldn't feel restricted. But there's lots of furniture available. There are curtains and shelves for these,' she waved at the recesses. 'Marigold thought you might want your own things.'

Pat paid the students, and sat down in the warehouse. Even her rocking-chair looked lost. When she unpacked it wouldn't be much better. Auntie Delia's things would look lovely here. All those monstrous vases, even that beaded curtain. Maybe she should send for them. They were all in the little house in Leicester. They would be hers when Auntie Delia died. Strictly speaking they were hers already, since she had rented the house out just to get money to pay for her poor Aunt in the nursing-home.

The rent covered the fees. The tenants didn't like all the overcrowding from the furniture but Pat had insisted the house should remain untouched since Auntie Delia *could* get better one day and *might* come home. She felt slightly disloyal thinking about taking Auntie Delia's treasures, but surely she couldn't live in a barn like this, while Auntie Delia lived in a world of her own, and the tenants lived in a house that they thought vastly over-stuffed with things they didn't like.

It was morning coffee time, so she gathered from the smell of fresh coffee coming from the kitchen. She was right, they assembled on the balcony, and had coffee from lovely china cups.

'I'll be sending to Leicester for my real furniture this week,' she said.

'We'll be dying to see it,' said Marigold, her china-blue eyes lighting up with excitement.

'And I must give you some money and everything,' blurted out Pat. 'I'm not much good at this you know, not having shared a flat before.'

'Oh, Joy will look after that,' said Marigold. 'She's so good with money, working in that office, where there's a lot of accountancy. She should have been a solicitor from the start you know, it's so silly to have waited until she's twenty-seven before starting her indentures.'

'I'd never have done it at all if it weren't for you,' said Joy gratefully. 'I'd still be working on there and taking my money each week.'

'It would have been pointless,' said Marigold. Her blue eyes looked out over the park, where people who weren't in wheelchairs jumped and played and ran about.

Pat sighed happily. It was so peaceful here and she had the whole week-end before facing the bank again. Nobody ever told you how easy it was to find a flat.

'Would you like me to do any shopping or anything?' she asked helpfully.

'Joy does that on Friday nights, we're very well

organised', smiled Marigold. 'We have a small deep freeze as well. It helps a great deal.'

While the rest of London sweated and fussed and shopped and dragged themselves through traffic jams or in crowded trains to the seaside, Joy and Marigold and Pat sat peacefully reading, listening to music, or chatting. By Monday Pat felt she had been on a rest-cure. She and Joy had done a lot of the washing-up, and preparing of things, rougher jobs like peeling potatoes and cutting up meat, and taking out rubbish.

Joy was friendly and eager to do everything, Marigold was gentle, serene and calm. Pat began to think that she couldn't have found two more perfect flat-mates.

On Sunday night she telephoned the people in Leicester and asked them to arrange to have seventeen pieces of furniture, some huge, some tiny, collected and delivered to London.

Nobody had telephoned the flat, nobody had gone out. Pat wondered what happened if you invited a friend in for supper. Would they all eat as a foursome? She saw no other way.

She gave Joy £80, and asked what to do about the tenner for food.

'I'll spend £20 this week, and you spend it next week,' said Joy cheerfully.

Pat wondered where Marigold's tenner came into it but said nothing. Why upset things? Things are not always so peaceful in life, it's silly to question just for the sake of questioning.

On Tuesday she rang Joy at work to say that she was going to the theatre so would not be home for dinner.

'Oh.' Joy sounded upset.

'But that's all right, isn't it?' asked Pat. 'Marigold won't start to cook until we get home anyway, so it's not a question of letting her know in advance. I'd ring her at home but I . . . well, I just thought I'd ring you.'

'Oh yes, it's better to ring me,' said Joy. 'No, no

problems. I'll pop home at lunch-time and tell her, it's not far. Don't worry.'

It all seemed very odd to Pat, but she put it out of her mind.

On Thursday her furniture arrived. Marigold was delighted with it. She whirled around in the wheelchair, stroking this and patting that.

'Lovely inlay,' she said.

'We must strip this down,' she said.

'What a magnificent curtain. Wouldn't it look lovely on the balcony?' she said.

So of course Pat, flattered and pleased, hung Auntie Delia's bead curtain up on the balcony, where indeed it looked lovely.

That night she asked if they ever heard from Nadia how she was enjoying Washington.

'No, we've not heard,' said Marigold.

'Nadia doesn't write many letters,' said Joy.

'What did she do, I mean what job had she?' asked Pat. Her slight jealousy of Nadia had disappeared, now she had only curiosity.

'She worked in an antique shop,' said Joy.

'Managed an antique shop,' said Marigold.

'Well, she worked there first,' laughed Joy. but Marigold told her she knew much more than anyone in it, and gave her confidence, so she ended up managing it for Mr Solomons.'

'She knew twice as much as Mr Solomons from the start,' said Marigold.

'Anyway Mr Solomons fancied her enormously, so that it didn't hurt,' said Joy with a giggle.

'Did she fancy him?' asked Pat with interest.

'Not until Marigold told her to have some intelligence and fancy him,' giggled Joy again.

'Oh,' said Pat.

Marigold seemed to think some clarification was called for.

'It always strikes me as silly to go to bed with half-drunk people, who forget it, or who feel embarrassed by it, or who do it so often that it's meaningless, and then refuse to go to bed with someone like Mr Solomons who would appreciate it, would remember it with affection, and would advance Nadia because of it. It just seems a foolish sort of thing to have a principle about.'

Put that way, thought Pat, it was unanswerable.

'But she left him all the same?' she probed.

'Oh no, she didn't leave Mr Solomons,' said Joy laughing. 'Mr Solomons left her. He had a heart attack and went to live in the country, so she managed his place for him, and took a share in the profits.'

'And had a very nice cut and first refusal on everything they stocked,' said Marigold, stroking the little mahogany cabinet beside her, almost sensuously.

'So why Washington?' asked Pat.

'She's running a little antique shop in Georgetown now,' said Marigold distantly. 'Very different kind of stuff, I'm sure.'

'She got sort of unsettled, and took the first job she heard of,' said Joy artlessly.

'Some silly business with a chap who used to restore paintings, very silly really,' said Marigold. And the conversation about Nadia stopped there. It was as clear a break as if 'End of Episode One' had been written in fire in the air.

Out of sheer curiosity, Pat stopped in Solomon's antique shop. There was no elderly owner type about, so she supposed that the good proprietor's heart could not yet have recovered from Nadia's exertions.

She asked how much they would give her for Aunt Delia's inlaid cabinet if she were to sell it. She described it very carefully.

'About five hundred pounds,' said the young man. 'Depends on what condition it's in, of course, but not less I'd say.'

That was odd. Marigold had said it was pretty but without value. Marigold said she should take great care of it because it might be worth fifty pounds. Imagine Marigold now knowing how much it was worth. A flaw in the lovely, graceful, all-knowing Marigold. A flaw no less.

'Is Nadia still here?' she asked on impulse.

'No, why, you a friend of hers?' the man asked.

'No,' said Pat. 'I just know people who know her.'

'Oh, she left here a few weeks ago. Kevin would know where she is.' He pointed out a young and very attractive, bearded, bending figure, who was examining the frame of a picture.

'It doesn't matter really,' said Pat hastily, thinking this might be the silly young man of Marigold's description.

'Hey, Kevin, this lady's a friend of Nad's.'

Kevin stood up. He was very handsome in a definitely shabby, ungroomed way. Pat could see that his nails, his unwashed hair wouldn't have fitted into the elegant furniture back in the flat.

'I was just looking around, and I remembered that this is where the girl who lived in the flat where I've just moved in used to work . . .' said Pat apologetically.

'Have you moved in there?' asked Kevin flatly.

'Yes, a few days ago.'

'Have you moved all your stuff in?' he asked.

'Well yes, yes I have,' Pat's voice trailed away. She felt unreasonably frightened.

'Did she tell you it's worth buttons, peanuts?'

'No,' said Pat defensively. 'Marigold said it's very nice furniture and I must take care of it. Why, anyway?'

'Will you tell her you've been in here?' he asked very unemotionally.

'I might, I might not. Why do you ask?' said Pat. She was definitely frightened now, which was ridiculous. She also knew that she would never admit to Marigold that she had nosed around Nadia's old place of employment and nosed out Nadia's silly young man.

'I don't think you will,' he said. 'Nadia never told her anything towards the end, she was absolutely terrified of her. So was I. It's her eyes, they're not human.'

'They're just too blue,' said Pat. 'She can't help that.'

'No, but she can help a lot of things. Do you know that she hasn't polio at all?'

'I don't believe you,' said Pat, feeling her legs getting weak.

'No, she hasn't, that's why none of them ring her at home. She goes out, you know, when everyone's at work.'

'Don't be ridiculous.'

'No, I saw her several times running down the stairs, and taking a taxi. I took a photograph of her once to prove it to Nadia, but she said it was trick photography.'

'But she's paralysed,' said Pat.

'So she says. It's nice being paralysed if you get everyone else to do all the work, pay all the bills, and live in fear of you.'

'Don't you think that someone would have to be mad to pretend to have polio, just to get out of carrying out the rubbish?'

'Marigold is mad, very mad,' he said.

Pat sat down on a reproduction sofa.

'Didn't you guess?' he asked.

'I don't believe it,' said Pat.

'Nadia doesn't to this day,' said Kevin.

'Is that why she went to Washington?' asked Pat.

'She's not in Washington, she's back in my flat. In Clapham,' he said. 'She told them she was going to the States, that was the only reason that Marigold let her go.'

'You mean she has no job, and just lives in your flat because she's afraid of Marigold?' Pat said. 'I don't believe a word of it.'

'Go down there and see,' he said. 'She'll be sitting

there complaining about the noise, and saying how little light there is, and how cramped the place seems to be. She doesn't even bother to get dressed properly, she hangs about all day complaining. That's what Marigold has done to her.'

'Does she want to be back in the flat?'

'She wants it so much I think she's becoming as mad as Marigold. "It was so peaceful. We were so gracious. We had such lovely music, not the neighbours' trannies." That's all she says, day in, day out.'

'Why did she leave it if she liked it so much?' asked Pat, almost afraid to hear the answer. Everything Nadia said about the flat was so true, there might be some truth in Kevin's whole terrible tale.

'She left it because I told her that she had given all her lovely furniture to this woman, that she had turned herself into a prostitute for her, that she had cut off her whole life for her, that she was working to support her. I told her to examine all these statements and if she thought they were true to move out. So she did and they were and she moved. But not without tissues of lies of course about Washington, which that nice silly Joy believes but Marigold saw through at once. Marigold didn't mind anyway, she had loads of stuff, hundreds of pounds worth, from Nad over the years, and she'll always get other slaves.'

'But Joy's normal.'

'She used to be, when she had a bit of a life of her own, and boyfriends, and big plates of spaghetti with the girls from work. She should have been married years ago and have three nice fat children by now, instead of trying to become a solicitor and earn more money for that Marigold.'

'You're very bitter about her.'

'I'm bleeding obsessed with her, that's what I am. She's ruined Nadia totally, she's turned Joy into a zombie, there was another one there too, I can't remember

her name, but she had to go out to bloody Africa as a
missionary or something to get over it all. Having left
some very nice lamps and some very good old cut glass
thank you.'

Pat's heart missed something of its regular movement.
She remembered admiring the lamps, and Marigold had
said they were from a dear friend who went to Africa and
didn't need them.

It was the end of her lunch-hour. She walked out
without saying anything. She knew where to find him if
she needed to know any more. He would take her home
to meet Nadia if she wanted confirmation of it all. She
was a free, grown-up woman, nobody could keep her
there against her will.

On the way back to the bank she passed an expensive
flower shop. It had unusual little potted plants. One of
them was very, very blue. It had a long name but Marigold would know it anyway. It would look lovely on the
balcony table. It would be so peaceful there this evening
after work. It was like a dream world really. It would be
such a misery trying to get everything out of the flat now
that she had just got it in. Anyway, why should she?
Kevin was just a silly young man. Jealous obviously
because Nadia had been so happy in the flat. Anyone
would be happy in that flat, it was so very, very peaceful,
you didn't need anyone else or anything else in the
world.

Lancaster Gate

It was funny the way things turned out. If she hadn't made that huge scene, and cried, and nearly choked herself crying, and admitted all kinds of weaknesses, she wouldn't be here now. She would be back in the flat, cleaning the cooker, polishing the furniture, ironing his shirts, so that he would think it was wonderful to have all these home comforts and value her more.

She would have gone to the cinema maybe, but maybe not. Films were so full of other people's relationships, and she kept identifying, and saying 'If I behaved more like her, would he value me more?', or wondering why some screen woman could be so calm when everything was collapsing around her. Lisa could never be calm. She could pretend at calmness very successfully, but deep down it was churn, churn, churn. Sometimes she was surprised that he couldn't hear her heart sort of hitting against her bones, she could hear it thudding as well as feel it from inside, she could actually hear the wuff wuff sound it made. But fortunately he never managed to hear it, and she could always fool him into thinking she was relaxed and at ease. Sometimes the nights that had started with her heart thudding very seriously had turned out to be their best nights, because she acted out the calm role so well. Lisa had often thought how extraordinarily easy it was to fool someone you loved and who loved you.

Or who sort of loved you. But no, no, don't start that, don't start analysing, worrying, your heart will begin the booming thing again, and you've got nothing to boom about. Here in London, staying in a big posh hotel, signing the room-service dockets with his name, putting the Mrs bit in casually as if you had been doing it for years and it was now second nature. She wondered how long it took married people to forget their single names. Brides were always giggling about it. She supposed it would take about three weeks, about the same time as it took you to remember each January that the year had changed and that you must write a different date.

And it was what they called a glorious day on the weather forecast, very flowery indeed for the Met Office, but that was the word the man had used, and she had run to the window to see if he was right, and he was. There were railings across the road and people were putting up pictures, and postcards, and souvenirs, to sell to the passing tourists. And they seemed to be shouting to each other and laughing. They must know each other from meeting every week-end here, and they didn't sound like rivals or enemies. They didn't look as if they'd mind if a passing tourist bought from one rather than another. They were unpacking little canvas stools as well, and some of them had flasks. They were old and young. Lisa thought it was a funny kind of life. She wouldn't be able for it, her old anxiety would show. People wouldn't buy from her because she would have an anxious face wanting them to buy, and the more they passed her by because of her anxious face the more anxious it would become. But then that was the same kind of vicious circle that everyone kept getting caught in. It was like the whole problem with Him. If she felt unsure of him and thought that he was losing interest in her, she became strained and worried and not the carefree girl he had once fancied, and so he *did* start to lose interest, and because she could see this happening she became more strained and worried, and he lost more interest.

But stop, stop. Not today, today is glorious. It has been defined as such by the weatherman on the radio, than whom there must be surely no saner, soberer judge. And today you don't need to act at being relaxed, you are. He's there in the bathroom shaving, he's happy, he's glad you're here. You've made love a half an hour ago, he liked it, he's humming to himself. You make him happy or happier than he'd be if you weren't here. You're fine really. Remember that. He didn't have to take you with him to London for the conference, now did he? He couldn't have been planning something else, something awful like meeting someone else, if he took you so readily.

Lisa smiled happily, thinking of how readily he had agreed to take her with him. She hadn't meant to ask at all. She had packed his case yesterday morning . . . was it only yesterday? Friday, it must have been. She had been polishing his shoes.

'You don't need to do that,' he had said, a bit embarrassed.

'I was doing my own,' she had lied.

'They're suede, funny face,' he had said, laughing.

What was it? It couldn't have been funny face, he called her that a lot, it was meaningless as an endearment, it wasn't even special. He called his daughter funny face on the phone . . . often. He called his secretary funny face. Once she had been holding for him on the phone, and she could hear his voice clearly as he crossed the office. 'Get me a cup of coffee, funny face,' he had said. 'I've got a bugger of a day.' It was probably because he knew she wore suede shoes. Idiotic, it couldn't have been that. Put badly it was really madness. What was it then? Why did two tears fall down onto the shining leather shoes in her hand? She could have hit herself with rage. It wasn't as if she knew it was going to happen. You always sort of know when you're going to cry but not this time. It was automatic, as if someone had tinkered about with her tear-ducts when she wasn't looking. And once started there was no stopping. She dropped the shoes and said a hundred times that she was sorry, she didn't know what was wrong. She tried to laugh through this appalling shower of tears, and that made her worse. She would sort of catch her breath and cough, and then it would get worse, and there were actual whoops coming out of her at one stage.

He was astounded. He thought he was to blame.

'What did I say, what have I done?' he had said over and over. 'You knew I was going away today, you *knew*,' he had repeated. He felt cornered, he felt she was blaming him. She couldn't even stop this terrible heaving to assure him that of course she knew, and that today wasn't any worse than any other day. He looked very wounded.

'The conference starts on Monday. I want to get into top form for it, I don't want to arrive exhausted. I want to be there and rested, and to have made my own tour of the hotel. I don't want to be thought of as your typical Northern hick who arrives all impressed by everything. It's important, Lisa. You said you understood.'

The use of her name maybe. She stopped for a moment. She actually had breath to speak. But instead of saying what she meant to, something like *of course* she understood, she heard her own voice betraying her, ratting on her. She actually said, '*Why* do you have to go away? We could have had this week-end together, just the two of us. Nobody would have known we were here, it would have been lovely.'

When the words were said, she decided that she had now lost everything, that the whole hard uphill race had been lost. She didn't know to whom she had lost, but she had lost. He couldn't stand people who begged, people who made demands. He had told her that was why he had left his wife, why the great love of his life (which had not been his marriage) had ended, because these women made demands. They wanted more of him than he could give, they saw something wonderful in a forced intimacy, they thought that the phrase 'just the two of us' was safe and reassuring. He thought it was threatening and claustrophobic.

And because Lisa had thought that she had lost him, she abandoned herself to the tide. It was a great luxury, like getting into a warm bath when you're tired and cold. She had said all the unsayable things, the whines, the moans, the loneliness, how hard it had all been on her. How she had given him, if not the best years, then all the fun hours of her life, and for what? Nobody could know they lived together. Nobody could see them out together. It was clandestine and anxious-making, and leading nowhere, and she, Lisa, who was free, was abandoning every other man, every other chance of happiness, and for what? For someone who didn't give two damns about her. Well all right, it was all right. She kept repeating the words 'all right' as if they were a magic charm. She had no idea what she meant by them, but they were safer and less final than saying something even more hackneyed like 'it's all over'.

He hadn't seemed relieved that it was all over or all right or whatever she meant; he hadn't seemed distressed, either. He looked interested, like he would have been interested in a farmer telling him about spraying crops, or a newsvendor explaining what margin of profit there was in selling papers. He sounded as if he might like to hear more.

'Come with me then,' he said.

He had never taken her anywhere before, it was too dangerous. He had always said that in his position he couldn't afford anyone to point at him about anything. Times were too tricky, things were too rough. He couldn't mean it now, he was just saying it to placate her, he knew she'd refuse for his sake. It was another ploy, another bluff. He had once explained to her why he won so much at poker. She had realised even then that the same rules that he used at the card-table he used everywhere.

As suddenly as he had asked her she accepted. 'Fine,' she said. 'I will. Where shall I meet you?' No back-tracking, no well-perhaps-not-this-time. He was on as well, that was one of the rules of the game. If you offer, you must follow through.

'Nowhere near the office, too likely to be seen. Take a bus to the big petrol station on the London road. I'll meet you there at . . . ten past four.'

'Right,' she said. He kissed her and said it would be great, he'd like showing her London.

'You hardly know it any better than I do,' she said.

No tears, no joy, no excitement, no gratitude. He looked at her approvingly. It was almost as if he thought she had gained a few housepoints. She had faked grief, she had got him to take her to London. Well done Lisa. He said jauntily that he wouldn't wait a minute after a quarter past four, and she said equally lightly that that was fine, and he left, suitcase in his hand, and she heard the car starting as he went off to work and to talk to the office funny face.

Lisa had felt light-headed, like the time she once went out in a speedboat, and nothing had been real. She sat down to steady herself. She must make a list. Obviously she wouldn't go to work. So what excuse this time? She didn't know how long she'd stay with him in London. The conference lasted four days, Monday to Thursday. She'd have to invent something that would take a week. Quick, she'd have to telephone in the next few minutes and alert the Head's secretary, before Assembly began and someone started looking for her. A death. Exactly, a death in London. Better than flu, a woman's disease, or a heavy cold. She dialled, she spoke, she waved her hands around in the air as she told the weary Miss Weston, the Head's tame dog, that an aunt, her nearest relative, was dying. She even got a bit sad about it as she filled in the form and details of this mythical aunt. No, there simply was nobody else, nobody at all, she had to go. She'd ring from London next week to tell them what was happening. She knew how terrible it would be trying to find a substitute at this late stage, but she had heard only just now, this minute, and she was going to London this afternoon. 'At ten past four,' she said meaninglessly but to make it more real in her own mind. Miss Weston said she would tell the Head, and implied that the job of telling the Head was far worse than saying good-bye to a favourite aunt. Miss Weston was never very good with small chat anyway.

Now, on with the list. Lisa had to get a smart case, she only had an old grip, not suitable at all, and what else? Take money out of the bank, get her hair done, ring her brother to make sure he didn't call her at school. He hadn't telephoned her for four months, but there was always the chance. Her brother was in his usual bad humour.

'You got me away from my scrambled eggs, they'll be all hard. Oh all right. No, of course I wouldn't telephone you, why should I? Oh very well. I don't know what you think you're doing. Have you read about the unemployment in this country? Where do you think you're going to get another job if you're fired? Sometimes I think you've no sense of responsibility. No, of course I won't say anything to anybody, but Lisa, I wish you'd tell me what you're up to. I was saying to Angela the other night that you are so secretive and you just ring me out of the blue to say the oddest kind of things. No, why the hell should I wish you a good time? I'm not able to run out on everything and everybody and dash off to London on some whim. Good-bye now, good-bye.'

No other friends to alert really. Funny after all the years of living in the same town. But she'd see Maggie at lunch and she'd tell her, and they'd have a bit of a giggle, and then Maggie would say, 'Make sure he pays for you, I think he's mean,' and Lisa would defend him to the hilt, he wasn't mean, he was careful with money, and that's how he got where he was and had all the things he had. She admired him for it.

It was a rush but it was a great day. There had been a few valleys. Maggie said she had heard that his wife was expecting another baby. Lisa said that it couldn't be true, he hadn't even seen his wife for six months. Maggie said it took nine months to produce a baby and this one was nearly ready to be produced. Lisa said it was all ridiculous, he'd have told her, and Maggie said sure, and anybody would tell you it didn't have to be *his* baby just because it was hers, and Lisa brightened. She darkened a bit at the bank when she tried to take out £60 from her deposit account and the clerk told her she had only £50 in it. She was sure there was over £200, but of course things like avocados were more expensive than the things she ate when she lived alone, and she did buy lots of little things for the flat.

She bought him a Johnny Cash cassette that they could play in the car, the kind of music he liked. It was a new one, they assured her. She was there at 3.30 and by four o'clock she knew every car accessory that they make these days. She bought a chamois so that the assistant wouldn't think she was loitering with intent. At five past four she got a horrible feeling that he might have been joking. She really should have rung him to make sure he meant it, but that would have looked humble and she didn't want that. Suppose she saw his car flying past. Suppose just suppose he did stop there for petrol and saw her, and hadn't meant to take her. That wouldn't be merely humble, it would be pathetic. Lisa shook herself, physically, like a dog trying to get rid of drops of rain, but she was trying to get rid of these hauntings and fancies. She seemed to have them these days the way people got mosquito bites, or dandruff. And then she saw him pulling in and looking around for her.

And the four hours, well it had been like a dream sequence in a movie. Or rather, like one of those sequences where they show you people making a long journey across America, and they cut from shots of the car on one motorway to another, lights from petrol stations and hotels flash on and off, signposts to cities pass by – and they were in London, and they hadn't talked much, just sat beside each other listening to both sides of the Johnny Cash over and over, and Lisa never asked where they'd be staying or how they'd hide from all the people from his company who were bound to be at the hotel, or what day she was going to be sent home. She didn't want to break the magic.

And when they came to London he looked a bit help-less because he didn't know which way to go, and he turned right once when there was no right turn and a taximan shouted at him, and Lisa was secretly delighted because he looked vulnerable then, and like a little boy, and she wanted to hug him to take the shame away, but she made no move, and finally after an hour of going backward and forward he found the hotel and suddenly he was his old self again. Because the world of hotels is pretty much the same everywhere, it's just London traffic that can throw you.

She had wondered what to do about a wedding-ring. He had never bought her any kind of ring, and she hadn't liked to get one this morning when she was shopping . . . well, in case he thought she was being small-townish about it all. Perhaps people didn't wear rings when checking in, perhaps it was more sophisticated not to. She had worn gloves anyway, it seemed a good way of avoiding doing the wrong thing.

The foyer was huge and impersonal, but full of people and shops, and newspaper-kiosks and theatre booking-stands. It was very different from the hotel that she and Bill had stayed in when mother was ill, and had suddenly been taken into hospital in London. That time they stayed in a small hotel near the station, and the woman who ran it asked them for the money in advance, and Bill had said they would have to sleep in the same room to save paying for two. And the woman who ran the hotel had turned out to be nice and kind when she discovered that their mother was dying, and had made tea for Lisa, and had told her how her own mother had died.

And it was different from the hotel that they had all stayed in when mother and father and Bill and herself had come to London for a week one October as a treat. That had been owned by a friend of father's, a North Countryman, and father said they wouldn't be robbed there like they would everywhere else. And it had been a vaguely unsatisfactory holiday for no reason that any of them ever understood and none of them ever dared say. Just a lot less than they all had hoped for probably.

But here in Lancaster Gate it was a different world and a different life, and he looked pleased that she was there and that was all that mattered. She smiled at him as the porter took their cases. She had bought one very like his, and got a cosy warm feeling in the lift because the cases looked like matching luggage, the kind of thing they might have been given as a wedding-present if they had been a normal couple.

And he must have ordered a room with a double-bed specially because she saw from the brochure she had been looking at in the lobby that most of the rooms had twin beds. And he gave her a kiss when the porter had gone, and said, 'There's nothing like a life of sin. Let's ring for a gin-and-tonic and let's go to bed.'

And they did, and then they went out to a restaurant where the Italian waiter asked them if they were married and Lisa said 'No' very quickly so that he wouldn't think she was trying to pretend in any way (except to the hotel) that she *was* his wife, and the waiter said he thought not, they looked too happy and too much in love. And Lisa's heart which hadn't pounded or thudded since that morning went into a little cotton-wool ball of happiness.

So it was indeed funny the way things turned out, she

thought again. Instead of losing out by behaving like a weak wife-type, clinging, dependent, she was being patted on the back and taken on a nice happy trip to London. There was a knock at the door and she leaped off the bed to answer it, thinking it was breakfast. It wasn't, it was a bowl of fruit and some flowers with a Compliments card. She gave the boy twenty pence and hoped that it was enough. He came out of the bathroom, all clean and young-looking, a towel around his waist. He was as excited as a child and nearly as excited as she was.

'Who's it from, who's it from?' she begged.

He tried to look casual. 'I always arrange little surprises like this for you,' he said, teasing her, and they opened the card.

It was from the President of the Company, an American gesture, he said, to make the employees feel they are part of a happy family, to make them pull harder because they think they are being looked after. He was very pleased, even though he wouldn't show it.

'Must have taken a secretary a long time to write out all these personal cards,' he said, not wishing her to think that he thought the President had written it.

'Still,' said Lisa. 'They did go to the trouble.'

She reached out for the card, and her heart became a big ball of putty and sank down in her body. It was addressed to 'Mr and Mrs' and hoped that they would both enjoy their stay.

'Is it . . . is it to tell you that they *know* you've brought a woman with you?' she asked fearfully.

He looked unconcerned. Not at all, the secretary had probably found out from the hotel which delegates had checked in with their wives and put Mr and Mrs on those cards. Just administration. He was putting on the cufflinks she had given him and he gave her a kiss on the nose.

She felt that the day was a bit less glorious and immediately felt very angry with herself for feeling that way. What had happened? Nothing. She was a cheat and a tramp, and a mistress, and illegally registered in the hotel as the 'Mrs' she wasn't. But that was all rubbish. The first night she had gone to bed with him she had rid her mind of all those labels, they didn't count in anybody's mind except the fevered minds of a long-gone generation. Why was a silly card upsetting her?

The breakfast arrived and they sat by the window reading the two newspapers that had been sent up as well. She touched his hand when she poured him more coffee. He smiled, and she hoped in a beaten sort of way that it was going to be fairly glorious anyway.

'What shall we do?' he said.

'I'd like to look at the pictures and things they're hanging up on the railings down there. Maybe I might buy a couple of things.'

'It's bound to be rubbish,' he said, not disagreeably, but as one who knew about such things.

'All the same, it would be nice to stroll around and then maybe go for a walk in the park,' she said.

'Perhaps we should move further away from the hotel,' he said. He was right, of course. It would have been idiocy to have hidden it for seventeen months back home, where such things were hard to hide, and then blow it in a city of ten million people, just by parading around in front of people who were bound to know him, and to know that she oughtn't to be there. Lisa agreed quickly.

'We can go anywhere else,' he said helpfully.

'We could get the underground to St Paul's and have a look at that,' she said eagerly, to show that she didn't mind being a second-best woman, a person who had to be hidden rather than paraded.

'Yes, we could do that,' he said.

'Or walk up to Oxford Street maybe, and look at the shops.'

'They'll be a bit crowded, Saturday morning,' he said.

She felt the familiar terror, the well-known realisation that she was losing his interest came flooding over her. You counter that with brilliant acting, she told herself smartly. You don't give in, you don't allow yourself to look beaten or sulky. You act.

'Listen my love, I'm doing all the suggesting, I don't mind *what* we do. It's a glorious day, even the man on the wireless said so. I'll do whatever you'd like, or anyway I'll discuss it.'

She smiled the bright bird-like smile that she felt must look so phoney. She always thought she must look like a model in an advertisement on telly who has suddenly been told she must act.

But no, as always, he responded as he would have done to a normal remark.

'Well, I'll tell you what I'd *like* to do,' he said.

'Yes?' Mask set, eyebrows raised, mouth in inquiring smile.

'It sounds a bit odd but, well, I've arranged to have one of these executive health check-ups. You know, we were talking about them. They have them on Saturday mornings. Do everything: heart, blood pressure, X-rays, blood tests, the lot. It makes more sense than spending hours and days at home.

'They have them on Saturdays so that executives can go without telling anyone at work what they're up to. When I thought I was going to be here by myself, I booked one for today, and sent a deposit. I could cancel it but you . . . you know, it seems a pity. It would set my mind at rest.'

The fluttering fear that was never too far from her heart came back and buzzed at her, it even got into her eyes.

'Stop looking worried, funny face,' he said, laughing. 'Nothing happens to me, it's because I do things like this that I'm so healthy. They won't find anything wrong. It's just wise to have it done at forty-five, that's all.'

She was ten years younger and a hundred times slower

in every way, in thinking, in walking, in making up her mind, in knowing what to say.

'Are you sure you don't have any pains or anything?' she faltered.

He was sure, and he was quite willing to cancel it. It was just that they didn't have anything like this at home, and you know that once you went for any kind of check-up back there, everyone knew about it, and they all had you buried before you came out of the doctor's surgery. Still, it did seem a pity to waste the nice morning, and she had been saying only yesterday that they didn't have much time together, just the two of them. Perhaps he would ring and cancel it.

She knew she was being manipulated when she insisted that he go. She knew he used the phrase 'just the two of us' in heavy inverted commas. She knew that he had never intended to back out of it for a minute. Anyway she thought it was a good idea for him to have the check-up. So it was on with the act.

No, nonsense, she would be very happy to stroll around herself. She'd meet him afterwards. She'd go down and look at those pictures that he didn't want to see. It was ideal really, they could each do what they wanted, and then meet for lunch.

He didn't know whether it would be over by lunchtime. But she thought that this was the point, that the check-up only took a couple of hours. Yes, well he hoped so but maybe they had better not make a firm arrangement for lunch just in case.

Oh act, act. Fine, that suited her too. After she had looked at the paintings on the railings, she'd have a quick look at Oxford Street, and then take the tube to St Paul's. She hadn't been there since she was a child, she'd love to see it again. Don't cling, don't cling, you mustn't appear dependent. Choose some very late time and he'll suggest earlier. He'll like you for saying you can manage alone, you'll like it if he says he wants you earlier. Don't ruin it, don't balls up the glorious day.

'Why don't we say six o'clock here!' Bright, light tone, utterly non-clinging, utterly ridiculous as a suggestion. His examination couldn't possibly take from eleven in the morning until six at night.

'That sounds about right,' he said, and the day went dark, but the voice stayed bright, and there were no give-away signs as she bounced cheerfully out the door.

The lobby looked less glittering and glamorous and Londonish. It looked big and full of people who trusted other people or didn't give a damn about other people. She looked at the house-phones on the wall. Should she ring up and just say 'Love you'? They did that to each other, or they used to a lot in the beginning. No, it was silly, there was nothing to be gained and it might irritate him. Why risk it?

She wound her way across the road, jumping this way and that to avoid the traffic, because it looked too far to walk to the pedestrian crossing, and anyway she was anxious to get to the other side. It reminded her of Paris, and all those thousands of water-colours of Notre-Dame, all of them exactly the same and all of them different prices, or so it seemed.

There was a young man with very red hair and a very white face looking at her.

'Scarf, lady?' he asked hopefully.

'I want to look at everything before I buy,' she said happily.

'Surprising more of you Northerners aren't killed if that's the way you cross roads up there,' he said good-naturedly.

He meant it nicely. It was to keep her chatting, she knew that. She also thought that he fancied the look of her, which was nice. She felt it was so long now since anyone had fancied her that she wouldn't know how to react. But somehow his marking her out as a Northerner annoyed her, she was irritated, even though she knew it was said in friendship. Did she sound provincial, did she look provincial, crossing the road like that?

Suddenly she thought with a violence that made her nearly keel over, that there was a great possibility that he thought she was provincial too. That could be the reason why he wasn't prepared to make any public announcement of their being together. Not announcement, she didn't really want as much as that, she wanted . . . a bit of openness. It was bloody obvious now that she thought of it. Living with someone, having it off with someone, having an affair, all this was accepted now . . . by everyone.

She stood there, not even seeing the blur of Towers of London, Trafalgar Squares, and Beefeaters that waved like flags from the scarf-rack. She could only see her herself years ago at supper-time, listening to her mother talking about people who gave themselves airs. Her mother had wanted Lisa always to remember that she came from good stock. They could hold their heads up with any of them, they were as good as anyone for miles around, they had nothing hidden away that could never be dragged out. Lisa and Bill never knew what brought on these kind of statements, they had never even known what she was talking about. Suddenly Lisa knew. It was the reassurance game, it was trying to say 'it's all right'.

Lisa felt like shouting it out aloud this very moment. She had an urge to tell the boy with the red hair that her father had been a local government official, that her mother had been a nurse, that her mother's father had owned a chemist's shop. She wanted to say it in a voice so clear and loud that he would hear it, before he left for his check-up, so that he would realise how lucky he was to have got a girl from such good stock, who was so willing to play along in a shabby game with him. That it was against her training, her background, her . . . well her kind of people. She wanted him to know, without having to spell it out, that she was better than he was, better in the way that older people valued things, that she had come from respectable people. His father had worked in the Potteries, that much she knew and only that.

Of course he had married into money, and why shouldn't he, a bright boy like him? Any family would have been delighted to have him as a son-in-law. Would her own family have liked him? Yes, her father would have admired him, her mother would have been a bit boringly embarrassing about stock, but she would have accepted him. However, she'd have liked him to know, if only there were some way of telling him indirectly, that her family wouldn't have fallen over themselves in gratitude . . . that he'd have had to make an effort to be accepted.

Lisa's head cleared and she looked at the boy again.

'I don't feel very well,' she said, feeling she owed him some explanation of why she was standing there looking at him wildly.

'Do you want to sit down, darling?' he asked kindly, and pushed out a stool for her. He looked a bit worried and even embarrassed. His customer had turned out to be a nutcase. That's what he must be thinking, Lisa told herself miserably.

He gave her a cup of very sweet coffee from his little orange flask. Over the rim of the cup she looked up at the hotel. Was there any chance that he would be looking out the window and would see her sitting down, drinking coffee there? Would he be worried, would he rush down to know if she felt faint? What would she say if he did? But as the hot sweet coffee went down inside her chest, Lisa had another feeling too. No, he wouldn't be looking out the window, straining for a view of her crossing the road. *She* did that kind of thing, he didn't. She was the one who would look hopefully out the window of the flat at home to see him turning the corner in the evenings. If she was the late one home, he was always reading or looking at television. He never stood at windows. He wouldn't be looking down.

'I feel much better, thank you ever so much,' she said to the red-haired boy.

'You still look a bit shaky, love,' he said.

'Could I sit here for a little bit?' asked Lisa, more to please him really than because she wanted to. She thought he would like to feel he was doing her a service. She was right, he was delighted. He moved the stool back against the railings and lit her a cigarette, while he talked to two Americans and sold them a wall-hanging with Big Ben on it.

'When they get home they'll probably have forgotten what city Big Ben is in,' he said. He didn't think much of Americans, he told her. Scandinavians were educated people, Americans weren't. He asked her if she was going to be in London for long.

'My husband is going to Harley Street for a check-up today,' she said cosily. 'It may depend on what he's told. But I think we'll be here a week.'

She wondered whether she was going mad, actually mad, at the age of 35. It did happen to people, they started telling the most fantastic, unreal tales and nobody noticed for a while, then they had to go and have treatment.

'Harley Street today, a Saturday?' said the red-haired boy cheerfully. 'Meeting some bird more likely. You won't find any doctors in Harley Street today. You'd better keep an eye on your old man, my darling, he's with some blonde.'

He smiled a big cockney grin, full of quickness and good humour. He liked most people he met, this boy did. He didn't particularly fancy her probably, he was like this with old dears of a hundred and with fellows as well.

'It's possible,' she said. 'Quite possible.'

The red-haired boy looked alarmed. She must look as if

she were going mad again; he must be regretting his little pleasantry.

'He'd be mad if he was,' he said. 'Lovely woman like you, no blonde could be any better. No, he'd need his head examined he would, if he told you he was going to a doctor and went off to hold hands in a park with a blonde.'

His face had a kind of transparency about it. It was watery somehow, with pale eyes set far apart from each other. It was a very simple face. It wouldn't disguise things, and look differently to the way it was feeling. It wasn't the kind of face that could smile and tell you that its health needed a check-up if it wasn't true. That face could never become troubled and talk about its marriage having been a sad sort of thing, better not spoken of, if in fact his wife were pregnant and it were planning to try and get the marriage revved up again.

'Are you married?' she asked him.

'No darling, never met a lady that was worthy of me,' he said.

'Neither am I,' she said.

She didn't care what he thought. She tried not to look at the flicker of puzzlement and irritation that came over his white, transparent face. It was because of his face that she had decided to tell him the truth, even though it would have been better in the short encounter between them if she hadn't.

She got up, folded the stool together, and placed it very precisely beside the railings.

'I really do feel a lot better, thank you. I might come back and buy something from you later on,' she said.

'You do that, my darling,' he said, relieved that she was going. She felt that even here she had stayed too long, talked too much, revealed a dependence. Was she ever going to be able to stop?

There was an opening into the park and she walked in. The grass was yellowish, there hadn't been any rain for a long time. A series of glorious days probably. She looked at the people. No delegates to the conference, nobody from back home had arrived yet; there was no danger of being seen by anyone. And even though he was careful about his health, it was funny that he hadn't said anything about the check-up before. And why had they got a 'Mr and Mrs' card with the fruit and flowers? He must have said all along that he was bringing his wife with him. And the room had already had a double-bed in it, before he had planned for her to accompany him. And what kind of fool did he think she was to believe he was having an executive check-up all bloody day? Or did he care what she thought? Was it just a case of it being more comfortable to have an undemanding fool of a woman who paid her own way and wasn't any extra trouble than not to have one, or to leave her at home sulking?

She strolled around idly, noticing that everyone in the park seemed to be with other people. There were groups of girls, and there were families, and there were a lot of pregnant women walking with that proud waddle they develop, hands folded oddly over the bulk in front, managing to look frail as well as huge, so that husbands had protective arms around shoulders.

And she wondered, did he have his real wife in London for the week-end, and was he in fact going to go back to her, and was it she who was pregnant or someone else? Maggie would say anything to get her nice friend Lisa out of this thing. Or did he have some other girl, who also had to be fobbed off with lies and hurried telephone calls? She knew how real his excuses could sound. She wondered whether any other woman in the whole world would have gone to live with a man who was not divorced and who went home every six months to see his daughter, but aparently didn't talk to his wife except about business matters.

She wondered if it was worth going back to the hotel to pick up the case. She thought not, really. It had cost £12 and that was a pity, but what was £12 compared to other things she had spent? She had her handbag with her and her money, there weren't many clothes at the hotel. She hadn't brought much with her in order not to appear too eager, not to look as if she was assuming that she was staying for the whole week.

She didn't make any plans about what was his and what was hers in the flat. She'd sort that out tomorrow or the day after when she got back, and she'd take what she felt like taking. She wouldn't take lots out of viciousness, or too little out of martyrdom.

She didn't even start fussing and worrying about what stations the trains went from and how to get there, or what times they were at, and how much they cost. She didn't even know whether she would go in to work on Monday and say her aunt hadn't died in London after all. It was strange, but she didn't even seem to be imagining how he would react when he came back at six o'clock and she didn't turn up. Would he contact the police? Would it embarrass him with the hotel and with everybody? Would he think she was dead? It didn't matter.

She always thought that things ended suddenly, that people had a big row, or they parted with clenched teeth and noble smiles like they did in old movies. And she stood still beside a seat which had a lot of old people sitting on it, and she took some deep breaths one after another as if she was testing to see how her heart was feeling, whether it was thudding, or if it was surrounded by that awful, horrible, empty feeling of fear like it so often was, when she thought he was angry or bored with her. And funnily it didn't seem to be in a bad state at all.

She wished she had someone to tell, someone who would congratulate her, someone who would be interested. If mother was alive . . . no, of course she couldn't have told mother about it, what was she dreaming about? Mother had been interested certainly, but you didn't tell mother about having affairs, that wasn't something people from our stock did, people who were busy holding their heads up with the best of them. And father, he might have liked the story if it had been about someone else. He used to listen to her tales about other people, and say, 'Fancy, aren't folk strange?' Maggie would treat it lightly, and probably come out with new stories about him, things she hadn't liked to tell Lisa at the time. And there was nobody in the staffroom she could tell, and Bill, well Bill and Angela would just have one of their worried conversations about her. She really had very few friends.

And that was the one cloud on her new freedom, she realised. That's what she'd miss, having him for a friend. In a few ways and some of the time, he had at least been a friend.

Marble Arch

These days she felt that the flower sellers, the men with piles of things that had fallen off lorries, the policemen and the road-sweepers were her friends. She felt they were all part of some kind of club, the only remaining English people in a sea of foreigners. It was a racist kind of thought perhaps, she said to herself, because if you started noticing how many people there were who smelled of garlic, or who wore face-veils, or head-dresses, then the next step might be to wish they weren't there. It would be better not to notice differences at all, to think that everything which walked on two feet was a fellow human.

Anyway she had no right to be anything but grateful to all the tourists. She reminded herself of this as an Arab thrust a piece of paper at her with an address down the Edgware Road on it, and she pointed him in the right direction. He was going to a chemist's shop, she noticed. She wondered whether it was for a prescription or to buy boxes of soaps and talcums. Without the Arabs her own business would have folded long ago. She sold hand-made handbags in a shop within a shop. They were quite expensive. Young Londoners didn't have the money young Kuwaitis did.

Sophie unlocked her little shop and started to hang up the bags. She then got a stool and sat out in the morning sunlight waiting for custom. It was much more expensive to have a street frontage, but it trebled business. She was glad she had such a good head for business. She really needed it because nobody around her seemed to understand the first principles of earning a living. She frowned with the beginning of a headache, and moved out of the sun. It had been a very late night.

It hadn't been night when she finally got to bed, it had been four o'clock in the morning. Eddie had brushed the hair out of his eyes and half-raised himself on an elbow as she left, but he was now back in a deep innocent sleep again and here she was sitting with a headache, trying to trap the tourists who came to Marble Arch, trying to keep awake and make a living for Eddie and herself.

She never thought of herself as earning a living for both of them. That wasn't the way the words or the ideas fell together. Only sometimes, when she had a headache or when they had talked long and without direction during the night, did she think wistfully how nice it would be if he was the one who got up in the mornings, and she was the one who could raise herself on an elbow and say 'Good-bye love, take it easy'. But that wasn't really considering an alternative, it was only thinking about things that would never be, like the way you sometimes imagined what it would be like to be a seagull when you saw one swooping backwards and forwards over a harbour.

Sophie thought a bit about last night's discussion. It hadn't been any different from the ones that had gone before, just longer. Eddie's dark brown eyes and their long black lashes looked dull with the pain of the world. They had lost all the flash and brilliance they had when he wasn't talking about the cruelty of the world. Dead they sat on his face as he spoke on bitterly about the producers who were pansies, the agents who were fairies, the script-editors who promised the moon, the misguided advice of friends who said, 'Well, why don't you just *go* to Framlingham or Fraserburgh or some ridiculous place and see what happens?'

Eddie wasn't going to just go anywhere. At thirty-seven he was too old now to just go to a stupid group of over-excited students or experimentalists and help them out with their productions. He had been in acting too long, learned too much, was too professional to give in, to sell the past. What had all these years been for if he was going to give in now? What would his love for Sophie mean if he was to allow that painted Jeffrey to feel him up and take him to that queers' pub as a possession, just in order that Eddie could get a part? No, life was cruel, and rotten, and the good people always lost out, and it was a plot, and you couldn't fight the system hoping to win, but at least you could try.

Sophie had never seen life as being cruel and rotten before she met Eddie, but she had always seen it as fairly difficult and tiring. She thought if you worked hard you made money, and then you had leisure time and you enjoyed that. If you were very lucky indeed you worked at something that wasn't awful, and then you enjoyed both work and leisure. She thought it must be very strange and sad to work in a world where there seemed to be steaming clouds of sexual desire and frustration, mostly homosexual, and that this was governing who got jobs and who played where and who succeeded or who failed.

It was so different to her own world. She had managed to leave the very dull, very depressing place where they had trained her how to sell cosmetics so well that she firmly believed she could sell lip-gloss to men with beards. She had always wanted to be in business for herself but with no capital it looked impossible. Her father hadn't wanted her to leave the cosmetic people. He thought she should thank her lucky stars day and night for the good luck she had got in life. Her father had never had much luck, there were more weeks when he collected money from welfare than from an employer. Her mother had worked regularly and quietly in a restaurant. She said that her one ambition was that Sophie should never have a job which meant walking and standing, and dealing with dirty plates and difficult customers. She was happy when Sophie was selling nice, fresh, good-smelling oils and paints for people's faces. She was worried when she seemed to become a person of no account sitting in a little stall shouting her wares to the public.

Sophie sighed, thinking how little everyone around her knew about business. If she had been her father, she would have kept a steady job; if she had been her mother, she would have demanded to be a cashier in that restaurant, where she could have sat in a little glass box near the door, rather than get varicose veins by walking and standing; if she were Eddie, she *would* take any acting job anywhere if she wanted to act, or more probably she would decide that if acting didn't want her among its ranks, she would take some other job and act in her spare time. Really she had made very little impression on anyone, with her own business-like attitudes. Nobody realised that it wasn't easy to be organised and disciplined, and to make money. It took a lot of time, and worry, and ate into all those hours you could be sitting around and enjoying yourself. Nobody ever got drawn into her little belief that people might be here on earth to work hard. Nobody but Peggy. Peggy was her one success.

Peggy had been a mess, and Sophie thought she would always be one, but she was so warm and friendly, that you looked through all this bamboo curtain of rubbish and saw a lovely, big, responsive soul inside. Peggy had been to the same school, had done the same useless meaningless course in 'Business administration'. Well, hardly done it, Peggy had barely attended a class there. She had been in chip-shops and coffee-shops, and places with plastic table tops where people ate ice-creams and drank fizzy drinks instead of learning Business administration or delivering bundles of dresses from the wholesale house to the retail which was what they were being paid for.

Peggy had a year of liberty, then came the storm. Her mother couldn't understand why she wasn't fitted for a wonderful job, some high business post. Gradually the tales of the chip-shops emerged, and Peggy left home under the darkest cloud you could find, a cloud of ingratitude.

Sophie had seen her from time to time. Usually she came to borrow a few pounds. More often than not Sophie got them back. Sometimes she came to grumble. This man had let her down, that man hadn't told her he was married, the other man had been perfectly nice for a fortnight and then it turned out that all he wanted was to beat her and for her to beat him. She worked in Woollies for a while and was sacked for stealing. She thought that this was unfair. Sophie thought it was also pretty unfair to steal from Woollies, and Peggy only grudgingly agreed.

She worked for a while in one of the coffee-shops of her youth. Sophie always had coffee there just to have a chat. Sometimes she thought it mightn't be such a good idea. Peggy looked weary, and dirty, and beaten, she seemed to resent Sophie's smart looks, essential for her trade, and her smart little car essential for bringing her trade from door to door.

But still Peggy didn't have anyone else, and when she was arrested the first time and charged with being drunk and disorderly, Sophie was the one she sent for. She sent for Sophie when she was in hospital, too, suffering, they told her, from malnutrition. Sophie came when she was charged with soliciting, and when she was finally sent to prison on her third charge, it was Sophie who waited for her three weeks later in the little car and drove her back home.

When Peggy immediately retrieved a bottle of barley-wine that she had hidden in the hallway of the depress-

ing house where she lived, Sophie decided she had had
enough. Quite enough. There they were sitting in this
filthy room, and she was refusing a glass of cloudy,
muddy-looking drink with the excuse that it was a bit
early in the day. Her old friend Peggy had become a
prostitute, a thief, and a near-alcoholic.

The years of dragging herself up and away and onwards were looking useless, if she could be dragged
down again so quickly by Peggy. She lost her temper,
and said all this and more.

'I'm not just dumping you, because I've become all
up-in-the-air,' she shouted eventually. 'Stop telling me
that I have ideas about myself. I've no ideas for God's
sake, I just work bloody hard, and it isn't easy and
everyone around me seems afraid of work or . . . or
sneers at it and at me. So now I'm telling you I'm sick of it,
sick, sick, sick. I have no more pity for you. I haven't any
more words, any more "Poor things" to say to you. You
can go whatever bloody way you like, I don't care if I
never hear about you again, because every time I hear
from you you want something, money, help, someone to
take you home from gaol. If you don't want something at
the beginning, you end up wanting something. You
drain me, and make me feel weak and feel nothing. So to
hell with you Peggy, to hell with you, I'm sick of you.'

And then it was Sophie not Peggy who cried. Peggy
was amazed. Not upset, just amazed.

The great cool Sophie was sitting there crying, the calm
Sophie had shouted. The mask had slipped. Peggy was
transfixed. Instead of the list of excuses, explanations,
and life's miseries that normally fell out unasked for, she
heard herself say quite calmly:

'What would you like me to do?'

'I'd like you to look after yourself for a change and not
rely on me to look after you. I'd like you to do something
quite extraordinary for you, that's go out and earn a
bloody living like most people in the world.'

Sophie gathered up her bag and her car keys and
banged out of the dirty room in the depressing house,
and went off and sold cream that took lines from under
your eyes to women who ran small dress shops. In and
out of her car she got, dragging display literature, explaining that people who bought dresses would like to
have unlined faces to wear with them. She went on and
on until the last late-closing shop had closed, then returned to her flat and worked on reports until midnight
and went to sleep.

Next day Peggy was at her door. A tidier Peggy, not
drunk, not hungover, not pleading.

'Can I come with you on your rounds?' she asked
simply.

Sophie was tired. 'Yes, if you don't talk,' she said, and
the day was much like any other, except for the vaguely
comforting feeling of Peggy sitting silently beside her.
They hardly spoke a word to each other until lunch-time.
Then Sophie offered her a drink.

'I'll have a coffee,' said Peggy.

During the coffee Peggy had asked intelligent questions about the kind of stores, shops and boutiques they
had been visiting. She wanted to know how much credit
they got. Since Peggy couldn't have had a pound note to
her name, Sophie wondered at the drift of the conversation. Surely Peggy couldn't see herself as a shop-
owner, even if she were going to pull herself together?
But anything was better than the kind of thing Peggy
normally talked about, so Sophie answered her sensibly.
Sophie was also relieved that no malice seemed to be
directed towards her for yesterday's outburst.

Peggy came silently in the car with Sophie for about a
week, except for the day she had to go and see a proba-
tion officer or social worker. She didn't have any tales to
tell about these visits, no theories about how women in
such jobs were sadists. Sophie began to feel quite optimistic about her, but didn't want to rock any boat by

saying it was a useless way to spend your days, sitting in someone else's car. Perhaps Peggy was just desperately lonely, she thought.

Then Peggy came up with her suggestion. She wondered, would these women in the shops buy handmade bags?

Sophie's first thought was that Peggy was planning to steal the bags, but no, she said, she had learned a bit of leather work once, and it turned out she was quite good at it. Would Sophie like to come and see some of it that evening?

The dirty and untidy bedroom was still untidy, but not with clothes, make-up and empty barley-wine bottles. This time it was with bits of leather and cord. Sophie stood transfixed.

Because the bags in all sorts of shapes and sizes were beautiful.

Some of them were soft pinks and blues, others were bold blacks and whites. They were made on a patchwork system, because Peggy had only enough money for scraps, she said. She looked shyly at Sophie, and blushed with pleasure at the evident delight and surprise she saw.

'I was wondering, could I earn a living selling them?' asked Peggy as timidly as a child. Sophie's heart was so full of pride and delight and resolution that she hardly trusted herself to speak. This must be the way teachers feel, or nurses when their patients get better, she thought; and they sat down and made plans for Peggy's new career.

Things moved very quickly after that; the only problem was that Peggy couldn't keep up with the demand. One boutique took a dozen, and rang up three days later for three dozen more. Sophie spent a whole Sunday with Peggy working out what they should do. If she were to get someone else to help her, they would have to halve the money. They had already seen the huge mark-up that shopkeepers put on the bags. It was time to define them as 'luxury items', as 'specialist work'. They got labels made with 'handcrafted by Peggy Anderson' on them, and they charged three times the price. They got it. And Peggy was in business.

So great was the business that Sophie decided she would abandon cosmetics for it, and that is why she was sitting in her little stall near Marble Arch. Not all the bags were Peggy's, no one person could keep up with that demand. But she sold six of Peggy's a week, and she paid Peggy ten pounds a bag, everyone was happy.

Now that Sophie had time off from the endless reports, and shop calls, and fights about commission that had made up her working life, she was able to have a social life. This was something she hadn't seen much of in the hard years of the cosmetic world. But it wasn't hard to find. There was George, silly, dull, kind George who wanted to marry her six weeks after he met her, and who took her to tennis parties and to drink outside Hooray Henry bars, where everyone talked about the last or the next tennis party, and what car everyone else was driving.

And then there was Michael, who was kind and dull too. And Fred who was far from dull, but also very selfish and made no bones about telling her that he would like a wife doing something a little more classy than working as a hawker on Oxford Street. And suddenly one night there was Eddie. At the theatre on a summer evening, when Fred had gone to get the drinks and they had started talking about the play, Eddie had asked if she was an actress, and on impulse she had told him exactly where her little shop was, hoping he would call there. He did, and they drifted into friendship, and an affair that became a real love affair, and then it seemed only right that Eddie should live with her, and now she couldn't live without Eddie.

It was for Eddie that she got up early in the mornings

because bills were bigger for two. It was for Eddie that she begged Peggy to make more bags, since the Peggy Andersons were the sure-fire sellers. It was for Eddie that she closed the shop for an hour and went off to the Berwick Street market to buy each night's dinner.

People told her that she had become nicer since she met Eddie. Her tired mother, whose veins were like knots of rope nowadays, and her sad-eyed father, both said she was more cheerful these days, but they put it down to her feckless life among the traders rather than to any love or warmth that had been added. They still thought her foolish to have thrown up her chances of real money.

Peggy said she looked marvellous, better than the days when she used to wear all the make-up she was selling. Love was great, said Peggy gloomily, for those lucky enough to find it. But Peggy didn't seem to like Eddie. She thought he was lazy and that he took too much from Sophie.

'I don't trust him,' she had said once. 'He's one of the takers. I should know, I used to be one. He'll take all you can give, and then one day he'll decide you are nagging, or not enough fun, or not sexy enough, and he'll go and take from someone else.'

Sophie had just laughed. 'Nothing worse than a re-formed drunk for telling you the evils of having a glass of sherry.'

Peggy simply shrugged. 'Don't say I didn't warn you,' she said, and went back to her leather cutting. She worked now about ten hours a day. Whenever Sophie called, she was either bent over minute pieces of leather or she was out. Looking for pieces from her various outlets, she said, or having a walk to clear her head. Sophie was amazed that she could change lifestyles so simply but Peggy said that she mustn't be naive. Occasionally she visited Mr Shipton in the afternoons, he had a couch in his office, and Mr Shipton was very nice about giving Peggy pieces of leather and suede from his factory, so Peggy was very nice to him from time to time on his office couch.

Sophie found that sad and a bit disgusting, but Peggy said rubbish, it was glorious compared to picking people up in the streets, and how else could she afford all the material, so Sophie tried to put it out of her mind.

But today her mind was troubled as she sat and smiled at the tourists and made the odd sale. She felt very restless and anxious for something to change. It wasn't just the heat and the headache, it was as if she had been getting ready for this feeling. Systematically she ticked off all the good things about the way she lived. She had Eddie, beautiful tender Eddie, with his big dark eyes that made her feel weak just thinking about them, like girls were meant to go weak at the knees over pop stars. Eddie was so moody and marvellous that you never knew what to expect when you got home in the evenings. But that's what made the evenings when he had bought her a huge bunch of lilac, and was waiting in his black dressing-gown to take her straight to bed . . . so magic. It quite paid for the other evenings when he wasn't in, and came in sulkily slamming the door, because yet another fairy casting-director had wanted his body, not his acting.

The only time they talked about the future was about Eddie's future. There had been that time he nearly got a part in a show going to the States, and Sophie had become so excited and said she must get Peggy working overtime to make enough bags so that she could sell them there. Eddie had been firm that she mustn't leave her place in Marble Arch, and that it would only be a couple of months' separation. She had loved him for being so solicitous about her work.

At school they used to have a teacher who always made them 'count their blessings'. Sophie remembered that it had been a hard thing to do in those days when she wanted to look like a model, and live in a house with a swimming pool. Nowadays it wasn't really all that much easier. Blessings should be accepted, not counted. So she had Eddie, so she had her health, apart from the odd bad headache. So she had a way of earning a living that she enjoyed. At the age of twenty-seven she was in business for herself, few other women could boast that. Even if Peggy became unreliable again, she still had plenty of other people who made bags. What could be wrong with her?

A couple stopped and picked up one of Peggy's bags. They examined the label and gave funny little cries of recognition.

'That's the girl we met at the theatre yesterday,' said the woman. 'Peggy Anderson, she said she made bags, these are lovely.'

'Do you know Peggy?' asked Sophie with interest. Peggy never mentioned anyone at all except the awful man whom she met on the couch now and then.

'Yes,' said the man, who seemed a nice chatty kind of fellow, but to Sophie's practised eye, a chatty fellow who would be nice to meet and who would buy nothing. 'We went to this lunch-time play yesterday, and got talking to a girl in the wine-bar, she was waiting for her fellow to turn up. Very good-looking girl, lovely red hair.'

'They are awfully dear,' said the woman sadly. 'But they are lovely. Are there any others of hers a bit cheaper?'

'What was the play?' asked Sophie suddenly, knowing somehow that they were going to say *The Table-lighter*, a silly little play which Eddie had seen yesterday. He had said it was a silly little play because he hadn't got a part in it. He had also said he had gone to it with Garry, a friend of his who was an agent, a useless agent. Peggy must have gone with Eddie, she didn't know anyone else, but why had neither of them mentioned it?

'It was *The Table-lighter*,' said the woman. 'This Peggy says she usually goes out at lunch-time, it takes her mind off work, and her chap is an actor, very good-looking fellow. He was late because he had been seeing someone about a job, I think.'

'It's a small world,' said the man.

'It is indeed,' agreed the woman.

'Oh very small,' said Sophie. 'Did they seem very close, Peggy and this actor? I just ask because I used to be rather worried about her, you know, she didn't seem to have much social life . . . I was wondering whether this might be something, well, you know, serious . . .'

Her heart was pounding, and she felt strangely outside herself as she asked the question. How great it was to be so cool and calm and not to panic, when the world was falling down. This is what she must have been expecting all morning.

'I don't think so, do you?' said the woman to her husband. 'Not a real thing going, they just seemed to be great friends laughing and joking without a care in the world. It's incredible to think that he's an actor and she's a leather worker like this. They didn't seem to have a care in the world.'

The nice man put the bag down. £20 was too much even for the work of someone he had met.

'That's right, I felt that too, sort of carefree. But then you know there are people who can be like that, and something sort of looks after them. It's like as if there were a big smiling God who says, "Go on Peggy and Eddie, amuse yourselves, I'll look after you".'

They couldn't know as they looked at the steely green eyes of the little girl in the bag shop that they were looking into the face of a big smiling God, who didn't know how to stop smiling.

Bond Street

The light was very bright when Margaret came out of the station. Everything seemed to dazzle her. Even the daffodils on sale in big baskets seemed too harsh a yellow. People's spring clothes seemed too loud, and the buses must have been re-sprayed recently. Surely they were never so aggressively red before? Or was it because there were so many of them in Oxford Street?

She was a little tired, she often felt tired before she began a shopping spree, it was tension she supposed Nobody liked shopping, places were too crowded, assistants not at all helpful, so many foreigners who didn't even attempt to speak English properly. Shopping was hardly something you did for fun. But then Margaret did shopping slightly differently from most people. She didn't actully pay for the goods she brought home. Her tensions and frustrations came not from trying to catch the eye of a shop assistant, but from avoiding it.

She made a list, like any conventional shopper would do. She took a shopping bag, she always carried enough money to pay for these listed items, but rarely if ever broke into it. She paused and window-shopped. She had coffee when her feet were tired, she got into little chats with other resting shoppers. In the evening she would go home again, sighing a little on the underground until someone would stand and give her a seat. Margaret had shopped in London like this once a month for nine years. Never in those nine years had she come into contact with a store detective, a security man, or anyone remotely suspicious of her.

Blinking slightly in the sunlight, she looked at her list.
Red towels.
Knives.
Tights.
Remnants.
Pendant.
Giant cup.
Table-lighter.
Jacket.

A lot of them could be 'bought' in Selfridges, but she
wanted a jacket from Marks, and she had seen a nice
table-lighter in a small souvenir-type shop on her last
visit. She might go down to Liberty's for the remnants.
She made sure that her wallet with the eighty-four
pounds in it was safely zipped into the pocket inside her
coat. You couldn't be too careful these days, with teams
of pickpockets coming to London from abroad. She
straightened her shoulders and went off to buy towels.

She had painted the bathroom last week. Harry had
been delighted with it. He said it looked really cheerful
with all that white and the window-frame red. He was
going to buy a nice cheerful red-and-white bath-mat, he
promised.

'And I'll get some red towels, when I'm doing my
shopping,' Margaret had said.

'Aren't towels a bit dear?' Harry had wondered with a
frown coming over his big kind face.

'Not if you shop around, they would be if you bought
the first good ones you saw,' said Margaret.

'I don't know what I'd do without you, you're a great
little shopper,' Harry had beamed, and Margaret felt
safe when she saw his frown disappear. She felt very
frightened when Harry worried, he looked so old.

The towels were easy. You pick up a big one, a middle-
size one and two small ones, you take them out under the
light to examine them properly, so that you have sepa-
rated them from the big piles where they are stacked.

Then moving slowly, and concentrating on them carefully, looking neither left nor right, you move farther and farther away from their original place. Put down your shopping bag and examine the corners of the towels to see that they are properly finished, drop the smaller ones into the bag on the ground, never looking around, that's the secret, then in a business-like way fold the big one into a small manageable size and put it in on top of the others, walking with the bag held out in front of you towards the desk where it says PAY HERE. Anyone watching you would think you are taking the items to pay for them, people at PAY HERE never watch anything at all. You then ask the PAY HERE people where curtains are, and if, suppose, by some terrible chance you are stopped . . . then you say, 'I went straight to the Pay place, and I got so absorbed in the curtains that I simply forgot.'

Margaret didn't know what would happen if she were caught. She assumed she would be able to talk herself out of it, if there were only one item in her bag, which was why she worked on the time-consuming principle of taking only one thing, and then checking it in as a parcel or in a left-luggage locker. *That's* what made shopping so tiring for her, all the endless walking backwards and forwards to luggage lockers, but it seemed only sensible. The day she was lazy was certainly the day she would be caught.

No problem either with the knives. Nice steak knives with wooden handles, Harry would love these. She would say she had found them in the attic, that they were a present for an anniversary, a present which must have got tidied away. They would laugh together over their good fortune in having found them.

The tights were a luxury for herself. She still had good legs and she hated the kind of stockings that looked cheap and hairy. Every month she collected four or five pairs of nice sheer tights, sometimes in what they called 'the new fashion shades'. She never mentioned these to Harry. He would occasionally say, 'You've got better legs than half these women on the television,' and she would smile happily.

The remnants were for dressmaking. She wasn't very good at it, but anyone could sew a pillow-case or a cushion cover, and it made Harry feel happy and comfortable, looking over at his wife sewing away contentedly while they watched television. She took enough to make a table-cloth too. That would only need a hem around it and Harry would never look at the edges, just at the nice bright colour on the table at breakfast, and he might say, 'Imagine you made that cloth yourself. I don't know how other fellows manage with their wives, I really don't.'

The pendant was a present for their son Jerry, who was away in the North at university. It would be his birthday next week. Jerry was a worry to her, he often looked at her very hard without saying anything.

'What are you thinking about?' she'd ask.

'Nothing, Mum,' came the invariable reply, but she felt that he was staring at her, and pitying her somehow and worrying about her. She didn't like that at all.

Once she had sent him a cashmere sweater for his birthday and he had rung up not so much to thank her as to protest.

'They cost a fortune, Mum, however did you afford it? They cost half what Dad earns in a week.'

Margaret realised she had gone too far.

'I bought it in an Oxfam shop,' she said, pretending to confess to a little economy, but her heart was pounding with fear.

'But it's new, it's all wrapped up in cellophane,' argued Jerry.

'Someone gave it away, a present they didn't want.'

'They must have been mad,' grumbled Jerry, still suspicious. From then on, it had to be gifts that nobody could put a real price on. The pendant would have cost about £7 had she paid for it, but she hadn't of course because she had asked the nice young man to show her some earrings and put the pendant in her pocket as he went to get an earring tray.

She and Harry. had seen a television play the other night where the husband had his tea out of a huge china cup. Harry had smiled and said wasn't it lovely.

'I've seen those in the shops,' said Margaret. 'Would you like one?'

'No, it's only silly, they cost a fortune and maybe my tea would get cold in it. It just looked nice, that's all.'

Margaret said she had a half-memory of seeing them in a sale where they cost about fifty pence.

'Oh well then,' Harry had said and went back to looking at the television.

The one Margaret took would have cost her seven pounds fifty pence, but when she was showing it to Harry tonight she would leave out the seven pounds. She thought it was a great deal of money to pay for one cup and saucer. Sometimes she felt aggrieved if the items she took were very expensive. She liked the best, but she liked things to be good value.

The table-lighter was a present for Harry's brother and his wife, who were having a twenty-fifth anniversary party next week. Harry's brother Martin never approved of Margaret, something Harry wouldn't and couldn't see in a million years. The families met rarely. A cursory visit around Christmas time, another in the summer. Martin's wife never had a cigarette out of her mouth, she never wore stockings, her hair was a mess, she had a loud laugh. Margaret was glad not to see too much of her. But she was always charming when they came to the house, and laughed insincere little peals when Martin said to his brother, 'Well, she has you rightly tamed, Harry, never thought I'd see the day when you'd be out planting vegetables and filling window-boxes.'

'Harry's marvellous at gardening, he grows a great deal of what we eat,' Margaret would say loyally.

'That's how you must be able to afford this place,' Martin had once said, looking around at lamps, ornaments, vases, and linen tray-cloths, all carried home from Margaret's monthly shopping trips.

'I don't know how you afford this style, I really don't.'

Martin had been far from helpful over that bad business years ago. Far from standing up for her and trying to keep up a good name for them, he had encouraged Harry in all that silliness.

'Never thought you had it in you,' he laughed coarsely, when Margaret had called a family conference to deal with the situation. 'A young lassie too, well that beats everything.' Martin's sluttish wife had let the cigarette ash fall down her stained cardigan with excitement. Old Harry, and a young girl from the factory, and a baby on the way. Excitements like that didn't come very often.

Margaret wondered whether the table-lighter was too good for them. After all they would have humiliated her, set her adrift if they had their way. Why should she get them anything? But still, it was all part of the scheme, the plan, the whole elaborate complicated business that made her victory assured. She had to be the perfect sister-in-law as well as the perfect wife. Only a perfect sister-in-law, herself a non-smoker, would be so thoughtful as to give something like a table-lighter. So quietly it went into the bag. Later she would get a really cheap box for it, they would assume it had a cost a couple of quid instead of twenty. They would be surprised it worked so well. Part of Margaret's good taste.

It would be a dull evening at their anniversary. Their children were loud too, and drank beer from cans. The lazy wife would make a small attempt at food, but it might only be sandwiches and trifle. There would be a lot of drink of course. And sometime in the evening Martin would nudge Harry and ask him were there any more little girls that he could pass on to his old brother, and Harry would look sheepish and silly and hope that Margaret hadn't heard.

Martin would love Margaret to have her come-uppance even at this late stage. He couldn't believe how well she had managed that business years ago. Looking back on it, Margaret herself often wondered how she had been able to cope with it.

There was Harry, all shuffling and foolish, and not able to look at anyone. There was this girl, small, fat, very fat now that she was five months pregnant. There was her father, a bit older than Harry, and even more shuffling, and everyone shouting about money, and rights and duties, and doing the proper thing, and not letting anyone get away with anything. Until Margaret had spoken.

'The only decision we have to make is this,' she had said. 'If Harry accepts that he is the father of this child, then he must marry the lady as soon as possible and give the child a name and a home. I will take our son and this house, and whatever it costs for both of us to live here. Harry must provide for two families, he will have no access to my home. I'm sure with overtime, he'll earn enough to keep us all.'

Her voice sounded so calm that everyone stopped shouting, and listened. Martin and his wife had been invited especially to give more support, but they sat open-mouthed through it all.

'If Harry thinks that he is only one of several people who might be the baby's father, then he should give the lady some money towards the upkeep of the child – a small lump sum, to thank her for his pleasure, and to acknowledge some limited degree of responsibility.'

The room was silent.

'And what about you Margaret?' asked Harry. 'What will you do?'

'If you leave our home, and go with this lady to some

room, I will never see you, nor allow you to see Jerry as long as I live. If you fail in your payments, I will get a court order against you. I have to look after *my* child, just as this lady has to look after hers. If you decide that you cannot be the sole person to be named as father, and you pay this lady a sum of money, to be agreed between you and her and her father, then when everybody has gone, I will make your supper as usual, and I will live here with you, never mentioning this whole incident again, unless you want to.'

'You'd forgive me?' stumbled Harry.

'It's not a question of forgiving, there's nothing to forgive, it's the bargain we made when we got married. I give you a comfortable home, and you give me your presence and loyalty, and support me. There's nothing unusual about it at all.'

And she had gone out into the kitchen to put some flowers in water, while their voices came from the sitting--room, and then they all left. Nobody came in to say goodbye or to tell her what had happened.

There had been no sound from the sitting-room, and she didn't know whether Harry had left with them. The five minutes were like five hours, the clock ticked, and the water tank burbled, loudly menacingly. But she wouldn't run in to see was he there, had he stayed, had she won.

She tore the stems of the flowers to little green rags as she waited. She knew this was some kind of test. It was too long, he must have gone. If she had lost, what would she do with the house. There was no point in scraping and saving to make it nice, just for a ten-year-old boy, and herself. If she had won, she would really keep her promise, she would make it a wonderful home for him, for them. Even if she had to steal, she thought, she wouldn't back-track on her word.

Then the door of the kitchen opened, and Harry, red-eyed, came in.

'I'm giving her £50,' he said.

'That seems very fair,' said Margaret.

She never asked why, or whether he had loved the girl, or whether she was a marvellous lay, or how and when they had met. She kept her bargain, and the next time she had gone to Oxford Street, she started bringing home little treats for Harry and herself. Her reward was his guilty devoted smile, his belief that he had married a Wonderwoman and nearly lost her through his own stupidity. That made her feel very good.

There was only the jacket left now; everything else, including her coat, was in the left-luggage office. She had a scarf and a brooch in her handbag. That was how she had got the jacket four years ago, the nice lilac one, that Harry had said made her look so young. This time she wanted black velvet.

She took one from the rail, and with one movement removed the price tag, throwing it behind the radiator, and pinned her own brooch on the lapel. The jacket was on her in a flash, with her scarf knotted under its collar. In seconds she had taken a different jacket out to hold it up to the light.

'It's nice,' she said to the sales girl.

'Nice cheerful red,' said the girl.

'And they wear very well,' said Margaret. 'I've had this one for quite a while, I was wondering should I get it in another colour.'

'It's a good idea to buy a couple if they suit you,' said the girl.

'But,' said Margaret, 'I think it's a bit extravagant of me really. I'll just go and do the rest of the shopping and if I've anything left over I'll come back later.'

'That's a good idea,' said the girl politely.

And she walked out into the afternoon sunlight to collect all the shopping from the left-luggage, and go home to Harry.

Oxford Circus

My heart sank when Frankie got a job in the BBC. Up to now all the disasters in her life had been reasonably contained among her ever-dwindling circle of friends. But if she were in reach of a microphone she might easily broadcast them to the nation. They might even become national incidents. Because Frankie was rarely out of trouble. I think it was only because I was such a boss, that I was a friend of hers at all. I liked the self-importance of rescuing her. I liked her undying gratitude and useless promises to be more careful the next time.

Clive didn't like Frankie, which was unusual because Clive liked almost everyone. He said she was brainless. Yet she had a far better degree than any of us. He said she liked getting into trouble, but he hadn't seen the tears pouring down her face as she sat in the police-station wrongly accused of starting a fight in a restaurant and causing a breach of the peace. Frankie hadn't started the fight, she had tried to stop somebody else's. Clive said she was vain. That couldn't be right either. Would somebody who was vain turn up at a dinner party in filthy painting clothes, because she had become so involved in doing up a neighbour's child's playroom that she had forgotten to look at her watch and just ran out to catch a taxi the way she was?

Frankie had recently disentangled herself from a particularly horrible man, who owned a restaurant and a bad temper, and who had beaten Frankie very badly on three separate occasions. The day she said she was leaving him, he had taken some of her best clothes and burned them in his incinerator.

She had taken nothing from the horrible man except a few bruises and a series of misunderstood memories. That was another fault of Frankie's, she never learned from anything. If she were to fall down and pass out six nights in succession because she had drunk too much, she never considered for one moment that there was an element of cause and effect. She just regarded each falling-down as a terrible happening to be deeply regretted. There would be other restaurant-owners who would throw all her clothes into the incinerator. I just hoped there wouldn't be many of them in the BBC.

'I want a reduction in the licence fee,' was all Clive said when I told him that Frankie was going to work at Broadcasting House. 'The thought of that woman's voice coming at me from the radio is enough to make me take sick-leave.'

Clive can be very silly once he has a bee in his bonnet about something, so I took no notice except to say that she would be doing research, not actually speaking on the air.

'That's a mercy,' said Clive. 'But the number of apologies for whatever she has researched for some unfortunates will be legion.'

For once we were having a quiet night at home, and I had cooked a dinner. Usually neither of us have much time, what with Clive giving evening classes and me taking them. For once we decided not to study but to stick photos into an album, and we had them all out on the floor when the doorbell rang. In London that's unusual. We hadn't invited anyone, and nobody selling bibles or double-glazing would ever climb the stairs to our flat, however great the commission in this world or the next.

It was Frankie.

'I'm not going to stay a minute, I'll leave the door open so that I won't even be tempted,' she said, blocking the door open with her handbag and creating such a draught that all the photos blew out of their little piles.

'Close the bloody door,' said Clive and I knew the evening was ruined.

'I just wanted to borrow one sweater, and one skirt. Until lunchtime tomorrow only. To go to work in, the job starts tomorrow you see, and because Bernard burned all my things I've got nothing to wear except this dress, which I don't think would be suitable for the Beeb.'

It was a lovely dress, cut to the navel, with rhinestones all around the bit of bosom it had. It would be unusual in the BBC but might just hasten on the disaster that was bound to befall Frankie. I said cheerfully that I would go and see what I could find.

Frankie sat on the floor, falling out of her rhinestones and oohing and aahing at the pictures.

'My God, didn't we all look foul at your wedding?' she shouted, and even through the bedroom door I could feel Clive bristling.

Then.

'Clive, that's not you. I don't believe it. With all the curls and the little toy horse sitting on a stool. It's beautiful.' She positively gurgled over the picture. I had begged him once with tears in my eyes not to throw it out, and had won only by such a small margin that I had always kept it hidden in the bottom of the drawer. I took it out to gurgle a bit myself over, privately.

I rushed out of the bedroom carrying my only good skirt and a new blouse which I had not yet worn.

'Would these do?' I said hurriedly.

Frankie was so far into the photos now that nothing would have got her out of them.

'Look at that picture of you and me and Gerry!' she exclaimed happily. 'Do you remember that night you went out with him and I had to pretend to your mother that you stayed with me? It was awful, I kept getting so confused about what I was meant to have been doing, or what we were meant to have been doing, that I'm sure I gave the game away.'

Oh she had, she had, then and now, but that was Frankie, so innocent, and hopeless. Always.

'I believe you have joined the BBC,' said Clive in a heavy overdone effort to save me embarrassment. It was as if he had flashed a notice saying let us change this unsavoury subject of my wife's past. I hated him for it.

Even Frankie must have sensed some tension, because she sort of gathered up her limbs, and breathed a few dizzy remarks about hoping she'd cope with her first day as a new girl, and snatched my clothes and ran.

Clive had put away the photos. The one of him with curls he had torn into eight pieces, and thrown into the basket. He said he had remembered he had a lot of study to catch up on. I went to bed in a sulk, couldn't sleep, so got up and did the ironing. Clive said I was behaving like a martyr, that I was only ironing to make him feel guilty. No, I said, harassed working wives love ironing, it keeps them sane, they use it as therapy in mental hospitals, everyone knows that. He said I was becoming as childish as my friend Frankie, and even more immature. I said his shirts were now a size too small for him, or a half size anyway, why else would all the top buttons be loose?

Oh it was a lovely evening.

Frankie rang me at work, nobody except Frankie ever rings me at work. The Principal hates it, and he's right, you can hear the whole form screaming while you're out of the classroom. I've told Frankie this again and again, but she never remembers. She wanted to meet me at six o'clock to give me back my clothes.

'I don't need them at once,' I said, furious to have brought the Principal's wrath down on me again for nothing.

'But I want you to have a little drink, just two little drinks in the BBC Club,' she said beseechingly.

There was no time to chat. I could hear a noise like a

tank division coming from my classroom. Anyway I'd always wanted to go into the BBC Club, that's what did it.

'Yes,' I shouted. 'Where is it?'

'Get off at Oxford Circus, and walk in a straight line,' she said. 'I'll have your clothes in a nice plastic bag ready for you.'

I hoped that she'd remember to get some replacements for herself. I could only too easily see her sitting there in her bra and pants drinking a pink gin.

The real reason I gave in so easily was that I wanted to avoid meeting Clive. We had parted in a mutual sulk that morning and I didn't look forward to apologising or waiting for him to. It would do him good not to see me waiting there anyway. We usually had a beer and a sandwich from the fridge at about six, before he went out to teach a lot of foolish self-advancing housewives all about economics, and before I went to learn Italian. I was doing a degree in Italian so that I could teach it in a school where the children were older, and more appreciative, and didn't scream like deprived railway engines.

Two little drinks at six o'clock, and the chance of seeing some personalities . . . it was a great idea.

The BBC Club was huge, and had two separate entrances, each with a porter's desk where you had to show an identity card before being let in.

'Perhaps your friend has signed you in,' said a porter kindly, examining the visitors' book. My friend hadn't. There was no passport to personalities for me at all. I felt very sad.

I waited on a chiar, feeling foolish, for about half an hour until Frankie arrived, breathless. She was desperately sorry but she'd been to the shops, it was late closing, and she'd got herself something to wear instead of my skirt and blouse.

She had indeed. It was an outfit of skin-tight black velvet pants and a sort of a big red handkerchief tied under her bosom. It looked great, but it didn't look like the kind of thing she could wear the next day at work. I had grave doubts whether it was even the kind of thing she should wear in this club.

We were about to sweep in when the porter asked for her card.

'But I work in the BBC,' said Frankie proudly.

'I'm afraid you have to be a member of the club though,' he said kindly.

Frankie was like a toddler whose ice-cream had been snatched away. I thought she was going to cry.

'We can go to a pub,' I said.

'I don't want to go to a pub, I want to go in here, it's where all the BBC people go,' said Frankie in a five-year-old voice.

At that moment a couple of men were waiting for the porter to finish so that they could go in, and they were amused by Frankie's predicament. They asked her what programme she worked on, and good-naturedly signed us both in, looking at Frankie's outfit appreciatively.

We were in. It was a big room, hot and smoke-filled, and crowded with people. I couldn't see anyone I had ever seen on television, and I wasn't near enough to people to hear any famous voices from radio either. I was a bit disappointed.

Frankie had wriggled up to the bar and got us drinks. There was nowhere to sit, nowhere to lean even, so we stood in the middle of a crowded room, like people at a party where we knew no one. I didn't like it at all.

'I have a purpose in coming here,' hissed Frankie, looking left and right in case anyone was listening.

'Oh my God,' I said.

'No, listen, you're always getting frightened over nothing. I think you don't go out enough, you and Clive. I mean poring over old baby pictures every night, it's not natural.'

'We won't be doing that again for a while,' I said darkly.

Frankie didn't notice any nuance in my tone. She was far more interested in her purpose.

'I'm here for a special reason,' she said again. Anyone who knew Frankie even slightly could see that trouble lay ahead. I who had known her since school felt weighed down with doom.

'You see there's this guy, my boss on the programme. He's absolutely great, very dynamic, people just do anything he says, and he was saying today that he thought I was getting on very well for someone who had just come in. I really did, you know. I used my initiative and brought many more files than they asked for, and we found a whole new line to go on . . .'

'Go on about the guy,' I said resignedly.

'Well, he said that what I needed was someone to sort of talk me into the programme, let me know the feel of the place, what they were at, where they were going, and what they wanted to do. And he said that I should try to live and breathe the programme constantly, thinking up new ideas, new ways of dealing with them, that's what makes a programme great he says. Martin says.'

'So?' I said.

'So I thought I should start doing it straight away,' beamed Frankie.

'Are we going to look for people from the programme and start living it and breathing it?' I asked in disbelief.

'No . . . not exactly. You see the one to tell me is this boss man, Martin. He really IS the programme. I thought I'd meet him here and get to know him, off-duty.'

'But if you're going to meet him, why am I here?' I said, hurt.

The two little drinks didn't seem such a good idea now I thought Frankie was going to dash off and leave me at any moment with over half an hour to kill before going to my Italian class.

But that wasn't it, there was more.

'No, he's much too important for me just to turn up

here and strike up a chat with him about the programme. That would be very forward. It's more complicated than that.'

I sighed.

'Some of the others were telling me that he has this utter dragon of a wife, a real Tartar woman, who won't let him out of her sight. She works in the Beeb, too, but in another department and she won't let him have any fun. She comes in here every night and stares across the room at him with awful eyes; then at seven o'clock she marches him home for dinner like a school boy.'

I automatically looked at the clock as if to count the minutes before this ritual took place.

'You've only got half an hour,' I said jokingly.

Frankie was utterly serious.

'I know, that's why I have to find her. I must strike up a friendship with her as soon as possible, so that she'll realise she has nothing to worry about, that I'm not after her husband. If she and I became friends then it would all be fine.'

I looked at Frankie, in her flame-coloured top and her tight, tight pants, her hair falling over her face like someone who had just got out of bed and was waiting, slightly tousled, for the next lover. I didn't think her mission was going to be possible. But there's no use explaining some things to Frankie so I offered to get another drink, and plunged into a sea of bodies around the bar.

When I came back Frankie was gone, or I thought she was, but she had only gone out to make a phone-call.

'I have to identify her first,' she said. At that moment someone was paged over the loudspeaker.

'That's her,' giggled Frankie.

'Where?' I scanned the room.

'We'll see. I went out to a public phone-box and rang her asking to speak to her. We'll just have to see who goes out.'

Like schoolchildren, we watched the door. Eventually a small blonde disappeared through it.

'That couldn't be his wife, not monsterish enough,' said Frankie firmly.

'Did they tell you he hasn't slept with her for years, but he can't leave her because of the children or her health?' I asked sourly. I was feeling very annoyed with this childishness, and hated being part of it. I also wondered whether Clive was worried about me. Maybe I should have rung him.

The small blonde came back, shrugging her shoulders at her friends. 'Nobody there apparently,' she said. 'The phone was dead.'

'It is her,' said Frankie in amazement.

'Now Frankie,' I begged. 'Don't go up to that woman and start one of your explanations, you know how people misunderstand your way of talking. It's always happening if you think about it. Why do you have to do it today? Let it go for a day or two. Please, Frankie?'

It was, of course, useless. I hadn't even finished speaking when Frankie had bounded over to the blonde's side.

I was too embarrassed to do anything except stare into my drink, and wish I were a million miles away, or about three miles away, at home with Clive, the row over, forgiven, forgotten, the two of us sitting there listening to records, laughing over it all, and making great plans about how we would see the world eventually. It all seemed so safe, and so much what I wanted compared to standing in this awful place with terrible things going on a few feet away.

I hardly dared look over for fear of what was happening. The small blonde woman was hauntingly familiar. Was she on a telly programme? Was she a film star? How did I know her face so well? Frankie had said something about her being a producer, you don't see producers' faces.

I knew it, I knew it, I was summoned over and introduced. Everyone seemed to be quite happy and relaxed, they always do with Frankie . . . initially.

'Is it your first day in the BBC too?' asked the blonde kindly.

'No, I'm not here, I mean I'm only here because Frankie asked me to have a drink with her after work. I'm just going off to my Italian lesson,' I said, wondering why did I always sound like someone who had never learned English but was trying to pick it up as I went along.

'I'm a teacher actually, in a dreary old school, nothing bright and glittery like this,' I said, wondering why I said it. I preferred the school a million times with its familiarity and chalk and noise to this strange place where you might be standing next to a news-reader and anything could happen.

The blonde seemed nice. Frankie had obviously told her some cock-and-bull story about being lonely and nervous in her job and wanting to get to know colleagues in the Corportation. This had endeared her to all of them. They said that it was only too rare that people admitted to knowing nobody, most people went around and knew nobody for ages because of this English trait of reticence.

One of the men bought us a drink, we were part of a group.

Frankie was making a great effort to convince the blonde that she was a serious, steady person interested only in her job.

'I'm not at all like my teacher friend, always flitting around,' she said. I didn't think anyone could have believed her. There was I in a jumper and skirt, while Frankie looked as if she was about to do a gypsy dance, and strip in the middle of it. They couldn't have believed her, could they? But it was important for Frankie's purpose that they did, so I went along with it.

'Yes, Frankie is always trying to get me to settle down. I couldn't give two pins for my work, just the holidays and the hours are all I could care about. Frankie likes to live and breathe her job, she puts in endless hours of overtime, silly I call it.'

Frankie smiled, the blonde frowned at me.

'You shouldn't stay in teaching, if you don't like it, it's bad for you and the children. I really do think it's a vocation, half my family are teachers, and the other half used to be. Those of us that didn't do it well got out,' she said.

Inside I agreed with her, but I had to go on, no use in being converted too easily. I'd never see this woman again, and she wouldn't judge Frankie by her hopeless, feckless friend, surely. I'd better make myself a really bad case, whom Frankie was trying to reform.

'Oh I don't know, it's a job the same as any other. Worse paid than a lot, but then you can always read the paper when the kids are doing a test, and our Head is a bit soft about things like doctors' certs. If I want to earn a few quid, real money I mean, in some other job, I just don't turn up for a few days. I get paid just the same.'

Never in my life had I done anything of the sort. One teacher had once, and we were all appalled and shocked. The Principal was a kind man who thought I was a bit flighty sometimes, but only because I did play with the children so much, even after school. His only real grievance was that my classes were too exuberant.

'I'm always trying to make her grow up, to tell her the joys of living and breathing her work,' said Frankie in a good-goody voice.

'Is it seven?' said the blonde. 'Damn it, I was having a lot of fun. Martin will be around in front of the building in his car, I must run.' She gave Frankie a warm good-bye, and wished her well, hoped to see her again. Barely glancing at me, she said she hoped I'd find a happier job soon.

'I'm really sorry to run,' she said to the others. 'It's just that we have to be home to change, we're going out tonight. My brother's having a little dinner.'

It was only as I saw her side-face on, that I realised why she was so familiar. She was like a twin of my Principal. My nice kind idealistic headmaster, who had, now that I remembered it, a sister who used to be a teacher but who was now a senior producer in the BBC.

Tottenham Court Road

A lot of the books seemed to be about lesbians, which wasn't what she wanted, however uninhibited and daring they might be according to the jacket descriptions, and then there were a sizeable number for gay men, with pictures of very beautiful muscled men on the covers, but this again wouldn't be any help. In horrified fascination she saw the section where Alsatian dogs and horses seemed to be people's partners, and about five shelves where people weren't naked at all but clad from head to toe in black leather and brandishing whips.

What she wanted and couldn't find was a book that would tell her how to be an enormous success as a woman in bed with a man. They didn't have any books for twenty-nine-year-old virgins. Such things weren't meant to exist . . . they were an embarrassment to society.

Oh the world was full of books telling twelve-year-olds not to be afraid of menstruation, and telling eight-year-olds about little eggs growing inside mummy's tummy, and assuring seventeen-year-olds that they would go neither blind nor mad from masturbation but that it wasn't as good as a healthy, meaningful, one-to-one sexual relationship. Julia was worn out reading helpful letters to people who complained of being frigid, advising them to relax and to be loving and to specify what they wanted. Who would tell her what she should want, and how to do it at her age without making an utter fool of herself? Twelve, even ten years ago, she could have put herself at the mercy of her seducer, virginity would have been an honour then, something to be treated with respect and awe and tenderness. Nowadays she couldn't possibly tell any would-be seducer that this had never happened before. If it weren't so sad, it would be laughable.

There were no men in raincoats in the shop, no sinister figures with moustaches and sun-glasses salivating over pictures in filthy books. In fact Julia found it very hard to find a book to salivate over herself. They all seemed to be wrapped in cellophane. She wondered how you knew what to buy. There was no way she was going to ask for assistance either from that man who looked as if he should have been a head-gardener in a stately home or from the tired, ageing woman at the cash-desk. She would have to hope that the blurbs, and the overwritten sentences about the material being uncensored, and straight from Scandinavia, would put her on the right trail.

The worst bit was over really, the walking into the shop and settling down with the browsers. She wore a head-scarf, which she normally didn't do, in some mad wish to look different, to put on a different personality for this reckless, sinful venture. She had given herself two hours to look for the right book, or maybe books. She had five pounds in her handbag. If it worked it would be an investment well made, and perhaps there was an additional gain, in courage. She would never have believed herself capable of setting off deliberately and examining the outside of pornographic bookshops. She had finally settled on the one which looked as if it had the biggest selection. Really, you could get used to anything, Julia decided. She had now stopped worrying about what the other people in the shop thought about her, and was no longer afraid that they were all going to jump on her and rape her because she had shown herself mad for it by going into a sex shop anyway.

She moved unhappily from the Oral Love section to a

small specialist area called Domination. Mainly women
in thigh-high boots with evil smiles, and men cowering
behind sofas. Disconsolately she leafed through one of
the magazines which was open – they had to leave
something for you to browse through in those kind of
shops – and saw sadly that it was Party Games, and that
you would need colouring pencils to work out whose
limb belonged to whom.

It was very depressing not to be able to find what she
wanted when she had got herself as far as this. Julia had
thought that the hard part would be making the decision
to find the shop, and going in, and perhaps even understanding the terminology of the book without anyone to
practise with, like you could with Yoga or wrestling. She
didn't know that her specific requirement would be
uncatered for. And it wasn't as if it was easy to know
where to go either. She had thought that Soho was the
right area to hunt, but fortunately she had been able to
ask people at work in a jokey way where they bought
sexy magazines, and a knowing guy had said anywhere
on Charing Cross Road, in the small places. Much better
than Soho, because not priced for tourists. 'Get out at
Tottenham Court Road tube station, and you'll be fine
then, Julia,' he had said, and the others in the travel-
agency had laughed. Because you just didn't associate
Julia with poking around in a porn shop. She looked too
clean and wholesome and well brought-up.

But they probably assumed that she had at least some
kind of sex life, Julia thought in a troubled way. She
didn't talk about having one, true, but then neither did
anyone else. They were fairly sophisticated there, or
even distant about things like that. Katy was married,
and Daphne was divorced, and Lorna wasn't married but
seemed to have a regular chap called Clive who was
mentioned casually in dispatches. They probably
thought that Julia met people at week-ends, and maybe
went to bed with them. If they knew she didn't, and

hadn't, they would have been mildly embarrassed and sorry for her rather than shocked. It was that kind of office.

But her two friends Milly and Paula would have been shocked, and horrified. They were heavily into going to bed with people. Milly regularly with the same, very unavailable man, whom she said she didn't love, but was irresistibly drawn to, and Paula with somebody new and hopeful-sounding every couple of weeks. Julia invented the odd holiday sexual happening, and would feel very trapped when Paul would ask, 'But was he good? I mean, you know, did he *satisfy* you?' Julia would say that some had and some hadn't and this kept Paula happy, and reflective about the differing abilities of men in this field.

Everyone plays games, even with friends, and Julia felt that she would have been breaking all the rules of the game if she had suddenly confessed that she had not known the experience and would they please tell her what it was like from start to finish. Paula and Milly would assume that she was having an early menopause, an unexpected nervous breakdown or had developed unhealthy voyeuristic tendencies that she wanted to indulge. They would never actually believe that such a thing could be true.

And really it was only too easy. Julia had been adamant about not going to bed with Joe, her first and long-lasting boyfriend. She was full of the kind of thought that said in letters of fire that you lost them if you gave into them. She had this firm belief that if she and Joe made love outside marriage he would never trust her again, and that he would assume she would be lifting her skirts for all and sundry. She didn't know from where she got this expression 'lifting her skirts', it was coarse and unlikely and had nothing to do with love. She must have heard her aunt use it about some serving-girl. Her aunt was like that.

Joe had gone to university and found a nice girl there.

When he told Julia that their unofficial engagement had now better be forgotten, Julia had asked in a pained way, 'Does she . . . er . . . sleep with you?' and Joe had laughed lightly and said that there wasn't much chance of actually sleeping with someone at university but they did make love of course.

So Julia, who was now twenty, decided that there must be other standards than her own, but for the next five years the only people who offered her the initiation rights were drunken people, or people who had been stood up or let down by some other girl, and who were using her as a substitute. And suddenly the years were passing, and she never knew what it was like to have the earth move, or to hear wild cries of ecstasy mingling with her own, and she felt frowningly that this was bad news . . . Still, there had been so much else to think about, borrowing the money, setting up a different kind of travel agency to anyone else's in a different kind of partnership, going abroad three times a year to investigate things like they all did, and there was getting a flat and doing it up, and keeping her aunt and her father happy by visiting them regularly with lots of cheery stories and bright dismissals of all their ills and complaints. And there was going to the theatre, and meeting Paula and Milly in each other's flats for great meals with lots of wine, and really it was hard to know how the years went by without going to bed with people.

But now it was important. Julia had met a very nice man indeed. He was in publishing and she had met him one evening last year when she was touring the night-clubs of a foreign resort with a notebook, writing down details of atmosphere for next season's brochure. Michael had been sitting in one of the clubs and had seen what she was doing. He offered her a bit of advice about excluding it, because the drinks were too dear and the floor-show was too touristy. Together they roamed several other clubs and at the end of a long night he suggested she come back to his room for a drink. Julia was about to agree when she suddenly realised with a horrible shock that she literally didn't know how to do it. There she was, twenty-eight years old, and she didn't know whether she was meant to lie down on the bed naked and wait for him to do everything, or if she should undress him, or if she should move up and down when it was happening or round and round, and it was all very well to say that she'd learn in time, but who could learn in two minutes what they should have been learning over the last ten years?

Lightly she said no, and refused for the rest of the week also, on the grounds that she didn't go in for holiday things. This sounded, she hoped, as if she went in for real-life things very seriously, and Michael seemed to think that this was reasonable enough. He didn't live in London, but he came to see her for half a dozen weekends, and for three of those she pretended she had someone staying in the flat and couldn't ask him to stay. Then twice she said she had too much work to do, and didn't want to ask him back. Finally, the last time, she had asked him to the flat for a meal, and when she was getting the usual excuses ready he had held her hand very gently.

'We get on well together,' he had said.

'Sure, very well,' she admitted, almost grudgingly.

'Then why do you close me out?' he asked. He had been so gentle and understanding that if she had said at that very moment what was worrying her she knew it would have been all right. Why couldn't she? Because she felt foolish. She felt that she was grown-up and intelligent in every way except this. She couldn't bear the vulnerability, it would show. She was even afraid that the whole thing might be messy and might hurt her. Because she was such an ancient virgin, it might be impossible to pierce her virginity. Think how appalling that would be.

She had bought time.

'The next time you come to London you can stay here for the whole week-end,' she said. 'I'd like that. It's just that, well, I'm not ready for it now, and I don't think people who are grown-up and equal should have to make excuses to each other, do you?'

He had agreed, and they had talked of other things, and he had his hand on her neck as they talked, and occasionally he kissed her and told her she was very dear to him. And deep down she thought that it would be possible to lose her virginity before he came back in a few weeks, and it would all be fine from then on.

It's harder than you think to find somebody to sleep with you, in a limited time, and for a limited time and with no strings, and with no build-up. Julia went to a party and behaved outrageously with a businessman who was in London for a few days, having what he said was a whale of a time. She even managed to get him home to her flat. Staring at herself in the bathroom mirror, she wondered whether it could ever have been so terrible for anyone as it was going to be for her. He was very silly and he kept laughing at his own jokes, and he was rather drunk. His idea of romance was to plunge his hand unexpectedly and painfully down the front of her dress. But Julia thought, brushing her gritted teeth in order to be nice and inoffensive for the beautiful act, it was better to learn on someone awful.

When she went back to the sitting-room, he was asleep on the sofa, and no amount of cooing or even shouting could revive him. Eventually she took off his shoes, threw a rug over him, and went in bed in a rage. Next morning she had to make him breakfast, assure him that his wife wouldn't be hurt in any way, and kind of hint that it had all been rather wonderful. She went to the office in a rage also.

In the next ten days she got two more men back to her flat. One was a friend of Lorna's and Clive's who told her eighteen times about his wife having upped and left with a teenager. She promised him consolation and a shoulder, even a whole body, to cry on. First though, there was the story of the wife, over and over, what he had done wrong, what he hadn't done wrong, how he couldn't blame her, how he'd like to throttle her, how he hoped she'd be happy, how he hoped she'd rot in hell. When it was bed-time and Julia got herself into and out of the state of self-pity and self-disgust about making love to such an unlovable man, he said that he would like to lie beside her all night, but that they couldn't make love as he hadn't been able to do that for a long time now. It was quite normal. Apparently the doctor had told him that thousands of men had the same problem.

The other possible bed-mate had been a really loud vulgar friend of Paula's who showed a marginal interest in Julia one night in a pub. Immediately she returned his interest a hundredfold. Since he had been making passes at her unsuccessfully for a couple of years, he was delighted. On the way home he told her what a splendid stud he was, that he wished one could get references for that sort of thing, that he loved women, big women, little women, young women, all women. Julia was nearly in a state of collapse by the time the taxi turned into her street.

'Do you like virgins?' she inquired hopefully.

He did, he loved them, he was very good with them. He hadn't had one for ages now, but he did like virgins.

It was half-way through the drink before deflowering that Julia remembered an article she had read the previous Sunday about veneral disease. It would be just her luck to wait twenty-nine years and then do it for the first time with someone who was riddled with syphilis, and then pass it on the next week to the only man she had ever really wanted. Suddenly she went all funny and said that she couldn't go to bed with him because she thought she had sprained her back. The remark sounded even more stupid than she could have believed possible.

'Let me do all the work,' he had said.

Julia had no idea what he was talking about, but was sure she would catch some disease if she allowed herself to find out. She shooed him out into the night, and decided it would have to be a bookshop.

She had told the girls in the travel agency that she was going to the Family Planning Association, so she would take a long lunch-hour. She had in fact been on the Pill for a month so that she was now protected. All she needed was someone, anyone, who would tell her how not to make an utter fool of herself and drive Michael away next Friday night. It was Tuesday now, for God's sake, she really didn't have any time to lose. She had suffered so many humiliations already, it didn't seem too much to ask the man who looked like a head-gardener for some advice.

'I wonder if you could tell me, do they publish any books, sort of manuals of instruction really, on how to make love . . . in an ordinary sort of way?'

'I beg your pardon?' said the gardener, and for one wild moment Julia wondered whether he in fact worked in some other shop, and she had done something unpardonable. No, of course he worked here, she had seen him directing people towards the shelves of their choice.

'Well, I was looking for something . . . to give to my niece,' she said triumphantly. 'She's . . . er, getting married soon, and I don't think she knows exactly what will be expected of her.'

The gardener looked concerned on behalf of the niece but didn't see how he could help.

'Couldn't you tell her yourself, madam?' he asked politely, but puzzled.

'Oh I have, I have,' Julia said. 'But only basic things really, and she wants to be sort of tigerish if you know what I mean. She feels she's going to lose out by not knowing the techniques that a man expects. She wants more than just clinical information, it's the response she's keen to learn really.'

'I don't expect her husband will want anybody to teach her that except himself,' said the gardener, a trifly hypocritically and pompously Julia thought. What was he doing running a porn shop, if these were his views? Oh well, I've got as far as this, she thought in despair, I might as well wade on.

'You see she's in an unfortunate position. This chap she's marrying, he's been around a lot, and my . . . niece more or less pretended that she had too, so she's going to feel very foolish when he discovers that she hasn't. I said I'd try and find a book that would tell her what to do.'

The gardener still looked mystified by it all. Oh why couldn't he understand, why couldn't he just say that there was such a book and sell it to her?

'But I don't see what she can learn from a book, madam,' he droned on, trying to be helpful. 'If I might suggest something, you'd be better off spending the money on a couple of bottles of wine, and sitting down with her and giving her the benefit of your own experience. If it's hard to talk about things like that, a drink often helps. She'd thank you much more for that than for just a book.'

Julia was now desperate, and desperate people say desperate things.

'I *can't* tell her anything,' she hissed in a low voice. 'I don't know anything. I'm a nun.'

'*A nun?*' bayed the gardener in horror.

'Well yes, we don't wear nuns' clothes these days, we work out in the world. You see, it all changed after that council in Rome, you hardly ever see nuns as nuns so to speak these days. Half the people walking around might be nuns.'

She wasn't even a Catholic, she knew only the vaguest things about nuns, but she was banking that a man who ran a porn shop might know less.

She was wrong.

'Well I never,' he said. 'My sister is a nun too. But she wears dark clothes, and a short veil like a scarf since Vatican Two.' He looked stunned at Julia's poncho cape and green trousers, at her sunglasses pushed back over the top of her scarf, and at her long, painted fingernails.

'I suppose that you Sisters must be getting more and more worldly all the time,' he said with deference.

'Well, it's so we'll look more normal at work,' Julia explained. 'Not to frighten off the other people, and make them think we are too holy or anything.'

'And do you teach, Sister, or do you work in a hospital?' he asked with awe.

'A travel agency,' said Julia before she could help herself.

'Why do nuns do that?' he asked with interest.

'It's mainly to help send people out on the Missions,' Julia replied, beginning to sweat, but thinking that in fact, it mightn't be a bad side-line for their own agency. If she ever survived this ordeal she would suggest it to the others.

'So now you see why I need that book for . . . my niece,' she went on briskly, and hoping to give the air of a worldly, business-like nun.

'Well, I really don't like to suggest anything, Sister,' he said fearfully.

'Nonsense,' Julia said. 'You must learn to accept us as we are, women working in the world, like other women. It's just that we've given up sex . . . or never taken it up,' she finished lamely.

'Perhaps a bigger store might have one of these books on preparing for marriage . . . by a woman doctor,' he said, trying to get out of it.

'I've been through those, nothing tigerish enough for my niece,' said Julia.

'Tigerish.' He thought for a while. 'We're out of tigerish books, Sister,' he said firmly.

'What would you suggest?' she begged.

'I don't think the fellow's going to mind at all, he'll like showing her around, if you'll forgive the expression.'

'But she's quite old, my niece. I mean she's in her mid-twenties, he'll expect her to know tigerish things.'

'Oh no, he won't, Sister. I'd go off and set her mind at rest about that. I mean it's not as if she was nearly thirty or something, he won't expect anything.'

Julia walked sadly out of the shop. The man who looked like a gardener rushed and opened the door for her.

'It was a pleasure to meet you, Sister,' he said. 'I hope we'll have the pleasure of seeing you here again . . . but perhaps not, of course. I'm sorry. And I'm sorry for suggesting all that stuff about the bottles of wine and the bit of chat. I mean I wasn't to know you were a nun, Sister.'

On the way back to Tottenham Court Road tube station she saw an off-licence. The gardener was probably right, maybe two bottles of wine would work better than a book. Maybe she could pretend to get drunk on Friday and see what happened, maybe she could make Michael a little bit drunk and watch what he did.

For the first time since the whole terrible problem had begun to obsess her, Julia saw a ray of hope. Perhaps it mightn't be as awful as she thought it was going to be. He was hardly going to get out of bed, put on all his clothes and say, 'You have deceived me.' It was laughable, really, and that was another thing. She and Michael did laugh together about a lot of things, they might even be able to laugh one day about the thought of a nun in cape and trousers running a travel agency for missionaries and visiting porn shops in her lunch hour.

Well, it was either believe that, or ask the good-looking Italian boy who was struggling with his map trying to find Oxford Street, whether he'd like to rent a hotel-room for the afternoon with her. And, really, Julia thought that for a twenty-nine-year-old virgin, she had coped with quite enough that day.

Holborn

Rita sat down to make a list of all the things she needed to do. Now that she had been such a fool as to agree to the whole ridiculous idea she might as well try and get through it as painlessly as possible.

She wrote LIST at the top of a piece of paper and stared at it in rage. Why had she agreed to meet them? Normally she was so quick and firm at getting out of things she didn't want to do, but his voice had disarmed her.

Ken had rung up last night and said he was in London, he and his new wife, they were still on their honeymoon, wouldn't it be nice if they and Rita and . . . er . . . Jeremy, was it, could get together for a civilised meal? It wasn't Jeremy, it was Jeffrey, he must have known. She knew that his wife was called Daisy, people didn't forget names, he must have done it on purpose.

She said hold a minute and she'd see if Jeffrey had planned anything. It was meant to be her excuse, she was going to come back to the phone and tell some lie.

'Right, of course,' Ken had said pleasantly. 'I hope he hasn't. It's our first time in London, and we'd love a bit of advice from a native.'

Jeffrey had said why not, it would be nice to meet them, he'd love to give them a bit of advice, he'd tell them about boat trips to Greenwich and he'd mark their card. He was full of enthusiasm. The fact that she had spent a whole year living with Ken didn't seem to disturb him in the least. What was past was past; they had both agreed that it was silly to brood.

She had come back to the phone and said it would be

.fine, where should they meet? Ken didn't know London at all, so he said he'd make his way to wherever she said. He wondered if they could make it straight after work or early evening anyway, because they'd want an early night.

'You haven't changed,' giggled Rita, with a small pang of jealousy that he still wanted to be between the sheets with his bird well before midnight.

'Oh, it's not that,' Ken said casually. 'It's just that we . . . well, Daisy gets tired easily. She's rather frail you know, we don't like too many late nights.'

So Daisy had turned out to be frail, had she? Marvellous, bloody marvellous, thought Rita. She was cunning to be frail, old Daisy. It meant she didn't have to go on all those wearying walks with Ken that Rita had endured, climbing hard sides of hills instead of easy ones, packing endless pairs of woollen socks for week-ends because you never knew when the next bout of walking fever would come on. How wise to be frail. Rita went back to her list-making.

Hair, she wrote. Yes, she'd take time off at lunch, an extra half an hour, and get her hair done. Silly to try a totally new style in case it didn't work, but she did need a cut and a conditioning treatment some time, so why not today? She decided that as soon as the hairdresser's opened she would ring round and get a lunch-time appointment.

She had another cup of coffee to celebrate that decision being made. Jeffrey was still asleep. Most of the world was still asleep. It was only 6 a.m., but Rita couldn't sleep.

Clothes, she wrote. They had arranged to meet at Holborn station of all places; it was the only possible meeting-point she could think of that was near Jeffrey's work, her work, and that Ken would be able to find. Ken really did sound bewildered by the size of London, not at all like the confident man she had known in Wales. Yes, clothes. She would wear her new skirt, the long patch-work one, and she would get a very simple sweater to go with it, in a matching colour, green maybe, or dark brown. She needed a new sweater anyway, it wasn't a question of buying anything specially for the occasion, that would be idiotic. What did she want to impress Ken for now? All that business was long over. She had ended it, she had left and come to London, she wasn't hoping he'd still fancy her. No, she needed a new sweater. Why not get it today? The shops in the Strand opened at nine o'clock, and she needn't be at work until half-past.

Photos, she wrote. She had a small pocket album of pictures of their wedding last year, it would be nice to show them to Ken. He would be interested, he would even recognise some of the people, her sister, her friends from Cardiff. And anyway, Rita thought, I look great in those pictures. After three months on a diet, naturally I look great. Why not let the frail Daisy have a look at me when I was two stone less than I am now? If they were still on their honeymoon, they wouldn't have wedding pictures yet, so she could be one up.

Handbag. Her own was a bit tattered, it didn't really go with the patchwork skirt, it didn't go with anything. She definitely needed one. At least twice last week she had been on the point of buying one. It had nothing to do with the fact that Daisy would probably have a frail little trousseau handbag with her either. No, she must get a handbag today.

She would borrow Lilly's cape. Lilly had a lovely black cape of fine wool with braid on the edge, which would be ideal over the outfit she was planning to wear. She must telephone Lilly at 8.30 a.m., before she left home, so that she could bring it to work with her. She had borrowed the cape twice already for parties and had lent Lilly her pendant in return. It was a gold pendant that Ken had given her. She still hadn't decided whether she would wear it tonight. Probably not.

It was still too early to talk to people, Rita grumbled to herself. She wished that people woke up sooner. Not that she could say much to Jeffrey, he would be busy getting out his guide-books to London, and his list of pubs that served Real Ale. He was so very confident of her, it would never cross his mind that she was excited about seeing Ken again, and that she was sleepless with worrying about how to present herself in a good light. Jeffrey would laugh tolerantly and say how like a woman. Jeffrey had a good comforting line in clichés when he wanted. Rita often thought he used them like warriors used armour to avoid having to meet any real thoughts head-on. Jeffrey was always pretty predictable.

Now that's one thing he wasn't. He was tiresomely unpredictable, you never knew what was going to happen. She hadn't liked it at the time and she didn't like it now, but that was the real reason she had got up so early. For all his protestations about having an early night, Ken might easily be persuaded to come back to the flat for just one drink. Jeffrey loved people to come back and so normally did she, but if Ken was going to see her home she wanted to look at it with an eagle eye herself first.

Coffee-cup in hand, Rita walked through the sitting-room. Ken would laugh at the coffee-table, not out loud but he would laugh. They used to use the word 'coffee-table' as an adjective to describe things and people they didn't like.

But what *did* you put things on, Rita complained to herself in irritation, if you didn't have a table of some sort? She just wished it didn't look so much like the kind of thing that held posh magazines and books nobody read. Well, she could cover it in things, ashtrays, knitting even. But God, how she and Ken had laughed at people who spent their time knitting. She hadn't known then that it was quite a peaceful thing to do while you watched television or listened to records. No, it might be pushing it to leave out her knitting, even though she was halfway through another great sweater for herself, and they only took her a week these days.

When she lived with Ken they had stripped down furniture and thought that the modern reproduction stuff was so ugly that it made you want to cry. She had no stripped-down pine in her sitting-room now; in fact, quite a few little desks and corner cupboards of the type they used to laugh at. Rita shook herself and reasoned that she could hardly refurnish the whole flat before 10 p.m. that night for a man who might not even see it, and for one whom she no longer loved. Yes, she knew that she didn't love him, but she wanted to think that he still loved and admired her. Having it both ways certainly, why not? A lot of people had things both ways.

Jeffrey, for example, had things both ways. He had his freedom to go racing, she never interfered with that, and he had his home to come back to. He had her as a kind of modern practical stepmother to his two sons who came to tea every Saturday. She never bothered doing the place up for them, she never wanted to impress them with tales that they could tell their mother when they got home. Funny that she never put on any show for these two silent big-eyed children, so that they could observe and note and tell their strange, silent, big-eyed mother, Jeffrey's first and foolishly ill-considered wife.

In fact she had met Heather on a few occasions and talked to her exactly like she would have talked to a client in the beauty-salon. She regarded Heather as somebody you made conversation with, it didn't grow naturally. A lot of the women she beautified were like that, they wanted nothing about you, nothing about them, but lots of cheery stuff on the weather, the price of shoes, the traffic jams and the wisdom of taking a holiday early in the season. Rita was very good at it. Heather had been easy.

So perhaps Ken and the dreaded Daisy would be easy

too. But she could never in a million years talk like that to Ken, she used to imitate salon-chat to him when they were living together, and sometimes he and she would make up a joke salon-conversation with each other . . . the kind of one where both sides were eager to find some harmless incontroversial middle-ground to speak about. If Ken caught a hint of that in her conversation tonight . . . an accidental little suspicion of it . . . she would die. Yes, she couldn't bear him to think she had gone over to the other side, to the enemy.

It was time to ring Lilly. Lilly grumbled and said it was raining and she was going to be taking her dry-cleaning anyway, but of course agreed. 'I love a bit of excitement over people's past,' said Lilly. 'You've always been so uneventful, happy, safe, married, never trying to pick up clients' husbands like we have. I'm glad there's a bit of drama here.'

Drama indeed! It could hardly be described as that. Much more a middle-class acquisitive wish to show off, Rita thought sadly, as she woke Jeffrey and handed him a cup of tea, because of some feeling that she was being disloyal to him by all this concentration on Ken. Jeffrey was pleased and touched, he looked very boyish and tousled sitting up in bed, drinking his tea as if it had been the most generous gift anyone had ever given him. Somehow this irritated Rita, and she said she was late and ran out of the flat.

She spent half an hour and almost a whole week's salary in a department store before she went into the salon. The sweater was far too dear and so were the handbag and the ear-rings that she felt she needed as well. They were all items she would have defined as luxury and out of her reach. She felt a low gloom come down on her after the initial exhilaration. A lot of eye-brow plucking, contour-massaging, skin-peeling and salon-chat went into earning that much money. She tried to tell herself that she needed a couple of nice things, but she felt guilty. The kind of people who bought handbags and sweaters at that price were usually debs or wives of tycoons. There would be problems at the end of the month when they came to do the hire-purchase repayments, but perhaps she could borrow something before then.

Lilly handed over the cape. They sympathised with each other again and again about working in the only beauty-salon in London that didn't incorporate a hairdresser's, and the day's work began. Between clients they had a giggle about how funny it would be if the dreadful Daisy came in to have a face-lift or something, and how Lilly would deliberately sabotage her.

Since she was already so much in debt Rita thought that it would be a pity to spoil the whole appearance by forgoing the hairdo, so that took care of the best part of a tenner and a half-hour over her lunch-hour. The afternoon seemed very long. Lilly wanted to know all about Daisy, but Rita didn't know very much apart from her newly-discovered frailty. She had been a nurse in the hospital where Ken ended up after one of his falls from a cliff, and had met Ken shortly after Rita left Wales. Rita had heard surprisingly little about her from the couple of friends she still had in Cardiff. She was said to be 'very sensible' and 'very good for Ken', two remarks which Rita always assumed were in the nature of mild insults.

'Well, whatever she's like, she can't look as well as you do tonight,' said Lilly loyally and admiringly, when the salon finally closed and Rita dressed herself up.

'I don't really care,' Rita said. 'But I'd like him to have a bit of a pang about me. It's only natural, isn't it?'

Lilly agreed it was totally the right attitude, and asked if she could sort of pass by the station too, so that she could have a look at them all meeting.

Rita didn't want that at all. It seemed too stagey. 'That's not fair,' complained Lilly. 'I've lent you my cape,

I've been excited about it all day. I want to have a look. I won't say a word, I won't pretend I know you.'

'Jeffrey will recognise you,' said Rita.

'No, I'll keep my head down. Oh go on, you can't stop me anyway. It's a public street, everyone has a right to be there.'

Very reluctantly Rita agreed, and they set off about thirty yards apart from each other.

It was a mild evening, and the lights of the shops were competing with the sunset as the girls walked towards the station. On evenings like this Rita felt that she had made London her own, she lost the impersonal side of it. It was like any big town, you had your own little quarters, the place where you lived, the place where you worked, the place where you shopped. It was a matter of breaking down a huge city and making it manageable.

Lilly was ahead. She stopped to buy a newspaper, and looked up the cinema times. This was her ruse, her cover for why she was hanging about. Rita saw Jeffrey there, looking at his watch. This irritated her too, because he was early, at least five minutes early, and there he was already fussing about the time. She could see no sign of Ken and his frail bride.

Just as she reached Jeffrey, who began to make delighted sounds at the way she looked, she saw Lilly talking to a woman with a walking-stick. They seemed to be greeting each other as old friends. Rita squinted. No, she didn't know the woman, and by her appearance she was hardly a client from the salon. You had to have a certain kind of chic and a certain kind of money before you could come in and have your face slapped by Rita or Lilly. Then, with a shock that nearly knocked her down, she saw that the woman was introducing Lilly to Ken. There he was, all smiles and grins and eager handshakes, the kind of overeagerness that meant he was shy. My God, that woman couldn't be Daisy. She was years older

than everyone, she could be Ken's mother. There had to
be a mistake. Daisy was around the corner, this was some
dreadful old woman who knew everyone, Ken, Lilly, half
of London perhaps. Wave after wave of sickness passed
over Rita, she actually thought she was going to faint.
Jeffrey was talking away:

'. . . really smashing, and you bought ear-rings too.
They do suit you. Love, you look like a magazine cover,
that's what you look like.'

'That's Ken,' Rita rapped out, pointing.

'And he's talking to Lilly,' beamed Jeffrey. 'Isn't that a
coincidence?'

He started moving over in great bounds with his hand
held out and Rita followed on legs that seemed too weak
to carry her. She kept well away from the edge of the
pavement, the slightest stumble she felt might push her
out under the traffic.

'Ken!' she said. 'And Lilly! Now who says London isn't
a village?'

'This is Daisy, Rita,' said Ken in the voice of a child
coming home from school with his first prize.

Rita looked at her. She was forty, she couldn't have
been a day less. She had stringy hair pushed behind her
ears, and she lent on a stick. She had a great big smile,
like someone's elderly and kindly invalid aunt.

'You're just the way I imagined,' beamed Daisy, and
with her free hand clutched Rita's shoulder and gave her
a sort of clumsy hug. She gave Jeffrey a hug too. Jeffrey
looked as if all his birthdays had come at once. A little
world of good-natured nice people had all gathered
together, he was as happy as a king.

Lilly was like someone with shellshock.

'Rita told me that she was meeting friends tonight, but
. . . well, isn't it absolutely extraordinary.'

'How do you know each other?' snapped Rita in a bark.
She was just recovering from the hug. She hated women
who embraced you, and particularly women who

embraced you from the awkward position of leaning on a stick.

'Peggy's an old . . . Peggy's a family friend . . .' stammered Lilly.

'I used to nurse with Lilly's mother,' said Daisy. 'And when Lilly was a child I used to come to the house and scrounge Sunday lunch. Your mother was so good to us, Lilly. We young nurses never had a penny in those days and there was always a huge meal there. It was really like home.'

Ken couldn't go to bed with this woman, Ken couldn't be on honeymoon with her. She wasn't frail, she was a cripple. What had he been thinking of? He must have had some kind of nervous breakdown? Why was she called Peggy and Daisy, and why was she standing there leaning on her stick in her shabby jacket and skirt smiling all around her and looking so horribly *old*?

'Let's all go and sit down,' said Jeffrey happily. 'There's a pub near here or we can go straight to the restaurant. Lilly, you'll come with us. Shall I get a taxi?' He was so excited by it all that Rita could have hit him hard with her new handbag.

'Oh no, I can't, I have to, I mean I'm going,' said Lilly, who, to give her some credit, thought Rita, looked wretched about it all. She didn't want to come and witness the shambles of an evening that it was going to be.

'Nonsense,' said everyone at once including Rita, and suddenly there was a taxi and the five of them were in it, four of them chattering like birds in a box, Rita trying to calm down her mind which seemed to be trying to get out of her forehead.

Why had nobody mentioned to her, even in passing, that this Daisy was an old woman? Very sensible, very good for Ken, what did they mean? Ken was fifteen years younger than her, at least. That might have merited a brief remark when Daisy's name came up. Rita looked at her. She was laughing and saying how exciting it was to be in London, and that she had already seen a man who read the television news, and an actor, and thought she had seen a woman MP, but Ken said it wasn't her after all.

'Why does Lilly call you Peggy?' asked Rita suddenly.

Daisy had an explanation for that too. Daisy had been her family name, like a nickname. When she was younger and worried about what people thought of her, she thought it was a silly name to have. So in the hospital she had pretended she was called Peggy. She had two identities now, the people she knew from those four years in the training hospital, who still called her Peggy, and her real name, which she had taken up again when she got a bit of sense, and decided not to upset her parents any more than she need by rejecting the name they had given her.

They got to the restaurant. Everyone fussed about Daisy. The taximan helped her out of the cab.

'Did you have a fall, my girl?' he asked her kindly.

Girl! Rita nearly laughed aloud.

'No, it's arthritis,' said Daisy. 'It's normally not nearly as bad as this. I feel such a fool with the stick, I'm always tripping people up with it. Most of the time I don't need it at all, it's just this week it's bad. I couldn't have timed it better, a wedding and a honeymoon and a stick, wouldn't you know?' The taximan was delighted with her. So was the waiter in the restaurant. He found her a chair with arms to sit on. Quite naturally, as if she had been the one who invited them all there, Daisy started arranging where they should sit.

'Rita, sit there by Ken, you have so much to say to him after all these years, and I'll take Jeffrey and Lilly here to tell me all about London.'

There was no fuss. They were seated. Rita raised her eyes to Ken.

'It's great to see you,' she lied straight at him.

'You look lovely, like a model,' he said truthfully, straight back at her.

'I feel overdressed and stupid,' she said, with honesty and feeling.

'You were always lovely to look at,' he said. 'But I think you've got even better-looking.' His voice had a simple quality about it, like the way he used to say that mountains were beautiful, or that some piece of wood they had been scraping and stripping all week-end looked perfect. Just objective, happy admiration.

'Jeffrey's in insurance, isn't he?' said Ken after Rita had just stared at her plate for a bit.

'Oh yes, he's with a company but he does a bit of free-lancing as well.'

'Perhaps we could get a bit of advice from him. We've got a small house. Do you remember Rodney Row? It's one of those.'

They used to laugh at Rodney Row and say they were doll's houses for doll people.

'I'm sure he'd be glad to give you any tips,' she said. 'Jeffrey loves helping people he knows, and not just to make a commission, you know.'

'Oh no I wouldn't think that, but of course we'd be very happy to do anything through him if it would help. I mean if there was any value to him out of it,' said Ken.

'I don't think he'd like to make money out of friends.'

'No, perhaps it's better not to mix work and pleasure,' said Ken agreeably, looking at the menu.

Pleasure. Pleasure. Had she remembered it all wrong? Was it she, not Ken, who was going mad? Perhaps he had always been the man who was destined to marry some ageing nurse with a walking-stick? Those wild months of freedom and abandon, and being sure with each other because together it was easy to reject other people's pretensions and nonsenses . . . had all that been real, or was it just in her head?

The others were laughing loudly. Daisy had said something endearing to the waiter, and he had brought her a rose. She put it behind her ear, in the middle of that lank greasy hair, and smiled a big smile with a lot of yellow teeth.

'Isn't this all great, Ken?' she laughed at him down the table.

Rita wouldn't let it go, there had to be something. There must have been something there, she couldn't have got it all so wrong, her memories of what they had. If they had nothing it would be like some kind of surgery, something would have been taken out of her.

'Look at those four over there,' she said desperately indicating a table where two middle-aged couples sat eating and making occasional little forays of conversation. 'Looks like a real salon-talk set-up, don't you think?'

Oh please, please, let him fall back into it, let us both start like we did in the old days. He might say 'One thing about the Italians is they know how to cook food' and she would say 'Isn't it funny the way all Italian restaurants seem to be run by families?' and he would say 'And they always seem to be so good-humoured,' it must be coming from all that sun' and together they would laugh about how people could and did talk in clichés from birth to death. Please, please, let him remember salon-talk.

Ken looked obediently at the four eaters.

'They don't seem to be having a good time, is that what you mean?' he asked.

'Yes,' said Rita flatly.

'I often think that people in restaurants must look over at other tables and envy them,' he said. 'They must wish they were part of a good scene like this.' He beamed down the table at Lilly and Daisy and Jeffrey and raised his glass to his travesty of a wife, and Rita wondered with a sharp pain whether she was going to be wrong about everything else as well. Had she never got anything right?

Chancery Lane

Dear Mr Lewis.

I'm sure you will think this very, very odd and you will spend the rest of your life refusing to talk to strange women at parties in case something of the sort should happen again. We met very briefly at the Barry's last week. You mentioned you were a barrister and I mentioned the Lord knows what because I was up to my eyebrows in gin. I was the one who was wearing a blue dress and what started out as a feather boa, but sort of moulted during the night. Anyway, your only mistake was to let me know where you worked, and my mistakes that night were legion.

I know nobody else at all in the legal world and I wonder if you could tell me where to look. In books people open yellow pages and suddenly find exactly the right kind of lawyer for themselves, but I've been looking in the windows of various solicitors' offices and they don't seem to be the kind of thing I want. They're full of files and girls typing. You seemed to have a lot of style that night, and you might know where to direct me.

I want to sue somebody for a breach of promise. I want to take him for everything he's got. I want a great deal of publicity and attention drawn to the case and photographs of me leaving the court to appear in the newspapers. What I would really like is to see all the letters involved published in the papers, and I want to be helped through the crowds by policemen.

But what I don't know is how to begin. Do I serve something on him, or send him a writ or a notice to prosecute? I feel sure the whole thing will gather its own momentum once it starts. It's the beginning bit that has me worried. If you could write back as soon as possible and tell me where to start, I should be for ever grateful.

I feel it would be unprofessional to offer you a fee for this service, but since it's a matter of using your knowledge and experience for my benefit, I should be very happy to offer you some of mine in return. You may remember that I am a tap-dancing teacher (I probably gave several exhibitions to the whole room that night). So, if ever you want a lesson, I'd be delighted to give you one.

Yours sincerely,
Jilly Twilly.

Dear Tom,
Thanks belatedly for a wonderful party last week. I don't know what you put in those drinks but it took me days to get over it all. I enjoyed meeting all your friends. There was a woman with the impossible name of Jilly Twilly, I think, but perhaps I got it wrong. She wore a blue dress and a feather boa of sorts. I seem to have taken her cigarette-lighter by mistake, and I was wondering if you could let me have her address so that I could return it. She seemed a lively sort of girl, have you known her long?

Once more, thanks for a great party.
John Lewis.

Dear John,
Glad you enjoyed the party. Yes, I gather her name is Jilly Twilly, unlikely as it sounds. I don't know her at all. She came with that banker guy, who is a friend of Freddy's so he might know. Pretty spectacular dance she

did, wasn't it? The women were all a bit sour about it, but I thought she was great.

Greetings to all in chambers.

Tom.

Dear Ms Twilly,

Thank you for your letter. Unfortunately you have approached the wrong person. Barristers are in fact briefed by solicitors in cases of this kind. So what you must do if you have a legal problem is to consult your family solicitor. If his firm does not handle the kind of litigation you have in mind, perhaps he may recommend a firm who will be able to help you.

I enjoyed meeting you at the party, and do indeed remember you very well. You seemed a very cheerful and happy person, and I might point out that these breach of promise actions are rarely satisfactory. They are never pleasant things for anyone, and I cannot believe that you would actually crave the attendant publicity.

I urge you to be circumspect about this for your own sake, but please do not regard this as legal advice, which it certainly is not.

I wish you success in whatever you are about to do, but with the reservation that I think you are unwise to be about to do it at all.

Kind wishes,

John Lewis.

Dear Mr Lewis,

Thank you very much for your letter. I knew I could rely on you to help me, and despite all those stuffy phrases you used I can see you will act for me. I understand completely that you have to write things like that for your files. Now, this is the bones of the story. Charlie, who is the villain of the whole scene and probably of many other scenes as well, is a very wealthy and stuffy banker, and he asked me to marry him several times. I gave it some thought and though I knew there would be problems, I said yes. He bought me an engagement ring and we were going to get married next June.

Because you are my lawyer and can't divulge anything I tell you, I will tell you privately that I had a lot of doubts about it all. But I'm not getting any younger, I haven't been in so many shows recently, and I teach dancing when I'm not in shows. I thought it would be fairly peaceful to get married and not to worry about paying the rent and all that. So Charlie and I made a bargain. I was to behave nicely in front of his friends, and he was to behave unstuffily in front of mine. It worked fine, a bit gruesome at some of those bank things. Merchant bankers en masse are horrific and Charlie did his best with my friends. I wasn't going to let him down in his career and he wasn't going to interfere in mine. If I got a dancing part, so long as I wasn't naked, I could take it.

And it was all fine until Tom Barry's party, and when I woke up Charlie wasn't there, he had left a note and taken my engagement ring, the rat. He said . . . oh well I'll make a photostat of the note, we'll probably need it as evidence. I'll also write out his address and you could get things going from your end.

I suppose it will be all right to pay you from the proceeds. I don't have any spare cash just now.

Warm wishes,

Jilly Twilly.

Photostat of note:

Jilly,

Now I've finally had enough. Your behaviour tonight is something that I would like obliterated from my mind. I do not want to see you again. I've kept my part of the bargain, you have failed utterly in yours.

Perhaps it is as well we discovered this before we were married. I am too angry to thank you for the undoubtedly good parts of our relationship because I cannot recall any of them.

I have reclaimed my ring. You may keep the watch.
                                        Charles.

Dear Ms Twilly,

You have utterly misunderstood my letter. I really cannot act for you in any way in your projected action against Mr Benson. As an acquaintance, may I take the liberty of reminding you once again of how unwise you would be to start any such proceedings? You are an attractive young woman, you seem from my short meeting with you to be well able to handle a life which does not contain Mr Benson. My serious and considered advice to you, not as a lawyer but as a fellow guest at a party, is to forget it all and continue to live your own life without bitterness. And certainly without contemplating a litigation that is unlikely to bring you any satisfaction whatsoever.

                                Yours sincerely,
                                John Lewis.

Dear John,

Stop telling me what to do with my life, it *is* my life. If I want to sue I'll sue. Please have the papers ready or I will have to sue you for malpractice. You have wasted quite a lot of time already. I am enclosing a copy of the letter where Charlie mentions my marrying him. It will probably be exhibit A at the trial.

Kind wishes and hurry up,
                                        Jilly.

Darling Jilly,

You must know that the bank can't put any money into the ridiculous venture you suggest. I didn't come to

America to meet show-biz people and interest them in your little troupe of dancers. I know that it must be disheartening for you not to get any backing, but in six months' time we will be married and you won't need to bother your pretty little head or your pretty little feet about a career. I love you, Jilly, but I wish you wouldn't keep telephoning the bank here on reverse charges, because I am only here for a conference and it looks badly to get several calls a day, all about something which we haven't the slightest intention of doing.

Look after yourself if you can,
Charles.

Dear Ms Twilly,
These Chambers will have no further correspondence with you about any legal matters whatsoever. Kindly go through the correct channels, and approach a solicitor who will if necessary brief counsel for you.
Yours faithfully,
John Lewis.

Dear John,
What have I done? Why is this kind of thing always happening to me? I thought we got on so well that night at Tom Barry's party. Did I tell you by the way that Charlie was quite wrong? Tom Barry was not one of his friends, he was a mutual new friend that we had met with Freddie who was one of Charlie's friends. So I didn't break any bargain by behaving badly.

I just thought that the publicity of a big breach of promise case might give me some chance of being noticed. People would hear of me, I'd get more jobs. You see without Charlie or my ring or anything I have so little money, and I was only trying to claw at life with both hands.

It's fine for you, you are a wealthy, settled barrister. What would you do if you were a fast-fading, poor little dancer betrayed by everyone. I'm nearly 26, my best years of dancing are probably over.

It was my one chance of hitting back at life, I thought I should grab it. Anyway, I'm sorry, I seem to have upset you. Goodbye.

Jilly.

Dear Jilly,

My letter may have seemed harsh. I do indeed see what you mean about grabbing at life, and I admire your pluck, believe me I do. What you need is not so much a court action, it's much more a good friend to advise you about your career and to cheer you up. I don't think you should get involved with anyone like Charlie, your worlds are too different. I only vaguely remember him from the party at Tom Barry's but I think he was a little buttoned up.

You need somebody younger than Charlie Benson.

Perhaps you and I might meet for a meal one evening and discuss it all, totally as friends and in no way in a client-lawyer relationship. If you would like this please let me know.

Cordially,

John.

Dear Monica,

I'm afraid I won't be able to make the week-end after all. Rather an important case has come up and I can't leave London just now. I know you will be disappointed, still we did agree that I should do everything possible to advance my career, so that is what I'm doing. I hope the week-end goes awfully well, looking forward to seeing you soon.

Love,
John.

Dear John,

I was sorry about the week-end. Daddy and Mummy were sorry you were kept in London. Daddy kept saying that all work and no play . . . you know the way Daddy does.

I came to London last Tuesday. You weren't in Chambers and you weren't in your flat, even though I phoned you there lots of times up to midnight. Maybe Daddy is right and although we all want to advance your career, perhaps it is a question of all work and no play.

Love anyway darling,

Monica.

Darling John,

How can I thank you for the lovely, lovely week-end. I always wanted to go to Paris and it really cheered me up. It was such a relief to be able to talk to someone so understanding. I'm afraid you must have spent a fortune but I did enjoy myself.

See you next week-end,

love Jilly.

Dear Monica,

I must say I thought your phone-call to the office today was hysterical and ill-timed. I was in consultation and it was very embarrassing to have to discuss my private life in front of others. I do not know where and why you have got this absurd notion that we had an understanding about getting married. From my side certainly we have no such thing. I always regarded you as a good friend, and will continue to do so unless prevented by another phone-call like today's.

You may check your letters from me to see whether any such 'understanding' was mentioned. I think you will find that nowhere do I mention marriage. I find this an embarrassing topic so will now close.

John.

Dear Tom,

I appreciate your intentions in writing to me with what you consider a justifiable warning. I realise you did this from no purposes of self-interest.

Still, I have to thank you for your intention and tell you that your remarks were not well-received. Ms Twilly and I are to be married shortly, and I regard your information that she has had seven breach of promise actions settled out of court as utterly preposterous. In fact I know for a certainty that the lady is quite incapable of beginning a breach of promise action, so your friend's sources cannot be as accurate as he or you may think.

Under other circumstances I would have invited you to our wedding but, as things are, I think I can thank you for having had the party where I was fortunate enough to meet my future bride and wish you well in the future.

Sincerely,
John Lewis.